Enemy Glory

Enemy Glory

Karen Michalson

TOR®

A Tom Doherty Associates Book   *New York*

ENEMY GLORY

Copyright © 2001 by Karen Michalson

This book is printed on acid-free paper.

Edited by David G. Hartwell

Design by Heidi Eriksen

A Tor Book
Published by Tom Doherty Associates, LLC
175 Fifth Avenue
New York, NY 10010

www.tor.com

Tor® is a registered trademark of Tom Doherty Associates, LLC.

ISBN 0-312-89061-3 (regular edition)

ISBN 0-765-30135-0 (first international trade paperback edition)

First Edition: January 2001

Printed in the United States of America

0 9 8 7 6 5 4 3 2 1

For Bill
For being there

Acknowledgments

Grateful acknowledgment is made to:

Jennie Dunham, my literary agent, for taking on this project and for working untiringly to see it to fruition. And to Donald Maas for recommending this project to Ms. Dunham.

David G. Hartwell of Tor Books for his always insightful editing, editing that helped to make this novel the best version of itself it could be. And to Jim Minz of Tor for his hard work and constant support of this project. And to Susan A. Warga for her sensitive and careful copyediting.

Fellow writer Leah M. Hughes, who commented on an early draft of this novel, but most of all because her willingness to speak truth at cost to herself helped to free this project from a destructive professional situation. Thanks, friend.

Enemy Glory

One

*T*he first time I saw the scarefisher I thought he was a compost heap. Pieces of sun-browned flesh kept falling off him and rotting away into the soft brown sand that surrounded his hovel. Lush reeds grew out of his feet and delicate daisies nodded out of his forearms. Strange white grubs crawled in and out of his soft permeable belly. So many waterflies drowned his chest that from a distance it looked as though his skin was growing the shiny scales of his prey. Two long gouges in his neck suggested gills.

Of course he couldn't speak. Of course he wasn't real. But he leaned against his hovel and slowly wove kelp nets out of wind. His weaving made me more nervous than the loneliness of the spot. You see, although I'm methodical by nature and used to feeling my way through slow bursts of logic, the slowness of his rhythms demanded that I slow my thoughts to match his, and I won't do that. Not for life itself.

Besides, it is especially dangerous to slow one's thoughts in the North Country. Here one is likely to mistake rabbit holes for oak trees and fall toward infinity while grasping for strength. Or oak trees for wrens and bleed on rough bark while caressing soft contradictions. Or wrens for weather. Or weather for dreams. Or dreams for all you've ever envied. Or a scarefisher, weaving down your thoughts, for the real thing.

Or, cruelest of all, here the sun might make you believe you are beautiful. And if you're not careful, you'll embrace the light and joyfully throw your life away to gaze at your deadly reflection. And then you'll die while the Northern light chants that it was all a trick, that you were really dust and maggots all along. I mean, I've made something of a career out of destroying beauty, enough to establish a reputation as an evil cleric, but here in the North the sun's cruelty could transform even me into a poet, the kind of poet who writes precarious verses as the sun destroys them.

I guess I am becoming a poet. The North does that to people. You begin to describe the North, and you're more than half gone. I watched the scarefisher weaving kelp out of wind for what might as easily have been weeks as minutes. The magic that animated him was still strong and sure; someday it would pull the world as I knew it through his resilient and formless fingers. In the meantime I would sit and catch the kelp as it turned darkly back to wind.

A heavily shod foot thudding into my back probably saved the remnants of my reason, although I've no idea if this was my attacker's intent or if I was grateful. An old fisherman leaned over me, roughly grabbed my collar, and tossed me to my feet, away from the scarefisher. The movement startled the waterflies into a spurt of confusion. I tried miserably to gain some balance on the slippery sand. My knees were traitors. My breath was stone. I fell and rose again unsteadily. The fisherman stood watching me through dull eyes, eyes of sticky amber that held a paralyzed remnant of his youth like a dead fly. In my heightened sensitivity I knew he had once been kind and innocent and generous and simple. I also knew that *something there is that punishes simple men,* for this was the phrase that swirled through my brain as I helplessly read his inner life. I groaned and heard the sun creating beauty on the water with tiny explosions of light.

"Isulde . . . ?" I gasped in explanation, immediately feeling my weakness intensify. What was I doing in this cold, charm-laden country, so far from the warm realities of southern climes? Nobody is real in the North. Even if one wanted to be real up here, there is very little the North Country will do to encourage such an ambition. My heart was splitting mountains and my stone breath was avalanching into pebbles of pain. Pain was real here. And Isulde, perhaps, could be real here. But what if she was really here, to see me like this?

"She ain't here." The old fisherman was sad and wistful. It was queer to realize that this was probably her foster father, this lonely beach her home. "How ye know Isulde?"

Hearing her name on his lips stunned me out of any reasonable answer.

"What's yer name, then?" the fisherman asked to prod my silence. He looked me over, his eyes and mouth narrowing suspiciously at my black riding clothes and the silver crescent moon that pinned my cloak. "Where ye come from? You either mighty sensitive or mighty weak to adapt so poorly to our Northern energies. Speak, boy!"

I lowered my eyes and stared through the impression I had made in the sand. It was dark beneath the surface. It usually is. "My name is Llewelyn. I come from . . . nowhere. . . . Sunnashiven in the south . . . the capital . . . I am a priest of Hecate, leastways I used to be. . . ." The memory of my horse sent me spinning into the sand again. "I think my horse became sea foam and I nearly drowned." Maybe I said this. Maybe I dreamed it.

"Yer nag is tethered in back, where I found and secured her. Ye had ridden her into a sweat. How do ye know my daughter?"

"I dreamt of her in the moonlight once."

A bitter smile tore open his leather skin. "Then enter and be welcome." He helped me to my feet and nodded toward the scarefisher. "Isulde made that one when she was a little girl. Still draws in the fish on a good day. Probably always will."

I nodded dumbly, leaning on his arm for support as we entered the hovel. Isulde was simply the best.

Of course, this was not her fault. The North Country bred magical talent, magic in these parts being as common as fish, and just as undisciplined. It's said that a Northern magician with the right training could rule the world with a smile, but again, try to train one. They'll have none of it, usually. And not from principle or moral qualms about the powers of chaos taking instruction. It's sheer laziness. Why build a fancy cottage when a makeshift hovel will do as well? Why hunt if food grows wild at your door? Why eat if the moon will sustain you?

The fisherman was handing me some porridge in a wooden bowl. He looked wistful again. I drank it eagerly. It was cold and sour and smelled of rotten fish. "Best of the house," he mumbled as I vomited porridge all over the sand floor. Tears of embarrassment scalded my eyes.

"I'm sorry. Maybe you can make it disappear?" I asked weakly.

"I'm not a wizard and my daughter ain't here to keep house." He took a little spade and began throwing shovelfuls of sand onto my retch. I watched helplessly, thinking how little I belonged anywhere north of the Drumun Mountains, how well that childhood curse against entering the North Country had held up. I would turn into something foul up here, a black squid squirting poison in the sand. I felt tentacles growing under my arms and summoned all my strength to wrestle away the illusion. The result was dry heaves. "Ain't often we get a priest of Hecate in these parts. Looks like yer monastic training ain't prepared ye too well fer survival 'round here. Or don't your goddess *want* ye wanderin' 'bout outside Sunnashiven?"

"I came of my own accord," I managed to choke out through splashes of chest pain.

"And no doubt expect a poor man like me to offer ye shelter because ye serve the forces of evil and claim knowledge of my daughter." He paused, then added softly, "The latter is enough." I could hear the scarefisher weaving. The roof creaked in the wind, and somewhere a wild dog barked. I could see through the doorway that the sun was slain and falling into the far shore. Soon it would be night. I began to tremble violently. Evil though I am, I feared the North Country darkness, a darkness more impartial and demanding than all the shadows my masters had nurtured me on into evil. Hecate would not protect me here. That dog was not her dog.

The rapidly cooling air allayed my sickness enough to let me observe my surroundings. The hovel was darker than the failing sky outside, and the fisherman had already lit a yellow candle and placed it on a roughly cut pine table in the middle of the room. I sensed that he recognized my fear and was clumsily trying to offer me a modicum of protection for Isulde's sake. From where I leaned in a corner against a pile of worn sheepskins I could look up and see all manner of crazy fishing nets and hooks hanging from the ceiling. There were no windows, and when my host closed the door the candle burned brighter in the absence of outside light. I noticed a fireplace and cooking tools on the opposite wall. The fisherman was throwing driftwood on the red coals, which he had probably used to light the candle. The wall to my left was bare and drafty, admitting a delirium of east wind. There were gull feathers stuck in insane patterns in the plaster. No doubt Isulde had placed them there.

I felt my left hand resting against something smooth and wet. Slowly turning my head, I saw a small black altar stone, long disused and covered with spray along the side that faced the door. It was probably Isulde's. The wind dropped tufts of gull feathers along its eastern edge. The far side was already glowing from the fire's warmth. On the side closest to me there was a thin hole in the stone, its bony darkness the slender blank of an ancient birth canal or an untimely grave. If she should come . . . if she should come . . . here would she claim her power and renew her spells; here would she sing to the Northern night and grow strong again.

And here would she think of me. It was with supreme effort that I tore off my riding brooch and placed it in the hole. In the flickering light the barest suggestion of silver betrayed its presence. The amulet would bless her altar with my energy and so she would know that I had been here. A dirty trick, I'll admit, but one born of desperation. My hand was light as a dying crocus, light as a lover's hint. My wrist plopped back on the sand like a dead thing. My brooch was a waning moon in a meager sky. It was my life for her to find.

After placing the brooch on the altar I noticed that along the wall to my right were some large storage chests which I guessed contained the old man's meager possessions. I suddenly realized this was the northern wall, and the thought sent my body into uncontrollable spasms. At the sound of my moans the fisherman, with some difficulty, dragged the table away from the fireplace, letting the light and warmth from the south wall engulf me where I lay. "Cain't do much more fer ye, evil one from the south. Like I said, Isulde ain't here, an' I ain't much of a healer. It's a nine-day wonder ye journeyed this far past the Drumuns and kept any life to ye."

The pains had returned and I was rolling on the floor, clutching handfuls of sand in agony. He sat in a rickety chair by the fire and spooned porridge into his mouth, watching my convulsions.

Every cleric, no matter what his moral or spiritual alignment, learns early on how to protect his body from magical attacks. A priest's body is a living temple of his deity. Beyond a certain level of training, a true priest's health depends as much on acting in accord with his deity's demands as on diet and exercise. But nothing I had learned in the service of Hecate was of use to me here. So I went back in my mind to a time before I became a priest and an adept at destructive power.

And what I found was that when I was a child, before I ever dreamed of Isulde or studied magic or knew anything of the gods save what nature told me, I suffered from deathly headaches because I loved beauty too much. Flowers were beautiful and so I loved flowers, and my love grew into a strange childish longing for the flowers to love me back. But every time I kissed a columbine or dragontongue, hoping that I could lick its colors into my dreams and that just that once the flower would sing and bloom and dance for me, the thunder-pain and nausea would roll through my body, menace me away, and reduce all loveliness to a grimy hallucination. Then one summer, sick with love, I made a blood offering to the fields around Sunnashiven. I sat among new flowers and dug a hole in my palm with a pointed stick and chanted a poem I made up as my blood ran into the ground, forcing my clumsy images through the flowery bursts of pain my childish love of beauty always seemed to bring on. The flowers did not love me, but when I kissed a day lily at the end of my poem my headache vomited itself into the ground, and as my head cleared I felt the bright and empty sky embrace me where I lay. Perhaps I once was a poet, before I knew better. I had used my own language, my first unwitting word spell, to stop my own pain. I tried this now.

Within three breaths I had succeeded only in making my feet numb.

But their numbness caressed them into a fine susceptibility to the fire's soft heat. The heat rose through my legs and torso and swallowed my head, bringing a light reprieve from the torture. I rolled onto my stomach and buried my face in my arms, desperately willing the pain to completely cease. My will has always been especially strong, but I could work nothing here. My anguish was merely dulled.

As the pain lessened I heard the fisherman scraping his bowl, followed by the sound of his chair creaking as if he was getting up to stoke the fire. I heard him settle back in his chair, sigh in annoyance, and grumble that *he* had not had it this bad his first time North, nor ever heard or knew of anyone who had. "An' I used to play with *fairies*," he said shrilly, banging his spoon against the table. Each bang made my liver fly into my mouth. He was clearly waiting for me to respond, and he would not let up his imbecile banging until I did. An evil cleric's liver tastes remarkably like owl meat and cardamom pods, which is what many of us dine on the eve before initiation. You have to rip open the owl yourself. I don't know where the tradition started, but it is not limited to Hecate's followers. Nearly all evil clergy follow it, even vegetarians such as myself, just as nearly all good clergy eat something equally unspeakable at their initiation. Anyway, when I spoke it was in the breathless woodwind shrieks of a tortured bird. My life was dancing out of me like a fuzzy baby owl in its death throes.

"Who . . . helped . . . you?"

"No one, boy. I played with *fairies*!" That was that, I guessed. After a short pause he added pointedly, "Fairies in the *south*!" I had no idea what he was talking about, but it was crucial to me that I understand. I was dying and he was my only link with Isulde. "Big fairies. Womankind. Ye know what they do. Hooo hooo!" I wondered if he was drunk, if it was indeed porridge he was drinking, or if porridge brewed from his Northern catch was naturally intoxicating. His supper clearly nauseated *me*, but that was no indication of how it might affect him. In or out of the North, a servant of evil must watch his diet as much as any other cleric. One priest's wholesome food is another's bane, and up here I had no way of guessing if the porridge was clean for me. Since I had been retching on my own food for three days, it probably didn't matter.

I waited for him to continue, but my patience was rewarded only with the sound of him rising from his chair again and swaying back and forth. I inwardly begged him to speak to me, to tell me everything he could about Isulde before I entered death. But my silent pleading turned my own throat to raw scabs and beetles, and he did nothing but hoot and bang his spoon.

If I hadn't been dying of my curse, getting him to speak would have been a fairly simple affair. It is a basic part of every cleric's training to calm and counsel in distress. We all know how to draw out the drunk, insane, and silent ones, how to entice people to speak their intimacies with us. We evil ones are less hesitant to calm an agitated person without his knowledge or consent than our good brethren are. Calm someone in a crisis and you make him ripe for conversion. Make converts and you rise faster in the profession. However, I am sure you will understand that in the present circumstances I was in no position to try any clerical magic. Merely hoping he would speak had turned my own throat against me. Actively attempting to influence him would involve drawing down my goddess's energy and invoking Her force through whatever conductive path I could create between my mind and his. The North Country is not the place for such magic because Hecate is a goddess who loves law and order and Her force tends to break up in the Northern chaos. I didn't want to think about what could happen to me if I tried to draw Her. A dying cleric is tender of his spirit, and I had risked too much of my spirit coming here in the first place.

Why did I come? The answer would be my doom and judgment once I brought it forth and owned it. Anyone with a farthing of magic in his shoes avoids the North Country like manticores avoid mice. Magicians such as Isulde who are *born* in the North bloom and thrive here, of course, but if your magic has another birth, the slow pounding of Northern energies will sooner or later wreak their havoc on you. Soldiers, merchants, farmers, fishermen—those who have no knowledge of magical arts—have little personal danger to fear past the Drumun range. An untutored woodcutter or a highly trained law interpreter, so long as he lives without magic in his heart and breath, will feel no ill effects here. Sure, he might see thistles turning into old men or onions into frogs, or hear colors arguing theology with the sunlight, or trip over a tree root and land back in his own root cellar. Such things frighten travelers and keep most folks south of the mountains, but such things do not kill. The ordinary traveler will not sicken and die here, except of his own fears.

Sometimes, though, the strength of the North is the strength of surprise. A merchant who never studied magic but has spent his life handling magical gems, a soldier who relies on magical weapons for survival, a child who pretends too earnestly at spells, might suffer here. Again, not to the point of death, but to various degrees of nodding acquaintance. Such people are also as likely to recover as to remain somewhat incapacitated during their stay. It is only wizards and clerics who are really vulnerable up here, but especially clerics. The closer you are to your deity the more you must safeguard yourself against outside forces anyway, because your power is in your god's protection. Yet nothing in the North is all that certain. I once read of a master wizard from Gondal who reportedly survived here for six months. The poor bastard did it with dandelions.

I once read a lot of things, none of them useful now. I was going to die . . . to die . . . to die . . . and none to know and heal me. I realized hazily there was a poem in that somewhere. Even Isulde, should she find my body split and wriggling, my corpse a hundred maniacal Northern fishes drying their gills before the southern fire, had no power to raise me from the dead, here or elsewhere. That would take a capacity for god energy and a formal discipline that no denizen of the North Country possesses. I wanted the strength of surprise. I wanted her to heal me. I wanted her to love me before I died as I once wanted the flowers to love me.

The fisherman was making buzzing noises. I turned my face toward him and could feel that the warmth in my mouth had reduced the beetles to sticky white eggs. I swallowed the eggs to clear my throat, threw up some white mucus with black buggy wings, and felt that I could speak again, although my head throbbed in seductive clouds of pain to express this new relief. I saw his mouth was ringed with purple, so perhaps he was drunk. I tested my throat with a moan, which came quite naturally and caught his attention. He sniffed and gagged in disgust.

"Yer ain't a fairy. Who ye be. Yer evil. I can smell it. Ye wanta woman. Ye wantsa fairy. Ye wasa fairy. I can smell it now. Bad!" He drank from a jug. "Ye die soon. I get fish."

"No doubt," I said thickly, then choked on my spit as he approached me with another bowl of porridge.

"Eats it down. Ye like. Ye wants. Good."

"No—" I lacked strength to scream loudly, and he had the loathsome mush down my throat and all over the front of my cloak. My gullet became a water snake, my heart a baby owl. When the serpent slid through my teeth my considerate host tripped over his feet and fell on me in fright. The owl's heart was now my heart. I told myself it wasn't real. It wasn't real. Nothing is real in the North. His fright was real. My pulse was a bird's—rapid and nervous and singing up a painful wind. My snake was a salamander. It found the southern fire and became a rainbow. My host slithered away in the sand.

And my language burned my tongue to half its size when I uttered the spell of revealing, "Ea Hecaatus somani caeribe." *To me, by Hecate, you write your heart.* By forcing his wretched sup on me he had placed himself at my mercy.

The North is a realm that loves not force. If I had tried to wrestle coherence out of him through magic, it certainly would have killed me. But since he had tried to force his will on me, I could bend his energy back on himself to prop up the spell without hastening my death by much. Simple mathematics. And I might score points with Hecate on the other side. Although under ideal conditions I would invoke Her blessing and power in the spell, the words themselves had an energy of their own that might be sufficient to waylay a drunk. I had no energy of my own to impart but I have always understood intimately the uses of words. His energy turned back on itself and he spoke. My tongue expanded to its former size, but my mouth began to bleed like his purpled lips. There is always a price for success.

"When I was a child," he began stupidly, haltingly, "I played with fairies."

"Yes, of course. Please go on," I said in my best nonjudgmental, clerical tone. If I could keep my voice this soothing, some of my monastic training was still worth something. How desperately my heart was cracking—the spell must hold.

He sat back on his haunches in the sand, a middle-aged puppy with eyes like moistening soil. "My brother and me" he grinned sloppily—"we used to like to fish, ye know. Back when we were kids." He wiped the back of his hand on his mouth and smacked his lips.

I waited. Nothing. The fire popped. *Speak, damn you, I'm dying!* "We're still kids, ain't we, brother?" I said softly.

"Yeah," he continued. "Weir kids in the river. We called 'em undines."

"An' we used to fish for undines?"

"When no one was looking. We weren't supposed to go fairy fishin'. We didn't have a license or nothin', and usually it wasn't legal. So we'd cross the river into the nomind's lands where they wouldn't bother ye."

Nomind's lands? He means unorganized territory. Where? It figured that his most significant memory was of lawbreaking. Laws are sacred to all disciples of Hecate, because laws are so easily used to strangle individual power into weak conformity and that is one aspect of Hecate's particular evil.

"Where were you born?"

"Near the river Kretch in East Angruk."

That's part of the Duchy of Walworth now. I smiled a little. Walworth was always one for laws himself, although he tried to hide it. I wondered what he would have thought of his own true love's foster father's proclivity for poaching, what he would have thought of the fisherman in general. *That* would have been a delicious meeting.

"We'd stolen some bass hooks, poles, the biggest ones we could get, ye know, we were just kids, and got them 'cross the river."

All the better to mangle undines with. I winced.

"An' we hid in the reeds like. An' we waited for dusk to see if we'd catch 'em singin'."

"And did you?"

"Yeah, we did. We did once! It was great." He wiped his sweaty forehead with his hand and smiled shamefacedly, like a tongue-whipped child afraid to say he likes something. But his voice was full of relish. I hated him thoroughly for that. The bastard didn't have to sound so enthusiastic. How in the name of Hecate and all that poisons joy had this dirty dim-witted son of an East Angruk ditchdigger gotten to hear the song of the water fairies when I hadn't even been able to get a flower to love me? I had been a sensitive child, too, with quite a fine mind. And I hadn't become evil yet. And I hadn't gone breaking laws. And I'd known how to love.

I should have been a high priest, or an archon at least, because despite the exquisite envy I was sampling I managed to keep my voice fluid and even. "And what did it sound like?" Being a lover of beauty I had to ask. I swallowed expectantly, prepared to interpret whatever confusion he threw at me, and thus die to something like fairy music. I was a swan. A black screaming swan.

The dolt couldn't remember the music but swore up and down it was great. I sighed and coughed. There is no justice. There is only fiction. Nothing is real in the North.

"We heard the singin' and we threw our hooks out." *Anything to spoil the cadence, the slob.* "Bein' kids, we didn't know." *How blessedly innocent. Was I supposed to applaud his ignorance? Excellent maestro; when I was a kid I "didn't know" either, but I never got to hear a fairy song, you bleeding jacka-napes!*

"And did you catch your prize?" I whispered kindly, while tears of outrage writhed over my bloodied lips like crushed butterflies. I knew from my studies what kind of damage fish hooks could do to fairy flesh. The child in me would have protected those beautiful, delicate creatures from such thoughtless violations, would have taken the hook in his own flesh first. I would have gladly drowned myself awake to hear such voices, not bait beauty with empty hooks like this half-witted cretin.

"I got pulled under. They caught me. 'Pretty boy' and 'lovercake,' they called me. 'Here's a golden ball to play with, from the frog prince to you. Here's a golden plate to share. Drink our sweet goo. Now eat with us and be our darling. Be our merman. Our luscious young man of the blue.' "

"And so you ate the food of fairy land?"

"They gave me candy and fins and told me I should be King of the Sandcastle. They called me sweet provender, and bale of good oats, and Bottom the waterbaby, and Tom o' the wisp, and said the caddis flies would sing for me every day and I would get great queens though I be none." He farted and belched.

"And did you . . . get great queens?"

"Ah—the womanfish, my mother, yes, she wrapped her soft white flesh between my legs, she blew bubbles in my nose and ears, she smiled upon my cheeks and licked my neck with her rough, dry tongue. I drank her clean milk and she drank mine."

I was now feeling faint and wet. I was losing consciousness and would soon die. In a voice of unassuming desperation I begged, "And Isulde, did she come soon after?"

"Isulde, yes, it was on the beach. They left me here, the sweet clean fishes. I cast my nets and wept for them. For years I wept." He sighed. Some coherence was beginning to creep back into his speech. "And one evening there was a little girl running to me on the shore, in the light of a full moon, rolling pebbles before her feet. I fostered her."

So this little girl was Isulde and she was indeed half fairy herself. Anyone who knew her would find the old man's story easy to believe, but I wanted more supporting evidence. The girl could have been an ordinary abandoned child, the old man's memories jumbled. *Question the source and die.*

I tried one last time to speak. The spell was thinning and my only hope was that his own drunkenness would keep the magic buoyant enough to impel him to tell me something more of Isulde. "Did you teach your daughter fairy songs when she was a little girl?"

"No, she knows 'em all already. She can sing 'em." He nodded his head in a curious gesture of awe and unearned pride. *I'll bet she can,* I thought ruefully, *and no thanks to your careful tutelage. Damn your eyes! If I had in my charge a student with half her abilities, her mind's growth would not be so abhorrently accidental!*

It was on the word *accidental* that my spell broke and I lost consciousness. Down went my spirit like a black feather falling in disgrace from the sun, helplessly yet logically drawn toward Hecate's portal.

And on my way to death I had a dream.

> *And somewhere in my dream a door opens and shuts.*
>
> *And somewhere a fine and noble voice echoes mine to ask, "Isulde?"*
>
> *And somewhere I am a bird of prey dropping closer to the portal. There is a scroll on the portal. There is an essay on the scroll. There is a poem in the essay and I tear the paper hungrily with my beak.*
>
> *A woman with three dogs, hunting dogs, bird dogs, gently opens the gate to let me in forever. She extends Her hand over the boundary. I perch there and croak something that seems to mean, "My love is darkness." The gate begins to close.*
>
> *And the voice that echoes mine comments wryly, "Then live and be damned."*

A violent surge split my chest and jerked me back to consciousness, where I hovered like a hummingbird between life and death, not moving too far in either direction. My eyes focused on a heavy sword poised sure and steady above my heart, a weapon I recognized, which caused me to raise my eyes with alarmed surprise to the cool gaze of its owner, the Duke of Walworth.

The duke's features were as steady and professional as his weapon of choice, but his eyes had an unnatural brightness and his brow was covered with the sweat of fever. I noticed his skin had a strange pallor and a soft smile briefly crossed my mouth in spite of myself. Walworth was a highly experienced soldier who had fought with and slept with and loved too many magical weapons to travel through the North Country unscathed. The North wouldn't kill him, of course, but it was having its effect. The magical sword he was holding me with now could not be healthy for him, and it was a rare event for me to see the duke look vulnerable.

Then I realized that his ability to use his weapon of execution to draw me from the point of death was a measure of his extraordinary skill and competence in everything he undertook. Only a highly superior, exceedingly disciplined fighter, perhaps only Walworth himself, would have the requisite skill and willpower to perform such a feat with a weapon created for other uses, and to do it in the confusing swarm of Northern energies no less. And the duke was clearly ill. My smile faded into an expression of utter neutrality, but I knew he could read resentment and envy in my eyes. Somewhere in the shadows the fisherman was clapping and howling, a drunken audience.

The duke's control of his weapon's power never wavered, but the noise drew his gaze to Isulde's altar, where he saw the gleam of silver from my brooch. Keeping the sword perfectly poised above my heart, he deftly released the moon from its hiding place and tossed it onto my chest, saying evenly, "Yours, I believe." He smiled with quiet amusement and added with pointed courtesy, "I should hate for you to lose something so valuable." I must admit, from a purely aesthetic perspective, it was touching to hear him admit his own weakness and love for Isulde in such an elegant turn of phrase. He actually feared having a conduit for my energy on her altar.

Anyway, I was alive now and my enemy and liege lord was responsible. I even felt the power from his weapon imparting to me enough strength to speak, although physical movement was out of the question. He acknowledged my condition with a gently mocking smile that shadowed his hardened, weather-beaten features. "You will not die unless I sentence you to death, Llewelyn, and I do not choose to do so yet. Even the meanest of my subjects is entitled to a fair trial before they meet the executioner."

"And you've ridden this far to give me one? I'm most obliged. Accuser, judge, and executioner at your service and pleased to make house calls. I shall remember this courtesy for the rest of my life, my lord."

"And so you shall." He sounded grave and concerned. "Be careful what you say, Llewelyn. You court your spirit's destruction to speak truth in spite of yourself. You could die blaspheming the powers you serve." A hint of smile softened the deadly earnestness in his voice.

"And high priest too? You mean I get a bonus? O lucky day!"

Walworth's face briefly softened to something approaching melancholy but quickly returned to its unyielding hardness. Once we had been friends. He was remembering. His sword arm swayed slightly but his weapon remained fixed. "Be careful. I move my hand a hair's breath and nature takes its course. I may be all that stands between you and damnation." His voice was most courteous and respectful.

He knew about the curse that had been laid on me in childhood. After all these years he remembered that as dedicated to evil as I was, I could claim no protection from Hecate in the North. My teachers had claimed they cursed me for my own "good," of course, to prevent me and any other young student with magical ability from hurting ourselves beyond the Drumuns if any of us was foolish enough to go. These were my earliest teachers, the ones who had charge of me before I adopted an evil alignment. The absolute certainty of dying here, which the curse ensured, was supposed to dissuade us from traveling to the North Country at all and potentially injuring ourselves. Not very logical, especially considering that Sunnashiven's citizens rarely traveled *any-where* and the North was little more than legend to most of us, but that was the sort of argument that caught people's imagination in Sunnashiven. And it provided work for the hack wizards in the school.

Speaking of catching one's imagination, for me the curse against traveling north was especially heavy because, except for very special circumstances, any cleric risked displeasing his deity and consequent damnation by willingly embracing death. My body was still Hecate's temple, and I *had* come here of my own accord. Not to mention how vulnerable I was in the North Country as a dedicated priest. Walworth looked at me with steadfast pity, as if he could read my thoughts.

"Bring me a vessel of hot water," he commanded the old man. The fisherman staggered over to us with his wine jug. "No, get a clean pot and fill it in the lake." Our host smiled dopily and disappeared. I heard the clang of metal followed by the door opening and closing.

"You should have asked for the house special, my lord. Our host brews a most excellent mush, one I'm sure you can't get at home."

Walworth grimly surveyed my cloak, quietly appraising the damage the fisherman's sup had done to me. His expression was severe. "Save your speech. You haven't the strength to waste on banter now and I'm losing patience. Remember, you'll need your tongue to plead your case tonight."

He had correctly assessed my condition. My last outburst had resulted in an explosion of weakness across my limbs, and it was all my enemy could do now to keep me conscious.

So we waited in silence for the fisherman's return, forming a most curious tableau. A young man dressed in clerical black lies helplessly before the altar of his love. His riding clothes are drenched with blood. The moon wanes upon his breast. A tall, imposing figure skillfully holds the younger man's life at sword point. His riding clothes are drenched with the sweat of fever, but his bearing is one of suprême discipline and his face is a study in concentrated attention. A tower of grace sheltering a black, crumpled wind. It is a broken flower that loves an ill moon.

It seemed like hours, but it could not have been more than a minute or so before the sound of the door told me that the fisherman had returned. The duke commanded him to warm the water over the fire and to do whatever he could to keep the flames blazing at their full power all night. The old man must have obeyed him because I soon began to realize that the room was growing warmer, although the heat was not helping me any now.

"There is a legend concerning kingship, Llewelyn, one I am sure you have encountered more than once in your studies. You have read of the peasant-king Aru, who banished the corn blight and became first true king of Arula, ancient capital of Gondal. You have read of the witch-queen Melga, who saved her people from the plague and became their first true sovereign. 'A true king is a healer' is a commonplace. What is not so common, and what learned scholars like yourself understand, is the meaning behind the legends.

Aru banished the blight so the corn could grow as it would. It grew more abundantly, so legend honors him for feeding his people. The truth is he freed the corn. Likewise Melga is honored for bringing prosperity, but the truth is she freed her people from sickness, and so many of them prospered of themselves."

He paused to glance toward the fire and then returned his gaze to me. "I have no reason to free you of your curse or to save your life, even if such a feat lay within my skill. But I think I can prolong your life a little, enough to let you speak your case. Do you consent?"

"With all my strength," I said wryly.

The fisherman came over to us with the steaming pot in his bare hands. I wondered at his flesh not burning and decided it must be another Northern mystery. He placed the pot in the sand near my chest and sat on the ground. Walworth tossed him a small brown leather bag while continuing to keep his sword motionless. "Empty the packet in the water." He did so and I could smell monkshood and kingsfoil. "Now stir the mixture with a burning stick." The old man sighed, went to the fire, grabbed a wine jug and then a stick, and returned to stir the brew. The odor grew increasingly pungent and I could feel a little strength returning already. "Now fill a small bowl and give it to him to drink. Do not sample it yourself. It isn't wine, and monkshood's a poison."

The old man put a little mixture in the mush bowl and held it to my mouth. I drank. Monkshood was Hecate's plant and I usually considered it a treat, although it was deadly for most folks. Kingsfoil was a healer and usually made evil clerics like myself slightly nauseated, but here the medicine appeared to be working. My sickness lightened considerably. Walworth noticed the change and firmly placed the point of his sword in the ground. "The effect will be temporary, but there's enough to get you through the night should the discomfort return. Also know that the more you drink the less effective it becomes. You are still dying, and your illness is still devouring your body. I've merely slowed it down a little."

I sat up slowly and once again noticed his fever-flushed skin. "Have some monkshood, my lord. Make a new man out of you."

"I'll live." This was probably true, all things considered. He smiled in cold appreciation and settled himself comfortably in a chair, his sword within arm's reach. "I, Walworth, Duke of Walworth and King of Threle—"

"King of Threle?"

"I won the war."

This was not encouraging news. I had hoped that he'd crossed the Drumuns to avoid capture or execution, to find Isulde and live in safe obscurity. When I'd fled from his duchy his side was losing. He continued, "I, King of Threle, do hereby charge you, Llewelyn, priest and scholar, with high treason against my person and people. To wit, with aiding Roguehan, our enemy, with using priestly arts to influence my critical judgment and that of my generals, and with the death of my cousin, Lord Cathe. The penalty for sabotaging our national defense is execution by the method of my choice. Do you wish to plead?"

"No, my lord. I wish to state that the border of Threle lies considerably south of the Drumuns and that the North Country has never had a ruler. I suggest that you have no authority to try me here, king or not." I succeeded in making my voice sound bored.

He seemed to consider, but I got the distinct impression that he expected this argument. "Man," he addressed the fisherman, "do you owe allegiance to any liege lord?" The fisherman looked uncomprehending. It was clear that the only allegiance he knew how to offer was to his wine jug. Walworth waited for an answer. The fisherman drank. "Who is your king?"

Our host waved his jug around. "The king of the fairies . . . no king at all . . . we are a free people."

"Then you are free to sell me your dwelling?" The duke tossed him a gold coin.

"Your currency has no value here," I objected.

"That coin has much value in my country, and it is our host's right to determine what the value be to him." Our host held out his hand again and Walworth tossed him another coin. "You can travel to Threle and live handsomely on those."

The fisherman looked at the coins and nodded dumbly.

"A match. Then I, Duke of Walworth and King of Threle, do declare this, my lawfully gained property, to be part of the Duchy of Walworth and under my sole jurisdiction." He looked gently at the fisherman. "You have my leave to remain here for as long as you please." He removed his sword from the sand and clapped him on the shoulder. "I appoint you seneschal of this property. Saving myself, here you are lord."

The old man murmured, "Lord."

"Good. I trust that takes care of your legal objections, Llewelyn?"

I was silent.

"The seneschal can stand in for a jury. With his consent, of course." He glanced at him and saw that he was almost passed out. "In the event that the jury cannot render a decision, I shall. Let us proceed. Do you wish to plead?"

I still refused to speak.

"Know that the court will allow you to plead your case. Because your life could be required, it is nothing less than your life that you may bring before us. You may tell us all your story and we will listen. You may also require us to relate our evidence against you." He waited.

"My life is little more than that yellow candle's, my lord. Because it is already forfeit, I have no desire to spend my last hours listening to your accusations. Yet I would satisfy the court's sense of fairness and plead my life if my lord would consent to a dying man's request."

"Which is?"

"If you find Isulde, you tell *her* my story."

"If she dwells on my soil, she shall have access to the trial records. That is Threlan law." He took writing materials from a large pocket inside his riding clothes, set them on the table, and held his pen like a second sword.

And so to this extent the law was on my side. I must tell everything for her. I might reach her through this absurd performance.

Settling myself comfortably back against the sheepskins, I looked boldly into the coolly questioning eyes of my enemy and began to speak my heart.

*S*et this down for judgment, my lord.

My earliest memory is of the witch who lived next door to my parents' house in Sunnashiven. Her name was Grana and she created my childhood out of sadistic fictions. I believed in her darkly, for her tales were wide and strange. I suppose I believe in her still, between my reason. Because even now, as I lie here dying on my own words, I choose to begin my tale in the voice of my childhood, as if I were once again beginning my life, as merciless and true as Grana once began it.

*G*rana was older than summer. She told me once that she used to keep the sun in her cottage at night and charge him sixpence for the privilege of keeping her bed warm. If he didn't pay, she made it rain the next day, and the day after, until he made good. And thus her garden grew. Grana always had a few warm coppers around to give me, so I began to like the sun very much and longed to meet him. Grana said the sun at night was not for little boys to see.

Grana also knew the north wind and got all the witch gossip from him. She used to keep him in her cookie jar when he came to visit, and once she let me hear him sing with delight as she shook the jar. "Poor man doesn't get many treats," she declared. "Be careful, Llewelyn, or he'll eat your bones." When the wind wasn't there she'd let me help myself to cookies. They were always sticky and cold and froze my teeth, but I didn't know better than to pretend that I liked them.

Grana had a cat named Grana and a goat named Llewelyn. They were just for us, and also had different names that I used to forget. When Grana showed me how to pet them they felt rough and shuddery. And when I was alone they turned into a dirty secret I felt afraid of having.

She also had a pack of dogs that lived in a big hole in the ground, but she said they were the dogs of the moon and I mustn't go near them. I was very much afraid of that hole and never did go near it. At night I lay in bed trying to keep my mind a blank lest the dogs of the moon hear my thoughts and come after me.

One night I went without supper to bring Grana some mutton to give to the dogs, hoping to get on their good side. She said she would tell them that the offering was from me. She also said she was sure that they would remember me for a long time. The next day she told me that the dogs liked my mutton very much and had told her to tell me to bring more whenever I could. I never ate mutton again, but eagerly brought it all to Grana, who would warm and spice it over the kitchen fire. She had to taste it for the dogs, she'd say.

She also taught me letters and symbols and let me read in her books. I learned to write *Grana* with double stars and to write the names of all her cousins the water sprites with *X*'s. But I was never allowed to write my own name lest the gnomes find it and eat it. We used to make up stories together, and anything I said was already in the book, which she told me was a gift from the gods and which someday I should use well. I was unused to gifts of any sort, so I was quite proud of having a "gift from the gods," even though I had no idea what a gift from the gods meant. But I did know that when I was with Grana I learned to think of myself as special.

We also had pictures to play with and a crooked mirror that told me my future, but I always forgot. The pictures scared me a little. A woman with horns was the priestess and that was me when she stood on her head. A woman pouring water would grant my wish but I mustn't wish too much or she might go away. A little boy hanging with the rope in his hands was me too but I mustn't touch the rope.

When the moon was dark Grana would go away on marvelous journeys that left me half enchanted and half in awe. Sometimes her dear friend the elf queen desperately needed her to check on last week's rainbow, who was ailing, or some powerful mountain wizard needed her advice on making magical jewels. Grana could raise exceptional storms, and so she was in much demand among the sylphs to teach their children her tricks. She knew the sylph king personally and often had a place of honor at his parties. She was also a dutiful daughter and frequently brought tea and oranges to her ancient father, a crystal cave in the North Country. She knew how to fly, and when the gods' messengers were especially busy Grana was happy to serve.

She would promise me all kinds of gifts on her return, the anticipation of which always got me through her absence. But despite her promises she almost always returned empty-handed. The elf queen had clumsily broken the magic drum she was making for me and was most sorry, or the mountain wizard had gotten some unexpected orders and wasn't quite finished with my toy sword yet. Sometimes she would describe in detail the wondrous toys and baubles that she herself had found for me in her travels: a packet of incense I could burn to summon up anyone I'd like to see, bright painted birds that would fetch me any food or drink I desired, a piece of night sky to wear in my heart. But she always lost these things "along the way," or the gnomes would steal them when she wasn't looking. I grew to hate the gnomes.

Once Grana brought me real mermaid's tears in her withered hands, which she said resembled pearls. When she opened her hands there was nothing there but mutton grease. She said the tears must have melted, as they do out of water, but just the same I should be happy she had brought them, as they took her much trouble to get. It wasn't easy to scare a mermaid into crying but Grana had managed it just for me, so I pretended to be happy just for her. I also remember a soggy fly-specked box of fruit pulp we ate with moldy bread. It was so sweet I had trouble eating it but she said it was a delicacy from good King Aru's court and would make me strong, so I forced it down.

It wasn't long after I started starving myself to bring her mutton that she said, "I'm off to see the king of the fairies to tell him what kind of a boy you are."

"What kind of a boy am I?" I was a little curious but mostly scared that the king of the fairies would learn something bad about me from Grana's report and convince her I wasn't really special.

"A lucky boy. It's not every boy the king cares to hear about."

"What does he say about me?" I tried to sound carelessly innocent over my pounding heart.

"That he's saving many beautiful things for you that you shall have when you are older."

"Like what?" Maybe it was all right. Maybe this time the toys would even survive the trip home.

"Oh—" her old-woman voice got low and seductive—"like trees that bear golden apples so high you can't reach them, and bags of jewels so heavy you can't carry them, and a crown of lightning that only a great king can wear, and a wand of starlight that only a great wizard can use." She was stirring some brown lumpy syrup for one of the sylph children, who was ill. "And remember, Llewelyn, my friends the sylphs are making beautiful books for you. Such books as would make you long your life away," she breathed. "Open one book and taste honey, close it and taste salt. You like honey and salt?"

I nodded. She gave me some. As I licked a foul taste off my hands she continued, "And no book will ever have your name on it. They are only books made by other people for you to look at and admire. Oh, and I will bring you a magic cap from my very special friend the winter queen that will make you invisible to all." She scooped some syrup into two rancid bottles and left the rest in the bottom of her cauldron to cake.

"Can I come with you, Grana?" I was sort of excited now. It would be great to meet the king of the fairies. Maybe he would teach me fairy songs or show me how to make a flower love me.

"No, Llewelyn. If you don't stay here and mind my garden, the dirty gnomes will come and steal my nice mushrooms and eat all my gold!"

"Then I'll throw rocks at them and kill them down!" I stoutly proclaimed.

"No, you won't. Killing gnomes with rocks is like swatting mice with a broom. They always come back stronger and someday they'll find you in bed and nibble off your feet." She showed me where the mice were gnawing hers. "You know what you're supposed to do."

"Let them nibble me to nothing so they won't get your gold." I was feeling brave lately because the dogs accepted my sacrifice of meat. Maybe Grana would think I was really special if I sacrificed myself on her behalf.

"Yes, that's exactly right." She nodded. "You're a smart boy." Then she put the bottles in a sagging wicker basket and hobbled away down the street, eyes brighter than a june bug's lust.

Llewelyn's stealing food!" crowed my sister Trenna. "I saw him put meat under his shirt." I had seen her stealing apples the other day, but since it was outside I couldn't say anything. Not that telling a tale on Trenna would have earned me much in the way of justice. My family pretty much ignored or hated me, so in return I pretty much ignored or hated them. Only Grana made me feel important and loved.

My mother, who had just been complaining of having nothing to do, lifted my shirt and saw a mess of grease. "Llewelyn, you've burned yourself and ruined your clothes. Now I have to wash them! Whatever possessed you to do that?" She sat back down and looked fierce. "What are you going to do now?"

"Put butter on the burn?" I said hopefully, remembering that Grana had taught me a song once where someone cooled a burn with butter—or was it that someone burned with longing for butter and died in the vat? I couldn't remember.

"Put butter on it and make your shirt worse?" She shook her head and sighed in exasperation. "Never mind about your damn burn. Give me your shirt. Now I'll have to wash again. Your other shirt was covered with grease yesterday too." I took off my shirt, feeling violated and worried. Even when Grana went away I always managed to leave an offering inside her garden gate when I went to mind things, just as a gesture to the dogs. What would happen to me if I forgot? "Look at your burn—that'll hurt for a week. I hope you're happy."

I wasn't, of course. I missed Grana, who promised me good things and never yelled. *I'm a smart boy—how dare they treat me like this? Wait until I get the wizard's wand Grana promised me. Then I'll show them.*

My father said nothing but continued to shovel food in his mouth. Even though he never let us forget that he was an undersecretary to King Sunnas and privileged to speak on all sorts of great matters at court, he never had much to say at home. Not that he ever seemed to notice much at home, but I always took my food with the horrible tightening fear that if he did notice me, I was sure to get punished for it.

Trenna delicately cut her bread into little pieces the way she'd heard the ladies at court did and slowly ate as if she were really one of them at heart and someday would marry a duke. She had a certain annoying air of being quietly justified for something through my downfall. I wanted to slap her but contented myself with kicking her chair and causing her to drop her food back on her plate. "Llewelyn, stop it!" she said in her habitual raspy voice. "Look what you've done!"

"Stop it Llewelyn!" barked my father, who clearly had no idea what I'd done but was finally disturbed by the commotion.

"I didn't do anything." Which was true in the simple way I thought about it.

"Well, stop it anyway, whatever it is. It's clear you're the troublemaker tonight. Where's your shirt?" he asked suspiciously. "Did the gnomes steal it?"

"Llewelyn stole food under his shirt and got it all greasy and now Mother has to wash it," offered Trenna eagerly. Now it was my mother's turn to act all quiet and justified, since Trenna had done her work for her. She waited expectantly for my father to punish me.

"You stole *what*?" My father's eyes bulged and his voice squeaked a little with panicked authority.

My mother waited for Trenna. "He stole food." Trenna offered no further explanation this time, knowing my father would think the worst without one. She kept softly chewing her bread as if she didn't care. I kept wanting to slap her.

"You stole food from where?" My father was not particularly bright, which didn't make his fits of authority any easier for me to bear. His neck muscles bulged and his eyes got bigger than horse troughs. He clearly thought I had committed some crime that would jeopardize his position, even though it was Trenna and her friends who stole combs and apples from the market. She was wearing a comb now. The wrong way.

"Why don't you ask Trenna where she got her comb?" I asked sullenly.

"It's my comb," said Trenna.

"It's her comb," said my mother. "Her friends gave it to her."

"I don't care about Trenna's comb. Don't change the subject, young man. It isn't fair. Are you stealing food?"

"I took some mutton from my plate and put it under my shirt." His job out of jeopardy, my father looked slightly relieved, but I still felt as though my desperate gift to my private life, to the only part of my existence they hadn't dirtied up yet, had been violated.

"Well, that might be a stupid thing to do but it's not stealing. Your mother will just have to wash it." He started to drift back into his perpetual fog but dear watchful Trenna wasn't about to let that happen.

"He brings it over to old Mother Grana's. I've seen him leave it behind the gate."

"Mother who?" His attention was back, however temporarily. "Who's that?"

"The old woman who smells funny and lives next door. I've seen her picking the ditches near the market and stealing combs." He mumbled something and closed his attention, but Trenna was rewarded with my mother's interest while my sense of violation sank deeper in my gut.

My mother prompted, "You mean in that rat-infested dung heap that ought to be burned? It always smells like shit when the wind blows." Her comment felt like a direct attack on the only beautiful thing I had ever had to believe in, and it gave me another reason to hate her ignorance.

"That's because she has this big pit outside she uses as a privy. I've watched her."

"Trenna, that isn't nice."

"Well, I can't help it. It's out in full view." My mother found this funny. "Besides, Llewelyn goes over there all the time, even when she isn't home. I saw them eating mud pies and grass last week."

"Is that how you got all muddy? What do you *do* over there?"

I was grateful that the subject of the meat had been forgotten, but resentful that my secrets were being pried into. "I don't know. We play." I hoped she'd be satisfied with that. The details were mine to cherish, and I knew instinctively that the more she pried out of me the less my experiences at Grana's would be mine. Once my family chewed over my poor private affairs I would feel dirty returning to Grana, as if Trenna and my mother would be looking over the garden wall and commenting on everything.

"I've seen them whirl each other around like a May dance in the weeds. Llewelyn couldn't do it right and he fell." My mother laughed approvingly. Any reference to my shortcomings always made her feel comfortable with herself again. I hated Trenna. It wasn't a May dance. Grana had promised me a ride to the sun so I could help drive his horses. Turned out I was too heavy to get farther than the cottage roof.

"Llewelyn, I don't think it's right for you to go May dancing with an old lady. You're too young. You shouldn't be over there bothering her at all. Why don't you leave her alone and play elsewhere?" Leave it to my mother to mask her fear of anything different with concern for others.

I had to think of something practical to justify my visits to Grana or the dogs might get me. Simply playing wasn't enough. I was forced to save myself by throwing out the best part of my life for them to pick over like vultures. "She's teaching me to read." My mother looked as though she didn't understand, which I took as a sign of disbelief. I had to continue to justify myself. "She's a witch and she knows how." Perhaps that would impress them into silence.

It didn't. Her voice was sarcastic again. "Llewelyn, she's not a witch! A witch wouldn't live in a dung heap like that! What's the matter with you?

Do you think a real witch would have time to go prancing in the weeds with a child like you? And teach you how to *read*?" Even though she had just laughed at Trenna's description of Grana, the thought of me having anything to do with a real witch threatened her. If my mother was too lazy to aspire to an education, it was just as well if I didn't consort with more motivated people who had. She might have to talk to one of them someday and then what?

I had to prove myself. I ran from the table and picked up one of my father's books, which was strictly against the rules. Opening it at random, I tried to read aloud, while my mother looked horrified and my sister looked pleased with herself. To my great embarrassment I recognized only a few letters on the page, but I bravely tried to pronounce them. Nothing came out but nonsense. My mother smiled and said sharply, "I thought so." I had made a fool of myself, so her world was right again.

When my father noticed what was happening, which took him a few minutes, he grabbed the book away. "What do you think you're doing? *You think you're smart?* Huh? You think you're smart? You know better! You want to burn the house down or send us all to fairy land? What are you trying to do?"

"Show I can read," I mumbled, feeling humiliated beyond their wildest hopes.

"So now you think you're a wizard. Think you can just pick up a book and read like a master. Why should I send you to school? You know it all already. You'll teach us! And if the house turns into a bale of hay or a bowl of sugar, you'll be happy then!"

Actually I probably would have been at that point.

"Oh, Sirle," broke in my mother, who could now afford to sound charitable. "That isn't a magic book, is it?" Her eyes sparkled with anticipation and her voice sounded hopeful that he would say yes and confirm the great danger I was placing them all in.

"No, Lenna, but any word can be mispronounced to sound like a magic word and any book can be dangerous in the wrong hands." My father knew nothing of magic but he liked to preserve his own sense of importance and he found my mother easy to fool. Even at that age I had a vague sense that he overplayed himself, but I had no way of knowing how. "Whatever possessed you to try to read?"

Trenna had been silent too long. "He says Mother Grana is a witch and taught him how."

"Mother Grana ain't no witch." He shook his head. All of a sudden he knew all about her. "She must be about ninety-five years old. I see her standing in the dole line every month, trying to sell handfuls of dirt out of her basket. She's the one been going up to my buddy Hara the guard and trying to see the king, claiming to be his mother or his aunt. Goes around saying she's the city's mother too." He laughed sharply. My father was always afraid to really laugh. "Llewelyn, you think she's a witch? Real witches have jobs and training. Real witches are out there healing kings and helping court wizards make the sun rise. Real witches write books and teach in schools. Grana ain't no witch. What are you, stupid?" I felt sweaty and shamefaced. Worse, the only thing I wanted at that point was to be next door sharing a story with Grana, but my want was now coupled with a strong feeling of guilt for wanting anything I might enjoy. My complex feelings dissipated into a general hatred of everybody.

"Well, Sirle, the boy's never been to school. You keep talking about it."

"He's still young."

"He's ten." My mother didn't so much want me in school as she wanted to argue with my father about sending me to school. She knew there was no possibility of my going anywhere yet.

"Well, what do you want me to do? Only nobles go to school that young. I can't just put him in until he's at least twelve. You think I'm a count made of gold pieces to put him in so young? You want me to lose my job through arrogance because Llewelyn thinks he's smart? You want us *all* to starve?" My hatred turned back into guilt, not over the possibility of my family starving but over ever having thought of myself as smart or special, even in the humble privacy of my heart. After all, I wasn't a noble and I wasn't in school.

My mother knew all my father's arguments but had to keep it up. Sometimes it's hard to let the feeling go. "Well, you could do something. *You* could start teaching him." She also knew that would never happen, and the question was calculated to irritate.

"When am I gonna teach him, Len? I haven't the time. There are food shortages all over Sunnashiven and the peasants aren't happy starving themselves to give up their meat and drink for the city dole."

"Well, if you were around more, Sirle—"

Now that the argument was picking up, I grabbed my greasy shirt, the mutton still in it, and made my way quietly to the gate, pausing breathless and shaken until I could feel the distance bringing in something resembling relief.

*I*t was to be our secret, Grana said.

I must have minded the garden well while she was gone, for I never even saw a gnome, and Grana was very pleased with me when she came back. She told me that all of her gold was safe, and that her mushrooms looked fresher and plumper than ever, although all I ever saw were the blackened toadstools under the juniper bush. She even gave me a unicorn's tooth disguised as a hard white pea, the kind that bruises princesses. And as a reward for my good behavior she was going to tell me a glorious secret, known only to herself and the king of the fairies. She had asked the king if she could tell it and he said it was all right to tell me but no one else. I was pleased and proud. She smiled importantly.

"I'm going to have a baby."

The only thing I understood as I clutched my gift was that something had been taken away and that somehow I was no longer good enough for Grana. "Why, Grana? Don't you love me anymore?"

"Yes, of course. Poor little fishie." She kissed me on the cheek. "Enough to want a smart boy like you to call my own and to let you help with it. I know how it will hurt you to fade away next door while the new bug takes your place, but that is the way of it, and you have made amazing progress in these things. Only a few months ago you started giving up your mutton to the hole each night to starve yourself in such a pretty way. Three days ago you decided to give your body to the gnomes to save gold you've never seen, such a boy as you are. Now help with a baby to take on your life and all's done and paid for. Wind up the charm. You are my sweet. You can do it." She was in a wonderful mood.

"Grana," I asked hesitantly, "can we give Trenna to the gnomes?"

"Trenna *is* a gnome, Llewelyn, and that is how it should be. But I see you are starting to learn, which is a very fine thing. I am most proud of my boy." She pinched some caked syrup from the bottom of the cauldron and put it in my mouth. "Candy mice," she said.

"How do you get a baby when you're so old, Grana?"

"With grass and bugs mostly, and the help of a smart boy to follow directions." She looked more tender than usual for a second and knelt down to my level. "Do you love the flowers, Llewelyn? Do you sing to them in the fields like you're supposed to?"

"Yes, Grana, but they give me headaches in the fields, so I come here to sing."

"My soft black bird. Sing and be merry. The headaches will end in a few years. Grana promises."

We spent the rest of the summer trying to help her conceive. Actually, it was Grana who did all the work. She grew the herbs, she made the potions, and I followed her orders and touched the drinking bowls with my hands. I also learned all the names of the plants and how to draw down the moon in a bowl of water without looking. By summer's end Grana told me she was pregnant and I mustn't ever come back to see or the baby would eat up my life. She gave me a few coppers from the sun to see me on my way and told me to eat well. My last memory of her is of an ancient hand stirring an empty cauldron.

*A*s I finished speaking of my early experiences with injustice I found myself glancing helplessly at Walworth's sword arm.

"Set this down also, my lord.

"I learned to hate punishment before I learned to hate anything else. Not because punishment is unpleasant, which is the reason most children hate it. I hated it because it was impersonal and therefore unfair, because it was never any clearly defined moral transgression that brought it on so much as my parents' incredible insecurities. If I demonstrated a hair's breadth of behavior contrary to anything in their narrow world, or chanced to let slip that I possessed anything resembling a definable personality, they needed to humiliate me to feel better about themselves, because humiliating a sensitive, intelligent child was easier than expanding their own minds and less threatening than listening to him plead his case. Like most Sunnans, they feared being responsible for their own lives, so they were going to make damn sure that I feared being responsible for mine. I grew up without ever feeling it was safe to claim ownership over my own existence, let alone over the tale of my existence."

I paused before adding slowly and carefully, "I never believed my words mattered."

Then I stopped speaking and studied Walworth's face to see what effect my words were having. Did *he* believe my words mattered?

My judge made no comment. He was good, I must admit. So far as he was concerned the game was still mine to lose, and my words—my life, I suppose—were still mine to tell, to prolong as I willed, until death from sickness or his inevitable judgment took me.

I felt the splendid pain of the Northern night press distantly beyond the healing broth I was drinking, and decided to return to the telling—assuming now a voice to match the tale.

*T*hree years later the old woman gave birth. The city records indicated she was over ninety, so nobody knew what to do. The city women discussed the event for weeks, the men looked frantically embarrassed when the women brought it up, and the king formed a committee to investigate.

The older kids made up dirty songs and jokes about it inspired by chaiaweed, dried flowers that were supposed to bring on visions or drunkenness or pleasant sensations—I was never sure which—when smoked in a hollow reed pipe. The flowers grew wild all over the city, and so when the authorities weren't poking into Grana's business they had quite a time trying to prosecute a pleasure they couldn't control. I remember that around the time Grana gave birth the bodies of a boy and a girl who had fasted for three days and smoked a good deal of chaia were found by a city guard outside Sunnashiven's northern gate. I also remember thinking with all the logic of childhood how safe chaia must be if only two people died out of the thousands who used it, how death came only if you were stupid enough to fast for days before smoking ten times the normal amount. But the government seized the ammunition it needed, declared that chaiaweed was deadly in "some cases," and poisoned all the city flowers. No one could smoke *any* flower without risking death. Three hundred people died. My father repeated the official line on how much progress we were making toward public safety.

Strangely enough, this summer of death was also the summer I chanted my poetry into the field and cleared my head.

But I also recall this summer as being overripe and deadly without the government's help. As if there had been a spill somewhere. As if the season were twisting itself apart, its hidden abscesses bursting open with the bloody pumping pestilence that fuels the underside of creation. Plague is nothing if not bright and insistent, and the colors that summer were ghastly bright. I didn't hear of anyone dying of plague, but it was a plague season nevertheless. Nature looked like a garbage heap, rotting and sickening her votaries with hues one chord above what should have been there. It was a ramshackle, crumbling kind of season through which I studied the cruelest spectacle of my early years—life's own machinery, insistent, bare, and wrought to the breaking point, achieving perfect god cycles at breakneck speed. That was the summer the strawberries bloated as soon as they formed, and collapsed into sagging skins and juice as soon as you looked at them. Wild grapes fermented on the vine. Flowers exploded in the seed. You could smell an apple rotting in your hand the moment you plucked it.

Outside the city the corn grew tall and plump two weeks after planting and while the amazed peasants brought offerings to the temple priests the corn rotted and fell to the ground for lack of harvest. The chaia came back after the poisoning, but a deep brittle red crept into the petals, something that never used to happen before first frost.

And everything else manifested a twisted fertility. The sky over Sunnashiven was pale and green for weeks, constantly threatening storms it couldn't produce. It leaned heavily over the ground and drew all the vermin out, more mice and bugs and rats than I'd thought the ground could bear. Dogs gave birth to puppies the size of young pigs, which promptly died. The sounds that summer were all wrong and premature, too. The heat was so oppressive that human voices were distorted like badly tuned lyres. If you paid attention, you could hear an echo against the city wall before you heard its source. Old men sounded like squalling babies. Women's voices cracked like the corn stalks falling to the ground. My own voice began to change, earlier than I had imagined it would.

My father would occasionally come home from work looking worried and complaining that the city wasn't getting its due and just wait until winter, the poor would suffer, but he usually lacked the energy even to mouth this much of the official line. My mother complained of having too much food to cook because she could find nothing else to complain of.

It amazed me that they could fail to appreciate the dogmatic weirdness of the season itself, but in this respect they were no different from anyone else in the city. The peasants in the countryside noticed, though, which is why there was actually plenty to eat after the first corn died. The peasants enjoyed several strange and abundant harvests during those months, and the court bureaucracy could not keep up with imposing taxes on everything for the dole, so they had plenty of corn to sell and the prices dropped. Even the poorer city residents could now afford to buy food.

I had long stopped leaving mutton at Grana's gate, or even thinking about her, but I had gotten into the habit of leaving my mutton on my plate untouched, my fear of the dogs having become a fear of some undefined punishment should I take too much food. No one seemed to care. I think perhaps that Trenna snatched it, for she often complained of growing fat, although in the context of the season it wasn't easy to tell.

At least, this is how I remember that summer. As I said, no one else in my family seemed to take much notice, and I said nothing because I feared the humiliation they'd heap on me for daring to imply that I had enough of a mind to observe anything on my own. Well, it wasn't so much the humiliation as having to endure the way my mother would take the only thing I valued, my intelligence, and turn it into a point of mockery, and nothing hurts more at a young age—or any age—than being mocked and reviled for failing to reach your ideals. Really, it makes you feel unworthy for life. I still remember the hot sweaty thigh-shaking feeling of being told in a sarcastic whiny voice, "You think you're smart? You think you know it all just because you've been in school for a year?" when the only private space I had to nurture a life that mattered was reserved for my intellect.

Trenna never had this problem because she never developed an intellect. She instinctively recognized that the easiest way to gain approval and favors was to become as ignorant as she was expected to be. By deliberately strangling off and killing whatever mind she once might have had, Trenna absolved her mother of her own uneasiness with life. My mother rewarded her sacrifice with a dirty sort of gratitude that passed for maternal love.

It was Trenna who saw the baby first, or so she claimed when the story finally reached even my housebound mother. It came in the form of some nonsense rhyme the local children were chanting in front of our house. Why they stood by our house I'll never know, but perhaps they feared going too near Grana's or they didn't recognize her dwelling for the mountain of weeds that now covered it and so they mistook ours for hers. Most likely they knew it was my house and were seizing the opportunity to taunt me. I had never been popular, and going to school at court made me the butt of a lot of the local children's jokes. Anyway, the rhyme went

> *Down in the market, down in the ditch*
> *Mother called Grana, called herself a witch*
> *Called herself a fairy queen, called herself a judge*
> *Called herself a merry queen, down in the sludge*
> *Had herself a baby, put it in a shoe*
> *Fed it lots of funny things and then named it Lew.*

Then they'd all run away, leaving my mother to ask, "Do they want something with you, Llewelyn? I thought I heard your name mentioned. Why don't they just come to the door instead of bothering people like that?"

Busy with my reading, I ignored her. I didn't know what it meant either but I knew if I spoke, I would implicate myself in the birth. Not that I feared the court officials investigating me, because maybe I would have learned something from that. I just wanted to avoid giving my mother anything she could use to make me feel wrong about myself.

"Trenna, do you know what that was all about? Llewelyn isn't speaking to us. He's too studious, I guess." Despite my strategy of keeping silence, my mother felt honor bound to lay on guilt for studying.

Trenna was quite the lady. "Well, Mother, that's what happens when you go to school. Just like Father." Trenna's bizarre comparison didn't make me feel any more confident about having a viable intellectual life. She had spent the afternoon leaning against the window waiting for the soldiers to go by. Somehow she always knew where they would be exercising and she always contrived to be there, which was why she was home for once. No longer able to read, I contented myself with pretending, which was not a bad state of mind to be in while the following conversation occurred.

"That old beggar woman who lives next door had a baby. Everyone's talking about it."

"What? Is she even still alive? I never see anyone over there. She must be close to a hundred."

"That's why everyone is talking about it, Mother. You should go out more."

"I can't go out with all the cooking to do this summer." She sighed a great martyr sigh, waited for some word of comfort from Trenna, got no response, and gave in to a curiosity made irresistible by her boredom. "How did you find out? Why didn't you say anything?"

"I've known about it a long time, Mother. Weeks. It's not the kind of thing one goes around talking about. It's disgusting, really." Trenna turned briefly from the window and looked pleadingly at our mother, clearly hoping she would ask her to talk about it.

"So you can tell *me*," Mother whined.

"Well, if you must know, old Mother Grana has been bothering everyone at market for months, asking for blankets and candles to consecrate her baby. Everyone laughed at her, of course, and Deeb gave her a corn-husk doll as a joke." My mother must have looked slightly disapproving because Trenna said, "Well, I didn't do it. I felt sorry for her, really. But it was kind of funny, because Deeb kept asking about the doll after that and Grana would kind of nod and blink and say the baby ate it."

"Trenna, you shouldn't hang around with Deeb. He's wild." She laughed as she said it.

"He's just a friend, Mother." Trenna always sounded so damn superior when she could claim friendship with a soldier. Never having trained for anything herself, she felt being around soldiers somehow made her as good as one, and she knew my mother at least would be impressed with her worldliness. "Anyway, three weeks ago Grana showed up at the market with a baby in her arms. She called it her goat and her kid and a thousand other things—piglet and filly foal and jack-in-the-shell and little prince and who knows what. We all thought she stole it somewhere because even though she had been looking rather big for a beggar we thought it was just fat, not pregnancy."

"Is she still big, then?"

"As a matter of fact, yes, absolutely bloated. You should see her breasts—like two pumpkins, and they give off this foul yellow milk when she squeezes them."

"Trenna! How do you know these things?"

"I just do, Mother. Everyone knows. The baby's about the size of a three-year-old already. Big and gray and lumpy. It really is disgusting."

"Aren't the authorities doing anything?"

"Deeb says there's a rumor that the temple priests are calling it a child of the gods and are going to raise it and give it an education. What else can they do?" she added cynically, glancing at me. "Oh, here come the soldiers."

Trenna positioned herself in full view in the window. I heard the loud steady *clop-clop* of marching feet outside and then a sudden unexpected silence. Trenna gasped and ran out the door. My mother turned to me, not ready to exhaust the topic yet. "Llewelyn, what do you think of someone going to school practically from birth? Marked already to be a temple priest? He'll get quite an education, don't you think?" she needled. "They'll make a smart boy out of him."

"I don't know," I said stupidly, quietly, noncommittally, trying to pretend now that I had no real interest in my book but had work to do nevertheless. I decided that if I could appear to be less committed to study than I actually was, my mother's stinging comparison between me and Grana's brilliant new child wouldn't draw the reaction she was looking for. She wanted me to show jealousy and thereby acknowledge not only my own inferiority but my own unreasonable desire, given the limited intellectual capacity she wanted me to believe I had, to be smarter than I really was. Her strategy worked because I felt an inner guilt and self-loathing anyway. I just covered it over in thin childish stoicism.

The sound of more passing soldiers gave me an excuse to leave for the shelter of my room, but my father walked in just as I was standing up.

He noticed me for once. "Where are you going, Llewelyn?"

"To do work." I couldn't get out of there fast enough. My stoicism might not hold. My room was a sanctuary for tears.

"You got work? What kind of work?" The question was an accusation.

"Reading."

"Oh." It was still news to him that I could read books now. He collapsed in a chair and my mother assaulted him with the question, "Sirle, did you hear about Mother Grana's baby?"

"Oh, yeah, the old woman who used to live next door. She's dead now, you know—"

Trenna ran in shrieking, "They're burning down her house! They're burning down her house! Come and watch!"

"What what what?" shrilled my mother, panicked at having to choose between two tidbits of news at once.

Trenna chose for her. "The soldiers are burning Mother Grana's house.

They've got torches and buckets of water to keep our side wet. They're using our well. Come and see!" She stuck her head back out the door. "Oooh, there goes her roof. Hurry, Mother, you'll miss it!"

This roused my mother enough to go to the door and look, but her attention was equally drawn to my father. "Did you say she was dead, Sirle?"

He slowly got up to join his family at the door. "Hara said they found her body in a ditch by the market this morning. Practically rotted away when they brought it up. Could be some new plague, who knows, but orders are to burn her house. We'll be all right, I'm sure." That was probably what they had told him. The news made me feel protective of my past relationship with Grana only because it also made me feel embarrassed. It was an awful feeling, much worse than something as clean as simple mourning.

"Trenna says the child is going to temple?"

"The child is huge. Looks nothing like a newborn. Might even be older, who knows? The priests have him now." I needed to be alone. The burning suddenly felt horribly personal and I was finding it difficult to breathe. The smoke was filling our house through the windows, and the doorway was blocked with Trenna and my parents. As I turned toward the back of the house I heard my mother ask, "And is he named yet?"

And my father absently reply, "Hara says they've given him an honorary title to designate his status as a child of the gods. They're calling him Lord Cathe."

"*Y*our cousin, my lord, the man I am accused of killing."

Three

*S*ix months before my seventeenth birthday the masters said they would be pleased to curse me. I was most happy to hear it, for I had worked diligently for five years to earn that privilege. Only the very best students got to be cursed, which was presented as a credential that entitled them to pursue the higher arts of wizardry. The preferred euphemism was "protection spell," but those of us who were smart enough to merit "protection" were also smart enough to recognize the spell for what it was. We were also flattered enough not to complain, and any uneasiness about the process was relieved through the laughter of false modesty. We were the chosen apprentices, far beyond our classmates in ability, so we could afford to laugh at the process while the others had to somberly prove their own seriousness. Being the only commoner who made the cut, I felt especially proud.

The process took all day, which was odd, because I'm sure I could perform an equivalent piece of work inside an hour or two, but government wizards are not the most efficient sort. Anyway, they put the six of us inside a small, barren room with no windows and left us alone. We joked with each other that the room, being so dark, probably doubled as an undersecretary's office. One young lady sallied that it probably wasn't so, as darkness could only improve the handwriting of her mother's clerk, and we all laughed a bit too loudly, to show each other that we were quite satisfied with ourselves and our new position. The solemnity of the occasion brought out an unexpected camaraderie for a few moments that I still look back on fondly, as the first time in my early years I could trace something resembling the workings of friendship.

That was exhilarating, the joking, because I had never been accepted as an equal among my classmates before. We were all going to be great wizards one day and I had visions of a stellar career in a famous court where I would hold mysterious consultations with my five classmates—my *colleagues*—on vital matters of state. The uninitiated would have to refer to us with grand mysterious titles in deference to our high distinction in the craft but among ourselves we would be on a first-name basis, enjoying that enviable familiarity among elites. I wondered how much longer I would have to address my fellow classmates as "my lord" and "my lady," and whether even now I could speak familiarly with them. Then I thought with satisfaction of how impressed my parents would have to be, and how even Trenna would have to show me some respect. After all, she was only a soldier's wife and had never even been to school. When another young lady, an earl's daughter, joked that she and I could put an illusion on the room to make it look like the king's chambers, complete with undressed king, I howled with delight at the novelty of actually being recognized and valued as one of them, even though none of us was capable of doing illusion spells. I even felt comfortable enough to notice how attractive she looked in the darkness by the light of her softly glowing robe. I was suddenly sure we would marry someday and be world-renowned wizards winning great battles together. I would even have a robe that glowed like hers. I confidently returned her compliment. "We could even put a disrobed Master Grendel in for good measure, that would scare the servants."

Everyone laughed loudly and it took me a few seconds to realize that Master Grendel himself was standing in the doorway with three chuckling master wizards at his side. He and I were the only ones not laughing. I was suddenly crushed with hot self-loathing at daring to go so far above myself and crippled with fear that my mother would gloat over my failure should Grendel throw me out of the circle. He was silently letting me know that as deep as my self-loathing went, it still wasn't intense enough to get back on his good side.

"Take off your clothes," he barked at me. Since I was the only one who couldn't afford a proper robe I had to go through the cursing sky-clad. Wearing nothing was considered better than wearing something improper. As soon as I had them off he threw them out of our circle with a look of disgust. The other students were too scared and impressed with what was about to happen to make any sign of noticing my nakedness, but I felt utterly worthless and humiliated before the softly shining lady of my dreams. Grendel drove that one home too by announcing that real wizards felt no shame of their own bodies and he had no intention of initiating anyone into the study of magic who couldn't control his feelings enough to avoid disrupting the circle.

I felt walls of blankness go up around the circle as we joined hands. No one was going to take a chance at being found out with the wrong feelings. I put up my own shaky mental walls and that seemed to satisfy him. The other three masters positioned themselves around the perimeter and Grendel walked around us with a white candle, muttering the traditional rune of opening. It was all quite hokey, actually, with all the usual stuff about the circle being the cosmos and the candle our protection and everything else you learn on day one. I would probably have dispensed with all that and gotten right down to it, but Grendel had to create work for himself to keep himself and his friends employed. When he got to the northernmost point he disrobed. I thought I heard a suppressed giggle from one of his colleagues.

"And so you are sanctified to the service of the great country of Sunna. Know that we bind you to the service of the state for the rest of your natural lives, a binding we exact as payment for your training," he droned. "Wherever you go, whatever magical arts you practice, you work for the glory of Sunna. And so, for your own good and the good of the state, we invoke four bans against your lives and enjoin you to know that death shall take you should you violate any one of them."

The wizard in back of me loudly yawned.

"One. You will not attempt any spell or divination requiring your full individual powers without our guidance and permission. The day will come when you may act on your own, and at such time we, and we alone, in council will decide to lift this ban. Until such time be wary of progressing too fast lest you become too enchanted with your own powers at the expense of what belongs to the state. To walk this path is death.

"Two. You must use magic only in the service of Sunna. To help another state is death. To work against Sunna is death.

"Three. This ban is related to the second. To help yourself is death, unless your ultimate goal is Sunna's welfare. It is death for the wizard to feed himself and death for the wizard to find herself drink. It is life for the wizard to save his life so that he might help his countrymen. Know yourselves and your own motivations in every spell you attempt.

"Four. It is death to travel beyond the Drumuns. Ye are novice wizards of the state and to the state ye shall remain wed. The North is a leaderless land and it is injurious to you now. The North is the land of chaos and it is death to you even now. We place this ban on you in perfect love and honor, to keep you safe from injury and to preserve you for our honor. Your powers are ours and it is death to lose them."

I felt the other three wizards driving the bans into us for about forty-five minutes, which I later learned was really more a factor of their officious self-importance and need to waste time than actual magical necessity. Under the right conditions a really good cleric could do the same thing in about fifteen minutes. Anyway, there was a good deal of chanting and candle waving and enough incense to choke a battalion of horses before they let us go. I don't remember feeling "cursed" or "protected" or different in any way except I somehow knew with pride that the spell had taken. I was special now. Initiated. Not everyone was capable of living, or could be trusted to live, such a guarded life as I would now have to under the bans. Although my shame crept back as Grendel watched me put on my clothes while the others left in silence, I felt the quiet glow of superiority spread over me when I was alone that night. I was now a novice wizard, of value to the state, and no one could take that away.

I suppose that is why it took me several months to admit that our "special training" was little more than elaborate repetition of what we had before. I finally had a reason to feel superior, and with the masters telling us every day how bright and talented we were it wasn't easy to give that reason up. The masters used our intelligence to justify their own slow progress with lessons, telling us we must review everything, everything, lest we forget one jot or one tittle of one half sound we'd been taught over the last five years. Since we were marked and banned and special and everything else we couldn't afford to forget things like ordinary students could. We had a responsibility to the state.

And so I learned little from my classes and had no contact with my classmates, whom I still addressed by title outside of school. Eventually I began to feel a little silly about the whole thing but I never let on. To my mother I was learning deep mysterious secrets I couldn't begin to explain. My father, of course, never asked and I wasn't even sure he knew that I was allegedly studying wizardry. Or else he was afraid to know lest I was acquiring enough of an education to see through his desperate pretenses at importance. Trenna came home only once. She sniffed at my books and acted bored.

Later, however, she contrived to talk to me alone outside. I was standing in the state-owned pumpkin field where Grana's house used to be, stretching my arms over the green earth and balancing on one leg, trying to look wizardly and to hear the vines stretching themselves toward fruition. There were food shortages again and I imagined myself as some unknown hero helping to make the fields grow for the good of the state. I was so caught up in listening for some affirmation from the plants that I got startled and lost my balance when she approached. I fell over and crushed the vines.

"Here, little brother, let me help you." Before I could protest in all my adolescent pride she had taken my hand. When she saw my look of annoyance she added quickly, "No, let me sit down there with you. I've always loved this place." She settled herself in the dirt, crushing three more vines with her skirt, and sighed as if she were full of appreciation for the natural beauty around us. I couldn't understand what there was to appreciate and thought that maybe I was missing something. It was an ugly patch. The weeds were already filling in one corner and the state had blocked off the property with a low wooden fence, which meant that from a sitting position we were not visible to anyone outside.

Trenna spent only a few seconds in her state of rapture before she suddenly looked at me, stopped sighing, and said, "My, what a man you've become since I've married and gone away. My little brother, the young adept of Sunnashiven's wizard school. I'm most impressed with you, Llewelyn. I tell all my friends about you. I really do. I hear you're at the top of your class. It's such a shame we don't see each other more often."

Since I had absolutely no feelings on the subject of "seeing each other more often," I felt a little guilty and confused, as though I had done my sister some wrong by not appreciating her. I had no idea of being at the top of my class but had always suspected this might be true, so I was willing to believe the absurdity of reports of my progress finding their way to the soldiers' station twenty miles east. It is wonderful to be flattered by one's own fantasy. Of course Trenna, who knew nothing of magic, would be impressed by anything I had done, and I was eager to let her know how special and adept I really was, just to soak in more praise. After all, she could not be aware of the tension between myself and Grendel, which was no doubt responsible for some of the aloofness on the part of the other masters. And perhaps the masters were all secretly impressed with me. However, the thought of Grendel chastened me a little, so I said in a voice that resonated somewhere between that of one who could do much if he chose and sheer terror, "It's nothing." That way, at least, I wasn't really boasting.

"Oh, no, I'm sure you are quite an adept," she said enthusiastically, reaching into her skirt and drawing out a small dry apple. "Would you like some fruit? Soldiers' families get first preference in times of shortage." Before I could answer she put it in my hand, and while my mouth was full she shook her head in wonder and said, "All those books and everything. The gods know I couldn't do it."

I was glowing but all I could think of to say between bites was another clumsy "It's nothing." I shrugged my shoulders and smiled jerkily at the ground, so uneasy in my pride that I was afraid to openly show acceptance of the praise she was giving me.

"Look at this, Llewelyn. My husband gave this to me." She dropped a plain gold ring in my sticky hand as I finished my apple. "It was engineered by a high priestess of Aphrodite," she told me dreamily. "Very expensive. If you wash it in rosewater when her evening star is visible, it brings out the best features of your own natural beauty, whatever they are. Dark hair looks darker, bright eyes brighter, that sort of thing. And if you wear it three days

running and throw it into someone's glass and they drink from it, that someone will love you completely."

There was a silence during which I felt she was looking for some response from me. I had to say something to show I was as appreciative of
her prize as she had been of my abilities, but I felt that to praise her ring
was somehow to admit that she had something beyond me and thus to
diminish her high opinion of my accomplishments. I asked with something
less than real interest, "Where did he get it?"

"I believe he won it at dice," she said. "It really works."

"You didn't look any different when you had it on." I felt mortified as
soon as I said it. I didn't mean to be peevish; I was just anxious about
proving my powers of observation and all I could think of saying was the
obvious.

"Of course not," she answered, and laughed pleasantly. "It's the middle
of the day, and I haven't washed it in rosewater."

"Oh, I forgot. I haven't studied much theology, and clerical magic is
outside of my discipline," I said defensively. I really felt stupid then. You
didn't have to be a high priest to know how sacred roses were to Aphrodite.
Trenna pretended my ignorance resulted from single-minded devotion to my
own arcane studies.

"Well, wizard, I'm sure you can at least feel the magic in it." She waited
expectantly, so I closed my fist over the ring and chanted the opening of an
identifying spell, which was all we had been taught in school. It *did* feel
warm, which was a sign of magic, but beyond that I couldn't go, nor could
anyone else in my class. It occurred to me afterward that I might have
violated a ban, but as I felt no ill effects, I gave it no further thought. Besides,
I was practicing to get better for my day of service. I returned the ring to
Trenna and said something intelligent like, "It's magical, all right."

"How clever! Llewelyn, I've got something else to show you. Tell me
what you think." She removed a small metal key with a red stone in the flat
part from her skirt and dropped it in my hand. I was still feeling the tag end
of the identifying spell and the key felt warm and then cool as the energy I
had summoned up dispersed.

"It's a magical key," I fumbled.

"It's a wizard's key," she said. "I know you know that. The kind that can
open anything."

"Where did you get it?" I asked enviously, resenting that Trenna, who
knew nothing of magic, had access to all these magical items and I didn't.

"My friends gave it to me. I don't know what to do with it, so I decided
to give it to you."

I brightened in spite of myself. A real magical item to call my own! I
had no idea if it really would open anything but it had to do something. It
did feel warm. "Trenna, are you sure?" I said to be polite.

"Of course I'm sure. I want you to have it." Then she added, "Promise me you'll keep it safe. Don't bring it to school or show anyone. It's just between us. Brother and sister."

"Well, sure," I promised awkwardly, overwhelmed with such an unexpected present. Why *would* I show it to anybody else? It was mine. "Thank you."

"Don't mention it." She stood up and hastily brushed the dirt out of her skirt. "I must go now, Llewelyn, Seth is waiting for me. But I'll see you again soon, I promise." I stood and she gave me a quick hug and ran toward the military wagon in front of our house, where Seth was leaning against one of the horses. Feeling more confident now, I waved at them and grinned and Seth waved back as if we really were brothers and not just related through marriage. Trenna got in the cart and they drove away. She made no effort to visit me again.

$\mathcal{I}$ never brought the key to school, but I did keep it in my pillowcase, along with the hard white pea Grana had given me and a piece of colored glass that I liked to look at. I saw no harm in going through the motions of impressing the key with my personal energy. It might make it easier to use later, once I figured out what I could use it for. And for that the library might help.

One of the privileges I had as a student of wizardry was unlimited use of one of the court's tower libraries. The other one was for clerics and their students and off-limits to us. The librarians were all idiots who constantly lost or misplaced books, but it wasn't a bad place to work once you learned your way around. I spent a lot of time there because I had no place else to go between classes and I rarely saw anyone else making use of the place, not even the masters. Besides, I would occasionally stumble across an interesting volume of history or mathematics or philosophy, which took the edge off the dullness of my classroom instruction. I got quite fascinated by philosophical proofs, so much so that I began to view class time as an intrusion on my real studies. Even though the library contained nothing really advanced, I learned enough from my casual reading to be able to outperform my classmates and show myself worthy of the honor of being educated in their school. My mathematics master even remarked once in surprise at how quick I was at finding the shortest geometrical proofs, a facility that would come in useful when we got to more advanced spells.

Which we never did, of course. Most of what I learned in Sunnashiven I taught myself and I learned to keep quiet about it lest the masters judge me overprideful in my own learning. There was a fine thread that divided superior classroom performance from superior performance generally, and I occasionally broke that thread to my own chagrin when I got caught up in some new idea from my reading. As long as I was proving myself equal to the lessons when my classmates weren't even bothering to study, the masters, including Grendel, seemed to quietly approve. My responses took up class time and seemed to justify the masters' own lack of preparation or to validate the abysmal level of their instruction, while my classmates' boredom indicated all too clearly their noble dissatisfaction with the masters' lack of ability. I felt many times that my abilities were used to defend my teachers' mediocrity, and I was a willing participant in the game. Anything to get that credential and justify my existence.

So after a while I began to feel a little nervous about spending so much time in the library, in case anyone did notice and decide that I went there out of purely personal ambition. I got into the habit of hiding in a corner behind a stack of books and listening with one ear for footsteps so that I could look like I wasn't working on anything too threatening should someone approach. This particular morning I had about three stacks of books around me, because was I was studying the library's worn copy of the *Wizards' Compleat Compilation of Magical Items* to see what I could find out about my new key and I didn't want to take any chance at being discovered. I had just determined that the *Compilation* was far from Compleat when I heard the door bang open and close, followed by heavy running footsteps and a soft indistinguishable sound of impatience as my table shook and one of my protective stacks of books crashed over. I slammed the *Compilation* shut and threw it away from me, which meant that I was now sitting there looking as though I was hiding with nothing to do. I looked up to see another student looking at me in surprise.

"By Ares' withered arm! I didn't know anyone was sitting here. Sea gods' granite gonads! I'm sorry! Here, let me get your books." She bent down to the floor and began loading her arms.

For the first time since the cursing ritual I laughed without self-consciousness. I'd never heard such language, even from the city poor who accosted me for bread crusts outside school and who were invariably threatening once I'd exhausted my slender supply. The incongruity of hearing such impious sentiments on the lips of another student struck me as wildly funny. All of a sudden the restrictions of school didn't seem real. I noticed her hair was hastily tied back without regard for fashion and that although her smock was finely woven, nothing except her absolute ease of manner marked her as anything but a commoner. She put the books on another stack, which swayed precariously under its own weight, and said seriously and earnestly, "I hope I haven't disturbed your studies."

"No, I'll certainly manage to continue," I said with a hint of self-importance. Then I collapsed a little. "Lady, is it?"

"Actually, it's General," she said proudly. I felt stupid, not knowing if she was testing my gullibility or if I should have noticed something. I had read about young military commanders, of course, but that was something for history books or princesses, and I didn't think she was a princess. Not knowing what to say, I said nothing.

"My father retired from military service and gave me his army so that he could give his full attention to the apple and wine trade." She looked at me as though I should have known that. "The growing seasons have been so strange for the past few years, in case you haven't noticed, that our county is suffering a bit of a depression." I must have still looked blank, because she insisted, "Apples and wine! Clion apples? The sweet kind that need a lot of rain? The legend of Clion, who planted serpents' teeth with his own blood and grew the most delectable multicolored apples this side of fairy land?" I grimaced involuntarily and she said, "Oh, I'm sorry. You're not an Athena worshiper or squeamish or anything, are you? My nurse used to read a lot and pray to Athena. Used to go berserk at the thought of killing snakes or owls, as she said both were sacred. I put a snake in her bed once— live. Didn't like that either. Want an apple? I have two pink ones. Best kind."

I started to laugh again, although a little uncertainly. The apple *was* delicious, fresh and pink like candied dawn, and I hadn't had really fresh fruit in months. She sat down nonchalantly on the edge of the table, swinging her legs and munching. A few books fell over. "It's the gods' own game getting them in here."

"Past the beggars, you mean?"

"No, past the librarians. The beggars I can handle. You roll one down the street—an apple, I mean"—I laughed, "and they all chase it and you run inside the palace quick. It's the damned palace librarians who won't let you bring food in the library. I swear by Venus's fat sow that Lady Justa looks for me just to confiscate them and eat them all herself. I put wormwood on one once, just to see what she would do. The next day she came in with a sore throat." I was beginning to like the general; I felt safe with her until I realized I could get expelled for eating in the library. The thought tensed me up and I tried to give back the part I hadn't eaten. "Don't you like it?" She sounded hurt.

"I'm a commoner," I was forced to explain, "and susceptible to punishment." I resented having to say this and jeopardize the friendly feelings that were starting to develop between us.

"Oh, posh, who cares? I give my foot soldiers more freedom than King Sunnas gives his counts. We'll just tell them you're under orders from me to eat."

She gave the rest of the apple back to me, so what could I do but take it? It would have been easy to dislike her not-so-subtle boasting about being a military commander, but she had such a pleasant, unaffected manner that I liked her in spite of myself. "Here, have another one before they go bad."

This one was yellow and tasted like a fruity mead. I couldn't get it down fast enough, and while I was thinking of whether I might ask her for another I noticed she had the *Compleat Compilation* in her hands and was browsing through it.

"You really understand all these symbols and stuff?"

"Well, not all of them," I said honestly.

"I wouldn't mind understanding even some of them, but not if I have to learn magic first. Wizards curdle my sword! I've never met a wizard yet that didn't look like a rat about to bite the cat's tail and win. That's why I come here where you never see them. Do you know Master Grendel? Every time he walks near me my apples sour. I'm serious. And Mistress Nage gives me the coughing fits. She's got eyes like a bug on chaiaweed. Witches are just as bad." My new friend made a face that sent me into paroxysms of laughter and she quickly hid the apples in case a librarian came over. "Oh, I'm so sorry," she said pleadingly while I was still laughing. "I didn't mean it. I see you're studying wizardry. How stupid of me."

"No, it's all right," I said between laughs.

But she continued, "I really have been rude. I forgot to ask your name."

"It's Llewelyn."

"You can call me Aleta. Since you're clearly a civilian I won't make you call me General. My father is Count Clio. My mother died in childbirth and I have no siblings, so I'm practically a countess already. We have a rather confusing history that nobody really understands, so we don't really belong to anybody," she boasted. "We even have our own language that nobody speaks." She sounded so earnest I laughed again and this time she joined me.

"As well as your own army," I said because I knew it would please her.

"Yes, my army, where I should be now, instead of listening to Mistress Nage repeat twenty times a day that soldiers used to carry kingsfoil for healing and chaia is bad for you. Bad for *you*," she said in a parody of Mistress Nage's voice, and stuck her finger toward my chest the way Nage did. I couldn't hold back my laughter if my life depended on it. "My father smokes chaiaweed and grape leaves all the time and nobody cares."

"And your soldiers?"

"That's where he learned it from. They call it *chana*, and it's more potent than anything you'll find here." She looked at me earnestly. "I really need to get back, Llewelyn. A general should be *with* her troops, not sitting at ease in some palace school. We had three raids against our orchards last year, so my father decided I'd be safer in Sunnashiven while the army looks after itself. Some strategy, huh?" Her good humor evaporated. "Sometimes I think he's more concerned about saving his precious daughter than about doing what's right for the land."

"Did your county repel the raiders all right?"

"Of course we did," she said defensively. "I led the first attack, when we were taken by surprise and my father didn't have the time to stop me. Killed three raiders." I was awestruck. She continued without noticing my reaction. "But then he sent me away. I get intelligence. I know the last two raids were successfully put down by our captain of the guards, the most capable Sir Perie, but *I* should have been there! I should have been there!" She banged on the table in frustration which finally attracted one of the librarians.

Since I was busily trying to recall what little history I had read concerning County Clio, so that I could have something intelligent to say to her when she finished, and I wasn't getting much beyond the doubtful legend that the area had once been settled by refugees from Glon, the tyrannical dwarf king, I didn't notice the librarian's approach. He caught me as I was starting to speak, so naturally I got the blame.

"And so the upstart boy from the wrong side of Sunnashiven is responsible for all the commotion." He whined the words in an irritating singsong voice, as if he viewed our conversation as a personal insult. "Is this how you repay our generosity? By hiding in a stack of books and making enough noise to fright the elves from fairy land?" I blushed at the allusion—not that Olin knew anything of my lifelong fascination with fairies and flowers, but some words have a way of hurting. "And you, Lady Aleta, consorting with him, a commoner. King Sunnas keeps distinctions and manners you would do well to learn." He grabbed her bag and emptied it on the floor. "I told you before! No apples in the library! They make a mess!"

Aleta, who was clearly still incensed by the thought of being kept away from fighting in her county's skirmishes, turned all her anger toward our persecutor. "Lord Olin, this man is not a commoner." He smirked but she continued. "He is a knight of County Clio and an official member of my honor guard."

"You have no honor guard here, my lady, and I know this boy for who he is. He is not one of your countrymen. But you certainly have interesting tastes." He leered at her breasts.

I thought she was going to kick him but she managed to control herself enough to say, "He is if I say he is and I just made him so. His name is Sir—" She looked at me, trying to remember my name. "*Sir* Llewelyn the wizard, and he is my servant and under my orders to pick up those apples." I was appalled, but I got down on my hands and knees and began shoveling apples in the bag so I wouldn't have to look at Olin. He was a duke's son and took himself most seriously as a court intellectual. I knew he would do his best to keep me out of the library from now on, and reading in the library was my only means to a real education. *Damn Aleta; she'd better be able to pull this off.*

Olin stomped on my hand and I cried out in pain. "I'm in charge of the library and I say the apples stay there!" He was probably planning to sell them on the black market himself, where they were worth quite a bit.

"And I'm in charge of my own servants and *I* say he picks them up. Not even King Sunnas would dream of interfering with a visiting noble's right to conduct her own affairs with her own retainers. I have diplomatic immunity."

"And I'm the king's second cousin," he began, but faltered, uncertain of his standing. I got the rest of the apples into the bag and gave it to her. "I want you both out of here now, and I don't want to see either of you here again causing trouble and disturbing people, for a long time." In my case that probably meant never. It didn't matter that there weren't any other people here. Good-bye studies. He roughly escorted us to the door, which he yanked open with a great deal more force than was necessary, and suddenly stopped in stiff surprise. There was Master Grendel on the other side, looking equally surprised at Lord Olin's pompous eagerness. Olin had to do something to deflect Grendel's attention, so he made his face smooth and inclined his head to me in quiet, innocent courtesy: "Good afternoon, Sir Llewelyn the master wizard of County Clio." He bowed low to Aleta. "Good afternoon, my generous Lady Aleta. I hope you can dispose quickly of your apples." Then he closed the door behind us and left us to our fate.

I could feel Aleta withering under the wizard's stare. She stared at her feet. If I could have died then, I would have gladly done so, but death wasn't an option, so I remained before him in a state of pure agony while he lightly searched my mind. "*Sir* Llewelyn the master wizard? Not much there, I'm relieved to report," he commented, probing and insulting simultaneously. "I should hate to think of County Clio being so desperate for help that they'd really hire you." He seemed to be disparaging Aleta as much as insulting me.

"It was all in fun," murmured Aleta. "I didn't mean it, and I didn't do it right anyway."

"I know that," said Grendel impressively, withdrawing his probe with a slap that made my head hurt. "My student here could suffer serious consequences if you had. Student wizards live under a ban not to help any foreign nation, no matter how friendly and well intentioned that nation might be."

Aleta went pale. "Llewelyn, I'm so sorry. I didn't know and it wasn't real anyway."

My anger with her was replaced by sympathy. "The ban is only against using magic. There was no danger, really. Was there, Master?" I mumbled, and looked at Grendel.

"Of course not, my lady," he said to Aleta with uncharacteristic gallantry. "But you really should take time to learn our ways. I shall recommend extra lessons with Mistress Shile." Poor Aleta! Mistress Shile would curdle *my* sword if I had one, and I was used to being around wizards. He looked in her bag. "Those apples *are* for personal consumption."

"They came from my father for me as a gift."

"The city poor might also appreciate them as a gift. Give them to me and I'll make sure they're properly documented and distributed." She reluctantly gave him the bag.

He put his hand on the door and said to me gruffly, "I missed you in class this morning. Don't let it happen again." He walked into the library with the apples. He probably wanted to extort money from Olin. I realized with alarm that he might see the *Compleat Compilation* I was browsing through and I walked away as quickly as possible to put distance between us. I had been so frightened of Grendel hearing me called "master wizard" that the thought of the key was knocked out of my consciousness when I met him, but I couldn't be sure what he knew now. What to do?

"Llewelyn, are you in trouble now?" Aleta interrupted my thoughts. "I'm so sorry. What can I do? Don't worry about the apples. I can always get more."

I quickened my pace even faster to get away from her, but she easily kept up. I spit my anger at her. "You have no idea what you've done to me, my lady. You might have just cost me my education and condemned me to a life of herding goats, but it's all one to you. You can go back to your army and estate." She kept following. I stopped and added coldly, "I must ask your leave to remove myself from your presence."

"Well, I said I was sorry! Herding goats! Don't be ridiculous. You're starting to sound like that obnoxious Lord Cathe, who always mopes around in such a wonderfully profound state of melancholy." She turned abruptly to go off to her rooms or something, but I was suddenly thrown into such an intense swirl of irrational fear that my anger was temporarily dispersed by morbid interest. I had not heard the name Cathe in four years, and even then it didn't seem real. Along with the fist of fear engulfing my body was the restless feeling of reliving a dream experience after having forgotten the dream. No matter what happened, I had to find out about this person.

"Lord Cathe?" I called. Aleta kept walking, and I felt my raised voice attracting attention to myself. I caught up with her. "Aleta, I'm sorry. I didn't want to offend you." She stopped and looked at me. "Who's Lord Cathe?"

"As if you don't know. You act just like him. You two would be great together." People were traveling back and forth through the hall and staring at us. I was terrified of being seen acting so familiar with her, especially after what had just happened, but I was more terrified of the name. I had to know more.

"No, I don't know. Please tell me who he is. Perhaps I should like to meet him," I pleaded.

"He's a prig the size of County Clio and Sunnashiven combined, that's who he is. He's not really a lord, either. The title is honorary, which is why he has to work extra hard at being a prig." A well-dressed lady looked us over with mild curiosity and kept walking.

"Please don't get me in trouble," I breathed.

"All right," she said sarcastically, "Nobody knows who the most honorable Lord Cathe is. There's a rumor that the gnomes stole him from the North Country and left him here, which I tend to believe, although you couldn't pay *me* enough gold to take him. There's another good story that he just appeared on earth four years ago and has aged into young adulthood already. That's what he likes to claim. He looks about seventeen and is a high priest of Habundia already. You'll see him skulking around the court-yard in the early morning pretending to bless the plants or whatever it is he does. He's quite impressed with himself."

Since I wasn't sure if this all applied to me on some level I said nothing. Taking my silence for anger, Aleta said stiffly, "It was nice meeting you, Llewelyn. May you prosper from your studies. I'm sure everything will be all right." She was off before she even finished speaking, leaving me to feel awkward and alone in the middle of the crowded hall.

---

*G*etting home was not easy that day, because my feelings kept causing my legs to give out and I was easy prey for the taunts and jostling of the street beggars, whose numbers appeared to have increased since morning. I neither ate nor slept, but spent the whole night going over and over the day's events and looking at my key in the moonlight. What did Grendel know? What would he do? Who was Lord Cathe? I had to see him, but the thought sent unexplainable paroxysms of fear through my chest. What would I even say to him? The whole situation was absurd. What if they didn't let me back in school? Even if I met Lord Cathe, would he say anything to me? He might not even *have* any connection to me. But those stories about him. Had he been around all this time without my knowing it? I supposed it was possible, as I had no social contacts either inside or outside of school to tell me of city affairs, and since the clerics kept very much to themselves in the temple, their affairs were rarely spoken of. I felt as though some dirty little secret I had nothing to do with had nevertheless been revealed and thrown at me for comment. I felt as though I had been caught in some crime.

With dawn came the resolution to try to find this Lord Cathe and see what he looked like. Not to speak to him or anything; just to see. So I grabbed my books and a little bread crust and headed out for the palace courtyard, where Aleta said he often went. There was nobody there, but I did notice that the flowers and shrubs looked exceptionally lush and beautiful, and even the pear trees were bearing fruit, although I didn't dare take any. After a while I got bored and began to read, but then the nervous anticipation of going to Grendel's class set in and I couldn't concentrate. I sat and watched the morning shadows contract until I knew it was time to go, marveling at the fact that no one had entered the courtyard all morning. The inside of the palace seemed strangely quiet and empty too, but all of the other students were sitting in their places when I walked into class, so things suddenly felt the way they were supposed to feel at this hour.

At least things felt normal for about five minutes. After twenty minutes with no sign of Grendel we all knew something was wrong but none of us dared bolt. After what felt like half an hour Mistress Nage ran in and breathlessly informed us that there would be no classes that day because the outer farms were under attack. As we all sat there in quiet horror she proudly rebuked us by saying there was no need to panic, but since all wizards were needed in council and we weren't real wizards yet we could best serve Sunnashiven by going home and keeping out of the way. Properly humbled, I maneuvered my way back home through the mauling beggars I had managed to avoid by coming so early, and sat in my room with another day to brood over Grendel, Lord Cathe, and my bright future as a goat herder.

It was because I was brooding over all the miseries of my life that I didn't hear my father come home early from work. That is probably one reason why the violent slamming of my door ripped the breath out of my chest. The other reason was that, small as our house was, my father never bothered or showed any interest in entering my room, so he really seemed out of place there, like an unwelcome guest I had to put up with. Since I had the key and the white pea and the colored glass spread before me on the bed I felt like he was intruding on my precious privacy but he didn't seem to even notice them. He was too conscious and proud of his court uniform, and too eager to get the unpleasantness of having to speak to another family member over with, to notice anything except my school-books, which clearly made him uncomfortable.

"No school tomorrow! Not till they tell me different." His duty done, he turned to go. I was supposed to make sense of that. My first thought was that I was being punished for something—the key, Lord Cathe, pride, who knew—and that my father expected I was aware of what I had done wrong and would save him the discomfort of having to tell me. I quavered and asked what he meant, which was more than I ever had occasion to say to him. "Just that. No school for anyone!" I felt relieved it wasn't just me. "That includes *you*." Relief vanished under what felt like an accusation. "There's a war on. You're coming with me tomorrow!"

"With you where?"

"To see the judgment and sacrifice. They're going to sacrifice some priest to make things right. Food shortages and all. It's our duty to be there."

I swallowed hard but could think of nothing to say except, "Do you know who is to be judged?" I tried hard to sound neutral so that he wouldn't get angry.

"It's got to be that smart one, Lord Cathe. The high priests all say it must be a child of the gods to appease the gods. Too bad, but it has to be. That's what comes of reading books."

My hearing was suddenly pitched to a fine sensitivity, for I heard my father walk away and my mother shrilly complain, "Llewelyn's going to a sacrifice? But he doesn't have anything to wear. What shall I do?" before I withdrew back into myself enough to realize that my hands, mechanically clutching Grana's pea in some mad bid for comfort, were growing cold and bruised.

Four

I entered the place of judgment on my seventeenth birthday. My father had not remarked on the significance of the day, but then it would not have been like him to do so. He had never noticed my birthdays, and now he was so busy standing and kneeling and rising and swaying and kneeling again on cue that he had no reason to speak to me. Occasionally a scribe would smile in his direction in a faint attempt to curry favor and he would briefly smile back the way he was expected to. Nobody spoke, but everybody was looking around to be noticed and to see who else was there.

I was grateful for the vastness of the place because it made it possible for me to feel separated from my father while I was sitting next to him. I needed that feeling of distance because part of me was in the throes of extreme self-consciousness as I waited for the ceremony to begin.

That's what comes of reading too many books. I hadn't slept all night for thinking of my father's inane remark on Lord Cathe. Not that I respected my father's opinion on theological matters, but I dreaded the possibility that he might compare me unfavorably to this young high priest, which was absurd, because my father only "thought" the way he was told to, and such subtle comparisons were really beyond his ken. It was I who longed to be like Cathe, I who longed to be considered worthy enough to be sacrificed. And so I sat rigidly in the place of judgment, fearing to show too much interest lest my longing manifest itself only to get trampled with the words "Do you really want to die?" or, worse, "So you think you're smart?"

What could I say to it? Lord Cathe had reached the pinnacle of high priesthood at the apparent age of seventeen. Only the highest and holiest clerics were chosen as sacrifices in times of crisis, a rare event that occurred once a generation, maybe. I had read about such things, but never had they seemed real to me. The most qualified servant of the deity that needed to be appeased was offered back to that deity in the best spiritual condition possible, which meant, of course, that a clerical judgment had to take place, a determination of the life of the sacrifice, of what was being offered. What little was lacking was supposed to be supplied by the other members of the order through whatever means were necessary. I thought it must be quite a special honor to be the focus of so much attention.

I also decided that Lord Cathe was about to be blessed into an enviable glory that I was being deprived of, for I had convinced myself during the night that he was indeed the child I had created for Grana and that I therefore bore some responsibility for his high status among the clergy. But my awareness of his physical proximity suddenly made me feel strange and sick about his existence, as if creating his life had been an act too horrible for words.

*"A*s if any life can be an act too horrible for words, my lord."

*H*owever, I was mostly nervous about my father making comparisons, and once I got used to the size of the room I became painfully conscious of him being next to me. I devoutly wished I was there alone, and thought I might even enjoy the whole experience if I were. He was kneeling again and pretending to read through a state-approved prayer book, copies of which had been distributed among the benches. He looked studious, which seemed to fool the scribes. I pretended to study the platform in front while I concentrated on the slow steady drumbeat that filled the place. Then I caught the fear that someone might think I was actually enjoying the drumbeat and therefore feeling good about myself. So I tried to look as if I didn't hear the drum at all by settling myself superfluously in my seat with motions deliberately out of rhythm to the drumming. I was also thinking how strange it was to be here and not in Grendel's class this time of morning. I didn't see Grendel anywhere, which was just as well. I also didn't see Aleta.

When the drummer stopped drumming and told us to rise I was so intent on trying not to be noticed that I didn't hear him, and it was only the sight of everyone else standing that pulled me to my feet where I couldn't see anything for the other people's backs. By the time we sat down there was a high priestess wearing the bright yellow robes of Habundia rustling some papers in the high seat of judgment. There were a few dead corn stalks in front of her. "Habundia's court is convened," she intoned. "Bring in Lord Cathe."

Enter one frightened, palsied youth who had to be helped to his seat by two guards wearing clerical yellow. His attitude bespoke such sheer terror that my own confused feelings leveled out to a steady low inner hum of fear, a fear that distracted me for a few minutes from realizing that this frightened squirrel of a youth was the Lord Cathe I had thought about all night. He was not a brilliant scholar going joyfully to his goddess to save us all from food shortages while we marveled over his talents. He could barely keep himself on his chair, and the guards were standing watchful by his side lest he try to move. I now felt personally embarrassed that my father might view all scholars as being as pathetic as Lord Cathe was and so see me that way by implication. So I pretended I had no interest in Cathe by turning my attention to the high priestess, who was beginning to speak again.

Her voice was viciously soft, cuttingly correct. My mind chafed and squirmed as she spoke, because I feared her placid tones would sacrifice my cherished intelligence into terrifyingly pleasant clouds of thoughtless agreement. She began by saying, "In the name of our Lady the Goddess Habundia, gracious queen of the blossoming fields and protectress of summer, do we publicly present our best and choicest offering. And here, Lady, according to your decrees, do we acknowledge what is wanting in our best offering and state how we will make it good."

"Make it good," the crowd murmured obediently.

"Lord Cathe is your child, created by the gods and given by the gods in a summer of plenty, and so he is that summer of plenty that we shall return to you in the hopes that you will give us more. We are hungry, Mother, and are giving you our best. Feed us."

"Feed us."

"And Lord Cathe, who is your best, we will return to you in a state of perfection. He has fallen from this state through pride, Mother, through pride in his great and considerable learning and advancement. To make him acceptable we will remove this learning—"

Cathe started screaming and the guards hit him with their clubs.

"We will remove his learning and hence his pride. He shall not have cause for pride as far as our power extends, and we shall use our power to make him miserable in any learning that he accrues in future lives."

Cathe rose unsteadily from his seat as if he would attack her and the guards restrained him. The high priestess looked as though nothing had happened and she continued in the soft voice that made *me* want to strike her in self-defense. "And thus it is to be for the good of the state and the welfare of the people of Sunnashiven." She turned to Cathe.

"One. Even now we have stopped your growth. Like the fruits that so rapidly fulfilled their blessed patterns of generation, blossom, and corruption during the season of your birth, you have attained maturity in the four-year time span of childhood. It would be your fate to continue to age and die in the time it takes the rest of us to reach maturity. As the brevity of your life cycle is the visible sign of your special status, we have slowed down your life processes to match our own. Sheer torture for you to be forced against your life's very nature, but necessary to show the goddess that you would give everything to her as our representative. We are starving and we thank you for the gift.

"Two. All clerical learning shall be magically erased from your mind. Your years of education are naught. This will be a difficult process, as you are a highly gifted youth and know much about magical defenses, but the state will spare no resources to accomplish this. You must give up the most precious portion of your life to Habundia to save us. Be honored.

"Three. You shall then have your heart and stomach removed from your body and buried unmarked in a cornfield, the remainder to be burnt.

"Four. We shall shape your next incarnation to please the goddess. It has been determined that your mind shall be born in hunger, craving knowledge the way a tender seedling craves the burning sun that dries and kills. The sylphs, although you'll never see them, will be your friends and playmates. They will whisper curses in your ear that you shall mistake for dreams. Your parents will be intellectual clods who denigrate your love of ideas, and so the only comfort you will find will be in the works of other scholars. Only your masters will honor your learning, and their honor will be joy to you, for you will know no other praise. The regard of the masters shall gift you with pride, serving to make you disliked by your peers, driving you deeper into learning and so earning more praise and increasing your pride. This shall be the cycle of your early life.

"We will then place the delicate curse of scarcity on you, for you will live at a time when work for scholars is scarce. For years you will not have time to watch the leaves uncurl in spring, or turn rainbow shades in fall, or even read the books you once loved, for if you break from your studies, you will fail at your chosen profession, so fierce is the competition. Your pride will fall to a stunning desperation. You will sacrifice all to complete your training in a discipline you have forgotten how to love. You will finish your studies with high distinction and you will be considered completely worthless by your society. Your pride falls lower and the sword of sacrifice is drawn. No monastery will hire you, for there shall be many competitors with better connections. No merchant will hire you, for fear your high learning shall unfit you for commerce. You shall earn your bread clumsily, tilling the soil or herding goats. You shall be scorned for your incompetence at peasantry and mocked for trying to be better than your visible station should you dare to show your book learning. You shall keep yourself alive in a long blessed hatred of yourself and the world. Your mind shall rot and go soft before your body does and you shall never forget what you were and what you are. You shall live to be a hundred.

"Your pride sacrificed completely, Habundia should be pleased, and beyond this point the court and clergy will not intervene. No doubt as a result of the experiences we are shaping, the life that follows that one will be one in which all learning is difficult for you, but that is a regrettable result we do not claim responsibility for. We shall begin the sacrifice tomorrow at dawn."

At the beginning of her speech Cathe was screaming incomprehensible invective at her, but the guards had beat him into silent submission and he was now whimpering like a dying animal. I wanted to scratch and kick the high priestess myself, not least because her voice was so irritatingly pleasant and soft throughout her list of recommendations, which set a tone of fairness and justice throughout the room, and because parts of Cathe's next life resembled my worst fears concerning my own. Even though I could sense awe and terror in the crowd at the severity and extent of the spiritual sacrifice required of Lord Cathe, I felt an equally strong certainty sweeping over people that it would be rude to question the judgment, even inwardly. The high priestess sounded so fair and compassionate. Although any archon or priest of Habundia had the right at such a proceeding to bring up opposing viewpoints, in the interest of covering every issue and ensuring a perfect sacrifice, I knew that no one would. Any comment that carried weight enough to move the hearing in another direction would necessarily sound argumentative against that simpering glassy voice and therefore be dismissed as prejudicial. Any opposing comment presented in an equally soft demeanor would not be taken seriously next to hers. Her style had decided Lord Cathe's fate, and as the guards led him away I noticed the faces in the crowd, including my father's, taking on an air of defensively righteous satisfaction, which was socially easier than resentment of Cathe's high spiritual status.

I also noticed between Cathe's renewed screams that he threw a magical pass that hit me in the chest, as if he were throwing a piece of his life into mine. I don't know if the pass was a random call for help thrown in desperation, but I do know it found its way to me, and I was engulfed with the certainty that this proceeding had nothing to do with Habundia or any other god, except possibly the god of jealousy, who grows stronger in times of want. Something spoke to my heart, chanting confidently that the gods do not require sacrifice and that something was very wrong here. It was blasphemous, but I also knew that food was not going to get more plentiful after tomorrow and that whatever the invaders destroyed of the farmlands was not going to come back.

I could hardly rise from my bench, and the only thing that helped me stand was my intense need to show that I wasn't affected by anything in the proceeding, to hide the intimate nature of my fear and disgust. It was with relief that I heard my father being told that he had to go to work that day, for he exited through one of the side doors into the palace, leaving me blessedly alone with my heartsickness. It wasn't until the crowd thinned that I was able to walk at all steadily, and so there were only a few people milling around in the street and asking for news when I exited the judgment place. I tried to walk swiftly along the low stone wall that bordered the footpath leading to the main thoroughfare, so that no one would stop me for news, but my progress was impeded by my need to lean against the wall for support. I lost all control of my legs when I reached a low gap in the wall and a strong hand roughly pulled me through to the other side.

It was Aleta. She immediately had her hand across my mouth until she was convinced I wouldn't cry out. When she saw there was no danger in that, she released me and urgently whispered, "Grendel is looking for you. For us, but I'm leaving. I wouldn't be here, but I feel partially responsible for what happened two days ago and a knight makes good any injustice she unwillingly commits." Aleta was dressed in traveling clothes, but I noticed some plate armor under her cloak. "A word of advice to pay my debt. Get out of the city and away from him. The outer farms are fallen and Sunnashiven won't hold. It's worse than they're telling you. Grendel will make a deal with the enemy, and you've got something he wants."

My head was a whirlwind. "How do you know all this?"

"There isn't time to explain. I just found out. Sir Perie heard of the impending attack and told my father, who wanted me out immediately. Sent him with an escort that just beat the invaders past the border."

"If what you say is true, how will you get out?"

"Trade secret. I've got to act quickly. I've done my duty by you now. Farewell." She turned to go but I grabbed her arm.

"Aleta, I hardly know you but I'm desperate and I don't know what to do. What you say about Grendel—you must tell me more. I think I know what he wants—I don't know. How can I leave—"

"Stop it." She shook me off. "That isn't my affair. I've already done more than I can afford to. I must go."

"Take me with you," I said without thinking, without even really meaning it, but not knowing what else to say.

She looked me over quickly. "Can you carry a weapon? Can you make yourself useful?" She decided for me. "I can't help you. Grendel has some kind of link to you and I don't need to risk having you in my party."

This time terror spoke. "Lady, don't desert me. I'll give you what Grendel wants. Perhaps you can use it."

"Not me. Not if it's magical and Grendel knows about it. I've got my own problems." But curiosity made her hesitate. "What is it he wants?"

"It's a key. A wizard's key. It will open anything," I said eagerly.

"Why didn't you say so before? Where is it? Let's go, soldier!"

I wasn't about to argue with or question her sudden change of attitude, so I said, "It's at my house, near the pumpkin field at the edge of the city. Come with me."

"No, it's not wise to be seen together. I'll send someone to meet you outside the city wall nearest the field at dusk. You can travel with us to the border but beyond that you're on your own, understand?" I nodded. She disappeared over the ridge that led down to the road, leaving me in the posture that best mirrored my thoughts: sitting with my back against the wall and my reason running like egg yolk through my hands.

I remained leaning against the wall for several hours. I really had no idea of ever leaving Sunnashiven. What did I even know about these invaders that nobody ever named, or anything except going hungry and studying books? If Grendel really wanted to find me, he would. Aleta was probably just looking for an excuse to go back to Clio and kill somebody and she found a good one with this week's border skirmish. Not worth throwing my life away on.

Then I remembered Lord Cathe and I felt myself drowning in tremors of uncertainty.

I remained huddled against the wall until the shadows cast by the city roofs began to lengthen and I had to make a decision. At any rate, I had to go home, and perhaps my father would have some more information about the state of affairs in the city if I could only bring myself to show some kind of interest in front of him. So I forced myself to start for home, but the city was quieter than it should have been, and the queer, almost public silence that surrounded each step moved me rapidly out of my desire to know something. Then, after a brief moment of comfort as my house came into view the way it always did, I stopped in midstride.

There was a tall member of the king's guard speaking to my mother while she frantically waved her arms around in what appeared to be a substitute for answering questions. The wind brought an occasional squeal from her voice in my direction. I was afraid if I moved away I would be noticed, and I knew that if I stood where I was, I would certainly be seen, so I continued walking the way I thought I was supposed to, straight up to the door, my heart in my mouth. My mother was squealing, "But what can I do? I really don't know. Would you like to come in and see?" until the guard noticed me walking up the path to the door and his gaze drew hers toward me in something like relief. "Llewelyn, oh, Llewelyn, I'm so glad you're home. This is Trenna's brother," she said to the guard. Then she turned to me as a defense against talking to him. "They're looking for Trenna; she and Seth just disappeared. She didn't say anything to you when they were here, did she?" And then to the guard, "Llewelyn might—"

"When did you last see your sister?" he interrupted.

"A few months ago, when she was here. Briefly." I said this with a voice on the verge of collapse. He looked me over and then faced my mother again. "I would like to come in and look around." She fell all over herself trying to get out of his way and followed him into our common area, where she immediately began emptying chests and drawers to assure him that everything we owned was his to inspect. I hurried to my room and grabbed my pillowcase. The key was still in it, with my other precious objects. I heaved myself up on the window and closed my eyes for the ten-foot drop, then ran back and stuffed my schoolbooks in the top of my sack so that I could continue my studies no matter where I ended up. The things we think of when pressed for time. *Back to the sill, throw down the sack, make the jump.* My legs took the sharp thrusts of pain as they hit the ground and I ran and ran and ran to the meeting place outside the city wall.

It was just past dusk. No one was there. I stood in the gathering gloom, afraid that I had missed Aleta's messenger, not knowing what to do next. Maybe I could find her, but I doubted this, as Sunnashiven has a rather long perimeter and I had no idea where to even begin to look. She was certainly in a hurry to get out; how long would her courier wait? Did he even know whom to look for, where to find me? Had plans changed and should I run back and give the key to the guard and tell him I found it somewhere? It was quite dark now and far too silent. There were no fires in the city. Something was wrong. I stood in the tall grass with the sack over my shoulder, looking around through the shadows, not sure what I was looking for and afraid to call out. The wind picked up a little and I thought I heard the edge of a voice in the distance, somewhere in the city probably. I turned instinctively in the direction of the sound and heard it again behind me, in the fields. I knew I must pay attention and not let my thoughts obscure whatever was out there. As soon as I decided to listen intently I heard a half whisper coming out of the grass near my feet: "Llewelyn?" I looked hard but didn't see anyone so I gingerly felt in the shadows with my hand and was immediately rewarded with a sharp cry and a tug that brought me down into the weeds face-to-face with the head and shoulders of an angry older man.

"Watch where ye put yer fingers! Aah! My favorite eye! I used to see well with it! Yer clumsier than sixteen goat herders in heat when the ale's free! Ye gods! My eye! My eye!"

"Oh, I'm so sorry." I tried to reach out with my other hand to help him but he quickly pushed it away.

"No, don't bother. Ye've been enough help already. Leave me one to see with, please."

"I didn't see you."

"No, really? Well, the way ye've been stompin' around out here and wavin' yer sack in the air, it's the gods' own luck if every guard on the city wall hasn't seen *ye*. Ye got the key?"

"Yes."

"Let's go." He took my hand and started to dart off with me through the weeds. After a minute or so my sack grew heavy, so I took my hand back to support it. He stopped abruptly. "Look, I can't keep up the illusion if ye insist on breakin' physical contact. Tie yer wretched pillowcase around yer neck if ye have to, but don't break my hand hold again or I leave ye here to choose between Grendel and the invaders, understand?"

I was out of breath. "All right, let me tie my sack to my belt. Why do we have to hold hands? Is it like a code or something?"

He sighed with impatience. "It's the only way I can keep us both invisible. Whatever ye've got in your sack is makin' it difficult enough—I don't need ye fightin' me as well."

"I've got magic books. . . . invisible? I—"

"Ye've got magic books. Terrific. No wonder there's a drag. Why in the holy name of common sense did ye bring them? Maneuvering with the key is bad enough."

"Do you want me to drop them?"

"And leave a trail? Give me yer hand again. We've got to get through it one way or another."

As we started traveling through the fields I asked hesitantly, "What do you mean, invisible? I've never been invisible before. I guess that's why I can't see you now. But I don't look any different."

"That's because it's dark, you idiot. Now, do ye think ye can keep your tongue still and yer thoughts shielded as we go past the guards in the northern gate—"

"Past the guards?"

"I said be quiet. One slip from ye and yer on your own, key or no key. Are you with me?"

"Yes, of course, but I have one more question. Why are we going back *into* the city?"

"How else are we goin' to free Lord Cathe?"

"What?" I nearly dropped his hand again.

"Didn't the General tell ye?" I heard him spit and stomp his foot. There was a brief pause, as if he was considering whether I was worth the trouble to bring along. "Look, there isn't time to explain—we need a diversion and Cathe's elected. Lucky man. If ye can think of a better distraction, let me know now. Otherwise mind yer tongue from here on in. Right?" I squeezed his hand in assent. I felt I was already committed, and in the excitement of the moment the thought of freeing Cathe seemed like a fine and daring and heroic thing to do. I had never been invisible before and was beginning to enjoy the whole experience.

"I know a shortcut to Habundia's temple from the north gate. The back of some row houses—it'll save us fifteen minutes," I offered.

"Good. Once we enter the city ye lead. Don't hit me with yer sack." We moved swiftly through the fields, Aleta's messenger pulling me in a strange uneven path that I assumed was supposed to obscure whatever trail our bodies made. When we got to within a few yards of the northern gate I felt him stop abruptly, so I did the same. I was bursting to ask him what we were waiting for, but I had to content myself with studying the cluster of guards who crowded the entrance. It slowly came to me that it was impossible for us to wend our way through the gate without physically running into someone, especially in the uncertain light of their single flickering torch. We remained perfectly still for about five minutes, until the faint but steadily increasing sound of horse's hooves caused my companion to jerk me forward again and begin running after the swiftly approaching horse. We were dangerously close to its back hooves as the guards parted for the mounted messenger, unwittingly letting us through the briefly emptied space. We were well inside the walls and had traveled down a few streets before I felt him stop again to let me catch my breath.

I felt his hand move roughly and quickly across my back, where he grabbed the bottom of my shirt and yanked once to let me know he was waiting for me to take him to the temple. I started off a little uncertainly, the streets being so dark that I wasn't sure of the shortcut anymore. My companion gave no indication that he knew we were lost, no shirt tugs or anything, but the second time I took him through the circular garden south of the temple I was sure that he must know I had made some errors and cost us time. I stopped and he stopped, waiting.

My fear of his impatience panicked me into a decision, so I started walking straight through the garden in the direction I knew the temple was in. No matter how thick or prickly the garden plants got, or how swampy the ground, the straight line would get us there, and I assumed he must be wearing thick pants and walking shoes and could stand a little mess below the knee. After yards of prickly bushes and an occasional marshy area we made it to the clearing behind the temple. Determined to make up for lost time, I ran quickly up the steps with him clutching my shirt. There were no clerical guards but there was also no light, so I tripped twice in my haste and he had to pull me back from falling.

When we entered the public area of the temple I stopped again. The realization struck me that I had absolutely no idea where Lord Cathe was being kept and I knew absolutely nothing of the building's layout. My accomplice was still with me, silent and waiting. The darkness was oppressive. Usually fires were kept burning in the sacred places but tonight there was nothing but the dark and the silence. I felt as though we could stand there forever like a living statue in the place of the goddess and nothing would change. How do you sacrifice a statue? By making it invisible. I felt the minutes passing. My partner's hand finally crawled up my back to my arm and down to my hand. He was taking the lead again.

We moved swiftly to the far wall and came up against a door I hadn't seen for the darkness. I heard my partner tap it softly and hiss, "Key." Another nervous period of wasted moments as I fumbled in my sack with my free hand. The key was on the bottom and I couldn't find it for the books, and he dropped my hand in impatience as I put myself in danger of any wandering guard with a torch by emptying the contents on the floor. By the time I found the key and had everything back in the sack, my accomplice had the door open himself and was pulling me through. When we got to the other side he closed and locked it, took the key from my hand, and continued to lead me down what felt like a close, dark corridor. Naturally I was full of questions at this point but didn't dare voice them.

It was clear that he didn't know the layout of the building either because we spent about twenty minutes circling and backtracking through what felt to me like the same passageways until a faint glimmer of light warned us of the approach of two clerical guards. We moved quickly against the wall to let them pass, and then followed, stealthily matching our footfalls to theirs. After about ten minutes of exceedingly confusing passageways we were rewarded with the sight of a miserable cell, dimly attended by two small torches and two bored-looking guards. We waited while the guards changed shifts and the first pair got decently lost.

My eyes adjusted slowly to the deceptive light, but eventually I was able to discern a figure huddled in the back of the cell, completely covered with a plain robe that blended into the shadows and hid his face and body. This had to be Cathe. To be so physically close to him filled me with such nervous anticipation that I could hardly keep hold of my partner's hand, but I didn't have to hold on for long, because the guards' attention was suddenly fixed by a large rock hitting one of them in the shoulder and a voice calling from somewhere down the corridor, "Habundia rots with the gray-ain. Habundia rots with the gray-ain and you eat sea gods' sheaths! Mmm, taste good, you," and the guards were off with one torch and we were in front of the cell.

We simultaneously dropped hands and by the light of the remaining torch I could see a middle-aged man about three feet high opening the cell with the key and whispering, "Cathe?" To my chagrin I noticed that his face was scratched and bleeding from the prickly plants I had led him through and he was damp to the knees. The figure in the robe moved cautiously toward us, his face hidden. "Happy birthday, my lord. Take a good look, take a good grip, and let's go." He removed the prisoner's robe and the prisoner looked at us questioningly. "Baniff the Gnome at yer service. Illusion's my specialty, thievin's my trade." I couldn't believe this. I was standing in the cell in an absolute stupor when Baniff quickly untied my sack and gave it to Cathe, who was expectantly extending his hand to his rescuer. Cathe dumbly tied the sack around his own waist, and Baniff grabbed Cathe's hand and threw the robe over me as they vanished from sight. Before I knew what was happening the cell door closed and locked with me inside. The fabric was across my face, blinding me.

"Wait a minute. What about me? You can't leave me here." I was trying to get the robe off without success. I heard a hand reach through the bars and felt it lift the material away from my face.

"Don't even try to speak or struggle. The fabric makes ye inaudible and ye can't remove it from yerself. I can't keep three of us invisible. Ye hold the fort." I heard the sound of footsteps in the distance. A voice caused them to stop and move off in the opposite direction.

"What about creating a diversion? With me here it will be the same as if we never came."

"Come mornin' when they remove yer robe before the sacrificial altar and see who ye really are there will be diversion aplenty. And that's when we'll need it most. Thanks for yer help." He dropped the material back across my face and I heard the faint sound of them moving off as I staggered with fear to the back of the cell where Cathe had been and assumed the huddled position we had found him in.

What would happen to me at dawn? What had I gotten into? Aleta might be miles away by now, and I had begun to doubt whether Baniff really had anything to do with her. A gnome! So such creatures existed outside of legend. I'd seen a gnome and now I would die. Not just die, but who knew what kind of torture would be created for me once I was discovered? I had been so stupid to act on trust. Why hadn't I done my duty and given the key to the guard at my home? Why hadn't I just stayed in bed? My parents would see me at the sacrifice; what could I say to them? What could I tell the priests? That I had traveled invisibly with a gnome who stole my pillowcase?

I heard the guards returning and positioning themselves outside the cell. After an uneasy silence one of them began to snore, which surprised me, considering the sanctity of their vigil. Then I heard the other one sharply reprimand, "Wake up! Do I have to do duty for both of us?"

"What's to do?" asked the other guard, reasonably irritated at having his nap disrupted. "Sun up isn't for two hours, and he isn't going anywhere." The guard's voice conveyed more resignation than reverence. I had the impression that he doubted whether the priestly sacrifice would do much for Sunnashiven but that he feared openly expressing his skepticism to the other guard.

"What's to do?" she repeated harshly. "You might stay alert for more trespassers come to profane the sacrifice." I found her concern ironic, considering she was now guarding a trespasser. "I'm the one that got hit with the rock, you coward, and I'm the one that went in front while you hovered like a green recruit at Momma's back."

"That was probably the last shift playing tricks," the other guard grumbled.

"We're helping to make sure the city will be victorious and well fed after tomorrow."

"If the city isn't razed after tomorrow."

"If the city is razed, would you be awake enough to notice?"

"If I were awake enough to notice, do you think I'd be here?" The first guard groaned in exasperation. After a while her partner began to snore again.

I had nothing to do but wait for dawn and the end of my life, but while I was waiting a curious thing happened to my state of mind. The cell was private and soothing, and the one guard's suppressed cynicism made me feel that the world was still normal whether or not I was tortured and executed. The guard didn't see me as a sacrifice or a high priest or a prisoner or as anything at all, which meant he really carried no expectations concerning me, and I felt I had nothing to prove to him. I could simply be myself in the delicious privacy of my cell, and I suddenly felt strangely content. No demands.

And then I thought of Grendel and school and my parents and decided that there was something infinitely more interesting in being executed than in going back to the life I knew before. Really, I wasn't giving up much.

But these were the thoughts engendered of solitude. When I finally heard the captain of the clerical guards arrive and kick the snoring guard awake, fear and anxiety broke my thoughts into dust and all I was aware of was my racing heart and the fact that I hadn't eaten in more than a day. He ordered me to be brought to him, and the two guards entered my cell and lifted me up by each arm to bring me into his keeping. He promptly tied my hands in front of me while muttering some nonsensical-sounding words. Then he began to lead me away as if I were a goat on a leash. I could hear the other two guards following behind.

It did not take us as long to leave the temple precincts as it had taken me to wander through the corridors and get lost on the previous night, but then my supreme fear of the impending ritual made time speed up. Before I knew it they had placed and locked me in what felt like a horse cart, because I was soon being jostled swiftly toward the place of sacrifice, which I remembered would be near or in a cornfield. I was grateful for the privacy of the cart again, but not enough to allay my fear, and every time we hit a hole in the road I thought my heart would rupture. However, that was nothing compared to the terror that all but demolished me when the cart finally stopped and I heard the guard dismount.

It took a long time for someone to open the cart, and as I lay there I heard nothing but the jingling of the horse being released and the rustling of the corn. I had read that sensitive wizards could train themselves to hear the sun rise, but I had no idea what to listen for and so I lay there hoping it was not quite dawn yet, not yet.

When the cart was finally opened two people, presumably the guards, pulled me out and led me unsteadily on my feet for a few paces before they cut the rope around my hands and left me standing alone. I waited for what seemed an eternity, unwilling and unable even to try to move, although my legs were certainly free, until I heard a rustle in the field and a low murmur around me, as if I was surrounded by a large crowd. The noise ceased as suddenly as it had begun, and the voice of the high priestess I had heard in judgment the day before sounded soft and clear. "Behold the sun who rises to kiss and make us fertile."

"Make us fertile," said the crowd.

"Now is the hour to give to the gods what we would have them return to us."

"Return to us, O slain one."

"Return in the corn to feed us, in the wheat to give us bread. O Habundia, most honored and most needed of the deities, for you we perform the supreme sacrifice, we give you back your highest priest, slain and torn in spirit and body. Give us back your blessing and abundance."

"Give us back."

There was a moment of silence. Then, "Remove his robe that he might face the sun."

The two guards violently tore the robe from my body, and while I was trying to shield my eyes from the harsh glare of the dawn sun, a stunned silence that sounded like a scream emanated from the crowd. The high priestess opened her mouth, looked at her assistants, looked at me, and cried, "Who are you? Where is the sacrifice?" Her loss of control sent shock through the crowd, and I saw people breaking ranks and running uneasily back toward the city walls. In the distance I also saw rising smoke and the sun glinting off armor. We were under siege, and no sacrifice would prevent that. No one seemed to know what to do, except the captain of the guards, who grabbed me by one arm, strode confidently up to the high priestess, and offered to bring me back to the temple for interrogation. She agreed and hastily shoved her ritual tools into her assistant's bag while shouting orders to the other guards to scour the city for Cathe. "He can't have broken through enemy lines! Find him! And yes, bring this youth to the temple immediately."

"Lady, I found this pillowcase on the west side of the city near the entrance to the palace school." He turned to me. "Is it yours, boy?"

"Yes."

"With all due respect, perhaps you could concentrate your forces in that part of the city—send your priests there with divination spells to begin tracking Lord Cathe. I'll bring the contents to you with this youth by circling round to the north gate to see if I spot anything."

"Yes, good. You'll be rewarded for this."

"I'm sure." He bowed his head and tied my hands to my sack, then threw the torn robe over me. I felt two guards hoist me onto the horse and then the captain mounting in front of me. We galloped and bounced into a fierce wind, so fierce that it puffed me away into a dead faint and I knew no more.

Five

So warm had life become the land was scarcely dry. I didn't write that. Someone else wrote it into my dream. That same someone held a burning rush light over my eyes, or a blindfold of incandescence, or something so bold and sure in its tepidness I wanted never to open my eyes again, only to relax into this comforting band of light and see darkly through my own closed lids. I could still hear something like the crowd rushing or sighing or gasping around me, but different now, the insistent whispers less expectant than the vulgar, brutal silence that had jabbed me that morning. I lay upon an immensity that felt both hard and welcoming. Something rough was probing my back and the point of discomfort increased to pain as I gained consciousness. The backs of my hands were being scratched and tickled and I felt something cool and moist caking them.

It is impossible to cling to sleep in a state of terror, and as I was rapidly approaching this state again under the steady guidance of my increasing heartbeat, there came a point not long after awakening when my eyes tore themselves open and revealed to me the source of all my own sensations. There was the midday sun in all his glory, standing proud and erect in the beech tree whose leaves were shimmering and murmuring over me and whose root was rubbing my back raw. My hands lay upon forest floor. Slowly turning onto my side to smoother ground, I saw that I was surrounded by a wild and beautiful forest with no other sign of human life. My sack lay beside me. I lay very still for a minute, afraid to move lest there was someone watching behind me, then very slowly and carefully pushed my hands against the ground and lifted myself to a sitting position. I still didn't notice anyone else, and I gratefully experienced that absolute, unexplainably confident feeling that wherever I was, I was alone. Had the captain of the guards left me here and would he return soon? I knew that I should run, that I should try to lose myself in the forest in case the captain had carelessly provided this opportunity to escape, but the foliage was so thick around the small clearing I occupied that I saw no way to move quickly, or even to move at all, without making a good deal of noise. Besides, almost as an afterthought to my feeling of solitude came a feeling of certainty that whatever had happened this morning was completely behind me. The air was different here. I knew that I was far away and removed from the events in Sunnashiven and that somehow the gods had been merciful to me. I had no thought of what to do next, of course, and as I became fully awake and my feelings gave way to thoughts, the only thoughts I could hold on to were those of curiosity, for I couldn't begin to put together how I had come here or where here was.

Out of both physical necessity and lack of anything better to do, I had begun to stretch my back and arm muscles as a prelude to standing up when I heard a loud thorny crash and snap in the bush across from me. Having spent my entire life in the city or in the cultivated lands, and being a rather nervous youth who had just passed through a passel of extraordinary circumstances, I wonder that the noise did not return my fear to me. By all rights I should have been frightened but I remember only being curious and feeling a strong sense of anticipation. I had no sense of being in danger. Danger is for people with something to lose, and people with something to lose generally have a past, and in that forest clearing I had no past. I was simply there like the trees, and like the trees I waited for the noise to reveal its source without my pushing for revelations or forgetting that mysteries exist.

After a short space of time a fat brown woodchuck wriggled out of the bush and into the clearing. He took no notice of me. I might really have been a tree for all the reaction he showed to my presence. He waddled across the clearing and circled behind the beech tree I was sitting against. I stood to turn and watch him. He stopped in front of a small boot that was attached to a leg that lay stuck out on the ground on the other side of the tree, and batted it roughly with his paw. The boot's owner woke up with a curse. It was Baniff. Kicking his leg away from the woodchuck, he rolled over onto his side and grumbled himself back to sleep. The animal waited until he was completely asleep and batted his boot again. Baniff cursed more loudly and kicked his foot in the vague direction of the creature, but the woodchuck avoided the kick by running up behind his back and butting his shoulder with his head. Baniff rolled back over and continued cursing while trying to grab the animal's head, but the woodchuck deftly wriggled over him and butted his back once more. The whole performance was really quite amusing.

The gnome finally sat up, yelling, "Can't a man get any sleep here? I've been pumpin' out illusions for two days straight like a rock dwarf comin' into heat." The woodchuck sat up on his hind legs and nodded as if he were in enthusiastic agreement with Baniff's displeasure or somehow identified with the rock dwarf in question. "What in the name of all that ills do ye want now?" he grumbled while grabbing his own feet to make sure his boots were still there. The woodchuck looked at him and clapped his paws together while uttering a strange little squeal. "Ye woke me out of a sound sleep to tell me *that*, ye overgrown sea pig? . . . No, I don't have any daisies for ye, and a lucky thing it is or I'd be makin' ye choke on them already." The woodchuck bobbed and clapped his paws again, as though he were most pleased or amused, and scampered away.

"Good morning, Baniff. You're looking fit." He was still covered with scratches, so I have no idea why I said this except that I thought it was the sort of neutral pleasantry that wouldn't draw fire in my direction. I was wrong.

"So yer awake are ye," he grumbled. "Here's another bad match on the Rialto, as they say. An alleged pathfinder through the intricacies of Sunna-shiven's city parks who has fewer uses than the lame horse who broke its neck at the bottom of a dry well and is about as pleasant to travel with as a cold wind in a privy at midwinter. No, make that a cold, wet wind in a privy at midwinter, and a horse with the plague. What the—" He had taken off his boots and was shaking them vigorously. A few prickers fell out, probably souvenirs of the previous night's rambles, and I could see the soles of his feet were bleeding. "They don't pay me enough, the gods know they don't pay me enough." He threw his boots against a tree. "Can ye do some-thin' useful, like conjure up a tankard of ale? I'd settle fer hard cider if ye could manage it."

I felt genuinely sorry about this strange little man's discomfort, but there was nothing I could do. "I'm sorry, Baniff, but I haven't studied materiali-zation spells yet. I don't know how to make ale. If there's anything else I can do—"

"There is, but ye don't want me to say it. Ye've been carryin' that dam-nable library on your back since ye left the city. Isn't there anythin' in any of those books?"

"No—I don't know—I mean, I can look but I can't use magic except to help the state of Sunna anyway and I don't think this would count." He rolled his eyes in annoyance. "Why don't you try an illusion, Baniff? You can look at my books if you think they will help."

He groaned and flopped back down on his back with one arm covering his eyes, shaking his head. "Because illusion ale isn't real, you dolt, and most of us have a hard time seein' our own illusions, let alone gettin' drunk on them. And right now I want to get drunk." He sat up again and leaned back against his arms, looking glum.

I was hesitant to say anything more, but his prolonged fit had prevented me from voicing my most pressing concern, and I thought he might be able to tell me something about how I had gotten there. "Baniff?" No response except a sidelong glance of annoyance. "Do you know where we are? After you left me in the cell the captain of the clerical guards came and took me to the place of sacrifice outside the city. I almost died; they would have killed and cursed me in the most unspeakably horrible manner." I began to quaver and feel a little self-conscious at the memory, especially since Baniff still seemed more preoccupied with his own sore condition than with any-thing I was saying. "And they tore off the robe and saw that I wasn't—"

"They saw that you weren't worth the trouble it takes to scratch off one's face in a briar patch, so they decided to haul ye in fer questionin' under the mistaken assumption that ye had anythin' intelligent to say, and ye made their sorry guess good by faintin'—which probably took more brains than I credit ye with to accomplish. And so here ye are, like the proverbial fool's dog that's swallowed his master's goose and wonders as he's bein' thrown across the room how he learned to fly."

"Baniff, how do you know what happened to me this morning? Were you there? Invisible? Do you know how I got here? Do you know what happened to the captain of guards?"

"I *was* the captain of guards, ye idiot, and a fine lot of illusion work that one took fer a fee that won't buy a quarter bale of horse barley. I saved yer miserable hide, boy, fer a sum that will barely clothe my own. Yer safe enough now and here's where my involvement ends. Aah, what a life, what a profession! I've got to get out of the business and do somethin' less stressful, like posin' as a dummy target fer joustin' practice."

Perhaps my uncharacteristic giddiness was a combination of my not having eaten in nearly two days and relief at my new freedom, but I began to laugh like a madman at Baniff's honest annoyance and at my own shortcomings. I was not laughing from some newfound position of maturity, however, but helplessly taking Baniff's own point of view toward myself. My laughter really was a kind of self-directed cruelty combined with an admiration of his ready wit that I couldn't shake off, but it was clear that it only angered my companion further; he seemed to think I wasn't responding appropriately to his insults. His ire stretched itself into a fine humorless silence punctuated only by constant rubbing of the soles of his feet and his face.

After several minutes of his silence and my ill-contained giggles at the memory of his delightfully easy manner of expression, Baniff exploded at me, "Ye *are* free to leave! Whenever ye like!"

"But you haven't even told me where we are," I said quite sensibly.

He scowled. "We're well behind yer enemies' lines, or rather, on the outskirts of their new territory, as they've probably taken Sunnashiven by now. If ye follow the path hidden by the blackberry bushes behind this tree for a few miles, ye'll end up back in what's left of yer city's farmland. If ye follow the path hidden by the bush in front of ye, ye'll soon be faced with all sorts of choices. They're all clear fer several more miles. Choose one and leave me in peace!"

I felt nothing but an odd sort of increased relief at Baniff's assurance that Sunnashiven was taken. No one would be looking for me, and I was safe here with my precious books. I was up to date in my own studies and perhaps I could continue my training somewhere with all the perfection and potential that accrues to clean beginnings. Life had given me leave to go anywhere, and I savored that feeling as I walked over to pluck blackberries from the bush and cram them in my mouth. "Want any?"

"No," he said crossly. "I want to be left alone."

I continued to pluck and swallow, pluck and swallow. I didn't even have to feel guilty about my parents missing me because for all they knew, for all anyone knew, I was dead and couldn't be expected to show up anytime soon. Then I realized that my parents might have heard or even seen what happened that morning and my relief twisted over into anxiety and the pressing familiar need to explain myself. Then, as my stomach filled, I thought of my mother feeding me and anxiety blossomed beautifully into the guilt I thought I had just overcome, tempered with a sneak attack of sorrow and loss when it occurred to me that my parents might be dead and I might be more alone than I thought. Bad as it was at home, it was all I knew. I stopped eating. I wanted to say something more to Baniff. There was a lot he hadn't told me, but I didn't know what questions to begin to ask him and I wasn't confident of getting any answers in his current mood. I was also afraid of him hearing the shrillness I knew would be edging back into my voice. I snapped off a blackberry branch and tried to sound casual. "These bushes are so thick I couldn't even tell they covered a path. How do you know the paths are all clear ahead? Did Lady Aleta and Lord Cathe find their way up there?"

"A wood spirit politely woke me out of a sound sleep to tell me we were safe."

I thought he was being sarcastic until I remembered the strange behavior of the woodchuck. I got all excited again. "You mean that 'chuck I saw batting your feet around wasn't really an animal? I've read about wood spirits taking forms that—"

"If he had been an animal, I'd be having him fer dinner. Real animals make me nervous or hungry, dependin' on how long it's been since my last meal. Of course he was a wood spirit—how else do ye think I was able to communicate with him? I'm a gnome, not a rodent." Baniff looked insulted. I guessed I had unintentionally said something really hurtful, and then I remembered having read that young gnomes were often mistaken for rats by clumsy gardeners and bludgeoned to death, so I bit my lip in embarrassment.

"Well, it was kind of him to take an interest."

He sighed. "They *all* take a bloody interest if they think they can get somethin' out of ye. He'd probably been watchin' us since we entered the woods. As to Cathe, he's long gone his own way and it's none of my affair where, thank the gods. That's done. The general's well on her way to County Clio by now to stir up some trouble. That is, if she hasn't gotten lost." He stood up, stretched to his full three-foot height, and smacked his lips. "Here, let me have some of those blackberries."

I gave him the branch I was holding and watched him take out a knife and cut off the prickers before he swallowed the branch whole. I noticed a few fresh scratches on his face but he was too deeply engrossed in his meal to mind my staring. "More, please." I broke off a few more branches and handed them over. He seemed satisfied with what I gave him, for he began cutting off the prickers again without any further requests. After folding and stuffing every last branch and leaf in his mouth and gulping nonstop, he exhaled loudly, patted his stomach, put his knife back in the little sack tied to his waist, and shoved his boots back on his feet. "Well, lad, here's where

I get off. Pass yerself a good life, stay to the high road, and never take a chicken by the beak. The luck of the gnomes go to ye!" He steeled himself to pass through the prickly bush that blocked the path in front of us, resolutely crossed the clearing, began to gingerly push aside the branches with his hand, and paused.

"Say, lad—Llewelyn—could ye give an old boy a lift over this miniature forest? I've gotten enough beauty marks on my maiden skin these past few days to drive a dozen princesses over the Drumuns."

"Sure." It was the least I could do. I gingerly placed a hand beneath each of his shoulders and lifted him until his boots were dangling before my face. I was not a particularly strong youth, but he didn't weigh much and I certainly wanted to do something to make up for the damage I had caused. I strode swiftly through the undergrowth, the prickers snagging my clothes here and there, and gently set him down on the path.

He looked up at me, then tightened his sack again. "Thanks. Well, I'm off. I assume ye've got someplace to get to?" The question was an attempt to clear himself of responsibility, with a hint of concern for my ability to survive in the woods on my own. My heartbeat hollowed out my stomach. I had no place to go and no confidence in getting there. When faced with the reality of my new independence, my recent sanguine naivete fled like the wood spirit into the bush. My instinct was to turn and follow the path back to the farmlands, back to something familiar, but I knew that was now an impossibility. I wanted to save face in front of Baniff, to let him know I had some sort of plan, and I had to move on, so I said, "I thought perhaps I would go to County Clio."

"Do ye know the way?" The gnome looked doubtful.

"No, but I was thinking I could follow you, since Lady Aleta has gone so far ahead."

"That's what ye get fer thinkin'," said Baniff. "I'm goin' to Threle."

"Oh." I paused uncomfortably. "So the general is sending you up north?"

"No. I don't take orders from the general."

"I thought you . . . you know, . . . thieved for her."

"I work for myself. That is, for whoever happens to pay. No, I just met the lady's party on other business, and she dropped a few coins in my hand to relieve her own conscience for somethin' or other and play the sterlin' knight of legend by buyin' ye an escort to safety. I usually charge more fer moonlightin', but I took the money and gave her my word because she told me ye had that wizard's key in yer possession. Which, by the way, I still have in mine. Which, by the way, I'd like to keep as compensation fer the trouble ye've put me through, seein' as the general didn't set any new records fer generosity. Of course, I've a mind to be fair with ye, boy. A bag of new gold would be equally appreciated and I'll call it even." He flicked his tongue across his lips.

I didn't know what to say. Baniff knew I had no gold in my sack, and that under the circumstances I could hardly refuse him the key. Not that I knew how to use it or had any present use for it now anyway. My tongue was also stilled with the realization of how profoundly alone I would be once Baniff left, and I knew that despite everything, I would return to Sunnashiven or whatever was left of it as soon as the gnome went his own way. I might have a few pleasant hours of solitude in the forest, but the fear would get heavier and heavier until I returned to whatever awaited me in the city. I was sad and mourning a little too, for I had come to like Baniff in spite of his contempt for me, not least because on some level I shared some of it. Also, I had eaten apples with a count's daughter who commanded an army and I had been invisible and gone temple robbing with a gnome and I had almost died and I had seen a wood spirit. In some ways, going back would be a worse death than if they had really killed me, which they still might for all I knew. I had a sudden longing to see Threle.

"Baniff, you can keep the key, I don't care, but it seems to me that the worth of a new bag of gold, for which you just now expressed a willingness to exchange the key, is much greater than the day's work you've put in on my account." He glared up at me. "Not to slight what you've done, of course, but I was wondering if the key might continue to buy your services as a guide to Threle."

"Whatever would ye do in Threle?"

I had no idea, of course. "That wouldn't be your concern. Just get me there. Or let me follow you. I have no place to go. Besides, I can carry you over bushes, and reach high branches for you, and keep the wood spirits away while you're sleeping." I was most impressed with my own boldness, so much so I wasn't even sure it was me speaking. Baniff looked a little surprised at my unexpected temerity. "And once I find work and start earning some money I'll buy you the biggest cask of ale you've ever seen." I was groping here, and he knew it.

"Yer not much of a woodsman and I travel quickly. Suppose I refuse?"

I swallowed emptiness and said truthfully, "Then I'll go back to Sunnashiven and I won't trouble you anymore." There was a weak face-saving sort of comfort in these words. I had nothing to offer him, really, and we both knew that, but I was letting him know that I would not rely on his charity or force my company upon him. I could also see in his eyes that he had no intention of letting me go back to the city, so I had the self-justifying feeling of fulfilling some sort of expected obligation coupled with the knowledge that I wouldn't really have to. There is always a slight uneasiness that accompanies this combination of feelings, but it was an uneasiness I was willing to pay for his services.

"It wouldn't set right with me fer ye to go back to the city after all the trouble it took to get ye out. Besides, I don't need to worry about yer tellin' folks back home all the juicy details concernin' yer great escape. All right, lad, I won't stop ye from hangin' 'round my back, but I'll remember me the cask of ale. Get your sack."

I plunged quickly back through the bushes into the clearing and grabbed my sack, which lay untouched, without even bothering to lose time checking its contents. I certainly didn't want him to change his mind. Within a minute I had returned to the path. As soon as he saw me emerge from the bushes Baniff turned his back and began to lead me northward toward Threle.

Getting to Threle via the woodland paths is like getting back to some familiar place you've never been to before. For me it was like reading a lengthy treatise by some famous wizard of yesteryear, a treatise so thick and heavily wooded that nobody reads it but everybody knows what it says because its shadows usurp so much of the landscape—the kind of book you don't want to bother reading because you *do* already know the major points and high places. But when you finally read it on a once-in-a-lifetime impulse on a hazy summer afternoon you discover that the leaves are a slightly different color from what you heard or remembered, the paths have moved, your map is accurate only in the outlines, and the details of the landscape surprise and delight. You're glad you've come.

What all of this means is that I had a rather agreeable journey for the first few days, because I felt free to admire the forest without self-consciousness. It was almost sexual, the admiration that insinuated itself as a weakness between my own heartbeats whenever I encountered particular spots of loveliness. I could slowly relish these pricks of pleasure because I knew that no one would punish me with them; no one would form a blunt instrument out of them to jam my pulse back to the terror that accompanies defense of one's vital psychic treasures. I had never been in a forest before, and it was so much like the geographical descriptions I'd studied that I kept expecting to run across something I already knew. But the subtlety of the various moods of greenery shading the festive crowds of wildflowers that danced for us in the clearings formed a physical argument that not only supported my earlier guesses but also sheltered and clothed them in unexpected finery. And I could enjoy my mind's new clothes in relative solitude, as Baniff kept his back to me for most of the time and did not attempt to initiate any conversation. Occasionally he would stop for half a minute and gaze upward at the leaves, but I was never sure if he was admiring them, as I was, or simply charting our course.

Even when we stopped at nightfall the gnome had little to say beyond explaining how to set up our camp. We used branches and twigs to form sleeping shelters and scattered the structures over the ground in the morning. Baniff knew how to call and attract small game, so we dined on squirrel the first two nights and on rabbit the third. On the third night I recognized a tangy herb called clivon growing wild at the foot of an oak, an herb I'd never seen outside of Grana's garden, so I gathered some to flavor our dinner. It hardly matched Baniff's contribution, for he had been generously creating nightly campfires believable enough to make my dinner warm my mouth while he, immune to his own illusions, had to experience the meat in all its rawness, but he seemed to appreciate the effort I was making to be useful. He really wasn't a bad sort, and once I'd gotten used to the idea of traveling with a gnome I grew full of curiosity concerning his life and profession and had to struggle with myself to refrain from asking questions. Not that I thought he would have been offended or anything, but he seemed rather tired and anxious to get to his destination and I got the impression that any conversation on my part might be viewed as an annoyance. Nor did I feel comfortable offering him any sort of commentary on the beauty of the woods. Such a critique would have been superfluous to a creature who could mine and use the woodland secrets for his own survival. There's something arrogant in a caterpillar telling a moth just how beautiful her means of flight really is.

So we traveled for four days in relative silence, and it was on the fourth night, as we finished up what remained of another large rabbit that Baniff had trapped, that he asked me again what I expected to do in Threle. "We'll reach the border on the morrow, lad, and as that's as far as I'm goin' this round I thought ye might like some advice. I've been thinkin' about yer situation some. Ye'll need to get set up doin' somethin'. Ye *can* read and write, of course. Do ye have a fair tongue at learnin' languages?"

"Fair enough, I suppose." I really didn't know, as the wizards in Sunnashiven did not instruct us in foreign tongues, but I had always had a feeling that I could learn languages quickly if given half a chance. The rudiments of magical languages seemed to come to me easily, but the only tongue I was truly familiar with was the one I was raised in, whose proper name was Botha. It was the official language of Sunna and used as something of a common language among the southwest kingdoms. I say something of a common language because there were still remote places in the southwest where people either didn't understand it or refused to use it. "I hadn't thought that language would be a problem in Threle."

"It's not. It gets used every day."

I laughed a little sheepishly. "I meant, I thought everyone still spoke Botha up there."

"Everyone does in the Duchy of Helas. In fact, that's pretty much all they speak there, but head further north and ye'll find tongues changin' faster than Krygon ale goes sour." I winced a little, as most Sunnans regard Krygon ale as their national drink. Sure, it didn't keep long, but it kept the ale makers employed, so nobody thought to complain. It was considered sort of a patriotic act to buy Krygon ale. Even my father indulged in it once in a while. That is, when he could get it free and pretend he was making a contribution to king and country. "Do you speak Kantish?"

"No. Why?"

"Because I know of a monastery just north of Helas, in the Duchy of Kant, that's often willin' to take in scribes. Don't know if ye've much of a religious bent, but they'll pay fer yer writin' skills and give ye board while you decide where to settle. Got a friend who minds the wine cellar there I could give ye a message fer. They might even have work for ye to copy in Botha, and be willin' to teach ye Kantish in return."

"Thanks, Baniff. I'm very grateful." I wanted to gush my gratitude, in part to reassure myself that he really meant to help me and in part because I was genuinely grateful for this lead, but it felt inappropriate. Baniff clearly just wanted to see me safely deposited somewhere so that he could continue on with his life. There was more selfishness than altruism in his offer. I also sensed that his life was one of exciting adventures in which I was merely a quickly forgotten event, and the contrast saddened me. Not so much because of him, although I had grown to like him, but because of his life. There was something full around him, if that makes sense, some context in which he had developed his capabilities to their logical, beautiful conclusion and claimed the rare privilege of being himself. I knew I wasn't worthy to see as much of his life as I already had.

But since Baniff had opened the conversation I felt bold enough to grub for whatever he could spare concerning his activities. So what if he shamed me by not answering my questions? It wasn't as if I expected to see him again after the next day. "There's something that's been bothering me since we started," I said hesitantly. "When I first regained consciousness on the forest floor you told me we were several miles behind enemy lines, but I was certainly in no condition to walk that distance and I don't imagine you carried me. How did we get there?"

"I traded the captain's horse fer a small pony. Much more manageable. Got a friend to help hoist yer body behind me and off we went. Ye were out."

"I thought the captain's horse was illusion. But if it wasn't, how did you manage to mount something so tall?"

"I climbed the wall of its stable and jumped. The grooms had saddled and prepared it and the real captain was out in back relievin' himself of last night's beer. Threw a sound illusion of jinglin' harnesses on the stable so they'd run around lookin' fer the horse to buy me time. Don't even know if the illusion held. It often doesn't if I'm not around to keep it goin'."

"How did you get past the enemy looking like a Sunnan guard?"

"I didn't look like a Sunnan guard by the time I got there," he said impatiently. Then he softened a little. "No tricks there. My papers show I'm a citizen of Threle. Why wouldn't they let me cross?"

"And no doubt being the daughter of Count Clio, Lady Aleta had no difficulty crossing either." Trade secret, she'd told me! As if she'd wanted me to think she was braving all kinds of danger.

"No doubt."

"And Cathe?"

"He was with me. I got him across earlier," Baniff said vaguely, as if he wanted to change the subject.

"What happened to the pony, Baniff?"

"It knew its way back so I gave it a slap and off it went."

"Why didn't you just keep it? You traded for it, it was yours. Maybe we could have traveled faster. Why give anything back to Sunna's enemy?"

He looked as though I had caught him in some contradiction or lie. "I guess in the heat of the moment I had no qualms about helping Sunna's enemy." His silence was uncharacteristically reflective. I had inadvertently reminded him of something he would have preferred to forget.

I pressed on. "Baniff?"

"I'm tired, lad, let me sleep."

"Baniff, I'm sorry, but I must know. A lot of things have been weighing on my mind these past few days. You told me that your purpose in rescuing Lord Cathe was to create a distraction, and then you used me to create a distraction in the morning long after he was on his way to safety. A distraction for what? The captain of the guards—you, I mean—made sure that the city's clerical and magical forces would be concentrated on the west side while the invaders attacked from the east by telling the high priestess you found my sack near the palace school. If I didn't know better, I'd say that your primary purpose in the city was to rescue Cathe and that you used me to create a distraction to help the enemy because you sympathize with them. Is it true? And then the wizard's key—not that I want it back, don't worry, but Lady Aleta wasn't even willing to help me until I told her I had it, and then she sent you. Were you looking for the key as well and is the general some sort of scout for you? Does she work for our enemy?" My heart was pounding wildly at my own presumption and boldness, but I think it was the knowledge that Baniff would walk out of my life the following day that pushed me into voicing my thoughts.

"I misjudged ye, lad. Ye've got a sharp mind. Ye'll do well in the monastery."

Any compliment to my mind emboldened me, so I continued. "Then am I right?"

He sighed loudly, nervously created some flickering fire illusions, and looked for all the world as though he was about to speak against his better judgment. I felt surprised and pleased with myself for having reasoned out something that he was clearly taking pains to hide. "How do ye feel about becomin' a citizen of Threle? Perhaps there's somethin' pullin' ye back to Sunna. I won't stand in yer way if ye change yer mind about crossin' the border."

"I haven't changed my mind." Then another thought struck me. "Baniff, our government likes to keep things close. We were never even told who these invaders are or what they want with us. I know Lady Aleta told me that her county has sustained a few attacks, and somehow I just envisioned troops of displaced peasants that can't feed themselves off the land anymore organizing and striking places at random. I know this sounds bizarre, but we're not fighting Threle, are we?"

"Yer right. It does sound bizarre. Threle is a peaceful nation and the Duchy of Helas would hardly sit idle while the king jeopardized its tradin' interests with the southwest kingdoms. Think again."

"I can't imagine, Baniff. There's food shortages all over the south. In

Threle too, probably. Nothing grows in abundance. Wandering hordes who want to fill their stomachs like anyone else are always attacking borders. Maybe they don't even have a name. They just form and disperse."

"Well, Threle's not so bad off right now. And the woods are full of growth, Llewelyn. Even ye've noticed that. It's true that the southwest has been producin' less food, but County Clio is still able to harvest a small surplus. At least, the general never tires of tellin' me all about it. There *are* loose, unallied troops about and County Clio's been hit. But that's not what's happenin' with Sunna. Since yer bound to hear the rumors when we get back to civilization ye might as well know that Sunna is fighting itself."

"What?"

"Yer 'enemy' are rebel peasants from the southlands of your country. Seems they're upset with King Sunnas's latest tax increase and unable to feed their own families let alone give up the better part of their produce to the state, so they've staged a takeover. Not sure what they'll do with the city now that they've got it, but they've got it. Fer now."

"And you had an interest in helping the rebels?"

"Well, let's say I got paid to distract King Sunnas's hired help. It's a livin'." He lay down to sleep. The woods were quite dark now. I heard animals rustling in the brush and somewhere an owl cried. I didn't want to bother my companion any further, but my mind was turning spirals and there was something else I had to know.

"Baniff, one more question." He didn't respond. "If Sunna has a new government now, even though it's really part of the old government, does it still exist as a state?"

"Try it again, lad. I have no idea what yer tryin' to say."

"I mean . . . I'm under a pretty serious ban against using magic for any purpose other than helping Sunna. But if the state of Sunna is different, or changed to a different government, do you think the ban still holds?"

"Yer askin' me?" he grumbled. "Yer the philosopher. Save it fer the monastery."

I knew there would be no more talking that night and that for me sleep would be impossible. The stars were dark and rude, laughing and winking at me as if they saw their way clear to pour me a sip of illicit pleasure. My thoughts were a ladder tipped drunkenly against the loudly setting moon.

Six

$\mathcal{W}$hen we crossed the border into Threle the midmorning sun was quietly insisting that the rapidly thinning woods share his brightness and strength. To my mind the woods seemed singularly unimpressed with the sun's entreaties, for the tree trunks coldly deflected his light while the leaves gleamed back mere politeness, seeming to prefer the night's dreamy darkness to the day's lively demands. Darkness still lingered on the shadow side of the thicker trees, where I thrilled to the power of the woods even as it succumbed to the easy explosion of bush and meadow. As we entered the fields that constituted the edge of Threle's territory the smaller plants and bushes appeared to hold back the enormousness of the southern wilderness with the strength of their lovely fertility. When I tasted the scent of their light sharpness after four days in the heaviness of woodland shadows I knew that the land itself formed a natural border that the Duchy of Helas merely pretended was its own.

As we left the woods bird sounds pulled my senses out of the wilderness with the abruptness of an undeserved compliment. There was no way to keep my thoughts on anything that Baniff had said since leaving Sunna when the meadowlarks were doing their heartfelt best to create their own border of natural emotion, rebuking everything I had ever felt outside these crowded fields. So this was Threle. Somehow I had expected a confusion of streets and markets and merchant's shops, the Duchy of Helas being a major southwest trading center. But we were entering via the little-traveled woodland paths, so I supposed we would get to more settled sections later. I didn't even see any guards or checkpoints, or dwellings for that matter, only rough meadows and clumps of trees. I noticed that Baniff had slowed down and was looking a little more at ease than I had seen him look before. He was no longer leading, but walking at my side.

As we crossed yet another field I happened to glance over at an intricate web of tree shadow that was struggling to subdue a proudly sunlit bush. If I hadn't been looking it would have taken me longer to hear the shadow singing, and even longer to discover the woman singing in the shadow, but my slow appreciation of the scene was more a result of my unfocused mind than any attempt on the singer's part to remain inconspicuous. Her voice carried quite a distance and as we got closer it grew loud enough to extinguish the sounds of the meadowlarks. I didn't mind, because her singing was so much better than theirs. It had no purpose and marked no borders and it absolutely charmed me with its utter lack of emotional generosity. You see, generosity springs from intent, and in her voice there was no intent—only music. Anything I felt from her singing I was taking for myself, and my takings were none of her concern, which made them feel solid and safe.

Her voice had an intangible rustic quality that reminded me a little of the peasants at home singing their harvest in, but with a foreign lilt that made it difficult for me to understand all of the words. Part of her song sounded like

time
to fly
to the end
of the
flower

time
to cry
at the end
of the
dream

none
to bind
my new heart
to his
power

none
to find
my heart's way
through his
dream

She gave no indication that she was aware of us. As we approached her she kept singing and harvesting what looked like elderberries from the bush. I saw that her arms were stained with berry and leaf juice and that she carried a large wicker basket full of herbs. Her hair was long and bits of twigs were tangled in it, as if she had spent the night sleeping on the ground. A woodchuck was sitting up at her feet, watching her, and I got the impression he was the wood spirit that had given Baniff so much trouble. Baniff greeted her, an unmistakable gleam of pleasure in his eyes.

"The best o' the mornin' to ye, Caethne, and better than the evenin' has to give fer a sweet lass that makes the journey's end worth thrice the journey's trouble. 'Tis always a fine thing to look at ye."

She smiled with pleasure but showed no surprise at his greeting and continued harvesting berries. "From the marks on your face I'd say you've been having a time of it, Baniff. Good thing I'm here, and better that the burdock's in bloom. I'll make you a balm for your wounds." She spoke Botha with a heavy accent I couldn't place, but I found her speech much easier to follow than her singing.

Baniff ducked his head a little and looked up shyly. "They're not so bad as they were, I suspect. From the burrs in yer own clothes it seems ye've had a bit of a walkabout yourself. What brings ye down from the duchy?"

"I wanted to see what that rogue brother of mine was up to." She snapped off another branch and handed it to the gnome.

"How'd ye know he was here?"

"One of the advantages of being a twin as well as a witch. Besides, his friend Mirand's easy enough to track."

Baniff chuckled. "I'm sure *he* doesn't think so."

"I'm sure he doesn't remember giving me his old robe to practice spells in, either. It gives me a stronger link to him than he probably realizes." Although she hadn't addressed me, I can't say she was ignoring me. Caethne was aware of my presence, aware I had nothing to contribute to their exchange, and perfectly willing to let me remain silent without indicating in any way that I had to speak simply because I was there. Which was refreshing, because in Sunnashiven people asked me about myself only as a polite offensive maneuver designed to save themselves the social discomfort of a natural silence, forcing me to take on the discomfort of telling all about myself to strangers who couldn't possibly care two figs if they had a hundred. But with Caethne I just stood in the sun and shadow, neither in nor out of the conversation, feeling neither forced to remain nor expected to leave. It was quite pleasant.

"Parents know yer here?" said Baniff, as if it was an effort to sound casual. He nibbled at the branch as though he didn't really care.

"No. And the location of your hideout is safe with me." She laughed reassuringly. He nodded and quickly ate the branch. The woodchuck pawed the air as though he wanted some and Baniff carelessly dropped him the last few leaves.

"So was yer twin surprised to see you?"

"Walworth doesn't know I'm here yet. I only arrived an hour ago and decided to take advantage of the morning before the dew dries, like it's beginning to now. Here, Baniff, accompany a hardworking witch to your lair and she'll make you elderberry wine to go with your face balm. There's a medicine I know you won't refuse." She shifted her basket to her other arm and playfully extended her free hand.

"I'll meet ye later, Caethne. Right now the lad here is on his way to Kant and I've got to show him the road and make certain he remembers where to put his feet."

"You look as if you've barely remembered where to put your own feet these past few days, judging from the condition of your clothes," she said. Baniff did look a mess, but that was more my fault than his. I was grateful that he didn't choose to tell her so. "It's a long road to Kant and you both look as if you could do with a more substantial meal than whatever you've been scrounging in your travels." The gnome looked a little put out, as if she were finding fault with his abilities. "Come, show me what you've got stockpiled in the way of food and I'll prepare you both a proper sup." She looked at me. "I daresay you haven't eaten well in months. If Baniff wants to watch his friends starve, that's his own affair, but I wouldn't be true to my goddess if I didn't offer to feed you before you went on. I can tell from your skin tone you're badly nourished." Baniff shifted his weight uncomfortably.

"Who is your goddess?" I asked, because it felt easy and natural to do so, and it seemed as though she had brought the subject up because she wanted me to ask. I didn't mind. I was naturally curious after my recent experience with religion and I was thinking about the monastery in Kant.

"Habundia Ceres." She smiled. "The gracious mother of abundance, and sustenance, and harvest, and food, which you seem to be in critical need of. The Lady of the Land, who smiles through the elderberry bush."

She smiled through the bush herself without a hint of self-consciousness. Baniff was clearing his throat and attempting to speak, or rather to stop her from speaking, but I had started to speak at the same time and it so happened that my voice won out.

"Are you a priestess, then, as well as a witch?"

"No," she said gently. "I celebrate Habundia the old way, the way the peasants do in my homeland. There She has no clerics, only creatures who give as She gives and who love the land as she does—"

I was utterly fascinated, but Baniff interrupted, "Llewelyn's from Sunnashiven, and I'm sure he's anxious to—"

"Sunnashiven's a nice place to be *from*," she said brightly. "Do you have time to stop for food, Llewelyn? I'm sure if my brother saw the condition you're in, he would insist on it."

The latter phrase was directed at Baniff, although she was looking at me. I had a strong desire to learn more about her relationship with Habundia, since she was so unlike the priestesses of my own land, and something in Baniff's manner told me I was about to discover another piece of his life he would have preferred to keep hidden. I couldn't resist prolonging my acquaintance with the gnome and his doings, and I got a strange silly impression that the setting moon had somehow heard my desires on the previous night and brought about this meeting. Anything Baniff was trying to hide had to be worth finding out about, and he was displaying an obvious desire to move on. Yet he also seemed a little in awe of this simple smiling woodswoman, so I knew he would do nothing to stop our visit if Caethne insisted we stay.

Baniff had his hand on my arm and was gently pulling me to leave when I spontaneously decided to throw myself upon the woman's strength. Extending my other hand to hers, I said teasingly, "Lead the way, lady of the land. And if you wish, I'll carry your basket."

She smiled so prettily at my words that I was tempted to say them again, just to see her smile again. Baniff released my arm and was impatiently rubbing his right boot into the dirt. The woodchuck was bouncing against his other leg, as if he was laughing or looking for more leaves or both. Baniff pushed him away.

Caethne slipped her basket over my arm and withdrew her traveling satchel from under the bush. "I may be a lady of the land but my friends call me Caethne," she lilted. "Come with me and be welcome."

"As you say, 'Lady' Caethne."

I was falling in love with the fun and banter, and thought it warmly amusing to give this attractive peasant woman a title in fun. She had this wonderfully easy manner that made shyness impossible, and the gift of making *me* feel special for complimenting *her*, as if she were lucky that I happened to meet her harvesting berries as the dew dried. I guessed she must be in her early twenties, around Trenna's age, but her manner made it hard for me to think of her as older, so I felt absolutely no novelty in the experience of an adult treating me like an equal. Such novelty, no matter how pleasant, would have carried something of a jolt, and the way we fell into conversation was too natural for me to feel as though I were crossing some kind of social barrier. I have since discovered that most Threlans are like that to a degree, that is, willing to take a person as he comes, but Caethne was more Threlan than most. Like her singing, she simply was.

Taking my free hand in hers, she led me lightly over the sun-dappled field, Baniff moving heavily and uncomfortably at my other side. By the time Caethne and I had run several yards Baniff was behind us and our arms were linked and we were laughing for no apparent reason except the day was fine and the wind was sharp and Baniff was panting to keep up. I felt we had some sort of special bond between us that the gnome couldn't share. Not that there was a lack of friendliness between Caethne and Baniff. They seemed to have a kind of special relationship too. But Caethne was the type of woman who seemed capable of establishing an exclusive friendship with everyone she met. She had a way of making you believe you were the only person in the world. She could heighten your sense of your own very best qualities and make you forget every fault you'd ever been punished for. I fancied she could even befriend a storm cloud or a blade of grass or the wind. She could certainly make a stone love itself.

We passed out of sunlight into the shadow side of a clump of trees that extended outward from the woods. There was a shadow in the shadow, a well-hidden entrance into a dwelling that looked partly chiseled out of the laughter of living rock and partly dreamed out of the hardened blood of dark trees. We ran inside without pausing, as if there were nothing to enter or recognize as essentially different from the woods that buried its existence. A skylight made the cooking area I suddenly found myself in feel light and airy. The dwelling itself pocketed emptiness and silence. There was a profusion of wildflowers covering a rough-hewn table, and the sun was beginning to creep through the skylight and kiss their petals into glory. I saw that they did not form a haphazard pattern but were sensitively and carefully arranged. The walls wore an uneven white plaster, and the dirt on the floor was so thick I couldn't tell if it was primarily made of soil or clay. There was a large fireplace with an iron cauldron that Caethne was already fussing with, and I noticed the woodchuck, who must have been following us, sitting up expectantly at her feet. She had taken back her basket and unceremoniously dropped her satchel on the floor, so I imitated her lead and dropped my sack. A few books spilled out, but she didn't seem to care or notice. She threw an old leather boot out of the cauldron with a look of benign disgust and began filling the cauldron with water from one of the clay jugs that stood against the wall.

"What do you think of my flowers, Llewelyn?" Her voice had enough of a hint of self-deprecation to be charming, as if she had arranged them in secret and was a little taken aback that someone as discerning as myself should happen upon them. Even though I knew she would have asked the question in exactly the same way of any stranger, her tone worked on me and I felt special and right.

"They're beautiful. I love them," I said enthusiastically, in part because they *were* beautiful and in part because her modest tone made me want to compliment her.

She blushed and softly hummed with joy, as if her cheerfulness were beholden to my good opinion, and bantered, "I'm sure the flowers love you too. They're love flowers, you know. Look at the way they shine in the sun." I was both pleased and startled to hear her accidentally refer to my childhood fantasy, as if she could have known, as if it were a spoken secret between us, but my surprise was quickly forgotten, for she immediately put me to work. "Come and help me stir in the elderberries. I've put a fermentation spell on the water, but I'm sure the wine will taste better if someone else stirs. The fire should hold now. Let me find you some bread and cheese, if the men haven't taken to getting all their meals in town." She started peering through cupboards and shelves. "Really, these shelves would shame a titmouse into moving."

Baniff entered on the word *titmouse* and stomped over to the fireplace, where he removed a large stone and took out a bottle of ale. The woodchuck vigorously pawed the air and Baniff skillfully led him back outside with the bottle, closing him out with a small wooden door I hadn't noticed that opened inward from the shadow entrance. " 'Tis good to be home, Caethne," he said as he drank, his words a hint that her reference to mice insulted him.

Caethne seemed to recognize his tone as an old trick to get her to apologize for a hurt she never meant, and parried by saying, "Sit, Baniff. Even mice have to eat." She brought down some bread and turnips from the back of a shelf, and drew a few potatoes and herbs from her satchel. "Good thing I always travel prepared. This will put strength in your liver, and then I'll make your balm."

"This'll put strength in my soul," said Baniff, admiring his ale. Caethne was wrapping the bread and vegetables in a white cloth, which she placed in the fire under the cauldron. I kept stirring the elderberry wine, which really was beginning to ferment. The gnome glanced at the flowers. "I see ye left yer calling card this morning."

Caethne gave a mock sigh. "And none to see or admire them except Llewelyn here. He says he loves them."

"He would." Baniff pulled off a flower and ate it. "They're not too bad, Caethne. Could use some—"

Caethne playfully slapped his wrist. "Wait for your sup, mouse. Wait till you see how my bread comes out."

"So now it's *yer* bread, is it? Better be a good meal—that loaf might have been counted on for tonight."

"It probably was, being the only loaf on the shelves. That's what happens when three men who can't keep a forest hideout secret from a poor witch such as myself try to set up housekeeping. If it weren't for me and Llewelyn, I swear by Habundia Ceres the three of you would be eating rocks."

"No, I need the rocks fer my head," said Baniff dryly, "but I'll kindly let ye know if yer cookin' pays for the sacrifice of our only loaf of bread." He smacked his lips. The bread began singing and Caethne took it out of the fire with a pair of sticks. She dropped it on the table and the cloth fell away of itself. She then reached up over the fireplace and took down three mugs, which no doubt belonged to the three inhabitants of the dwelling.

"The wine should be ready now. Here, Llewelyn, fill these and let me know if my magic is a match for natural fermentation." She looked over at Baniff, who was contentedly filling his mouth with bread and turnips. "You should thank Llewelyn first. He freed me for cooking by stirring the wine."

I handed Baniff a mug of wine. "I thank 'ee, lad," he said through a full mouth while reaching for the drink.

"You've earned half the bread," Caethne said to me. "Please indulge yourself and don't let Baniff steal what's yours."

We all laughed at this sally, and I sat down across from the gnome and ate. The bread was superior. So was the wine. We were both so famished that we ate and drank our fill in silence while Caethne kept replenishing our mugs and watching us with obvious satisfaction. I wasn't used to drinking and the wine went straight to my head but by the time I noticed I didn't care.

When Baniff was finished eating he swung around in his chair and resumed his good-natured teasing. "Ye let in a woman and there's a mess to be had already. Just look at the refuse ye've got littered over our finely swept floor," he mock-complained. "When are ye goin' to get down on yer pretty peasant-girl knees and give it a scrub, Caethne?"

She gave him a merry look, as if she took his words for a compliment, and bent her knees in playful curtsey. She had managed to spread the contents of her satchel and basket over quite an area in the course of her cooking, and the loose books from my own sack weren't helping to neaten the place any. Caethne started to gather up her own belongings but one of my books caught her attention and she picked it up instead, as if the subject of housekeeping had just been closed. Her voice was suddenly tender.

"You read Grima. *Greening the Sun: Philosophical Investigations into Magic and Reality*. I love that book. I must have read all of Grima's works at least once when I was a student. What a wizard she must have been! Wouldn't you love to have known her? There was a time when Grima's writings inspired me to take up theory and become a wizard myself, but then I looked into my heart and decided I wasn't really a theoretical sort of person and loved playing with the natural forces too much, so I became a witch instead. If I ever write a book, I want it to be like one of hers." She sat down on the floor and started thumbing through the pages.

Baniff rolled his eyes and drained his mug, murmuring to me, "Here we go."

Caethne continued as if she hadn't heard him, "Grima's books are wonderful. Her theory *feels* like a natural force, which I suspect is why so many witches fall in love with her. By the time you discover it's all made up you're wishing with all your newfound powers that it's real, and when you put down one of her books you'd swear on all you hold dear that nature is wrong and Grima right. That's because she writes her theories as if they were songs, the same way I believe the gods write us. She fools you through divine imitation."

Baniff idly made his mug disappear and reappear, but Caethne was in too high a rapture to notice.

If I hadn't been so drunk, I would have been surprised at this charming, simple-hearted peasant woman's running commentary on what I knew to be a difficult treatise, but as it stood I was too drawn in by her insights for my feelings to move anywhere. It seemed to me also that Grima was the most poetical and appealing of the theoreticians I'd read, but I'd never thought about why this was so. I knew I liked her style, and I had read the entire book over several times, even though there were only two or three sections we had been required to memorize at school. I'd read nothing else by her, as our library didn't have any of her other works, but I knew of them from commentaries.

Caethne was browsing through my copy and singing passages at random, but she suddenly stopped in the middle of a line and exclaimed, "Llewelyn, I would love to hear you read to me! I've never seen this translated into Botha before and your accent is much better than mine. Do you know the passage about the serpent and the eagle locked in flight? The one that begins, 'If you should take your own true form'?"

"Yes, it's one of my favorites." It was not one of the passages we'd learned at school, but I had read it over so many times that I had memorized it without even trying. We loved the same words. I discovered the meaning of joyful astonishment.

"Then please come honor me with a reading. I must hear what it sounds like in proper Botha." I got up from the table and sat on the dirt floor next to her. Baniff gave us both a look that seemed to say *It figures*, got up to refill his mug, and left the room.

Caethne smiled at me as if we were once again sharing a marvelous secret and handed me the book already opened to the passage in question. The wine had completely obliterated the shyness that Caethne's warm personality had weakened, so I began to read aloud to her expectant face without a trace of quavering or hesitation. I felt power in my voice and was so charmed with the feeling that I almost didn't hear her stop me after the first two lines. "Let's cast the circle for this poetry. It is too beautiful for anything less, Llewelyn. Since I feel as if I am between the worlds when I hear it, I want to be between the worlds when you read it." She put her hands palms outward in front of her and I put my hands firmly against hers. She began,

> *O east and south and west and north*
> *In air and thought these words bring forth*
> *In fire and desire make them burn*
> *In water and friendship may they turn*
> *To earth and mystery.*

I felt a soft spiral of protective energy rising around us, rising around my words as I dropped my hands from Caethne's and began again to read. A boundary was forming around us, around the poem, protecting the images from all external corruptions, keeping the language pure. And I read the language thus:

> *If you should take your own true form*
> *For any natural thing*
> *Then bind your limbs in blackened thorn*
> *And lick the adder's sting*

> *As her strange light seeps through your tongue*
> *Drink hard from blackened pool*
> *And sing the words from which you'll run*
> *Invent the adder's rule*

> *Once an eagle took his flight*
> *Serpent pulled him down by night*
> *Without a dream of rule or might*

"They mock the flight they close." A steady voice from outside the circle finished the poem.

"Your voice, my lord."

Walworth slightly inclined his head to acknowledge the words we had once shared, so slightly that perhaps I was merely imagining that he remembered. He paused in his transcribing and looked at me questioningly.

"Set this down. My words. Because I am speaking for the court record, for others to one day read and judge, I ask leave of your patience in recounting events in which you were a participant, leave to speak *of* you, from a critical distance as it were, rather than *to* you."

As he looked for all the world that I might speak as I may, I continued.

Caethne bounded to her feet, the energy dispersed, the boundary ruptured, and I looked up to see her eagerly embracing a weather-beaten young man of curiously noble bearing. He was wearing a brown travel-stained cloak and battered walking boots and he carried a large, delicately carved sword under his belt. His face resembled her own, as did his accent, but his smile lacked her easy spontaneity and his eyes had quieter depths than hers. His glance was constant and still and even whereas Caethne's dark eyes were always full of dancing brilliance, cloud shadows chasing the sun. I knew at once they were twins.

"O my sweet wandering brother, how good of you to come here and pay me a visit," Caethne teased, stepping back from him. "I'm not sure I should let you in. You might track mud on the floor, and I hadn't planned on having another guest for dinner. Really, you should learn some manners and send a message ahead to let one know when you are coming."

"It seems I already did." He looked at the flowers on the table and then at Caethne.

She laughed merrily and hugged him again. "I am glad to see you. It's been months since you left the duchy."

His lips betrayed a hint of amusement. "Mirand will be here soon."

"Mirand will be here soon. Mirand will be here soon. As if I journeyed across an entire kingdom to see Mirand."

"Didn't you?" He smiled.

She sighed in mock annoyance and smiled back into his eyes. "Come," she said, taking one of his hands, "meet my supper guest, Llewelyn from Sunnashiven. He's on his way to Kant and he reads Botha like a wizard's dream."

"I know. I heard him." He extended his hand to me and I rose without taking it, being busy shoving my books in my sack.

"Llewelyn, my brother, Walworth, the future lord of the land."

I was too drunk to understand her words as anything but a jest on the title I had playfully given her earlier, and I was still high on myself from the poetry reading. So once I was on my feet, swaying a little from the wine, I raised my hand in a mock salute and, solemnly winking two or three times, as if we shared an intimate jest I extended my hand and said jokingly, "My lord."

"It's Walworth," he said, looking at his sister. There was a short pause in the conversation, during which Walworth's eyes rested briefly on the mug I was holding, which bore a *W*.

Caethne broke the silence by explaining, "Baniff was showing Llewelyn the road to Kant, and I couldn't let a fellow scholar pass through here in his condition. He looks as if he's learned to live on starvation—"

"Being from Sunnashiven he probably has."

"—so I took him in and fed him. He's repaid me with a poem. I knew you wouldn't begrudge a loaf of bread."

"No, of course not." He kissed his sister's cheek indulgently. "Not if it makes you happy. I forgot your penchant for adopting strays."

She laughed again.

"So when did you leave Sunnashiven?" Walworth asked me.

"About four days ago," I started to answer, when the door opened and a much older man, whose black hair was peppered with gray and whose clothes were even more tattered than Walworth's, entered the cooking area. The woodchuck was at his heels. The man's face was tired and careworn, but his eyes could outstare a hawk's. Indeed, they would have been a hawk's if they hadn't looked so kind and intelligent. They missed nothing. You could feel his energy crawling inside your clothes when he looked at you. Even the woodchuck seemed a little subdued.

"Look who's here," said Walworth cheerfully. It wasn't clear which of us he was referring to. Probably all three at once. The newcomer, whom I guessed was Mirand, did not answer immediately. Caethne motioned to the woodchuck.

"Come, Pourra, come have some elderberry leaves. Come look sweet for me." Her voice was slightly weaker than usual. The woodchuck gave a low whistle and waddled over to her outstretched hand. She fed him leaves from her basket. "At least you have a tongue to speak to me, which is more than my old master seems to have at the moment. Aren't you surprised to see me, Mirand?"

"Surprised? No. I felt your power interfering with mine for at least a week. Watch your aim, my lady. You damn near gave me a headache two nights ago." His voice was that of a teacher telling a student who was accustomed to praise that she had somehow failed his expectations.

Caethne looked absolutely crushed but she quickly recovered her poise. "Yet you're looking well enough now. Perhaps I can make you a healing balm for your head. I already promised Baniff some for his face—"

"I can heal myself," he said irritably. He crossed the room without further ado, looking as if he just wanted to be alone to rest. Caethne held her mug out to him, which she had barely drunk from and which bore an *M*.

"Would you like some wine, Master? I brewed it myself."

Mirand stopped and gently took the mug from her. He then politely kissed the rim as if he was sorry for his rudeness, swallowed the wine in a gulp, and handed the empty mug back. "Lady," he murmured in thanks, and continued to cross the room. Caethne stood looking at his back.

Just as he was passing through the doorway into the rest of the living quarters Baniff stopped him by reentering the cooking area. The gnome looked up into his haggard face, raised his empty mug, and said, "Welcome home, Mirand. Looks like the party's all here." Mirand nodded, and Baniff continued, "Time to show Llewelyn how to get to Kant. Ready to leave, lad?" I was still swaying unsteadily on my feet. Mirand was leaning an arm against the doorway and searching me with his eyes. "Need to be back by evenin' to catch up on all the news," Baniff said pointedly to Walworth.

I tied my sack to my belt and made my way slowly to the door that led outside, as I really didn't want to leave yet but could think of no good reason to linger. Also I was still feeling light-headed from the wine. Baniff got halfway across the room, Mirand idly watching him, when Caethne suddenly called out, "You mustn't leave yet, Llewelyn. Let me read you your cards for your journey. You're still a stranger to Threle and it cannot hurt to be forewarned even when traveling familiar territory." She hastily bent down to the floor and withdrew from her satchel a packet covered by a black embroidered cloth. "Come, sit with me at the table." She cleared an open space among the flowers.

I did so, even though I wasn't sure if she was more interested in helping me or impressing her teacher with her skill. I did see her glance in Mirand's direction once or twice, as if to make sure he was watching. He was, but his look was one of patiently resigned interest. He was tired and wanted to be alone. Walworth had come closer to the table and was standing on the opposite side of me from Caethne. Baniff was somewhere behind me, no doubt impatient for the reading to start and finish so he could send me on my way to Kant and be back by evening.

"I have no yellow candle," Caethne began, "so I will make use of the sun." She opened the cloth and withdrew a folded piece of yellow parchment and a pile of divination cards whose worn backs told of long and frequent use. "I learned on this set," she said to me. Holding the cards to the skylight, she invoked the sun's energy into them, saying, "Sunna, bless this son of Sunna and speak to him of his journey." I felt as though it were just she and I in the circle again, two users of magic with a secret to share. Then she placed her own hands over them, divided them into three piles, and told me to choose one for its warmth. They all felt warm to me, whether from the sun or her hands or the residual magic in the pack, so I chose the center pile. She put the other piles aside and began to turn over the cards I'd chosen.

"And first the blessed sun," she said, naming the first card. "This card is a pun on my invocation, no doubt, an insurance of my accuracy. And of course you come from Sunna, the land of the sun, and so the child who is depicted here driving a white stallion is a clear journey symbol. No surprises." She turned over another card, which showed a pale young man sitting with bowed head in quiet contemplation, unaware of the three pinecones swelling above him with fertility, the three glowing bowls at his side, or the hand extending a fourth bowl like an unseen present from a cloud. "There are great gifts around you, Llewelyn, if only you would take notice of them. Sometimes your thoughts usurp your promise. You still have promises to claim." She turned over a card picturing a woman with horns who sat in state between two pillars, a scroll in her hands.

I was suddenly so busy struggling through the wine to read the symbol I didn't hear what Caethne was saying. The horned woman was a priestess reminding me that I had seen this pack before, or one like it, that the system wasn't foreign. Where had I seen her before? At Grana's as a child. I instantly knew I could read them. The next card was a burning castle tower with a pair of figures falling to the ground. Caethne silently drew another and placed it between myself and her twin. A dark-haired lady whose eyes were bound in white cloth sat with her back to a raging sea and a rising first-quarter moon. Her arms crossed over her chest, and each hand bore a sword. "Decisions, decisions. I see someone here who—"

"Caethne, what about the torren?" I called the tower by the name Grana had given it. She looked at me questioningly. The wine was still making it easy to speak. "The card of changes crowns the decision card and should be read accordingly, doesn't it—if I can guess the system you're using. May I look at your parchment?" I was speaking like a drunk and eager to show off for my colleague, so I unfolded the paper before she could say anything. It was covered with magical symbols, and I had no trouble recognizing them, for here was the language that Grana had once taught me. The language I had forgotten I ever knew. Reading it aloud was like coming home.

And when I finished reading, the silence in the room was like the silence I'd sometimes experienced after inadvertently outperforming my masters and classmates at the wizard school. An acutely insistent silence that only occurs when expectations and curiosity hum so loud that no one can speak. Caethne was the first to break it. "Where did you learn to read Amara? I didn't think anyone else knew that language."

"A witch taught me when I was a child," I said, feeling quite pleased with myself. "She was a neighbor of mine on the east side of Sunnashiven."

The silence continued for so long that I was starting to feel a little awkward despite the wine when Walworth said breezily, "Well, I'm sure there are at least half a dozen families or so who still speak the old tongue."

"At least," said Mirand. "Comna le nomin fre wice?" What was the name of the witch? he asked me in Amara. His accent was different from how I remembered it.

"Sa nomin e Grana. Esa comna lemond sa nomd." Her name was Grana. 'Tis what everyone called her, I replied, the words coming back to me as easily as a childhood song. I continued in Amara, "She was quite old when

I knew her. She brought forth a child. I was there at the beginning, aiding her." I don't know why I said this, except that Amara is a language that wells up and compels one to speak, unless one has learned to master it, which I hadn't. I was still flowing with the words and letting them master me. Amara's words have life in them, which is why the language is so effective and so dangerous when used for magical purposes. If you don't know what you're doing, the words could turn against you as likely as not. Anyway, the words had brought the memory of Cathe back to my consciousness, as well as all the harrowing events of the past few days. I started to feel soberness trickling up under the wine and my habitual self-consciousness returning. At that point I ceased speaking.

Mirand probably noticed that I started to look uncomfortable because he spoke to me in Botha. "And what business do you have in Kant?"

Baniff saved me the trouble of answering by briefly explaining the high-lights of our journey, including the key. "Kant was my idea," he said, looking at the floor. "Seein' as the boy came up with me from Sunnashiven's wizard school and needs to find some sort of work, we thought he could put in as a scribe in a monastery I know up there."

"Is that what you want, Llewelyn?"

"I would like to finish my studies somewhere eventually. I don't mind starting as a scribe."

"But Baniff says your background is in wizardry. You won't find that kind of training at a monastery."

"No," I said shyly, "but it's a beginning." There was another pause. No one was helping me continue. "A place to start," I said helplessly, in an effort to sound as though I had some viable plan for my life. "To get settled some-where. Then I can look around or maybe study some myself." Another pause. "If they'll have me. If they need a scribe." The wine was really beginning to ebb now and I felt as if I were facing Grendel in one of his ill humors, except that I could sense no cruelty in Mirand, only cold, pragmatic sensi-bility. Also Mirand frightened me more than Grendel ever had. He had an air of supreme competence that knew nothing of admiration or contempt. My abilities would be taken as a given and therefore would not impress him one way or another. He had a way of throwing you back on yourself.

After another pause, during which Mirand kept looking pointedly at me, he said unexpectedly, "Would you consider staying here with us for a while?" From where I was standing I could see Walworth look at him sharply, but he remained silent, as if he had implicit faith in Mirand's judgment. "Now that Caethne has gone her own way I am in need of an apprentice. Would you accept me as a tutor?" *Would I?* His humility certainly impressed me. "We can easily begin your studies from wherever you left off."

"I . . . don't know." I looked around the room. "I would love to stay, to apprentice myself to you . . ." I remembered the bans. "But in Sunnashiven they placed a ban on us against using magic for any other reason except to aid the state of Sunna."

"Ah, yes, the bans of Sunnashiven's wizard school. How do you hope to escape them in the monastery?"

"I don't know," I said lamely, feeling caught in some shortcoming.

"I can remove that ban."

"Just like that? Just off the top of your head?" *What a stupid thing to say.*

"Well, it's a fairly scholarly head."

"I also have a ban against using magic to help myself, and against attempting any spell requiring my full individual powers, and against traveling north of the Drumuns."

"Yes, I know. As to helping yourself, I would prefer to think of using your tutelage to help me. But I can also remove that one if it will set your heart at ease. It's hard to teach a student in a constant state of fear. I don't imagine we will come anywhere near using your full individual powers, and I never travel north of the Drumuns myself, so we needn't concern ourselves with those. At least not now."

"All right . . . Master. I should like very much to stay and learn from you."

"Good. We'll begin tomorrow. Now I must beg your leave to sleep." He really did look tired, and I said nothing as he turned and passed through the door into the rest of the living quarters.

There was another pause as the cooking area recovered the relaxed, homey atmosphere Caethne had given it before Mirand arrived. She lightly embraced me and said warmly, "Well, I shall have to go to town and get extra food for tonight. I am so glad you are staying with us. I shall have someone else to practice Amara with. It will be just like having two brothers." She said this last statement while looking to Walworth in an attempt to gauge his reaction.

"There is kinship between myself and all of Mirand's students," Walworth said graciously. "You are welcome. Mirand has much to teach."

"Thank you."

He lightly pressed his sister's hand. "I must to sleep myself. We'll talk later."

"Of course," she said softly, but he was halfway across the room when she said it.

After Walworth passed into the rest of the dwelling Baniff went over to the cauldron and refilled his mug. He toasted me with "Welcome home, lad," but he was looking over at the mess of cards and flowers on the table. "Ye never finished yer reading."

"Another time," said Caethne. "I thought Llewelyn might like to come to town with me to get food before it gets much later. The markets of Helas should be a treat after Sunnashiven. Would you like to come with us, Baniff? Or would you prefer to keep a careful eye on the mess I've created?"

"Someone's got to guard the homestead. Besides, I need a nap."

She laughed at the incongruity of his statement and promised to find him some leeks. At the word *leeks* Pourra, who had been sitting quietly for some time, ran to the door leading outside, as if he was anticipating an outing. Caethne emptied the rest of the elderberries out of her basket into a pile near the fireplace and took my arm in hers. "Guard well, gnome," she said, laughing again, while Baniff relaxed in a chair, mug to his lips.

When we passed outside the land was still dappled, but now there was more sun than shadow. It was a temporary patchwork, the sun having crossed the sky border of the meridian, but I knew that the day would hold itself together, and that Caethne and I would be running down those places where it held itself fast for now.

Seven

*T*he wildflowers on the table took six months to die. When I asked Caethne about their longevity she told me that her love kept them alive, and since I thought that was as good an explanation as any, I believed her. Once she gave me a handful of the flowers to take to the room I shared with Mirand, but they withered within a few hours, so I fed them to Pourra. He didn't seem to mind. A few leaves from the wildflowers would sometimes find their way onto Mirand's plate before he sat down to eat, but as he never remarked on their presence, nobody else did either.

Mirand was an effective teacher. I learned more from him in six months than I had learned in my previous seventeen years, and despite his austere exterior we soon got on comfortably together, at least on the surface. Mirand was far too observant to fail to notice my lack of confidence and far too wise to pretend my insecurities didn't exist. In this way he differed from Caethne, who didn't recognize my shortcomings at all. When Caethne smiled and greeted me in the morning she was speaking to my most cherished image of myself, to a fellow scholar whose insights she respected and who might be bleary-eyed and a little disoriented from staying up late the previous night with his books. I would later learn, in the course of my monastic training, how to trick people into bonding with me by pretending not to notice their worse qualities and seeming to endorse their own fantastic images of themselves. But that was much later, when I had achieved a stronger, more charismatic personality and had begun to seriously study the ways of evil.

Caethne was not evil. She knew nothing of politeness. When she asked me about my studies, as she frequently did, it was out of genuine interest. Her manner with me was not consciously contrived to put me at ease and so I had no sense of being tricked into acting confident, which would have fostered resentment rather than liking. Few people enjoy being made fools of, even if others occasionally mean well.

Mirand never said anything directly, but he acknowledged my insecurities by letting me know that he had neither the time nor the patience to indulge them. If I made a mistake in an exercise and nervously laughed at myself in an attempt to reassure him that in no way had I expected to get it right in the first place, he would watch me with a stony expression until I had finished putting myself down and then pick up the lesson again as if nothing had happened. The effect was devastating. I knew at once that he had absolutely no sympathy for my self-doubts, and I quickly began to feel ashamed of showing any skittishness in front of him, as if my awkwardness would be viewed as a cowardly plea for him to lower his standards. The end result was not the death of my shyness, although this might have been part of his intent, but rather the birth of a strong desire to pretend to be confident in front of him to avoid disapproval. With Mirand, as with so many wizards, the acting was all. But after a while the acting grew most enjoyable. My pretended confidence was a brave and gaudy mask that drew life from my fear of displeasing my new master, and I was finally learning to love life.

In short, it was from Mirand that I first learned to lie.

And I learned a lot of magic. In fact, once we got used to each other, or rather once I got used to him, we had excellent conversations on all sorts of intellectual topics. At first, however, it was rough going. I remember spending the first night in a chair by the fireplace in the cooking area because I lacked the courage to ask for anything better, and keeping myself awake until dawn with my own thoughts and fears concerning my new apprenticeship. Just after I managed to fall asleep Caethne woke me to tell me that Mirand was waiting. She was wearing a crumpled sleeping shirt that I guessed was her brother's and her hair looked even more tangled than it had the day before when I first saw her harvesting elderberries. She handed me a bowl of warm porridge and I quickly swallowed its contents, but the food did little to make up for my lack of sleep and I knew that I was in a wretched physical and mental condition for beginning an apprenticeship. My hand felt grimy as I clutched my sack.

She led me through bare living quarters that were partly built into a cave. She had made a bed for herself in the far corner out of two worn pieces of mat and a wooly brown blanket, and I couldn't help thinking how uncomfortable the hard stone floor must have been for her during the night. She was using the clothes she had worn the day before for a pillow. Pourra was still asleep, curled up inside the blanket with only his little brown head and the tip of one paw visible, looking for all the world as if he owned the bed. He twitched a little as we walked by and Caethne whispered, "Look, Sweetness is dreaming for me."

We climbed some stone steps to an upper level where Mirand's room was located, just above her own bed. His door was open. He was sitting on a plain, narrow bed, and he was dressed in a simple purple robe and studying a scroll. He looked quite refreshed. His hair was combed and he had washed and shaved. The scent of new rushes on the floor mingled with that of burning frankincense, which added to the effect of readiness and order. I stood in the doorway in the sweaty clothes that I hadn't changed in almost a week, my sack of books in hand, and waited uncertainly. When I looked around for Caethne she was gone.

He continued reading long enough for me to wonder if he was aware of my presence. When I began to agonize over whether I should interrupt him or risk having him think that I was late to my first lesson, he looked up and said kindly, "Come in, Llewelyn. This is to be your room as well as mine. I have always shared my quarters with my apprentices."

I entered, hardly daring to breathe lest I make myself unwelcome by taking too much air. Even with my limited magical training I could feel the periodic pendulum swings of power in the room. Power in enclosed places often feels the way a river current might feel if rivers ran alternating currents of mood and tone instead of water. Since I was not particularly advanced in my studies, I immediately realized that Mirand's power had to be exceptionally heavy for me to feel it.

I noticed there was another bed that matched his own, and he motioned toward it to indicate that it was mine. I stood in front of it and he indicated that I should sit, so I sat down and rested my sack on the bed. The bed felt firm and hard. Mirand continued reading, and while he was occupied I looked around and noticed all manner of books and scrolls lining the walls, so many books the room felt like a small library that happened to have two beds in it. There was a writing table and a three-legged stool in the corner that weren't visible from the doorway. The table was covered with stones and crystals and parchments. A small black mirror in an amethyst frame was also on the table, propped against the wall. There were other tools, most of which I didn't recognize, on a low table between my bed and his, including three or four small wands and inscribed candles, but I knew nothing of their uses at the time. A cage containing two gray cockatiels hung over the writing table, and there was a window cut into the cave wall over the table between our beds. The censer of burning frankincense was on the window ledge. Mirand continued reading for the space of a few minutes, while I sat there painfully trying to determine if he was testing me to see whether I was discourteous enough to interrupt him or lazy enough to let him continue so that I wouldn't have to do any work.

Those few minutes seemed half a morning, but he finally looked up. "You may avail yourself of any books that interest you." There was an undercurrent of slight reproach in his tone, as if I was needlessly wasting time by watching him. I had thought we would discuss my previous studies or my new duties as his apprentice, and I was a little overwhelmed by his unexpected invitation to make myself free with his books. I had trouble accepting his generosity because I didn't want to start our new relationship by imposing on him in any way, so I removed a book from my sack to read. He shrugged and continued with his own studies, and I realized with dismay that my insane need to please had just cost me a morning of browsing through some of the most intriguing and tempting volumes I had ever seen. If I put my book down now in favor of one of his, I would risk looking indecisive and ill disciplined.

We read our separate texts in silence. My mind occasionally wandered back to the reading I had shared with Caethne on the previous day but I had no trouble focusing my thoughts on my book. I was grateful for the way our first "lesson" was going because I didn't trust myself to make intelligent conversation with Mirand and our solitary readings gave me a legitimate reason for not speaking. I expected that soon he would ask me about my reading, or maybe even give me a test, so I was especially intent on memorizing difficult passages and finding weaknesses in the arguments so I could impress him. After about an hour filled with the sounds of a rising household, the subdued shrills of the cockatiels, and the crackling of our papers, Mirand put down his scroll and stood up. "I have other business to attend to today, but first we shall deal with your bans." He walked over to the writing table, picked up two clear stones, and brought them over to me. "I designed these myself. Your hand."

He seemed to mean my left hand, so I extended it to him, palm upward. He put the stones in my palm and firmly grasped it in his own hand. I was again aware of how sweaty and dirty I was, and I felt a little ashamed. "Is it of your own free will that you consent to have all bans removed from your working magic without reference to helping Sunna and from your working magic to help yourself?"

I was a little frightened, probably because I realized that consenting would constitute a permanent break with my past, and as little as I cherished my past, it was in some ways all I had. The change was really going to happen. Now. I also knew we both could be executed if we were doing this in Sunnashiven, and Mirand's matter-of-fact tone gave me the impression that he did not take this as seriously as I did. It was probably natural for me to feel a bit fearful under the circumstances. Yet I also knew that there was no way I would refuse his offer, because I felt beholden and attracted to the entire strange household and I was as much afraid of appearing ungrateful as I was of losing my past. I wanted him to think I was serious and that I thought enough of him to trust to his protection as my new master. I murmured, "Yes," and devoutly wished he had just done the thing without bothering to ask for my permission.

I felt pressure in my palm, and then he quickly released it. "Keep the stones about you. In three days they shall turn black. That is how you will know the bans have been removed, for the bans shall then be in the stones. At that point it would be wise to bury them."

"All right, Master."

"Mirand. You don't smile enough to call me by my title." I smiled, not at his familiarity, but to make up for not having smiled before. I really wanted to get it right. He pointedly refused to respond to my belated expression, but abruptly stood with his back to me and relit the incense, which had gone out. "Frankincense is excellent for hex breaking and not a bad thing when dissipating bans." He showed me a little pouch on the window ledge. "Use as much as you feel you need to, and keep the censer burning as long as you feel comfortable with it." It was clear that he wasn't referring to my emotional feelings but to my sense of the effectiveness of his magic. I was to pay attention to when the incense had ceased to be useful for me by paying attention to my own magical responses to his spell. It takes some discipline for a novice to be able to do this sort of thing without guidance. Of course he would know from what remained in the pouch how much I had burned. So this was my test.

"Mas—Mirand, would you like to talk about my reading?"

"No. Would you?"

"I . . . don't know. I thought maybe—maybe you might like to see what I've been studying."

"I've already seen it." He handed me the scroll on his bed. To my surprise it not only contained all of the words of the text I was reading, but the words of my own thoughts as I tried to find counterarguments to those in the book. "It's clear that you understand this treatise as well as anybody else does, and possibly better than the author himself. I happen to agree with your assessment. Therefore there's nothing to talk about." He started to leave the room. "In three days, when those stones are safely black and buried, I shall read and criticize some text of my choosing and you shall manifest the words on a blank scroll. It's a good technique to practice in preparation for materialization spells, and a useful trick to know should you ever decide to go in for scribe work. I'll use no thought defenses. Those will come later."

He was leaving the room when I said hastily, "I'm not sure how to begin with something that advanced. Will you be returning soon to teach me?"

"No, I won't." He started to step into the hallway but stopped himself and turned his face toward me. "The collected wisdom of hundreds of wizards lines these walls, and you've got three days to exploit it. You might even discover that a few of them actually knew something worth knowing. Research. At least get the theory down. Until those stones turn black I won't expect you to practice." Then he left.

I pocketed the stones and listened to the cockatiels for half a minute. I was not doing well physically, and my fatigue made the bed look more tempting than Mirand's books. I wouldn't let myself lie down, however, because I still felt a little like a trespasser in Mirand's domain. I also had the shamefaced feeling that my teacher thought I was too stupid to have considered researching the problem he set me. I, who had spent years in the library! I damned my own ineptitude and slowly got up enough resolve to empty the entire contents of my sack on the bed so that I could organize my belongings and begin my work. I wanted to display my books somewhere so that Mirand would notice how well read I was. Perhaps they would counteract the negative impression I feared I had given him. At least I wouldn't look as if I was waiting for him to tell me what to do, which seemed to be the way he wanted things.

I gave my sack a final shake and a small white wand that my colored glass and hard white pea had stuck themselves to fell out. The wand was carved in a long flowing script I didn't recognize and was studded with blue sapphires. I had absolutely no idea how it got there. My first thought was that Mirand had materialized it as some sort of clue to help me with my first assignment, but the instant I grasped the wand it burned a hole into my palm the size of a gold piece. My screams brought Walworth, who found me on the floor where the force of the wand had knocked me.

"I'd come in but it looks dangerous," he said pleasantly from the doorway.

"Come in anyway," I said, rising. After all, I wasn't about to tell him he couldn't enter what I still thought of as Mirand's quarters. I stretched my wounded palm to the air because it now hurt to clench my hand. This was a mistake, as the pain began to throb in time with the power surges in the room. Once I was standing I noticed that Caethne had come up behind her brother. She was fully dressed now and carrying Pourra.

Walworth walked toward me with all the graciousness of an invited guest entering a new dwelling for the first time. His manner made it clear that he regarded this space as my room, but far from putting me at ease, it increased my discomfort. I felt somewhat dishonest telling him to come in, knowing that he had probably been in here dozens of times and that I was the newcomer. I was glad that Caethne followed him.

"That isn't one of Mirand's toys." He bent down and looked appreciatively at the wand, which had fallen on the floor. "Such craftsmanship. How did you come by it?"

"I don't know. I found it in my sack. I don't know how it got there."

He looked strangely at me and said, "You have an impressive talent for acquiring magical items."

Caethne knelt next to him and set her familiar down. "Let Pourra play with it. Wood spirits aren't sensitive to power alignments." The woodchuck was already batting the end of the wand. His weight flipped up the opposite end and as it fell back toward him he caught it in his teeth and shook it. No ill effects.

Walworth gingerly removed him, being careful not to touch the wand himself. "I would hate to see your friend's sharp teeth mar those beautiful carvings," he said to Caethne. He took a black cloth out of his pocket and, using it as a barrier between his hand and the wand, picked it up for closer examination. I had forgotten that using a black cloth barrier was the proper way to handle any unfamiliar magical item, as black will absorb energy without transmitting it. A black cloth has the added advantage in some cases of combining in itself your own energy with the item's, which is useful for acclimatizing yourself to a particular tool. Grabbing wands at random could result in injuries like mine.

"If it is an alignment problem, why did it injure me?" I asked Caethne. "I've never allied myself with any particular god force, and I'm certainly no cleric."

"That may be the point," said Walworth. "The wand didn't recognize you as one of its own. Pourra can handle it because nature spirits are universally recognized by magical items."

"The same way nature is," added Caethne.

I felt chagrined that Walworth had to remind me of the obvious. I knew these things, of course, but I had forgotten them because I was busy focusing my mind on how the wand had gotten into my sack. Now Walworth would think I was stupid, as Mirand probably did. A trickle of blood was running down my palm to my wrist. I turned my hand palm up so that my blood wouldn't drip on the new rushes.

Caethne stood up with Pourra under one arm and took my injured hand in hers. "I've made that healing balm I promised Baniff. Come with me and I'll put some on your palm."

"Yer balm doesn't work, lassie. I put a gallon on my face and I'm still sober." Baniff was in the doorway. His scratches had disappeared. "We've got a courier here," he said hastily to Walworth.

"May I show this to Mirand?" Walworth asked me quickly. I nodded and he started for the door with the wand. At the last minute he turned to Caethne, "No more sleeping on the cave floor, soldier. You'll be no use to us with the ague. There's extra space in Baniff's quarters."

"Look who's giving me orders, twin."

"Yes, look," he said with a smile, but I could tell he was serious. "That disease trap is no place for my second in command. The lady who shares my authority had best not take unnecessary chances with her health."

"Oh, you must mean Mother. She's never been one for jeopardizing her health. I'm sure she's seen about as many dirty mats as you have, embroidering fine linen napkins with her ladies-in-waiting at home while they all cluck and worry about her wayward children." Caethne lightly dismissed his concerns and turned her attention back to my hand.

I couldn't fathom what these last statements meant, so I assumed they were a private joke between Caethne and her brother and I pretended I hadn't heard them. "When I noticed your bed I thought you must be terribly uncomfortable," I said to Caethne.

Walworth smiled at me as if we had suddenly become partners in a conspiracy. "Listen to Llewelyn. Those musty mats are fit to be burned before they spread plague throughout the household. So burn them. That is an order." He left with Baniff.

She stuck her tongue out behind them. "Want to watch me cleanse a mat with fire?" I started laughing so hard I forgot my pain. "Come on, I'll cleanse your clothes too, and show you where we bathe. The men actually built a bath here. Not that you'd ever guess from the floor in the cooking area that a little dirt bothered them. Guess it must be my alignment." I don't know which of us was laughing more loudly.

"Do you have an alignment, Caethne?"

"Are you kidding?" She laughed and made a grim-faced gesture that reminded me of Grendel. I broke up. "Most witches are above that sort of thing. I think alignments are for certain childish wizards and clerics, mostly male, I might add, who don't know how to live without a set of rules. I like Habundia Ceres, at least the Habundia I know. I like aligning myself with natural forces who know no stupid handed-down-forever-from-the-gods-and-jump-three-times-boundaries. I'll create and disperse my own boundaries as they suit me, thank you, and I'll harm none doing it. And I'll sleep on a cave floor if I like." She turned toward the door as she said the latter. "Have you ever met a religious person who was truly free?"

I thought a bit. "No, I guess I haven't."

"Case closed."

We ran down to the cooking area, Caethne giving her bed a disdainful glance along the way. She took some golden liquid about the consistency of honey out of the cauldron and rubbed it into my palm, telling me to take my clothes off and wait. Then she ran out and returned with her bedding, Pourra running in front of her as if he couldn't wait for the fun to begin. She stripped off her own clothes, bundled them together with mine and the mats, wrapped everything in the blanket, and tossed it in the fire. "Watch this!" We were both still laughing and getting quite silly. She uttered some words in Amara with a few extra flourishes for fun, got serious for a minute as she pulled the flame toward her by slowly curling her arms toward her shoulders to flex her biceps, and said, "That'll cleanse now."

She lit a torch from the fire and led me back through the living quarters and toward a narrow stair leading down that I hadn't noticed before. Neither of us had a stitch of clothing on and neither of us seemed to think anything of it. "An underground river flows near the base, the water is usually fairly warm, and there's even soap. Your clothes will be ready in twenty minutes, sir." She handed me the torch and mock-curtseyed. "Don't get the balm wet."

I descended through the darkness, torch in hand, and was delighted to find that the steps led directly into soothingly warm water and that there was a handy hole drilled into the last dry step for the torch. I splashed around for a few minutes, admiring the stalactites that tripped all over themselves on their way down from the roof, some of which joined into a rock column on the other side of the little pool the river formed at this point. After a while I noticed a strange little gray-and-yellow spotted fish, and then another, and then a whole underwater cloud of them, so I amused myself catching fish in my good hand and letting them go. I was so fortunate. What a wonderful household, really, especially Caethne, who I began to wish was really my older sister. *I must learn more about witchcraft*, I thought. Baniff was a fascinating companion, and Walworth was certainly kind and courteous enough, and I was sure that once I got back upstairs feeling new and cleansed I would surely be able to research my eyes out and make a good impression on Mirand. To have all those curious books at my disposal! And in three days, when the stones turned black, I would be free to—

The stones! The stones were in my pocket, and Caethne was burning my clothes in witch fire, and who knew what her magic would do to them. Mirand had told me to keep the stones with me! I leapt out of the water, grabbed the torch, and ran dripping up the steps and into the living quarters, where Baniff happened to be crossing the room from the cooking area with an ale bottle in his hand. He silently raised the bottle in salute and ascended the stairs, and I rushed into the cooking area hoping that Caethne would be there alone. She was, and she was still nude. She looked at me understandingly and said, "Don't pay any attention to him." The fire was low now, practically out. She took out the bundle and unwrapped the unsoiled blanket.

I quickly put my clean clothes back on to avoid more potentially embarrassing encounters, and Caethne did the same, although her hurry seemed to stem more from her anticipation of the next stage of her project than from any sense of shame. The mats now looked as if they were newly woven. I took the stones out of my pocket. They had both turned a deep, rich black, and one now had a fine crack running through it.

"What have you got there, Llewelyn? Let me see."

I gave her the stones and explained what they were for and how I feared Mirand's reaction when he discovered how careless I had been. "Do you have any advice?" I asked disconsolately.

"If these were natural stones I might be able to do something to repair the damage, or at least determine exactly what happened to them in the fire, but since Mirand made them himself I have no idea how to begin. And I've never worked with bans. That sort of thing is for wizards. But don't despair, there must be something in one of his books."

I thought about all the other work I'd been assigned and panicked at the thought of having more research to do than I could possibly accomplish in the next three days. The morning was already half gone. Caethne, having been a student herself, instinctively recognized my concerns. "Look, if there is any damage done, I'm partly responsible, so I'll do what I can to help you. But first let's finish up here."

She took a small piece of white birch from near the fireplace and a broken stick with which she engraved the words *Burned, sir* on the wood. Then she made two small holes in the wood with the stick and murmured, "Enough magic for now." She took some daisies from the table, called Pourra, and made a little daisy-chain collar for him, from which she suspended the sign. "I'll give you something better if you promise not to eat them." He nodded. She took an ale bottle from behind one of the fireplace stones, picked up the bedding, and said, "Come."

The three of us went up the stairs and down the hallway past a room that was on the other side of the hall from Mirand's and farther down. I got the impression that this was the room that Caethne would soon be sharing with Baniff. We stopped before a slightly open door at the end of the hall. Caethne started to push it open wider, but the sound of an unfamiliar female voice speaking in flawless Botha stopped her. "Sunnashiven is completely under the control of the rebel forces now, although Count Sina is quickly becoming a problem."

"But Sina was one of the rebellion's prime instigators," interrupted Baniff. "He's been plottin' against King Sunnas fer two years."

"Yes, but that was never his intent," responded the woman. "Let me give you some more background."

"Please," said Walworth, his tone lightly rebuking Baniff's recent interruption.

The woman drew an audible breath, as if to make sure the floor was really hers now, and continued her report in a voice hard with hesitation. "Count Sina's peasants were so badly off two years ago that they would have overthrown him if he hadn't started pointing their anger toward the capital and sweet-talking them about how he was their true friend in liberty and hated King Sunnas's taxes as much as they did. He even strolled about the town markets in peasant garb to show his solidarity with the farmers, and he lowered the county tax to mollify them."

"We certainly thought he was sincere," interjected Baniff again. "Ye generally don't incite yer people against yer king if ye generally don't mean it."

"Well," responded the woman with dry impatience, "we all thought he generally meant it."

"Sometimes truth outweighs illusion," added Baniff poignantly.

I glanced toward Caethne, who smiled a little at Baniff's comment. Of course I had known nothing of this intrigue in Sunnashiven and so I was helplessly fascinated. And as Caethne wasn't attempting to get me to leave, I decided not to encourage her to do so.

"When Sina lowered the county tax, his guards nearly mutinied over a rumor that the reduction in county income meant a similar reduction in their pay. Sina responded to this threat by collecting more money in the name of the king than King Sunnas actually demanded, so he could pay off his guards and meet a few other expenses with the difference."

"Didn't the guards wonder where their pay was coming from?" asked Walworth.

"Of course. Everyone had questions about Sina's ability to continue to spend county money after apparently reducing the county tax income. So Sina tried to turn things to his advantage with another lie by claiming he was paying salaries out of his own personal treasury. His popularity at home increased."

"I see," said Walworth coldly. "And thus is a rebel made. Continue, Mistress."

"And thus is a rebel made, Commander," she wearily agreed. "Whenever Count Sina claimed that King Sunnas was demanding a new 'tax increase' he was careful to feed his people pretty words about tyranny while feeding Sunnas secret messages of loyalty that explained how he feared being overthrown. As long as Sunnas was getting his share of loot he did nothing to discourage Sina's tactics, but you can bet the king kept an eye on him. To make things more uncomfortable, Sina's creditors also began to keep an eye on him. If he had enough gold in his personal treasury to pay his guards, surely he could start making good on his debts. The count had inherited two or three generations of public and personal debt when his father died, and he had gotten into the habit of borrowing money from all the other southern counties just to keep half a flush ahead of his creditors."

The woman paused as if she was expecting to be questioned, but as nobody spoke, she continued in her stiffly hesitant voice, "You should know that Sina's biggest creditor was King Sevalas."

I gathered this was a rum state of affairs, because I heard one or two loud sighs of impatient surprise at this piece of news.

The woman tried to mollify the impact of her report. "King Sunnas never would have stood for any of his nobles borrowing independently from foreign nations, but it happens all the time, as you know firsthand, Commander. King Sevalas probably knew that Count Sina would never repay his debt, but Sevalas wanted a plausible excuse to set up a military base in County Sina, in the heart of the Kingdom of Sunna, and he was threatening to do just that by making Count Sina's debts public and marching across the border."

"Of course," said Walworth, sounding vaguely appreciative of Sevalas's strategy. "Who would stop him? King Sunnas's army couldn't even withstand a handful of well-trained, determined peasant soldiers, as we've seen."

"And no other power in the world could really condemn Sevalas's action, the debt being real," added Mirand, speaking for the first time.

"Well," answered the woman, "Sina put everything he owned and then some in hock to raise the money for King Sevalas, but he could come up with only half the amount. Sevalas took it, of course, knowing that the count would then be utterly destitute, owing gold on gold to all his peers, and in a mood to make deals. The deal was horrible. To avoid a catastrophic invasion from Sevalas, Count Sina was to pledge his oldest son, Franko, in marriage to Sevalas's youngest daughter, signing the county over to them and making the little princess the county's nominal ruler."

"An agreement of questionable legality without King Sunnas's consent," commented Mirand mildly.

"Yes," agreed the woman, "but it was the piece of paper Sevalas needed to ensure Sina's complete compliance. In effect it was Sina's death warrant. If King Sunnas didn't kill him for treason, the other counts surely would for making their own territories vulnerable to a foreign power. Sina explained Franko's absence by telling people he was studying for the priesthood at a monastery in Sevalas. The truth is that King Sevalas was keeping Franko a virtual hostage. The point is, Count Sina has been most cooperative in instituting Sevalas's people in his county, and it was Sevalas who really made a 'rebel' out of Sina."

There was a brief space of quiet, exasperated sighs. I had grown so intent on catching every word of the woman's report that I had ceased to notice Caethne, but my new friend had grown as quiet as I was. We mirrored each other's intensity as the woman continued speaking.

"You see, to the count's horror, his people had begun to interpret his impassioned anti-tax speeches as encouragement to refuse to pay any tax to King Sunnas. As a result, the count's farmers felt emboldened enough to start growing only enough to feed themselves, to avoid the tax. Soon the peasants in the other counties followed suit. Sina's economy was the first to crumble when the farmers no longer had any profit money to buy things from the merchants, or surplus food to sell to traveling marketeers to bring to Sunnashiven. Everyone who wasn't a farmer became one. Then the strange weather patterns that have been plaguing the southwest kingdoms for years wiped everything out and Count Sina was forced to go, cap in hand, to King Sunnas to ask that his county be put on relief."

"Sina must have needed all of his oratory for that meeting," interrupted Baniff.

"He needed more than fine words," interjected the woman, sharp with impatience to continue. "King Sunnas refused to help him unless Count Sina put his county's and his personal treasury in trust to the kingdom. The king also threatened to make public the count's secret pledges of loyalty if Sina refused to comply. You see, the king had been biding his time with Sina. Sunnas knew that if the count was revealed as having been the king's man all along, it could have a dampening effect across many of the more rebellious southern counties, and if Sina was assassinated by a disappointed rebel for his loyalty to the king, well, all the better excuse for exercising martial law over County Sina and plundering all its resources for the capital. Teach the would-be rebels a lesson. But Sunnas miscalculated. Sina promised him everything he wanted, returned home, and ran to Sevalas's people for instructions. That's when he threw himself into the war effort, with Sevalas's backing. He actually had the cheek to hope that his war 'contribution' would be accepted by the other counts as payment of his debts to them." The woman paused before asking, "That isn't Krygon ale, is it?"

"No," said Baniff, "this is drinkable."

"I only ask because the distillery in Krygon was ransacked and destroyed at the same time Sunnashiven was taken."

"Good job," said Baniff. Everyone laughed.

The woman continued, her voice killing off the laughter. "Anyway, a week before the march on the capital, the rebel counts, including Sina, met in council and drew up a charter for the new government. There were several peasant representatives present, for show. They had no real voice in the charter. One of those representatives was my contact. I learned from her that Count Sina is to be made temporary lord protector of the State of New Sunna whether he likes it or not."

There was a chorus of groans, and Walworth asked, "Out of fourteen rebel counts, what did Sina do to deserve this honor?"

"People like his speeches. The southern farmers love him. King Sevalas sent a few sham representatives to stir up sentiment in his favor. Most important, nobody else wants the job, as nobody seems to think now that the new regime will last, and Sina is afraid to refuse. King Sunnas left almost nothing in the treasury and the country's debt is staggering when you realize that he was financing everything on credit from proposed tax increases. Two of the rebel counts have already disappeared. Sina's terrified that King Sunnas will return and he just wants enough money to disappear somewhere himself, but he's equally terrified of King Sevalas. He knows the country couldn't sustain a counterattack should King Sunnas return with help and that his own life will continue only as long as Sevalas supports him in office. Sina never really sympathized with the people's complaints in the first place, but he can't back away from his golden oratory now. Besides, to refuse the office would be to compromise the only protection he has."

"I see," said Walworth coldly. There was a pause for thought. The air felt dense around me and Caethne. "What is your sense of Count Sina's popularity in Sunnashiven itself?"

"My sense when I left the city two days ago, Commander—by the way, I gave my charger the gods' own workout galloping here along the trade road in two days. The forest paths wind around so much I didn't trust myself not to get lost in them, and I'm sure my horse appreciates the extra feed— my sense was that he has little support in the city. The other counts are prepared to publicly acclaim him lord protector in front of a crowd of imported southern peasant-soldiers to put on a show of popularity. I believe that Sina will then use the office to milk whatever he can to finance his escape to obscurity."

"Sounds sensible," quipped Baniff.

"There's more. Just before I left Sunnashiven I received word that King Sevalas has now offered King Sunnas and his followers protection. I am sure that Sina does not know this; if he did, nothing could induce him to remain where he is. As it stands, King Sevalas now rules the Kingdom of Sunna through Count Sina. However, the country is in such a mess that it won't be long before people start clamoring for their king again, and Sevalas has done his bit to hasten the collapse by having his lackeys give orders to their soldiers to burn the fields around Sunnashiven when they invaded. The only food getting into city is coming from Sevalas, but Sina is telling everyone it's surplus from his own county and no one wants to question him before he's safely made lord protector. Sevalas wants no competition, so traders from Helas have been turned back at the border."

"Yes, we've heard," acknowledged Walworth.

"In sum, my lord, when things get miserable enough, my guess is that Sevalas plans to support King Sunnas's return to a country devoid of a rebel opposition, and seat his own people throughout the south counties and around King Sunnas. Whatever happens, King Sevalas is now and will remain the real ruler of Sunna, which means of course that despite our efforts Roguehan has acquired another state."

A stiffly delicate silence greeted her words. I took it that the woman had finished her report and that Walworth did not wish to offer any more comments on it at present. "Thank you, Mistress," he said quietly, dismissing her. "So it seems we've befriended our enemy."

Caethne glanced sharply at me and gently drew me back from the door. I now noticed that while we were listening she had put the mats on the floor and placed Pourra on the mats with the sign *Burned, sir* displayed around his neck and the open ale bottle between his paws. I followed her swiftly down the hall as she whispered, "Why waste a good practical joke?" When we entered Mirand's room Caethne was in a rushed kind of vagueness. "I'll get all the gossip later," she said somewhat apologetically. "Right now you've got an assignment to do, and I promised to help you research those stones. Besides, that balm is long overdue to come off." It had dried to the consistency of plaster. "Mirand should have some water in here. We must wet your hand now." She began to move objects around on his writing desk.

"Caethne . . ." I paused uncomfortably. "If you need to 'get the gossip' now, it's all right. I won't say anything."

She turned and looked at me for a long time. It was most embarrassing. All of a sudden my "older sister" had disappeared and neither of us knew what to say. She continued to fumble through the objects on the desk, found a jar of water behind the mirror, picked it up and went to the door. She held it in one hand as she looked down the hall in the direction we came from, then softly shut the door. She came over and sat next to me on the bed.

"It's all supposed to be a big secret and everything," she said. "But Mirand has his reasons for asking you to stay, and I, for one, detest secrets." She dipped her fingers in the jar and began to rub the balm, but I could see she wasn't really paying attention to what she was doing. "My brother, with the help of the Duke of Helas and a few friends, has been running a wildcat operation to aid your country's rebels. Helas will do anything to keep his southwest markets viable, and the Helan merchants have been losing trade income as a result of Sunna's internal problems and the general falling-off of production in the southwest kingdoms over the last several years. The king knows nothing about Walworth's operation and our parents would die if they knew. Our monarch is a good king, a man of peace, and his policy has always been one of noninterference in other countries' internal affairs. It's a good policy and has worked for Threle for many generations. The king understands, as Helas does not, that we have no right to tamper with other governments to protect our trading interests. My brother agrees with this in principle."

"Then why is he helping Helas?"

"Because there's more at stake than trade. No Threlan had anything to do with the peasant rebellion. That happened without our prodding, as you've heard. But once talk became action, Walworth and Helas agreed to lend their support. They had learned that King Sunnas was secretly sending tribute to Sevalas, protection money, and Sevalas, of course, is a front man for Roguehan."

"Who's Roguehan?"

Caethne briefly smiled her older-sister smile as if the whole thing were really silly and she wished to make it a private joke. Then she looked serious again. "His father was a soldier of fortune who was granted a small duchy somewhere in the western part of the Kingdom of Furnesse, a duchy that Roguehan has now inherited, but I understand he's never there. Apparently he's also inherited and collected a dangerous coterie of unusually powerful companions who have gone into the land acquisition business. Either they've got something over Sevalas, although I can't imagine what, or Sevalas feels he can use their talents to secure his own troubled kingdom and realize his own imperial ambitions. Whatever it is, Walworth says that Sevalas takes orders from Roguehan. Now Sunnas and Sina do, too. Not bad for a young duke."

"Who is Roguehan's king? Does Roguehan have his support? I know nothing of Furnesse, except it's very far away."

"The king's name is Furna, and nobody seems to know what he thinks. Furnesse *is* very far away. Some say it lies so far west that it touches the end of the world. I don't know anyone who's been there." She absently spilled more water on the balm, which had practically worked itself off at this point. I peeled it off myself and it quickly disintegrated. I let my hand drip water into the rushes on the floor, and I gave her my full attention while she continued.

"One of Roguehan's companions is his former tutor, Zelar, whom Mirand studied under at one time. Talk about alignments. Mirand says Zelar is evil, that he worships evil gods, and he's convinced my brother that Roguehan's ultimate design is to consolidate the southwest kingdoms and invade Threle. That's why Walworth wanted to see the peasants in power. There hasn't been time to find out more. Also, we are of peasant stock ourselves, our titles go back only a few generations, and my brother tends to sympathize with—"

"Your what?"

"Our titles. Well, I suppose you must know sooner or later. Our parents are the Duke and Duchess of Walworth, the northernmost duchy in Threle. I'll tell you all about our family history sometime if you really care to hear it"—my mouth was open—"but perhaps you'd rather research something more interesting, like magic."

"So you really are a lady of the land." I trembled and knelt. "*Lady* Caethne, please forgive my—"

She looked hurt and raised me to my feet. "I thought we were getting to be friends, Llewelyn. What's changed? The only person who ever called me by my title at home was my old nurse in a fit of anger as she tried to teach me manners. Besides, in Sarana, my native language, the proper word is *cae*. Lady is a verb. It means 'to act' or 'to lie.'" She was clearly hoping I would laugh at the incongruity of our languages, but I only felt more mortified at my ignorance.

"In Sunna . . . in Sunnashiven we never—"

"Well, Llewelyn, I guess you're not in Sunnashiven anymore." I was silent. She certainly had a point. "I have an idea. Why don't you call me *cae*? Between us it's short for Caethne, but you can think of it as meaning 'lady' if you really need to."

"What shall I call your brother?"

"Call him Walworth, like he told you to. Everyone else does."

"But what is his proper title? I should like to know it."

"It's *caen*. Lord is a nonsense word. But please don't use his title. He really doesn't like it, and he'd probably end up killing me, or you, and we wouldn't want that to happen. Come on, that was a joke."

I finally let myself laugh and everything was fine. "All right, Cae, I—*cae* is an Amara word too, isn't it? It means 'sister.'"

"Yes, that's right, 'sister.'" She smiled and hugged me. "You may certainly call me 'sister' if you like, since we're fellow scholars." She stepped back and held both my hands in hers, smiling and sighing and darting her eyes, being her old self. Everything was comfortable and friendly again, and we held hands until her glance rested on the censer. "Come, let's to work. When I was Mirand's apprentice it was one of my jobs to keep that burning."

I turned. "Oh, no, the frankincense! I was supposed to pay attention to its effect on the bans." Caethne showed me how to start the flame back up, and I threw on some more incense. "I'm afraid you won't be able to help me with the sort of self-study this exercise requires."

"Probably not." She smiled. "Ban removal is pure wizardry. But I can help you by explaining to Mirand how it went out when I dragged you to your badly needed bath. I'm sure he'll appreciate that. What is he having you research?"

"How to manifest words and thoughts on a blank scroll. I've got three days to find out how to do it."

"I should have known. He always starts with that. The formula's in Mirga. Here." She handed me a volume. "Page two hundred and two. Memorize this and he'll be happy."

"Thanks. You've just saved me the hours I've lost."

She was so eager to help she didn't respond. "Also this." She pulled down another volume. "Rihe is one of Mirand's favorite theoreticians, and you'll really impress Mirand to no end if you read the chapter on wordplay and adapt Rihe's technique to Mirga's formula. Know how Rihe derived and tested his argument, anyway. Finally," she said, handing me a tightly wrapped scroll, "Mirand's own complimentary critique of Rihe. It's in Sarana, but the formulas are in Amara, and I'm sure he'll be pleased to tell you what it says. Trust me."

"Thanks. I already do." We smiled at each other.

"Now that you've got plenty to start with, I'll see what I can find on those stones." The sound of voices and footsteps and Pourra's high-pitched squealing told us that the meeting was breaking up down the hall. Caethne started looking through the shelves and I began reading near the censer. A minute later the door opened and Mirand entered alone. "Really, Master, can't you tell we're having a class?" said Caethne playfully. "Your apprentice has learned enough information this morning to keep us all wary, and now needs some quiet to digest it. Your blessed cockatiels make less noise at feeding time than you do entering a room." I looked up to be polite, although I would have greatly preferred the safety of my book.

"And less mess," said Mirand, looking at the half-empty jar and the now soggy rushes on the floor.

"That was my fault," said Caethne quickly. "I needed some water." She started to explain as she bent down to pick up the jar and wipe the moisture with her skirt, but Mirand lifted the jar first and held it toward the light.

"I'm certain you did. Otherwise you couldn't say so. This jar contains an infusion of something new I've invented that I call truespeak. The name is self-explanatory."

Caethne giggled. "Congratulations. It really works."

"Good." Mirand closed the jar and put it back behind the mirror. He picked up a scroll from the desk. Since he had said nothing to me and I was shy of addressing him, I went back to my reading. I did hope he would be impressed. "Caethne, there is much we need to discuss with you."

"I shall join you all shortly, but first I must fulfill a promise to Llewelyn." She explained to him about the stones and the time lost from watching the censer, but she didn't mention our eavesdropping. I looked up nervously from my book as she was speaking.

"Let me see the stones." I took them out in my good hand and he examined them. "The witch fire's heat intensified and speeded up the absorption process. They probably took in the laundry dirt. Keep them about you for the three days anyway, at which time I'll test for the bans. Keep the frankincense burning." He picked up the packet, which was almost full. "Must have been a long bath."

"I kept Llewelyn longer than I should have," Caethne said truthfully. "He hurt his hand badly on that wand, and the healing balm needed to harden."

"Can you use your injured hand now?" I thought he was concerned about my ability to write words or practice spells and therefore be useful to him, so I hastened to assure him that I no longer felt any pain, and I stretched my injured hand slowly open and closed. He seemed to study my palm intently for a few seconds, more intently than I thought the situation warranted, as my hand now felt perfectly normal. "An extremely unfortunate injury," he said softly and regretfully. "Some wands are dangerous to handle without taking proper precautions." He turned and left the room, Caethne following. She merrily winked a silent good-bye to me as they went out of sight.

When I was alone I examined my hand. The hole had healed beautifully, but in its place, where Caethne had inadvertently doused it with truespeak, was the universal symbol of evil, Hecate's symbol, the distinct outline of a waning crescent moon.

Eight

*T*hree days later Mirand pronounced the bans removed. Just as I had felt no different after the wizards in Sunnashiven drove them into me, I felt no different after Mirand's stones removed them. I had kept the frankincense burning for two days. Thanks to Caethne's help I didn't have to spend time tracking down the reading materials for my other assignment, manifesting Mirand's thoughts and reading on a blank scroll, so once I'd memorized Mirga's formula and studied Rihe, an afternoon's work, I had an entire day to browse. I learned from browsing that two days was probably about right for the frankincense to achieve its full effect, and since Mirand said nothing when I let the censer go out the morning of the third day, I assumed it was all right.

I had made an honest attempt to meditate on my own responses to the incense each evening after studying, but my thoughts alternated so rapidly between fear of Mirand's success and fear of his failure with the bans that I found it next to impossible to achieve a meditative state. Not that my other thoughts helped. I still had no idea how that wand had found its way into my sack. Mirand had said nothing about it, but then I rarely saw Mirand during those first few days, and when I did see him, he spoke little. For my part, I was reluctant to bring the subject up lest Mirand think that I resented Walworth's showing the wand to him or that I wanted it back. I also feared drawing his attention back to the symbol of evil that now appeared to be permanently etched into my left palm.

Neither Mirand nor Caethne had mentioned the symbol since Mirand first remarked on it. Caethne, of course, might not even have noticed it, in the same way she never seemed to notice any of my flaws, but Mirand was clearly aware of it. And since the waning moon is one of the most publicly recognized and widely used symbols of evil in the world, I didn't want to seem unduly interested, so I pretended there was no dying moon on my palm, that I was gifted with nothing more sinister than plainly scarred flesh. Besides, I knew I wasn't evil and I certainly had no reason to consider my scar as prophetic. I treated it as an occupational hazard, deciding that if I couldn't adopt as clinical and distanced an attitude as Mirand seemed to have about such occurrences, then I didn't belong in the business. Lesson one: Accidents happen.

Mirand tended to leave the room very early in the morning and return late at night. Nothing but my own shyness prevented me from wandering through the dwelling or going outside to find him, but shyness is a powerful restraint, and tracking him down in the midst of his other affairs felt like the height of impertinence, especially since I was supposed to be attending to my own work. I couldn't even bring myself to wander down at mealtimes, if there were mealtimes, for I wasn't sure if the household even took food together. Caethne would bring me things to eat at odd intervals, which gave me the impression that the members tended to eat pretty much when they happened to feel like it, so there was no reason for me to leave the room unless I wanted to bathe.

I always bathed in the morning, and as I never ran into anyone else at this time, I began to feel quite literally as if I lived alone. I rather liked this state of affairs. It reminded me a little of the stories of fairy palaces Grana and I used to enact together when I was a child. You knew you were in a fairy palace when food appeared on your plate and golden drink in your cup, when you heard voices and laughter in other rooms, when you had freedom to do pretty much as you liked, but you never saw the fairies themselves. Of course, I did occasionally see the members of this household as they passed by my door and threw me a quick greeting, but I spent such long stretches in solitude and was learning so many curious things that those childhood stories weren't a bad analogy to my present situation.

So when I wasn't studying or browsing I had plenty of opportunity for reflection. I kept thinking that Mirand's offer to apprentice me made no sense in terms of the secrecy of this military operation. I was from Sunnashiven, and I suppose if pressed to it would have had to consider myself loyal to King Sunnas, although I honestly felt no deep allegiance to him or to my country. If anyone in the household knew that my father had been attached to Sunnas's court, they would certainly consider me a potential enemy, if not a prisoner of war. Yet here I was, living at perfect liberty in what I could only assume was one of the command posts of the rebel army, and their master wizard himself had told me to make myself free with his library.

It was also strange that Caethne had made no attempt to draw me away from eavesdropping until after the damage was done, and I marveled over how little prompting it had taken on my part for her to tell me everything she knew, although perhaps the truespeak had eased her tongue. Walworth himself actually called her his "second in command" in my hearing. Even if he was rightly assuming I wouldn't understand the allusion, it seemed like fundamentally bad policy even to make the allusion in the first place. Even Baniff, who had been comparatively circumspect before we arrived, was anything but secretive about there being a courier on the premises, although perhaps he intended me to interpret the word to mean a traveling merchant from the Helas markets. I would have thought they'd be more careful with what they said. I wondered if their easy frankness was in some way responsible for their recent reversal of fortune, and I worried a little about this, as the more I learned about the members of the household the more I started to care about them, especially Caethne. I thought about approaching Walworth the next time he walked by my door, since he was obviously the commander here, and telling him everything I knew about him, everything Caethne had told me, and how I didn't want to see him or anyone else here in danger and that I thought he might want to be more secretive around strangers about his activities. He had already misplaced his trust in one Sunnan noble; perhaps he would appreciate being warned about watching whom he took into confidence.

But as I said, these thoughts occupied my time when I wasn't reading, and I was so set on learning as much as possible to impress Mirand that I did more studying than speculating. Even though I resolved to speak to Walworth, he always seemed so intent on his own concerns when he walked by my door that I lacked the courage to do anything more than look up from my book in quick acknowledgment of his passing greetings. I was perfectly confident about my next session with Mirand, however. I had learned from reading Rihe of another source that contained a description of a technique for manifesting my own thoughts or written words on someone else's blank scroll. I wondered if this technique could be adapted to a scroll that already contained words, and I spent an hour or two working out a possible formula for extra credit. I also familiarized myself with Mirand's Amaran formulas so that I could ask him questions about his treatise.

So when I returned upstairs after my bath and a quick bowl of porridge on the morning of the fourth day, I felt prepared for anything. Mirand usually took his frugal morning meal in our room before leaving me alone for the day, so I had grown used to having only the cockatiels for company when I returned from bathing. It was probably this daily solitude that strengthened my confidence, because it is easy to believe yourself talented when there is no worry of being contradicted. But as soon as I saw Mirand quietly waiting for me I suddenly feared that my performance would be inadequate, and I wished I had had another day to study alone.

"Good morning, Llewelyn. Are you ready to begin?"

"Yes, Mirand, I am." This wasn't exactly true, of course, given my suddenly nervous state of mind, but what else could I say? I showed him the stones, which were still as black as when Caethne removed them from the fire, and he took them over to the table under the window, where he lit a small white candle. The stones gave off a distinct gray aura in the flame. He laid them on the table and snuffed out the fire with his fingers.

"You're free to practice magic now, Llewelyn. Show me what you've learned." He took a volume down from one of the shelves and sat on his bed. "This book is a basic text written in Botha. No tricks, no hidden messages, and no power words that might interfere with your ability to draw. I'll read and comment on a passage at normal speed without attempting to obscure my thoughts—" He broke off and looked at my empty hands. "Are you going to try this without paper?"

I really felt like an idiot then. I quickly crossed the room, took from the writing desk some blank parchment that I knew was too large for this exercise, and breathlessly returned to sit across from him. "I'm ready now, Mirand."

"Let me know when your thoughts start pushing against the blankness of the parchment and when you're ready to receive." Nervousness interferes with concentration, so my performance anxiety increased with the fear of my anxiety's effect on my performance. This combination formed a high-energy thought spiral that my eagerness to please shot out of control. The result was that I rushed into a receptive mode so quickly that I found my thoughts slipping over the power surges in the room and manifesting waves on the paper before I could signal my readiness to begin. Once I did signal with raised hand, the first words threw me off balance, but I caught the rest of the passage for dear life, as a drowning person catches floating objects in a storm. When Mirand's thoughts started arriving, the storm became a steep mountain I was running down so fast that stopping would have thrown me headfirst over the edge. I didn't dare stop. I brought up his thoughts fast and furious, so furious I found myself pulling rather than receiving, pushing deeper into his mind than common courtesy allowed. He responded by increasing the tempo and I increased my copying speed past anything I would have thought possible. We continued at this rate without letup for about a page, and then he increased the speed again. The language at first came out as gibberish but I managed to grab an edge of text and fill in the blanks, which felt like cheating, as I wasn't sure whether I was still receiving from him or simply guessing from context. After the gibberish I got a sentence or two of thoughts that didn't seem to connect to any text at all, and my power broke like a sharp pen held too hard against a rough surface.

There was a pain in my head, there were ink stains on my hands, but, joy of all joys, there were words all over the paper! I'd caught something! When I looked up at Mirand I saw that his book was closed and that he was watching me, waiting for me to show him my work.

What I'd caught was a passage as crystalline and clear and true to its original as fear could make it. The writing was a little messy and blotched, but it was readable, and it matched the passage Mirand showed me.

"You've gotten down my thoughts without distorting them," he confirmed, "which is a most unusual talent among wizards who work with words. The nonsense phrases are a result of my skimming the last few pages, which you obviously didn't expect, but you adapted to the situation and picked up words from the book when I wasn't deliberately throwing them at you. The last two sentences were pure thought that had nothing to do with the rest of the text."

I grew very excited. Even if he was deliberately making his thoughts easy to catch, I had never come close to doing magic this advanced before, and I was certain that I must be making a wonderful impression. I was certainly impressing myself. Thank the gods for Mirga and Rihe!

"That's a pass." His tone was understated enough to be a compliment. He tossed my papers back to me. "Practice manifesting passages from books when nobody is reading them. Rihe's technique, which you've learned well, is far more difficult to use when there's no reader to draw energy from, but that's the way you're most likely to use it, as the great majority of books go unread a large part of the time. Learn to manifest your own thoughts as commentary when you read. It's good discipline, especially with the more obscure texts. Creating commentary on books that nobody reads requires almost as much strength of spirit as writing such books in the first place. Both exercises will develop the considerable discipline you'll need for the higher arts."

I was completely taken aback by the casual way he spoke to me of magical practices that I had thought would take me years to accomplish in Sunnashiven. Even though manifesting words on blank paper was a fairly standard magical practice, my other teachers had always done their best to convince us we weren't ready to learn this practice yet. We needed more life experience, they'd say. Or, sure, we could all manifest words if we tried, but it was such a common talent among wizards that we had no business wasting our time with it when so many great magical theorists existed to be studied. Then I'd go to the library and study the theorists and see life experience become an absurdity. Even more restricting was their insistence that any words worth manifesting had to express ideas that either were derived from everybody else's studies or fit into other people's work. I'd learned to fear word magic because I was taught to feel inadequate concerning it, and I'd always suspected I'd end up being harshly criticized for writing my own words, especially in forms that the school considered unwizardly. But here Mirand was telling me to manifest *my own thoughts*, as if that was the most logical and natural next step in the world!

"Mirand . . . I hesitate to bring this up . . ." He waited. I got up the resolve to show him the extra work I'd done. "I did find an essay on manifesting one's own thoughts, I know it's considered by some to be presumptuous to do so at my stage . . ." I didn't want him to think I was so full of myself that I'd taken the liberty to read about this technique before he told me I could, but I was so encouraged by what he had just said that I had to show him.

I paused in awkwardness and he studied me impassively. The sound of the cockatiels made me suddenly aware of time passing. Since it was clear that he was not going to offer any opinion and I felt I was wasting his time with my uneasiness, I tried to compensate by saying in a voice that I hoped sounded confident, "I will show you what I've read."

He smiled. "Please do." I took down the volume with the essay in it and got more parchment from the writing desk, which I offered him. He took it and immediately signaled his readiness. I sent him a page of text and commentary, after which he signaled me to stop and then put down the paper in obvious satisfaction. "Interesting. Your thoughts feel low and steady and cool. I wouldn't have expected that in one of your temperament."

I didn't know if this was a compliment. He said it like a statement of fact, but since he had lost the expressionless impatience of a few moments ago I decided to continue. "I worked out a formula of my own." That was daring and my heart raced as I said it, but I spoke as calmly and matter-of-factly as he did.

"All right, read it to me." I did so, and when I had finished he showed me a used piece of parchment with the words from my formula appearing at odd places in the text. "It works, although it could use some refinement. You might find it useful to take another look at the formulas in my treatise." He looked over at the table, where he saw that I had his treatise out.

"Mirand . . . I already have, and the third one . . . which I really liked . . . gave me the inspiration for . . ." I sounded completely unsure of myself, which is exactly how I felt, because having admitted that I'd read his formulas and still come up with one of my own that needed refinement was like admitting incompetence. He let me continue faltering and when I finished he stood up.

"Read them again—closely, if you're really interested in pursuing word working. There's a Sarana-Botha grammar on the second shelf that might help you with my text. Let me know when you're ready to manifest words without a reader, and we'll proceed to materialization spells. Any more questions?"

"No. Thank you for your time."

He nodded and left. Alone again, I surveyed his books and mentally reviewed our lesson. *That's a pass*, he had said, as if I were a fellow professional and didn't need the flowery praise one usually reserves for students. In retrospect, his simple manner seemed a compliment. At least, it was easy to believe that I had made a good impression on him, because he had told me to proceed to more complicated techniques. Surely he wouldn't have encouraged me to manifest my own words if he didn't think they were worth manifesting. And even if my formula needed refinement, *it had worked*, and Mirand was willing to make his own research available to me as if I were a colleague, as if I was smart enough to understand it with nothing more than the grammar to guide me. The grammar! He didn't even bother to explain it; clearly he thought I was capable of teaching myself. That was a compliment, too. I would greet him in Sarana next time and learn to speak it with him and the rest of the household. Why not? If I was going to live with them, I might as well learn their language.

But all these good intentions felt hollow. What if I greeted him in Sarana and he answered with a phrase I didn't understand or laughed at my clumsy accent? I knew my fear of failure would move me to outstudy Apollo himself, but that same fear would also cause my nerves to fail in front of my master—if not out of self-doubt, then out of fear of not being able to keep up my progress. The force that caused me to excel also caused me to falter; I literally couldn't do one without the other.

I resolutely took the grammar down from the shelf and sat before Mirand's treatise. I had just worked out how to greet people at various times of the day and resolved to surprise Caethne with a Sarana greeting the next time I saw her when the sound of sure, even footsteps coming from down the hall told me that Walworth was about to pass by my door. If I was really going to live up to my resolution, I should greet him, tell him all the things I knew about him, and warn him about his openness. So, swallowing hard and ignoring my racing heart, I plunged bravely into pretended confidence the moment he came into sight.

"Planten srine vocamen baurra. Si srine vomesse on?" May you call yourself blessed before the dawn sun. Does the sun find you so? A bit formal, I admit, but it was all I had found in the book so far. Besides, I hadn't forgotten that I was addressing a *caen.* I then realized that I was completely committed to going through with what I had planned to say to him. Since he always greeted me first, my greeting was a practical admission I had something to say, and since he seemed to be in a hurry, I knew immediately I had best say it without delay.

He stopped in midstride and smoothly responded, "*Planten srina.* 'Dawn sun' is accusative." His tone was gracious, as if he were complimenting rather than correcting me. "But, yes, I suppose. Si srine memesse on, sce mecamen baurra en ma livey ent en mas ressen. Ata vo?" Since it was painfully obvious that I had no idea what he had just said, he translated to save me the embarrassment of fumbling. "The sun finds me so, for I call myself blessed in my life and in my friends. And yourself?"

"Mecamen baurra, too." He looked genuinely pleased, for which I was grateful. I continued, hiding my self-consciousness behind a smile and an unfamiliar tone of self-teasing, "I guess I know how to ask the right questions, but I haven't yet learned how to interpret the answers."

"I'm sure that ability will come with time. Your accent is impressive. Any of my countrymen would have understood you easily. However, we usually shorten it to 'Vocamen?' and the respondent simply says 'Baurra' before stating his name." I laughed at the pun, and Walworth smiled. "It used to be considered quite the witticism, but it is now merely the standard informal response. The form you learned is perfectly correct but archaic. I have heard it used among older people or when addressing someone of higher stature."

"Then I used it correctly, *caen*."

I couldn't believe I had the nerve to say that, but he seemed to accept my self-mocking tone as if it were directed at him rather than me, for he replied lightly, "I suppose you did."

His casualness was all the courage I needed to continue, although his easy familiarity somehow humbled me into faltering again. "Walworth—I would like to tell you that Caethne and I have been . . . well . . . talking." I hesitated, because I couldn't bring myself to directly mention the eaves-dropping.

"That's your problem," he said pleasantly. "I can't help you there." I found myself laughing at his unexpected response. "I'm sure I owe you a debt of thanks for your service. Mirand used to say that keeping up with Caethne in conversation was an act of valor. I say good thing it's not a crime to talk."

"Not here, anyway." I was thinking of Sunnashiven, but he chuckled quietly, as if I had said something particularly amusing.

"Yes, well. Not here. I see Mirand showed his usual excellent judgment in apprenticing you."

"I've learned quite a bit these past few days—from Caethne, not from Mirand, although I've learned a lot from Mirand, too. But Caethne has talked to me about . . . a lot of things." I briefly made eye contact before shyly looking at the floor. "And I'm most grateful for everything you and Mirand and Caethne have done for me. If there is ever any way to repay you, I will, ten times over. I just want you to know that." *Damn it! What happened to all my resolve about warning him to be more secretive?*

"Noted," he said gently, and turned to leave.

I knew I was about to lose my opportunity to say what I wanted, so I said nervously to his back, "I mean, I don't care if I am from Sunnashiven—I want you to win."

He turned around. His face looked puzzled and amused. "Win what?"

"Whatever you're fighting for. The Duke of Helas's trading interests, stopping Roguehan from controlling the southwest kingdoms and invading Threle, helping Sunna's peasants overthrow their tax burden, replacing Count Sina with someone who'll stand up to King Sevalas, whatever is nec-essary." *Oh, no, that was stupid. Now he would know I eavesdropped!* "I realize I shouldn't know these things, but I want you to know that I know. I mean—I want to help you. I'd become a citizen of your duchy in a minute, a citizen of Threle, forget Sunna. But what I want to say is . . . what if I didn't feel that way?"

He considered my words with interest. "If you didn't feel that way, then we wouldn't be having this conversation."

"No, I suppose not. But if I didn't know about your activities, we wouldn't be having this conversation either. I just wandered in with Baniff four days ago, and if I were really loyal to King Sunnas—I could be a spy or anything—I mean . . . I really want to help you, but what if I didn't? I worry about you, and about Caethne, and about everybody."

"Clearly."

"I wonder if you'd be less vulnerable to betrayal if you were less open about your affairs." I was afraid that he might be offended at my implied criticism, but he looked deeply touched, as if I had just paid him a very high honor.

"You do know how to ask the right questions. All right, what if you were my sworn enemy?" As soon as he said this I felt ridiculous. "What if you were a spymaster for King Sunnas and felt strongly enough about his government to do anything you could to put him back in power? What sort of threat do you see yourself posing to us?"

"Well, none, but if I were a spy—I already know what books Mirand studies, what inventions he's working on, who you really are, and where your command quarters are. That might be valuable information to some people."

"And no doubt is. How would you convey that information if you were so inclined?"

I thought for a minute. "I don't know."

"Why do you worry about what you already know about Mirand rather than what Mirand already knows about you?" I had no answer. Walworth continued, "I have no power to grant you citizenship in my duchy, but either of my parents may do that if you truly desire it. However, it is quite far from here, and different from Helas and the rest of the southwest, so perhaps you would like to see it before you make that decision. As to becoming a Threlan, the Duke of Helas has authority to grant you citizenship here, and you already speak the language. If you would like me to, I will tell him of your desire."

"Please. I should be grateful. I want to do whatever will help you and Caethne."

"Then why not remain a citizen of Sunna, whatever that means right now? I can foresee your being more help to us if nothing marks you as one of us." He said this kindly, as if his advice was an acknowledgment of my loyalty.

"All right, but please know that 'my heart is in Threle,' as they say." This was a line from an old folk song I'd heard once, and I managed to say it with a smile, so I didn't sound as cloying as I felt.

He clapped my shoulder and laughed appreciatively. "Then study hard, soldier. I should be proud to have you in my ranks. Perhaps we will have need of your magical abilities at some point. And please feel free to talk to Caethne as long and often as you like. I see there's no harm done." He turned and left quickly, and once his footsteps faded I took advantage of my solitude to think about his questions and about my position.

Perhaps I had been approaching the problem the wrong way earlier. *Was* it naive trust that motivated them to accept me? When Mirand had first invited me to stay, to the obvious surprise and discomfort of both Walworth and Baniff, he knew I spoke Amara and he knew I had given Baniff that wizard's key. The key was probably important to their cause; at least it was important enough to induce Baniff to give his word to Aleta that he would rescue me. True, I happened to fit beautifully into his scheme to free Cathe, but there had been absolutely nothing to induce him to return the following morning except his own sense of honor. Or maybe his own natural caution. As long as I was wearing that robe, which Baniff likely still had, I was inaudible, but what would have happened if I had been taken in and questioned by the high priestess? Baniff no doubt had very good reasons to avoid the risk I would pose by talking about Cathe's escape, and he had even said as much. I also wondered why I had been able to do an identifying spell on the key with no ill effects from my bans, and decided that I might be able to ask Mirand about this at some point.

As to speaking Amara, Walworth had said that a few families still spoke this language. These families included his own, obviously. In my drunken state I had read Amara symbols readily enough, and for all Mirand knew I was prepared to go spouting off Amara words all over Helas and at the monastery in Kant. I had seen Walworth, I could describe him, and I had no reason not to talk about my recent adventures. Walworth had left his parents' duchy months ago, so I'm sure the absence of the young *caen* had been noted, although I got the impression he did a lot of wandering and his absences weren't considered unusual. But why risk having a Sunnashiven refugee wandering about who could call attention to one's secret hideout? I was clearly less of a risk inside the household than outside it.

It all began to fall into place. Mirand's generous offer to remove two of my bans was also added insurance. It would be death for me to return to Sunnashiven in such a state, even with the rebels in control. Their quarrel was only with taxes, which meant that the laws against removing loyalty bans would still be in effect, and as the son of one of Sunnas's undersecretaries, I could not look for mercy from Sina's regime. Seeking out King Sunnas would be absurd; his people would take my information and then kill me, because I'm sure it wouldn't take much for another master wizard to determine that the bans had been removed with my full consent. Finally, and perhaps most important, Mirand instinctively recognized my strong desire to excel at scholarly pursuits and was cleverly providing a powerful hook for me to stay. With all the books I had access to here, why in the name of any god would I care to return to Sunnashiven's wizard school? Not to mention that there was actually enough food to eat in Helas.

The more training Mirand gave me the more he would learn about me too, and of course there was no question as to who was the stronger party. And unless he decided to remove the ban against using my full individual powers he would always be the stronger party. He would quickly develop exact and intimate knowledge of what my magic could and could not do. Mirand's thought processes were fascinating. By taking me into their household, by taking me into their confidence to an extent, Mirand and his friends had effectively disarmed me with a smile and a greeting and a promise of sweet hospitality. Not a word or gesture of force had been used, but I was in a position to reveal about as much as if I were still a prisoner in Sunnashiven and silenced by the robe.

I longed to be fully accepted as a friend and comrade of Baniff and Walworth, to be included in their adventures. I admired their cool, easy manner. I wanted them to like me for myself, but logic dictated that their friendliness was merely strategic, and I feared that if I named the situation for what it was, I'd lose the illusion of growing comradeship that was becoming everything to me. I had to pretend to confidence in order to be accepted. Only with Caethne was there no pretending. It was because I could contrast my responses to her with my responses to the others that I had become aware of how much I was pretending and how friendship and well-meant pretense seemed very much the same in Threle.

Of course I would study hard, of course I would make myself as useful to their cause as possible, and of course I was flattered by the possibility of one day using my magic to help, the way Baniff and Mirand already did. In my youthful enthusiasm I resolved I would be with them all forever, in victory or defeat. After all, how glorious and romantic to be on a first-name basis with the future Duke and Duchess of Walworth, to be privy to a secret organization with the power to send old King Sunnas scurrying, if only I didn't let go of the illusion and act as the tactical houseguest I really was. Pretense carried enormous rewards. I would attach myself to their court when they came into their office—a "brother," as Caethne had practically called me. We would take on the world together—no, we would even make new worlds together.

I felt as though I had just gotten permission to be my true self. I ran over to the table and picked up the blackened stones, looking at my former bans with a sense of wonder. Bury them, Mirand had said. Well, here was the real test. Could I bury them, pretend they didn't exist, act bold and free, as befitted a soldier of the army of—of—I didn't even know if the army had a name, but that didn't matter. *I am a member of this household, and I have no choice but to make myself free.* I sauntered down the stairs. No one. Through the living quarters. No one. Through the cooking area. No one. Outside the house, where I stood alone in the tree shadows that obscured the entrance, I felt as if I belonged, as if I had come home. I ran along the path Caethne had led me down a few days ago, looking for a place to bury the bans, as far from the dwelling as possible.

I got out into a field and Pourra's high-pitched squeal unexpectedly grabbed my attention. The woodchuck was sitting on a large rock and waving his paws in greeting, and I saw a large clump of tarragon growing wild and gray and wonderful in front of his perch. *If Caethne didn't plant that, she should have*, I thought admiringly.

Grana had once taught me that tarragon was a wonderfully protective herb, and I had read that magical items buried under tarragon did not leak their energies back to the earth but retained them. So I decided to bury the bans here. The stones were magical and could be of use again someday. I might discover exactly how they worked and find a way to remove the bans from them without destroying the stones' usefulness. I might even be able to use them to remove my other bans, with or without Mirand's knowledge. I started digging with my hands and Pourra jumped down to help, throwing dirt on my face and squealing excitedly. When I dropped the stones in our hole he pushed at them and sat back and clapped while I covered them up and spread tarragon back over the spot. I suddenly felt close to Pourra, as if that moment made him as much my familiar as Caethne's. So when I rose to brush the dirt off my clothes I immediately bent down to pet him, reveling in the novelty of freely acting out this strange new feverish fit of friendliness. And his eyes sparked with pleasure, as they always did for Caethne, until he saw the mark of evil on my hand. Then his eyes got big and he ran away.

"So be it," I resolved. "If Pourra wishes to mistake appearance for reality, he is as free to do so as I am." I walked back to the dwelling to return to my studies and as I approached the entrance I saw Walworth and Baniff and Mirand entering in front of me. My heart's pace belied my intentions, but I forced my legs to run until I was beside them, and then I pushed my breath into something I hoped sounded like a joyous announcement: "I've buried the bans."

There was playful applause and a few cheers. The attention mortified me but I knew that to walk with them back into the household I had to keep up the sound of cheerfulness in my voice. "And I have three solemn riddles for three wise men—riddles the earth gave to me."

"And you stoppeth one of three to ask them?" said Walworth, quoting from a well-known old Botha poem I was surprised he knew.

"If you are next of kin, then the mariner hath his will," I finished the quote, and since my Botha accent was better than theirs, they laughed appreciatively.

"And does yer first riddle concern why yer keepin' us all busy with our work out here when we should be wastin' our time inside quotin' poetry?" asked Baniff good-humoredly. Everyone laughed again, including me, for it was laughter that covered the stab of uncertainty his question raised. I held on to my laughter as tightly as I had held on to the text Mirand sent me earlier, and I was proud of myself for breaking off laughing at the instant my companions did.

"Well, Baniff, my riddles in part concern your work. The first concerns the wand I found in my sack and what it is and how it got there."

"It's a wand of evil, lad, in case ye haven't noticed." They all looked at my palm and laughed, so I laughed again.

"Well, of course, and it was foolish of me to grab it—" *No, better stop that tack.* "But it isn't every day one finds a wand of evil, and I'm so curious as to how I came by it."

"So are we," said Mirand. "If you wish, it would be most helpful to us if you allow me to work magically with you to determine its origin."

At the word *helpful* I looked up at Walworth, who I imagined was considering our earlier conversation. He seemed to indicate approval. "Yes, of course, Mirand, anything to help," I said eagerly. "My second riddle concerns your work more indirectly. Baniff told you when I first arrived here that I also came by that wizard's key. The key was a gift from my sister, Trenna. But when Trenna first crossed my palm with it"—I noticed Mirand's eyes widen slightly, but I continued as if I hadn't—"she asked me to do an identifying spell, and of course the key felt warm, but I felt no ill effects from my bans, and since I wasn't helping Sunna, I should have felt something."

"Like what, death?" quipped Baniff. We all laughed heartily at this.

"Well, I'm not complaining. I'm more—like curious."

"It's simple," said Mirand. "Your sister had to be working for whoever or whatever constituted the state of Sunna at that particular moment, and if identifying the key induced you into accepting her gift, then accepting it must have constituted an act of helping the state. I'm more interested in why you would risk your life to please or impress Trenna."

"I don't know. . . . I guess that's the way things are in Sunna." My chagrin was audible, so I tried immediately to change my tone back to its original buoyancy. "Trenna's husband is a soldier loyal to King Sunnas. His name is Seth. I remember her showing me a ring of beauty, a love charm, that she said was created by an Aphroditian high priestess. She said that Seth gave it to her. I identified that too. In my palm." Mirand nodded slightly. "But perhaps that was her way of letting me know she had real magical items, of piquing my interest before tempting me into accepting the key or something."

"Or charming you into doing whatever she asked. Sounds like Trenna wasn't taking any chances that you would refuse her gift."

That was the moment in which my teacher led me to my working definition of heroism. Heroism is sounding confident when your audience has just pointed out that you've been a fool. It's as painful as the gods' own hell. I laughed so hard my stomach hurt. No one else was laughing, so when I stopped I had only pain to propel my third riddle. My words got there first, before my sagging feelings could catch them, and thus my speech formed a shield around my inner explosion. "Well, friends, as three times pays for all, the bringer of the three mysterious gifts of the wand, the key, and the robe begs leave to ask the final question."

"He may ask," said Mirand, quietly smiling.

"And may he answer?" I pushed rhetorically. "You have agreed to help me find the information to answer the first question. I supplied you information to answer the second. Now I shall answer the third. Of all the citizens of Sunna, whatever that means"—I smiled at Walworth while using his phrase—"who is the one to be watched and guarded and kept track of more than any other. That is, who now poses the most immediate danger to Threle?"

"Tell us, Master," said Mirand, still smiling.

"Why, Master Wizard Grendel, of course, and I will tell you why. Before I left the city Lady Aleta of County Clio, a fine soldier herself, told me that Grendel was looking for me, that I had something he wanted, and that he was about to make a deal with the invaders, that is, with the rebels. I would have riddled you about what Grendel's deal was, but the answer to that one is fairly clear. What he wanted was the key; it was the only object I possessed that was of any value. There was even a guard at my doorstep looking for Trenna and searching the house, and I had been keeping the key in my pillowcase and impressing it with my energy, not to mention researching it in the library. Grendel had been in my mind once or twice, and in the library at least once"—there was laughter, so I knew I was redeeming myself with the library comment—"and so had ample opportunity to discover I had the key. If he knew Trenna had it, he would have had particular reason to determine whether or not it was in my possession."

"How did he know Trenna had it, and how did she come by it in the first place?" asked Walworth.

His question threw me and I faltered a little. "I don't know. But I know the court wizards keep their spies. . . . I'm guessing," I said recovering. "The important point, though, is that the only way I could have been helping the state of Sunna by accepting that key was if the key was a threat to the state while it was in Trenna's possession. She gave it to me to keep it hidden, knowing she could easily get it back. She knew that someone, logically an enemy of the state, perhaps a rebel, knew she had it and was about to take it from her. Grendel had to know she had it and 'lost' it. I don't know exactly how," I said to Walworth, "but he had to know or he wouldn't have paid attention to me. Perhaps he sent someone to steal it and it wasn't there."

"That happens," said Baniff.

"So Grendel's deal with the rebels involved that key." I stopped uncertainly, another question threatening my argument. "I don't know how Aleta knew that a deal was going to take place."

"How does Aleta know anythin'?" asked Baniff. "Count Clio keeps his own spies, and Sir Perie's a fine gossip when he's on the weed."

"All right. So logic dictates that Grendel believed King Sunnas's regime was ready to topple, and he decided to save himself, not unlike Count Sina," I said bravely. "Anyone who knows Master Grendel knows that he has no real sympathy with the peasants, but he would do what he could to save himself. He's not above using the city poor as an excuse to rob people of their belongings and line his own pocket with the spoils. I've seen him in action, stealing Aleta's apples."

"Yes, she told me that story," said Baniff. It appeared that Baniff had already told everybody else. "Grendel's tactics give honest thieves a bad name."

"Well, Grendel's in trouble now, if it's any compensation. He has to be. If the guard that searched my house was loyal to King Sunnas, then Sunnas knew about Grendel's intended treachery and was trying to beat him to the key, which means Grendel can never go back to the king. Sevalas would also know that Grendel is completely untrustworthy, for Grendel had to be aware that Sunnas has been taking his orders from Sevalas, and yet Grendel would have handed a powerful weapon over to the rebels to save his own neck. Grendel would not have known that Sevalas was backing both sides, any more than Sunnas did, or in the interest of self-preservation he would have run directly to Sevalas for protection. Now Grendel's a traitor. On the other hand, even if the guard was secretly working for Grendel and Sunnas knew nothing about it, Grendel's in trouble. Since Grendel didn't deliver the key to Count Sina and the rebel forces, it's safe to say he's not a favorite with them right now either."

"I'm fascinated with your analysis, Llewelyn," said Walworth intently. "But isn't it possible that Grendel knew that Sevalas was backing both sides before we did, and that his deal was made on orders from Sevalas? Sevalas could do worse than keep a loyal master wizard close to the rebel government."

"I have more faith in your intelligence than in Grendel's," I said stoutly. "I've studied with Grendel." Laughter. "And you—*we*—just got word of the real situation. Besides, even if Sevalas is backing Grendel in this deal, Grendel has still lost the key as far as Sevalas *and* the rebels are concerned. His predicament is no less real."

"Excellent point. Continue." My audience was completely enthralled.

"There is only one person he can possibly turn to for protection right now."

"You mean besides us?" Baniff sallied.

"I mean Roguehan. He's the only person in the drama with the power to protect Grendel from Sevalas, Sunnas, and the rebel counts. But what can Grendel, who's proved himself completely untrustworthy to all sides, offer him in exchange for his life? Roguehan has wizards, better wizards than Grendel. I say that because Zelar was once Mirand's master, and if Mirand is any indication of Zelar's prowess"—I nodded slightly in my master's direction—"then Grendel would do better to offer himself as a street sweeper than as a magician to Roguehan. It takes Grendel half a day and three helpers to drive bans into six novices." Mirand chuckled. "But the key, if he had it, sounds like the sort of payment Roguehan might accept. After all," I went on, turning to Baniff, "it was enough of an inducement for you to put yourself at considerable risk and through all sorts of trouble to help me out of the city."

"Almost enough," said the gnome.

"It was valuable enough for Grendel, who is as close to King Sunnas's court as anyone, to attempt to buy the rebels off with. The rebels hate everything associated with Sunnas, so that key would have to be extremely valuable." An inspiration struck me, "Perhaps it is even an object that Grendel knew would be a powerful protector for the rebels against Sunnas's return. No, that's not it. If Trenna was working for the state of Sunna, and I wouldn't be here if she wasn't, why would she have a key to something that could make Sunnas vulnerable? Surely Sunnas didn't give it to her. It couldn't be any safer in her possession than under guard in Sunnas's own quarters. I know I wouldn't let out of my sight any weapon that could be used against me. But someone—someone like Grendel, who sensed which way the wind was blowing—could have had it stolen and given it to Seth or Trenna for safekeeping. No, not Grendel, he'd keep it for himself."

I thought for a while and became aware of the sun and shadow forming patterns over the dwelling and over my companions' faces. Pourra waddled out of the undergrowth and joined us. They were all waiting for me to continue, but I had suddenly lost my way in the morass of what were becoming political conjectures based on guesses, and I hesitated to speak beyond what I knew firsthand of Grendel and Trenna.

Walworth saved my embarrassment by speaking first. "Your speculations are essentially correct, but they don't go far enough. It's clear that someone who knew the key's value stole it from Sunnas and gave it to your sister. It's also clear that both the thief and your sister had to be working for the *true* state of Sunna, or we wouldn't be having this pleasant conversation." He said this with an easy gallantry.

"What is the true state of Sunna, then?" I asked.

"Sevalas or Roguehan," he replied unhesitatingly.

"And whose key is it?"

"Ours," said Baniff practically.

Walworth smiled a little and spoke again. "Sunnas probably had the key stolen in the first place as protection against them, although Sevalas no doubt had it stolen first as protection against Roguehan, as the key holds immense power against him. It's my surmise that Sevalas believed that as long as he had the key, he could use Roguehan's power for his own ambition without being used by Roguehan. Now that the key's gone, Roguehan will do anything to retrieve it, Sevalas is at Roguehan's mercy, and Grendel has no choice but to do whatever Roguehan bids. So yes, Llewelyn, Grendel is the one to watch."

Everyone looked impressed by the accuracy of my initial suggestion, with the exception of Pourra, who was sitting up pertly and watching me with his bright eyes.

"Well, lad," said Baniff in a complimentary teasing sort of voice, "ye put our spies to shame."

I beamed. "Just manifesting words." I looked at Mirand. "Lesson one."

"No defenses," said the wizard graciously.

"And no secrets," said Walworth, taking a parchment out of his pocket. "We learned just now that Grendel left Sevalas's court almost immediately after arriving there and started south toward one of Roguehan's strongholds. Please come in and join us. I should be most interested in hearing all your old school stories. Come, tell us about your teachers, about Grendel, about Trenna. I promise we won't be bored."

It felt wonderful joining in their good-natured laughter, and so as we passed into the dwelling together, a merry band of brothers, I hardly noticed it when Pourra dashed in front of me and I tripped over the threshold. Caethne, who was working in the cooking area, noticed, for she sang out playfully, "Good thing that's your second entrance. 'Tis ill luck to trip when entering your home for the first time."

" 'Tis also ill luck to miss meetings, twin. Come join us upstairs."

Caethne picked up Pourra and a handful of grass from her basket. She held the grass to her familiar's mouth and he ate. We went upstairs and as we passed by my room I thought briefly of my next assignment and how much more exciting real life was than studying. Caethne was humming a little. Pourra was squealing happily in response. The caged birds were singing. I was practicing believing I'd come home.

Nine

Coming home is always an act of belief. That is a Helan folk saying that the Helan merchants are always mouthing when they want you to think you've made an especially fine bargain. "Coming home" is a kind of local idiom for "agreeing on a fair price." The saying is supposed to mean, "If you believe you've made a fair bargain, you have." The irony is that you almost never hear it said unless you've spent more on an object than you know the object is really worth, and so for me the saying always sounded as though I was being cajoled into believing I'd "come home" after I'd spent more than was necessary. I learned this quickly, though, so I always did my best to haggle whenever I went to market with Caethne. After a while I got so good at striking bargains that she started sending me to market alone, providing me with gold pieces to spend on household needs. I suspect I was relatively successful with the merchants because my command of their language was better than hers.

Anyway, even if I hadn't been regularly included in all the household discussions, my thrice-weekly trips to market would have provided me with much valuable news concerning the southwest kingdoms, and Sunna in particular. I watched the price of local produce fall steadily from week to week, and I listened to all the market gossip, so I knew that the Helan merchants were still being turned away at Sunna's border, causing an immense surplus of locally grown crops to hit the stands. Due to the weather patterns affecting the southwest harvests, Helas had for years been exporting more food than it imported, so the farmers suddenly found themselves competing with the crops intended for export. All the exporters to the southwest were forced to sell their goods at home or to compete for the markets in the rest of Threle's duchies. Clion apples were also cheap and plentiful. The apple merchants had to lower their price to compete with the abundance of local elderberries and blackberries that normally got sold in the southwest. I wondered how Aleta's county was getting along with its markets being so severely restricted. I always made it a point to buy Clion apples.

King Sevalas was officially admitting no imports either, although rumor had it that there was still a hefty black-market trade between his kingdom and Helas. Imported goods from Sunna were nonexistent, and there were no crops from the Kingdom of Sevalas, which told me that King Sevalas was still in control of Sunnashiven's food supply and using whatever of his own crops he could spare to keep Sunnashiven directly dependent on him. I suppose I should have felt something like pain when I saw food intended for Sunnashiven rotting in barrels, but to be honest I felt nothing.

Oddly enough, a few bushels of black-market corn occasionally made their way up from the deep southwest, outside of Sevalas's purview, but it was usually blasted and mildewed and nobody bought it. I concluded that the weather had remained unforgiving in the far reaches and that the corn was probably ruined before it got here. Roguehan no doubt had better things to think about than stopping the black-market trade in inedible foodstuffs from the hinterlands.

I once saw a few expensive bags of semiprecious stones on display and recognized the insignia on the bags as belonging to a well-known Sevalan jewel exporter. I concluded that Sevalas needed money and was allowing some products out of his country in return for hefty export fees, or else the black market was thriving as it ever did, and there was increasing risk associated with getting goods out of the country. Our intelligence said it was a little bit of both. Roguehan was interested in choking off Helas's southwest trade as much as possible, but Sevalas needed a supply of money that Roguehan didn't know about, so some of his border officials felt comfortable looking the other way for a hefty fee when certain merchants wanted to get their goods to Helas.

So Helas was not a bad place to be while I was there, although even with the discussions I was privy to in meetings and the market gossip I heard on my frequent trips into town, I didn't understand all the forces affecting it at the time. Food was plentiful and inexpensive, and despite the fall in prices the farmers didn't suffer too much because buyers from Kant and points north came down and bought up the surplus. The other merchants grumbled about their southwest markets being cut off, but the scarcity of southwest goods drove their own prices up, and the extra coins people saved on food made it possible for them to meet the merchants' demands, so the grumbling quickly disappeared. If Roguehan was trying to upset Helas's economy, it seemed to me that he was going about it all wrong.

Since Caethne insisted I make myself free with her purse I had a field day buying little gifts for everyone in the household: local crystals for Mirand, a cask of ale for Baniff to fulfill my promise, an intricately engraved dagger for Walworth. The last of these was expensive, but I knew he would appreciate the artwork. I also bought a homespun peasant blouse for Caethne, since I knew she favored them, and new walking shoes for her rambles. I always bought treats for Pourra, who quickly learned to follow me whenever I left the dwelling.

Choosing and buying luxuries was a novelty to me. Caethne kept insisting that I buy whatever would bring me happiness, so long as it was something I wouldn't have been able to get for myself in Sunnashiven—which was just about everything. Necessity dictated I buy some changes of clothes, and I did so, yet when I wandered by myself through the streets and shops and colorful market stalls of town I wanted nothing. I was alive, the streets were noisy and vibrant, the merchants knew my name, and over time the faces in the crowds grew familiar enough to smile at. Could I buy these sharp early autumn breezes and azure skies? Could I take the merchants' delightful patter and the leisurely autumnal expectancy that I grew to love in the Threlan people? What was to buy, anyway? Could I buy friendship from Walworth, natural friendship that didn't spring from Mirand's studied decision to keep me close, where I could do the least damage to their secret operation? Could I trade pretense for certainty? Would I? My daily pretensions to freedom and confident goodwill were becoming dangerously comfortable. After a few weeks I had to make a painful effort not to get taken in by the sweet illusion of friendship they bought for me. Yet when a middle-aged farmer at a market stall I frequented asked me where my sister was, meaning Caethne, I felt I had "bought" enough real happiness to last a week. The farmer believed I was really Caethne's brother and therefore presumably Walworth's despite our different accents. That thought charmed me so much I bought three bags of pink Clion apples from her and gave apples away to the next three strangers I saw.

The lovely accidents of day-to-day life in the markets took on the coercive force of one's first love affair. I often saw an old man who came to town with a white dog. The dog always had a red kerchief around his collar and stayed close to his owner. I never spoke to either of them but I grew used to seeing them at market and I quickly grew attached to them without their knowledge. I wanted to know where and how the man lived, what his work was like, how he spent his evenings, and who his friends were. When he bought corn and bread and tobacco I liked to imagine his homey cottage in the evenings with the food cooking and the smoke filling the room and the dog at his feet and maybe a few friends to gossip with. Yet I never talked to him. His presence and my quiet imagination satisfied me. Besides, the more I practiced pretending I was free and genuinely valued at home, the more I learned to fear reality. Reality dictated that I was in the household as a security measure, no matter how warmly fraternal my own feelings toward the other members were. If I discovered the old man really lived in a crowded garret over a closed shop somewhere, my trips to market would surely lose some of their charm. So the picture he and his dog created for me tutored me in the pleasures of belief.

I saw an orange cat who wore a pink ribbon and slept in the window of a weapons shop every afternoon, and that cat became something I had to see every trip. An old woman sold homemade rutabaga pie from a stall and greeted people so pleasantly that the intonations of her "good afternoon" became a refrain I had to hear over and over. I never bought her pie, just as I never spoke to the old man, but it grew important to me to see other people buying her wares and speaking with her.

There were enticing book shops to wander through. One always smelled of cinnamon and cloves, and the owner was kind enough to let me browse through his collection undisturbed. Once on a cold and rainy afternoon he lit a fire in his shop and gave me a pale blue bowl of apricots and figs. I ate them as I read a book of local history that contained a fascinating account of the Duke of Helas's ancestry. The owner told me he was a distant relative of the duke, and we struck up a pleasant late afternoon kind of friendship, the kind of friendship that lives only an hour or two on dark days before the light fails, and never lasts longer than a season. I loved his stories.

I grew enthralled with the way the afternoon light brought out the brightest hues in the apple carts. Sometimes I'd stand in front of a jeweler's and silently bless the late-in-the-day emptiness that formed in front of the window as the gems threw off the light. It was the rubies and garnets that drew me, for through my increasing magical sensitivity I could feel their warmth across my wrists and lower abdomen merely by looking at them. By the time the leaves started to turn I could feel along my spine the echoes of the trees withdrawing into their own impressions of death without even expending effort. There was an oak at the edge of town whose leaves turned bright red, and once in the cold yellow sunfall of early evening, when I was sure I was alone, I applauded long and loud until I was startled by Pourra staring at me in wonderment.

Sometimes I would follow a group of locals to listen to them gossip about people and events I had no connection to, and hearing their voices at a distance became important to me. But I had no desire to be with them or to trade banter, for I proudly thought it was an act of loyalty to Walworth to keep aloof. One of them might ask me questions about myself and who knew what I could inadvertently give away. Then I would catch myself in the weakness of thinking that perhaps I did share a friendship with Baniff and Mirand and Walworth as deep and as genuine as the one they shared with each other. But when I spied close groups of friends going together through the town streets, I had to steady myself for half a minute. These scenes abruptly brought me back to my true position in the household. I was now privy to all intelligence reports and my input and presence at meetings was warmly welcomed by all, but I knew that I was merely following my new companions in the shadows. I was playing at friendship and willing it to be real. In reality I was very much alone.

"*I*n my defense, my lord, if I did occasionally forget my true position and embrace illusion, you and your companions did nothing to discourage me."

I sipped some broth and gazed thoughtfully at the yellow candle. The flame hurt my eyes where I felt it, like a dagger of light ripping into my mind. Walworth would neither discourage nor endorse these particular memories, and I was trying to know, for my own obscure reasons, how much his neutrality hurt. But when I set down the bowl I felt only how much my pain lessened, believing in the shadow of relief like a young prayer.

"Perhaps you recall this time in a different way," I continued. "I shall say that my own recollection is tempered with a strange pain that you are probably indifferent to. Be that as it is, I shall continue to speak *of* you, as if you do not know my tale. For I am speaking for the clarity of the record, for others to read. Please honor my deathbed honesty; it's all the truth I have to give the court."

His pen poised, I continued.

*B*aniff included me in his crusty, cynical humor as often as he included anyone else, simply because I was around. We even had good-natured drinking contests together, which, despite his smaller size, he always won. As my studies progressed we'd try to see how drunk we could get and still produce results with our respective branches of magic. Mirand was as unfailingly professional with me as I sensed he had been with Caethne and Walworth when they were students. In fact, I sometimes flattered myself that my teacher and I shared academic interests the others didn't, as Caethne had left wizardry for witchcraft and Walworth's study of magical theory had quickly become specialized into the study of magical weapons. Both Walworth and Caethne appreciated words and thoughts and the reasons behind the reasons certain spells worked or failed, but neither had chosen to become a wizard. So if Mirand and I got into an intellectual discussion in front of the others in the evening, as happened more frequently over time, there were moments when I caught myself believing that my thoughts on some topics were valued even over Walworth's. Of course Walworth himself was no slouch in intellectual debates. Mirand had trained him well and he had a naturally sharp mind, so I found it flattering when the *caen* listened and commented on my insights as if he was favorably impressed with my thought processes. I suppose I hero-worshiped Walworth to an extent, but my feelings concerning him had an odd way of turning back on myself. That is, the more Walworth rose in my estimation the more I rose in my own. I was most impressed with the way my short life was turning out, in that I could relax and joke and drink with a young *caen* before the evening fire as if we were equals.

But even in our most familiar and easy moments I could never forget that Walworth was the joint heir to a duchy and one day would have a court of his own and practically unlimited power over his domains, while I was a commoner.

The same was true of Caethne, of course, but Caethne was always so playful and earthy it was sometimes possible to forget that she was a future duchess. Walworth was unfailingly courteous and could play the charming host, but there was always a tinge of melancholy in his eyes and around his mouth, a melancholy that Caethne lacked. Even when we arm-wrestled in jest or he let me handle his sword, there was a distance that colored his familiarity, a profound sadness that, despite my access to all incoming intelligence, I could only guess at. Even when everyone was singing or laughing or chattering to me in Sarana, which I was picking up quickly, I would sometimes catch him staring into the fire with a look of heavy contemplation. Mirand noticed also, and as my magical sensitivity increased and I grew acclimated to the way Mirand thought, I was aware that the master wizard was deeply concerned for his former student.

Walworth had his playful moments too, but they were rarer than his sister's, and perhaps for that reason more memorable. When Walworth was in an especially genial mood he would tell entertaining stories of his own youthful adventures in Threle, and until the stories ended I would feel as if I had partaken of his adventures myself and that my life in Sunnashiven was a bad fiction. But these were rare occasions. Mostly he matched wits with Baniff and Caethne, and later with myself, and he would end up leading riotous evenings of riddles and teasing and wordplay. Only Caethne was really a match for him at these times, but he occasionally managed to out-riddle even her. When I got brave enough to jump in the fray I usually lost unless Caethne came to my rescue, but he was so gracious in victory and so adept at turning his final, killing phrase into a compliment that I never felt defeated. And when we bantered in Amara the margin was usually quite close, for I was working spells for Mirand in that language on a daily basis and I had become quite adept with it.

I do not know exactly when I let down my defenses and succumbed to the charm of actually believing, rather than pretending to believe, that a natural friendship was beginning to exist among the four of us, a friendship as real as the one that blossomed between me and Caethne.

First came the mornings when I actually felt comfortable initiating magic skirmishes with Baniff. After I learned how to manifest words from closed books and foreign languages and went wild for a few days manifesting my own thoughts all over everything, Mirand introduced me to materialization spells. As soon as I learned how to turn the word *stone* into a real stone, and then how to work with plurals and make piles of stones, I sent pebbles to both Caethne and Baniff at night that spelled their names. She was delighted and saved them in a little bag, to which she added more stones. The next day she manually spelled out *Llewelyn, master wizard* in stones across everyone's plate. Baniff had to respond by sending an illusion of an avalanche of rocks to my room by night. Being illusion, it did no real damage except for annoying Mirand, who tripped over his robe and hurt his foot when he got up in the morning and thought he was running into a small mountain. I let Mirand in on the game and in a rare fit of humor he materialized a clear cask of real ale in Baniff and Caethne's room that couldn't be opened. Baniff grumbled so loudly over "damned wizard tricks" all day that Caethne asked Mirand when he was going to remember her with midnight presents. That night he sent her a cabbage.

There was something sad about the cabbage. Caethne, poor, smiling, irrepressible Caethne, responded by serving Mirand cabbage soup for a week while everyone else got treats. There were many jokes about this, as you can imagine, because sometimes Caethne would flavor the soup like Mirand's favorite dishes and sometimes she'd flavor it like dried leather, so he never knew whether to drink it or not. But the morning after the cabbage first arrived I saw her crying a little and kissing the leaves before she threw them in the pot. My heart went out to her in sympathy, but I never said anything. It was the only unspoken secret between us.

Caethne sometimes set up elaborate practical jokes, such as brewing a nonintoxicating sorrel soup that tasted remarkably like ale, so we all could watch Baniff drink himself silly while he wondered why he wasn't getting drunk. One time she arranged all his ale bottles in the shape of a gnome and hid them in his bed, throwing a blanket over them. Another time she caused the stones over the fireplace to seal themselves tight, and everyone had a good laugh as Baniff went cursing to his room, convinced that he was cut off from his drinking supply. The curses got louder and more colorful when he was convinced that someone was sleeping in his bed, and the whole household had quite a laugh when Baniff drew his short sword, tore off the blanket, and stood there holding his ale supply at sword point. Then, of course, Caethne loosened the stones, and the rest of us pretended not to understand why Baniff was choosing to sleep with his ale.

Baniff did his best to respond to Caethne's ribbing, but it wasn't easy for him. Witches are so used to handling natural forces and elements that they simply see through and don't respond much to illusions. Baniff tried valiantly to hold an illusion of a giant mushroom growing out of Caethne's bed, and he purposely left their door open so everyone could see it and anticipate her reaction. I told her what he had done, and she said she hoped it was a pretty mushroom, one that matched her shirt. Caethne disappointed

Baniff by going to bed as usual that night, as if nothing were amiss, but you can bet she served him a basket of real mushrooms, harvested at dawn, for his breakfast the next morning. And for weeks after that Baniff complained of his ale taking on a mushroomy flavor.

One afternoon, not long after Mirand materialized the clear cask of ale for Baniff, I found myself sitting in Walworth's room and listening to one of our regular couriers with the delicious feeling that the courier was an outsider to the household and I was an insider. That the five of us shared intimate jokes and experiences the visitor knew nothing about. That the courier was treating the five of us, me included, as a tight command unit he had to report to. My feeling of inclusion was probably encouraged by the fact that we had that evil wand with the blue sapphires in it on the table before the courier arrived. The moment Walworth suggested that we hide the wand, there being no reason for "outsiders" to know that we had it, I was completely taken by the belief that I was "in." There is nothing like being privy to a secret, except being privy to an important secret, for believing yourself among friends.

Despite Mirand's best attempts and my full cooperation, the origin of the wand was still a mystery. At Mirand's request I had willingly put myself in a light trance while he questioned me about my travels, and together we determined that there were two times when my sack had not been with me: when I was in the cell at Habundia's temple and Lord Cathe and Baniff had it, and when I left it briefly in the clearing while I lifted Baniff over the bush and persuaded him to take me to Threle. I held the colored glass and the hard white pea in my hands, for they had attached themselves to the wand, but neither Mirand nor myself could determine anything meaningful concerning their length of exposure, as I had kept them in my pillowcase for several days after my mishap.

I remembered that Pourra had been in the woods with us before Baniff and I started for Threle, and this was something of a breakthrough, for Caethne was then able to determine that her familiar had indeed planted the wand in my sack. How he got hold of it in the first place was anybody's guess. Caethne said all he would tell her was that his animal friends gave it to him and that he put it in my sack "to help."

Mirand was able to determine that the wand amplified the directed energy of its user in such a way as to cause objects to explode into nothingness. Evil wizards had a euphemism for it; they called it a Wand of Surprises because if you were facing the wrong end of it, the wizard only had to discharge it once and surprise—you were dead. Technically, it was a will amplifier designed particularly for deconstructing the component elements of objects until the elements destroyed themselves in a kind of magically induced sadomasochistic fury.

Helping Mirand identify the wand was memorable, but perhaps the most memorable incident of that time occured one evening when we were all pleasantly intoxicated around the fire, except for Walworth, who could drink even Baniff under the table without showing any noticeable signs of drunkenness. There was a good deal of poetry that evening, poetry we got into via politics.

An intelligence report had arrived in the late afternoon indicating that Sunnas's return to Sunnashiven was imminent, and my friends were seeking my opinion as to Sunnas's real popularity in the city. King Sevalas had reduced the food supply he was sending into Sunnashiven by a little less than half, and three more rebel counts had quietly disappeared in the night with all they owned and everything they could steal. Lord Protector Sina had long since stopped trying to explain where the food was coming from, and it was now obvious to the city's populace that it was coming from the southwest, from the Kingdom of Sevalas. King Sevalas's agents started a rumor in the city that the food reduction was due to the peasants in the southern counties, who were waylaying the traveling merchants and stealing the food for themselves. They also let it fly about that King Sunnas was safely ensconced in the Kingdom of Sevalas and had nobly done his best to persuade the Sevalan people to send whatever food they could spare to help his loyal subjects in Sunnashiven. The rumors were readily believed, and demonstrations against Sina and the rebel government were breaking out all over the city.

I was eagerly explaining why these rumors would be so readily believed in Sunnashiven and simultaneously reflecting on my own eagerness in offering explanations. People love to talk about their homeland, even if they hate their homeland, because it is one of the few opportunities most people have in life to be an expert on something without having to work for it. Simply by virtue of being born and raised there, I knew more about Sunnashiven than my friends did. Only later, when I was alone in bed and Mirand was softly breathing across the room while gray clouds of wizard dreams formed over his head and softened the darkness, did I remember that I should have felt guilty for not openly acknowledging that my superior knowledge of Sunnashiven was solely a matter of chance. I had spent nearly all my time at home or in the fields or in the library at school, and had any of my friends been born in the city their more adventurous temperaments would have taught them more about Sunnashiven in one day than I learned in a month. Even Mirand, for all his studious nature, no doubt would have observed more than I. But for an evening I was an entertaining lecturer—witty, bright, charming, and confident, and I still remember this comfortable, familial night as one of the happiest in my young life.

I drained my ale and felt its sweet warmth spread up to my eyes and out the top of my head. "Of course, in Sunnashiven the people engage in a strange sort of double belief. I want to say that they believe with their mouths what the government tells them, but some of them believe with their minds that the government is lying."

"You mean Sunnashiveners *have* minds?" teased Baniff. And oh, blessed stars, it didn't hurt a bit.

"Well, besides me and Grendel, who we all know is a real genius, some of them do. Except I lost mine when I came here." I grinned.

"Then have another ale, lad. It helps."

"Thanks, comrade." Baniff was playing at dice with Walworth, who seemed to be winning, but both were listening intently to whatever I might say. Mirand was sitting on a low stool against the wall. Pourra had crawled into his lap, and the wizard was idly petting him. Mirand had been carelessly strumming a small harp, but the music had attracted Pourra and now the harp leaned silent against the wall while the wood spirit basked in the wizard's attention. Mirand's feet were bare under his robe. Despite the situation in the south, he was comfortable with his life. Caethne had seated herself opposite Mirand, close to the fire. She was busy sewing a pouch for herbs. She never once looked over at her familiar, but she occasionally glanced up at me and over at her brother. She had a scrying glass on her lap. I reached across her to refill my mug from the cauldron and briefly caught the reflection of my scar in the glass. I continued speaking. "Take the southern peasants, for example."

"Take their worthless leaders," said Walworth dryly.

"And hang them," added Baniff. He gave his dice another throw.

"In Sunnashiven it is common to think of the southern peasants as ignorant provincials who'll follow anyone with a silver tongue and a bright promise," I said.

"It took the whole city to figure that one out?" asked Baniff. "I guess there is a mind or two in Sunnashiven."

"Well, it took the five of *us*," I replied, and laughed.

"That just means we're smarter," said the gnome.

"Especially since we now have Llewelyn working with us," said Caethne. "Please tell us more about the peasants."

"Well, Cae, since you ask . . ." I sipped slowly on my mug. She had made an oaken one for me with an *L* carved in it. "I was describing them as an example of double belief. For although the peasants are seen as greedy, selfish louts who lack the ability to understand why the state should claim everything they produce, they are also seen as representatives of an attractive, older way of life that the city inhabitants have lost. The same people who deride the peasants for their ignorance elevate them like a city god for their rustic ways. I can't even begin to describe it. You have to be there. You'd still never believe it."

"Then use these," said Baniff, tossing me some oddly shaped dice and promptly withdrawing a new set from his pocket. It was clear that he had lost another round with Walworth and was trying to change his luck. I admired their bright colors in the firelight. "Illusionist dice, lad. They'll improve yer powers of description like nothin' else. Roll them and help us believe it."

"You're giving illusion dice to a young wizard?" asked Mirand. "Aren't you afraid your dreams will go up in flames?" He was gently teasing.

"What dreams?" said the illusionist.

"Baniff's more afraid of finding ale in his bed," said Caethne, deftly pulling thread through the cloth for her pouch. "It might be the kind of ale he can actually open. And then he'd have to drink it. And then he'd get drunk and miss Llewelyn's treatise on double belief."

"Or at least be able to understand it," said Mirand softly, almost as though he was extending me a compliment.

"Ah, it's Llewelyn who ain't drunk enough to be understood."

"Then I'll match ye mug for mug, Baniff," I said, draining mine.

"Yer on it," he agreed, draining his own. "Besides, those dice are really pretty worn. They're good only fer gamin' now, lad."

"No, they're not. You just lost."

"Well, that's the way of it, but I've rolled up small objects with them in the past, illusionist goblets and daggers and such. No tellin' how they work with words, but you might as well give them a try." I refilled my mug and Pourra jumped down from Mirand's lap and waddled over to the fireplace. I gave him a sip. "No cheatin,' lad. Drink it all." Baniff got up to refill his. I filled my mug back to the brim and crossed the room to the table, where the wildflowers were just beginning to show signs of age. I remember thinking, *They brighten as they die.* Then I was sitting on the table among the flowers, one foot on a chair, putting my mug to my lips, and turning to face my audience. Here was my crown and my glory. Pourra was sitting upright near Caethne. It was dark where I was, as I was farthest removed from the fire, and it occurred to me that I could see my friends better than they could see me. Darkness is a mask. I rolled two dice with a flourish and began to speak.

"Well, let's say the five of us are in Sunnashiven right now, and that you are all wearing clothes of Sunnashiven make that I've provided for you out of the gold you brought along—a bag each. So you don't look too out of place, although you carry yourselves slightly more confidently than most Sunnashiveners do, and as soon as you open your mouths your accents betray you as foreigners. Baniff will get some looks, as gnomes aren't commonly seen in the city."

"What if I put an illusion spell on everybody to change their accents and make myself seem taller?"

"You can try it. Or you can trust me to guide you and do most of the talking."

"Lead the way, Captain," said Walworth.

"Be careful what ye say," said Baniff. "He just might."

"I intend to. By the way, it is the dark side of dawn, and we each have a crust of bread in our pockets, because I've been starving myself for five days to provide you all with something. It is all the food I can spare."

"Damn nice of ye, lad."

"Well, actually it is. One of the things you'll have to think about in Sunnashiven is getting food. Since I'm used to going hungry and you're not,

I'll have something of an advantage. Now, you also have whatever weapons and tools you normally carry, and you're standing near a meager pumpkin patch on the eastern edge of the city. Where would you like to go?"

"Back to Threle," said Baniff.

I rolled the dice for effect. Pourra squealed. "The loudest thing you can hear is a pale streak of light across the sky. To the east you can hear the silence twisting itself into a thick, hungry hole. That's where the pumpkin patch is, only nothing grows there now. Beyond is the city gate, where the silence dies into something unnameable that opposes and devours sound. To the west is the city, where silence dies into sound. Which do you choose?"

"You sound like Grima," said Caethne appreciatively.

Perhaps my face flushed slightly at her compliment, but I'm sure they couldn't see this in the dark. Fully conscious of my role now, I remained outwardly impassive while I waited.

"Which way do you usually go?" asked Caethne softly, hypnotically.

I sat in silence a minute and rocked back and forth. "I go west when I have to and east when I can. I'm much more comfortable in the east. I can think there." I was working myself into a trance; there were power surges in the room, or were they in my own heartbeat? I could see that my friends were coming along for the ride.

"Yet the city is west and we need information," said Walworth. "Will you lead us there?"

"Of course. West it is. West." I rolled the dice again. "West we travel a dirt lane that winds among some empty gardens and cottages. There is a faint but unmistakable sour-sweet stench in the air. Good thing we haven't eaten, because we all feel crests of sickness when the breeze picks up. How are we walking? The lane is wide enough for the five of us to link arms." No response. "All right, we're linking arms, then, five comrades in arms looking for adventure in the city. Baniff, have you decided to try to look taller through using illusion?"

"No, lad, yer doing fine work in that line without my help."

"Right, then. The four of us are linking arms, and you, being smaller, are in front. We're walking swiftly, since there's nobody else using the lane. The sky is growing lighter as we walk."

"Is there nothing in the cottage gardens?" asked Caethne.

"Nothing but a few dried twigs. There's a graceful black circular motion in one of them, though. The crows have come for their morning feed."

"On what?"

"Take a look."

"I'm peering into the garden now."

"And you see impressive glossy fat birds tearing the meat off something that looks like a child's hand. As your eyes adjust to the gore, you see another hand almost devoured and then part of a white torso in a dead bush. The garden is as sterile as the others. One of the crows takes flight with half of a little limp foot in its beak."

"That's horrible!"

"Yes. We're passing beyond the gardens now and into a cobblestone street where the cottages are closer together. The stench increases, so strong now that the smell disrupts the perfect morning silence. There's the emaciated corpse of a middle-aged man sitting in a doorway. His face is ravaged by disease and his right cheek is bloated and bursting with pus, which trickles down to his torn clothes. His clothes seem to be moving, but on closer inspection you see that they are crawling with vermin. A rat runs out of his collar and up his face and then jumps down with a startled plop. A crow lands and starts tearing at the man's exposed belly, which is covered with red, ragged sores. The flies are starting to gather too, it being a lovely morning, but you can't hear their song. It's too early for that. You see fat juicy miniature bulbs of black making lazily intense curves as they wander to their work, and your mind fills in the *bazzz, bezzz, buzzz* you know should be there." I paused to drink.

"Well, lad, guess yer takin' us down the scenic path."

"Thought you'd like to see the way I usually go to school. Now, all the doors and windows to the cottages are closed fast, but the silence we pass through marks and strengthens the first sound of the city coming to life— the sound that penetrates one of the cottages, the sound of a woman wailing as if her heart would burst."

"Let's stop and listen," said Walworth.

"All right." I paused and then wailed, "The rats got my bread. Heuh hih hih heuh, the rats, the rats, the rats ate my food." And I screamed, "The rats got my lovely food. And they ate my lovely baby. My-y-y ba-a-by. My baby is all gone. My kit-*ten*." Then I said placidly, "Would you like to continue?"

"No," said Caethne. "I'm invoking my deity, Habundia Ceres." I rolled the dice. "I'm unlinking my arm and taking bread out of my pocket. I'm walking to the door. I knock."

"No one answers."

"I call to her that I'll give her food."

"No one answers."

"I call to her that I'm leaving food at her door."

"And do you?"

"Yes, of course. Food and three gold pieces. I turn to leave."

"As you're walking away you hear a light scuffle."

"Then I turn towards the sound."

"You see rats eating the bread and carrying away the gold pieces." I drank a long deep draught from my mug.

"But I invoked Habundia," protested Caethne.

Mirand broke in. "You forgot that in Sunnashiven Habundia is an evil deity who requires sacrifice and loss. Llewelyn is being consistent—the deity heard you."

"I don't like Sunnashiven."

"That's all right," I said. "Neither does anybody else, but nobody likes to say it, as nobody likes to go to jail. Shall we continue?"

No objections. "West. Well, a few more paces and Caethne starts to feel a light, frantic clawing somewhere inside her blouse, against her stomach."

"So I take off my blouse," said Caethne.

"Right there, on the city street?"

"Why not?"

"All right." I rolled another die. "Just as you remove your blouse you feel a sharp biting pain under your ribs. There's a rat clinging to your flesh, and warm blood trickling down to your thighs. Your screams of pain are attracting the attention of a group of locals."

"I draw my dagger and knock the rat away," said Walworth. I rolled the dice again.

"You're more than skilled enough to accomplish that. Caethne is slumped on the street, bare-breasted and bleeding. No one is helping her, but an old man grumbles that the city should really do something about the rat problem. A few people are staring curiously at Baniff."

"My sister always carries healing herbs. I pick up her blouse and immediately take out a handful of powdered dragonwort to stop the bleeding."

"In your haste you spill a few gold coins and the crowd pushes forward to grab them."

Baniff hooted. "Then I make myself look like a giant menacin' rat."

"And the crowd runs."

"Does it take much illusion for you to look like a rat or are you just accentuating your natural capabilities?" teased Caethne.

"Well, lass, if ye've got what it takes, ye've got what it takes," said Baniff proudly. "Did the crowd drop anythin' interestin'?"

"No. But they grabbed a few gold pieces. Caethne is strong enough to stand now. I offer her my arm. Shall we continue, sis?"

"By all means. I suppose I shall keep my shirt off and expose my wound to the air."

"We walk a few hundred feet and see a knot of figures dressed in yellow approaching us."

"Clerical guards," said Baniff. "How are you feelin', lad?"

"Just another fine day in Sunnashiven."

"I thought so. Good ale."

"I suppose we would keep walking," said Caethne. "No reason not to."

"They're branching out to our left, so unless we turn and head back east we will run into them." I drank the rest of my ale and got up to refill my mug as Baniff went to refill his.

Returning to the table, I threw the dice again. "They're on us now, and there's ten of them. The king's guards have been greatly diminished after the revolution, so the clerical guards have usurped many of their peace-keeping functions."

"How do you know that? You haven't been back to Sunnashiven since the revolution," Caethne objected.

"I'm making it up. My words are true in spirit only." I paused. "They are wearing the insignia of the corn sheath, Habundia's symbol."

"Then I greet them," said Caethne. "Hail to thee, brothers and sisters."

"Their spears are out and they're surrounding us."

"Breaking spears is a simple matter," said Mirand.

"Wait," said Walworth. "We may learn something." Then he said, as if speaking to the guards, "We come in peace. If we have unknowingly violated any of your laws, we are sorry for it and would make amends."

"Then give us your weapon. You may not carry it inside the city," I said in the belligerent fashion so typical of Sunnashiven's guards. "What happened to you?" I queried Caethne harshly.

"A rat bit me. My brother healed it with dragonwort."

"The guard lightly jabs Caethne's wound and it opens up again. She doubles over in pain," I said. "It is illegal to heal yourself without a city license. What is dragonwort?"

"Shall I just break their spears for them?" asked Mirand.

"No," said Walworth. "We're here to learn. Let's follow it through. I give their leader the dagger I wear outside my clothes."

"Keeping the one you always wear inside your shirt?" I queried.

"Of course."

"All right, I'll try to comfort Caethne. The crowd is chanting, 'They have gold, they have gold. Make them give up their gold.' The guards ignore them. Their leader tells Caethne, 'You may not walk bare-breasted through the city. Mocking a high priestess is another crime.' You're in too much pain to answer. I take your shirt back from Walworth and manage to get it around you. You can stand a little if you lean against me. The guards are forcing us to walk at spear point through several twists and turns of city streets until we come to a large white flat place. The guards hustle us up some steep white steps and then it gets shady and cool. High-vaulted ceilings. Baniff may recognize this place as the public area of Habundia's temple. We are taken through a narrow door, along several dark descending passageways, and into a cell. Slam. Lock. The guards leave. Alone at last, my friends. The air in the cell feels close and damp. The rats smell our bread crusts and they're coming for us. I hope none of us have bare feet." I looked pointedly at Mirand.

"The lock breaks," he said.

"And out we go," said Baniff. "Thank ye for the courtesy, master."

"No problem," said the wizard. "I also think it's time I conjured up a pair of shoes for myself."

"Noted."

"Let's say I lead us up through the dark corridors," said Baniff.

"Let's say you do," I agreed. "And let's say you get us outside the temple and into the light. After we blink for a few minutes in the brightness, our eyes will adjust to a cityscape that helplessly moves and throbs as the nerves of a dead animal do. A city that simply buzzes with the low slow flattened hum of a dying mathematical equation. Poke a muscle and the reflex thanks you, with or without the brain's permission. The towers peel themselves inside out with darkened pulpy edges. Have you ever seen a building rot while still in use? A few of them are pale and green. There are people ghosting the life that's already fled. I'm thinking of an image of a ratty little animal skillfully hacked to pieces, with each piece somehow being kept alive and functioning separately from the rest of the pieces, so the same animal's life force parodies its own natural need for death. I'll leave blank whether it is an intelligent animal that can feel and know that it is being deliberately kept in this nightmarish state, a state that could drag its slow ratty scaly length for years and years as easily as not. Anyway, that image is for the sort of life before us, which pulses irregularly in and out of sight, in and out of the decomposing towers, as people don't quite walk to wherever they're not quite going."

Baniff looked as though he was about to lose his ale all over the floor when I mentioned the ratty animal, but he put a brave face on it. "Careful with the imagery, lad, ye'll scare the lady."

"No, he won't," said Caethne. "Llewelyn's doing fine." She continued to nonchalantly sew her pouch. I noticed that even Walworth looked a little pale around the eyes, as if his own natural courtesy was struggling with a desire to tell me to lighten up the story, but he was still listening intently. Mirand looked a little too analytical, even for him, so I knew he was experiencing discomfort. I felt I was accomplishing something. Isn't art supposed to move people? And weren't these *real* emotions I was creating?

I seized the power with alacrity, drinking thoughtfully while my words took effect. While I was speaking, the moon had become briefly visible through the skylight over the table, but she had now hidden herself again. "Well, with all of civilization's delights laid open before us, do we do some exploring or stand around and wait for the guards? By the way, Mirand might be feeling a little sick from the nature of the power surges that leak and wash from the city."

"I can protect myself," he said. "And so can you."

"Right. Well, as we're taking in the view, a heavily braceleted woman erupts from the temple. She's annoyed with us for blocking the entrance. Do you wish to speak to her?"

"No," said Baniff.

"Hail, mistress," said Caethne.

"She stops and blesses you with a face of permanent annoyance. Then she pushes past you and in doing so drops one of her bracelets."

"So I stoop down to pick it up and give it to her."

"And your wound opens up, with a great deal of pain. The blood on your shirt draws her attention. Her face spreads into a soft mask and her mouth forms something that passes for a smile. She cajoles, 'Oh, there you are, my lords and lady. There you are. There's been a horrible mistake, and we're so sorry, but what could we do? You didn't tell us who you are. My mistress would love to see you now. Please come with me, my good lords, please come, my lady. Tsk, such a wound. My mistress will cure that, please come.' " I drank again. "Do we follow her?"

"I suppose," said Baniff. "Anythin' to shut her up."

"As we cross a large meeting area and ascend some stairs, she chatters, You're a gnome, aren't you? Huh? That's really great. I've never seen a gnome before, but that's fine. If you don't mind my saying, you don't look anything like a mouse, but I suppose you're older. Gnomes are welcome here. Everyone is welcome here. Oh, here's my mistress's chambers. Please go in.' She opens the door and smiles and nods vigorously to someone, and then runs away."

"She also has two large ass ears growin' on the top of her head."

"Baniff, that's cruel," said Caethne.

"No, it's not. Illusion isn't permanent."

"Are we entering the room?" I asked.

"Might as well."

"The room is grand and formal, as befits the chambers of a high priest-ess. Carved oaken ceilings show the yearly sacrifice of Habundia and the harvesting of the grain. Marble statues of the goddess in her death throes. Piles of expensive carpets litter the floor, so soft and pliant you can barely walk on them. A pure gold sheaf of corn stands on an ivory table, near bowls of real food and drink. The high priestess crosses the room to greet us and she is short and simple and unassuming. Her hand is extended toward Walworth. You want to like her."

"No, I don't," said Baniff.

"And she speaks. 'My good Lord Walworth, I am so pleased to receive you and your entourage. We all want you to be comfortable here, to enjoy your visit to the city you have given so much help to. When the guards brought me your dagger and I recognized by the engraving whom it belonged to, I was most embarrassed over our mistake. We had no idea who you were, and we can only apologize to you a thousand times over and do our best to make amends. You will want to meet Lord Protector Sina, and I should be happy to accompany you to see him.' "

"I ask to see my dagger."

"And she replies, 'Yes, of course, I have it here and I shall certainly keep it safe for you until you leave the city, my good lord.' "

"I want it now."

"It is here, but it is not safe to carry weapons in the city. You might get stopped by the guards again. Sunnashiven is a violent city, my lord and sad to say, people are still being stabbed to death every day. We made weapons illegal in the interest of safety."

"Given the circumstances, I should prefer to carry mine in the same interest. Is my weapon in sight, Llewelyn?"

"Yes, it's on the table. I should have mentioned it."

"I take it up and put it in my sheath. Diplomatic immunity."

"All right, I guess that would work."

Caethne put in, "I am so curious about the statues, which all portray the Goddess's dying aspect. Priestess, I am also a devotee of Habundia, but at home our practices are different. I would learn why it is her sacrificial aspect you revere at the expense of all else here. Not as a point of difference, but as two daughters of the Goddess sharing insights."

The high priestess smiles indulgently. "Our customs are simple ones, my lady. We sacrifice ourselves for the good of others. It is our version of perfect love. We ever strive to make Sunnashiven a city of sacrifice, no matter who is running the government. My lord protector and the rebel counts may seek to eliminate taxes, but we at the temple are always here to insure that people are made to sacrifice something of themselves. That is why I would encourage your brother to sacrifice his weapon. We understand your concern for your safety, my lord, but we believe our guards are adequate protection against violence, should such protection be needed. Trust us. There are too many weapons in the city now, and they are almost always used against our innocent populace. I'm sure you understand."

"No, Priestess, I don't. How can these weapons be used against innocent citizens if the guards are adequate protection, as you claim? Having experienced the sort of 'protection' your guards offer, I choose to trust in myself."

"Let's not argue, my lord. I'm sure your intentions are good, but we would ask your cooperation in reducing city violence by leaving your dagger here. Suppose someone should steal it from you and use it in a crime?"

"The way I see it, someone already has."

I spoke as myself. "The priestess has a point. Leaving your dagger here might very well reduce city violence. If you let the temple disarm you and make you vulnerable to physical attack, you might very well be killed in the streets. But if you fight to defend yourself, there's a chance that both you and your attacker will die, thus increasing the level of violence. The city of Sunnashiven holds all life to be sacred and so would rather see you die than see you and somebody else who might be trying to kill you perish."

"What makes you think I'd lose?"

"I think the priestess would remind you that good people like yourself do not kill under any circumstances and choose death over self-defense. Am I correct, Priestess?"

" 'Being a native, you understand our ways better than your friends do,' the priestess says, and smiles."

" 'May I eat, priestess?' I ask respectfully. 'I've gone hungry for five days so that my friends might have food.' "

"Yes, of course. Those bowls contain temple offerings that we now require the people to make. It is difficult for some of them to meet the quota, but we must do everything we can to feed the clergy, to ensure that the temple's business continues. We minister to the spiritual development of the populace, and we feel that we do that well. One of our goals is to change attitudes toward violence so that violence no longer exists, by stressing that we all are born to serve others."

"I'll remember that when we're gettin' robbed," said Baniff.

"Another of our sacred teachings, as I'm sure you know, is that as long as no one takes for himself, everyone benefits, and he who gives up the most and takes nothing in return is most blessed."

"Then the corpse we saw in the cottage doorway must be held in truly high esteem," said Mirand. "He looked as if he had taken nothing for himself in weeks, and he was still giving of himself to every life-form that crawled along."

" 'Oh, there are always corpses in the doorways. We can't help that, especially lately, as I'm sure you understand. The poor always suffer by the greed of the rich. Come, my lady.' She sweetly takes Caethne's hand and leads her before one of the statues. 'This is a particularly rare statue showing Habundia with knife to breast, shedding Her blood on the growing corn. It cost a great deal, so we choose not to display it publicly. It is my favorite example of self-sacrifice. See how the greatest of the deities would tear her living heart out that the lowliest of her creatures, the simple corn, might live.' "

"Who is that ugly little man peering from behind her robe?"

"His name is Christus. He is her younger brother, and our true deity and savior. The people have never really accepted him, but you can still see his spirit all over the city. It has always been Mother Habundia that the people adore, so we use her name and image. Christus is just for the initiated priesthood. He's special. You *are* initiated, aren't you?"

"No, not in the way you mean. When I fell in love with Habundia—the *real* Habundia, if you don't mind my saying so—I spoke to the corn in the fields and initiated myself."

"Well, that's a new one on me. No wonder you're so ignorant of doctrine. Don't you know that only an initiated priestess can initiate you into Habundia's worship? I hope you won't tell me that your grandmother drew a circle in her kitchen and brought you into her worship when you were a child, or that you are an heiress to a family tradition stretching back through antiquity, or that you suddenly discovered that the universe is feminine, or any number of things being claimed by witches today."

"Well, actually I did have a great-aunt who claimed to know an old woman who initiated her grandson, so I can play with the forms and stories with the best of them. But I prefer honesty, and in honesty I claim only to have heard the stories and discovered myself. In my homeland Habundia has no siblings. She *is* the corn, so it is meaningless for us to speak of sacrifice."

"Does your corn never die?"

"I suppose we look at death as change into something else. The corn becomes the living earth, or the energy that kindles our bodily actions, or the sound of a young calf lowing for his mother." She turned to me. "How am I doing?"

"Not badly," I said honestly. "But I'm not convinced the priestess would understand those images."

"So I continue," said Caethne. "To us the corn just does what it does, and for it to do otherwise would be evil. To deny the self is evil. I am Habundia because I naturally give of my work and my life to others. If this were not naturally so, she would not be my deity. It isn't like a conscious adoption of doctrine. I listened to my heart and heard Mother speaking."

"My dear child, none of us is the Goddess. We can only strive to be like Her in small ways. But I appreciate your enthusiasm. I'm sure you are a generous lady, but we must ask ourselves in good conscience what would happen if everyone did as they liked. Most of us would not be as good and gracious as you are, and the poor would starve. Surely you would not deny your obligation toward the poor?"

"Obligation? What is the nature of this obligation?"

"Lady, surely your family's great wealth obliges you to give to others. Since you've been given more than most inhabitants of this poor earth, you owe something to those who are less fortunate. A true servant of Habundia—of Christus, I should say—understands the principle that each of us must give according to our wealth to others according to their needs." I made the priestess's voice sound caring and self-righteous at the same time.

"No one ever gave my family anything. My grandfather was a simple peasant who earned a duchy from the king through his own efforts. In his day he risked his life and fought bravely against the raiders who threatened our northwestern borders. He used his skill to invent better weapons and shields that defended our people and saved their lives, and the peasants were thrilled to see him earn the title of duke and protector."

"A symptom of their own oppression, no doubt. With all due respect, my lady, has it ever occurred to you that most people are not as brave and clever and lucky as your grandfather? Most people aren't capable of inventing better weapons, or I should say better ways to kill. It seems to me your grandfather bought his duchy through manufacturing instruments of war, not peace."

"The people were most grateful for his protection. Plowshares are little comfort when facing an army that wants to slaughter you and take your land."

"Well, I guess I find it a little silly to fight over land. The land doesn't care who owns it."

"And neither does the temple," said Mirand. "Which will receive its offerings from frightened people no matter who owns the land."

"Why should anyone own land? Can land really belong to anyone?"

"The land is Habundia," said Caethne. "And the Habundia I invoke gives of herself through those who love the land and know how to work it, just as other gods manifest themselves through other talents. If I work the land and produce an abundant harvest, shall that land be usurped and trampled upon by someone else because the land does not *really* belong to me and that other person wants to destroy my work?"

"Caethne, child, I'm sure you're a fine agriculturist, but producing too much might make other people jealous, and that's how wars begin. Even if you gave all your produce away and starved yourself like your friend here, someone else who owned land might be more selfish. Perhaps we need a temple to ensure that nobody takes from the land more than they need."

"Since your land isn't producing anything now, that shouldn't be difficult," said Walworth.

"Well, that will change. We've outlawed private gardens to force people to work the temple lands, and we are sure the lands will bloom again. We've become rather successful during the present food shortage in making certain that no one in Sunnashiven ever takes or receives or owns more than physical need requires."

"Except the clergy," said Mirand.

"The priestess ignores you. 'We are proud to see the spirit of the Sunnashiven people change in hardship. Poverty is a wonderful teacher. You can't learn unless you suffer. Besides, my guests, I speak only in peace. If no one owned land, there would be nothing to fight for and war would end.' "

"Your words are truer than you realize," said Mirand.

"Don't those who have talents bear an obligation to use those talents to help others without seeking personal gain? Caethne, don't the grandchildren of the peasants who knew your grandfather have just as much right to a duchy as you and your brother do? Perhaps even more right, because they didn't have clever grandfathers to give them advantages in life?"

"My grandfather did use his talents to help his countrymen; that's why the king made him a duke. Do you mean to say that duchies should be given to people because their grandparents *didn't* have them?"

"I'm saying that we're all human, we're all servants of Habundia Christus, and we all deserve equal treatment," said the priestess softly. "In point of fact, you are no more deserving of your good fortune than any poor child is."

"Since we're all human and all equal, then I'm no less deserving either. Although I'll admit that in my case desert had less to do with it than the accident of my birth. Or am I less deserving than others because my grandfather was brave and clever?"

"Should a poor child suffer because his grandfather wasn't brave?"

"My grandfather was once a poor child himself. And believe me, the peasants in my homeland don't suffer. If they did, my parents would be out of a job and we'd have a new duke. Our populace is armed and informed, a combination I suspect would be rather dangerous to the government in Sunnashiven."

"But who takes care of your poor?"

"A lot of our people celebrate Habundia and simply take care of each other in hard times."

"Caethne, Caethne, I thought you had a good heart. Look at the misery and squalor around you here. So much needless suffering. Perhaps you've been more fortunate up north, but our people can barely help themselves, let alone each other. Is it fair for anyone to inherit half a duchy while others are starving? Isn't it our obligation to end all suffering? This is the whole secret and mystery of Christus, and the basis of our laws, which even Lord Protector Sina is beginning to see. We are all one, we are all the same, we are all born to serve others. You are nothing in yourself, you are everything through others."

"Does that mean no one really exists as himself?"

"That's exactly what it means," said Mirand. "It's kind of like being fictional."

"Or being dead," said Baniff.

"You are only worthy insofar as you give of yourself," I continued in the voice of the priestess. "To that end, we allow no wealth in Sunnashiven, even under the new government. We take from all and give equally to all, each according to his needs. It is well to speak of private acts of charity, but charity that is enforced and publicly administered, gives the poor some certainty that their needs will be met."

"To Habundia, forced giving is a perversion of charity," protested Caethne.

"I'm proud of you, student," broke in Mirand. "I've trained you well." I noticed Caethne's eyes were glowing in the firelight. Clearly her performance had been for Mirand as much as for me.

"Yet Christus tells us we're all responsible for each other," I said as the priestess.

"How am I responsible for the mess in Sunnashiven? I didn't forbid the people to grow food for themselves during the present shortage, or turn back Helan farmers at the border, or insist on taking offerings from people who can barely feed themselves. How am I responsible for that child's corpse I saw being torn apart by birds? Or for that woman I heard bewailing the loss of her baby?"

"Don't you care about human suffering?"

"Of course I care, but your strange policies tell me that you revel in it."

"The priestess smiles at your outburst."

Caethne continued, "I cared enough to leave her my only crust of bread, and if it were up to me, I would let her grow and keep her own food and let her use whatever means necessary to protect it. But I can care about people without feeling responsible for their misery, and I wonder why you equate responsibility with caring, as if one cannot care about another unless one feels guilty about another's condition. Or is guilt the sacrifice you exact from true love and compassion lest some individual somewhere feel too much love?"

I spoke again as the priestess. "Fine words. But if everyone were allowed to grow their own food in the present situation, no one would work the temple lands and the community would suffer. We must think of the common good, which always overrides the good of individuals."

"But it's only individuals that suffer. That is why I direct my charity toward real people and not abstractions called 'common good.'"

"You call yourself Habundia and you repudiate sacrifice and helping others. Yet look at your side. Wouldn't you like someone to take care of you, to cure that?"

"My brother already did. With dragonwort."

"Dragonwort? That's illegal here. Only licensed clerics can heal, and not with dragonwort. That's a dangerous herb if you don't know what you're doing. No wonder your wound is such a mess."

"My wound is a mess because your guards forced it back open with a spear thrust."

"Well, you can't blame them for carrying out their duties, my lady. I'm sure you and your brother are perfectly capable of using dragonwort properly, but what would happen if a passerby, or a child even, saw you two using it and wanted to try it himself and poisoned himself from an overdose? It's really better for you to bleed a little and suffer some pain so someone else who lacks your herbal skill doesn't have to suffer. Besides, you look like you're better able to handle pain than the average person. By the way, I'm qualified to cure that."

"The priestess lifts your blouse without asking permission, looks at your wound, and crosses the room to pick up a black jar. She returns and opens the jar, revealing a yellow jellylike balm."

"Didweed! That doesn't cure. It merely saps your strength so you don't feel any pain and after a while you just get dependent on it."

"'It's state-approved,'" says the priestess. "'We use it all the time, and it won't poison you.'"

"That depends on what you call poison. I wouldn't use that on a sick cat. With all due respect, Priestess, I'd rather bleed."

"Caethne, Caethne, my dear lady, you sound so young, child! Honestly, do you think we would let you bleed? According to law you must be cured, for your own good."

"I thought my own good didn't matter."

"How would it look if we let you wander the streets of Sunnashiven in that condition? Besides, you might infect someone else with that open sore. You must be cured whether you like it or not. You have no right to refuse treatment here. Your own good is the good of all."

"But you also told me that my own suffering and sacrifice is for the good of all. How do you reconcile those statements?"

"It's called double belief."

"Punch line," cried Mirand appreciatively. "An excellent performance. Although your rendition of the high priestess was really a caricature. You could have presented her as a more challenging and worthy opponent. Stretch your talents. She was too easy." His words were meant for me but he glanced at Caethne as he said them.

"Someday I'll get her down exactly right. So right you won't even recognize me."

The door flew open and the wind gusted dry and crackling leaves all over the floor and into the fire, which flared enough for my audience to see me and made the room feel very much like autumn. I got up to close the door, suspecting the wind had come at Caethne's bidding. "And that is my sister's rendition of pathetic fallacy."

"It's pathetic all right," said Baniff. "I've seen more impressive winds underground."

"Real winds don't blow underground," said Caethne.

"That's the point. Hey, I've matched ye two fer one, lad." He held up his mug.

"But Llewelyn's won the game," said Walworth. "He got us all intoxicated on his words."

"So that just means he drank less than all of us. Keep the dice, lad, ye've earned them."

I jumped into the center of the room and bowed to all, including Pourra, who had fallen asleep and looked to be dreaming. It was a fine moment. Mirand picked up his harp again and started playing a merry round. Baniff began dancing a drunken jig and Walworth and Caethne started clapping for rhythm. I sat in the shadows, watching them, thinking that it was good to be home.

Ten

It was Aleta who brought us news of Sunnas's reinstatement to the throne. She arrived one bright and barren morning with Sir Perie, her arms laden with bulky sacks of apples and pears and her breath churning clouds in the solid air of early winter. I was surprised and pleased to see her. Caethne had run to market that day, and I had left my studies in midmorning to check the fire in the cooking area and boil some water for tea when I heard a loud, insistent thump against the door, as if someone were trying to kick it in. At first I thought that Baniff was playing a trick, so I ignored the pounding, but when I heard a muffled voice say, "Nobody's home. Hold these," I crossed the room and opened the door, thinking it might be a courier.

Aleta had turned to hand off her sacks to her companion, who was standing empty-handed behind her, so I was able to swallow my surprise and merely look gracious and hospitable before she turned and saw me. The effect was wonderful. There I was, casually leaning against the doorpost with my shirt open to the waist in that comfortable, at-home, among-friends style I had come to adopt. I held my mug in one hand, which still contained a little tea from breakfast, and I made sure I was sipping it when she first saw me. The room itself was warm enough for her to feel the difference from where she stood. It was Perie who saw me first, for he drew back a little and cleared his throat expectantly as the door opened. When he said attentively, "My lord," Aleta noticed the change in his demeanor. She was handing him a sack, but she started to turn around while speaking quickly, so her vision was partly obstructed by the parcel.

"Finally, Commander. We've been waiting here longer than a Titaness's gestation—" Silence. Stunned, wide-eyed, flabbergasted silence. Then— "Llewelyn? Is that really you? I don't believe it! You look so different! I thought you were Walworth! You live *here* now? Aphrodite's golden beard but you've changed! You *are* really Llewelyn, aren't you? Remember me? We met in Sunnashiven last summer, before the fall? The revolution, I mean? Remember Sunnashiven? What a mess! I didn't even recognize you. You look older. This is Sir Perie, the captain of my guards." He nodded and so did I. "I was looking for Walworth. Is he here? I brought apples. Pears too. Seedlings from Kant. They grow well in County Clio, but the apples are better."

"I'm sure they are, General, and I know that both will be greatly appreciated. Please come in. Both of you." I motioned airily with my mug. They crossed the threshold and I closed the door. "Walworth is upstairs. Until Cae returns from market I'm afraid I can offer you only tea. It's chamomile. I made it myself."

"As long as it isn't mugwort, I don't care." Aleta dumped her sacks on the table, where the wildflowers were clearly much closer to death than life, and then gasped and did a double take. "So Caethne is here too, is she? I might have guessed. Some of those summer flowers are still green and it's winter! Some are blooming on dead stems! Some of the dead stems have juice! Perie, take a look at this!"

"Quite unusual," he remarked dully.

"They're dying," I explained. "Not even witchcraft lasts forever. Cae should really burn them one of these days." This time I emphasized my use of her nickname. Sir Perie cautiously put his own sack on the table and promptly looked uncomfortable, as he no longer had anything concrete to do and nothing to say. I gave him tea to keep his hands busy. He murmured his thanks and held the mug tightly in both hands, drinking gingerly lest he finish too quickly and find himself in the embarrassing position of not knowing what to do with his mug. Aleta sat down and swallowed her tea in two gulps. Then she banged her empty mug noisily on the table, sighed loudly, and looked around.

"What's that?" She was looking at the dirt floor, where Caethne had been scratching symbols as part of a word game on the previous evening.

"A little bit of night magic. Cae got a little silly. But she did save the flavor of the chamomile on the table before it completely died this morning, and so we have tea."

"What?" Aleta's cheeks bulged bigger than her face. "You mean I just drank a witch brew? Why didn't you tell me?" Captain Perie put his mug down on the table uncertainly and stood awkwardly with his hands behind his back.

"I did, sort of. How else could we come by chamomile this late in the season?" I couldn't help but laugh at her obvious distress. "I am so sorry our humble fare isn't pleasing to you, General. Perhaps you and the captain would prefer some ale?" I magically transferred two bottles from behind the fireplace stones into my hands. To Aleta it would have looked as if they appeared out of nothing. "It's fresh."

"N-No. I would prefer something normal, something without a lot of magic in it."

"Then what are you doing here?" I grandly teased.

"I have a message for the Commander. Important news from the outside world. Something I'm sure he'd like to know. It took the gods' own persuasion to get my father to let me come, so finally I just came anyway. He doesn't even know I'm here. How did you learn to just—just make ale like that?"

"I didn't make the ale, Cae did. It already existed. I just moved it."

"Oh. Let me see it, then." I offered her a bottle. "No, I don't want it. But let me see it. Is it real?"

"Real as anything. Captain?" Perie walked over and looked closely at the bottle without touching it.

"Very clear, very rich-looking," he murmured. "Fine shade of amber."

"Would you like some?" I opened the bottle.

"Oh, no. Oh, no, I'm fine, really. No, thanks. Had some this morning." He waved his hand in refusal, ducked his head, and backed off.

"Ah, go ahead. It'll put a tongue in yer mouth, Cap'n. Sweeten yer speech." Baniff had entered just as I opened the bottle, and he took it from me. "Mirand said ye were thinkin' of me, lad. Thanks." He started to drink.

"Always am. If I weren't thinkin' of you, I'd study too hard and give Mirand something to think about. And then where would we be?"

"In a heap of trouble, seein' as Mirand don't like to think."

I politely offered the remaining bottle to my two guests, but as they both declined, I drank it myself. "Sounds like you need my help upstairs," I said to Baniff.

"Think maybe *ye* can straighten 'em out?"

"We came with intelligence for your commander," said Aleta.

"Good, I think he needs some," quipped Baniff. "I see ye came with apples too, lassie," he said approvingly, choosing a green one and swallowing it whole. "Ah! 'Tis almost as good as drink."

"Best of the lot," said Aleta proudly. "As much as our pack horse could carry through the forest."

"Why use a pack horse? Send on a message and the lad here can work the ether." Aleta looked a little puzzled and put out. "Perie, my man, got any of that Clion chaiaweed on ye?"

The captain quickly inhaled deeply through his nose twice and bounced a little on his toes while patting his chest pocket. "I have a little, yes. For winter camping."

"That's my buddy." Perie shyly took out an enormous packet and put it on the table. He and Baniff began stuffing their pipes with the contents.

Aleta looked surprised. "I didn't know you had any left! You've got enough chana there to stone the Hydra's dam and her twelve sisters! I thought we traded it all for the horse. We could have used that to trade for a better steed."

"I like to keep a supply on hand." He looked a little uncomfortable. "For health reasons, you understand."

"Of course," said Baniff. "Same reason I drink. If 'taint one thing, 'tis another." He lit Perie's pipe with illusion fire and then lit his own. We glanced knowingly at each other. Baniff clearly had no intention of succumbing to anything stronger than ale right now, and he wanted Perie to feel at ease without risking that the chaiaweed would really affect his memory for details. I nonchalantly turned away and drank from my bottle. "So come along upstairs and tell us your tales."

"Baniff, must you always do that?" said Aleta.

"Do what?"

"Create fire out of nothing. It's more nerve-wracking than finding a plate of scorpions in your jousting armor."

"What should I create fire out of? Rock salt?"

"In Clio, if we *must* be deliberately mysterious, we just use a code, like 'three sisters and two sticks'—"

The door flew open and Caethne tripped merrily in, her basket piled high with market supplies and Pourra riding tall and proud on top of her purchases. Pourra was wearing a bright red ribbon around his neck and looking rather elegant. Caethne had managed to get her hair more tangled and windblown in a few hours of walking than Aleta had in several days of riding through the forest. She put down her basket among the dying flowers and touched them tenderly, murmuring, "Poor children." Aleta looked uncomfortable and stood up swiftly with her hand on her sword. Caethne showed absolutely no awareness of her discomfort. "What *are* the three sisters?" she asked with breathless sweetness, pushing back her hair. "Corn, beans, and squash?"

"Carbon, sulfur, and saltpeter," said Aleta a little stiffly.

"That'll work," said Baniff, puffing on his pipe. "Especially if ye don't mind the mess."

"Of course it works." Aleta turned to Baniff. "Perie and I figured it out ourselves. Ye gods, it works better than Hephaestus mocking Ares from the volcano's mouth. Better than illusion, even. Louder and more persuasive too." Perie nodded, his mouth too occupied with dragging on the pipe to offer any comments. "The first time we started a fire with that my father thought it was old man Uranus himself come down from the sky to pay a call. He was so angry he wouldn't let me out for a week, and I had to tie my bedclothes into ladders so that I could sneak out at night and keep experimenting. That really scared the servants. My stupid nurse actually wanted to bring in a cleric to exorcise the land of wood spirits. I didn't think rational people even believed in wood spirits. *She* certainly had no reason to fear them, seeing as she had a face that would slay the Gorgon herself, never mind a harmless wood spirit, even if they did exist. Father got used to the noise, though, and now he insists on starting all the fires at home himself."

"*That* would scare me," said Baniff. "Lose any chimneys?"

"Three," said Aleta proudly. "But we've got the right proportion worked out now."

"I see your mug is empty," said Caethne. "I'm sure I can get more tea out of these plants for you before they expire."

"Don't do me any favors, Caethne. I really should deliver my message now." She started to move, but her gaze was arrested by Pourra. While Aleta was speaking he had crawled over to the hearth and taken out a pawful of fire, and he was now fiercely batting it around in the air and across the dirt floor like a little ball. "What is he doing?"

"Playing. Wood spirits do that sometimes," I explained.

Aleta shuddered impatiently. I wasn't sure if she believed me or just couldn't think of any other explanation for Pourra's seemingly odd behavior. "It's really time Captain Perie and I went upstairs and gave our report."

"Would you like some ale?" pressed Caethne graciously.

Aleta looked at me and Baniff. "No, thanks. I'll just have an apple." She speared one with her sword and started eating it as she made a motion to leave.

I started to show her the way when Captain Perie spoke up unexpectedly. "I'll have myself an ale if you don't mind, milady. Been a while since I've had anything but birch beer and apple wine. Ever since the southwest stopped exporting to us it's been nothing but homegrown, and a man can do with a little variety now and then." Clearly his belief in the chaiaweed he wasn't smoking had put him in a conversational mood. Caethne started to open a chimney stone but I materialized an ale bottle for him to save her the trouble. Aleta scowled at me. Perie continued unabashed. "Yes, sir. Been so long since I've had a spot of good homebrew ale, I'd settle for Krygon if I could get it."

"Poor man," said Baniff.

"Ta." Perie drank and smacked his lips. "Hits the old liver like Athena crashing her old man's head—pardon the soldier talk, milady."

"I'm used to soldier talk." Caethne smiled.

"Yes, hmmm, very good stuff indeed. Smooth as a dragon's fist."

"Dragons don't have fists," said Aleta.

"I think that's his point," I explained for Perie.

"You might say the same of the chana," said Baniff.

I chuckled discreetly. "Shall we go? I think it's about time, and the general looks impatient."

"Well, *I'm* going," said Aleta, who started through the door to the living quarters. "You can all follow me." I caught up to her while the rest followed, Perie commenting nonstop on how well constructed our dwelling was and how much it reminded him of an old fort he had played in as a child, while he frequently stopped to rap on the cave walls and ceiling. As we passed my room I couldn't resist pointing it out to Aleta, not least because the table under the window, which was littered with impressive-looking magical items, was visible through the open doorway.

"Would you like to come in? I share it with Walworth's old tutor, Mirand. I know he wouldn't mind."

"No, Llewelyn. Not now. Later, maybe. It's nice. You're really lucky," she said hurriedly. We all reached Walworth's door and she hesitated and whispered to me, "Is Mirand in there?"

"Of course. What's wrong?"

"Nothing. He curdles my sword, is all."

"Come in, Lady Aleta," cried Mirand gaily from behind the door. "There's nothing to fear. I've hidden my face and withdrawn all my magic into a locked and guarded nutshell. Not even the elf-king himself could pry it open while you are here." Aleta rolled her eyes in annoyance.

"Have to be a pretty small nut or the rattling would scare away the elf king and his army," I countered, opening the door.

Baniff and Caethne laughed, but Aleta looked at me in horror. She took a breath, steadied her eyes, and bravely pushed the door all the way open with the hilt of her sword. Mirand was sitting in consultation with Walworth, a map and a candle between them. "And if it please the general's sensibilities, I'll even pretend that my crystal didn't tell me she was going to arrive with an important message today." He smiled. Mirand was certainly in a strangely jovial mood, but then, he occasionally and unpredictably got that way. This warm and lovely household certainly never lacked for strange moods.

"Your sword still looks straight," I teased Aleta.

She sheathed it and gave Walworth a formal military salute, which he politely returned with a shade of amusement in his eyes.

"Commander."

"Commander."

"My captain of guards, Sir Perie."

"Commander." Perie was holding his ale bottle as he saluted. Baniff and I doubled over laughing.

"At ease, Captain." I could tell that Walworth also found their insistence on military formalities to be a little silly under the circumstances but that he respected Aleta's earnest enthusiasm too much to let her in on his real feelings. Besides, she positively glowed when he addressed her as "Commander" in his best no-nonsense officer's voice. She threw back her shoulders and stuck out her chest in the most genuine and touching display of pride I'd ever seen. Soldiering clearly brought out her best self, and her best self responded with a simple soldier's grace and dignity that made even formalities sound genuine and fresh. I knew instantly that she had no need of the *caen*'s approval but that it was crucial to her sense of calling to earn his respect. I also saw that Walworth had already earned her awe and respect as a highly competent military leader, and that her presence here in spite of her father's objections was the highest compliment she could pay him.

She began, one soldier addressing another, and all her unease vanished into the confidence of competence. "We have come with an intelligence report for you, my lord. Concerning the movements and activities of one Master Wizard Grendel; one Sina, former Count of Sina and former lord protector of the State of New Sunna; and one Franko, Sina's eldest son."

"Proceed."

"You are aware, of course, Commander, that the State of New Sunna no longer exists. All of the rebel counts who still held office six weeks ago have vanished, and it is known that Counts Gren and Santh committed suicide. Their bodies were found in their palace chambers ten days ago with notes wishing their loved ones a good life."

"Yes, I am aware."

"As you also know, Sina disappeared immediately after, confirming the collapse of the rebel government. Sevalas's agents had done their work well. Celebrations broke out in the city along with opportunistic riots, which were quickly held in check by the city guards. The agents kept the guards organized with promises of higher pay and more privileges should they support Sunnas's return, so martial law was enforced while a delegation of soldiers started toward the Kingdom of Sevalas to ask for their sovereign's reinstatement. They unexpectedly met him halfway, for Sunnas had heard of the rebels' collapse and had started back for the city with his flank of Sevalan troops. My informants tell me there was quite a dramatic scene, with fat old Sunnas falling to his knees and symbolically embracing guards from Sunnashiven, repeating the whole performance at the border and kissing the ground, and repeating it again before the city crowds, kissing babies and promising a new age of prosperity and wealth for all. He's safely on the throne again and busy organizing the instatement of Sevalan nobles across the southern counties. No one in the south is daring to complain."

"Yes, we've heard as much," said Walworth gently, "but we thank you for your added confirmation." He didn't want to dampen her enthusiasm by dwelling on the fact that her report was dated. "We are anxious to hear of Master Wizard Grendel and Sina and his son."

"Yes, Commander, for that is what I came to tell you. I saw all three of them traveling together. In County Clio. Four days ago. I rode immediately to tell you. I thought you would want to know." She saluted briefly to indicate the end of her report.

"Did you speak with them, stop them, question their activities?" I interjected.

"No," said Aleta. "Grendel knows me, and I thought quiet stealth and timely intelligence were the better part of valor."

"That *is* news," said Baniff.

Aleta gave him a dirty look and turned back to Walworth in a posture of full military dignity, waiting for her commander's dismissal.

"I meant yer report," offered the gnome apologetically, which only made matters worse. Baniff took another drink, shrugged, and shot me a what-can-I-say look.

"We are extremely grateful for this information, General," said Walworth graciously. "Did they appear to be hurried? Could you tell what they were carrying? What direction they were traveling in?"

"They were riding nearly identical gray horses, not too fast. A rather leisurely pace, now that I think about it. It was the middle of the afternoon in the marketplace, within sight of my father's castle. I don't know what they were carrying, but they all had rather large saddlebags. The odd thing is they were wearing merchant's clothes, as if they were trying to disguise themselves."

"Why is that so odd?" quipped Baniff. "If I were Grendel or Sina right now, I wouldn't want to be tellin' the town crier's brother about it."

"No," said Walworth, helping Aleta, "but you wouldn't be riding in daylight at a leisurely pace through a public market either. If Grendel's party wanted to avoid recognition there are faster and much less traveled forest paths between the southwest and County Clio."

"What the general means about oddness," interrupted Perie, who had been floating off his own belief in the chaiaweed's effect and now saw his chance to speak, "was that their accents were Helan." The gods bless Baniff for his wit! He had known Captain Perie as the shy type whose perception and recall of details had served him through life as one of his chief defenses, and Baniff's use of illusion was producing facts that Aleta, for all her sanguine derring-do, had missed. "Old Grendel kept flattening his *a*'s, so *apple* came out 'ahpple' and *cat* came out 'cot.' I know it was intentional, because young Franko occasionally forgot and his father would elbow him and talk loudly so that nobody would notice. You see, I come from one of the few areas of Clio that still speaks the old language, so I didn't learn Botha until I joined the military. People sound pretty much the same to me across the southwest, but I once knew a fella from Helas who definitely pronounced words differently than the way I was taught, and I remember that. Their clothes were southwestern, but they wore Kantish-looking shoes. Paid for bread and corn in Threlan coins, I noticed, and I kept wondering to myself where they got them. That's the oddness the general means. When Grendel opened his sack to pay I saw it was filled with expensive-looking crystals. Kept wondering how he got those too. Didn't seem too eager to hide his wares."

"It's odd that Grendel didn't recognize Aleta," said Mirand.

"I wasn't about to get that close to a wizard."

"Oh?" said Mirand in mock surprise.

"I was standing behind another stall," she explained. "Once I saw Grendel I had no desire to look that closely at anyone in his party."

"Shall we conjure up another stall for you?" asked Mirand.

"I noticed something else," said Perie, bringing our attention back to himself. "Grendel kept loudly asking for southern produce. Said he knew a black-market shipment of Sevalan corn had arrived, when of course I knew there was no such thing. Our marketplace is rather small and something like that would be noticed. It was as if he wanted everyone to know he had come up from the south. Made quite a to-do about telling everyone his horses were from Sunna. I suspect they weren't. Too well fed, and the saddles and equipment looked too expensive. Also told everyone in sight they were looking to buy lots of food. Demanded lodging for their horses and said they would pay in Threlan currency. Then they were going to head east for the markets."

"For Helas, no doubt," said Walworth, looking at Mirand. "Did you see them on your journey?"

"No, but we came posthaste on a semisecret path the general and I once discovered," said Perie. "We didn't see anyone."

"When did you leave?"

"The same day we saw them," said Aleta. "I went straight to my father and told him, and when he refused to let me go riding off I just came, as I told Llewelyn. He wanted to send a regular courier. For all I know he did and we beat him."

"Or Grendel encountered him on the road," said Mirand.

"Come here and look at this map, Commander," said Walworth to Aleta. "I greatly value your opinion. If Grendel were on his way here, what do you think would be his most likely route?" Aleta traced a line with her finger and explained that the shortest route besides her own, assuming Grendel knew it, would bring him into Threle within the next two days if he left the morning after she did. "If he increased his riding speed maybe sooner."

"That will be all, Commander. Unless you have more to add."

"Can I convince you to stay for sup, Aleta?" asked Caethne.

"No, Caethne, you can't convince me of anything except what I already know, which is that we must return to Clio right away. I'm sure my father has turned the whole county inside out by now looking for me. It wouldn't surprise me if there were scouts on the road even as we speak."

"I'm sure there are," said Mirand with a touch of ire in his voice that I made a note to ask him about later.

"Aren't you concerned about running into Grendel on the return trip?" pressed Caethne.

"Not the way we're going. He would be heading east. We're going to start south toward Sunna for a day and then cut west and cross the trade road. It will take longer, but that will put Grendel considerably north of us."

"Thank you, Commander. Captain." Walworth saluted in dismissal.

"My pleasure and duty." Aleta saluted. Perie put down his bottle and saluted correctly, then they both turned to leave.

"Let me see you out, General," I said impulsively, joining them as they started through the door.

"As you wish," said Aleta. I sensed that she was in a hurry to leave, so I walked quickly with them down the stairs, through the living quarters, the cooking area, and out. I noticed with some disappointment that she didn't even glance toward my room as we passed by it.

Once we were outside Perie nodded to me and went off to attend to their horses like the well-trained soldier he was. From his reticence I guessed that he believed his pipe of chaiaweed was wearing off. Aleta started to take her leave of me. "Well, if I don't see you again, may the gods keep you tight, as they say," she said stoutly, turning in the direction of the horses.

"Aleta, of course you'll see me again. Many times," I said breezily. "There's much work to be done, and I don't foresee either of us losing interest in the outcome of the upheavals in the southwest." She looked a little taken aback by this statement, and I decided it was because she was still getting over the shock of seeing me in Walworth's command headquarters. I immediately felt sorry for her, because she had clearly ridden long and hard and risked her father's wrath to help us, and Baniff and I had returned the favor by having a little fun with her fear and distrust of magic. I softened my voice into what I hoped would be a pleasing combination of apology and gratitude, a combination that would accurately convey what I was sincerely thinking and feeling. "I came outside to thank you, General. Both for your timely intelligence and for your persuading Baniff to get me out of that accursed Sunnashiven. If not for you, I wouldn't be here, and I'll never forget that."

"I owed you a favor. It's done. Thank Baniff." She turned again toward the horses.

"Of course. I already have." She was walking away when I drew her attention by speaking again. "General, it might be a dangerous trek for you going back. Mirand has a scrying crystal he lets me use, and I'm sure I can find a charm for you to carry that would help me see you. Would you feel better if you knew someone was watching?"

"No, I would feel better knowing you weren't using magic to spy on me. I'll be all right, and even if I'm not, there isn't much you can do at a distance besides watch. Is there?"

"No," I said shamefacedly.

"Llewelyn . . ." She looked hesitant, but then plunged ahead. "I truly hope you prosper in your life. I can see you'll make a fine wizard someday, and Mirand is generous to train you. I'm glad you're happy. I must go now. Like you said, there is much to do, and Perie and I will be taking a longer path back."

I felt a stab of resentment under my rib cage when she said "someday," because I had already come to consider myself a wizard. True, I was still under a ban against using my full individual powers, but Aleta didn't know that. Besides, Mirand had mentioned in passing the other day that I had progressed further with word magic than either Walworth or Caethne had chosen to, and I knew myself that I had made so much progress in the past several months that I no longer thought of myself as a novice. Mirand himself now trusted me to manifest secret messages on paper at several miles' distance. Aleta was clearly no judge of magical ability. "I could invest you with a word of power, something to get you through the return trip—"

"No, I don't need it! Llewelyn, I don't mean to be rude, but I must go. It seems that Walworth has assembled his usual assortment of odd companions, and I'm happy you're a member of the club, but—"

"Wait a minute. Who's odd?" I sounded more pleased than defensive. I had come to regard the shared eccentricities of myself and my household as a mark of superiority, so I accepted Aleta's remarks as a perverse sort of praise.

"Who's *odd*? You have to ask? You all are! Caethne isn't odd? I don't care if she is Walworth's sister; she's got a smile that would scrape scales from a mermaid's bottom. I've known her for two years and I still can't figure her out. I've never once seen a morsel of food pass her lips, yet she's always trying to pretend she's some kind of mother goddess with a sacred mission to feed the universe. Her waist isn't much bigger than a large serpent's. Have *you* ever seen her eat anything?"

"Come to think of it, no. So what?"

"So what? If she's such a fine and mighty grain goddess, where's her belly? I've seen scarecrows with more substance. I feel hungry just looking at her. Besides, I would think that a future duchess would want to spend her time studying military strategy and learning how to defend her people, not extending plant life to make herbal teas and taming woodchucks to act like wood spirits."

"Pourra really is a wood spirit. Besides, Caethne is devoted to the goddess Habundia. In her case what you call pretense is really lack of fear to be herself."

"It's a lack, all right. A lack of foresight. As capable as her brother is in battle, he isn't immortal. Once her parents die, Caethne is one sword thrust away from being sole ruler of her duchy. What would she do should Rogue-han ever attack Threle? Sit up north and get everyone drunk? And then there's Baniff. The gods only know where he came from. I don't think he really means any harm, although he could learn to take some things a little more seriously."

"Baniff is very serious. He just has his own way of doing it."

"And then there's Mirand. Does he always look like he's passing judg-ment on the most intimate childhood memories in your mind or is that just what passes for courtesy among master wizards when they receive couriers?"

I laughed. "Believe me, Mirand wouldn't just spy on your thoughts, and if he did, you wouldn't be able to tell from his looks. You'd have to be another wizard to even begin to feel him probing your mind. He's a profes-sional. He's just exceptionally alert to what's around him and he's very good at reading people. Without magic," I added. "Besides, he wouldn't tease you like that if he didn't like you."

"Look, it's not for me to question the commander's judgment and I really don't care what company he keeps while he whiles away the waiting period. When the action starts Walworth will be ready for it and that's all that mat-ters to me. Right now I have orchards to patrol."

"What do you mean, when the action starts? We've seen plenty of action already."

"Where? Here? In Helas? You mean you saw a couple of merchants roughing it up over the price of squash? There's action in Sunnashiven! There's action in my county, where we've been hit again by raiders, in case you haven't heard! There's action in Roguehan's steady acquisition of the southwestern kingdoms! There's intelligence reports and strategy meetings and occasional orders issued here. Here it's all words!"

"That's not a bad thing," I said weakly. "Besides, what else can we do right now? The King of Threle doesn't even know Walworth is conducting this operation, and we stand to get no support from him unless someone actually attacks Threle's borders. Even Helas's duke has grown lukewarm about our presence, because despite Roguehan's attempts to strangle trade here, the economy has improved somewhat and the merchants are happy. Believe me, Walworth is completely aware of the danger the southwestern kingdoms now pose to us, and all of our intelligence gathering will be in-valuable when it does come to war. But it's not for Threle to invade another kingdom without direct provocation, and we haven't been invited to stave off Sunnas's return. The Sunnan people want him back, so what can we do? Tell them we don't like their choice of tyrant? That in itself would be tyr-anny."

"You sound like a Threlan. No offense meant, of course," she added hastily.

"What should I sound like?"

"Yourself."

"Don't know if I can handle that one, but I'll try to please my lady," I said cheerfully.

"No, never mind."

"When the rebels needed and wanted help Walworth did what he could for them."

"Yes, and I see he was richly rewarded for his efforts," she said sarcastically. "Look, this is not an academic policy question for me. County Clio is self-sufficient. We have a stalwart, loyal army and we know how to feed ourselves in even the worst of times. And we've always maintained a foreign policy of neutrality, because every time you make friends you make enemies, and why make enemies? But we are a small county, and under the present circumstances we may have to make friends with somebody. I should like it to be Threle, because I would rather die than see Clio become another Sunnashiven. Of course that is still for my father to decide, and Walworth is hardly in any position to broach the subject with the king right now, who wouldn't be too thrilled to learn that some upstart *caen* from the north has taken it upon himself to organize a secret intelligence-gathering force."

"King Thoren will be grateful someday that Walworth had the foresight," I said coldly. "The king won't be in any position to view our commander as an upstart when he's depending on his work to defend Threle's southern border."

"Don't get defensive, Llewelyn. I have nothing but respect and admiration for Walworth and what he's doing, but I doubt very much that these feelings will be shared by King Thoren. Threle is a large country, and the king is far from Helas, and even in Helas the people are relatively complacent concerning the southwest, even though their borders are the most vulnerable. My father's couriers have already told me that the duke is quietly trying to extricate himself from involvement in this operation. That tells me that he senses further involvement to be unwise or even dangerous."

"Unprofitable is more like it. Helas was in it to protect his trading interests. He's feeling secure right now, so he sees no reason to get involved in the southwestern mess. He hasn't asked us to leave his duchy yet."

"Why should he? Officially he doesn't even know you're here. What a laurel leaf in his pocket if he should suddenly find it convenient to 'discover' your presence and turn Walworth over to the king. Or over to Roguehan."

"Roguehan?"

"It's an arrow from a dark bow, but it strikes me as exceedingly odd that Helas's economy is booming when everyone else in the southwest is barely scraping by. I'd worry about the Duke of Helas keeping your activities secret. What will you do with your beloved commander in prison? Personally, I think Walworth is too clever to let that happen, and Mirand will certainly use his considerable powers to protect him, but damn the gods' rotten teeth, Llewelyn, I don't know how long I can wait before I ask for Thoren's protection, and when I ask, I'll have to explain where I've gotten my intelligence from. It would be better if Thoren heard it from the *caen* first. Put yourself in the king's place. An envoy from a foreign nation shows up one day to tell him that the son of one his warlords has taken it upon himself to set up a secret military and establish his own foreign policy—for the good of Threle, mind you—because the king himself, in this same young lord's opinion, isn't doing his job. 'And by the way, Your Excellency, Clio would like your protection, and we would really appreciate it if you would let this relatively unknown underling of yours fill you in on the state of the world.' Do you really believe the king will be grateful? If Roguehan sends Sunnas over the border, Thoren might not show his outrage with the *caen*, but you can bet he'll feel chagrined that Walworth was right to break Threlan policy. He'll reward him in public all right, and then he'll find a way to contain him privately. You can bet your life on it. Perhaps you might even have to."

"Perhaps I already am," I mused.

"And think about this. If Roguehan gives up his imperial ambitions and goes home, which I highly doubt, Walworth may find himself breaking rocks at the king's pleasure. Which may happen anyway if Helas is a traitor and gets to the king before any of us do."

"What are you suggesting we do, General? Pack it up and go home?"

"I'm not sure you haven't already done that by sitting here in safety as the rebel government ran its course. You've done your research, the time for action is clearly fast approaching, and you need to position yourselves for that. Walworth must go to the king and tell him everything—now, before someone else does. That's the only hope he has of ensuring that Thoren gives him anything remotely resembling support. Walworth has enough facts to be able to present a convincing case now, especially with Grendel heading toward Helas. Let him bring Mirand, who is exceptionally skilled in argument. Thoren will be angry, but Mirand will certainly be able to convince him that the *caen* needs the freedom to act and organize troops openly and that he's the only warrior in the kingdom with the intelligence to do that effectively. I don't think the king will refuse him, and his anger will be mitigated by hearing about it first from the source. Then I can safely approach Thoren for help, for the king will know how dangerous the situation is and I needn't supply more information than that we've been attacked by raiders and need Threle's help."

"The horses are right ready, Commander," called Perie.

"If the situation seems to call for it, I'll even be sure to compliment the king on his wisdom in allowing Walworth to gather intelligence secretly, making it sound like my couriers and I think it was all Thoren's idea. I'll say whatever Walworth thinks would be helpful, but I won't wait much longer to say something. My first loyalty is to my county. Will you speak to Walworth for me?"

"Of course, but why didn't you mention these things yourself?"

"Because I don't trust Caethne."

"Caethne? Caethne's my sister in spirit. She has a very good heart."

"She makes my—"

"I know, she makes your sword curdle."

"No. She makes my liver run like serpent sweat."

"But then all magic does." I'm sure I sounded impatient.

"Be careful of her. Promise me you'll talk to Walworth alone. Tell him I fear greatly for the safety of my land. He'll understand that. Thank him for his help."

"All right, Aleta. I will. Straightaway. Have a good journey home."

"Enjoy the apples." She left me for the horses and I watched her deftly mount, take up the reins, and ride away, Captain Perie at her side and the pack horse following. The tramp of the horses sounded serious. I watched their hooves assault the frozen ground with wretched gasps of almost-sparks.

When I returned upstairs the others were waiting for me, including Caethne, who was now holding and stroking Pourra. I immediately reported on everything Aleta had just told me, including her distrust of my most beloved sister. Cae laughed indulgently, saying, "Well, 'tis typical. And I can't say but that I understand. My brother is the only fighter I've ever known who doesn't have a healthy distrust of magic. Which is much to your advantage in this company, twin."

"Having had Mirand for a teacher is much to my advantage in that school," said Walworth. "Other soldiers have not been so lucky."

"Other soldiers have broken gourds for heads when it comes to magic," said Baniff. "I thought her sword really would curdle when I lit those pipes."

"Didn't it?" I joked. "I definitely saw it curl."

"Must have been a magical sword, then," joshed Baniff. "Felt yer piercin' gaze."

"Or fell for her enchanted soldier," I replied.

"Or enchanted itself into somethin' useful," continued Baniff. "Its blade looked so dull I'd feel safer fallin' on it than using it in battle. Its workmanship was almost good enough fer Sunnashiven make."

"Then let's hope she hasn't need of it during her return trip," said Mirand. "If I know Count Clio, he's got so many scouts on the forest paths looking for his daughter that Aleta would have bought more secrecy giving her report to Grendel himself. It's a certainty now that he's encountered one or more of those scouts, if not Clio's regular courier. We have to assume he knows that we're expecting his arrival."

"How much information would Clio share with his scouts?" I asked.

"Enough to be dangerous. When it comes to his daughter's safety the count cares nothing for security. I'm sure Grendel could extract plenty from a scout's mind and surmise the rest. Damn her for doing us a favor! Didn't she think I was capable of tracking Grendel's movements without her blessed 'help'?"

"When I offered to track her movements back through the scrying crystal she wanted nothing to do with it." Mirand looked at me stonily. "I thought she would feel safer if I offered. Aleta doesn't think in terms of magic, you know that. It probably didn't even occur to her that you could track Grendel, and she thought she was doing her duty by warning us. Besides, none of us even knew that Grendel and Sina were headed our way until she came. Now that we know, you *can* track them. You know where to look."

"Mirand did know Grendel was coming before Aleta arrived," said Walworth quietly, motioning toward the map between them. "Now we have to deal with the plain fact that Grendel knows we know."

"All the more reason to break camp," said Mirand in a tone that implied that this had been the subject of the morning's disagreement to which Baniff had alluded earlier. It seemed that everyone had known Grendel was on his way but me.

"How did you know we'd been discovered?" I asked Mirand nonchalantly.

"The wand you brought into the household developed a noticeable draw last night. Noticeable enough to wake *me* out of a sound sleep, anyway. Someone has been tracking it, and that someone has to be relatively close for me to notice the effect. I don't think Grendel is skilled enough to follow the draw himself, which greatly concerns me, but his bag of crystals concerns me more. He has to be getting help, and it's likely that Roguehan has given him some sort of tracking device. He's probably aware by this point that you had the wizard's key in your possession, and the scar the wand left on your palm doesn't exactly hide your location from a highly adept wizard like Zelar. My impression is that Grendel's tracking the wand, but Zelar could just as easily be using that to track you."

"Why don't we just throw the wand away someplace?" asked Caethne. "It's not as though it was designed with any of us in mind."

"Why not just give it up to Roguehan himself?" shouted Mirand angrily, pounding the table. "Don't you realize what we have here? I'm not sure that even I could create a wand this powerful, and I happen to know a little something about wands! As outstanding an imbecile as Grendel is, I have no intention of turning over to him something that could destroy us all with a wish and a promise!" When I saw and felt Caethne's heart shattering like an early robin's egg through her eyes I could have hit Mirand for his outburst. "Let's stop aiding and abetting the enemy and start containing the damage! After all, that was our original reason for setting up these quarters, wasn't it? To gather enough intelligence to contain future damage. Or have we all forgotten that?" No one dared speak, although Walworth looked as though he had heard and considered these sentiments earlier. Mirand continued in a quieter tone, "I shielded the wand earlier this morning, but I fear that Grendel already knows where we are. Remember, his miserable life—and Sina's too, no doubt—depends on their finding the key for Roguehan. That's a powerful motivation, even for a Sunnan." I was conscious of not wincing.

Since Mirand was looking at me when he finished, I spoke up first. "Were you able to determine exactly how the key holds power over Roguehan?"

"Of course," he said, as if I had just insulted his prowess. "The key holds power over his chief wizard. Besides unlocking just about everything, it also unlocks the cask that holds Zelar's most cherished power talisman, his name stone. I saw the key many times when I was his apprentice, and I always wondered that he would invest so much of his personal energy in one place. I believe his reasoning was that by having a well-hidden energy source— and believe me, it is well hidden—he would become practically invulnerable to direct attack. I'm sure he never counted on having the key stolen, or if he was concerned, he never much cared, knowing that no one would be able to get through the other defenses he's placed around his stone. I'm sure he even has other keys. He might even have assisted in the theft of this one, to provide Sevalas with a feeling of false security that would induce him to work with Roguehan. Certainly he never expected it would end up in our possession. Grendel would be as likely to eat it as use it correctly, but Zelar knows I could certainly be a threat to his liege lord's imperial ambitions. And key in hand, I undoubtedly would be."

I had a fleeting, strange, uncomfortable feeling that all of this had been known by my companions for a long time and that I had been intentionally excluded. I also wondered why Mirand hadn't told me that he knew of Grendel's approach so that I could help track him, but since he had just found out late the night before, I said nothing. Not that the silence now in the room was at all conducive to speech.

"I hate to say it, Commander," said Baniff with uncharacteristic slowness, "but given the certainty that Grendel knows we are aware of his approach, he'll be well prepared for any surprises we can think up at the border, and we have no idea what sorts of evil toys Roguehan has armed him with. It's certain he's well prepared to do what he came to do, and it's a damned good assumption that he and Roguehan already know the location of our headquarters. Now that the wand can't be tracked it makes sense to disappear back into the world for a while, to act as if Helas never existed. Why fight him for the key if we already have it? That is, if we end up fightin' him at all. Grendel may be a fool, but he's such an obvious fool that Zelar would be sure to give him so much firepower that he needn't rely on his limited wit to succeed. And I don't see much charm in watchin' my vision break loose from my last dyin' eye while Mirand duels it out over our corpses in a battle he can't win. No offense, Master, but Zelar's been preparin' for this one longer than ye have."

"I'm not sure we'll have to fight him at all," said Walworth.

"Now yer talkin'. I vote we ride up to Loudes and seek audience with Thoren. Aleta's right fer once. He'll rant a bit, but we'll be right as rabbits once we tell him that Grendel and Sina have entered Threle. Now is the time fer action, and now is the time we must seek the king's support in organizin' the real military to repel an invasion."

"Mirand, pack your books." The wizard looked visibly less tense. I felt his mind relax slightly. "Caethne, find the most ragged, shoddy clothes you can."

"She already has," said Baniff, looking at the habitual mess she wore.

Walworth didn't smile. "Not good enough. You need to look like you've been traveling—at an unhurried speed—for several weeks. Buy yourself a little wagon and have Mirand shield it so that his tools don't draw Grendel's attention. You're not to look as though you're running from Helas, but rather as if you've been on the road longer than Grendel has, like a peasant woman making her usual round to Kant with her wares. Too many locals know you and we need to limit road rumors. Once you're well into Kant I trust you to travel with all speed back home. You needn't tell Mother you've seen me."

"How shall I explain arriving with our esteemed tutor's paraphernalia in my wagon, twin? Or don't you think Mother will notice?"

He considered. "There's a chance we'll overtake you on the road anyway, but there's no telling how long we'll be with Thoren. It's the better side of caution not to have it widely known that I'm planning to show up again at home at this particular time. That could be another flag to Roguehan that we know about Grendel's movements and I would prefer to give him something to guess about. A delay at Thoren's will confuse any of Roguehan's people who might be watching for me. Tell Mother I'm well, I'll see her soon, and I'm anxious to tell her all about my adventures myself. Give her this ring and ask her to say nothing of my impending return until I do return. She'll balk at that, but I must trust to your excellent conversational abilities to keep things discreet. It would be helpful if you set up Mirand's study for him so that it's in working order when we do arrive."

"Speaking of my excellent conversational abilities, what good is a disguise once I start speaking Botha in my northern accent?"

"Try not talkin'," said Baniff. "Ye might even enjoy the experience."

"I could go with Caethne," I volunteered. "I've listened to the merchants for so long I probably sound Helan by now anyway." I was thrilled with the prospect of seeing the rest of Threle, especially Walworth's duchy.

"No," said Walworth. "I want you with us for now." Something beyond thrill pushed up along my back. My friends had need of me! They probably felt I had valuable insights to offer to the king. "Baniff speaks wisdom. Don't feel you have to greet every traveler you pass on the road. Keep moving and your accent won't be a problem. Keep your familiar hidden."

"Shall I take the wand and the key with me too, for safety's sake?"

"I'll keep the wand for safety's sake," said Mirand. "And we'll need to show the key to Thoren."

"All right," she said brightly, standing and picking up Pourra, "If that is how it is to be, I'll go work on my disguise now. Shall I pick up supplies for your journey north when I buy the wagon?"

"No," said Walworth. "I didn't say the rest of us were leaving."

"Ye didn't say . . . what?" exclaimed Baniff, dropping his ale. "I know *I'm* leavin' before Grendel gets close enough to give us a taste of Zelar's wizard fire. You know, the kind of fire that melts rocks."

"*I* know," said Mirand. "But I think my former student here needs a reminder."

"I understand what we're up against," said Walworth. "But Grendel won't risk destroying the dwelling if he thinks the key is here. Right now he's doubting the crystals Roguehan gave him because the wand is shielded and they can't track. We gain a little time while he tinkers and asks for instructions. Zelar will understand what Mirand's done, and Grendel will assume when he finds this deserted headquarters that we've cut our losses and run."

"A fine assumption," said Baniff.

"A fine way to ensure that unwanted guests show up in my duchy and all over Threle," Walworth answered. "Remember what Mirand said about *containing* damage. It's clear that Grendel and company are planning to set up shop here for the long term, or they wouldn't be in disguise. It would be much faster and easier to remain inconspicuous, travel quickly, do the job, and get out. Roguehan probably feels he can offer them protection from everyone in the southwest who would like their heads if they stay in Helas, and perhaps he views our quarters here as just the place for them to set up their own counteroperation. It was clever of him to arrange for Franko's release from Sevalas. If the southern counties ever do rise again, he's got the son of their old hero to throw them as a sop. Grendel certainly wants everyone to think they're Helans with southwestern business connections, which may be a cover for future visitors from the southwest in Helas. It seems to me it's our job to make sure that doesn't happen."

"How? By greeting Grendel at the door and asking him in for a drink?"

"By rendering him powerless," I interjected. "By making sure he's more afraid of us than he is of Roguehan. That will send a message back to where it counts, a message that will buy us time to garner Thoren's support. Walworth's right. We can't just leave Helas in a state of vulnerability."

"We can't stay here," Baniff insisted.

"No," said Walworth. "But we can take disguises and take rooms in town for a few days. An abandoned dwelling will give Grendel every reason to believe we have left, and with the wand shielded he may be drawn to Llewelyn here. Mirand can use that to attempt to interfere with his toys. You won't get them all, Master, but I know you can do enough damage to make him worry. It's the last thing he'll expect, and confusion will buy us time."

"I have a better idea," I crowed. "Mirand can drive death bans into Grendel against using magic to help the state of Sunna or to help himself. One action on behalf of the enemy and he's gone. That would send a proper message!"

The room was hushed, as if I had said something offensive. Baniff shook his head in his hands and Walworth looked expressionless. Mirand finally broke the silence. "And how do you propose I do that without my tools and without his knowledge?" he asked icily, "even if I did lack your seeming moral qualms about bans?"

I had to invoke my mask of confidence to continue in the face of Mirand's uncharacteristic sarcasm, but continue I did. "Well, Master, it just so happens that the two black stones you graced me with upon my arrival—"

"Should be long dead and dissipated in the lower regions of earth."

"I buried them in a tarragon patch."

Mirand looked at me sharply. The only sound in the room was Caethne's laughter. "Well done, brother. Tarragon will hold in the magic like nothing else. If you all want your devices of destruction to play with I'm sure I can soften up the frozen ground for you." She patted Pourra's head. He had curled himself into a furry ball and fallen asleep on her lap.

"Where was this patch?" asked Mirand, ignoring her. I started to describe its location but Mirand interrupted me by angrily banging the table again. "I didn't realize you missed your old master so much that you'd put up a signpost for his arrival! Didn't it occur to you that the ban against working magic to help a foreign state was *designed* to be tracked? If the Sunnan government feared that its wizard students might use magic against Sunna, why wouldn't it fear them plain old working against Sunna? That ban was the government's way of keeping track of you! Now Zelar may have a permanent lock on me!"

"I don't understand."

"I've buried fragments of my own energy source in that patch, never dreaming that anyone would bury death bans there. I've scattered crystal fragments from *my* name stone all through that soil." I started feeling sick. "After being with the bans all this time those crystal fragments can, and no doubt are, being used by Zelar to track me. It's also not beyond his capabilities to ban me through those fragments, although that would take some doing at a distance. But Grendel—" He didn't finish the sentence; he didn't have to. Grendel might very well be prepared to ban Mirand. He sighed and ran his hands through his hair. "There's no help for it. We must remove the bans from the patch and destroy everything else."

"Master, do *you* need a reminder as to what you are suggesting?" asked Walworth urgently. "I cannot permit you to sustain that kind of damage to yourself. Your powers are too valuable to us."

"My powers are a hazard so long as Zelar can shadow my magic through those crystals. Fortunately I keep the heart of the stone elsewhere, but Zelar might easily be able to find even that through the fragments. Right now I'm a liability."

"Why didn't you bury the stones where you knew they would dissipate?" Walworth asked me evenly.

I looked steadily at him. "I thought I was demonstrating foresight in guessing that we might have uses for the stones someday."

"Well, lad," said Baniff darkly, "Yer a genius. It sounds like we very well might."

"If I'm to do any damage to Grendel's weapons, I'll need to be in full command of my powers," said Mirand, as if he were stating the premise of a geometric proof. "I will keep the crystal fragments with me, for if I'm being tracked anyway, that won't matter. After I do the work I'll explode the crystals at a safe distance from town, which will result in extreme damage to my body and most likely my mind—"

"Mirand, no, you mustn't do that!" Caethne looked as though she wanted to embrace him, but she held herself in check.

"I'm open to other suggestions."

There weren't any.

"Let me meet you outside of town with the wagon," insisted Caethne. "I'll take care of you. Tell me what you'll need to heal, to recover. I'll get it. I'll force the earth to yield all her secrets to me—"

"You'll force nothing. I must help plead our case to Thoren, and perhaps my sickly condition will be more eloquent than my words. I shall have to trust myself to the wisdom of the court wizards."

"And if you fail to live through the journey?" asked Walworth.

"Then show them my blessed corpse," snapped Mirand. "Perhaps that will persuade the king. As long as Zelar has a means of tracking me we're all in danger, and right now we're Threle's only hope."

There was another long silence, which Walworth finally broke with a heavy voice. "Then so be it, Master. We shall keep your horse between our own and ride with all haste to Thoren."

"I'll ride ahead and warn the court wizards, prepare them for your coming. I'll bring them out to you, Master," I offered, but my words were greeted with a new silence that suggested that the topic was now closed. There would be time to decide on my offer later. Now we needed to put feelings aside and plan for Grendel's arrival. "Mirand," I pressed eagerly, "shouldn't it be possible for us to drive the bans out of the stones and into something drinkable? Caethne could make an ale or spice some water to make it receptive, and I could let Grendel find me when he comes to town and make him drink it." So much for Aleta. Now was the time for real action, and I would be part of it.

"*Make* him drink it?" asked Mirand in a deliberate tone of utter bewilderment that would have devastated me six months earlier. "Are you suggesting that 'we' collaborate to send a fellow wizard to his death?" I kept my eyes steady. "What has he done to deserve your sentence?"

"What hasn't he done? He certainly poses an imminent threat to us."

"The lad may have a point." Baniff sighed and squirmed a little.

"Grendel is acting to preserve his life, and wretched as that life might be, it is not within my wisdom to decide to close it. He's injured none of us yet, and I can't justify taking anyone's life out of fear of what he might or might not do. I should think wreaking havoc with his magical tools would be enough. If I can do damage to Zelar's setup through Grendel's crystals, we'll give them all enough to think about. If we must stay local for a few days, I vote for implementing the commander's idea."

"I have no ethical problem with Llewelyn's proposal," said Walworth unexpectedly. "As I understand it, Grendel has been driving death bans into young students of wizardry for years. I see a natural justice in having him partake of his own magic."

Mirand considered. "Grendel's students willingly accept those bans as the price of admission into school. That differs from slipping Grendel certain death without his knowledge. As much as I despise him, I cannot be a party to his death unless he does attack us. And I say that with the sad realization that waiting for him to make the first move increases our vulnerability."

"Speaking as one of Grendel's students"—I saw Mirand nod slightly to acknowledge my words—"I must say that we never receive the education we are promised in return for accepting the bans. It was you who taught me everything I should have learned in the Sunnashiven wizard school. By not making good on their end of the deal, it's as good as if they did curse us without our consent. Isn't it, Master?"

"All right," he said evenly, but his eyes grew dull and seemed to be focused on something far away. "How do you propose to carry out your plan?"

"Grendel likes luxury. So does Count Sina, I suspect. Anyway, Grendel made it clear in County Clio that he intends to stay in inns. He'll be in town, I'll find him. Besides, he's probably looking for me anyway. I'll be friendly, I'll confuse the breath out of him by dropping all sorts of misinformation, I'll offer to get them drinks, I'll manifest the banned ale, I'll watch him drink it, I'll meet you outside, and we'll ride to Thoren." A real adventure! I couldn't wait! And I would get a chance to do something heroic, such as save my teacher's life!

"Shall I soften the ground for you, Master?" asked Caethne, a touch too brightly.

"Wait," said Mirand. "How does my apprentice propose to pull off this intricate stunt without having Grendel read his thoughts?"

"I can shield my thoughts from Grendel and manifest ale at the same time."

"He's clever that way," offered Baniff.

"Right. Can you shield your intentions from Zelar as well?"

I hesitated, and Walworth answered. "No, Mirand, but you can. Even if Zelar is tracking you, you can shield your thoughts from him. Baniff can cloak you in invisibility and Grendel would never think you were in the same room. You could then safely help your apprentice in whatever way seems appropriate, and ethical, to you. I will be in the room as well, in case Sina offers trouble."

"Then Baniff will have to throw illusion over you also to make you unrecognizable. Remember, Zelar will have shown him what we all look like.

And with all that illusion floating about the room even Grendel is sure to feel something, not to mention that Llewelyn and I would be working magic under a handicap. And where are the key and the wand during this time?"

"They would be as safe with us as anywhere else," I said. "Perhaps it would be better for you all to wear physical disguises, just as Grendel's party is, so that our magic is unimpeded."

"I can think of no objections to Llewelyn's plan," said Walworth.

"Nor I," said Baniff, but his voice was solemn and resigned.

Mirand was silent. "Master?" said Walworth. "Now is the time to speak your final thoughts on the subject."

The wizard sighed. "My apprentice and I shall murder one of our own kind to contain damage to Threle. Then I shall damn near murder myself for the same reason. I am content to do what must be done."

"Then 'tis decided," said Walworth, looking gently at his teacher.

Caethne smiled reassuringly. " 'Then 'tis time to make the ale. Come, Pourra." Pourra woke and stretched, chattering softly and sweetly in Mirand's direction. It was a testament to the master wizard's strength of spirit that he could smile a little mysterious smile in return. The rest of us just sat heavily, looking as blank as sun streams in a frozen wind.

Eleven

Melancholy begins where work ends, and Caethne had spent the previous afternoon and night at work. She had softened the ground and dug up the bans and the fragments of Mirand's name stone. She then made a bottle of ale that captured the essence of the bans. She bought herself a little wagon and loaded it with all of Mirand's belongings. I worried about the cockatiels catching cold and dying but Caethne said there was nothing easier than keeping caged birds warm. She also created disguises for herself and my companions out of tender flax which she used a witchworking to charm and rip out of the dead ground, and magically weave into cloth. I busied myself doing what I could to help her and to help the others pack what we needed for our journey north. Then there came a moment in midmorning when the work ended and we all knew there was nothing to do but part company. I still had no disguise. That would come at night, when Caethne and I would meet in silence to work magic, a bitter, profound magic during which we could not speak to each other. She would draw me silently by the strength of our bond and I would willingly accept the trance, running to her call. A witch knows the best place and time for her magic, and Caethne insisted that we make my disguise in secret, by night and by wind. If all went as planned, I would have the most contact with Grendel and therefore need the most protection from him.

So any farewells had to be said now. Caethne would spend the day sleeping in the wagon with Pourra to restore her strength. She said she could do this best in the woods. A witch can sleep well in temperatures that would kill most anyone else, for her power resides in nature and is nature. Her heart can beat as slowly or as quickly as Mother Earth's.

And so she put Pourra at the reins, which seemed to make him feel important, and stood before the wagon in a state of melancholy that would have turned dried gourds into butter. With typical Caethne humor made all the more poignant by the moment, she knelt in the frost, gave Baniff a light hug, and managed to smile as she extended him a bottle reading *Krygon Ale—The Drink Beyond the Pale*. It contained nothing but a single daisy that she had somehow found the time to steal from the dream of a seed in the ground. "If ever you have need of anything, and be it for health or wholeness, then wish upon this flower and eat of it and it shall be yours."

"I shall, my lady," said Baniff, quickly returning her hug. She started to cry a little, so Baniff tried to lighten the mood by tying the bottle to his belt and proudly pointing to the word *Krygon*. No one laughed. He untied the bottle and put it quietly in his sack, saying, "Even dressed in rags as ye are, no one could but mistake ye for a real duchess." She touched him on the shoulder and turned to Walworth.

Their parting was much more solid and formal. Walworth kissed her lightly on the forehead and took her hands in his. "Speed well and safely, twin," he said in Sarana. His tone was not so much a wish for a successful journey as a reminder of the business at hand. Caethne kissed his cheek and smiled a wan version of her usual reassuring sisterly smile.

"Trust me. I know what needs to be done. There is no separation between twins," she murmured. Then she turned quickly to me and Mirand. "We must not have words together during the work tonight," she said to me. "So now," she continued to us both, the tears flowing unchecked, "now must suffice for all, for the time that intervenes between now and our next meeting." I found it painful to observe that her sadness had no discernible effect upon Mirand, who I knew was its chief cause. It chastened me to feel Mirand shield the black pouch that carried his name stone fragments as he hung it around his neck, but it nearly destroyed Caethne, who pointedly turned her back on him to embrace me with all the fervor of spurned affection.

I thought it was tactless of him to shield his pouch in front of her. At this point in time no shield could do more than obscure Zelar's ability to track Mirand for a day or so. Zelar's lock on the name stone fragments would be too strong. And yes, the intensity of his shield would provide that day or so of confusion we needed to ensure safety in our new lodgings, but Mirand could have waited until Caethne had already left. It looked too much as though he was closing her out, and I felt her hurt well up in my own mind.

When she turned to her former teacher, however, Caethne completely eclipsed my bravery. She looked at him in unflinching wordlessness for a long time through her tears while he looked back stolidly. Then she suddenly and hungrily kissed his black pouch, sucking and licking and caressing it while he stood there unmoved. Finally she broke away to throw her arms around him in an embrace of excruciating intensity. He let her hold him for a short time, then finally hugged her lightly in return, but it was a damnably faint hug that probably hurt more than his practiced indifference. Caethne couldn't see his eyes briefly close and his mouth quiver a little as he hugged her, but I could, and I decided to tell her about it at the next possible opportunity. I also decided to say something to Mirand, to sound him out about Caethne, if the chance arose. He released the embrace and we released her to her tears and her responsibilities. I shielded my bad palm. Then we shouldered our packs and departed silently for the footpath that led north around town, where we would seek a night's lodging and swift horses for the trip.

We took rooms just north of town, on the upper floor of a withering old cottage let by a crumbling old couple who reminded me very much of two walking lumps of moldy cheese. The man was partly deaf due to the fact that he was missing one ear, and the flesh had healed over in pale raised swirls that looked like the long curling lines of hard blisters. Like bad cheese, he really did have an oily green mold growing over part of his face, which sweated a disgusting substance like sticky whey. His forehead had a horrendous-looking wen, which he kept absently fingering when his wife wasn't yelling at him. Half of the backs of his hands were covered with boils and half with dull red indentations where he had bitten his boils off. The woman was blind in one eye, and her good eye was all but buried in a bright purple carbuncle. Her cheeks were flaky and yellow and covered with juicy-looking warts and tufts of hair. The couple stank of sour ale, the man more so. It seems they had once run a considerable farm, but now they rented their land for pasture and took in guests. They said they raised squirrels for food, but all I saw was empty cages.

Supper was insufferable. Caethne had made us packets of food, and I was all for staying upstairs and eating in peace, as something about the couple and their cottage made my throat and stomach feel like dried honey. Mirand agreed, but his mind was on more important matters, such as whether or not he would be alive in a few days, and he was not up to insisting on anything, so I decided to plead illness for both of us. I was immediately shouted down by the old couple, who harshly ordered us to sit at their rickety table and let them wait on us. They spoke Botha with an odd lisp and an accent that none of us could place and occasionally they lapsed into a language that none of us, including Mirand, recognized.

Once Walworth graciously agreed to supper, it immediately became clear that their insistence on serving us was not some misguided attempt at hospitality but an often-used ploy for keeping guests captive during a meal.

What the couple really wanted was for us to have to listen to them boast about their dead daughter, and listen we did. Without end.

It seems they once had a daughter named Genna who was the very last thing in daughters but who drowned herself for love in a pond just west of town. The old couple swore up and down that nobody in the world had ever been or ever would be as beautiful and wise and good and worthy as Genna. Genna was a regular brick. No one could eat like her, no one could kill fish like her, and no one could take off her shoes and sit like her. And no one could amuse the cows as nicely as she did. The old man kept asserting, "She didn't even smell up the cows! She didn't even smell up the cows! The cows loved her all the time. They did!"

"And made her milk," added the old woman. "She milked and they milked! A long time—so! And you should have seen her have her period. Like a goddess she did—at the new moon it came and went away. And those cows—they *would* see! Chomp chomp!" The woman vigorously nodded. "Chomp chomp!"

I doubt that even Caethne would have taken that one up. Certainly none of us was about to. I wondered if Walworth had known what we were getting into when he chose this place, and then decided that he had had his reasons. The couple was clearly dotty, and there was no way they would recognize any of us from town or be able to report our movements to anyone. It just seemed so wretchedly sad that this could be Mirand's last meal with us, and I thought he deserved better company than this.

Walworth tried to change the subject by offering to help with the meal preparation, but he was loudly and sanctimoniously spurned with much bellowing and hand waving. It seems that no guest was permitted to make soup, because that used to be Genna's job and no one except the old woman must defile the cracked and blackened spoon that Genna used to stir the broth with. No one could tend the fire except her mother, because that too had been Genna's job and no one ever did it right except her. Our napkins, which were yellow and disintegrating, had been embroidered by Genna's very hands, so we weren't to touch them, only look, and we couldn't light more than two candles at a time because Genna always liked things on the dark side. Genna also had been a natural genius and knew more about magic than half a dozen court wizards. She could and did turn glowing embers into mice. If we found mice in our rooms, we mustn't kill them because of course they might be descendants of Genna's mice, and on and on and on until I began to appreciate why Cae preferred sleeping in open fields.

Baniff drew ire by inadvertently sitting in Genna's special chair, a chair that seemed placed for the express purpose of inviting unwary guests into making such an error and thereby giving the couple an excuse to tell how Genna used to hold her little gray kitten in that very chair every night and sing to it. And how she had loved that kitten, which died of ague a week after Genna drowned. The couple had thrown its corpse in the pond. This was supposed to be very sad, but the old woman shared this family intimacy with us in such a self-righteous tone of voice that I finally asked her pointedly why she didn't just wear the dead kitten around her neck for old times' sake. I said in a voice that oozed tones of technically perfect politeness, "I, for one, would like nothing better than to see what would be left of Genna's most beloved pet after its corpse had lain so many years against your sweet maternal bosom."

The old woman replied in a squeaky, defensive little voice that sounded like she was apologizing for some personal shortcoming, "Wouldn't it have started to smell?"

"Probably not so you'd notice," I said. "After all, Genna touched it herself, and her presence so permeates this room with eternal life and youth that it wouldn't surprise me if the kitten kicked up its heels and began to meow for blood."

Walworth looked at me sharply and Mirand closed his eyes and bowed his head as if he was embarrassed, but I noticed a hint of a smile on Baniff. Perhaps I *was* being rude, but I was angry at the way this couple was demanding that we mourn Genna when we were all facing a much more important loss. Who cared about Genna and her damned mice? Give me a broom or a sharp stick and I'd cheerfully make short work of Genna's alleged magic! As far as I was concerned, Mirand could outperform any court wizard who ever lived, let alone some childish oaf begotten (shudder) of these imbeciles. Surely my master merited some respect, some honor, on this night of all nights. Before he shut out his own life, was he supposed to make obeisance to the memory of their strange offspring taking leaks in the cow pasture? I wanted to destroy something.

"Do kittens eat blood?" asked the woman uncertainly. "I know squirrels do. Except sometimes they starve on it. Here is fine squirrel."

"Fine squirrel," shouted the man, smacking his lips.

The couple began giving us bowls filled with dried twigs. Baniff started eating his with a why-not-it's-food look. Walworth and Mirand thanked our hosts kindly and did nothing with the bowls. Some mourn in silence and some mourn in anger. I decided to make a scene.

"Would Genna call this food? Look what you've done, dear mother. The skin is dried and covered with warts and surely we can't eat that."

"Can't eat that last night, no, sir," said the old man. "Try again for now." He was tossing the twigs in his bowl like a salad.

"Haven't you a knife for the belly?" I asked. "A sharp knife for the squirrel's soft belly? A knife for the meat of the thing? A knife to eat Genna and her kitten with? Surely Genna had a knife—"

"Are you truly ill?" interrupted Walworth in an effort to silence me.

"Let him continue," said Mirand.

"I could eat your daughter's knife and all her strength before the squirrels eat her blood."

The old couple was swaying rhythmically to my words. Incredibly, they started chanting immediately. My magic had never been this strong before, but I'd never tried to work a spell from the depths of anger before, either. I considered my instant success a compliment to Mirand's training. The old woman began harshly, insistently. The man alternated.

"Genna was a squirrel."

"Genna was our squirrel."

"We ate her."

"Then she drowned."

"Where's her knife?" I asked.

"We drowned it with her kitten for it growled."

"And none but us to love her now."

"I carried a stone in my womb until the goblins brought us beauty. Then I bled in ecstasy for a month."

"For two months and a day," said the man, biting his thumb.

"And my husband loved me then, then for always, for her sake."

"For whose sake? Genna's? But Genna's gone now, as you know." Piercing animal cries and wails. Good. Now for the kill. "And others merit deeper grief. None mourn Genna but yourselves, but all should mourn and wail the loss of one greater. Turn your grief to us, to present loss, if grieve you must. We will not be commanded to weep for some cretin girl we never knew, when our own—"

"Enough!" commanded Mirand. He looked deep into my eyes, which were drowning in grief and rage despite the power I was raising. "I understand your pain. More than you know. But they have naught to do with it. Break your hold!"

I did so, but I let them down slowly with what I hoped was a gentle compliment to their insane obsession. "I am sorry about your daughter. The man who spurned her must have lacked the intelligence to wake up in the morning without divine intervention."

The swaying stopped for a second, then all the depths of Hades suddenly broke loose. "It wasn't a man! It wasn't a man!" they screeched. "It was nothing human! It was the pond! She loved the pond! She threw herself in the pond because she loved it so! She made her kitten out of that pond!" It was very important to them that we understand this. Mirand stepped swiftly over my confusion to pick up the shattered spell.

"Easy, easy," he chanted. "Not so quickly, then." Within two breaths he had brought his mind against theirs. "So, so, Genna loved the pond. We know that now. It takes skill to make kittens out of water. Was the kitten warm to hold?"

"Oh, yes," said the man. "As warm as a dove's beating heart."

"As warm as moss," said the woman, quiet now.

"As warm as Genna's eyes and ears," said the man again. I sighed audibly and shook my head in disgust.

"As warm as Genna's love for you both," said Mirand. "She was a young girl. She was only seven when she left." *Seven!* How did he ever get that?

The couple had said she was menstruating. I logically had assumed she was older and I hadn't bothered to get a fix on her. "Genna came to you warm from the pond."

"The lovely goblins brought her to my breast."

"How rapid her growth. How nourishing your milk." The woman softly cried and smiled. Her tears formed a kind of muck over her carbuncle. It was absolutely disgusting. "In seven years she came of age and returned to her home. Somewhere she dreams of you and remembers your milk."

"Yes."

"Take my hand, foster mother. Take my hand, foster father, and tell me—easy now—tell me of Genna's love. Of its taste. Of its smell. Of its sound."

A pause. Piglike snoring breaths. Then poetry. Incredible, improbable poetry, in the deep shuddering voice of a wounded beast.

> *Genna's love?*
> *Its taste? . . . well,*
> *Say it quenched the flame it couldn't kill.*
> *Genna's love?*
> *Do clouds have scents*
> *Which weary air they never fill?*
> *Genna's love?*
> *Sings holes in music.*
> *In stillness I dance.*
> *And am still.*

"Are you dying, weary, dancing in stillness?"

"Yes."

"What do you need?"

"To know that Genna was here. For you to know. For everyone to know."

"I know. Feel my heart? How strong it is?" I gagged. How could Mirand stand letting those ugly little demi-trolls take energy from him? "I will always know your daughter. She shall live in my memory too. As long as I *have* memory. She is real and living to me. Now and always."

"Thank you," sobbed the woman.

"Thank you," murmured the man.

"Your dearest wish is fulfilled. Blessed be." He gently lifted the spell. I was so impressed. Even on the eve of what could be his own death, Mirand had chosen to heal the grief of two strangers, and two utterly obnoxious strangers at that. *He must live through our journey to Thoren! He must!* I would die to get him to those court wizards in time. I would offer to absorb into myself whatever damage I could when he destroyed the name stone fragments. I was sure I was capable enough.

Mirand rose and excused himself to head upstairs to our rooms. The couple just quietly nodded at him, and as he turned his back and ascended the stairs I took the opportunity of leaving the table to follow. I wanted to compliment him and perhaps put in a word concerning Caethne. But most of all I wanted to throw my arms around my dear master in sheer love and admiration. I followed in his footsteps up the stairs. I stepped when he stepped. Breathed when he breathed. Tried to shape my thoughts to his. "Mirand . . . Master." He stopped but kept his back to me. "I've never told you how much I've learned from you. You gave me magic when I had nothing to choose but death in Sunnashiven or slow intellectual death scribing to foreign gods in some cloistered monastic den. You made a wizard out of me. I'll always remember that. In fact, you've taught me everything I know. Not just magically, but politically and ethically. Why, between your instruction and Caethne's—" I heard him swallow and I felt a wave of discomfort pass from him followed by a shield. It wasn't the time to bring up Caethne. "I want you to know that I will be with you throughout our entire journey. No matter what happens. I will do everything I can for you. In some ways I owe you my life. Mirand, if any master ever deserved the love and loyalty of his students, you do. I want you to know that you have my love and loyalty. Always. I would do anything for you. Name it."

"Never use magic in front of me again."

"Mirand?"

He turned sharply. His eyes shone in the semidarkness. "Never use magic in my presence. You are no student of mine! Whether I live through the next few days is my own concern, not yours and not Caethne's." So he thought I was speaking entirely for Caethne! "Stay or leave, take dictation or advise great kings, return to your city or haunt market stalls in Helas— do what you will, so long as it doesn't include me. Your education is no longer my affair."

As practiced as I had become in faking confidence, I withered under his wrath, so it was in all honesty that I said, "I love you, Master."

"I know." He turned to leave.

"I sincerely meant every word."

He turned again. "If I didn't think you were being completely honest with me I would blast you where you stand. What is love, Llewelyn? What is loyalty? What *have* I taught you? To use your power to compel a helpless old couple to forgo the only genuine feeling they ever had in favor of your own sorrow?"

"They tried from word one to compel mine. To compel ours."

"And of course you thought none of us capable of resisting their chatter without coming to our rescue by showing off how much magic you have at your command. I'm most impressed with your sense of fairness. Tell me, does no one have the right to mourn a loss save yourself? Or must all the world grieve because you do? Isn't there a poem about a tyrant who weeps millstones to crush the skulls of smiling babes?" His words felt like millstones themselves.

"I acted out of loyalty," I choked.

"You acted out of intolerance. Is it so hard to believe that someone else fails to share your values? That other varieties of suffering exist? And you call yourself a wizard." He sighed and stared briefly into the darkness before looking back at me. "And so you are. I'll not dispute that. In six months' time you've mastered my spell books and learned all the theories and shown all and sundry what a brilliant mind you have for magic. You've outperformed all my other students and you've learned your share of witchworkings as well. Yes, I've seen you with Caethne. I've also watched you lording it over the market merchants and playing tricks on the local youths and terrorizing poor Aleta out of her chain mail. And I've watched your insecurities fade into the smiling cheerfulness of a young killer who praises himself for finding arguments for murdering a colleague."

"Grendel—" I could hardly speak. "Mirand, there is no other way. We discussed it. Walworth agreed."

"And if there was another way, would it matter to you? If there were no reason to kill Grendel and involve me in your revenge, how long would it take you to invent one? If you must weep, weep for the act we are both about to commit."

"You agreed that we would work together."

"We are not working together. I agreed to kill to defend Threle. You decided to kill because Grendel doesn't have as brilliant a mind as you do and you resent the fact that he never recognized your considerable talents. Just as you decided to try to kill our hosts' grief because you felt it didn't deserve to eclipse your own! I know your heart, wizard. But you know nothing of my values and I cannot teach you those."

"I would learn anything you would teach. You speak of tolerating different values, yet you reject the values you call mine. . . ."

"And so I do. Toleration does not imply acceptance. You are free to go your own way. I do not interfere with your life or compel you to change. Nor would I, though it lies within my power."

"Mirand . . . I'll never practice magic again. I'll give it all up, if that would please you."

"Give what up? Your power? Your intellectual abilities? Do you think I am some Sunnashiven priestess to be pleased to see you spill your brains in a bloody mess at my feet? What *is* magic to you, Llewelyn? How do you profit from my instruction, which you claim to hold so dear?"

He waited. I had to answer. "Magic is the art of manipulating universal forces through the power of mind and will."

"I've read the books too! For many more years than you have! Tell me what you think. Say it!"

"Magic is a path toward self-development."

"Closer! Try again!"

"Magic is—I don't know. A study, a practice requiring . . ." I couldn't finish.

"Intelligence? Discipline? Sensitivity? Special talent? Superiority? Not everyone can be a wizard, can they, Llewelyn? Not everyone possesses your superior gifts? Not everyone is as good as you? To be a wizard is to be better than everyone else?"

So you think you're smart, huh? You think you're smart? There were raised sensations across my face, as if I were being slapped. My own reactions were causing them. I gagged. "No."

"Admit it. Admit your motives. I see them. Magic is your gateway to the praise and admiration of others."

"And so I admit it," I said defenselessly. "But I find no evil in learning to love myself."

"Learning to love yourself." He shook his head. "By *compelling* another's praise? By sacrificing others' natural feelings to your own glory? A wizard earns his honors. I find much that tends toward evil in your willingness to sacrifice others' feelings."

"Shall I sacrifice myself, then?" I shouted. "Perhaps you *would* like to see my brains at your feet! Perhaps it would do justice to your own *true* teachings. You, who always taught me that self-sacrifice was the greatest evil and yet walk steadily into your own destruction without a backward glance for me—for any of us!"

Mirand could not have looked more hurt and surprised if I had hurled a dagger into his chest. It took him a moment to respond. "I always taught you to honor the self," he said quietly. "Your own self and the selves of others. If your own self cries out for giving to what it loves, to hold back is sacrifice."

"Does anyone really want to die for a country?"

"I do. If necessary, I will." I felt his shield throbbing. "You account it hurt and loss to die for anything, and ascribe virtue to pain. That is why you are so eager to give up your magic, as if forgoing your own abilities would somehow make you more acceptable to me. Since you do not understand or share my love for Threle"—that hurt me so much I put up my own shield—"you cannot imagine anything but intense pain in what I choose to undergo. So you define acts of heroism by how much they hurt in the performance and think to make yourself a hero in my eyes by hurting yourself. What's next? Teaching other people they must hurt themselves to be acceptable and destroy themselves to be good? Is that your path? And hence our hosts are only worthy insofar as they destroy their own natures and inclinations in favor of yours? Aleta is only your friend so long as she swallows her natural fear of magic to admire you? You call me 'master' and 'teacher' only as I walk into death? Why do you think I stand here teaching you on the eve of my own destruction, knowing full well how little you care for the lesson?"

"Master—you are generous, and I am not worthy—"

"Haven't you learned anything, scholar? My 'generosity,' and your worthiness have nothing to do with it! I teach because that is who I am and what I do. I am a teacher, not a martyr!"

"Mirand, I would give anything to you."

"You have nothing to give that I would take. Your heart is not that way." With that he turned and ascended the stairs, leaving me in a crumpled heap of misery. I could not follow him and I could not descend back to the eating area with my emotions in such a mess. I could not bring myself to explain to my other companions what the shouting had been all about. I gasped for steadiness. I stood and grasped the rail. I tried unsuccessfully to harden myself for the descent. I had to meet Caethne. I had to give myself to her silent draw. I had to listen for silence. We still had magic to work, and that would take some discipline, for I wanted nothing more than to throw my arms around her and ask her to make everything right again. But this night of all nights I couldn't ask for her sister love. This night we couldn't speak.

I began to put one foot down on the step in front of me, then another, breathing heavily, my anxiety at facing Walworth and Baniff increasing with each movement. I heard chairs scraping and the sound of voices rising, as if my companions were leaving the table. I froze. There were footsteps on the floorboards. Good, they were going into another room. The eating place was empty. *Now! Run! Down! Down! Down!* I heard my feet hit the floor but felt nothing. My empty abdomen was pushing them into motion. Through the empty eating area. Out the door. Across the field. *Run! Run! Run!* Until finally, in the gratuitous shelter of darkened trees, my breath gave out and physical distance made my feelings safe. I could see light from the cottage. It was good not to be there, not to be exposed. Did they all hate me for what I was? *Come, come, it's all right. Mirand was speaking under pressure. He knows you're his prize. He called you a wizard, didn't he? And scholar? It's all right. Go to Caethne. Do your job.* The cold got intolerable, and I was tempted to conjure up some warm air, just enough to surround myself. *No, don't use wizardry! Not now. What would Mirand think? How can you casually care for your own physical comfort after the poor impression you've made on him? If you took his words seriously, you couldn't possibly be thinking of warmth. Run through the cold to Caethne and do your work. Feel the pull? She's out there. Take the trance. Who do you think you are?*

I did run and run and run through the bitter cold, and ice droplets formed through the material of my shirt, hardened, and cut my chest. My blood was warm and then quickly scabbed and froze. My only surprise at seeing her standing in front of our now abandoned living quarters was that the path back home was so straight and sure.

*T*he practice of magic is the practice of madness, for you must be willing, at least for the duration of the spell, to perceive mundane reality as if you and the visible world had just been introduced and don't quite trust each other yet. You must navigate the unfamiliar edges of habitual thoughts and perceptions; you must see into and speak from the hidden life of things. That is why working particularly powerful spells can craze the heart and mind for a short time. And the spell I worked with Caethne was both powerful and crazed.

Caethne made me a cloak out of silence and tears. It was a beautiful graying, clouding, falling-night cloak that made me look like the back corner entrance to a rainy evening. The cloth was the midnight smoke of burning leaves. The leaves were oak and ash. Caethne sang them out of hard ground and ice. She sang them from the stiffening kiss of winter. She sang them out of the barren enchantment of their own deaths while I guarded time and played to the stars with an aspen branch. I felt the pull of the stars that night, and the sharper pull of winter darkness in leaves rising slowly and reluctantly for miles around at her call. I felt frozen leaves crawl out of the ground and refuse further movement. Caethne changed the pitch of her song and I danced and pulled the leaves with the strength of my heart. There are twists and wrenches in the magic that brings back the dead, starts and stops in the fitful spells, chants in the forms of ruin. The mirrors run and crack, and time must be carefully guarded lest your own life run backward and you find yourself choking on that old red sickness of birth. Witches draw the dead roughly or not at all, and with full appreciation that every being brought forth into life spins another into death. That is the way of things. Our furtive harvest would no doubt slow the growth of many trees next spring. I thought of Mirand.

Her song went home and the leaves broke themselves and crumbled. Their parts danced madly to the shrill tune of a heavy yellow wind and I danced with them. It was Caethne's wind and it too kept time. Then I felt the wind thin and go taut as the leaves gave up their ghosts for life, as the leaves split their veins and shrieked their curses and charged like torrents of young colts into our waiting sacks. We pulled the strings and secured the pulsating captives before our sacks could wriggle out of our determination and back into our dreams. We beat the wind to the threshold, where Caethne turned and spun thread from its tortured orgiastic cries before beating it back to the hidden place of all winds.

Only then, in the unfamiliar stillness of the cooking area, in a fire burning the edges of abandonment off our newly emptied living quarters, did Caethne burn the leaves. She wrapped the yellow thread around her arms and the thread became as black as the smoke that was the leaves' new billowing life-form. And just before the smoke dispersed into clear air Caethne had to catch and hold it with the thread. She turned and pulled and cajoled and made love to that smoke, caterwauling and sobbing and moaning until the smoke became cloth and the cloth became a cloak and the cloak was presented to me. Then we ran from our beloved home without a backward glance. We ran through dark ice fields and silent woods and the sedentary tones of the moon on the wane. We ran through the solitary cries of a lonely owl and the distance of suddenly strange stars and our own tearing sense of profound change. We ran up against the hidden homespun wagon and there the trance began to fade. I stopped short and felt the eager natural wind turning my eyes into ice. Caethne jumped into the seat, pulled on the reins, and drove off for her distant place of birth without a word.

Also without a word I put on my cloak and walked slowly north toward town. I was grateful for Caethne's parting gift, as it would probably take me an hour or two to walk across town, and the cloak would keep me warmer than my own life blood. She had created the cloak to hold in my body heat and other energies, so no wizard could trace me, and she had attached a hood and scarf to cover my face. I could smell black licorice when I wrapped the material around my mouth and I could hear tree branches cracking their winter lives open under ice when I held it near my eyes. No one could follow this cloak or me in it, and that was the whole idea, for it was to be my protection and disguise when I scoured the town for Grendel on the morrow. I noticed that Caethne had also attached fingerless gloves at the end of the sleeves to cover my palms, so my scar wouldn't draw Grendel's attention. Wearing the cloak made me think and move like fog against a grimy window, a window whose cake of dirt hides intimations of comfort. Wearing the cloak, I became the dark of a winter noon.

I swiftly paced the cold ground, saying a silent farewell to the special forest places I had come to love. The warmth of my cloak did not comfort, because the warmth reminded me of Caethne, who of course had not spoken directly to me since she parted from us this morning. The magic we had worked together that night was a purely collegial, impersonal affair that demanded all of Caethne's affections and attention. To speak to me was to risk losing her hold on the wind, and so we did our work and left. There could not even be words of parting lest the newly made cloak revert to smoke. So before dying to new, the moon had pierced nothing but a pale young student of the arts leaning heavily against a dead oak tree, watching a now unfamiliar wraithlike witch goading her horses into the dark. And that was all. My hurt was still my own.

I was therefore grateful that my night walk would get me back long after everyone had retired. Even taking the shorter way through town would get me back late enough to miss everyone, and perhaps I could bring myself to rest a little before dawn at the rickety table before leaving to scout. I doubted whether I would actually sleep. It seemed to me I didn't deserve to, and I feared Mirand would find me indulging my bodily senses like that. There was still much work to be done, and taking time to sleep wouldn't prove my capabilities or loyalty to my friends—what friends? I sat on the ground by a thorn bush and pulled off my hood and began to slap myself in the face over and over and over until my skin and cheekbones crawled with stinging pain. This was good. It would make up for my weakness in taking warmth from the cloak, which I also didn't deserve. I was stupid! *Slap!* Stupid! *Slap!* Stupid! *Slap!*

I wanted to hurt! I now knew my wonderful "friendship"—my wonderful "family"—had never been anything more than a stupid fantasy on my part, a dangerous strategy for adapting to my new situation. I had started off in control of my damn beliefs. I had started off with some semblance of a real perspective, some semblance of distance. *I thought I was so damn smart—no?* Well, I had started off distrusting and weighing every word, afraid even to say good morning to Walworth, afraid even to make the suggestion of intellectual laxness in front of Mirand. What the Hades had happened? Was I so "smart" I had forgotten why they took me in in the first place? I had started to believe in my own private illusion, like an idiot! I had been right to be shy and distant in the first place—how had I come to think I deserved to apprentice with a master wizard, joke with a future duke, call a future duchess "sister"? *Who in the name of the gods did I think I was?* Why didn't I just go offer myself into slavery to Grendel right now if he'd take me? No, I could end up betraying my fr—them! What could I call them?

What could I do? I wanted to die. If the ground sucked me under, I would be grateful, although I panicked at the thought of nature or anything else fulfilling any wretched desire of mine. I tore open my cloak. I should freeze! I should freeze my bones to dust! I should suffer! I couldn't stand it! I screamed and screamed to the ground and sky, "I hate myself!"

"Yourself! Your strange old self? What self?" wailed a young girl's voice in intonations that perfectly matched my own. My self-loathing became anger. Couldn't I even be allowed the privacy of despair? Whom was I hurting? I wanted solitude. Something cold and tender thrust itself inside my cloak. It felt like a hand. "Are you warm, then, in my dream?" I was terrified and stood up, trying to get the cold hand out of my cloak. I did so and pulled the material around me. "Nay, then I cannot come to you. For I am only in a dream and need your energy to stay."

I opened the material a little. Fear commands obedience. My heart was pumping fast enough to drown despair, and my legs barely supported me. "Who are you, then?"

"Genna. Let me in before I wake up."

In the darkness I saw the outline of a young girl about my own age. I opened my cloak wider and said mechanically, "Enter my heart, then . . . Genna." The outline got more distinct, although the details of her face were obscured in the new-moon darkness. She placed her hand upon my chest again.

"So . . . there you are. Warm again, Llewelyn."

As far as I was concerned, her hand wasn't getting any warmer. "How did you get my name, maiden?"

"I don't know. I just did. Ah, slow and strong, then, and finally strength has no slowness, no motion at all. First there's heat and then there's rock. I like the rock. With others you feel rock first and then the warm soup. With others the rock forms last and cracks easily when you stick your hand through it. With you it's hard from the first forming—it's the heat that runs in rivulets."

"I'm flattered that my character amuses you. Would you care to tell me something of yours?"

"No, you tell me." She leaned her head against my chest. Her head felt like a cold stone with soft hair.

"I'm tired, Genna. I don't wish to use any power now. Who are you and what do you want?"

"What do *you* want? I heard you earlier. When you pulled the grief clouds out of my other parents I caught something of you, and I happened to be dreaming, so I followed you through your magic and I came."

"Dreaming where, fetch? Of what?"

"Dreaming beyond the northern mountains. Dreaming of my other lives. I lived here once. Between the water and my home. I liked what you said about my life and youth—or was that an echo?"

"I said it, ghost."

"Call me Genna here. Here it is Genna."

"And elsewhere?"

"In the North it is Isulde. When I wake, I mean. I am not a ghost. I am dreaming you now—and holding—so. When I'm awake I do not even remember Genna. Or her speech."

"Or me, probably." I let out a long slow breath of disbelief. I let myself hold her, mostly because I didn't know what else to do but partly because I'd never held a dream before. After a while she warmed with my body heat. I was so curious I didn't know what to ask, and as I stood there looking for the right questions I became conscious of her breasts pressed against my chest. *Damn it! How can I be professional and learn anything when*—I felt ashamed of my own feelings. I didn't deserve to hold this beautiful girl, this dream, when I—

"You want to kiss me." I was terrified, but she immediately pressed her lips against mine, brief enough to start pressure in my mouth and the suggestion of pressure in my knees and lower thighs before she pulled away. "Or like this." She kissed me hard and long that time, and the pressure rose and peaked through my thighs and lower back and my face and throat. I let myself respond to her, kissing in what I hoped was a hard and forceful way. She was so intent on pressing her mouth to mine I couldn't tell if she liked my kiss, so I broke off and bravely pressed my mouth back on hers, just to let her know I *could* kiss if I chose, even though I'd never done it before. I had to stop within a few seconds because I was so scared of her reaction that my heart was racing and I needed to breathe. She was clearly experienced and I didn't want her to find me lacking. The result of my stopping was a coughing fit. I felt her watching me with concern. She put one hand on my arm. " 'Tis all right then. 'Tis only a dream. Hold me warm, Llewelyn."

I recovered and kissed her hard again, putting my tongue in her mouth the way I had once read about in a poem. I didn't much like the sensation. I felt like I wanted to go clean my tongue on dry leaves or something, but

Genna threw herself into it. She swirled her tongue around mine and pulled me tightly against herself. I broke off the kiss and noticed that she was slowly rubbing her pelvis against mine. So I held her, afraid to do anything, not knowing what to do, not knowing what she wanted me to do, but helplessly feeling my penis get hard. She continued for about five minutes, and I went through an agony of working up the courage to touch, to just feel, her breasts. My hands were on her lower back. I took a breath and raised them to find her breasts, then panicked and let them drop around her shoulders. The slow grinding continued. I slowly moved my hands down her arms. She didn't stop. I stopped. My penis now thoroughly stiff, I straightened my body to separate myself from her and felt unable to continue standing. She took my right hand and placed it on her breast. I left it there as it rose and fell gently below me with her breathing, then slowly, awkwardly, I began to lightly pull at her nipple.

She brought her hands behind my neck and pulled me down on the ground so that I lay on top of her, where I kissed her hard again and let myself put both hands on her breasts, still scared but also a little exhilarated as I felt her body relax below mine. I was overpowered. Despite my self-loathing, my death wish, my feelings of unworthiness, lust got the better of me and I lifted her shift. I remember wondering at her being in these cold temperatures in just a shift and then remembering it was all a dream as I clumsily entered her and just as clumsily withdrew, coming all over the ground and my thighs and my cloak. I felt sticky semen run down my knees and turn cold in the night.

When the climax ended, she was gone. I turned to a nearby tree and tried to wipe the semen off my legs by rubbing them on the rough bark but I succeeded only in making my skin stick on the ice that had formed in the bark's ridges. I had to pull so hard to get my legs away from the tree that I tore my skin in several places and began to bleed. So I stood there in the absolute solitude of the winter woods in the dead light of hollow stars, feeling my blood and semen harden and freeze, my pulse and breathing gradually slow, and my guilt at allowing pleasure to take me rise to full force. I had just been effectively disowned by my master. I had once again remembered and forced myself to own up to my true status among my friends—companions—*them*. I had just faced up to and swallowed and screamed and bled and cried my utter worthlessness to sky and earth and frigid air—

And I had just lost my virginity to a soft, cold dream.

The woods are silent only in the center of a winter night. I let out a long, slow breath and its sound startled me and made me listen at fever pitch to whatever was around me. That is how I recognized a change in feeling, a certain spreading of the tone, that bespoke the woods' readying themselves for the fragmented, isolated sounds of winter dawn. The sounds would come and then the light. *I have to move—do something—get home,*

I mean back—soon, now—there's still work to do, isn't there? No matter what *they*—what Mirand thought of me, I still had to prove myself worthy. There was a plan; they were counting on me to play my role.

So I walked as quickly as fear and determination permitted through the newly pregnant woods, over a small frozen field, and into town proper, where I rested a few minutes trembling against a low wall. It would take every bit of acting I'd ever learned to face Baniff and Walworth in the quietly confident demeanor of pretending nothing had happened, that we were all still excellent friends, that there could be no ill will among us, but I had to do it. I was determined to prove myself by saving Mirand, by helping where I could, by giving my all to them to show my loyalty. It was my job to scout, and dawn was coming.

I ran across the silent town, past shops drawn into themselves and small dwelling places that smelled of sleep, the only smell permitted by the winter air. I passed the bookstore I used to visit and marveled at how much it looked like a discarded box at that hour before morning, and how warm it would be to enter the store forever and curl up in those books. The jewel shops were dark. The weapons shop felt bald, there being no orange cat presiding in the window. I rested breathless from my running here and by the harsh light of the stars noticed a pattern of cat prints held tightly across a small pile of snow. I stared at those prints for what felt like forever. Damn it but I loved that cat! And that was real and had nothing to do with self-glory. I was capable of love. I loved my friends and Helas too—no, damn it, I hated them, especially Mirand, for not seeing my true meaning and intent.

But it was only Mirand who had released me, and he did say that he knew I loved and honored him. I was still one of them. I would do my job and it would all be all right. I had to get back now, get back and concentrate on the matter at hand. Rest a little, even, and forget about that stupid cat!

So I made my way through the rest of town and saw candles being lit in windows as I entered its northern environs. I saw activity in a bakery and watched for a minute, trying to decide if I should try to buy something to eat in order to avoid imposing myself on my friends by eating with them at the cottage. I couldn't bring myself to speak to a stranger without quaking and time was running out, so I moved on, running and running and walking quickly and walking normally as the field and cottage came into sight, and slowing down to trembling steps as I approached the door. The cottage was dark and quiet, but still I leaned on the door a few minutes before summoning the courage to open it. I put my hand around the door handle, clenched my fist, pulled against the hinges to minimize squeaking, and pushed with a devout wish for silence. It rattled like stones in an empty bucket. It was locked.

I stood there for a few minutes not knowing what to do. I had to get inside to assure Walworth I was prepared to go scouting, to let him know that Caethne had left and I had a safe cloak and I was still here and ready to work, but the last thing I wanted to do was wake anyone up, especially Mirand. What if Mirand answered the door?

As I stood there in a quandary the door itself startled me by softly opening and I swallowed in preparation of apologizing for my intrusion when I noticed it was the old woman who had come to my rescue. I gratefully entered the eating area as she closed the door behind me, happy to be where I belonged, prepared to rest at the table and leave a written message for *them* before they got up. A message explaining I was off scouting and would return soon with Grendel's whereabouts. Everything would be fine. I would redeem myself. Bless the old woman.

The old woman closed the door, locked it, and immediately started screeching at me for disturbing her rest. "And here I had some dream of cake, you nasty boy—of cake! And then you come and wake me up. *Wake me up!* You wake us all up to wake the dead! Now!" She lit a candle from an ember in the fireplace and put it on the table. Then she lit another candle from the first.

I heard movement upstairs. I heard footsteps on the stairway. "And so here they come now!" yelled the old woman. "And do you like that? What do you think of it?" She turned and stomped back off to her room, leaving me in terror of facing Mirand again.

It was Baniff who came down the stairs. Alone. He leaned against the entrance to the stairway. I couldn't tell from his expression whether or not Mirand had said anything to him, whether or not he too condemned me. He looked the same as he always looked. "So ye've come home. Some of us have been gettin' worried. How'd the work go with Caethne?" He glanced pointedly at my semen- and bloodstained cloak. "Never mind, lad. I'm not sure I really want to know."

"It was successful."

He looked at the stains on my cloak again. "Let's hope so."

"It will be light soon, Baniff—"

"No kidding."

"And I came to tell you that the work went well, that Caethne left last night, that the cloak seems to work, that is, it *does* appear to hold in my energies, and I'm going scouting now. I'm not tired. I'll return here as soon as I have something. Please tell the others."

"Will do. We'll be eagerly awaitin' yer intelligence." He turned and went back upstairs. There was nothing more to say. Clearly there was nothing for any of them to do until I returned. I stood staring down at my stains, tempted to magically erase them, fearful of using magic in the same dwelling as Mirand, wondering if using magic on the cloak would affect the cloak's ability to mask me. I decided that the stains were somehow necessary, that I needed to wear them for now. Later I would wash them in snow or disguise or remove them. They certainly wouldn't affect my ability to go forth and drift anonymously into the morning crowds, and that was my job now. *Get the job done, soldier.*

I crept across the room and softly opened the door, stepping hastily outside into the winter dawn and closing the door again without a sound. Then I ran like a broken bottle of wine over the lightening field and into the now defined patch of woods that led back toward town and waking.

Twelve

*B*y the time I got back to town the shops were opening. Everywhere I looked there were candles burning holes in window frost and new light falling into the hungry streets. The day would be dark. The streets would be darker. I usually felt content and even cheerful on dark days. I usually felt a rousing sort of lethargy as I walked slowly through the day-long dusk, stopping frequently to sample the private, small-town, just-us feel of little shops in dark, wet weather. I loved dark days. I loved reading books in warm firelit rooms while the windows created comfort out of gray rain or snow. This was the sort of day that would have compelled me to get my studies done by midafternoon so that I could run to market and chat with the man who ran my favorite bookstore. This was a day on which to buy warm pasties to surprise the household. This was the sort of day on which the entire town never quite opened into full awareness of itself. A day on which shopkeepers conducted business with their earnestness subdued and their friendliness intact. They were lovely to watch. In rain or dark snow all small towns and most large cities expose their hidden recesses to you. On dark days it doesn't matter if you take ten minutes to stare at the bricks in an old wall or at a gray roof quietly sweltering into a grayer sky. On sunny days it matters a great deal. Try appreciating the charms of local architecture on a sunny day and strangers will keep interrupting your revelry to ask you if you're lost. I still don't know why this is so, but it is. It is like a rule.

But there are so few rules in Threle that the ones you find you find forever. I mean they stick. So accustomed had I become to Threlan ways that it suddenly felt odd to think that this town I had grown to love so much didn't have a name. It is an unwritten rule of the Threlan people, north and south, not to name their smaller towns. This trading community, along with three or four others, was simply known within this southern region of Helas as "the town." It was distinguished from its sister "towns" by being closest to what passed for Threle's southern border. So when Helans needed to designate this particular trading place they referred to it as the "border town" and everybody around here knew what that meant. In Threle, it is only the larger cities and the duchies that have names.

I have no idea why I was trying to find rules as I walked toward the center of town. The gods know I had more immediate things to consider, but I suppose I needed to keep my mind protected from my emotions. It's strange, the kinds of unrelated thoughts that will intrude on even the purest despair. I wondered how the Threlan custom of not naming towns evolved, and decided that having a town name implied having a town government. Threlans don't like to bother with more government than their duchies already provide. Threlans gather to trade. Little communities form. That's that. Sometimes committees of volunteers assemble to deal with local needs as they arise. But as long as the duchies provide courts and military protection and sheriffs, the smaller towns see no need for local organization and make it a point of pride to resist it.

I really loved Threle, the improbable way it worked, the way you could be yourself here and not be bothered. Could *I* be myself here? My thoughts chilled and broke.

It is a sad thing to want to love something yet be afraid to. I walked along, suddenly aware of an odd, deadening sort of buoyancy in my step that resulted from a potent combination of nerves, physical distance from Mirand, and anticipation of having to return to the cottage with news of Grendel. All the homey places I had become familiar with and learned to love now looked like errors of judgment. The weapons shop was too dark and still had no cat. I suddenly felt as though my favorite bookstore was too far to walk to. There was a man setting up to sell hot mead from an outdoor market stall who shouldn't have been there. There should have been more people walking the streets and heading for work at this early morning hour. It was a bit too cold.

Yet there were spaces of perhaps half a minute when my strange new morning perspective vanished. I was struck into steadiness by the comfortable crannies of town life that still endorsed my memory of what living should be like. There was the right number of horses standing outside the barrel maker's, stamping their hooves in the morning frost as they always did. The light from the weaver's was still the brightest on the street, as it always was. The spice shop still perfumed the morning with lavender and dried rosemary when the door opened, and the candle maker's bell sounded the same as ever, despite the temperature. But these things took my attention only for brief spots of time and left me feeling worse for having experienced them from the depths of my misery.

I kept falling under the spell and familiar mystery of the dark town and then remembering Mirand and feeling awkward as I strode through the streets. It seemed strange that the people I saw *didn't* know how in disfavor I was. That I could approach each one with a smile on my face and none would recognize my innate "intolerance." Yet I held back from smiling out of fear that someone would see my unworthiness. What if it got back that I was friendly to some passing stranger the morning after my disownment, as if nothing had happened? What if Mirand heard of my smiling and greeting another human being as if I had nothing but goodwill in my heart when he had just called me on my tendency to evil? Wouldn't he think I really was unteachable or insensitive? Wouldn't he add hypocrisy to his list of my faults? Could I *be* a villain and smile?

And so I used the cloak, and by willing to be unnoticed and anonymous I found that I was. No one smiled or looked at me. I wasn't invisible. I was simply unnoticeable, unmentionable. Anyone who happened to look in my direction would keep his eyes still moving until they lit on a wall or a crack in some bricks. I simply couldn't command attention unless I chose to.

The jewelry shops were closer to the center of town than they should have been, meaning that I passed them so quickly that I didn't even realize they were behind me until I came up against the alley leading to my first stop, a quiet, studious little tavern called Jango's. Jango's was the prize at the end of the alley, a warmly serious snow-filled alley that stretched itself luxuriantly along the backs of several trinket shops. You had to walk around unexpected bends and breaks in the walls to find the tavern's entrance. I walked long enough through the wet snow for the bottom of my cloak to get damp and my self-consciousness to shake itself into a thick fever. I hugged my cloak tightly around me, not caring whether the damp increased the chill in my legs. All I knew was that I didn't want to be here but that I had to go through with it. Jango's let a few rooms over the adjoining trinket shop and if there was any chance of Grendel being there I had to find out. I kept reminding myself that Grendel couldn't notice me in the cloak unless I let him.

The alley was devoid of other walkers, which of course only served to heighten my uncomfortable sense of myself. Even though Grendel couldn't notice me I didn't really want to see him in my present loneliness, and for all I knew he had spent the previous night at Jango's and was now checking out and walking in my direction. I hoped the tavern wouldn't be open this early or that it would be closed for the midwinter season, to save me from having to go inside. I waited a long time by the dark entrance, staring in trepidation at the upper floor of the adjoining shop, before prodding myself into trying the door. Jango's didn't look open, which gave me the courage to pull at the handle. I wanted to assure myself that the little tavern was closed, that I had done my duty, and that Grendel wasn't here.

To my disappointment the door opened easily. The tavern was empty of visible life, but I heard the sounds of glasses clinking as if someone was working in the back room. Each table had a small lit orange candle on it and nothing else. No one was behind the bar.

I stood there not knowing what to do. If Grendel was here, would he, or had he already, come down? Should I just go upstairs and see what I could find? Was there a guest list I could steal a look at and would Grendel even use his real name? After a while a young woman came out of the back room to set up tea mugs and breakfast dishes on the tables. I stood in the corner by the door, willing not to be noticed. She continued her work as if she were alone, humming an incongruously cheerful tune. I debated whether or not I should just ask her who was staying here and decided not to draw any attention to myself unless I had to. I waited and watched for several minutes as she made her rounds of the room before I decided to go to another inn. No one was coming down the stairs, and Jango's was a small, semihidden place known mainly to locals. Chances were good that no one had stayed here last night.

As I turned to leave, a footstep on the stairway drew my attention. I stopped and waited breathlessly, watching every detail of the stairway until I was relieved to see a heavyset older woman emerge into view. Grendel probably wasn't here. I should go elsewhere. I reached for the door, failing to notice the cheerful table setter who was now reaching behind my back to pick up some firewood. She knocked into me and dropped the logs. "Ah— huh—oh, aw, I'm sorry," she said brightly, shaking her fingers as if to shake out clumsiness, while the logs rolled and bounced against my feet. "I didn't see you standing there. Can I help you? We'll be serving breakfast and yar- row tea in a quarter hour."

"Uh, no. Thanks." What could I say? I didn't want to sit down to break- fast. I had to find Grendel. But what if he was upstairs here and I missed him? I had no choice but to ask. "Um, I'm looking for a friend. Three friends. I thought they might be staying here."

"What are their names?"

"Uh . . . I don't know, I mean, they're business associates . . . I mean, I'm supposed to meet them for a job."

"He's looking for a job! Someone here for a job?" she called out loudly to the older woman, who just shook her head.

"He's an older man," I said quietly. "A merchant. Heavy thighs and a grizzled beard. He would be traveling with another man and a youth. But I don't need to see him now. I just want to know if he's here. You don't have to tell him anyone asked about him." She shouted my words across the room again.

"There was an older man here last night," called back the older woman. "Said he was a teacher. I think he's on his way down to breakfast. Could that be him?"

"I don't know." I shrugged nervously, glancing between them.

"I'll go get him," called the older woman, trying to be helpful. I was about to ask her please not to bother him when she said, "Oh, no, here he comes. He's coming down now. Well, good morning, sir," she called up the stairway as my heart gave out to the sound of descending footsteps. "There's a youth here to see you."

An older man in brown emerged tiredly into view. It wasn't Grendel. "I—I have to go. Wrong place. Made a mistake," I stammered, and hurried out the door, back into the cold, where I stood for a minute collecting myself before pushing on.

Calm down, calm down, I commanded myself. *No one can notice you unless you let them. Pay attention to the streets. He could be anywhere. He could even be back in Jango's for all you know. You might have to come back later, when you're calmer. Be careful.*

I emerged from the alley to the sound of the mead seller crying his wares and pushed quickly across the little square toward a place called the Prancing Goose. The Goose was an affable, steady sort of establishment that never opened for service until noon. I knew I would be remiss not to stop there, but I had no idea how I would get inside at this hour, and my anxiety wasn't helping me think clearly. There were more people in the square now, which twisted my anxiety into an empty, pulsing panic, a panic that apprehended every detail of every passing face but which caused me to forget to renew my will to escape notice. For the space of three minutes I was utterly exposed to anyone in the square, and anyone in the square could be Grendel. I did not remember to activate the cloak until I saw a young man nod at me as he left the Goose, and even then my fear slowed down my reaction by several seconds. The door to the inn had swung closed behind him. I tried it. It was locked from the inside. I leaned against the wall and watched him cross the square in the direction of the mead seller. Then I waited a little while, anxiously studying passing faces, until two elderly ladies startled me by banging open the door and ladling themselves into the street with a good deal of creaking and huffing. One leaned on a cane and was being helped by the other. They moved so slowly that, despite my shaking nerves, I managed to catch the door before it closed and propel myself inside.

Before me was a knot of people paying their accounts and preparing to leave. I felt awkward, as if I had just cut into the wrong side of a piece of fabric. I quickly made sure I was still unnoticeable. There was no sign of Grendel, but I saw two or three youths slightly older than myself standing in line. Any one of them could have been Sina's son Franko. I waited and watched, but the youths all appeared to be in the same party. They left together. As I stood there watching the knot of people disperse bit by bit through the door, I also felt time dispersing and running by. The longer I stayed in one place the greater my chance of missing Grendel someplace else and the greater my fear of actually seeing him where I was. *Stay calm, stay calm, he might not even be here.* Two more people left. Nobody new joined the line. When a woman stuck her head in the room and reported, "House clear," I bolted with grateful fear.

Back to the square, keeping anonymous. Should I try Jango's again? There were still two inns I had to scout, but they were both across town, and if Grendel was at Jango's, I risked missing him. I went back to the alley, briskly started down, and stopped. *Wouldn't the women have told me if there was a party there that matched the description I gave them? Jango's is a small place. You know he's not at the Goose. If you go back to Jango's and Grendel is there, the servers will certainly tell him you're looking for him. Try The Copper, or Mock's. If he isn't there, then you know he has to be at Jango's or still on the road. This time keep yourself unobservable.*

I galloped through the snow, back out of the alley, and into the square. I stopped briefly, swallowed cold wet air, which hurt my chest, and walked quickly by the mead seller. I made sure to study his customers and everyone else I passed. *All right, keep going, swiftly now, down a long dark road of shops. Look in the windows. Keep moving. He could be anywhere. I began to feel hungry but quickly buried my hunger in a hill of nerves. Walk. Walk. Faster. Run. You don't want to miss him, wherever he is. Slow down. You don't really want to find him, do you? You have to find him—how can you go back if you don't?*

I ran in starts and stops across town until Mock's came into sight. Mock's was a large wood-and-plaster affair that sprawled effortlessly near the main road coming from the west. It had a reputation throughout Helas for friendly hospitality and it attracted many travelers. But there was also the Copper across the lane, which was a large newer establishment and competed fiercely with Mock's. Which one? I was so tired from running. I wished I had a horse. Would my cloak be effective on a horse? Could I even manage a horse—*Wait! Damn it!* I suddenly remembered that Aleta had said that Grendel's party was riding nearly identical gray horses. *Damn it again!* Why hadn't I remembered this before and thought to check out the stables at the other inns instead of wasting time waiting for people to check out and getting into dangerous conversations with servers? I should have gone all the way through the alley to the cross street, where Jango's kept a few horse stalls. I should have gone in back of the Prancing Goose to see the horses stabled there instead of wasting time inside. I puffed into sight of Mock's. *I'll just go to the stables. Quick and easy. Three gray horses. Three gray horses. Then I'll check the Copper.*

Mock's stables were locked and closed. I tried to look through cracks in the wood and cracks in the door but I saw nothing. I grew aware of the horsy smell that always surrounds stables, and in the cold air the smell felt warm. I heard a horse's high-pitched shuddery voice yelp once, then the thud of a hoof kicking the wall. I leaned impatiently against the door, listening hard, wondering if I should knock or wait for it to open and then dash inside. I heard a few more thuds but nothing that would indicate the presence of stable hands. Someone *could* come at any minute. I could lose time by leaving. Minutes dragged. There was a pile of straw on my left. It wasn't wet or frozen. Someone had recently put it here, and that someone would be coming back to feed the horses—

I looked around and my eyes lighted on the Copper in the distance. Its stable looked open. I agonized over whether I should give up my post here. Someone could open the stable in the next minute, and I would lose time by crossing over the lane. More minutes came and went. It occurred to me that I was probably wasting more time worrying about missing Grendel than actually looking for him. I ran and stopped for breath and ran again over to the Copper's stables, trying valiantly to ignore the pain in my side. A stable girl was bringing a roan mare out to a hurried-looking woman. I went inside, willing not to be noticed. There were about a dozen horses, including four light gray ones and one dark-gray-and-white one. Two of the light gray ones had nearly identical white markings on their backs, but one of them bore brown markings around its hooves. The other two were perfect solid gray matches. It was possible that Aleta, peering from behind a stall, would perceive any combination of these horses as nearly identical, especially since the white back markings on the first two would be covered by saddles. Now what to do? Should I wait here or go into the Copper? I waited a few minutes, then decided I had to check out the inn. *No one can notice you if you will it so.*

I went inside, my heart beating in my throat. I saw and heard no one as I went up some stairs and down another hall. Then a door opened and I froze. Two men in merchant dress, one a youth, walked past me on their way out. Sina and Franko? I watched their backs and started to follow, then heard light footsteps running behind me. A young girl, who appeared to be the merchant's daughter, joined the group before they went downstairs, leaving the hall to silence and emptiness. Not them.

So far the Copper seemed like the likeliest place to find Grendel, given those horses. What was I to do? Knock on every door and quickly blend into the wall when someone answered? Should I go stand by the entranceway?

I ran back down in time to see the merchant family paying their bill. The merchant walked out. No one else left. After a quarter of an hour he returned with three horses, one of them gray.

Time was running out. I had to check out Mock's, just in case. I knew that Grendel could still be at the Copper, but I also knew I could check the stables again on my return. So back over to Mock's it was, and by now it was getting closer to midmorning. What if Grendel had been there and left already?

There were a few people eating at tables when I entered Mock's, and once again I renewed my will to be anonymous. No one was checking out. I went quickly upstairs, not intending to spend a lot of time here lest Grendel be at the Copper and I lose him.

I heard nothing but the sound of somebody pushing a bed over the floor of one room, so I turned to dash back to the Copper, feeling it was something to have at least been to all the inns. Grendel was probably at the Copper anyway if he was anywhere. Those horses probably belonged to his party. I would wait inconspicuously by the stable. No, I would go back inside. Perhaps he wouldn't leave for a while. I was nearly halfway down the hall when a door abruptly opened and a breathy, fretful voice in a south Sunnan accent disrupted my plans.

"All right, I'm going." I heard a loud exhalation, some shuffling, and a very long pause. I stood still, shielded myself all over again for good measure, renewed my will to be unnoticeable, and crept closer. "But I'm only saying they *could* know we're in town, what with all those scouts!"

The door abruptly closed again, as if someone had slammed it. "Damn the scouts, Count." Grendel's muffled voice rose in tones of annoyance through the door. My heart started racing. "Pull yourself together. We haven't seen *any* scouts for the last twenty leagues." I found his accent unconvincing.

"H-How do you do that?"

"Magic," said Grendel impressively. Despite my fear of discovery I wanted to laugh. Grendel couldn't be more than a few feet away from the door. It would have taken him less energy to just physically lean over and close it. Was this his way of impressing Sina, or scaring him? I wished Mirand had seen this; he would have found it amusing. Then I remembered that Mirand and I would not be sharing amusement again, and the pain made me drop my shield for a second. *Back up! Shield up! Ignore your emotions, wizard!*

"W-Well," stammered Sina in a fearful, accusatory voice, "I wish your magic worked consistently."

"I wish your accent did."

Sina sighed. "I didn't think it mattered, being alone." He sounded Helan now, more so than Grendel. "But don't you think that if there's any chance they know we're here, we would do well to lie low for a few days and wait for Zelar? Once we explain to him about the scouts—"

"He'll take us both for a couple of incompetents who ought to get our heads lopped off for showing we can't handle a simple job ourselves. Even if *you're* not in a particular hurry to go back, I would just as soon get the miserable job done *before* Zelar arrives, like he told us to." I heard another heavy sigh and the door handle weakly rattle, as if Sina was deliberately moving as slowly as possible. *No one can notice me. No one can notice me.* "Believe me, Count, there's nothing to fear."

"Except failure." I heard him moving away from the closed door.

"*We* won't fail. The kid-cleric might run into some problems, but that won't be our fault." Kid-cleric? Sina had once told everyone that Franko was studying in a Sevalan monastery. Was there some truth to this? Had he been engaged in some kind of monastic study during his stay with Sevalas? It sounded as though Franko wasn't even there. Where was he? What if he came back? Would my cloak and wizard shield hide me and my thoughts from a well-trained cleric? Grendel was still speaking, and I tried to pay attention. "I know what I'm doing, you know what you're supposed to do, and believe me, there's nothing their damned wizard can do for long to block the energy Zelar's crystal here is putting out." I heard something heavy being slammed down on something hard and found myself wincing instinctively at what I took to be Grendel's cavalier treatment of a delicate magical instrument. "Remember, Zelar trained him. He knows his mind, and he engineered this crystal specifically for his energy. The crystal's energy is battering his shield even now. A few hours, a day at most, and whatever he's using will be as good as an open window."

"That's what those other crystals told you two days ago too." Sina was desperately needling him.

"These tracking crystals are experimental," said Grendel impatiently, "and the kid's damned invocations were inadvertently warping my aim and changing their structure."

"Hey, it wasn't the boy's fault, you know. He's a nice kid. He's trying his best. Besides, remember Lord Roguehan wanted—"

"I know, I know, and whatever Lord Roguehan wants—" Something fell with a crash. "I'll be glad when this damned thing is over. But I told you, that's all one now. We know where their command quarters are and that's all that matters."

"All I know is you had a fix on this all-important wand and lost it. And it's still lost, 'window' or no. Now you've lost your fix on that wizardwhad-dayacallit—name stone, as well. Yet you told me yesterday that this almighty crystal had a lock on Mirand's name stone. Forgive me if I'm losing faith, Master." *So Zelar didn't determine it was fragments and not the whole stone.*

"Look, it doesn't really matter where the name stone is. The crystal does have a lock on it, and unless Mirand has moved his stone out of town in the last day, it's in range. The only thing we have to worry about is getting him alone when the shield around the stone fails, which *could* happen at any time. Speaking of which, are you collected enough to go into town now?"

"What if I run into him accidentally?"

"Who, Mirand?"

"Yes. We've met before and he knows what I look like. Frankly, the guy scares me. Won't he know what I'm thinking?"

"I doubt it. You worry too much, Count. I'll throw a magical disguise over you and even if you did pass him in the street, he'd never recognize you. Stay in the crowds and come back quickly. He's not going to try to read every passing stranger on the street, even if that were possible."

"But if he does know we're here, wouldn't he be out there looking? I mean, he knew enough to shield himself. And wouldn't he sense magic around me if I was disguised?"

"Then go out as your miserable self and stop quavering! He *doesn't* know we're here! Wizards are always shielding themselves and their stones for one reason or another. For all we know this shield bought us safe passage into town. If Mirand were tracking us, he sure as Hades wouldn't have a shield up. That would be like trying to follow weather patterns through a brick wall. Look, I know for a fact that some kind of power was being raised near their command quarters last night, which tells me that they *don't* know anything about our movements. It was as if someone was doing everything possible to *flag* those command quarters for us. That's how clear the power was. Even if we didn't already know their location, we'd know it now. In fact, if I didn't know better, I'd say they were extending an open invitation to any magic user in the area to drop by. They probably never did get a message from Clio."

"Or they did and it's a trap."

"If Lord Roguehan didn't have plans for their little outpost and we didn't need to search it for the wand and the key, I'd give it a good washing of wizard fire right now, which shows how little I fear a trap. End of story and we all go home. Lord Roguehan believes in stocking his new bases well. We've got enough fire power in this sack to take out ten square miles."

"Yes, well, we'll see. Don't miss and take out the neighbor's cow." I started to suppress laughter before I was sobered by the sound of the floorboards creaking, as if Sina was approaching the door again. Then there was silence. "Uh, I thought the kid was picking up all the supplies. How much cloth should I get?"

"Enough to haul Mirand's carcass into the woods so the brother can do his bit and work his miracle."

"You don't sound too hopeful of his success. Are you quite sure you want to rush things? And are you sure the kid will be undisturbed in the woods? It's my understanding that there are always people going in and out of that place, not to mention the people who already live there. And it's quite cold, in case you haven't noticed."

"I'm not hopeful, but orders are orders and, unlike you, *I'm* in no position to argue." Sina sighed loudly at the implied criticism. "Look, if the kid insists that he does his best work in the woods, there's nothing we can do to persuade him otherwise. I understand that winter is not the best time to draw upon the grain goddess for a resurrection and that being outdoors will give a lift to the brother's invocation, and in my opinion it *is* a precious waste of minutes dragging the body out there and it makes for awkward strategy. But hey, he's the cleric, even if he is becoming a prima donna about the whole thing."

"Well, he's young, you know, proud of his first—"

"He's also our scapegoat if the plan fails. All I know is that Zelar wants *me* to make sure his former student is good and dead."

"Well, dead, anyway," corrected Sina.

"And Zelar entrusted *me* with this crystal to make sure it happens. If it weren't shielded, I could hit Mirand's name stone right now. But I need to feel it myself through the crystal and the shield is preventing me."

"Perhaps that's not the only thing," said Sina reproachfully.

"Do you doubt my abilities, Count?" Silence. Then, "Once his shield fails I just have to direct the crystal's energy. I don't even have to get to the heart of the stone or even the stone itself. Hitting ten feet away is close enough to drain energy, and once it affects any part of the stone it sets up a magical induction in all parts." *Magical induction! Then it doesn't matter that the stone's heart is elsewhere.* Mirand! Mirand! I had to warn him, even if he did hate me, but I couldn't leave without finding out more. What to do? "It'll kill him all right. It will also completely destroy his spirit, but that's for the brother to worry about. I'll do my job and that's all that matters. And no, I'm not convinced the brother's efforts will succeed. Even if he does bring him back, working a conversion spell on him to change his alignment will be no small feat. We'll see. The key and the wand I can understand wanting, but there are so many master wizards who do decent work I don't know why Zelar insists on having Mirand back."

"Because Mirand's smarter and potentially more useful to the cause than you are," tossed off Sina, opening the door. *No one can notice me. No one can notice me. Shield up.* "Oh, have you decided how to deal with his friends? They may have objections to us dropping by and killing one of their own." He closed the door again.

"If all goes well, Mirand will deal with his friends for us. Later. After Zelar arrives to reorient him as to what's needed to be done. That's the plan. Let the *caen* continue to be a watchdog, not suspecting that his beloved tutor is spying for us. Let Mirand persuade them to move camp so that we can move in. Besides, if the brother fails, it's not our problem. We simply wait for orders. You know that," Grendel said irritably. Even though my cloak was keeping in all my warmth, I felt so cold and sick I forgot to be nervous.

"I know that things will go more smoothly if we can do the job without having to fight his buddies, which means getting him alone before you fire on the stones, and getting him alone somewhere where the kid can start working immediately. Even I know that the longer he's dead the smaller the brother's chances are of bringing him back. Since the hideout appears to be occupied, it seems to me we might take some time to figure out an alternative strategy, like getting Mirand alone in the woods and persuading him to get the wand and the key for us after the boy brings him back from death's gate."

"And if the boy fails in his clerical duties? Trust me, I know my job. Zelar gave me a wand that will stun anyone who happens to be in those command quarters. I go in blasting, I increase the pain level until they tell us where the wand and the key are, then you get them. I throw a sleep spell over everyone—which will be easy after weakening them all with the wand—then I explode the name stone and we drag Mirand's corpse into the woods. I make sure the spell holds while the brother works his miracle. Then we all come back here and wait for Zelar, who should arrive in the next few days."

You couldn't throw a sleep spell over an oak tree without missing, I thought ruefully.

"Yes, I know the plan." A pause, then, "Grendel, once we get hold of that Wand of Decon—whatever, Surprises, couldn't you just blast them all? What if your spell doesn't hold and they come looking for us?"

"My spell will hold. Roguehan doesn't want to give King Thoren cause for concern, and an assassinated *caen* is of no use to us. An aspiring young warlord in charge of a state-approved counteroperation is, though, if his trusted tutor is a spy. No unnecessary killing. Lord Roguehan said it was important to him to watch the enemy working hard to destroy the very thing they love and wish to protect."

What a stupid plan! Is this the best Grendel could come up with? Grendel the master wizard? Roguehan certainly has a compelling sense of aesthetics, but as to cold hard practicality . . . even assuming we were still in the command quarters, what makes Grendel think that Mirand wouldn't have that place protected against heavier forms of magical attack than a stun wand? Grendel would have to get inside unnoticed and work one on one for any stun wand to have an effect, and I doubt he has the skill to calibrate it to different energies quickly enough to succeed. He clearly has no idea who might or might not be inside, and he doesn't seem at all concerned about keeping his magic from rebounding on himself. If I were in his position, I'd listen to Sina and wait for Zelar. Zelar is the only one of them who has a real chance of getting through Mirand's defenses. Why can't Zelar just throw a shield around Franko that Mirand wouldn't be able to detect? Not that it would be easy, but Zelar is supposed to be extremely powerful and, being a cleric, Franko could bolster it with a clerical shield that might fool Mirand. They could then send Franko to us with the crystal on him and some story about having escaped and needing protection. We'd take him in—ye gods, we'd take in anybody. As soon as Franko happened to be alone with Mirand he could destroy the stone fragments and go to work. If Grendel could manage the crystal, a cleric could certainly be trained to. Then he and Grendel could stay in the household, get the wand and the key, and wreak all kinds of havoc as hidden allies of evil—

The door opened again while I was critiquing Grendel's plan. I dropped my intellectual exercise and instantly pushed myself into a more extreme degree of unnoticeability, thickening my shield further than I ever had before. I moved quietly toward the other side of the hall, at an angle from the door. *I am the wall, I am the wall.*

"Stop!" said Grendel. Count Sina, a heavyset man with delicate features, turned sharply.

"What?"

I clutched my cloak and stood absolutely still before realizing with horror that Grendel was pointing toward a large mirror that hung on the wall of his room, and there, clear as life, was my reflection. The mirror was not animate. It could not fail to notice me. I panicked. I lost my concentration. I ran about six feet before I felt a rough hand on my shoulder and a foot slamming into my lower legs, and then the hard floor as I fell. Sina was grabbing me and pulling me into the room, where Grendel slammed the door closed without using magic. I was immediately pushed into a chair, and I felt the point of a dagger against my throat as the count violently yanked back my hood. "Who are you?"

It was more fear than common sense that renewed my shield under my cloak. That is why Grendel had no idea I was shielding myself as he turned and saw my face, because my cloak was keeping my energies inside itself. I was terrified, as I knew that it would only be a matter of time before he noticed that I had no energy around me. He was staring, clearly unable to decide what to do next. I noticed a large jagged clear crystal on the window ledge.

I spoke. "Master Grendel . . . I . . ."

"At ease, Sina," he said uncertainly. The dagger was withdrawn from my throat but Sina was still brandishing it close to my neck. "It was thoughtful of you to pay us a visit, Llewelyn. I'm pleasantly surprised. Nice cloak."

I wasn't sure whether he knew it was a safe cloak yet. "Thanks, I made it myself." *Come, I must put some thoughts through my shield so he doesn't know the shield's there. He mustn't probe through my mind or all's lost. Remember how you used to pretend confidence for your friends? Remember how you used to keep thoughts and attitudes uppermost and act on them even when you knew they weren't true? It just takes slightly more steadiness and resolve to manifest stable, solid thought energy outside yourself. Slow your breathing and concentrate. The cloak will hide your body changes. Lie now! Lie for your life and theirs! Forms! Create forms!*

"You know each other?" asked Sina.

"I was once a student of the master's," I said cheerfully, with an invisible catch in my throat I hoped Grendel wouldn't detect. "Back in Sunnashiven." Grendel looked as though he hoped Sina would be impressed. *I must get that crystal away from him. How? Keep your thoughts up and obvious. Come on, can you conjure up a replica under your cloak? Just a little more difficult than moving ale. Use the Amara word for crystal—assal, assal—damn, I've never done this from thought before, it's easier if you can say the word, use the sound of it—breathe, lower now, he can't tell, you're shielded, safe—*

Grendel said gruffly, "But I understand you're not Sunnan anymore. I know that two of your bans are buried in the earth and we both know who removed them."

"Bans?" said Sina.

Come, come, . . . assal, assal vetu—got something, don't lose the thread, keep it up, catch it.

"Magical incentives against certain forms of behavior," Grendel said grandly. "So tell us, how go the lessons with Mirand?"

Got it, got something, it's here, it's here—

"With Mirand?" interrupted Sina. "You mean we've got one of Mirand's apprentices here? Ain't *that* special? Hold the carrying cloth. All we have to do is persuade—what's your name again, boy?"

"Llewelyn." I smiled and nodded affably, afraid to speak at length now. It was difficult to keep my voice cool and to respond to their questions while holding my shield and manifesting thought forms as a decoy, let alone creating a physical replica of the crystal without speaking the word. The fact that my true emotion was sheer terror and my residual feelings about Mirand were a knife's edge from playing havoc with my concentration didn't help. Had I really bragged to everyone the other day about being able to shield my thoughts and manifest ale at the same time? I thanked the gods for Mirand's training.

"All we have to do is persuade Llewelyn here to send out a call for help once his master's shield breaks down. Have him tell Mirand he's got himself entangled in a bad situation, which he has. Have him ask his teacher to kindly show up alone in some nice secluded grove of the cleric's choosing, with the key and the wand, if he values his student's life. Job's done." He put his dagger briefly against my throat again. "You'll do it, won't you, kid?" He turned uncertainly to Grendel. "Don't apprentices always have some kind of direct link with their masters?"

"It depends. Some do and some don't. My guess is that Llewelyn here does or he wouldn't be playing the spy on us. How about giving your master a shout, boy?" It was at that moment I decided that I would rather die. This was not a heroic decision, or even an admirable one. It had nothing to do with my love for Threle or my resolve to protect Mirand no matter what he thought of me. It was purely a consequence of my cowardice at asking Mirand to sacrifice himself and Threle's interests for my sake. He wouldn't come, of course, but his dreadful apathy toward me would certainly turn to contempt. I hated admitting the meanness of these motives to myself but there it was. Death was preferable to shame because I wasn't strong enough to live with shame. Had I been stronger I still would have chosen death, but at least it would have been for the right reasons. The worst part of this reflection was my knowledge that it was all moot anyway. Logic told me that Grendel had no reason to let me live.

"I won't do it. I mean, I know it wouldn't work. Besides, if Mirand comes, which is doubtful, he'd be likely to use that wand you're looking for against you."

"You talk as if he already *can* use an evil wand," said Grendel. Sina chuckled nervously. "We're well protected against that wand, even if your master has been able to modify it. Rest assured, he won't be able to use it without taking you out first. We'll make sure of that. And he will come if you're convincing enough. I understand that Mirand has a soft spot for all his students. Sounds like we've got the best plan so far. Funny how those bans still hold up on a mundane level. Work against Sunna and you still end up dead. You should have known better than to get mixed up with Threlans." He brought a large crystal over to me and held it near my head. I could feel its warmth through my shield. *Damn my sensibilities. Hold steady! Hold steady!* "Yes, this one should take enough of your energy for me to shape into a convincing call if you should be uncooperative. I have my own path to your master."

I wanted to kill Grendel. It was a wonderful, all-consuming feeling. It slew my confusion and fear and gave me the strength and steadiness to speak at length while keeping up my elaborate defenses. "He wouldn't come, master. That's why I'm here. I want to help you, but Mirand won't come for me. Look, look deep into my mind, I've nothing to hide." I threw out memories of my disownment on top of my shield, including Mirand's calling me on my tendency to evil. I suppose it was a bit base of me to pretend my faults were virtues, and I knew that Mirand would have created a strategy based on the strength of his virtues alone, but hey, I was desperate and my faults were all I had to work with. Any dog in a storm.

Grendel took the bait. He put down the crystal. "Good job, kid. Now, how were you planning on helping us?" He sounded genuinely interested.

I didn't want to sound too informed. "Any way I can. You tell me. What do you need done?"

"We need the key and the wand. Can you get them?"

"Yes," I lied.

"What do you know about Mirand's movements—"

"Does he know we're here?" interrupted Sina anxiously.

"Believe me, he has absolutely no idea that you're here." Well, that was true, he didn't know they were in Mock's. "I do know he's in the habit of spending his mornings strolling by himself in the woods and reading." This was true, too, of course. I hoped throwing this tidbit out would delay their plans for at least a day—enough time to warn him, to get out of range, to do something.

"Llewelyn, boy, it's admirable of you to help us. I should like to give you a crystal through which you can communicate with me—you *can* use a crystal, can't you?"

"Sure."

"Good. Then you can tail him and let us know when he's alone in the woods tomorrow?"

"Of course, Master, I'd be happy to." *How to make the switch with Zelar's crystal? It must be done!*

"Then here is the deal." He put a small iron chain with a black globe attached to it around my neck. Sina looked puzzled. "Meet us downstairs two hours after sunset with the wand and the key and I will remove this charm, as you cannot. Anyone who attempts to tamper with it will die. Should you fail you die. Should you succeed, I give you a crystal and you report to us on Mirand's movements tomorrow."

"Sounds fair to me," I said lightly. How to switch crystals? I knew nothing of illusion, of creating distractions. I had to get them out of the room—but how? I stood up slowly, not wanting to leave without making the switch. Suddenly, providentially, there was a loud crash outside the door that I knew I had absolutely nothing to do with. I spoke with all the cleverness of earnest instinct. "Better check that out."

Neither stopped to think. They both pushed carelessly into the hall, and while I was making the switch with trembling hands I heard Grendel say, "My fair Brother, you must be more careful. Of course we will store your supplies . . . You have to go get more rosemary water *now*? When did rosemary become requisite?" After a minute Grendel and Sina came back into view, Grendel's arms laden with sacks. He was complaining, "*Rosemary water* for hand washing? Who does he think he is? The crown prince of clerics?"

"As long as he's happy, I don't care. A happy cleric is an effective cleric," sputtered Sina.

Grendel looked at me. "You can go now, Llewelyn. We'll see you tonight."

"So be it, Master." I bowed my head in a gesture of humility, which seemed to please him. "I'm looking forward to it."

I was out the door and down the stairs and out of the inn and two miles through winter air into the center of town before I collapsed in the middle of a crowd, clutching Zelar's crystal and praying words of thanks to Habundia for her clumsy cleric and my day of reprieve.

I should also have prayed words of thanks for the darkness of the day. I'm sure it was the darkness that let me lean shaking against a shop wall for a quarter hour without being disturbed. It wasn't the cloak, because as soon as I was away from Grendel nervous relief threw all my magical defenses to the winds, and I walked in complete exposure. I knew I was getting calmer only when I physically realized that I was supremely hungry and tired, which led me to remember I hadn't eaten or slept in nearly a day. I forced myself to walk with quick leaden strides in a northerly direction, taking a different route back, hoping that this was a shortcut, wanting only to get out of town. My ramblings lost me more time and it was early afternoon before I found myself on the lane that led out of town toward the cottage.

I had no idea what Mirand would do with Zelar's crystal, of course. I had vague ideas of him disarming it, alternated with idle, childish thoughts of killing Mirand myself to impress him with my power.

The sad truth of the matter was that I hoped beyond hope that Mirand would be so impressed and grateful for what I had done that he would grow to like me again. I was still afraid to face him, and the closer I got to the cottage the more I worried about how or if I could approach him. Sure, I had probably saved his life, but I had done so through lies and deception and theft and the cold consuming desire to kill. If I hadn't ever considered myself "superior" and "special" enough to show off my wizardry, I wouldn't have been practiced enough to pull off the multilevel magical stunt that I just had. Besides, as Mirand had pointed out, my desire to magically destroy our host's grief and my desire to destroy Grendel were practically moral equivalents, and it was my desire to kill Grendel that had gotten me through the ordeal more than anything else. Mirand could be such a purist—would he even want his life back under these terms?

Life? As I emerged from town into woods I became conscious of the death charm banging against my chest. I tried to remove it. It was impossible. Now what? Perhaps Mirand knew . . . *Damn!* Tired and hungry and emotionally exhausted, I sat on the ground. For all my efforts I had accomplished absolutely nothing. I was still a hostage. I was still in the shameful position of having to crawl back to Mirand and ask him to risk himself for me, or else to jeopardize Threle's interests by giving me the key and the wand, which Mirand had in his possession. The only difference was that the choice between shame and death was entirely my own now. Grendel wasn't going to force the issue with his crystal.

So instead of running into victory I had merely slouched toward some charming failure to succeed. I had won for myself the right to choose, and that was all. *All right, I won't tell Mirand. I'll put the charm inside my cloak in case I run into him. I'll give him the crystal—no, I'll give the crystal to Baniff to give to him, and I'll make my peace with the gods and go take a long walk toward death. My gift, my sacrifice for Threle—and if my death helps, does it matter if my motives are wrong. Soon it will all be over and none of this will matter and no one will be able to accuse me of having a tendency toward evil or feeling superior.*

I could feel the early afternoon wearing around me as I came in sight of the cottage. The sun was sweet. It would be my last sun. Baniff and Walworth were outside loading up the horses, no doubt preparing them for the long ride to Loudes to see King Thoren. I wouldn't be with them. I would be dead. I didn't see Mirand anywhere and for this I felt something like relief.

Baniff called out to me as I approached, "Well, lad, it's about time. Ye've been gone so long we were beginnin' to think ye'd been kidnapped."

"I was," I said without thinking. "Grendel and Sina are at Mock's. Franko's a cleric now. They'll be downstairs two hours after sunset." I then explained everything that had happened this morning, including Grendel's plan to get Mirand alone in the woods but excluding the death charm. As my story unfolded the coolness I had sensed from Walworth on the previous day dissipated into warm surprise and genial gratitude. I could tell he approved, and when I got to the part about replicating the crystal he smiled.

"Well done." It was clearly difficult for him to speak. "There isn't another of Mirand's students who could have done better."

"Better than well," said Baniff in a tone of awestruck surprise.

"You did say to me once that my magical training might be useful to the cause," I said to cover up the awkward pause. "So here, I've got a present for Mirand. For the cause. Uh, would you mind giving it to him?"

"Why don't you give it to him yourself? I'm sure he will be most grateful to you. As we all are. He's meditating in the woods in back of the cottage."

"And he's alone," said Baniff lightly. "Go talk to him, lad. He'll probably raise ye a degree for this one."

"I'd prefer not to disturb his meditation." They both looked at me strangely.

"Wizards," sighed Baniff, shaking his head. "If I live to be five hundred I'll never understand."

"It's-j-just," I stammered, then collected myself. "Tonight will still take some doing, and I'm exhausted at all levels. I must go restore my own energies."

"I'll give it to him," said Walworth understandingly.

"Thanks." I started to go. "I guess you'll have Mock's all spotted tonight, and I'll arrive at the appointed time—"

"Lad?" said Baniff. "What will happen when ye don't show up with the key and the wand?"

"I thought of that already," I said in truth. "Uh, when I recover I'll create replicas." That was a brilliant idea, considering that it was off the cuff.

"Don't ye have to worry about gettin' the right power levels in the objects to fool Grendel? Wouldn't it help if Mirand gave ye the real objects to work from?" I looked dismayed, as though I'd been caught in a lie. Baniff noticed. "Sorry, lad. What do I know? Yer the wizard."

"Don't bother Mirand about it. I'm sure I can manage." I smiled weakly.

"Again, lad, I'm no wizard, but won't Grendel recognize that the duplicate crystal is a dud when he can't get any readin's on it?"

"Grendel can't read his other tracking crystals either. He'll just blame Franko, or grumble about it being experimental. Maybe it will force him to wait around for Zelar, and Zelar will punish his incompetence." Baniff had a point, and I knew my responses were nonsensical in terms of our plans.

"Llewelyn," said Walworth, "it just occurred to me that you had to have been impressively persuasive to get Grendel to trust you with this mission."

"Uh, I guess I was. I had a good teacher."

"What did you say to Grendel?"

"Nothing, I—" Hadn't Mirand told him? How could I tell Walworth all about my being disowned? I was so ashamed. *Here's your choice!* "Grendel doesn't exactly trust me. He gave me a . . . it's like a tracking device sort of . . . I mean, he'll keep track—it's fine, I know how to disengage it," I lied.

"Let's see it," said Baniff.

I took the death charm out of my cloak. Neither of my companions appeared to recognize it for what it was. "I'm letting him think he's tracking me. Lull his suspicions. It will disengage tonight." The latter statement was true, anyway. "I must go recover. Good night." I walked away.

"Good *night*?" I heard Baniff saying quizzically to Walworth.

Whatever, I thought. *I'm tired. I was thinking "good-bye forever" or something—it doesn't matter. I've done what I can. Time to go upstairs and make my peace.*

When I reached our rooms I tore hungrily into one of Caethne's food packets. I tasted nothing but felt it destroying the emptiness in my belly as I threw myself on a pile of blankets, commended myself to Habundia, and tried fitfully to sleep.

Thirteen

I woke to night and took my waking slow. This was another garbled line from a dream somewhere, whispered and chuckled by some foreign poet. It did not come from me, and I had nothing to do with it. What did come from me as the dream left was the drowsy surprise hastening into panic that comes to any sleeper who rises to unexpected pain. The room was dark. *Damn! What time is it?* Grendel had said two hours after sunset, and it would take nearly an hour to get to Mock's via the shortest route. Wait, I was supposed to have a pony, wasn't I? Outside? Half an hour, then, but for all I knew it was midnight and all was lost. How long would he wait for me?

I stumbled to the window and noticed with relief that the snow and trees and sky wore the pinkish, elven glow that lives only in the brief light of winter sunsets. All right, I would still make it—but what about the key and the wand? I knew I'd never conjure up believable replicas now. To replicate objects that magically complicated I needed to see the originals, as I had seen the crystal that morning. It didn't matter. All that mattered was getting Grendel to drink the ale. *The ale! Wasn't I supposed to manifest it under my cloak? No, that was my idea, my clumsy attempt to put more magic into something than needed to be there. To Hades with magic! It makes more sense just to carry the bottle with me and make sure I don't drop it. I must invent a story. I must persuade Grendel to drink. Then I can die knowing I've done something right.*

Die? I felt for the death charm and noticed it wasn't there. *What the—*It was supposed to be there. I *was* alive, wasn't I? This frightened me more than the unexpected darkness. Strange how utter confusion cries for light—not that light helps, but it seems to be instinctual to want to see in order to be able to think. I bumbled down the stairs and took a lit candle from the table, ascending back to the rooms to the sound of the old woman singing, "Bill's paid, twiglet. Bill's paid now to leave."

By the light of the candle I saw that my sack had been disturbed. The bottle of ale was standing next to it, as it should have been, but the top of the cloth was turned down. *Damn the old woman! Did she go through my things?* The candle caught the glint of something glittery and blue and as I emptied the sack I saw with amazement that it was the wand that glittered. The key fell out and rang against the floor among the thud of my books and childhood trinkets. *What? Mirand would never—are they replicas?* I did a quick identifying spell and the key felt warm, as it should have. I put my scarred palm gingerly against the wand, knowing the scar would protect me somewhat from another blast, and steeled myself for a reaction. There wasn't any. Was I really evil now, or was the wand a replica? Or did my scar offer more protection than I had thought it would? The warmth from the key told me only that it radiated a certain amount of energy. It could be magical, or it could be a replica designed to fool.

I put everything back in the sack and stood up. The light from the candle fell across the pile of blankets I had slept on and caught a cold metallic spark. There, lying in the blankets, was the death charm, and holding together the now broken chain was a thin strap of green cloth. I picked it up carefully by the green tie and felt the weight as it dangled back and forth. With the chain broken I could wear it in safety; the charm's power would have no circuit through which it could set up an induction to kill me. I put it over my wrist and took it off without a problem. I put it around my neck and took it off again.

Then came an exquisite explosion of humiliation. Only Mirand would have been able to disarm the charm without killing himself. Mirand—why? He hated me, didn't he? How had he even known about the charm?

Walworth must have told him, described the "tracking device," and recounted my story. Then Mirand must have come to my room while I slept and—but why hadn't I woken up? *Come, you can't stand here speculating, there's work to do.* I put the charm back around my neck, stuffed the ale bottle in my cloak, and picked up my sack again, conscious now of its heaviness.

It doesn't matter whether or not the wand and the key are replicas, I told myself angrily. *They're life savers. Use them! Don't waste time. . . . No, I have to know.* I headed down the stairs as quickly as I could without extinguishing the candle's flame. A real wizard's key would unlock anything. That was how I would know. The old couple was sitting by the fireplace now. It wasn't lit, but there were a few red coals the old woman was poking with a stick. "Woman. Host." She turned her wrinkled face to me. I noticed that her carbuncle was oozing and that one of her lower teeth was caught on her upper lip. She very much resembled an ogre I had once seen in a picture book. I suddenly felt very alone and knew once again, this time in the coldness of my bones, that I had stayed too long. "I'm leaving. For good. Please lock the door behind me."

I wasn't sure she understood, but she waddled over to me and shouted, "The door will lock you out for good. To lock now! Or pay!"

"Yes, good night." I gave her the candle and went outside, hearing the door pushed closed and the bolt slammed fast.

I put the key in the hole and turned it. Nothing. Mirand had made replicas.

The pony was standing placidly in front. I mounted and rode off in a westerly direction that would take me around the town. I would get to Mock's in time; the sky and ground still showed a trace of pink being swallowed into an olive-gray fading glow. I wanted a little time to think.

Removing the death charm had to have taken extremely delicate work on Mirand's part, work that anything could have disrupted—especially my own rage-laden emotions about him and everything else. My own natural resentment at having to be saved by him would have bordered close to anger with myself, and this combination would have been exceptionally dangerous to work around and would have served only to strengthen the charm. Mirand was certainly disciplined enough to put his own feelings for me aside and work his magic, but his chances of success would dramatically increase if my thoughts and emotions were put out of the way—so he had probably kept me asleep to protect himself. But Mirand would never work magic on anyone, no matter how much he despised him or how strongly he believed the magic was for his own good, without his consent. He just wouldn't do it. Perhaps he had seen that I had chosen to sleep anyway, and so he just held me there, but . . . would he have known that before coming upstairs? Had he actually been planning on talking to me after what had happened the night before? But why bother with me in the first place if he didn't care?

Because there's still a job to be done, stupid, that's why. You can't do your bit for Threle without those replicas, so he gave them to you for Threle. What would you *do in his position? You, who consider yourself a Threlan loyalist?*

But why had Mirand risked himself to remove the charm? If Walworth had told him everything, as he clearly had, wouldn't Mirand have been able to surmise that the charm was Grendel's guarantee of my cooperation, that Grendel would remove it so I could continue to follow orders the next morning? And even if Grendel had merely delayed the reaction until later, what did Mirand care? He knew I was not worth risking his life for. I wondered if it could be a kind of payback for the crystal—an acknowledgment in kind. Perhaps he had been able to disarm the crystal and everything was going to be all right. Perhaps he had forgiven me my "tendency to evil." Perhaps he was grateful. Perhaps he was even favorably impressed with the way I had handled the situation. Perhaps I had proven myself to him now and I was redeemed. Perhaps it was another pass.

I couldn't wait to get to Mock's. I urged the pony to go faster. After all, I was playing the key role tonight and I had been something of a hero already. My *friends* would be so proud of me, I thought, and Mirand and I would reconcile and maybe even laugh about the legendary anger of wizards and we would all ride up to Loudes to see King Thoren and get his support and have lots of adventures and save Threle and I would get to tell Cae all about—

Stop. Better think about Mock's and the work at hand.

What did I know about Mock's? I had never been there before that morning, but of course I had often heard about it listening to conversations at market. Mock's was an inn of dangerous merriment and soft confusion born of sweet drunken pleasures. Old Mock had been dead for several years, but the locals still called the inn she had run for two generations by her name. Her nephew Berra, who now owned it, had unsuccessfully tried to rename it the Pocket of Darkening Coin, or simply the Pocket, in the hope that his patrons' pockets would grow dark and empty as they spent their coins there. The name never took. Mock had once named the inn the Silent Dell, because it was easily the most boisterous drinking place in town, but this name never really took either, despite the conspicuous way it was carved in red letters over the entrance.

Even in this morning's cold dark weather I had found Mock's to be the most bustling of all the inns, the only inn in which I saw people taking a morning meal. Apparently Mock had been quite a comedienne, and her quick-witted humor and good-natured impersonations of well-known locals had attracted a large and loyal following. Then she had brought in wandering jesters and jugglers and illusionists and poets and musicians and dancers and her tavern became not so much a tavern as an institutionalized nightly party, a party that had continued at twelve-hour intervals for more than fifty years. As I rode up to the entrance it occurred to me that I had never been to a party in my life, and silly as it sounds, I hoped I'd know how to behave.

My pulse clutched and throbbed a little when I glanced through the lit window and saw the crowd inside. Grendel and Sina were in there somewhere, waiting for me. I dismounted on shaking legs, thankful for having to take a few minutes to tie my pony before going inside, thankful for the space to steady myself. As I fumbled with the rope I became aware of music escaping through the walls. I also became aware that every time I made a proper knot the knot uncoiled of its own accord, and I began swearing against every god I think of until something harshly tugged at my cloak.

"Don't look," breathed Baniff, who was invisible. "Pretend to tie the rope—fer *the fourth time!* I'm keepin' the horses loose fer a faster exit, in case that hasn't occurred to ye." I remained silent, absently fingering a loose knot. "Ye've got the ale?" I took it out of my cloak. He grabbed it into his own invisibility lest anyone see, and I noticed a pale outline of the bottle glowing in the dark air. "Ye gods, ye didn't put a shield around this, ye put full armor. Relax, everythin' will be fine. Y'er covered inside and out."

I let out a breath and replaced the bottle in my pocket. I took the wand and the key out of my sack, putting the key in my other pocket and the wand under my cloak. I remembered to hide the green tie holding the chain together under my collar. My instinct was to use the cloak to become unnoticeable, but this was not an option, as I wanted to appear completely open and trustworthy to Grendel. I needed to make my entrance as if I had nothing to hide. This meant shielding my thoughts under my cloak and manifesting safe thoughts for him to read outside my cloak, just as I had done that morning, only I was much more nervous now because I had had time to anticipate doing it. Also, I was more fearful of Mirand's presence than I was of Grendel, because I knew that Mirand would be watching and judging every move I made.

"The gods go with ye, lad. Half an hour and all's done." I swallowed heavily and nodded, and felt a soft slap of encouragement on my left shoulder.

I took a deep slow breath, exhaled, and walked whistling and trippingly into the light and laughter and music that was Mock's, swaggering full and proud like the bursting midday sun. I had decided that my attitude should be a mask of overconfidence. I wanted to flatter Grendel into thinking that all my youthful bravado was a result of having the great good fortune to work for him, that I was oh so proud to be his lackey. And if I really put it on, he'd have to think I was just plain stupid, considering the circumstances, and so he would be more likely to trust me. *Yes, Master, anything you say, so eager to serve.* So I strutted to the beat of the music past a few men who were lounging and gossiping near the doorway, forcing myself to do little jumps and pleased-with-myself bows in case Grendel was watching. I was visually searching the people in the crowd as if I owned them all, bouncing upward on one foot, stretching my back, and extending my arms a little as if I were actively seeking notice when a voice from the doorway called, "You there, kid. Three coppers to enter." Without rupturing the mask I turned smiling, sauntered over to the doorkeeper, and dropped the coins in his palm. "That ain't an ale bottle, is it?" he said, looking down at the bulge in my pocket.

"Why, yes," I said loudly, without thinking.

"Can't bring it in here. Private establishment. You want to drink, you buy from us." He was friendly about it.

"What if we pretend I bought it from you?" I said easily, giving him two more coppers. He nodded and let me in. That's the way of it with Threlans. They are usually inherently reasonable about things like that. The inn was in business to make money, understandably enough, and being private, it certainly had the right to exclude people from bringing in their own ale. But as long as Mock's was making the money it would have made had I bought ale from the bar, there was no problem. In fact, Mock's was making a good profit on me, because I wasn't depleting their overhead.

A sharp prodding against my cloak reminded me that I had forgotten to put up my shield. Mirand had picked up my speculations and was reminding me to be careful, that my own train of thought was irrelevant to the situation at hand. This chastened me so much that I briefly lost my cheerful, naively self-assured demeanor until I got my shield up. I looked through the crowd of dancers, trying to find Grendel, but I didn't see him anywhere. I could not make my way across the floor until the song ended, so I stood there swaying to the music, hoping he might notice me. I didn't actually see Mirand anywhere, but there were several tables out of view from where I stood. I did see Walworth, dressed in traveling clothes of dark green, which reminded me of the green tie holding my chain together. There was a tall mug of ale in front of him, and he was leaning back in the corner, watching the room from the shadows. He reminded me of a character in a very long story Grana had once told me, a story about a band of adventurers and a disguised king. Grana had said it came from another world, from the pen of an author whom I should never touch. I loved this story. There was a death ring in it and a big eye that saw and knew everything. I thought Walworth slightly raised his mug to me in encouragement, but he kept his attention focused on the room, watching the patrons rather than the band.

There was a lot to watch. There is nothing in any world to match an assortment of Threlans hell-bent on having fun, and when Helan merchants dance, they *dance*. The band was playing folk songs from a Threlan duchy called Reathe, and even though I didn't understand a word of what they sang, the music acted as a sensitive and compelling translator. The dancers were actually singing along in Botha, all of them making up different versions. Some were clumsily trying to imitate what I supposed was Reathen folk dancing and the band members were occasionally leaping onto the dance floor to lend encouragement. An old man in a ponytail kept rolling his eyes in ecstasy, showing absolutely no self-consciousness about expressing his joy of movement. He kept dancing with men and women at random, with anyone who wanted to keep the energy flowing. And there was energy flowing here, sweet, warm, and lifting. I know it would have been easy to let myself get pulled into it if I wasn't shielded, and I wondered if Mirand was at all moved.

So it wasn't until the music stopped that I was able to make my way across the dance floor, weaving among couples and threesomes and fivesomes and eightsomes all clutching each other and laughing breathlessly and crying for more. Someone playfully threw a looped bunch of blue and purple ribbons at me and I tied it jauntily around my neck where the colors brightly contrasted with my dark cloak, and turned to dance a few steps in the break of the music with whoever happened to be close by. No one took me on as a partner, but a few people moved back and forth a little to acknowledge my gesture and the crowd opened a little to give me room, so I kept up the beat longer than I intended to. This situation resulted in the musicians picking up their instruments and playing a tune to match my dance steps, and the other dancers resuming their own movements, thus catching me in the middle of the floor, where it was next to impossible to push myself out through the press of bodies.

I knew the energy being generated between the musicians and the dancers would be sharp and seductive if my shield let me experience it fully, and the thought of my shield reminded me to start manifesting thoughts for Grendel's benefit. *Grendel is a brilliant wizard and so wisely fair*, I began. *I am so happy to please him, my true master*. . . . The dancers were spontaneously linking hands and forming circles within circles, and I was being helplessly carried along in the moment's movement, whirling and pulling and spiraling faster and faster because I could do nothing else. I reached the outermost circle in a state of utter dizziness that threatened to play havoc with my shield, regretting that my back was to the tables and I couldn't see across the room for the other dancers, when I was harshly yanked out of place from behind and jerked down onto a bench by a table partially obscured in shadow.

It was Sina who did the jerking, and I found myself sitting next to him and facing Grendel across the table. Next to Grendel and diagonal to me was a young man dressed in clerical yellow. He looked politely inquisitorial. It was Lord Cathe.

Recognizing Cathe slowed down the dispersion of my dizziness somewhat, so I heard but failed to respond to Grendel the first two times he asked, "Where are they?"

On his third repetition I asked stupidly, "Where are who? Oh—you mean the key and the wand. *Them.* Got them," I said, bringing back the veneer of confidence and patting my pocket. "Got them right here."

"Where's the Wand of Surprises?"

"Right here, under my cloak." *Damn, if I open my cloak, he'll be able to tell I have a shield on! I know he's searching me.* "Uh, here's the key." I slid it across the table to him. "It's warm. I checked it myself."

Grendel was already identifying it. "It is warm. It had better unlock our room tonight." I looked blank and innocent. "It'll be the gods' own luck if you haven't damaged the wand with all your imbecile swirling and dancing. A wand is a delicate magical instrument, in case you didn't know."

"Of course, Master. That's why I've kept it carefully wrapped inside my cloak—so it wouldn't get cold or wet." I smiled proudly, even though I knew water and temperature had no effect on any sort of will amplifier. I thought the lie was a brilliant touch of earnest naivete. I saw Cathe smile slightly, as if he was secretly laughing at me.

"Well, let's have it then."

Cathe interrupted. His voice was sententious and high-pitched and childlike all at once. It was one of the most irritating voices I had ever heard. "I should feel better if he *didn't* wave the wand around so close to my body. I can feel it pulsing under his cloak now, I assure you, and I greatly prefer not to have my sensibilities upset tonight if I am to do the work tomorrow. It is quite enough of a strain to be forced to stay in the same room as your wretchedly abundant bag of crystals." He fanned his face with his hand as if he was trying to cool himself down.

I was terrified that this high priest could feel anything underneath my shield. The wand was a replica and I certainly felt no pulsing. What was he picking up on? I forgot to keep up safe thoughts, and I felt something pull at my shield as if it was trying desperately to pull out thoughts—Mirand again. I threw out memories of grasping the wand and injuring myself. The pulling stopped. "I'm not too eager to grasp it again myself, Master."

"Yes, I see," said Grendel. "Why don't we all go upstairs, unlock the door with our fine new key, and have you take your cloak off? I'll handle the wand."

I dropped my shield completely for the four seconds it took to take the wand out of my cloak with my bad hand. I heard Mirand mentally exclaiming, but in the moment it seemed wiser to take the risk. I had no intention of going up to their room and seeing the key exposed as a fraud. Fortunately, as soon as I opened my cloak Cathe clicked his tongue loudly and impatiently and whined about having to go up the stairs again, and this served to distract Grendel enough to complete the action in safety. As soon as Grendel grasped the wand Cathe started moaning and exclaiming that the pulses were too much for his delicate flesh to handle and that he simply had to change places now with Count Sina.

"I don't feel anything but a low steady hum, Brother," said Grendel.

"Oh, you know I've been fasting and praying for three days," he whined. "Ooh, I am so sensitive now. It hurts my head a little. I must move."

Sina got up to change seats, looking stupidly sympathetic. I strengthened my shield to full force—the last thing I needed now was a high priest sitting right next to me. Cathe got quieter and calmer all of a sudden and seemed to withdraw into himself. He looked as though he might be meditating, and I wondered how someone so irritatingly "sensitive" could pull this off while surrounded by loud music and swirling dancers. Grendel inspected the wand. I tried to concentrate on the music. I noticed Sina looking at me with a touching, desperate sort of friendliness that made me feel pity for him. He was convinced we were allies now, and he didn't want me to feel too frightened. By befriending me he was convincing us both that things would be all right. "Looks like the kid delivered what he promised," said Sina hopefully. "That'll make things easier."

"We'll see," said Grendel, looking disgustedly at Cathe, who was now deeply and loudly breathing with eyes closed like a novice, calling attention to his ability to meditate.

Sina looked cautiously at Cathe through slanted eyes and then back at me. "Have you seen Mirand?" The question contained a strange sort of anxiety, strange because the anxiety was meant for me as well as for himself.

"No, but I know where he is."

Cathe started loudly smacking his tongue, as if he were dreaming of some divine feast. Grendel pointed the wand toward him in annoyance. Sina looked alarmed. The cleric did not appear to react. Grendel looked puzzled and pointed the wand again. Still no reaction.

"Where is he?" asked Sina uncertainly.

"With his friends. Where else would he be?" I said brightly. I could feel Grendel starting to probe me, so I put up more thoughts of music, slightly out of sync with the beat in the room, hoping to confuse him. "He'll be alone tomorrow. We'll get him then."

Sina nodded nervously. "Would you like to call it an early night, then? I'll buy you an ale. For doing such a good job. They've got good ale here. Not like Sunnashiven. Then you can go back while we wait for your call tomorrow morning."

"Yeah, sure, I'd like to have a drink," I said eagerly. Cathe was delicately moving his jaws up and down and loudly smacking his lips as if he were indulging in the most glorious repast.

"Grendel, the kid—Llewelyn here,—" Sina nodded at me. "—would like to have a drink."

"Let's go upstairs."

"But Lord Cathe here—"

"Screw Lord Cathe."

Sina looked bewildered and anxious. "But Lord Roguehan said—"

"Where's your death charm, boy?"

Cathe stopped making noises and started daintily raising his palms and spreading his fingers in front of him. "Yea, verily, Habundia, thy visions are most wise and wonder-giving." *Sweet gods, what does Cathe know?*

"Where's your death charm?" Grendel shouted, the tail end of the music dispersing into crowded silence as he finished speaking. Cathe startled himself into awareness. I stalled for time by pretending to watch the dancers leave the floor as the musicians started their break, but this only gave me a clear view of Walworth across the room so I forced myself to concentrate on Sina's offer of an ale rather than risk giving my commander away.

"Uh, it's right here, Master," I said reaching for it. "Under my cloak. Under these ribbons." It must have worked its way under as I danced. One stupid detail like that and all was nearly lost.

Grendel reached across the table and tore the ribbons off me, pulling the charm out of my hand. He was holding the globe. Cathe picked up a few strands and was holding them up to the light, admiring and murmuring about their colors with childlike earnestness. I realized with horror that Grendel would find the green tie holding the chain together behind my neck. "Don't you find it strange that I couldn't feel the charm's power until now?"

"You couldn't feel the crystal's power all day," said Sina.

"Shut up! That too. So you made that cloak yourself, did you? Open it! Or I will." His hand was on my collar. Out of the corner of my eye I saw Walworth put his hand to his short sword and edge over to the side of his bench.

"Of course, Master. I hope there's nothing wrong." I slowly began to open the front of my cloak, dispersing my shield as quickly as possible and forcing my surface thoughts into a facade of perfect trust, which wasn't much protection against a probe but was now all I had. I heard Mirand shouting in my mind, "Turn the tie to a chain! Turn the tie to a chain!" something I should have done earlier but didn't think of. I didn't dare attempt magic now with Grendel sitting in front of me. The shock of quickly unshielding myself in such a loud and vibrant place sent me spinning a little. I hoped Grendel wouldn't notice.

So I exposed my thin shirt to him and looked up into his eyes with a puzzled but eager-to-please puppy stare, pleading and begging on the surface to check my mind, all of it, just so *I* would know there was nothing wrong.

I added a touch of nervousness and youthful apprehension at the possibility of there being anything wrong. I felt the tie across my neck shrivel itself into a chain but sensed no surge of power. *Bless Mirand for his skill.*

Grendel fell for my bluff. He didn't probe below the surface, but he did take the globe back in his hand. I felt a surge around my neck that turned my stomach lining into vomit. He threw it back against my chest. "I've re-adjusted the charm. If you make good on your promise tomorrow, I'll remove it. Otherwise, you know the consequences. Try to take it off."

I did so and couldn't. Whatever Mirand had done Grendel had just undone. Grendel looked satisfied. "Here's the crystal." He slid it over to me as I closed up my cloak. "Put it in your pocket." That way he would know immediately if I tried to shield myself. I put it in the pocket that had contained the key and smiled proudly, as though I'd just been given a marvelous gift. I let all my energies disperse through the cloak so that Grendel would be sure to feel the crystal. "I feel better having a direct link to you, Master," I said to cover up the awkwardness.

"Do you still want an ale?" asked Sina in a tone that would have been conciliatory if it hadn't been so fearful. He really didn't want any hard feelings between us, and I thought he kind of needed me to like him for him to feel all right about himself.

"Huah, an ale! And I have been tasting the Lady's blessed delights in Paradise," whined Cathe. "So blessed and thorough I was in ecstasy. Aware of nothing and no one save Her." Grendel studied him uncertainly. "And now must feel a rough old ale against my tender palate. I shudder at the thought."

"Of course you don't have to have one, Brother," said Sina.

"Oh," Cathe said softly and childishly, as if he was hurt. "But I mustn't not drink alone. To be left out is never good for the spirit." With horror I felt his hand reach under the table and into my pocket, grasping the bottle, which was no longer shielded. Sina flagged down a barmaid and ordered four house brews.

The musicians resumed their places again, so I studied the dance floor with a look of repressed boredom, like any good Sunnan would, while wondering what Cathe was up to. He was staring expectantly at the musicians too, as if they were going to play solely for his amusement. And to think I had once rescued this traitor and been envious of him. Now I just wanted to kick him and bite off his wretched hand. I didn't know what else to do. *May Habundia and all the gods damn his life forever. Perhaps the high priestess was right.*

The drummer started abruptly with a sharp, unpredictable rhythm that threw everyone in the room off balance, including Grendel. My head was doing double loops, and I barely recovered before the mandolin player ruffled some chords that made me feel as though I'd already drunk a bottle of ale. As I settled out into the music's startling and rapidly changing energy levels I noticed that the bottle in my pocket had disappeared.

Cathe didn't have it, but he had removed his hand and was now looking impatiently over the dance floor, which was filling with people. "Eating Habundia's food never quite fills one, nor Her drink. Of course none of you would know about that." He seemed to exclude me from this statement, as he was looking across the table at his two companions. "My reward for fasting is visions of food-laden tables, tasting of emptiness and groaning to be consumed."

"Here's the ale," said Sina stupidly, partly because the barmaid was making her way toward us through the dancers and partly because Sina felt he had to make some response to Cathe's statement and wasn't sure what to say. Not that I had a clue, either. The fact that all four bottles looked exactly like the bottle I had been carrying wasn't helping my conversational abilities any.

Sina reached eagerly across to pay the maid and hand round the bottles. He felt secure when he was doing something familiar, and buying ale seemed to be a familiar act to him. Cathe sniffed at his bottle and held it to the light. "Too heavy." He sighed and licked the top a little. "No, no, too heavy. I'm afraid I can't swallow this one."

"They're all the same," said Grendel.

"To you perhaps, but I can feel the very moment when each was created, the very thought and heartbeat of each, and to me they are distinct." Grendel sighed and rolled his eyes in annoyance. "After all, ale is of the essence of the grain, gentlemen. May I sample yours?" he asked Sina.

"Of course," said the Count. They traded bottles.

Cathe sniffed and studied and licked. "You see, also heavy. I could not drink this one either without feeling positively bloated. I'm sure I'd start singing dirges." He looked pleadingly at Grendel. I was beginning to understand. Cathe was there to ensure that Grendel got the right bottle.

"Here, Brother, try mine." I gave it to him as though I were extremely impressed with his sensitivity. He didn't trade bottles but he sniffed and tasted mine. "You see, this one is too uneven. It has a fine commendable sweet taste, but the bubbles speak to me of salted ground. Somewhere the root and stock took poison." He gave it back to me. "*I* should not drink from it, but then, it isn't mine." He looked back at Grendel, who had been staring at Cathe with a hard glaring impatience throughout the whole performance.

"Please, Master, let him try yours."

"Why?"

"Because this is so interesting. About the different bottles, I mean. I'm learning something." Cathe kicked my foot under the table. I smiled and bobbed my head excitedly.

Grendel sat back and sighed as though he didn't care so long as Cathe was quick about it and we could all retire soon. The cleric went through his routine and pronounced it a fine bottle, as I knew he would, keeping it for himself and giving the bottle he had taken from Sina back to Grendel. "To Habundia, the Living Womb of Plenty. Let us drink deep and rejoice." Cathe

slowly and deliberately drank the entire contents of his bottle and I immediately followed suit. Sina followed our lead, swallowing in one long smooth
mouthful all the ale in his bottle, drinking that way because he probably
thought he was supposed to. Then Grendel drank down his ale in two gulps,
burping in between, because it was all he could handle.

Sina banged his bottle enthusiastically down on the table and let out a
sigh of contentment. "Good ale."

"Job's done," I said, putting down my bottle with a flourish. I felt another
kick from Cathe. "I mean, drinking the ale in one fell swoop like that," I
nodded vigorously. "Good job."

"Good job, indeed," said Sina, holding up his empty bottle.

"Not every day you get to *kill off* a bottle of ale," I couldn't resist adding.
This time I felt Cathe dig something sharp into the flesh of my calf. I decided
it was time to cool it.

Cathe stood up. "I must go for a long stroll in the light of the waxing
moon," he announced. "I cannot drink the fruit of the Lady without blessing
Her abundance."

"We know," said Grendel, clearly annoyed and tired. "Why don't you see
Llewelyn safely home? Make sure he doesn't get lost."

"I intend to," said Cathe. He looked impatiently at me and I stood
up, too.

"Well, see you all tomorrow," I said cheerily.

"Won't you be cold, Brother?" asked Sina.

"Never in Her light," said Cathe humbly, bowing his head. Sina looked
impressed.

We made our way as quickly as possible through the chanting shaking
bodies on the dance floor. I saw Walworth get up to follow, and I knew that
at one of the hidden tables Mirand was doing the same. Everything was
going to be all right now. We had succeeded, and Mirand would remove the
death charm again, only this time I would help, and he would wreak havoc
with Grendel's crystals just to drive the point home to Zelar, and we would
laugh all the way to the king. And Lord Cathe was a wonderful secret ally.
Nothing like having an ex-Sunnashiven cleric for a friend. I gave the doorkeeper a friendly nod and a wave as I emerged into the night and started
running with Cathe for the horses. I saw Baniff appear on top of his pony
as I ran to mount mine, which Baniff had kept unhitched like the others.
Cathe mounted a full-grown mare next to my pony, and Walworth leapt on
his charger, bringing it around to lead us. Mirand emerged from the door
looking exhausted and joy splintered every thought in my head. I wanted to
dismount and run to him with open arms but this was hardly the time. He
climbed upon his own sturdy horse and rode up to Walworth. Then they
sped west out of town at a gallop, the rest of us following.

When we reached the edge of town, which took us only a few minutes,
Walworth and Mirand left the road and charged up a snow-covered hill.
Baniff split off from us to follow them. Cathe motioned me to stay with him,

and he led me up a smaller hillock a little below the rest of the group, from where I had a clear view of the lights of town to the one side and of the outlines of my friends on the other. I saw them pull their horses up short. Cathe and I did the same.

Mirand dismounted, walked slowly to the edge of the hill, and raised his arms against the sky. Now Zelar was in for it, I anticipated. Mirand was pulling up a blast that would rupture the frozen sky into starry shreds, a blast with enough force to terrify a cyclone, a blast to cause the winds themselves to bury their soft heads in the ground and weep for mercy. Even sitting on my pony I could feel the ground rumbling and snarling beneath me like an angry ocean kindling up death storms for hire. I couldn't wait. This would be a firestorm Zelar would never hear the last of. The shuddering ground was making our horses nervous, so I patted my pony's neck. Cathe tied a rope through the pony's bridle. I saw Walworth dismount from his charger and come up behind his tutor, so I assumed that the horses on the other hill were probably also having quite a time of it. I wished I were over there and wondered why Cathe had insisted we separate.

Then came the chanting, in exquisitely beautiful Amara, in sounds and thoughts I heard more clearly in my mind than with my senses. The words formed a five-pointed sigil, and each of the points held words of knowledge, life words for Mirand's own path of study, words of strength and protection. Within each point was a word picture of a presiding spirit of some branch of learning, and yet not the spirit itself, but Mirand's own experience with the spirit and with the learning.

And so in the northeastern point was an intense young boy experimenting with simple magic and working through physics problems. The boy was moving knives and cups with wishes and the spirit was raining softly and falling through weights and pulleys and picking itself up and falling again. It chuckled in hail-fellow-well-met tones and rubbed its own belly as though well fed and satisfied. The boy was not aware of its presence but heard something warm and right in the beat of the rain outside.

In the southeastern point was an older youth experimenting with more complex magic and playing with alchemy. The youth turned objects out of themselves and into other things. He made candles whose essence was water. He drowned them and they burned. He coaxed casual equations out of mild young flowers whose petals were numbers speaking steady poems. The poems revealed their primal seeds as winter mountains. He turned sunlight into snow. The spirit turned itself colors, from red to blue to yellow to clear to black to red again. The youth poured rainbows in and out of jars and turned haze into liquid and liquid into living rock. The spirit sang and blushed.

In the southwestern point was a young man working with an older wizard. There were books and books and the spirit sat quietly upon them in contemplation as the younger man wrote.

In the northwestern point the spirit stood tall and proud and unmoving.

It was dressed in white. This time the man, older now, sat still in contemplation before it, trying to grasp the spirit with his mind. But the spirit wouldn't move nor could the man grasp even the hem of its robe. Sometimes the man's breath brought the robe close to his face, and then he nodded.

In the northernmost point the spirit was a woman. She wore a helmet and carried an owl and a snake in her left hand. In her right hand was a rod encircled with olive leaves. She was looking ever upward and away—and her father was the sky god and his head lay cracked and bleeding.

And the waxing moon was setting her bulging crescent behind the hill.

And her light was the light of the crystal Mirand held aloft.

And the chanting increased in intensity.

And the ground swallowed and rolled.

And the crystal exploded.

And my master crumpled into himself and to the ground like a spent storm.

And I heard myself screaming my disbelief. "Miraaaand! Noooo! Noooo! Noooo! Let me die instead! Mirand! This wasn't supposed to happen! Nooooho-ho-ho! *Noooo!*" Cathe was jerking at my bridle and trying to force me to ride with him back toward the town. "No, let me go to him—let me go—"

"There's nothing you can do!" Mock's exploded in a fireball so loud and intense I could feel its heat from where I was. And in the same instant the death charm broke around my neck and a hole ripped into my side, and my screams for Mirand became screams of physical pain. "This way!" yelled Cathe, forcing my fearful pony to canter behind his in the direction of the flames.

"It's burning, it's all burning, oh oh, the town is burning! Oh, I'm hit. Oh, Mirand! Save him, Cathe! Save him! You're a cleric! You must save him!"

"What? And change his alignment?" he shouted, pulling my pony toward the dreadful choking rivers of smoke that were quickly filling the west end of town. The smoke was clogging my eyes and the more air I swallowed the less I could breathe, but still we continued into the destruction. My pony's fear rose to an animal numbness that thrust mechanically in whatever direction Cathe pulled. As we reentered town the smoke stung my eyes so badly that I had to close them, and even so my lids stuck together. Smoke also scratched sharp lines in my throat but there was so little good air I found it impossible to breathe except through swallowing whatever air I could through my mouth. I felt soot on my teeth and tongue and tried to spit but my need for air was stronger, so I ended up swallowing ashes. Every breath cost me coughing fits, which intensified the pain in my side.

I heard mighty crashes and explosions that caused my pony to rear in terror but Cathe kept pulling us along and the animal didn't resist. I heard roofs crashing around me and flames bubbling and ringing like glass bursting against glass—or *was* it real glass? Sharp fragments of something kept shattering against my face, but there was so little good air that I didn't dare protect myself with my hood. The heat was intolerable. I felt like even my bones were sweating. The soles of my feet were damp. I heard men and women shrieking—and the shrieks terrified me because there wasn't enough air for more than one shrill before a deathly coughing cut it off, There was coughing everywhere and the ghastly stench of burning flesh. I heard other horses screaming and felt my pony being jerked abruptly around a corner; I bounced so wildly I had to grasp its neck with both hands and open my eyes instinctively for balance.

The smoke was burning my eyes, but I kept rubbing them on my pony's mane so that I could see something, and when I finally braved using sight again through slit lids I saw that the roofs of the shops on both sides of the street were all on fire, and people were running and pushing in a north-easterly direction. Being mounted gave Cathe and me an advantage in that the crowd had to get out of our way. But it was still slow going and panic knotted the crowd into an impassible mess at the sound of yet another explosion somewhere behind us.

"Push on! Push on!" yelled Cathe. Someone was grabbing at my leg, and by hastening my pony forward I shook off his grip but trampled someone else. Cathe was beating someone away from his horse with a small staff. The second floor of a shop directly above us crashed down, showering everyone in our vicinity with jagged pieces of burning wood. I saw a woman's hair catch on fire and people beating her head frantically to put it out. I clung to my pony's neck and urged the poor beast forward, relying more on the pull of Cathe's larger steed than on my own horsemanship. Another roof crashed down. Our horses jerked into a panicked gallop that dispersed the crowd around us and got us to the end of the street, but as soon as we turned into the main road heading northeast we found the way blocked by a fallen building and piles of burning and gasping debris. Turning around in the press of people was impossible without crushing someone. The crowd kept pushing forward, the people in back unaware of the fiery obstacle in front. I saw people fall underfoot and not get up. I knew they were being trampled to death. "Push on!"

"I can't!"

"Now for it!" Cathe pulled my pony toward the lowest and least fiery pile of debris. The smoke was fiercer here and smelled foul and acrid. It made my head swell with a bruised ache. Even with my eyes closed again I knew we were trampling over fresh corpses and soon-to-be corpses. Then I knew we were starting to jump the pile, and I did nothing but cling to my pony and pray to Habundia for an end as it obediently left the ground. It squealed as its back hooves landed in embers. This was the only way I knew we'd landed at all, for I still felt our dash along the main road was all part of one long jump. There were fewer people for a while, but we soon encountered crowds again. Every building was in flames, but for some reason the smoke here was slightly more tolerable.

I saw a little dog with its flesh burning and thought its yelps were my own. I saw a trampled child wriggling her way into death and felt the skin along my own thighs pinch and convulse. I saw shops whose carefully crafted identities were forever destroyed by fire and I named them again in memory. I saw a blind old man battling the crowds and closed my eyes and felt my head throb as he got pulled under for the last time. I tasted the dark side of my love for the town.

My side was still bleeding, hot and sticky. We pushed on and on through all the sights and scents of horror, and I had to take in every detail of my beloved town in its death throes. And I thought of the dancers in Mock's, and those damnably seductive musicians, and the merchants I'd watched and never known, and the woman who sold rutabaga pies, and the cat who kept the weapons shop, and the kindness and stout goodness of the Helan people, and Mirand, and poor Cae, and how she would grieve when she heard about it and how I would grieve too—for the rest of my life.

I don't know how long it took us to make our way through this place of destruction, but there came a time when the air felt colder and the coughing stopped and there was no smoke. The road was dark and unfamiliar. Our horses slowed. I think it was the slackening sound of their hoofbeats that first brought home to me that our surroundings had changed. I never felt us leave the town, but all in a moment I knew that the town was behind us. Turning in my saddle I saw the sickened beauty of flames feeding the night sky as they enticed the darkness to stake its claim on the newly opened land. Then we took a bend in the road and I saw nothing.

I untied Cathe's rope from my bridle and rode up to his side. The moon had set and I could only see his outline by starlight. Cathe was caroling high-pitched, childish laughter as though he had just heard the very best joke in the world. "Woooo—wheeee, by'r Lady, what a glorious mess is ours to behold tonight! I do wonder how cousin Walworth is going to explain this one to King Thoren, let alone to the Duke of Helas. He'll need three dozen silver-tongued wizards and then some just to persuade the king's footman to let him in the door. Heeee heeee, Lady, what a night!"

I didn't know where to begin. I honestly didn't know where to begin. I felt as though I had just lost everything I ever cared about and this clown was laughing and chortling as if it were was all a grand game. "It's not funny," I choked out.

"Don't be absurd. Everything's funny in the right way." He was still chuckling.

"Including having your intelligence sacrificed at the whim of some council of jealous clerics?" I said, just to be cruel. "You weren't laughing then, as I recall."

"No, but then neither were you."

His answer made absolutely no sense and I decided he had to be mad. "I wasn't having my life judged. I was safe in the audience. I didn't even know you. What's your point?"

"What's yours?" He sighed happily and threw back his head. "Just look at those stars—the Lady's plenty burns. Oh, I'm sorry. Just taste those sweet spicy globes of delight, mmmm—and isn't this moment as blessed as it comes?"

"No, this moment isn't anything of the sort! The town is destroyed, the cause is lost, and Mirand—Mirand is—"

"Dead? Yes, well, a pity, but what can you do? Makes things a bit more dicey on the other end." I started shoving and pummeling him on his horse. Cathe looked only a few years older than I and he was lightly built. I wanted to throw him to the ground. I wanted to make him hurt and hurt. I only succeeded in making him laugh and laugh. "Oh, please, Llewelyn, it isn't as if you've never wished the same on him." Guilt paralyzed my arms. "Come, you rail against getting your wishes and refuse to call that funny. Here." He stopped his horse and reached over to put his hand against the wound in my side. "I've got something for you." I felt my flesh close up and the pain subside. "Feel better?"

"No."

"Good." He started to ride slowly again and I kept up with him. He was still chuckling softly.

"Where are the others? Why did we separate? Why did you lead me through the town?"

"I guess I thought you'd like to see everything. The others are on their way to Loudes, presumably."

"And where are we going?"

"Kant. Sweet succulent savory Kant. Lady, look at those stars—"

"Why was the town destroyed?"

"For the same reason your tender side was ravaged. Mirand couldn't disarm the crystal you stole for him, so he did the next best thing, which was to reverse the direction of induction back toward Zelar. Mirand effectively set up an induction in every one of the crystals Grendel was carrying, which *all* had something of Zelar's energy guarding them, Grendel being woefully incompetent in such matters. I believe you had one of those crystals in your pocket. Grendel's dead now, of course, and hence the breaking of your death charm. I'm sure Zelar took his share of damage as well, if it's any consolation."

"It isn't."

"Of course." He started humming.

"I thought you were Franko."

"Disappointed?" He was amused again.

"How and when did you get involved with our operation?"

"After you and Baniff were kind enough to rescue me—you know, snow is much more brilliant by starlight than by moonlight; feel how rhythmic the sparks, smell them, ah, yes—well, I made my way to Lord Roguehan's camp and offered my blessed services."

"You what?"

"I made my way—"

"I heard you. You mean you just walked into the enemy's stronghold like that? After we got you out of enemy hands?"

"Why not? Never be afraid to take it upon yourself to be a hero. Roguehan was glad to have me. Remember, there's nothing a wizard can do that a high-level cleric like myself can't do nine times as well and three times as fast. Why play havoc with theory and abstractions when you can take your power straight from the gods themselves? Yes, I've been part of this affair much longer than even Walworth knew. Saved *you* this morning with a well-executed distraction. And when I approached my cousin this afternoon with all I knew, everyone was most glad to have my help. Good thing I was there tonight to shield the bottle while Mirand moved it."

"How were you able to find us?"

"By the Lady's guidance and help."

"I didn't even know Walworth had a cousin."

"Well, we're cousins of a distance. Related through the northern branch of the family, as you might have guessed."

"Then Cae's your cousin too." I used her nickname deliberately, to show my familiarity and take the edge off his uppityness. "She lets *me* call her sister."

"She lets me call her wife. We're married. Ah, the wind tastes slightly sour when you lick its cold breath, don't you agree?"

"Funny *she's* never mentioned it."

"Mentioned the taste of the wind?"

"No, being married."

"Well, since she wouldn't, let me explain. About a year ago, before all this nastiness, my dear lady came walkabout to Sunnashiven on her brother's business and so there was a time in play—in play, mind you—when we skipped out upon the dying fields and pledged our troth for fun and I called my goddess for witness—and so it sticks."

"Then you're not really married."

"My dear Llewelyn, how sweet of you to care about my personal life. But we are joined in the eyes of She we called upon, and Caethne called as clearly as I did. And I did marry us with mine and Habundia's authority. We are as married as—as—salt water and sand. Oooh, feel the night weaken and snap, there is natural light again somewhere in the world, it's crawling through my veins, lovely, lovely..."

"I don't care. Why are we going through Kant to get to Loudes? Isn't Loudes on the western side of Threle? Kant is northeast of Helas, isn't it?"

"Well, that's the way of it, of course, but there's a monastery in Kant I think you'll like. A safe place to be until the trouble dies down. But forgive me—I must just...just..." he started sucking at the fleshy part of his palm. "Yes, to take the light from my veins is just right here—a certain tartness to the sour old wind—ah, and so my tongue is licking in Paradise."

I wanted to cut his tongue out. "I don't want to go to a monastery and hide. I want to go to Loudes and help Walworth."

"Such a boy as you are, Llewelyn. And there's nothing you can do in Loudes, of course." The singsong quality of his voice made me want to strike him again. His tone both pointed out my helplessness and mocked my heart-felt attempts to do something useful for the cause. I was condemned for my condition and condemned for trying to change my condition. Cathe was parceling out his words in such a slow cadence that I had to dig my fists in my pony's neck and squirm around to avoid hitting him; if I did, I'd have to put up with his irritating laughter again. "But we'll put you up in a nice quiet monastery—for a period of time, you can stand to lose some time—"

"No! I'm going to Loudes. Time is all I have to lose, and Walworth needs me now. To help explain to the king." I spurred my pony forward to get away from his irritating voice. He caught up easily.

"Llewelyn. Come and think with me. You are a citizen of Sunna. You've been assisting an illegal intelligence operation in Threle that has resulted in the destruction of a fair-sized border town. Your master is—well, I won't say it, but you did play something of a role in that piece of business." I went dead and dark inside. "The *caen* is going to have quite enough to account for without explaining why he saw fit to include an ex-student from Sun-nashiven's wizard school, the son of an undersecretary to King Sunnas, in his camp. Don't you think that in the interest of saving face you would be the scapegoat for what happened here? Someone will have to be blamed, I assure you."

"Then let them blame me if it will help."

"Oooh, I do love your spirit—but unfortunately it won't help. Walworth may have to cast blame on you to save himself, to save his credibility with the king and to save Threle. He'd do so with all reluctance, of course, but he'd do so if he had to, you know that. For Threle he'd sacrifice a friend. Look at the equanimity with which both he and Baniff approached your late master's expected demise, and they both loved him."

I screamed in fury, "No, not equanimity as if it didn't matter. It mattered, but they were strong and philosophical and dedicated and knew what needed to be done."

"And loved Threle more. Face it, Llewelyn." Cathe sighed gently. "I'm sure my cousin deeply grieves the loss of his old tutor. But he's probably hurting more for the damage done to Threle. Now he must lose another friend—yourself, for his country. To save the cause he loves, he must watch you condemned for dedicating yourself to the country and cause he loves. Just like Mirand."

"Oh no!"

"And you would ride up to Loudes to make sure that happens. To study how far equanimity stretches before it becomes empty pain. An interesting study, I suppose. You would enjoy watching your friend suffer more—"

"No—Stop it! Noooo! Please, I'll die first!"

"Well put. I like that. Llewelyn, monasteries are protected places in Threle. They belong to the gods, not the state. Not even the king can touch you there. Lie low in Kant. Claim sanctuary among the priests and priest-esses. I'll speak for you. Walworth can then blame or use you as he has to without sustaining a second loss. When the time is right you can go to him again. And of course I'll be with you when I can."

Somehow this didn't feel comforting, but I wasn't sure that anything would feel comforting right now. *Well,* I thought, *if the best thing I can do for Threle is to disappear, I'll disappear.* Baniff had spoken of a Kantish monastery before. He had originally wanted to bring me there himself. So I'd hang out there for a little while—a few days, a week—assess the situation, and move on. Perhaps I could still help explain things to Thoren, or ride up to Walworth's duchy and lend a hand there. Walworth needed to sort a lot of things out now and so did I—we'd reunite when there was a clear plan, and then we'd smash Roguehan.

"All right, Cathe, I'm yours. Show me the way."

"My dear boy, I already have—and isn't that the most delectable crunch and crush of new snow and wrinkly old oaks you've ever sucked? Suck it now, into your stomach, through your pony's hooves, and out of the hotly anxious press of the stars—they do get hotly anxious just before dawn, don't they, the bitches? Ah, a bit early tonight, girls, but then the sweetly gnarled oaks are tasting even now of—of sour baby pumpkins, do you think? To match the wind? Oh, delight is in the heart. . . ."

I sang a wordless tune, softly, in rhythm to his words, to discourage him from speaking to me again and disrupting my thoughts. It seemed to work, for he made up hymns to Habundia and to the night sky, using my singing as accompaniment, and so he did not speak to me directly for a long time. In my thoughts I was grateful not to be going back to Sunnashiven. That was all I could come up with and all I had. I heard Cathe weaving my awful gratitude into a hymn of praise to Habundia as the cold new sun rose heavy on my heart.

Fourteen

Cathe brought me breathless within the walls of the monastery, my tired pony plodding behind his surefooted mare like a slow obedient shadow lumbering back into darkness. I saw the morning wind smearing the light of a dead and bloodied sun all over the tops of the walls. A hole in the wind brought the smell of decay, but for the most part the cold air sheltered and swallowed the miserable morning I was leaving. If I breathed through my mouth while looking at the rotting light spread out across the walls, a faint taste of mold flowed between my teeth and around my tongue. I was coughing frequently, which made it impossible not to breathe through my mouth. I took in morning air and coughed up something foul and watery.

Cathe was still singing blackened, beggarly hymns. He sang to his goddess the way a cheerful mongoose might sing to a ripe baby cobra.

> Let me crush you in the egg, my dear
> Let me eat away your early entry
> Sorely do I love you
> Sorely do I love your uncreation

There was more. There had been hours' worth. He sang with a sublime sort of cockiness, the cockiness of one who had measured his goddess's power and found his own to be greater. Even when his words were meek he adopted such a swaggering tone that anyone might think *he* was Habundia and Habundia merely his serving girl. Sometimes he would break off his singing and threaten his deity with all kinds of elaborate tortures to be done to her sacred images at particularly holy times and places. Then he would smile encouragingly at me as if inviting me to join in the fun.

I would say nothing, of course, and invariably the singing would pick up again, sometimes in Botha and sometimes in languages I didn't care to understand. This bizarre performance had been going on all night and all morning, and I was still refusing to get drawn into it. I hadn't eaten well in the past three days, and I had repeatedly exposed myself to the wet and cold. Stress had been my constant companion, and with the exception of the previous afternoon's surprise at the strange cottage, I had hardly slept.

All of these things were now announcing themselves in the flush of fever I felt slithering under my cheeks and rattling in my throat. The inside of my neck was sore down to my shoulders, caked with a thirst that licked insistently into my lungs. My head was steadily lightening with creeping sickness, and so when his singing did come through, it came through weakly, like dead bees pattering into the dried sleep of a dream-deadened hive. There was no impact. It was quite beyond my power to be impacted. I could not hold any thought steady except *So here we are; what now?*

I noticed that the tight gray monastery walls enclosed a good deal of land. We rode slowly past shabby patches of dead winter gardens interspersed with smoother patches of brilliant snow. Cold yellow smudges of ghastly sunlight lay splayed across the face of the western wall. I noticed a few barren trees whose wind-lashed, cringing limbs served as crutches for icicles. There was a large stone building in the center of the enclosed land, which I took to be the monastery itself, and there were several smaller buildings scattered around whose function I could only guess at. Pillars of ice winked and flashed between the flat roofs and the ground. Although it was bitterly cold I didn't see any smoke rising from any of the structures, and I wondered briefly how the residents, if there were residents, kept themselves warm. But I didn't wonder for long. Fever has a way of thinning out wonder.

Cathe reined in his horse and so did I. He looked over the silence and the dead land, sighing loudly and smacking his lips with an air of intense satisfaction. "Well, Lady be blessed, you're home at last. Dismount, dismount, and take your things." I slid off my pony's back, landed stiffly on numb feet, and untied my sack. Cathe remained mounted. As soon as I was finished he clicked his tongue and my pony obediently walked up beside his mare, where he tied its bridle. "Go, go, go!" he said to me encouragingly, motioning toward the large stone building with several flicks of his hand.

I started uncertainly and then turned. "Aren't you coming?"

"And what can this ripe an' rippin' ol' bag of sanctified flesh do for you here?" I looked up at him, feeling utter physical repulsion. "Oooh, you'll miss me," he said caressingly. "I'm touched, really I am, but surely you know I shall be back. Never you mind yourself about it." He turned the horses. "But please go along now. I know you know the way. For now. And for good."

I kept staring at him through fever and disbelief, the way one helplessly stares at a mangled arm or leg.

"Be bold, Llewelyn, be bold and beautiful, and such as you are, the world is yours. To have." He looked back toward the large building and raised the three middle fingers of his right hand to his lips in a tender kiss, closing his eyes as if to fix his attention elsewhere, as if the coldness commanded all and nothing else existed. I watched him because there was nothing else to do, and because I felt reluctant to let my last link with the only fellowship I had ever known ride off, no matter how much I detested that connection. After about a minute he opened his eyes, took up the reins again, and added, "Go now. Really, it's all right. You're quite safe here." Then he kicked his mare hard and cantered off with my pony in tow.

The sound of the horses' hooves vanished into a sharper loneliness. A new silence swung hard through the grounds, pulling my fever with it. I stood still in unfamiliarity, feeling the lightness in my head arch itself into the iron-blue line of wall and broken horizon. I stood watching the edges of dead trees pulsing. Branches meddled with the hard sky. After a while the edge of the ground also began to pulse, especially where it fought for space with the gray walls. I knew the pulsing was really fever distorting my vision, but I held to those pulses as I would have held to a friend. My fever had its origin in actions that involved my friends, and therefore constituted something of a tangible connection with them. So I stood there cherishing my sickness. What can I say? I had never felt more alone. There were no words here. Only the fever spoke, and it kept hissing into heavy head clouds. My thirst kept increasing. My thirst kept licking deeper into the cold bilge that swelled painfully in my lungs. There was nothing for me in the ground. The solid sky locked out thought. Winter was different here, a foreign season. It caught me with a foreign cold.

I didn't even know where I was, really, except that I was standing on the grounds of a monastery somewhere in Kant. I supposed I should approach the large building, ask for sanctuary, and offer to make myself useful. I could go in for scribe work for a week or two, just until things settled somewhat. Surely a monastery would have a library. Surely a library would have maps. I would earn some traveling money for my services, plot a course for Loudes, and get the hell out and back into action. Besides, news would certainly travel here and soon I could get some kind of message to Cae. Or, depending on circumstances, perhaps it would be better if I didn't go to Loudes and just joined Cae up north in her duchy. At any rate, I wouldn't be here long. That I knew.

Nothing moved or hummed and so my slow walk toward the large building felt like a violation of some secret rule. At least it would be an experience to hang out with monks for a while. At the very least I'd get some evening stories out of it, and there was no telling what I might learn that would be useful later. Perhaps I'd even get a little physical space of my own where I could mourn Mirand in solitude.

I sorely wanted to sit still in my fever and think about him and say a silent good-bye. He had never spoken to me of his deity or of his own alignment, but I knew from the previous night's vision that his life had been one long celebration of Athena, the goddess of wisdom and learning. If any of Athena's clerics resided here, I would ask them if I could attend one of Her rituals and offer private prayers or whatever one usually offered to Her. I supposed I could leave the books in my sack on Her altar. I didn't have anything else, and books seemed an appropriate offering to Athena. As much as healing hurt, I had to heal and recover, if only to be strong for Cae and Walworth and for the cause. The cause was all. Mirand would have wanted it that way.

I rapped on the bronze door without realizing it; only after I felt the skin tear off my knuckles, which had frozen against the metal, did it strike my consciousness. I did not hear the sound of my own rapping. I knew the pain would have been louder had the air been warmer, and that the lightness in my head would have throbbed in slower cycles. No one answered for a long time, so I stood endlessly in the cold and in the throbbing.

I had raised and clenched my fist to knock again when the door opened outward and hit me squarely in the knuckles, knocking me a little off balance. A short paunchy bald man was holding the door and smiling up at me as if to say, *What can I do for you?* I noticed his eyes were bright and blue and warmly expectant. I entered into a little hallway that intersected a corridor at right angles. The door closed behind me. The little man was smiling cordially and bobbing his head, so I began to speak, to create a story that wouldn't compromise Walworth.

I was an apprentice witch from Helas, I began to the doorkeeper. I knew something of herbs and divination. I could read and write a fair hand and wished to put in for scribe. My mistress was a poor peasant woman and could not keep me through the winter. I had no money but could work in return for a season's protection and sanctuary.

Every word dug puddles of soreness into my throat, and I struggled mightily against my rattling cough. The little man kept grinning and bobbing. I finished my story with the realization that he didn't understand a word of it. After I had finished he seemed to wait for me to continue, his silly smile unchanged, his blue eyes friendly and eager. I had no idea what to do except begin all over again. I had gotten almost all the way through my story for the second time when a tall middle-aged woman in clerical garb ran up to me, took my hands in hers, bent her frame down to my height, and gazed earnestly into my eyes. The little man turned his stupid smile in her direction as she approached, content to let her take charge of the situation and make everything right. She was speaking to me in inflections that sounded like questions, but her language was harsh and strange and I didn't understand it. I assumed she was speaking Kantish.

I responded in Botha, but because of the soreness my previous speech had exacerbated in my throat I couldn't have enunciated more than a few words, including *sick*, *shelter*, and *scribe*. I contented myself with coughing and pointing to my throat. She put her hand to my brow, nodded, and left. The doorman was still grinning. He motioned me toward him. His eyes were still bright and friendly. When I got close, he stuck both of his forefingers inside his fat lips and pulled his mouth open wide. His teeth were pointed like a dog's. His tongue was missing. It had been neatly cut out, and he wiggled a blackened stump at the back of his throat for me to see. I recoiled and he dropped his hands. He grinned and bobbed and pointed at me. Then he made bird motions by linking his hands and fluttering his fingers, swaying his arms upward in a wide arc. He looked as though he wanted me to do the same.

I turned away from him in disgust, hugging my cloak around myself and looking up and down the cold corridor that ran perpendicular to the little entrance hall. There were closed doors. There was no movement. I thought about leaving, about hiding somewhere in Kant where not even the king could find me if he wanted to, but I knew that leaving would mean being invisible to Walworth as well. Cathe was going to tell him I was here, and I knew it was important to be in a safe place where my commander could quickly send for me if he needed my help. But it was so cold here, colder than outside. Even my cloak did little more than an ordinary blanket would have done in a blizzard.

I heard the doorkeeper stomping from foot to foot behind me, and then the sound of footsteps down the corridor. The priestess was returning with a much older cleric, a man. He smiled and addressed me in the same unfamiliar language the priestess had used, only the sounds were softened by his genial facial expression. I coughed again and pointed to my throat. He looked interested, took some crumpled parchment out of his pocket along with a reed pen, and offered them to me. I scribbled out in Botha the story I had created for the doorkeeper and gave the parchment back, watching him as his lips silently formed the words I had written.

"You are from Helas?" he asked in such thickly accented Botha it took me seconds to interpret what he was saying. I nodded again. "Do you speak Kantish?" I shook my head and coughed. He looked at the priestess and she spoke to him in Kantish. He spoke back to her and smiled benevolently at me. "Go with her. Work later." His accent was horrible, and it was clear he could not construct more than simple sentences in Botha. I wondered if he even understood my note. I began to walk with her down the corridor. "What is your name?" he called behind me. I told him. He mispronounced it. "Luvellun. Good."

I guessed I was in. Soon I would have some blessed privacy in which to recover from my sickness and plan my next move. *Don't they ever light fires here?* I wondered. The clerics showed no sign of feeling the cold. She led me along the corridor of closed doors and around a corner, where she stopped and spoke to a youth who appeared to be around my own age. He looked respectfully at her, then blankly at me. She motioned me to follow him, so I did. He led me down some stairs to an underground level, which felt slightly less cold, and into a large room filled with cots. There were several boys huddled in groups on the floor of this room. It reminded me of a large holding cell in a prison. He said something in Kantish and pointed toward a stained, sagging cot in the middle of the room near a cluster of young boys. I took the cot to be mine. He walked away and joined a group of older boys sitting on cots in the far corner.

The room was full of chatter. Each group of boys was huddled in a circle for warmth. In some of the circles the boys had thin blankets wrapped around their shoulders and over their heads like cowls. The older boys did not have blankets. I dropped my sack on the cot, sat down, and pulled my cloak around me, but even holding in all the natural heat of fever did little to keep out the relentless cold. I did so want to be warm. And alone. I wanted to lose my sickness. I wanted to meditate on Mirand. But it was good now just to be able to sit somewhere uninterrupted. I hadn't had that luxury in days. I closed my eyes and entered my own fever. Under the circumstances, this was the best way I knew to separate myself from my dismal surroundings. If I could only be still and conjure up some warmth, I now had a space of time in which to smooth out my thoughts. I had to get my strength back. I needed to eat. I thought about Aleta and Perie. Had it really been only three days since I'd last seen them? So much had happened it seemed like months. It was strange to think that they probably hadn't even gotten back to County Clio yet, taking the route they'd planned. They probably knew nothing of the previous night's catastrophe.

I managed to manifest a little warmth out of my fever, enough to blunt the cold. However, as the warmth left my fever and entered the air around my body, my skin broke into a chilly sweat that the warm air couldn't combat, a sweat that bloated my pressing thirst. So much for using magic to help myself. I felt so miserable I idly wondered whether I was still banned against such an action.

As I fell into another frigid coughing fit, sweat bursting and freezing my clothes into my skin, I heard a loud low buzzing noise. The noise sounded like a fat black winter fly determinedly smacking out its life against a hard surface. The boys with blankets quickly folded them on the nearest cots and stood stiffly, raising their hands at right angles to their sides in a ridiculous gesture that involved spreading their fingers wide and staring fixedly at the far wall. A few glanced guiltily toward the door before restricting their gaze. The older boys slowly broke their blanketless circle and stood in a line, arms crossed over their chests, hands flat against their shoulders. I remained seated, not caring to participate in whatever absurdity was going on.

One of the younger boys, whose head had been covered with a blanket, let his gaze wander longer than the others did before throwing his blanket under a cot and clumsily starting to assume his stance. Suddenly he noticed me. His eyes got huge. He howled in rage, frantically flinging his arms up and down while jumping in place. No one reacted. If I hadn't been so sick I probably would have thought the whole thing quite funny, all these boys standing in this preposterous formation while one of their own carried on like a madman. The boy ran up to me, pointed at my chest, and howled and bounced in a frenzy. He glanced desperately back and forth between me and his companions as if he wanted them to come and look at me. None of them paid him any attention. They all kept their gaze fixed on the wall.

The boy was utterly disgusting. He had a grimy face and his teeth were covered by a sticky yellow film. He had foul breath and his clothes smelled distinctly of feces. In quiet deference to my rising illness I covered my face with my hood, willing not to be noticed and shutting out this nauseating disturbance with a shield. As soon as I did this I heard the older boys laughing in back of me, which told me that some of them were sensitive to my magic.

The fly sound buzzed again, sending the boy bolt upright. He ran back and forth between me and the others as if he couldn't decide where to position himself. The laughter stopped immediately. When the door opened and a young male cleric entered, the boy found himself halfway between me and his little group. He jumped twice, whimpered, fell over his own feet, looked terrified, stood up, and fearfully assumed the stance that conformed to the others'. The cleric, who was carrying a large staff, walked briskly up to him and pointed his staff toward the spot where the boy should have been standing. The boy ran back to his place, but not without looking up fearfully to the cleric and whining and pointing toward me and the older boys.

The cleric failed to notice me, but he barked something that sounded like a question toward the far corner. I noticed the little boy's face. It was an absolutely repulsive combination of self-satisfaction, terror, and anticipation. The older youth who had brought me here walked over to the cleric and pointed to the blanket the boy had thrown under the cot. Fury broke free and easy all across the cleric's face, while everyone else in the room except the angry and frightened little boy stiffened into themselves like the trees outside.

The boy cowered and whimpered on the floor while the older youth returned quietly to his position. The cleric fiercely wrapped the miserable blanket around the end of his staff. He began poking the boy in the stomach with it and bellowing at him in Kantish.

I wasn't sure whether the issue was that he had not folded his blanket like the others or that it was forbidden to wrap oneself for warmth. I decided from the guilty looks I had seen earlier and the lack of any heat source in the monastery that it was probably the latter. I wrapped my cloak tighter in quiet defiance. As I did so I noticed that my cot was the only one that didn't have a blanket on it, and it dawned on me that my cot probably belonged to the boy. His rage was justified, erupting from having the only thing he had seized from him and given to a stranger. He had taken the only recourse that appeared to be available to him, appealing to the authority figure for justice against his tormentor. The older youth had retaliated by singling the boy out for a punishment that the others equally deserved, and since it was clear from the earlier laughter that the younger boy was not the most popular kid in the room, the older youth probably felt safe fingering him. In fact, the youth's own social standing was probably enhanced. I pitied the boy as much as my own sickness allowed.

Anyway, the sense of fear in the room was now palpable enough to increase the rate at which my head throbbed. The little boy was crying and shaking so much he couldn't even whimper anymore, just gasp and choke. I didn't understand this, as the cleric was now placing the boy's hand on the edge of the staff and his own hand over the boy's, as if he were going to guide him to do something. The fierceness in the cleric's manner was subsiding, and he merely sighed and looked impatient, as if there was a job to do that needed doing. There was no suggestion of any sort of punishment in store. The blanket was on the floor again and the two of them pressed down with the staff. I saw they were directing a cutting current of energy into the blanket, for the staff was neatly cutting the material up into little strips. The cleric occasionally wrinkled his nose and coughed in disgust, but considering how badly the boy smelled, I didn't much blame him.

Once the blanket was in strips, the cleric said a few words in a harsh tone and the fear in the room reached a breaking pitch. The little boy was on the floor again, only now everyone was helplessly staring at him. He was taking off his clothes in the wretched cold, shivering and trying to double over in a futile attempt to keep some warmth to himself. He was so scared of whatever was about to happen that he lost control of his own urine, which steamed in the cold air. The cleric repeated the words in a harsher, more insistent tone. The boy then picked up a strip of the blanket, which was no doubt as dirty and foul as his own body, and began to roll it into a ball. He ate it tearfully while the cleric watched.

This was too much for me. The blanket was probably all the kid owned in the world, and he had been made to destroy it. He had also been made to completely expose himself to the deathly cold. Now he had to eat the damn thing in front of everyone? Why? I was probably partly to blame. I didn't even want his damn cot, or sanctuary with this insane lot. I made up my mind to leave as soon as I possibly could and still ensure that Walworth would be able to contact me. But in the meantime I wasn't going to sit as silent audience to this absurdity.

So I burned the blanket. Right there on the floor, in front of everyone, I caused the damn thing to explode in flames, which warmed the room to its furthest corners before dying down. No one knew it was me. I dropped my shield, sent the fire, then put my shield back up. I made sure I couldn't be noticed. Then I watched the fun.

The boy jumped back from the blast, eyes wide and skin singed, looking dazedly up at the cleric. The cleric's robes were also singed, but he said nothing. The rest of the boys were jumping and laughing and shouting something that sounded like "Soonraytun! Soonraytun!" grabbing their blankets and huddling together for warmth, this time standing. When I turned around I saw that even the older boys had blankets now, and they too were huddling and shouting for joy. The cleric said a few more words—which were greeted with the rousing shout of "Soonkin! Soonkin!"—and then used his staff to create a large genial fire in the middle of the room. All the boys ran over and warmed themselves at it—all except the miserable one who seemed to be the center of this whole bizarre business. His clothes were thrown in the fire and he was made to stand away from the flames in the coldest corner of the room while everyone else was having an absolutely marvelous time dancing and hopping in a circle around the fire. I sent some heat in his direction out of pity but stopped doing so as soon as the door opened again and the priestess entered the room. She watched the singing and rejoicing with a sweet smile and looked questioningly at the younger cleric, who pointed toward the corner and spoke to her at length. She watched the festivities, clapping her hands and calling out cheerful-sounding phrases, and then the two of them left together. I sent more warmth over to the boy, who was shuddering like a cow with the ague. I hoped the clerics had gone to get him something warm to wear.

When the clerics returned they brought half a dozen or so priests and priestesses with them, two of whom led the boy away. The other clerics gathered up the rest of the boys and led them out in a shouting group, chanting, "Soonraytun! Soonraytun! Soonkin! Soonkin!" After the crowd left I considered staying behind in the solitude, just to be alone somewhere, but curiosity got the better of me, so I followed at a distance, leaving my sack behind on the cot and willing to be unnoticed. As the shouting mass passed down the empty corridor doors flew open and fires were kindled. Good, I thought; soon the place would warm up.

I followed them all outside through the bronze door. An equally joyous mass of shouting, chanting girls came up behind us and I found myself in the middle of the crowd, casually making my way unnoticed to the front to get a better view. I thought there was going to be a party, the way everyone was carrying on, but I was getting concerned about the boy, who was being carried stark naked by two clerics through the winter weather. His skin was turning a horrible mottled pallor in the cold air but no one seemed to notice or care. He had ceased crying, but his whole body occasionally gave a piteous deathly shudder. For some reason I thought briefly of my own sky-clad initiation into wizardry. Couldn't they at least give the wretched thing a robe?

The two clerics suddenly stopped. I could feel them measuring the sun's angle. They strode deliberately over to one of the pillars of ice that had formed between the ground and the roof of an outer building, one that the sun was directly hitting. Then they tied a black cord around one of the boy's wrists and tied the other end around the ice pillar, so it acted like a leash that gave him a little room to move about. The female cleric said a few words whose cadence sounded like a binding spell and tested the knot. Apparently it couldn't be untied. The boy huddled himself into a ball. Everyone ran back clapping and shouting into the monastery, where I could now see smoke billowing out of the chimneys, leaving me alone with him.

It was clear to me that the boy would not survive exposure to the bitter cold for any length of time. He already looked half dead. I tried a witch-working Cae had once taught me, to raise the temperature of the air around him. His skin turned ugly red and then normal color. He looked up at me from his huddle. I made eye contact while the warmth messily dissipated into winter air. I raised the temperature again and tried a wizard shield around it so that he would stay warm. It seemed to work. He looked at me again as if he understood I was trying to help him.

"What's your name?" I asked, because it was something to say. He didn't respond, and I remembered he probably didn't understand Botha. I could certainly have used wizardry to drag his name out of him if it mattered that much to me, but it didn't. I reached in the pocket of my cloak, where there was some stale bread from Cae's food packet, bread so hard I couldn't eat it. I gave it to him. He sucked at the crust as if he'd never seen bread before, then he sucked at the pillar of ice for drink. I looked at the knot in his tether and decided not to tamper with the magic that held it together. When he saw me inspecting the knot he cried and grabbed the cord away from me as if it were a precious possession. *All right, whatever.* I'd done what I could. Cae would have done no less. I had more important things to do, such as gather information and make plans for leaving.

I turned to go. He squealed like a hungry piglet looking for its mother.

"What do you want, then?" I said harshly, not really asking, knowing he couldn't understand me. I saw that the bread was gone and he was pointing toward his mouth. "I'm hungry too. But conjured food isn't as life-sustaining as natural sup. At least mine isn't. I can get your gut filled, but it won't strengthen you any." He kept looking at me. Finally I shrugged; I had to eat something too. Being sick and all, I didn't want to fill my own belly on a conjuring, so I had been holding out for something nourishing, but hunger was getting the better of me. "You like apples?" No response. "Bread and apples. Warm bread and baked Clion apples." Why not splurge? I used the Amara words, substituting *pleasure* for *Clion*, there being no Amara word for "Clion." I needed something to bring up the delicious nature of the fruit. "Pleasure apples"—the kid was going to have a feast! What the hell, we both were.

The food materialized on my second try, to the boy's wide-eyed amazement. I gave him most of it, keeping some bread to stave off my hunger pangs until I could find some natural food. Cae would have been proud. "Enough?" I turned to go while he was stuffing his face. He cried out and grabbed at my hand as if he didn't want me to leave. "Gotta go, kid," I said, taking back my hand. "There isn't any more. Really." I needed to save my strength. "The heat will last through the day. As long as the shield does. Have fun."

I started walking away, but the child started crying so loudly that I crossed back into his shield, against my better judgment, to silence him. "Stop it! I'm probably not even supposed to be here. There's nothing more I can do." He stood up in that ridiculous posture the younger boys had assumed this morning. "What do you *want*?" He looked pitifully up into my eyes and then down. His odor was causing my stomach to twist against the warm bread I'd just eaten, so I turned and walked quickly back toward the monastery, willing to be unnoticed, and shutting out the sound of his cries.

When I got to the bronze door I pushed it open without knocking. The doorkeeper wasn't there, but the priestess I had met earlier was standing in the corridor engaged in earnest conversation with a young clerical student. Neither noticed me. There were also more people walking through the corridor, and more doors open, and I smelled pungent wood smoke filling the building. The corridor now felt considerably warmer. I thought about wandering through the building on my own in search of the cooking area, but I was in such dire need of a decent meal that I decided it would save time to try to ask the priestess about it. I willed myself back into noticeability and stood waiting to be spoken to.

She saw me immediately and smiled and cajoled softly, motioning me to join them. "Luvellun," she said warmly, and then spoke rapidly, addressing both the student and myself as if she was making introductions. The student's name was Rebe. That much I caught. She was older than I and she smiled patronizingly in my direction, evidently trying to show her priestess how nice she could be to strangers. Then she inclined her head solemnly toward the priestess, as if to show me she had grand affairs to attend to that lay beyond my simple ken, and left. I looked up at the priestess and noticed the band of yellow around her collar, proclaiming her a servant of Habundia. I started to speak but she smilingly raised a finger to stop me and looked over my head down the corridor. Turning, I saw another cleric walking briskly over to join us. The priestess said a few words to him, including my name, and he began to speak to me, O joy, in lightly accented, perfectly understandable Botha. He even got my name right!

"Llewelyn, is it?" He extended his hand. "My name is Brother El. Good day, yes? Brother Styrn gave me the note you wrote him this morning, and as it turns about I do have need of a scribe who is fluent in Botha. Preferably in both Botha and Kantish, but I'll take what I can get. You are from Helas, I understand?"

"Yes," I replied in my recently acquired Helan accent. "Botha is my native language, but I'm sure I can learn to speak and write Kant here in no time." I laughed familiarly at the pun, for in Botha the word *Kant* sounds almost like *cant*, that is, academic nonsense. El smiled stiffly and politely. I could tell he liked neither the pun nor my clumsy attempt at familiarity.

The priestess tried to smooth over what she sensed as an awkwardness by speaking rapidly to the priest.

"Good, yes. Sister Elwyn reminds me that you are suffering from fever, and I can see for myself that you aren't well." His tone was sharply charitable, a reminder that he was conscious of his own generosity in finding a reason to overlook my recent impudence. A warning not to presume so far upon good taste and his own good nature again. "She says you are hungry." *Bless Sister Elwyn!* I thought fervently. "Now that the sun has returned I was about to break my own fast, and although I'm not accustomed to sharing bread with applicants, this happens to be the most convenient time for me to explain the work to you. Will you come with me, then?" he said formally and quickly.

I nodded humbly and tried to act as though he was doing me the greatest service in the world, which in some sense he was, although I resented feeling that I had to pay for my meal with fake humility. I followed him along the now busy corridor, up a narrow staircase that opened up into a wide common area, and into a wing that appeared to be where the clerics lived. His own apartments were well appointed, with beautifully crafted furniture and carpets and a huge cheerful fireplace blazing to full capacity. An older clerical student with tangled hair that kept falling in his eyes was feeding the fire. He had a slightly twisted back and a crooked mouth. There was an owl perched on his shoulder. Brother El said something to him in Kantish and he left.

"Cristo will bring us something to eat. Now sit down, Llewelyn, and tell me why you want to put in for scribe work and claim sanctuary here. Sanctuary from what?"

"Uh . . . from the cold. I meant, I need a place to stay. As I said in my note, my mistress is a poor witch and cannot keep me through the winter."

"Mmm, yes, right. Never known a witch who couldn't keep herself and anyone that mattered to her through the cold season."

"Well, true, she could have kept me but I chose to leave. To make things easier for her."

"Were you happy studying witchcraft?"

"Yes, I loved it. I'd go back and study more if I could. I love nature—and magic."

"Good. Then do I understand that you came here because you gave up something you loved to make it easier for your mistress to get through the winter?" He leaned back in his chair and put the tips of his fingers together.

"Yes, you could say that." And on one level I suppose it was even true. I was here so that Walworth and Cae could get through the difficulties ahead.

"Admirable, admirable. It's not often one finds such noble sentiments in one so young. Good. And so when do you plan to return to her?"

After the story I had just given him I couldn't exactly say "in a week or two," so I said, "Next season, when spring comes again." El was silent for a while, seeming to consider something. During his silence Cristo returned with two bowls of sorrel soup and some warm bread, and then left us. I thanked El and gulped down the soup. He spoke while I was drinking.

"The goddess Habundia is my mistress. She keeps her servants well through the winter, yes?" Although this comment was tossed off absently, it changed the meaning of our preceding dialogue. Now I wasn't sure whether he had been talking about Habundia all along or about my fictional mistress. "I'm not interested in a scribe who plans to leave when the weather changes. I wonder, are you strong enough to entirely forsake your work for ours? To reside here as my personal scribe for the long term?"

I was certainly strong enough to tell him whatever he wanted to hear. "My mistress is so very poor, I'm sure she would be pleased if I chose to stay here indefinitely." There—if he was thinking of Habundia, that statement would give him something to consider.

He seemed to be considering. "You write a neat, fair hand. I'm looking for a scribe to copy correspondence quickly and neatly for me, without error. Also to compose letters and reports for me in Botha when I am too busy to do so myself. You must be capable of setting down exactly what I tell you to without embellishment or change. I want a scribe, not a poet."

"Of course."

"I suppose you could copy Kantish characters."

"I suppose."

"I shall expect you to learn our language eventually, but I don't count it a half-bad thing to have a scribe who can't read half my letters, at least at first, while I'm getting to know you, if you understand my meaning. Anything you copy for me or anything I say in your presence is strictly confidential, you understand that? And you are at my call at any time, day or dead of night, yes? And you do not leave my service until such time as I release you. Monastic law, you know." I said nothing, which he seemed to take as assent. "Now, I need to ask you, as one officially under the protection of Kursen Monastery in the Duchy of Kant, Kingdom of Threle"—it felt strange to hear him say "Threle," though I don't know why—"do you wish to try a calling to serve any particular deity while you are in the house of the gods?"

"No," I said too quickly, and then softened it with, "I like Habundia, of course, and Athena and Thoth, who looks kindly on scribes, but I have no calling now. Is it necessary?"

"No, not necessary, but I had to ask. Besides"—he laughed emptily, and his tone got lighter—"today is Sunreturn, a time when many of our younger residents find themselves in the mood to make vows to one deity or another. By the way, did you catch the excitement this morning? The Sun King has returned, manifesting himself in the person of young Devon. Who would have thought?" He looked at me pointedly. I looked blank and mildly interested. "And if Devon survives the day, he shall have the right and privilege to rule over all the other nonclerics here for the next year. Which is something, of course, you should know about." He looked at me searchingly again. I smiled as if I cared. "We have a tradition here each Sunreturn called Finding the King. On Sunreturn some extraordinary event designates one lucky student as the new year's embodiment of the sun. Often the event involves the sun. One year a young girl found a packet of cinnamon under her pillow; cinnamon being a sun spice, we knew she was chosen. Another year someone found a square of red cloth bearing sun symbols sewn in his shift. Before this event occurs, and it could occur at any time during the day, there is no warmth or food or fellowship. We are dead as the god is dead. Once the event occurs there is merriment and rejoicing to welcome him back. The student is presented as a sacrifice, that is, as an offering to the cold. If the offering survives what remains of the day, then it is Sun King and rules for a year, to be offered again next Sunreturn and so on every year until death. Or graduation."

"What if the sacrifice dies?"

"Then there is no Sun King that year. The king is in exile, disguised, his head hidden in sorrow from his people." He didn't like the question. "We have our own rules here. You'll do well to learn them." Another pause. "I suppose you think us cruel. Did not your own mistress teach you the doctrine of sacrifice?"

"Well, not exactly. Not in the same way. She didn't work with the sacrificial aspects of her deities. Not in a formally religious way, that is." I wondered if I was saying too much. "I guess I'm really just naive about these things. Doesn't the Sun King rule the clerics as well?"

He swallowed and pulled at his collar. "Well, we couldn't very well require that. Not all of the clergy here are sun worshipers." *Neither are all the nonclergy,* I thought. "Besides, it's only symbolic, and we feel it teaches humility to the students, having to take orders from one of their own, often from one less experienced and knowledgeable. Anyone who refuses obedience on any matter is expelled, losing all his or her years of study. We destroy all records, leaving the ex-student to find work without being able to account for the years spent here. No one wants to give up eight or ten of their best years only to become a field hand. And also obedience is part of any cleric's training. Of course, sometimes it works out that the Sun King is about to take priestly orders after years of study and due to his or her senior position the others don't mind taking orders as much. Sometimes he or she merely arrived that morning looking for scribe work."

"So do the clerics mark students they wish to be Sun King with ritual objects? Students who will really drive in the humility lesson?" I asked in a tone that suggested approval of the practice.

He looked annoyed. "Not exactly. There are ritual objects and they show up according to the god's will."

I'll bet, I thought. My burning Devon's blanket was no doubt an "unusual event" they couldn't ignore, so Devon had become Sun King much to everyone's surprise. I wondered what would happen now when the real "chosen one" found an orange or a box of cloves or a red candle inscribed to Apollo in his soup. That would be amusing.

"In Devon's case I understand his blanket spontaneously combusted. Interesting, yes?" Brother El looked at me again.

"Interesting," I repeated.

"And so we'll check Devon at sunset. Now to other matters. Here's some paper and ink. Take this down. You can write at the table over there." This meant turning my back to him, which was just as well.

Sunreturn
My liege Lord of Helas,
Greetings in Her name. Your courier arrived this morning with the news. I see no reason why you should not turn destruction to your (and our) advantage. You certainly have enough material now to concoct a story of high treason, for which I can assure you my lords will continue to protect your duchy in the manner they have already done. You might even be rewarded with a certain northern piece of Threle at some point in the future. Two casualties—enough, but not much loss, then. I don't think there will be much concern on either side, but if you need martyrs, well, two innocent crystal merchants are as good as any, and better than most; as your people are largely merchants themselves, they may take it personally. Who knows? I shall be sure to instruct my sources to start a rumor in Sunnashiven concerning Sina's having killed himself somewhere in the southwestern reaches. Grendel won't be missed, of course. I can get witnesses to claim to have worked with the caen in an attempt to

overthrow Helas. *Whatever kind of conversation you find useful to report, I'll coach somebody to be believable in. The loss of a town is regrettable and unexpected, of course, but I'm sure that Lord Roguehan will not be unhappy with the turn of events when you help him establish his own base there.*

I look forward to the day the northern peasants are speaking Botha.

El

"What do you think of all that, Llewelyn?" What was I supposed to think? I was too busy manifesting a copy of the note to send to Walworth to think of anything. I chose the second sheet in the pile, so El couldn't see what I was doing. What an absolute stroke of luck! Perhaps Cathe wasn't a bad sort after all. He had deposited me directly into enemy hands, and from here I could do all sorts of good for the cause. *Wait until Walworth gets a copy of this. Wait until King Thoren sees it.* El leaned over my shoulder, inspected my work, and signed it. I made sure to manifest his signature when he walked away.

"Postscript: This note is written in the hand of my scribe, who arrived here this morning claiming to be a citizen of your duchy. And thus is also signed by him." He paused. "Sign it."

Damn. If the Duke of Helas was in league with Roguehan, he didn't need to know I was here, scribing for El. I'd sent him enough messages for Walworth that he'd probably recognize my hand anyway. I signed it sloppily, hoping to obscure my name, and magically changed the slant of the characters. Better.

"Let me see." El inspected it, and while he was reading I pulled the copy I had made into my cloak and manifested the postscript—there. "Mmmm." He pulled out the note I had written this morning. "Your penmanship has undergone a bit of a sea change."

"My fingers were stiff and cold earlier. I feel better now. The food and warmth helped."

"All right, then." He folded the note and sealed it. "Cristo," he called down the hallway. Cristo emerged out of nowhere. "Bring in the courier."

"She's here, Master. Now."

"Good." I heard light footsteps. The courier entered the room. The courier was Trenna.

Trenna stopped in midstep and flushed a little when she saw me but instantly recovered her composure. "Take this back to the duke," said El, smiling. "Immediately."

"Yes, of course, Brother," she breathed, looking at me. "Hail Habundia."

"Hail indeed," echoed El. I noticed that Trenna was wearing bright yellow riding clothes that stylishly resembled a clerical robe. "Meet my new scribe. His name is Llewelyn. He wandered in from Helas this morning looking for work." He related to her the entire contents of my earlier note, including my having been a witch's apprentice. I felt her hanging on every word.

"Such a pleasure to meet you, Llewelyn from Helas." She extended her hand to me. Her voice was cool and bright. I noticed she was still wearing the ring of Aphrodite she had shown me months ago but not her wedding ring. I ignored the gesture and she withdrew her hand.

"Llewelyn will be scribing our southwestern correspondence."

She smiled and inclined her head in acknowledgment. "I'm sure the Duke of Helas will be pleased," she said politely. "But now I must go if I am to return to him tonight. I shall need help with my horse. Is Llewelyn free?"

"Go with her," said El affably to me. I was only too eager to do so.

Trenna and I walked silently and rapidly through the halls of the monastery and out onto the grounds. I saw Devon in the distance sitting cross-legged in front of his ice pillar, arms spread to the sun. I quickly checked his shield. It still held. He looked comfortable enough. Trenna spoke first.

"Apprentice witch from Helas!" She was laughing pleasantly. "Really, Llewelyn, what a stroke of luck to find you here. Now, am I right to assume that this is what I am to say to the duke, if I am to say anything at all?"

"What else *would* you say?"

She took some rose-colored apples out of her pocket and began eating them while looking at the sun, making me wait for her answer. "Pleasure apples," she said. "Every time I eat them I look at the sun and think of Sunna. Makes me feel love for my country."

"What country?"

"Oh, Llewelyn, I don't know. Don't be so analytical. They just give me pleasure. What's wrong with that? Aren't we all supposed to feel love for everything all the time? That's all the apples do. Make us feel what we're supposed to feel anyway. Everyone should eat them. They come from somewhere out west." Yes, from Furnesse, no doubt, Roguehan's birthplace. "Would you like one?"

"No." Pleasure apples—love apples! *Oh, no, poor Devon.* I'd made a grand mistake there. That was why he whined for me. Why hadn't I thought of that before? Trenna delicately slapped her hands together to clean them. "They're delicious. And very good for you. Quite an addiction, really. It's gotten so I must have them all the time. Now, where were we? Oh, yes. Thank you, sun; thank you, Sunna, for your pleasure; thank you, sweet Habundia the Slain One, and all of that. Oh, and Aphrodite, my love to you," she finished mechanically. "*Now*, where were we? Let's see. I could tell Helas nothing or I could tell him your story. Then again, I could tell His Excellency who you really are. Do you think he'd like to know?"

"I really *am* an apprentice witch. I took up in Helas with—"

"A witch named Lady Caethne, I know, and scribed for her brother—Walworth, is it?—and composed many a letter for my lord on behalf of your friends. And for all I know you are still working for them, hence your story.

Look, I don't much care, but surely it's worth something to you for me to keep silent and pretend we've just met."

"Why don't you just keep silent and pretend out of the love you claim to feel for everything?" I asked reasonably. "Am I not I included in your benevolence?"

"Well, yes, of course. Of course you are. Everyone is. But I still have a price."

I calculated the damage she could do. If the Duke of Helas was trying to pin a treason charge on Walworth, my letter could save my commander's life and Threle. But if Helas learned my true identity, it would certainly lend credence to Helas's claim that the note was a forgery. El would get believable witnesses to testify against Walworth. More likely I'd never see the outside of the monastery again. I wouldn't put it past Roguehan's people to force me to testify against my friends. I'd be the perfect witness, and I really didn't have any defenses against clerical magic. That was exactly the sort of thing the enemy would love to see.

Of course I'd die first. I'd kill myself if I had to. I knew how. But then I thought about what Cathe had said about Walworth's sustaining a second loss. Also, if I were dead, El would have no difficulty producing believable testimony on my behalf. *Damn!*

I thought about binding Trenna so that she could not speak about me. Perhaps I could use those apples as a trigger for forcing her affections in my direction, but she seemed clearly bonded through them to some vague concept of Sunna. It would take more skill than I possessed to wrench what passed for her heart from Sunna to me, considering I didn't even know what Sunna *was* anymore or what it meant to her. I wasn't even sure *she* knew what it meant to her, beyond feeling good. Also, I had no way of knowing if the spell would hold or for how long. A ban would be best but not very practical under the circumstances, because I lacked the materials and time for something that complicated. *Bind her tongue anyway—you've got nothing to lose.* "Trenna, Trenna—let me warm your sweet throat with my hands."

"Why?" She sounded scornful and puzzled.

"Because it's cold, so cold you can't speak properly . . . ne voxe lamen . . ."

"What's the matter with you? Can't you talk right?" she said impatiently. "Or are you just showing off by speaking in some language no one can possibly understand? Really, Llewelyn, I can't stand it when Helas's wizards do that. Why can't everyone just speak in plain Botha?"

"When Helas's wizards do what?"

"Every time I come and go one of the wizards mutters and fusses no end over me. Sometimes for hours. Really, I can't stand it." She sighed loudly, the way our mother often did, and shook her head. "It's *so* annoying. I get *so* irritated. I wish they'd stop. Really I do. You'd think I was royalty or something, the way they fuss over me." She was bragging more than complaining. I supposed she wanted me to think her special for being the frequent center of attention of Helas's wizards. They were probably just putting up the routine defenses any courier traveled with and checking them on her return. So much for my binding spell. Also, I was sure she didn't act so "irritated" around the wizards.

"Gee, Trenna, you're so humble. I admire you so much when you pretend through irritation that you don't think yourself good enough to consort with wizards. Helas's lackeys must be terribly stupid to make such a fuss over *you*. How silly of the poor chaps! Don't they know you're just a simple girl—I mean, young woman—from Sunnashiven and that you don't need or want their attention at all? But then, perhaps all these powerful people can't help but recognize how inherently wonderful you really are, and I'm sure they want nothing more than to do everything for you, even though you yourself are just so simple and natural and humble that you can't see your own special qualities for yourself. Life is just so good to superior people. And I suppose you've told them all exactly how you feel, being so simple and unassuming and all."

"It's all right, really," she snapped at me. "I don't mind *that* much. Besides, Helas says it's for my own good, my own protection. It's just—"

"That you feel you have to act humble. And because you don't really feel humility, the tension between act and feeling comes across as an irritation that you'd never express to the wizards for fear of losing the attention you can't admit that you crave. Which really *is* annoying. By the way, how's Seth? What does he think of your new exalted status?"

"Seth's dead. The duke had him killed after His Excellency started sleeping with me."

No false humility there. Trenna sounded proud enough for anyone's taste now. Which was equally annoying, because I honestly couldn't imagine the Duke of Helas having anyone killed for Trenna's sake. In fact, I couldn't imagine *anyone* having anyone killed for Trenna's sake. Seth had probably died in a skirmish somewhere or simply disappeared, and Trenna was vain enough to believe the duke had done something dramatic and romantic for love of her, just like a princess in a storybook. I knew through my own sources that Helas had a penchant for sleeping around and that he wasn't too particular, but it was still a bit of a shock to realize that he was bestowing that sort of attention on Trenna. Trenna, a duke's mistress! It was my turn to sound humble. "What's your price?"

"Llewelyn," she said sweetly, "I should so much like to be able to read. I should so much like to be educated. To know things. To be able to converse with people. I meet people and hardly know what to say."

"You want me to teach you?"

"Well, not exactly. I'm too old to learn now, I suppose. I don't have the time it would take. I would be happy if you would promise to read things to me. And write notes for me. In your beautiful handwriting. And since I know you know something of magic, a few favors once in a while would be appreciated."

"Like what?"

"Oh, I don't know yet. Nothing immediately comes to mind. But I do come to the monastery often, and if you can arrange to be available for me and do favors for me while I'm here, I won't tell Helas you're my brother and the same scribe who worked for Walworth. I won't interfere in anything you feel you need to do so long as you help me whenever I ask. And so long as you don't leave. You leave, I talk. And I talk quickly—to Brother El, to the duke, to everyone I know. And I'll reach people before you will. You know I will."

I considered Trenna's sudden foray into blackmail. Her motives eluded me, especially since she was so mindlessly infatuated with Sunna. Whatever unnamed favors she needed me for clearly had more sway with her than the love apples. I decided to make her wait for my answer.

"When did you leave Hala, the capital?"

"Sometime between midnight and dawn. It's not a long journey and I'm used to it. Why?"

I was calculating how long it took her to ride the distance, how quickly she could talk to the duke. This led me to thinking about the contents of El's letter and how incredibly fast news of the town's destruction had traveled. I knew that it would take a fast horse at least six hours to reach Hala from the market town. Aleta had been right. Helas was clearly a traitor. Did he have messengers around that Walworth wasn't aware of, and had one of them managed to survive the destruction? "When His Excellency gave you your message, did you notice if he had recently received another courier?"

"No, he came to my room, woke me out of a sound sleep, and bade me dress and take a message. I have no idea about it—why?" she asked impatiently. "Are you going to help me?"

I thought for a moment. "Why did the duke have to come to your room if you normally sleep with him?"

"Oh, Llewelyn, you can't take pleasure every night." She sounded uncertain. "Besides, he's been busy with the gods know what lately, and I hate to disturb him." I knew from her voice she didn't like the question, so I pushed on with one she'd like less.

"Why would a man who would order another man killed for love of you resent you disturbing his business affairs?"

Trenna suddenly went stiff in her riding cloak. Her voice got shrill and defensively exasperated. "Look, you don't know anything about it. His Excellency loves me," she insisted. "*I'm* his mistress, for Habundia's sake. But like most men, sometimes he can't help himself when women are always throwing themselves at him—and they always are, just because of his rank. He needs me to protect him against unscrupulous females—he really does. It's only for his own good that I know what his messages say, and who's writing to him, and that I'm able to send a few messages of my own if the need arises. And not just for him," she added unconvincingly, "but for Sunna and the rest of the southwest, too."

So despite her Aphrodite ring she was worried about losing the duke's favor and thought she might keep it if she made his personal affairs her business.

She continued speaking, "Last night he seemed to be listening to some wild-eyed tale told by a peasant woman who looked as though the wind had blown her in over the Drumuns. Why the duke is giving audience to commoners who have no more consideration than to wander in at any hour they please is beyond me! And she was wretched-looking—all torn clothes and tangled hair, as if she combed her hair once a year with a blackberry branch."

"Your concern for the Helan people is touching."

"I'm concerned, Llewelyn, I really am, but not in the middle of the night—and His Excellency is so busy with real problems anyway. Besides, she wasn't Helan. I don't even think she was from the southwest. Maybe she was Threlan, but who knows? She spoke Botha in an accent nobody could possibly understand. And she was disgusting. She carried this dirty little animal in her arms like a baby, and she kept hugging it close and crying. And it was the middle of the night, for the gods' sake! The animal looked like a woodchuck and it squealed to wake the gnomes out of the north. Who knows what her problem was? I didn't get too close to her, as she probably smelled or had some kind of terrible disease. But she was right there, whimpering to her—her—thing, while the duke wrote out the message. I'm sure she wanted money. They all do. Really, there ought to be a law."

So Caethne had not gone to her duchy the way we had planned. She had stayed around—sleeping in the woods, no doubt—waiting to see the end of things. I should have known, we all should have known, that she would never leave Mirand under the circumstances. Since she could not have made the journey in half a night by wagon she probably had unhitched one of the horses and left the wagon well hidden in the woods. But why was she going to the duke at all? Did she know that Helas was a traitor? Suddenly I remembered how her magic had served as a flag to Grendel concerning the headquarters, and I felt a sickness that had nothing to do with fever. No—Caethne was one of us, she had to be, I was sure of it. Almost.

"Come, Llewelyn, let's be friends as brother and sister are supposed to be. I need you. Will you help me and do whatever I say?"

"All right, Trenna. Deal."

"Good. Now, first favor. Read this note to me." I opened the seal and did so, then magically sealed it again. "Thanks." She paused. "That's awful, 'the loss of a town' do you know anything about it?"

"Yes, it's awful, and no, I don't."

She looked puzzled. "You'd better not, because if I find later that you do . . . I won't be lied to."

"Trenna, it was a market town on the border that exploded last night. That's all I know."

"The town near where His Excellency was sponsoring Walworth's little operation?"

"Yes."

"What *do* the northern peasants speak?"

"Sarana."

"What northern piece of Threle?"

"Walworth's duchy. What are you going to do with this information?"

"Oh, I don't know. I just like to know. I'm really so glad we've met again."

"Are there a lot of couriers arriving here?"

"I don't know," she said, as if she was threatened. "I'm the main one from Helas. Why?"

"Let's say I wanted to send a letter—home. How would I do that?"

"You wouldn't. Not from here. This is a cloistered monastery and the only missives in and out go through me or some other appointed courier with the permission of the clerics. Some of the students bribe people to take letters to town. But monastic residents aren't supposed to use the duchy's mail service."

"Why not?"

"Well, the Duchess of Kant probably wouldn't mind the extra income, as she runs the thing as a side business, but Threlans are extraordinarily scrupulous about respecting monastic rule. It's all part of separating religion from state business, you know. The various governments here respect monastic rules and refuse to interfere with them. Not like Sunna. So the duchess's mail drivers never come here. Monasteries are established to keep residents out of the world. You're not supposed to be contacting people on the outside." She sounded most self-righteous, thoroughly enjoying lecturing to me about some rule she had learned only as a consequence of her courier work. She really warmed to her subject. "Why, do you have a message to deliver?"

"No, I just had a passing thought about writing home sometime."

"Look, sweetie, I don't mind taking letters to town for you. Really I don't. Just tell me where to tell the coach driver to deliver them." *Yeah, right, so you can find a way to get the coach driver to read it to you.*

"I don't have anything now." Pause. "Trenna, do you have any pleasure apples left?"

"Two. Why?"

"Can I have them?"

"I guess so. Sure, brother, sure. Anything you want. What do you want them for?"

"To eat with the sun." I forced myself to smile. She gave them to me and I helped her mount, still smiling, glad as a lark's song to see her go.

It looked as though I really was going to be here for a while. At least until Walworth got this present trouble behind him and obtained Thoren's permission to openly organize the military against Roguehan. I'd have to be very careful. Even if my commander had gotten clear of the prior night's mess, I was in a vulnerable position. He couldn't just openly send for me without admitting I worked for him. And then, of course, I'd *never* get out of here. Cathe must do something, I thought. Cathe—now *there* was a reliable figure to pin my faith on. Damn Cathe, but what else did I have besides myself? I had to believe he would tell my commander I was here, for whatever good that might do. It wasn't as if I had any friends or allies here or a position of power to work from. I didn't even understand the damn language.

Clearly it was time to pay respects to next year's Sun King. I ambled over to Devon, who clapped his hands and greeted me with a broad smile. "Hungry, friend? These are on me." He swallowed the apples in three gulps. "Now, Devon, is it? Devon, Devon, Devon," I chanted softly. "King Devon, King of the Sun, Sun King, Sun King, powerful one . . ." The words were mostly nonsense to him but I knew the magic was there and that it would hold. I thought guiltily of Mirand but kept it up anyway. If Devon was going to run the place this year, why should I not run it through him? It could come in handy, and I might well need the extra help. Anything to get El's letter to Helas into the proper hands.

I'd never done anything like a love spell before but the kid was so stupid he was easy to work on. I'd need help getting messages out of the monastery to Walworth. I'd rule through Devon, just enough to get done what needed doing. And he'd be happy with it. Done. The kid loved and admired me. I was his hero. I just needed to keep feeding him apples when I felt the spell weakening.

When I returned to El he asked me what had taken me so long. I told him I had made obeisance to the Sun King. He sighed. "We'll all do that soon enough. Well, I have nothing more for you to do." He looked as if he was waiting for me to help him out.

"Brother El, where is the library?" He explained that there were several and that the students normally used one located in the outbuildings.

"You're not a student, of course, so you have no privileges here. Why do you want them?"

"I'd like to learn Kantish," I said brightly.

"If you wish to use the library in your spare time, I see no harm in that, so long as it doesn't interfere with your primary responsibility to me. Here's a permission letter." He scribbled something in Kantish. "I shall expect to find you there if I send for you. In fact, I expect you to keep me informed of where you are at all times, yes? I *don't* expect to have to pull out of you where you've been." His last statement could have come close to passing for a joke had his voice been brighter. As it was, he sounded tired.

"Yes, of course, Brother El."

"Llewelyn, since you *are* working for me, I don't object to being called 'master' once in a while. This *is* a place of respect, and familiarity doesn't look as good as it might elsewhere."

"Certainly, Master. Thank you so much for your permission. May I go now, Master?" I really put it on for him.

He waved his hand in assent. I sped back down to the underground room. No one was there. My sack lay on the bed where I had left it. As I opened it something red caught my eye: a square of red cloth tied with a red cord and embroidered neatly with black sun symbols. It was a packet of cloves. In the center was a piece of paper. It was signed *Love, Cathe.*

So my questionably aligned "savior" had crowned me Sun King. I dully supposed that if his plan had been for me to rule the monastery, he would have informed me of it, so I could only conclude that Cathe wanted me dead—sacrificed to the cold on monastic grounds where the Threlan government could neither investigate nor interfere. Like poor Devon, who through no fault of his own was now in my place, just as through no particular merit of my own I had once nearly been sacrificed in Cathe's place. Cathe probably hadn't counted on my ability to combine a witchworking with a wizard shield and so survive the day by keeping a little heat for myself. And if I were to strike off on my own toward Loudes, Trenna would destroy what slender hope I had of saving Walworth from a trumped-up treason charge.

Keeping Cathe's signature for future use, I burned the damn rag and tearfully watched the flames leap and die at my feet, riding my thoughts softly against the fierce margins of disbelief, riding my feelings hard against the knowledge I was trapped.

Fifteen

It was six weeks before a way presented itself to get the letter into Walworth's hands—six weeks of scribing for El and trying to gather as much incriminating evidence as I could against him and the Duke of Helas, six weeks of cramming as much Kantish as my infinite spare time would hold. Infinite in the sense of always approaching zero, that is, like two scrying surfaces throwing each other's reality into infinity, for when El didn't put me to work on his personal correspondence there were household accounts to copy or student records to maintain or a hundred other trivial tasks he seemed to think up to keep me busy. I was also expected to take care of his apartments, clean his clothes, make his dinners, polish his boots, run his errands, and help Cristo with anything Cristo didn't want to do for himself, which was most things. It even fell on me to care for Cristo's owl, an ill-tempered bird that was in the habit of biting.

I couldn't figure out Cristo or what his function was, and my Kantish was so poor I couldn't ask. At first I had thought he was an older student, because of his dress and because whenever I went about my chores I often saw him engaged in friendly conversation with other older students. However, I never once saw Cristo engaged in anything resembling study. His main work seemed to be seeking out and finding people to talk to. Not necessarily people who would listen to him, just people to talk to. Which is not a half-bad way to spend your time if you can manage it, I suppose. He seemed to especially like talking to Sister Elwyn, probably because Sister Elwyn had a marvelous trick of looking sympathetic and delightfully interested in anything anyone happened to say to her even as she was walking away to attend to something else. It's a useful talent to be able to look enthralled by people even as you ignore them, and Cristo seemed to be its chief beneficiary. So Elwyn got to practice her charms and Cristo got to talk to somebody, and in that sense it probably worked out even. Besides, Sister Elwyn was a good catch in that she seemed to attract large numbers of students. When Elwyn closed a door she usually left three or four students cluttering up the hall behind her who had nothing to do but wait for her attention and be talked to by Cristo. And as the composition of the line changed every quarter hour or so with new people, Cristo usually had it made for the better part of an afternoon if he could stake out Elwyn say, just before lunch.

And when that amusement wore thin there was always the doorkeeper. The doorkeeper appeared to be something of a last resort for Cristo, to be made use of only when no one else was available. But Cristo could go quite a long way on a last resort. After all, the doorkeeper was there, and the doorkeeper certainly wasn't going anywhere, and I suppose it's a fine thing to have something steady in your life you can depend on. I would spend an afternoon running errands to various outbuildings and Cristo would remain planted near the door, intently chattering away until even the keeper grew tired of grinning and bobbing. Night would fall and it would come time for me to take the wretched owl, and still Cristo would talk. I half expected him to pull up a cot and stay there since the doorkeeper was so amenable.

I'd seen him chattering away with some degree of gusto to a circle of young people so deep in trance they'd be hard pressed to hear a horde of hungry dragons chewing thunder cuds three feet overhead. And if no new opportunity walked by as the circle dispersed, Cristo would smoothly latch onto someone newly emerged from trance and blithely continue his conversation until a door stopped him. And then he would shift his weight, scratch his owl, look lost, stare up and down the corridor, and wait for the sound of footsteps, which always brought relief back to his face and motion to his tongue.

I once passed by Cristo on my way to clean the stables and thought I heard him speaking quite volubly to the remains of a god figure that the younger boys and girls had set up in the snow for Devon. And I don't think he was praying to the figure, which might have made some sort of sense. He was *practicing*. For as soon as I passed by him he followed me to the stables, uttering precisely the same sounds as he watched me work. And the strange thing was that the horses actually seemed used to him, for they kept nodding in affirmation as he spoke.

Anyway, I knew he wasn't a scribe, because he seemed to have a lot of free time. Yet El often gave him things to copy and Cristo occasionally took it upon himself to do El's household tasks, usually when El appeared to be working on something that required all his concentration, which allowed Cristo to make the most efficient use of his penchant for annoying people. Crashing logs and banging pots isn't nearly so much fun if you don't have someone's work to disturb with the performance. It's probably sheer ecstasy if you can claim to be offering "help."

I didn't think Cristo was a cleric, but El was forever giving him student papers to comment on, which I then had to copy. Also, I was greatly surprised once when I walked by a classroom and saw Cristo addressing younger students as if he was teaching, and the students dutifully taking notes. Also, Cristo would simply disappear for weeks at a time, only to reappear with a bundle of papers at the precise moment El was getting ready to retire for the evening.

I eventually learned from El that Cristo was a student slowly converging on priesthood. It wasn't obvious to me that Cristo was "converging" on anything, except maybe a good long life in monastic limbo.

Since El always spoke to me in Botha I did not have the advantage of being immersed in Kantish for the better part of my days and evenings, so the accounts I copied were gibberish to me. I could enter one of the students' libraries, but I was restricted to the library used by younger students, and I did not have permission to remove books. The other libraries were strictly off-limits to scribes. I found a Kantish-Botha dictionary designed for beginners that laid out the basic rules of Kantish verb conjugations and syntax and a Kantish grammar written entirely in that language, so I struggled through these when nobody else had them out and I could steal time away from El's endless tasks.

And then there was Devon, the new Sun King, whom I made it a point to keep well fed and happy—not that I could communicate with him yet, seeing as we had no common language. I painfully constructed a note to him in Kantish once, with the help of the dictionary, asking him to borrow the books for me, but Devon, being dumb as a stone, couldn't read it. I don't think he could read anything, but he looked up at me as if I were going to enlighten him as to the mystery of writing. I read the note to him in my horrible accent and he only looked confused, so I burned it, much to his delight. Since I wasn't supposed to have books out at all, I didn't think it wise to try to get another student to read it to him. It once worked out that

I had an opportunity to bring Devon with me to the library, and I was able through hand motions to get him to understand that I wanted these books. He eagerly took them up to the cleric who acted as librarian, and threw them down in front of her with such insistent ferocity that several students looked up sharply from their work. Devon was already used to being in charge. The cleric, however, promptly took the books away and sent him out the door. It seemed that Devon didn't have library privileges either, and it occurred to me that even the youngest students I saw using the library were slightly older than himself. He'd probably have to learn to read first. Clearly it would be a while before I could use him to get messages out.

But Devon had his uses. Whenever he could escape from his classes he would follow me about my chores or wait for me to emerge from El's apartments, and if I needed to deflect Cristo's attention away from me Devon was happy to tug at Cristo's shirt and be talked to. I never even had to explain what I wanted. The kid seemed to know instinctively when I needed to be alone, as the pleasure apples I created or got from Trenna made him uncannily aware of my moods. I felt a little guilty about manufacturing loyalty and admiration in him where none naturally existed for me, but hey, that's war; Threle was more important than one emotional casualty, and once I left the monastery and he was without pleasure apples the effects would most likely fade into a pleasant childhood memory. I couldn't let myself be touched by his devotion or think about the tears that would come in my absence and also give my full attention to the business at hand.

When Trenna made her routine stops, which averaged two or three a week, I had to keep her happy by reading notes and explaining things to her that I'd rather she knew nothing about. Whether through ignorance, spite, or caution, she provided me with no news, and it quickly became obvious that her interest in the messages extended only as far as their use in keeping rivals away from the Duke of Helas. Cathe did not return, nor to my knowledge did any of my friends attempt to contact me, so the only information I could glean concerning outside events came from copying El's Bothan correspondence, which I dutifully manifested copies of for my own purposes every time I took dictation, grateful for the cloak that hid my magic, always careful to disguise my writing lest Helas recognize it.

One night I created a stack of paper and brought it into the library with me for the express purpose of manifesting copies of the Kantish books so that I could keep them with me at all times. I performed the manifestation successfully at the cost of losing my only study time for the day, then shoved the copies into my cloak and hurried back to the main building through the darkness, willing to be unnoticed lest anyone stop me. When I returned to my wretched underground cot I noticed to my great dismay that my sack was missing, so I stashed my copied books under my blanket and spent the night damning the scrupulous honesty of the clerical community. Leave anything of value for any length of time in a monastery and someone will steal it, sure as peacocks have wings. I woke up in the morning with a bruise in my side only to notice that the thief had dropped the hard white pea I always carried—Grana's gift from childhood. So I put it in my pocket and grimly went to work cleaning El's floors and making his fire before he appeared with more work for me to copy.

That morning he gave me a stack of kitchen accounts, and after I had sat at the table for the better part of an hour copying the Kantish characters, he spoke into the silence. "Llewelyn, you should know that it isn't proper for a scribe to seem more studious than a clerical student. *Our* gods are pleased with decorum. Use the library if you must, but be discreet about it, please. With all those books you carry around, anyone might mistake you for a student, if you get my meaning." I did. Therefore I wasn't surprised to find my Kantish books missing when I returned to my cot. So El now knew I could create paper and manifest words. I didn't think he knew about my cloak, but from that day on I took precautions not to manifest *anything* in his presence. I would walk out with Trenna if he gave me permission to, or ask to go to the privy before she had put too much distance between us, and then do the work. Getting those letters down was the only thing that got me through those six weeks.

The reason I didn't just carry the manifested Kantish books around with me was that I was saving all the room in my cloak for the letters, which I couldn't leave unguarded under any circumstances, and the books were bulky enough to show. I certainly didn't need to be asked to open my cloak and reveal its contents to El or to anyone else.

I knew that Walworth's life, and possibly the future of Threle, literally depended on my success. I learned that Walworth had arrived in Loudes three or four days after the border town exploded, a journey that should have taken about a week according to the maps I was able to read in the library. He and Baniff must have ridden night and day, taking turns sleeping on their mounts. As soon as the Duke of Helas received El's first letter he made the trip to Loudes himself, arriving three days after Walworth and promptly and publicly accusing him of treason, that is, of attempting to incite a rebellion in the Duchy of Helas and plotting to overthrow King Thoren in order to claim the throne for himself. All absurd, of course, and at first I was confident that anyone who knew Walworth would never believe these things. I also took comfort in knowing that the *caen* had had a solid three-day lead time in which to present his side of the story to the king. It would be all right. It had to be. Then I thought about Caethne and my certainty softened.

It fell apart as I learned what a cunning case Helas was helping the enemy construct. The duke was prepared to deny ever giving the *caen* permission to run his operation from his duchy, which was to be expected. I was gratified to learn that El did not consider it worth the risk to bribe Walworth's regular couriers to lie. Most feared arrest and couldn't be found, for news concerning the upcoming trial had spread all over the kingdom. All were fiercely loyal and couldn't be relied on in court. The Duke of Helas had people of his own who were prepared to claim to have worked with Walworth and to testify to his secret plans to start a military invasion of the duchy and blame it on the peaceful southwestern kingdoms, which had never had anything but goodwill toward Threle and besides, were suffering enough internal problems to make invasion unlikely. Helas was going to claim that none of these people were really rebels but were instead his own spies, whom he had put into place when he discovered this northern intruder running an intelligence operation in his territory. They had forged documents in Walworth's handwriting showing that he intended to launch a propaganda campaign alleging that His Excellency was lax in his duchy's defense, and thereby gain the loyalty of the Helan people. There were more documents proving that the *caen* intended to make himself commander of the Threlan army by inventing evidence of some alleged infiltration of Threle sponsored by some relatively unknown warlord from Furnesse named Roguehan, whoever *he* might be. Some of these documents proved that Walworth had created a plan to convince the king that this infiltration was the prelude to an invasion and therefore constituted a clearly aggressive act. As commander of the Threlan army, he planned to stage an overthrow of the capital and make himself king. He and Mirand had destroyed the border town themselves to make their claims more convincing.

Worse, Walworth's claim that Sina and Grendel had already entered the Duchy of Helas as agents of a hostile foreign power intending to establish a secret base there was going to be refuted through the testimony of young Franko. Franko had agreed to claim that he saw his father in the Kingdom of Sevalas in a state of deep depression two days after the town was destroyed, and that Sina had committed suicide. King Sevalas himself was prepared to make the trip and confirm Franko's story if necessary. Cathe—dependable Cathe—could certainly testify to having traveled with and seen both Grendel and Sina, but the thought of Walworth's life depending on Cathe's testimony did not inspire confidence. I also learned that Zelar had survived the blast he had taken, ridden his horse to Hala, and taken up residence with the duke while he recovered. I had no idea if he would be at the trial. As best as I could tell, Roguehan wanted a conviction, which, under Threlan law, would put Walworth's inheritance directly under Helas's control. If Caethne was in league with the enemy, and I still couldn't completely bring myself to believe that she was, Roguehan would have gained control of both the southernmost and northernmost duchies in Threle without having to spill one jot of blood. A rather civilized form of warfare, I must admit.

And so I had to get those letters to Walworth, some of which bore El's signature as well as my own obscured hand, and some of which bore the duke's, for I made it a point to manifest copies of everything Trenna delivered. At the end of six weeks I had quite a packet. All I needed was a secure way to deliver it.

It was Brother El himself who presented me with the opportunity I needed, about a week before the trial was to be held. I entered his apartments with my habitual servant's smile. My arms were weighted down with a wicker basket of Cristo's clothes; I had just spent the morning cleaning the incense smell out of them after some strange ritual of the previous night. Cristo promptly grabbed the basket and pushed his dirty flapping owl into my morning's work, muttering as he shuffled through the door. There was the remainder of a stack of student reports on the table that I hadn't gotten all the way through on the previous day, so I sat down to another dismal day of copying. I had gotten through half a page when El came out of his private chambers, stood in the doorway with his hands behind his back, and stared at me for about a quarter hour. I kept up the copying and pretended to ignore him, although the unexpected close scrutiny terrified me.

"Hmmm, Llewelyn. Good morning. But we are a bit slow today, aren't we? Hmmm?"

"Slow, Master? I'm sorry I haven't finished the reports yet. I'm doing my best."

"How disappointing. But then, surely you don't think I'm talking about the reports? Students are used to waiting. The best of them will wait for years to begin their lives, so the worst of them will certainly wait a few days for their modicum of compliments. Like 'winter fish waiting for worms,' yes?"

"Pretty phrase, Master."

"Yes. It's not original, of course." Nothing in a monastery ever is. "And it doesn't translate as well as it might. In Kantish the poet employs a wonderfully cheerless onomatopoeia, 'schincherpas hashamcher schuchen schensch.' Brilliant, really."

"I'm sure. Is schincherpas 'fish'?" I asked politely.

"Sort of. Four centuries ago it punned with the word for 'student.' Schensch was both 'worms' and an exclamation people used when a lover's promise proved false. It also meant 'a little death,' or the base feeling that bolsters disappointment. Hence my point. Students will wait—forever, if need be." He entered the room and sat at his desk. "Anyway, come. I only meant to say that surely you've ascertained that today is the day we ride for Loudes, and that you and I are to be at Caen Walworth's trial. You really do disappoint me. I thought you were sensitive enough to the business' at hand to know without being told that you should be packing for our journey already." It was an effort to keep copying, to keep up a silence that felt like mild chagrin at my oversight and nothing else. "Or do I sense an admirable reluctance on your part to see your old friends again?"

"Master?" I said with all the naive brightness I could summon up over my rising pulse.

"Your old *friends*, Llewelyn." He paused. I became acutely conscious of the scratching of my pen. "I mean in a general sense, of course. Fellow residents of Helas, yes? I thought that since you were from the duchy you might be eager to see justice done in the case of this would-be traitor from northern Threle. But who knows? Perhaps you really hold no love for Helas; perhaps you prefer to have nothing to do with the place, thank you, and would rather stay here quietly and . . . copy things. Which, of course, is admirable. Quite admirable."

"I would like nothing better than to see justice done, Master."

"Yes, right." I heard him shuffling papers. "Or even to see your old mistress again, perhaps."

"If she's there," I said nonchalantly. "She doesn't travel much."

"No, of course not." He laughed his odd empty laugh. I swear that all high priests must receive formal training in laughing as though they had a reed pen stuck through their tongue. They would have to take lessons to get it down right. "And how *do* you feel about watching the trial, I wonder. After all, it is in part the result of your hard work here. When we gain a successful outcome you shall rightly be able to congratulate yourself for your part in easing the communications path." I felt him studying my back intently, so I shielded myself under my cloak. "Turn around and look at me, Llewelyn."

I did so. Slowly. "Master?"

"Let me put this proposition to you. Better, let me *say* to you that you are to testify at the *caen*'s trial next week. You are to stand before king and court and swear your soul upon the truth, that you were once an apprentice to Walworth's old tutor Mirand, that you have often scribed treasonous letters for Walworth himself, that you were present at secret meetings when the destruction of the border town was discussed, and that you have often heard the *caen* discuss his plans to usurp the throne. In fact, you shall be given several letters in court to identify as authentic. It's nothing to me if you wish to maintain your Helan identity. Your accent is certainly convincing enough, and claiming to be acting out of loyalty to the Duchy of Helas would not be a bad thing. In fact, a few well-placed patriotic tears for Helas and Threle would be a most impressive touch, if you can pull it off. *Now* tell me how you feel." He leaned back and delicately placed the tips of his fingers together, studying me.

"Fine," I said evenly, dropping my accent. "I'll do it." And of course I would stand up and read the letters I was carrying, and that would be that. Good-bye Brother El.

El looked slightly surprised, an unusual expression for him that consisted mainly of slightly widening his left eye. "Fascinating. However, I must admit my utter perplexity. Do you like it here so much—wasting your fine mind in tasks that an animated rock could perform almost as well—that your loyalties have suddenly shifted?"

"No, I hate it here," I said simply, surprising myself with my cleverness. "I detest the monastery, the work, and yourself. I'm better than any of this. You know it. And Walworth knows it." Unexpectedly bringing up Walworth was risky, but since El had just revealed he knew of my past relationship with the *caen* and was willing to use that relationship as a weapon in court,

I decided to chance appearing as if I bore Walworth a personal grudge. Perhaps if El thought I was genuinely cooperative with his plans, he would refrain from probing into my mind.

"Yes." He seemed surprised and pleased. "Go on."

"I wouldn't even be here, slaving away at this animated rock's work, as you call it, if it weren't for Walworth's damned cousin, Lord Cathe. He's the one who deposited me here six weeks ago and told me to take sanctuary, may he rot with the grain in the belly of a dead rat!"

"Ah, so you blame Cathe for your unfortunate condition and wish to exact vengeance on the entire family, yes? Llewelyn, you astonish me! Does your hatred truly know no bounds?"

"None." I was really working up a heat now. "Besides, Walworth is just as bad as Cathe. He's spent six weeks under guard in some comfortable royal tower, with more resources at his disposal than the gods have time, I'm sure, and one would think that with all his couriers and connections he could have seen fit to get some kind of message to me, to send for me. He could have sent Cathe. Or Caethne. Or anyone. You and I know that the king hasn't prevented him from communicating with anyone. But of course he's forgotten me. I'm a Sunnan commoner, so who cares? I only left country and kindred for his personal ambition and glory, so that he could set himself up as some Threlan folk hero saving his people in secret—like some king out of legend. Yes, and I didn't even get paid like a lowly mercenary. Not a cow's farthing! And the way I see it, if that's the way it is, if I'm to clean privies here at his pleasure and dream for the rest of my life of once having had the high and holy privilege of shining his armor, we'll both hang. I really don't care."

"Wonderful! This is easier than anyone thought it would be. Excellent, indeed. Unexpected, but excellent all the same. Hmmm. Well, you won't hang; Helas will say he knows you, that you were working for him all along." *Terrific*, I thought, *just the sort of thing I've been working six weeks to avoid.* "Of course, some of us had hoped that you still harbored a little loyalty toward your old commander. Enough to make it painful for you to testify against him. We had thought of using a little clerical force, mouthing words through you while you inwardly denied them—but perhaps this will do nicely. The former would have taken some work and risk."

"I like your idea about pretending loyalty to Helas and Threle. Threle is Walworth's weak spot, and I'm sure it will hurt him greatly to see his old servant from Sunnashiven come across in court as more loyal to Threle than he is." I grinned what I hoped would come across as a conspiratorial, twisted smile. El seemed to believe me.

"Hmmm, perhaps. Not a bad angle. Well, if you're skillful enough, I shall reward you myself. How would you like student privileges in all the monastic libraries, and two hours each day to study Kantish?"

"You are generous, Master. Count on me to make my loyalty a sticking point in court."

"I will, my boy, indeed I will." He still seemed a little taken aback by my unexpected enthusiasm. "Well, then there's nothing more to say, is there?" El scribbled something. "Here's a note asking the cooks to give you a week's supply of food. For three. I have decided that Cristo will accompany us, as I wish him to take an academic interest in the kind of personal dynamics at play here." He studied me as I eagerly took the note. "You realize, of course, that I have not dismissed the idea of using clerical force on you should it be necessary after all."

I nodded and shrugged in feigned nonchalance.

"So be it, then. When you return from the kitchen you will help Cristo pack what is needed for our journey. We will leave as soon as practical."

"Yes, Master, of course. Anything you say."

*I*t was a long tense journey to Loudes. El was clearly timing things so that we would arrive just before the trial was to commence and not a day sooner. We kept an excruciatingly leisurely pace on the road, stopping in small inns and monasteries every night. Since El was a dedicated high priest of Habundia and scrupulous about restricting his diet to fruit and grains, and Cristo was aspiring toward his own dedication to Habundia's priesthood, the three of us ate only from the food packets we brought with us, which made the inns an especially painful experience around dinnertime. I had been living off moldy potatoes and cabbage and watery sorrel soup ever since I entered the monastery. Having to content myself with dried pears and corn kernels while watching Threlans dining on stuffed trout, warmly ostentatious pasties, bread-and-plum puddings whose dangerous sweetness clawed at me from six tables away, and all manner of curious local dishes that changed from duchy to duchy was, well, a *schensch*, a little death.

It takes an organized priesthood to convince people that the goddess of abundance is best served by abstaining from abundance, but then, it takes an organized priesthood to make most absurdities believable.

I silently vowed to gorge myself in honor of the old Habundia Ceres with all the food and drink I could find after this whole dismal business was over. I promised myself that as soon as I was reunited with my friends after the trial I would indulge my appetite with fish and chicken and cheese and rutabaga pie and all the delicacies Threle had to offer. I'd definitely get drunk. And stay drunk. For as long as possible.

The only thing worse than stopping in public places and seeing Threlans laughing and eating while I had to remain a virtual prisoner of El was having to watch Cristo pretending to laugh and enjoy his food packets in a pathetic attempt to prove that he wasn't a prisoner of El. At least, *prisoner* is my term for it, for Cristo was clearly afraid of his teacher.

When El laughed Cristo made polite ingratiating laughing sounds, always a second later and always intent upon stopping and smiling when El stopped. Cristo was definitely afraid of humor, for he never said anything in a tone or with a facial expression that suggested levity, and El never greeted his words with a smile. He never initiated conversations but seemed to feel bound to drone on in a tone of interminable anxiety whenever El asked him anything. He ate at the precise instant his master ate and stopped before El took his fill, as if to impress him with his ability to abstain from food. Then he would secretly devour the remains of his food packet late at night when El was sleeping, which was sort of sad. Cristo never even went to the privy unless El did it first, and even then he'd look guilty about it. I noticed too that whenever we stayed in inns Cristo was inhumanly fastidious about sitting stiffly attentive to his master and not paying attention to our surroundings, unless El happened to point something out to him, which he seemed to do frequently.

Cristo's shuttered intensity was too bad in a way, because we traveled through almost a dozen duchies and every one of them was fascinating in its own right. The people didn't just dress and speak differently in each one, but they kept different spaces about themselves and sat differently at table and walked at different speeds and took different periods of time for exchanging greetings. Threle charmed me in patches. My six weeks in the monastery had deprived me of witnessing so many of the ordinary occurrences of life that I found myself jealously devouring every mundane particular moment of living I could steal around El's watchfulness. And I learned that the stolid charm of the border town I had loved in Helas does not exist anywhere else in the mercantile duchies of southern Threle. Charm does not translate. Charm has a thousand varieties, of which all speak out on their own terms in their own locales or not at all.

In the Duchy of Medegard I watched a charming game being played by the children of guests at an inn. The children light the inn candles when dusk falls and the other guests make a game out of giving them candles to hold to the main fire. It seemed that no child could light a candle until he or she came up with a word that rhymed with a word one of the guests pronounced. But once having made a rhyme, the child could hold up the light for all to see. The game cheered me a little because it reminded me of the word games I used to enjoy with my companions, and so I decided it signified my success in the trial, which of course would be one grand word game. I was also charmed to notice that all Medegard towns have a tree in the center surrounded by a low stone wall and that people throw coins at the trees as they pass. Sometimes people stand on the walls and make speeches and then gather up the coins. The practice felt in spirit like the candle game, and I was intrigued to see one speechmaker actually hold up a candle in fun after she gathered up the coins. *May her victory be mine*, I thought.

When I walked the streets in the towns of the Duchy of Glamisson the very stones and buildings talked to me. I was startled to hear the noises, and El explained that there was a local legend concerning a wizard who wanted to build a living monument to his witch wife's beautiful voice and so constructed singing streets and walls in each town. I guess not everyone hears the singing streets in Glamisson nowadays, even though it's something tourists listen for. You have to be sensitive and the conditions have to be right.

El seemed sort of impressed that I heard Threle singing here, and I grew a little nervous wondering if my ability to hear the music betrayed my love of Threle, because I was sure the two were one. So I resolved to keep the rest of my impressions of the kingdom safely to myself, to carefully guard the borders of my heart.

But even so Threle had a way of reflecting my heart's resolve. Most Threlan duchies do not mark their borders, but a few of them, such as Sengan and Medegard, do as a formality. In Sengan they welcome you with an acorn and a kiss. Cristo did his best to avoid the kiss and looked so confused concerning what to do with his acorn that I took it off his hands. Cristo seemed to be confused by all the duchies, but Sengan appeared to be an especially difficult prospect for him. I decided that was because aesthetically the entire duchy felt very much like an acorn and a kiss, an odd juxtaposition of barren rocky mountains, which split southern Threle off from the rest of the country, and seductive snow-covered valleys, which led gently north to the Midlands. Everything in Sengan was hard or soft. For me, everything reflected the extreme division between what I truly felt and what I dared show for El.

And then there's the Midlands, where it hits you as soon as you emerge from the mountains and cross out of Sengan's extremes that there is a good deal of emptiness. In the Midlands there are no small towns; there are only plains and immense cities. And unlike the small towns of southern Threle, they all have names, such as Disenward, Elasak, Ingnothum, Threlanche, and Loudes. It can take days to cross some of them. Once you cross through Threlanche—which is a small city by Midlands standards, as it only takes about twelve hours to cross—you ride over sparsely populated plains for two days before the red towers of Loudes suddenly break upon the distant sky.

Threle is really an absolutely fascinating kingdom. I found it odd that an aspiring young scholar such as Cristo wasn't in raptures of curiosity concerning all the new things around him. But he seemed to fear curiosity as much as he did humor. He acted as if any show of interest in the world around him was tacit admission of so much energy not put into his studies. He seemed to regard curiosity as personal failure. I never once heard him say anything that sounded like a question.

Only the monasteries remained pretty much the same, and Cristo always made it a point to look admiringly at whatever tattered and broken relics adorned their walls. I presumed this was calculated to show off his "seriousness" and single-minded devotion to the priesthood.

Yet, in all fairness, we were not traveling under circumstances conducive to easy sociability, and I myself was careful not to appear too curious or intrigued by what I saw lest El find my interest worth remarking. Also, much of what I read from Cristo was guesswork, as he and El only spoke to each other in Kantish, although after a few days I got the impression that El found Cristo's practiced myopia a bit wearisome, as he would often repeat explanations to me in Botha after failing to elicit more than a brightly empty attentiveness from his protégé.

On the night before we were to enter Loudes we were staying in a monastery somewhere in the plains outside the city, and El appeared to be lecturing to Cristo in Kantish. I heard him say something that sounded like a question; Cristo, apparently as a response, stood up, bowed his head slightly, and left the room. I had been tending the fire and thinking about the next day's events, hardly able to believe that by this time the following night everything would be as it should be, as I would have it be: El and the Duke of Helas would be facing trial, and Walworth and Baniff and Caethne and I would be organizing an army. In my fantasy Caethne had reassured me of her loyalty. We were all living and working together in Loudes with the king's blessing, and Aleta was making frequent visits, and all was right with the world again. I wasn't even thinking of the trial ahead, for in my mind that was already won. I was impatient to get on with it. To not have to live on dried pears anymore. To see the only people in the world I cared anything about.

El sighed, linked his fingers together, and stretched his hands toward the fire. "Ah, yes. Cristo is a good kid—means well, he does—but frankly, it's about time he was out of here. The monastery, I mean. You'd think he'd want to get on with his life. Well, who knows?"

I didn't know how to respond to this unexpected bit of familiarity, especially since I wasn't sure whether El was testing me for a reaction. Something in his tone seemed genuinely wistful, which was passing strange until I remembered that evil clergy were expert at adopting agreeable if not deferential voices to encourage confidences. I had no idea if he was deliberately adopting this tone with me to gauge my reaction or if there was some unexpected dimension to his personality that I was suddenly privy to. I responded brightly, "I thought students will wait, Master. Like 'schincherpas hashamcher.'"

"Hm? Well, yes, I see you get my meaning. But it's a shame, really. Not that it's for me to sound paternalistic. Cristo's a big boy." For the first time since I'd known him I was reminded that El was a Threlan, for despite his religious bent he was loath to interfere in Cristo's sluggish life. Then he shook his head and his next words destroyed my passing thought. "Well, so long as he wishes to waste his life in Kursen pursuing a calling he has no aptitude for, I suppose it's my calling, in service to the Goddess, to encourage him. Waste is waste." He said this in a tone I can describe only as sadly sardonic, as if he simultaneously both regretted Cristo's lackluster scholarship and relished the opportunity to please his goddess by wasting a life. "Don't know what he's going to do at the trial tomorrow. Not sure he knows either. Not even sure his Botha is good enough to understand what's going on."

Threle has no official common language, and since the principal participants in the trial spoke Botha, that was the language the court was going to use. Which meant, of course, that Helas and his people had another advantage over Walworth. Especially since Walworth no longer had Mirand to speak for him. "So Cristo speaks Botha, Master?"

"No, he reads it. So he says. With a dictionary. It's been a while since I've seen any from him. At one time he was interested in Sunnan history but that seems to have fallen off the cotton wagon too. I just wish he'd finish his paper. Sometime."

"What is his paper about?" I ventured to ask.

"I'm not sure. It seems to change with the seasons. I had suggested he compare the aesthetics of treason to the aesthetics of loyalty, but now he tells me he wants to write on why Glamisson women don't wear jewels. And the class was two years ago. I hardly remember it at this point myself. Aah, what can you do?"

I laughed because the situation was funny and El seemed to want me to. Or want somebody to. Like I said, it was very strange. Also, my mood was lifting as the trial got closer.

"Was it a class on treason?"

"No, oh, no." El laughed. It was a genuine laugh, the first I'd ever heard from him. "It was a class on self-sacrifice. The Aesthetics of Murdering One's Life, it was called."

"Guess it worked. I'd pass him." I bit my tongue as soon as I said this, for fear that El would rebuke my familiarity, but he seemed to appreciate it this time. Maybe after being a week on the road with Cristo he was lonely for a receptive audience—I don't know.

I do know there was an unexpected current twisting through his laugh, as if El didn't merely enjoy the simple pleasure of wasting the lives of willing dunces such as Cristo but relished it beyond the requirement of his profession. I decided it was personal, that it was his private revenge on those students who insisted on taking clerical orders while failing to meet his rigid academic standards. He loved his calling to evil with the same intensity Mirand had loved his calling to teach. I still hadn't forgotten how Mirand had been capable of simultaneously disowning me and teaching me. El was capable of encouraging Cristo to murder his life in pursuit of an occupation he had no talent for by gustily teaching him. But at the same time I think he would have been overjoyed had Cristo suddenly demonstrated a real aptitude for clerisy and a genuine calling toward evil.

I also decided that he was hungry for intellectual companionship and that for some reason I couldn't yet fathom he found it hard to come by in Kursen.

However, he made it clear by standing up that he wasn't going to discuss

Cristo's lack of progress with me any further. He took a brightly colored scroll down from a shelf and motioned me toward him.

"Here, Llewelyn, look at this. Copied from the work of one of your countrywomen. Extraordinary color and proportion, yes. The copier doesn't quite do justice to the original, which hangs in the king's palace in Sunnashiven—have you seen it?—but he got the red pools by Her wrists and feet perfectly. Uncanny, really. It's almost as if Habundia's blood casts a shadow here, hmmm? But it's a shadow the weeping children turn to as if for comfort—none of them quite look toward the sun do they?"—I shook my head. "And their bodies so pale and cold one would think their very desire for warmth would draw them there, it beckons so sensuously through the broken wall."

"Perhaps it's their desire for warmth that draws them to Her blood. They're so intent on catching it in their chalices that they can't see Her hair, which really is what draws the viewer's eye first and forms the eternal crux of the painting and the universe: Is the Goddess's hair blocking the children's only source of warmth or is it the divine burnt offering that makes all sustenance possible? I love the ambiguity." I was getting all excited now. "And of course, nothing is clarified by the young cow with the corn stalk in her mouth. She's facing the sun but she's closing her eyes against it, so is she really shutting out the sun or drinking it in? Likewise, is she eating the corn or spitting it out, feeding herself or fasting? Was the Goddess eaten and thrown away as wanting or does She want—or is She Want? And are the children bathing Her in Her own blood to restore life and warmth to Her or bleeding Her into some hardened divine oblivion?" I could easily have gone all night with it—I'm sure I could even have outtalked Cristo on this one— and El sat listening to my lecture with a look of sheer delight and pleasure.

"Yes, I see that, and so Llewelyn, tell me—since I listen to you and feel like I'm standing in Sunnashiven and seeing the original painting again for the very first time—if the cow was giving milk, what would the milk taste like?"

"To whom?"

"To the children, to us—to anybody, say. Since you read this painting as a comment on the universe, I'm not sure the point of view, or of taste, I should say, would matter. It would be a constant, wouldn't it?"

"I'm sure one could argue that each child or viewer would taste the same thing differently, since each approaches the Goddess from a different angle. So let's just say their identical appearance and differing approaches provides another example of the painting's ambiguity. Given that assumption, then, the milk wouldn't have a taste, at least at first. It would scald and freeze the tongue, and then the veins, and then the body, and then, tragically, this being a visual work, the eyes. And once the alternations reached a beautiful pitch of intense violence, it would probably taste like tastelessness—like fine gray dust. But the artist put no milk there, Master."

"Hmmm, true." He turned the scroll. "I wonder, though, if that was—"

Cristo walked in and spun the room into silence, a new and strange experience for him, no doubt. He was carrying a pile of blankets. El said something to him in Kantish and Cristo spread them out on the floor before joining us to look wordlessly at the scroll. As I turned back to tend the fire El was speaking to him in a buoyant tone while Cristo fished around for paper. Then I saw Cristo politely taking notes. It was incredible. Even his enthusiasm was polite. Nice enthusiasm from a nice kid. He clearly didn't understand day one about the painting, but he did understand that he should look attentive and take notes. How would he ever think and feel without El?

It was a passing question, and it would be amusing to find out sometime, but I didn't plan to be around after the next day and it really wasn't worth a great deal of my attention. In a short while El would be dead, I would be dedicating my mind and magic to saving the kingdom from invasion, and Cristo—well, Cristo would be talking to the doorkeeper. It promised to be a happy ending for all.

Sixteen

El had timed our arrival beautifully, for I had barely been seated next to the Duke of Helas in the section reserved for his witnesses when Thoren made his entrance, grunting and panting his way to the top of the dais with the support of his queen, Freda. The king did not look as though he particularly wanted to be there. He was clearly experiencing a good deal of physical discomfort, and he had audibly grumbled twice at Freda's difficulty in getting him up the platform. Freda responded to his grumbling with what sounded like a sharp admonishment that got laughter from the spectators and annoyed looks from Thoren. The king rolled his gaze over the ceiling and stared resignedly at the main entrance as the hoots and chuckles spread through the first three rows and his queen nodded with vigorous contentment.

Thoren said something tiredly to a young man who was standing near him on the dais. The young man responded by loudly swearing at the queen in perfect Botha, which elicited a good deal of laughter from everyone in the witness section, including Helas. I took it that this was the king's translator. Now it was Thoren's turn to look satisfied.

The six judges, who I understood had been selected from the Duchy of Helas because of the need for fluency in Botha, hadn't bothered to stifle their laughter during the translator's outburst. I wondered what they thought of life in the capital. The courtroom certainly possessed a rather alarming informality, and I wasn't convinced that this would work in our favor. Would Thoren even listen to Walworth, or would he think about his physical discomfort and how irritated he was with his wife? I also wasn't convinced that a slate of Helan judges would work in our favor, even though I was aware they were powerless to do anything but make recommendations to Thoren.

The bench reserved for the accused was empty. I hoped Walworth wouldn't be brought into the courtroom in chains like a common thief, and I began to heartily resent the tone of the whole thing. Walworth would be pleading for his life, and for Threle itself, really, and the Threlans he faced execution for trying to save were now laughing and placing bets on who would win the latest royal marital squabble. One fellow was waving a white handkerchief around and taking coins. Freda proudly gave him two. She was going to win, and no mere treason trial was going to start until she did.

I studied the other spectators who were crowding the room. El and Cristo had been seated near the back, as they were not going to be testifying, and I hoped that there would be guards at the door to prevent El from escaping once I read the letters. That worried me a little. The Duke of Helas looked impatiently confident. He knew he was going to win, but he clearly wished the business was behind him, for he would occasionally glance quickly between the judges and the back entrance and his chest shuddered a little as he breathed. I tried to imagine what Trenna saw in him besides his title. Then I tried to imagine what he saw in Trenna, and gave up. It must be sex. With all the manufactured evidence to support his accusations, I found it fascinating that he didn't look as relaxed and affable as El, who was leaning against the back wall and studying the marble tracery across the ceiling. I decided that Helas was a bit of a coward. And I decided that cowardice probably accounted for much of whatever was going on between him and Trenna, Trenna's Aphrodite ring notwithstanding.

Somewhere a bell rang. I was relieved to see two or three guards amble through the doorway by which Thoren had entered and make their way to the back entrance. They did not close the entrance door right away but chatted with some of the spectators in the back. They even tossed some smiling comments to El, who nodded affably and waved seconds before Cristo did. It seemed an eternity before the guards finally did close the door, only to abruptly open it once more and admit a breathless Lady Aleta with Sir Perie at her heels.

Aleta looked searchingly over the heads of the spectators. When she saw me sitting next to Helas in the witness section her glance broke; shock shattered her rushed intentness into a jelled loathing as she and Perie clumsily made their way to the middle of the seated spectators, where I noticed for the first time a familiar mess of hair that had been hidden behind the shoulders of a tall man sitting in front. O sweet gods, Caethne was there, and why wouldn't she be, but it was excruciating to see her and not be able to speak to her. Aleta's loathing I could deal with, knowing that soon all would be set right and I could probably tease her about it for months, but I couldn't bear Caethne's thinking ill of me for even a minute. Then I wondered why she wasn't on trial with her brother, and I thought of her secret visit to Helas and found myself swallowing sticky lumps of uncertainty. She did not look in my direction.

Caethne was seated between an elderly couple who made room for Aleta, and as they shifted their positions on the bench I got a better view of them. I knew immediately that this was the Duke and Duchess of Walworth, Caethne's parents. The poor duchess was miserable, shaking and trembling so badly that Caethne had to keep holding her arm to keep her on the bench. The duchess was crying and drying her face in her sleeves, and Sir Perie reached over and gave her a piece of cloth, which she promptly buried her face in. Perie sniffed and stared in the distance as if he felt he had been impolite to notice her tears and was now making up for it by pretending not to notice anything.

Aleta looked concerned, but she was also doing her best to distance herself from Caethne as much as the crowded bench would allow. The old duke's cheeks were gray and puffy and he held to his daughter the way I realized I was holding to the letters. *Soon, now, soon,* I wanted to say, *and all your tears will be for naught.* I wanted to try to throw a thought at Caethne, on the off chance that before focusing on witchcraft she had once learned enough wizardry from Mirand to receive it, but I didn't dare because of El and whatever wizards Thoren might have about. My defense was worse than useless if it came out that we knew each other, that I was a "spy." I not only had to read the letters but prove they were original. I worried that Helas might try to argue they were forgeries concocted by one of Walworth's people; it was bad enough that he was going to claim that I worked for him, because of course at one time I did, and seeing as El clearly knew my real history, there was no reason to believe now that Helas didn't.

The bell rang again and I thought they were finally going to get on with it, but the guards opened the door and a pudgy, uncomfortable-looking man entered and made his way straight over to Aleta. He was also out of breath, and Perie stood up straight as he entered, sitting only when he sat. This had to be Count Clio, Aleta's father. *Nice of him to come,* I thought. *Perhaps his daughter has finally convinced him to take Roguehan's threat seriously.* The guards then closed the door, formed a row in front of it, and nodded to Thoren, who was looking most impatient. He banged a short rod three times on the table in front him and silence fell upon the room with the exception of the Duchess of Walworth, whose sobs were now audible to all.

Enter about a dozen guards through the king's entrance, flanking the accused. It was not until the guards removed themselves to stand at the further wall that I got a clear view of Walworth. He was seated in the section directly opposite me across the open floor space, before the judges. We caught each other's glance for an accident of a second before Walworth impassively looked to Thoren as if I didn't exist for him. Right now I was just one more of life's little hurts.

Sitting next to Walworth was Baniff. He kept his gaze on me for a few seconds, then pulled his legs up onto the bench and twisted his body around to gaze ruefully at the wall behind the dais. He looked to be blaming himself for something—for *me*, probably—and his expression was as close to a look of guilt as I'd ever seen on him. He also looked sober, which I'm sure didn't help his mood any.

I looked around the courtroom and saw that Caethne was again blocked from view and that the duchess had stopped sobbing as soon as her son came into sight. Cristo was taking notes. Then my gaze fell back to the opposite section again and there, shredding the day out of reality, coming in between two guards and being seated next to Baniff, was—incredibly—Mirand.

But Mirand is supposed to be dead! That was my first thought before astonishment leapt over what should have been joy and fell bleeding upon the thorns of resentment. Resentment for the king and court, that is. Resentment for Thoren's wizards, who had saved Mirand from the brink of death only to bring him to stand trial for his life!

"*I* mean, my lord, when you think about it, how damnably unnatural."

Walworth remained impervious to the irony I was baiting him with. His studied neutrality infuriated me.

"I mean *aesthetically*, my liege! How needlessly overdone! How shatteringly baroque! How jejunely melodramatic! How unnecessarily complicated and flatly redundant! How *wordy*! Justice should have a simple, even beauty about it, don't you think? Justice should be as balanced and steady as a Helan merchant counting his lots, as the several varieties of truth. Justice should not be radically imposed upon intimate natural processes for the cold satisfaction of some legalistic state-approved system. How typically and irritatingly Threlan!"

My judge glanced coolly at his sword arm. It was his only comment.

"Set this down. Seeing Mirand temporarily destroyed the real context of the trial for me, which should have been the opportunity I now had to save him with the truth of my words. Instead, I found myself in the sickly throes of the academic argument I was confronting, for you see, my lord, the question in my mind, which I would have put to the court if I could, and which really had nothing to do with the matter at hand, was, why torture the poor man into life only to watch him justify his actions and existence for someone else's satisfaction? Wasn't it philosophically inconsistent of the Threlan government to interfere with anybody at this most intimate point of existence, given that Threlan governments, under almost any other circumstance, practically make it a state religion not to interfere with *anything*?"

Determining if justice was available to me was suddenly more immediate than creating my argument. My voice rose again. *"Can I obtain justice from an inherently inconsistent government? No matter how skillful my words?"*

I don't know if Walworth looked at me for an answer. Pain took me, and I refused to meet his glance.

*T*o continue, then. Since Thoren had to speak through a translator it will be clumsy for me to report both speakers, so let it be assumed that when I say the king said this or that, it was said through the second party of the young man. And everything anybody else said was repeated by the young man in the king's language. And Caethne appeared to be translating the procedure for her parents throughout. So the trial began, and justice, unlike charm, would have to exist through translation or not at all.

The king spoke. "In the name of justice let us begin. I, Thoren, King of Threle, do sit in judgment upon you three, Caen Walworth of the Duchy of Walworth, Baniff the Gnome of . . . of . . . I can't read this, and Master Wizard Mirand, who does not put down a place of origin. You three stand accused of high treason. To wit, of attempting to incite rebellion in the Duchy of Helas, of destroying a border town and killing scores of innocent people to garner support for such a rebellion, of interfering with Threlan foreign policy by attempting to cast blame upon the southwestern kingdoms and thereby lead Threle into war, and with aspiring to take over the Threlan army with an eye toward overthrowing me and usurping my throne." Freda mumbled something that drew quiet chuckles from the spectators and dirty looks from Thoren. "Do you wish to plead separately or together?"

"Together," said Mirand, standing.

"And I understand that you are speaking for all the accused?"

"Yes."

"Caen Walworth, I must ask for the court record: Does Master Wizard Mirand have your consent to speak for you, and do you therefore agree not to exercise your right to speak on your own behalf?"

"He does and I do." The same was asked of Baniff, who nodded his assent to both questions.

"Master Mirand, do you wish to plead? Because the penalty for high treason is execution, you have the right to speak to the court for as long as you wish on any topic you wish, yea, even to tell us all your very life, and we will listen. You may also require us to relate our evidence against you."

"I do not wish to plead at this time. I wish to hear the court's evidence." Mirand sat.

"Very well, then. The court calls the Duke of Helas to present his case." Helas stood up, with a sharp intake of breath that did not prevent his stomach from quivering, and made his way across the open floor. "My lord of Helas, the court must recognize your right to call upon any witnesses you choose in the presentation of your argument. However, under the principle that 'your story is your story,' the court cannot compel you to call any witness you do not wish to speak for your side. That is, we cannot and will not interfere with your case. You may speak for as long as you wish to."

"Your Majesty." Helas bowed low, which elicited a few titters from the spectators. He really was becoming a Sunnan or something approaching it. "And my fellow Threlans." He inclined his head slightly. I think he would have bowed to them too if it hadn't been for the laughter, and so he began his story by positioning himself outside of Threlan cultural expectations. I looked over to make sure Cristo was getting the notes on this one. He wasn't.

"I have nothing to say that Your Majesty has not already heard, seen, and read for yourself. That is, I have nothing original to add to the documents Your Majesty has perused, but I shall be happy to repeat my story for the court records." Helas paused for breath. "As everyone now knows, one of my border towns was brutally destroyed on Midwinter Eve. I did not lose scores of people. I lost hundreds. Children—" His voice cracked a little. I looked at the duchess, who was listening to Caethne translate. "Well, what can I say? Families. Good men and women who plied their trades and made their lives in their own fashion as they would—good Helans all. I lost a family member myself in the destruction—a gentle man, who ran a fine book store and loved learning."

Damn, not him too.

"So much loss—so much labor and effort and lovingly created businesses utterly destroyed. There are 'ashes where the ashes grew,' as we say at Helan funerals—as people in the southern region *still* say of the destruction. Excuse me." He turned his face into his collar. "I still weep for my people."

The judges of course let him go on weeping, and the space of time was just long enough to focus all the courtroom's sympathy on him. He stopped when their emotions were most open and vulnerable. The queen gave him the white handkerchief that had belonged to the fellow who had been taking bets earlier on her public bickering with Thoren and which she had apparently won without my noticing. Helas thanked her profusely.

"Yet 'my heart is in Threle' as the song says, and much as I weep for my duchy, my beautiful peace-loving duchy, I weep more for my kingdom when I see it endangered." The spectators were nodding approval. "And so it is with great sadness, fellow Threlans, and sorrowful reluctance that I feel bound to accuse three of my countrymen of treason. And yet, I will not permit myself the luxury of silence, knowing what I know. And what I *know*, and you judges and Your Gracious Majesty shall make of this what you will, as I hesitate to draw the ugly conclusion I fear I must, is this. That last Midwinter Day but a year, Caen Walworth, Baniff the Gnome, and Master Wizard Mirand established a secret intelligence base just outside the town in question, near the border of my duchy, or should I say the border of Threle. . . ."

Need I repeat everything? The duke went through his whole prepared argument, including his allegations that Walworth had created the fiction of an infiltration of Threle by two hostile foreign agents, namely, Count Sina and Master Wizard Grendel, to justify his own illegal intelligence operation to the king, and that Walworth had destroyed the town himself to bolster his claims of a southwestern invasion. There was a goodly amount of tears and coughing and shudders and pauses. I didn't think Helas had that much high drama in him. The duke broke off in midsentence to call his witnesses.

He began with several alleged scribes and couriers with forged letters and stories of treasonous conversations that never happened, stories laced with cloying protestations of loyalty to Threle. He and El really had done it up nicely. When it came time for the part about the town's destruction, Helas even brought out two tearful survivors who had lost children and spouses, which brought all the hatred in the crowd home to my friends. Then, to ride the hatred hard and really make it count, he brought forth three more "couriers" to dutifully testify to having seen or scribed letters proving that Walworth and Mirand had created evidence of an infiltration of Threle by Lord Protector Sina and a master wizard named Grendel from Sunnashiven's wizard school. As the judges were passing the forgeries around, my anticipation increased because I knew I would be called soon. I was supposed to be one of Helas's plants, and so now would be the logical time to call me to witness, and then, well, it would all be over.

But Helas paused, as if the shock of the testimony were too heavy to live through, and then respectfully led Franko, Sina's timid son, to the floor. Franko was not impressive. He looked as though he had just woken up. It was an effort for him to speak, and not from manufactured emotion. He was too lazy to talk. Sevalas's daughter, Franko's young wife, was with him, a sad little willow of a thing who knew how to look to her milk-shod husband with a powerful combination of weakness and wifely support. It no longer needed to be a secret that they were married, I supposed, and the trial was probably a fine way for her to garner some loyalty among the southern peasants of Sunna by making a public appearance wearing mourning for Count Sina. They had seen Franko's dear father three days after the blast. He had given them his blessing, walked off and drowned himself, distraught over the suffering in Sunna. The funeral had been private, just themselves and King Sevalas, who sent his very best wishes to Thoren. They knew nothing of Grendel or even who he was, of course.

After they sat down Helas called another witness. She claimed to have been a student of Grendel's. Grendel had gone into isolation for a period of intense study and meditation over the calamities befalling his country, poor man, and would not make a public appearance, but sent this letter as a token of his well-being and good health.

At that point Helas thanked the court profusely for their time and closed his argument; he had no more witnesses to call at this time. And so he sat down. I absolutely had to hide my outrage. Did El know my plan? Had they merely placed me in the front row for show? To use my presence as an instrument of torture for my friends? So Cristo would have something interesting to take notes on?

"But I have letters to identify, my lord," I whispered.

"Not now," he whispered hurriedly. *Later, then? Damn them all, but I will speak before the trial is over, protocol notwithstanding.* One of the judges harshly told us to be silent.

"Your story is ended, my lord of Helas. Have you anything to add?"

"No, your honor."

"All right, Master Wizard Mirand, you may speak. Do you wish to plea now, or call upon your witnesses?"

"I wish to speak. I have no witnesses to call."

"Proceed, Master."

Mirand stood upon the empty floor and faced the spectators. Walworth and Baniff were all attention. So was I. I noticed the top of Caethne's head; it wasn't moving. The duchess was not crying, and neither was the old duke. They were too busy hating their son's tutor, blaming him for everything. Directed hate was their only way of coping. It was awful, really.

Mirand's voice contained no tears, no emotion, no histrionics. He simply stood and spoke his plea. And his simplicity was devastating.

"We are guilty. I am not here to defend our actions. I am not here to seek mercy. Let that be understood. I am here to speak of our guilt." His words were greeted with hisses and groans. The king called for order. I myself wanted to slap Mirand. What the hell was he doing? "Did we run an intelligence operation? Yes, we did. I should be happy to show you all the very spot. Did we destroy a Helan border town? Yes, I did so single-handedly and would do so again. Did we plan to incite a rebellion against Helas? After listening to today's testimony, I must confess that indeed we did, although at the time we were not aware that we were working toward this goal. Did Walworth plan to make himself commander of the Threlan army? Once again, yes, although planning to make oneself commander of anything is not a crime. What we stand accused of under the law, we are guilty of under the law. And we deserve to suffer the full penalty of the law.

"Now, you are all aware, as competent judges, that one of the basic principles of Threlan law has always been that motivation does *not* diminish guilt, save in cases of self-defense. If a man kills, he is guilty of murder. It is no matter that he claims to have killed in anger or in drunkenness, or that his intention was only to injure and not cause death. Likewise, a man who steals a bag containing one hundred gold pieces, thinking that he only stole fifty, is still guilty of stealing the hundred. Or if he thinks himself justified in stealing the hundred because his motivation is to give them to someone in need, he is still guilty of theft, for he has injured and placed in need the person he stole from. I bring up this common point of law because it is our motivation that buttressed the actions of which we are guilty, and so it is our motivation I would discuss. But only as a matter of historical record. I do not wish my speech to be regarded as a plea for mercy, for we are guilty. Under the law we are guilty.

"Last Midwinter Day but a year, Caen Walworth, Baniff the Gnome, and myself established a secret intelligence base in the Duchy of Helas, with the full knowledge and financial support of the Duke of Helas himself. Thoren has letters indicating that such support indeed existed, letters that Helas now alleges are forgeries. Walworth had learned, via intelligence gathered and sent to him by his distant cousin Lord Cathe, a young cleric from Sunnashiven, that Lord Roguehan of the Kingdom of Furnesse was quickly installing himself as the true power ruling the far southwestern kingdoms and was preparing to acquire the Kingdoms of Sevalas and Sunna as well." *So it was Cathe who got them all involved in the first place?* "Lord Cathe chose not to attend the trial today, but his letters are also in Thoren's keeping. If the judges will accept the written testimony that Master Grendel is in seclusion and choosing not to attend and that the recent Lord Protector of Sunna had a private, sparsely attended funeral, then I suppose you must accept the existence of Cathe and the authenticity of his letters, for the evidence on each side is equal. And yes, the letters may be forged, but forgery in this case, on either side, is entirely a matter of belief."

The letters were passed and read into the court record. My sense was that Helas had done his job so well that no one really believed in their authenticity.

"I am aware that it is not the business of Threle to involve itself with the internal affairs of other countries. Nor should it be. So it was not as agents of our government or representatives of the kingdom that we took it upon ourselves to monitor the situation, but as private citizens with something more than an academic interest in foreign affairs. We were not even acting on behalf of the Duchy of Helas in any recognized or official capacity. But we were acting. We were gathering intelligence and sending spies and accepting foreign couriers and reporting all we knew to my lord of Helas. And we were doing so for the future defense of Threle. But motivation does not matter. Law alone matters. I am not aware, however, of *which* law matters in this particular circumstance. You judges, is it forbidden to talk to people and exchange ideas?"

"No."

"When we were asked to lend our support to the peasant rebellion in Sunna, we did so because, as the evidence Thoren has in hand indicates, evidence he may show the judges if he pleases, we knew that King Sunnas had become little more than a front government for Lord Roguehan, as had King Sevalas. The Kingdom of Sunna is only a few days' ride from Threle, from the Duchy of Helas. And so we thought it good to lend support to Sunnas's overthrow, to push Roguehan back deeper into the southwest and form a buffer state if we could. The rebellion enjoyed temporary success, Count Sina was instated as lord protector, and you all know the rest. And yet our support of the rebellion may indeed have violated Threlan law in that Threle has a clear policy of nonintervention in other countries and we took it upon ourselves to act in violation of that policy. Although I know of no law forbidding a private citizen to act or speak against national policy unless such actions constitute a clear danger to Threle."

"Nor do we," concurred the judges. "But you do not stand accused of running a private operation; you stand accused of using this operation as base for overthrowing Helas and eventually usurping the throne."

"I stand accused of having a treasonable motivation, not of breaking law. Let us be clear."

"And of destroying a border town."

"Ah, yes, the town. I did destroy a border town. I do not dispute that. And in doing so, as Thoren knows, I destroyed myself." Mirand explained how he knew that Count Sina and Grendel were going to cross the border and set up their own base in the duchy, how he had tracked them through his crystals, how he had come into possession of the key and the Wand of Surprises, which Thoren now had in his keeping, how he tragically miscalculated the damage his own destruction of Grendel's firepower would cause the town, and how his action resulted in a reverse induction in his own name stone fragments, which caused him mortal injury. I noticed he did not mention my role in any of this. The wand and the key had been given to him by one of their people. The king might show them if he would.

Thoren did so, letting one of his wizards carefully handle the wand so that the judges might see it. Mirand was still speaking. "Thoren knows in what condition my body arrived in Loudes. I understand that my physical processes were not detectable. I was not breathing, my heart was not beating, and since I remember nothing of that journey, my mind was dead. I am told that my spirit was drawn back because the heart of my name stone existed, and it was through delicate searching and calling for the stone, through what little remained of the exploded fragments, that the king's clerics called my spirit and his wizards made me whole again. But I remember nothing of death. I do not think the nature of things permits such memory. And indeed, Helas's witnesses claim that Sina and Grendel could not have invaded the duchy. And perhaps they would have you believe I tasted death for my own glory. Others have. But motivation is irrelevant. I was intent enough on wielding destruction to take my own life in doing so.

"And so Walworth presented not only our evidence, written and otherwise, but all our other signs to Thoren. And indeed, since Thoren decided to overlook our legal transgressions in favor of the urgency of the time and, I might add, in full understanding of our motivation, and since we were not to be prosecuted in any court but rather to enjoy his protection, we were not guilty. But now there is new evidence—new letters cleverly wrought in Walworth's hand, new tales of intrigue cleverly told with many tears and sighs—and the king cannot ignore it. Roguehan bides his time. And so we are guilty. Not of 'planning' or 'desiring' or 'plotting' to do anything, but of breaking the very laws we broke in the first place. It is only the motivation you ascribe to us that makes what we did treason or heroism, but in this case either is punishable under the law. Throughout history good people have died for both. I have already died for one—you decide which.

"Thoren, the penalty for high treason is death, and should you accept the argument of the other side that is what, in fairness, you should offer. But my lord of Helas merely offers treason as a motivation to his argument; plotting to usurp the throne is not the same as having attempted to do so. And clearly we were imprisoned before any such attempt could be made. However, motivation aside, we are guilty of the following, and I put to you, Thoren, now, publicly, to state what you feel the penalty for each crime should be." He paused. "One. We ran an unauthorized intelligence base in the Duchy of Helas."

Thoren looked confused and quietly asked his judges something before speaking. "There are no precedents for that particular crime, if it is a crime. There was a Reathen duchess tried for something like it four hundred years ago, when she was concerned about the Angrukan invasion, but the Angrukans did invade and so the queen rewarded her."

"How?" asked Mirand.

"By making her commander of the Threlan army." There were uneasy titters from the spectators.

"Two. I destroyed the town in question."

The titters were strangled by somberness. "The penalty can be no less than death."

"And since I am solely responsible for the actual deed I am solely in peril of my life on that count?"

Thoren looked to his judges. "I suppose so."

"How many times can a man pay the death penalty?"

"Once."

"Well, then, I submit it is paid."

"I submit it is," said Thoren. Walworth's parents were beyond amazement. El's eyes were popping out of his head. The spectators were absolutely stunned, but it was from disbelief rather than admiration at Mirand's brilliance in exploiting the technicalities of Threlan law. And I felt much hostility underneath their amazement, for many were still convinced of his guilt in spirit if not in fact, although a few were wavering.

"Three. Caen Walworth attempted to incite the guards to rebel against Helas. Whether he did so through lying in his letters, as the other side alleges, or through his zeal to save the kingdom, which couldn't help but constitute a rebellion against a duke with clear southwestern sympathies, is irrelevant. Motivation is irrelevant. The *caen* is guilty. What is the penalty?"

"Death . . . but," said Thoren, "if a real invasion had taken place, then the *caen*'s actions could only constitute a defense of Threle, no matter what his motivation."

"You have our evidence for a real invasion and you have theirs," said Mirand. "Which do you believe?"

The king was silent. A judge said, "Are you finished with your argument?"

"Yes." Mirand sat.

Now it will be our turn again and I will read my letters. I couldn't wait.

"My lord of Helas, have you more witnesses to call?"

"None, Your Gracious Majesty."

"Master Wizard Mirand?"

"None."

"But *I* would speak! Now! I have something for the king to hear!" It was Aleta who said this before I could. She was already standing, with Perie. Her father looked scared.

"You are out of order. Under Threlan law, no one speaks save as a witness for one side or the other. And both sides have closed and dismissed their witnesses."

"I am not a Threlan. I am Lady General Aleta, commander of the armed forces of County Clio, daughter of Count Clio and sole heir to the county, and I would address the court as an ambassadress of my country and a friend of Threle."

"Proceed, my lady. Let it be noted that your remarks are not formally for either side, and that you are permitted to speak only as a diplomatic courtesy and that the court reserves the right to silence you at any time."

"As you wish." She went to the floor with Perie. "King Thoren. Before you make your decision as to whom to believe, I think you should know that there was an infiltration of Threle. I believe there was, because my captain and myself saw Master Grendel and Count Sina in my county, disguised as merchants, on their way to Helas and we rode to warn Walworth of the impending invasion. Mirand said he had evidence in his crystal before I even got there, but I did see them."

"Are you claiming involvement with their operation?"

"Yes, and I'm also claiming diplomatic immunity from prosecution."

"All right. If Count Sina and Master Grendel were disguised, how did you know them?"

"I know Grendel. I went to school in Sunnashiven, but not for wizardry."

"Yes, but the court cannot speculate on the motives of disguised travelers in your county, which lies several days' ride west of Helas. But please continue. How did you know Sina? Had you seen him before?"

"No. But he was with his son Franko."

"And you were previously acquainted with Franko?"

"No . . . Your Honor."

"My lord of Helas, may we question your witness Franko?"

"Please do, your honor."

"Franko, were you in County Clio at this time?"

"My wife can attest that I wasn't."

"Lady Aleta, did you see them enter Threle?"

"No," she said quietly.

"You may be seated."

This was my cue. I leapt up. "I would speak too, Your Honor. I have important evidence to give."

"I have called all my witnesses," objected Helas, "I wish to call no more."

"I cannot let you speak for Helas then. Are you claiming yourself as an ambassador of a foreign country?"

"I am from Helas." That brought titters from the spectators, including the queen, and a visible wince from Walworth. Perhaps I had overdone it there, but my first thought was that claiming to be Helan was safer than potentially having to explain the circumstances under which I had left Sunnashiven, which at all costs I wanted to avoid. "But if I cannot speak for my lord of Helas, might I speak for Master Wizard Mirand?"

The judge looked to Mirand. Mirand's eyes locked on mine for an instant. "Since my opponent is so intent on stopping him, I see no reason why I should cooperate. Let him speak."

I ran to the floor. *Time to stick in the knife.* "Your Honors, Your Majesty. My name is Llewelyn, and I am a scribe in the Monastery of Kursen in southeast Kant, but I am Helan by birth and loyal to the Duchy of Helas. I speak to the court as one attached to the monastery, as one under its official protection. It was through my scribe work for Brother El, in the back there, that I was asked to write some of the following letters. The others are copies of correspondence received by Brother El from the Duke of Helas. Let me read them for the court record."

And I did so, for forty-five minutes, solemnly handing each one to the judges as I finished it. When I finished Walworth was leaning back and beaming at me, Baniff was laughing out loud, and even Mirand was gracing me with a hint of a smile. The duchess had been listening intently to Caethne's translation and now Caethne had to restrain her from climbing over the benches to hug me. The old duke was slapping his knees and already on his way to see his son. It was wonderful. I didn't even look at Brother El. Helas was having convulsions, and the guards were already moving toward him. The king was in a state of happy disbelief.

Helas managed to speak. "Your Majesty, the young man made an impressive performance, but I submit that every one of those letters is a forgery that he created himself, that he is one of Walworth's spies, and that he was planted among my people. True enough, I didn't want him to speak, for I happen to know, and my people will attest, that this is the same Llewelyn who often scribed for the *caen*, that he is, or was, an apprentice of Master Wizard Mirand, and that indeed he is Sunnan, not Helan at all, and that he is lying to the court. He himself was involved in the operation. In fact, his sister Trenna works for me."

"What does Trenna do?" asked one of the judges.

"She's a courier to the monastery," I answered. "She delivered many of these letters." The spectators were laughing.

"She's a courier," said Helas. "And if she were here she'd testify to the same."

"So this Trenna who provided some of the letters is your sister?" asked the judge.

"Yes." I had to admit.

"And she is from Helas?"

"No, Sunnashiven," shouted Helas's witnesses. "I know her. She's Sunnan."

"But you said you were Helan."

"I . . . live in Helas."

"But you also said you live in Kant." The judges were understandably confused.

"I am a scribe in Kursen Monastery."

"That is your official, legal designation?"

"Yes."

"When did you scribe for the *caen*?"

"I didn't. I've never met or worked for any of the accused. It is true that I am Sunnan by birth, but I have been so long in Helas, I consider that my birthplace and my home, and it was out of loyalty to the Duchy of Helas and Threle that I brought these letters into court." There was a lengthy discussion among the judges.

One of them spoke. "When you claimed to be a native-born Helan you lied to the court once. Even if you did so out of zeal for the duchy you've adopted, the court has been eloquently reminded today that motivation does not diminish guilt under Threlan law. The penalty for perjury is a fine of two gold pieces. Do you wish to plea?"

"No. I wish to pay it and get on with it if I could. But I am a poor scribe and have no money."

"I shall pay my scribe's fine," shouted El from the back, much to everyone's surprise, including my own. "On behalf of Kursen Monastery."

"Llewelyn, do you wish let your monastery pay the fee on your behalf or do you wish to plea?"

"Let them pay it," I said. Why not? I had no idea what El was up to. A sharp glance from Mirand, which I pretended not to see, told me I had made a misstep, but I wasn't sure why.

"All right," said the judge, taking the money from Cristo, who smiled and bowed his way up and down from the back. "Be careful what you say in the future, Llewelyn. Since there is much riding on the authenticity of these letters, we should like to question my lord of Helas."

"You may," said the duke uncertainly.

"If you knew that Llewelyn here was involved in the *caen*'s operation, why did you not bring charges against him?"

"It's obvious: He took sanctuary in a monastery, where the law couldn't touch him."

"And came here with Brother El to sit in *your* witness section?"

"Well, his letters would lose a lot of credibility if he sat in theirs. He's a spy claiming to be acting out patriotism for his *native duchy*, remember."

Thoren spoke. "I have in my keeping several letters from one of Walworth's people, who also calls himself Llewelyn, which is a common name in the Botha language, my translator tells me. It is a simple matter to see if the handwriting matches."

And of course, thanks to my magic, it didn't. And Helas's writing matched perfectly. "Innocent," said the king. "Would my lord of Helas care to plea or accept the king's finding of guilt of high treason?"

"I have no plea. I accept your finding," said Helas mournfully as the guards led him away. The king rapped the table in front of him to indicate the close of the trial. More guards came and led away the witnesses, including Franko and his wife. I guessed that would all be sorted out later. I wondered what would happen to Trenna and then decided I didn't particularly care.

The spectators fell into a paralyzed sort of celebration as Helas was led away. Walworth's parents were already hugging him and Caethne was crying and laughing and Aleta was looking stalwartly pleased and Perie was stiffly bouncing on his heels and ye gods but I wanted to join them. And yet I couldn't. Not there. Not then. My friends' innocence was very much a factor of us not knowing each other and a public show of friendship at this time could very well undo everything. So I understood why none of them, with the exception of the duchess, so much as looked in my direction. And I understood why Caethne appeared to be doing her best to dissuade her mother from approaching me, which was a simple matter under the circumstances, as the old duchess was so thrilled to be with her son. I heard the king publicly declare Walworth commander of the Threlan army and state his readiness to support the *caen* as he organized against a planned invasion. The day was won.

Yet I noticed when I looked to the back that El seemed strangely unaffected by the whole affair. He was pointing out the marble tracery to Cristo, who was, of course, taking notes.

Freda started to help her husband down clumsily but two of the judges waved her back. So she stomped over to Walworth's mother, waving her arms and sputtering. The judges were earnestly trying to tell Thoren something, and the king sharply rapped his rod on the table as they cried for order. Everyone sat; the duchess had both arms around her children, happily oblivious to the queen, who was still grumbling.

The king rapped again for quiet and called El forward. "Brother El, even though there has been much evidence of your guilt of treason presented today, you know as well as the court does that we cannot touch you, as all of your crimes were committed within monastery walls. Therefore we send you back to Kursen Monastery under king's guard with the warning that your life is forfeit should you ever leave the monastery. That is as far as the law can go."

"Yes, of course." El didn't seem at all upset. If anything, he seemed amused, as if he regarded the trial as a fine show and had no complaints concerning the quality of his entertainment. He was an appreciative audience, a smiling critic about to pass his own easy judgment.

"Llewelyn," said one of the judges, calling me forward, "I presume, after the testimony you have just given, that you would prefer to return to the Duchy of Helas? Or should I say the south portions of the Duchy of Walworth, as under Threlan law the Duchy of Helas is now under the Duke of Walworth's control." There was some laughter. "Perhaps to see your sister."

"I would prefer to make myself useful to Threle's defense. I would ask if His Majesty is in need of a scribe who reads and writes Botha?" The king chuckled and shrugged after the translator finished, as if he was saying, "Why not?" I was so happy I could have pulled the moon out of the sky and danced with her right there. I could even have danced with Aleta. Hell, I could even have danced with Cristo!

El spoke. "Your Majesty, I wish to raise a point of monastic law. My scribe here has publicly and officially declared to the court that he is under the protection and sanctuary of Kursen Monastery. That is true. He is my scribe and bound in service to me. I have not released him from this service. Also, I submit that if my scribe removes the fingerless glove that covers his left palm, it will be seen that he bears the sign of the waning moon, a sign that clearly marks him as belonging to our order."

I had absolutely no idea that El had ever seen my scar, as I *always* kept it covered. Did he know about the uses of my cloak all along, then, as he had known my true background all along? And did he know about the letters? Then what had been his point in bringing me here? Of course there was no way I could bring in the real cause of the scar without revealing my relationship to Walworth. *Damn clerics, and all their breed!*

The judge asked me to remove the glove. I did so, and each judge inspected my palm. El continued, "Also, since my scribe accepted of his own free will that the monastery pay his perjury fine on his behalf, under Threlan law he belongs to the monastery and is subject to monastic law."

"That is true, Brother," said one of the judges.

"I submit that Llewelyn must return with me, under guard. I also submit that until such time as we give him permission to leave, should he ever attempt to leave Kursen Monastery he would be in violation of our laws and under monastic agreement with Threle must be returned to us by the king's guards."

All of the spectators were as silent as sunshine in a midnight storm. Except my friends. Their silence was not the silence of a forgotten sun. It was too full and pale and bloodless. The silence on the lips of a corpse would have been pure eloquence beside it.

Thoren looked helplessly outraged and tried to speak to the judges. The judges busily whispered among themselves for several minutes. When they broke their huddle, five looked uneasily resigned and the sixth said woodenly, "I am afraid you speak truly, Brother. Llewelyn, you must return to Kursen Monastery under guard with your master."

Couldn't Mirand do something? Walworth? Any of them? But none of them could argue too vociferously on my behalf without jeopardizing the verdict. And it would take more than a feeble protest to get me out of this one. The duchess was making a protest in Sarana, but none of the judges understood her and no one was translating. It was clear that though Thoren's sympathies lay with me, even he could do nothing. Freda ran over to me and gave me the coins she had won. I decided the queen had a good heart. She was trying to do something for me and the gift of money was all she could think of. The king rapped on the table, the guards surrounded El and myself, blocking my friends from sight, and that was that.

*T*he North Country night felt suddenly personal, as if it was weighing its terrible dark against the storm of my sickness, as if the dark and my ban were holding themselves in cosmic balance like a strange laughing promise of cosmic justice.

I paused in my recitation, or my sickness did.

"I am not here to speak in your defense, my lord."

We caught each other's glance for another accident, another impassive hurt, but the pass quickly ended into the measured scratching of pen on empty parchment, like a dutiful sword cutting into blank flesh. I supposed it had to. Having accepted my preference to speak of him as if he were not present transcribing my tale, Walworth was too much the judge to react to my taunt. And so I suffered myself to continue speaking, wrenching words out of my mind, knowing that my judge could not exist for me any more now than then, but that I had to defend myself against his verdict all the same.

*A*s the guards took us through the courtroom and out the front entrance, it occurred to me that the very thing Cathe had brought me to the monastery to avoid had come to pass. I remembered his words: "To save the cause he loves, he must watch you condemned for dedicating yourself to the country and cause he loves." And it was Cathe that got them all involved in the first place. It probably was Cathe who had gotten me involved in some unknown fashion as soon as he threw thoughts at me during his own clerical hearing in Sunnashiven . . . no, as soon as I helped Grana conceive whatever it was that eventually became this abomination. Was something of his spirit directing me even then? I should have tampered with the birth magic that brought him forth in the first place. Cathe would have made a wonderful frog.

El cheerfully congratulated me on delivering a first-rate performance. Cristo came forward and shook my hand. I was absolutely convinced that the clerics had been arranging this spectacle for months as a form of grand entertainment!

And as if to bolster my conviction, Cathe was outside, smiling and clapping as we emerged through the door. He even had the whole crowd clapping, although none of them seemed to know why. I bowed sarcastically, to which he responded with ugly doggish yelps, and then all clapping stopped.

I felt my friends emerge through the door and enter the crowd somewhere behind me. Cathe ran over to them in high good humor and kissed Caethne on the cheek.

"Catching fishes in my tea. Dead or alive?"

"Dead," said Caethne.

"Oh, and what ails my oyster girl, my pale spring-violet wife with hair so windy blue?"

"Life."

"Ah, moondown, moondown—all around. Life does ail indeed. Lady, but our northern nursery songs *do* sound different in Botha, now don't they? Come, tell your sweet husband all—" At this point the guards led us away to our horses and our journey back to Kant, so I did not hear the rest of Cathe's line. I suppose that was a distant piece of mercy.

Seventeen

*W*e returned to Kant in a strangled monastic silence. I stared past the late winter stars and tried to get myself to believe I would be returning to Loudes with the king's guards, tried desperately to grasp at thin hopeless dreams to shelter me from the world's realities. But as Mirand once taught me as he faced almost certain death, belief is not a choice. No comfort returned to me from the undreaming winter wind.

I was sure I would be killed. There was no incentive for El to keep me, not even the pleasure he might feel watching me waste my life the way he took so much pleasure in watching Cristo waste his. Surely I wouldn't continue as a scribe, and my servant duties were unnecessary make-work. El had certainly been roundly pleased with the aesthetic experience of the trial, with the opportunity to relish the pain of Walworth and Mirand and to imbibe the backward energy in the tragic rise and fall of my hopes. But the show he had helped put together was over and I couldn't imagine what further use I could have for him. His demeanor was now as inscrutable as the distant glint of the night sky.

I decided that if it came to dying, I would give the monks something to write home to their gods about. That I would spite them by becoming the author of my own demise, by devising an original piece of work that generations of Kursen clerics would be forced to memorize and analyze and spit back at their masters. It would be a free-will offering of my bright contempt for them, a daring and beautiful curse. It took days for me to nail myself to this resolve. But once I did so, the journey couldn't go fast enough for my taste.

So when the guards finally left us inside the monastery walls, I turned to El, spread my arms like an all-giving Sun King, and refused to move. El was clearly unaccustomed to open disobedience. He stood a full thirty seconds and "hmmmd" and "hummed" and looked mildly at Cristo, who looked attentively back at him. Then he made a dismissive hand gesture and Cristo walked obediently away from us and into the large central stone building. Then El spoke, for the first time in a week, and it was in Botha.

"Do you do well with choices, then, Llewelyn?"

"Exceptionally well, Master." I grinned and bobbed like the doorkeeper. El looked toward the sun, which was quickly being swallowed behind the building. The roof reflected traces of pink. "The monastery blushes far too lightly to be convincing, don't you think, Master? A true virgin should flush and burn in her chastity, devouring herself in redness like Habundia Herself, commanding attention while crying, 'Touch not!' But the monastery stones are not so chaste, are they? The sun penetrates and licks their every hole and crack until the sky is drowned with the scent of their lousy rut. They house no virgins. They'll kiss and cloy before they'll cloister"—El's left eye was bulging in anger but I kept pushing—"just like a high priest whose only pretense is his claim to being chaste while he grunts and pumps and grinds his way to witness the rarest and most sublime of life's little performances. Friendship killing itself. How . . . exotic! Was it good for you, Brother? Was it really good—the elaborate tricks and lies and sharp thrusts and withdrawals into and out of bleeding, quivering justice? The performance cost you a lot of time and effort so I sincerely hope it met your expectations if not your needs. And didn't the marble tracery just . . . just leave you dry—"

El slapped me hard across the face.

I still kept at it. "I'm sorry that Franko didn't have more mournful energy around him, to really bolster up the crescendo, but his wife did a flawless bit of work—"

El slapped me again. "You think you're smart? Make your choice!"

"What is my choice, Master?"

"Accept our training into the priesthood of Habundia, the virgin goddess of denial and sacrifice. But I suppose you are not strong enough to take that way, yes?"

"Are *you*, Master? Really?" El looked impatiently toward the now nearly invisible sun. "But you mentioned a choice. Is there another way to take, Master? What is my choice?"

"Accept our training or accept our mastery. Become our student or remain our servant. I open the path to the Goddess to you. It is your own path, so I do you no favor."

"How blessedly humble of you, Master."

"Enough! Will you become a novice student of the priesthood and un-

dergo the rigors of monastic training, tending your soul and spirit to Habundia's keeping?"

"I'd rather shovel shit. Master."

"So be it." He shrugged and started nonchalantly for the main building.
"You know where the stables are, and the horses need to be bedded. When
you change your mind, let me know." He shrugged again. "Later, yes?"

I blew kisses at the newborn evening dark.

As a servant of the monastery, I was no longer attached exclusively to El
but was at the beck and call of every cleric in residence. I lost my meager
library "privileges." According to the rules, I should have been removed from
the luxurious comfort of the cot-filled common room where I had first been
installed. Servants were supposed to be housed behind the cooking areas in
two of the outbuildings. But Devon raised such a ruckus during the first
night I spent with the servants that the clerics decided to break the rule on
my account and put me back with the other scribes and younger students.
Apparently one of the other scribes had told Devon that I was gone for good
and Devon had responded by kicking over all the cots and running screaming down the hall. He grabbed the first clerical student he could find, ordered
her down to the room, and commanded her to burn all the cots with her
magic, and of course, Devon being the official Sun King, she couldn't refuse.
The smoke must have been terrific, for the boys went coughing and gasping
out of the room and they had to be housed with the clerical students that
night. I understand Cristo was blessed with two of them. The upshot was
that I got returned to the common room and we all got new cots and blankets. I also achieved a good deal of popularity, or should I say respect,
among my roommates, as there was now no question as to who really ran
things.

And I wasn't shy about openly exploiting my position either since I no
longer had anything to lose by doing so. I decided that the monastery rules
governing servants had absolutely no reference to me. Barring considerable
use of clerical magic to force my will, which I didn't sense was worth the
trouble it would take, the clerics had no way of enforcing them—especially
since the usual punishment for disobedient or lazy servants was to let
them go.

The one thing I wanted to do was to get fluent in Kantish and make my
grand gesture of dying in a foreign tongue. And this was much easier to do
in my present position, even though I was now technically barred from all
the libraries, than when I was scribing for El and had limited access to
teaching materials. I had all kinds of study time. I needed only decent books
and a competent tutor. And I could now use Devon to help me get them
without any fear of consequences should I get caught.

There is a library within the main building of the monastery that is
restricted to clerics and clerical students. The first morning after returning

from Loudes, I walked boldly with Devon into the clerical library. There was a student on duty who, strictly according to the rules, should have stopped us, but after the previous night's fiasco no one was about to stop the Sun King. I smiled pleasantly, Devon smiled, the student smiled uneasily, and we were admitted. I strolled through the stacks until I found the section on foreign languages and I took down all the Kantish–Botha grammars and dictionaries that I could find. Then I found the section on southwestern history and literature, where there were several shelves containing Botha-language books, sat down at a nearby table, and began working on Kantish verb conjugations, not caring who saw me. I created a pleasure apple for Devon, even though eating in the libraries was against the rules. Creating things for Devon seemed to keep him amused. Devon watched me work, a look of hero worship in his eyes that would have been touching had it not been magically induced.

It took three hours for my tutor to come into the stacks and start reading the Bothan books. He did not know he was my tutor when I first approached him, but he was bright enough to grasp the facts of our new relationship fairly quickly. His name was Salan. He had a job lined up teaching in Sunnashiven and was scheduled to be initiated into Habundia's priesthood in three months. His specialty was Sunnan history and he had studied Botha for years.

"Good," I said cheerfully, "you'll do nicely."

"I'll do *what* nicely?"

"Teach me Kantish. Three months should be about right if we settle on, say, three hours a day of intensive practice. At your convenience, of course. Morning, noon, or night, I don't much care. And we can break the time up if you'd prefer. I'd hate to interfere with your studies."

"Who *are* you?"

"Llewelyn. I'm a servant of the monastery. And that's my friend Devon." I pointed to the table. "The Sun King. I'm thinking that Devon and I could move in with you, as your rooms are probably much nicer and quieter than our current living arrangement. After all, Devon tends to spend more time with me than he does in class, and he could stand to learn a little reading and writing himself." Hearing his name, Devon came over to me.

Salan told us both to get lost.

I corrected his attitude. "Salan, you don't understand. I really would hate to interfere with your studies, but I've recently developed more than a passing acquaintance with hate. And more than a passing interest in Kantish. Now, the way I see it, until you are an initiated priest you will lose everything you've worked for here if you disobey His Glorious Majesty of the Sun. And being so close to initiation, you've certainly got plenty to lose. I suppose being a swineherd has its attractions for some."

"Look, I don't know who you are, but in three months I'm out of here."

"One way or another." I glanced at Devon. Salan started swearing under his breath. He was more eloquent than the king's translator. "Either I'm fluent in Kantish by the time you take initiation or Devon helps you make a career change."

He looked down at Devon, who was smiling because I was. Poor Devon had no idea what the conversation was about, and I wasn't sure I would even be able to communicate my threat and desire to him, but his presence was enough to win Salan's attention. "How much Kantish do you know?" Salan asked me uncertainly.

"A little. Simple verb conjugations in the present tense. Three or four handfuls of naming words."

"And you expect to be fluent in three months?"

"I'm a quick study."

He looked at Devon again. "All right, Come to my rooms around six. Promptly. I haven't time to spare." Turned out he now shared rooms with Cristo. He had moved in during our absence. He grabbed some Bothan books and started to storm off.

"Oh, Salan?" I stopped him. "Would you mind taking out these language books for me? You can leave them here, of course, as I happen to be using them, but it would be most convenient if I had exclusive use of them. Just put down your name so no one else can touch them. His Majesty here will go with you."

And of course Salan had to do as he was told. I felt bad for him in a way. I really had nothing personal against him and I knew I was being a bully—but I also knew that the monastery left me with no other option except remaining ignorant of the spoken language around me. Besides, Habundia's clerics were all supposed to embrace humility and self-sacrifice, so I supposed I was rewarding him according to his beliefs with a practical lesson in clerical obedience, a warm-up for life in the temple in Sunnashiven. I resolved to inconvenience him as little as possible. In fact, I decided I would make it up to him by cleaning his rooms or proofreading Bothan papers for him or any other little thing I could do to save him the time I would cost him over the next three months. And when my Kantish improved I would use Devon to arrange some kind of nice reward for his trouble.

In ten weeks I was fluent. Not that I could have done a magical working in Kantish, or written an epic poem, but then, who would want to? Kantish, or "cant" as I thought of it, is not a particularly beautiful language and has absolutely no magical properties, but it is a wonderful language for academic nonsense, and also contains a good many Botha cognates so it is not that difficult to learn. So I didn't read a lot of poems. I worked through my language books and read Salan's theology books and papers and had lengthy conversations in Kantish with him at night. Salan had a rather testy personality, but anyone would have, under the circumstances. He had to live with Cristo and his owl. And then he had me for a student and me and Devon for roommates. I could study my language books in peace all day and practice my speaking skills at night. And the irony wasn't lost on me that now that I had fallen to servant status I was living the life of an advanced clerical student. And even though El had to know all about it through Cristo, no one tried to stop me.

I kept Salan's fire going and his rooms in good order so that he never had to lose time to housekeeping. I made him tea at night and let him use Devon to run his errands. In fact, Salan learned quickly that Devon and I were quite willing to do anything he asked of us so long as my lessons weren't interfered with. And I wasted no time getting right down to business during our lessons. Once he learned that I was as anxious to get through the tutelage as he was, his voice lost some of its sharpness. I even threw silencing spells on Cristo for him, as Salan was reluctant to use his own magic against a fellow aspirant to Habundia's priesthood. This alone scored me points. Salan also viewed me as a resource on Sunnashiven, and I was happy to tell him all I knew about the city in which he was going to spend the rest of his life. He never really warmed to me but after the first two weeks he did settle into a cool tolerance.

Devon did not learn the written language from Salan as well or as quickly as I hoped he would, but you can't have everything. Since Devon had no problem listening to me for hours, I taught him how to write and read as soon as my own skills were strong enough, and through his desire to please me he became semiliterate, but that was as far as we went. Devon lacked genuine interest in book learning and I needed to conserve my time for my own studies.

I did manage to use my friendly influence to get Devon to start washing regularly and I was able through wizardry to clean and mend his tattered clothes, so he began to look more presentable. I was also able to persuade him to keep his Sun King tendency to terrorize and bully the other students in check most of the time, although my record wasn't perfect here. Not that I was particularly qualified to provide Devon with social guidance, but I did what I could. He had been abandoned at Kursen, neglected by the staff, and constantly tormented by the other boys his age. This sad state of affairs had naturally resulted in Devon's developing some unattractive personality traits, such as bullying his peers and destroying physical objects, but I believe I was able to smooth a few of the rough edges off his personality, or rather bring out some of what would have been his personality had he not been given over to Kursen. I don't believe he was naturally evil, just unlucky. That much we had in common.

It wasn't a half-bad arrangement, although every moment when I wasn't studying I was thinking about my friends, wondering what the state of the world was, and hoping beyond hope that they would find some way to contact me or get me out of here without jeopardizing their cause. There were times when I didn't want to die. There were nights when I couldn't sleep and I would lie for hours trying to convince myself that Mirand was taking weeks to construct some brilliant legal argument that would win me my freedom and that any day now the king's guards would arrive and tell me I could leave. Or that Walworth's parents were so grateful to me that they were using their influence as nobility to work something behind the scenes. Or that Baniff was planning some elaborate escape to a secret hideout, or maybe even to County Clio, where I could work without the king's knowledge. But each day passed like the one before and the one after. I had no news of external affairs and no reason to believe that my friends had even considered my plight in the midst of their now considerable duties.

Salan took his initiation and left for Sunnashiven in late May. I stayed in his rooms with Cristo and read books that Cristo dutifully brought me from the library. And that was my life. I didn't even get out of bed if I didn't feel like it. I ate sparsely. I drank only weak tea. Sometimes I felt something like deadened love for the sun, because I lived with its rays falling across my bed every day the way I might have lived with a lover, and I would spend hours watching its every change of motion or mood. Genna came to me twice in sexual dreams, if it was her and not my own memory passing out of life. And then watching the sunbeams hit dust motes became as important to me as watching the sun burning rubies in a Helan jeweler's shop once had been. Cristo talked to me at night—about all the papers he had to write, mostly—and Devon brought me little trinkets that he stole from other students. I don't think either of them knew I was dying. And my grand symbolic gesture of dying in Kantish, the gesture that I had worked so hard to achieve, was also lost on them.

I think I read Kantish textbooks and wasted away for about three weeks after Salan's departure. I knew it was getting close to Midsummer. I remember I was thinking one morning that there would be something aesthetically pleasing about touching death on Midsummer Day when Devon interrupted my reverie by running breathless into my room and jumping on my bed. I was weak enough to see the ghosts of the objects around me echoing their sources, so Devon's words sounded like the slippery language of a vision. "Luvellun, you've got a message! From a *gnome*!" His eyes were big.

"I've got a—*what*?" Hail sweet life! I was out of bed and dressed in less than a minute. "Where, Devon? Where is this gnome?" *How long will Baniff wait?*

"In the wine cellar. Right away."

As we ran through the building and across the yard to the outer building that housed the stairs leading down to the wine cellar, I remembered that Baniff had once told me he had a friend who minded the wine cellar in a Kantish monastery. Bless his old soul—he had found a way to get through without arousing suspicion. Perhaps he even had news of a legal way to get me out of here. Poor Devon, but what could I say? Feelings are the first casualty of war.

I was so out of breath when I got into the cellar that I couldn't speak. Which didn't matter, as I didn't see anyone down there besides ourselves. After I caught my breath I asked Devon how he knew about the message.

He told me the wine keeper had seen him playing in the grass and had told him. All the servants knew we were best friends. "How did you get to know a *gnome*, Luvellun? Can I meet him?"

"Sure," I said absently, looking for some sign of movement. Could Baniff be invisible? That would be like him. There was a footfall behind me. I turned. "Baniff?"

It was the wine keeper.

"Luvellun? I could lose my job for this." The wine keeper gave me a sealed letter, which I promptly stuffed in my cloak. "I'm supposed to tell you that the messenger will be back at the same time in three days. Naturally, I know nothing about it. Got my pay."

"Understood." I reached into my pocket and took out a few of the coins Queen Freda had given me, dropping them in his hand. The wine keeper nodded and went back to work. Devon and I ran back to our rooms.

"Tell me what it says! Tell me what it says!" shouted Devon as I closed the door.

"Only under secrecy," I said seriously. That was our code. Whenever I had used Devon to do things for Salan that Salan didn't generally want known such as stealing extra food from other students, I told Devon it was to be done "under secrecy." He respected that. "All right. I'll read it first, then I'll read it to you." He settled back on the bed and waited.

It was from Caethne. It wasn't dated. I kissed the paper, trembling with anticipation for the first time since my return to the monastery, and began to read.

Dear Brother,

And may I still call you so? For that is how I think of you. And may you still live to read this.

Oh, Llewelyn, how utterly brave and daring you were. I don't think that even Mirand, for all his carefully planned legal pyrotechnics, could hold a dying candle to your splendid achievement. After all, Mirand had six weeks of untrammeled leisure time in which to plan his course, and you were working—well, under much more difficult circumstances.

I must tell you that Mirand was most impressed—we all were. I know he thinks of you. I'm sure he's far more impressed with your actions than with mine. You see, our beloved master didn't know this at the time of the trial, but I had a hand in saving his life, too. Remember the morning we first met, when you and Baniff arrived in such a cat-bedraggled state and I was gathering elderberries? You know I had tracked Mirand through his old meditation robe, and so of course I knew where his name stone fragments were buried and well—what can I say—I gathered some of the fragments that morning, before you put the bans in the ground.

Why? So I could have them. Oh, Llewelyn, I wonder what you think. I can't begin to explain some things, and yet I really do think of us as siblings, and so I know that I needn't explain everything. Since the fragments could be tracked only through the bans, these fragments were fairly safe. And since most wizard energy is so full of itself and its own intentions (sorry—I don't mean this personally) I was sure that natural forces could protect them, or at least hide them from Zelar if he should determine where they were through the others. And so I made Pourra eat them, and then I rode to Hala, where I gave Sweetness a brew to bring up the contents of his belly and begged a very good wizard friend of mine to do what she could to keep Mirand alive. It was work getting past Helas, but there you have it—I preserved Mirand's life like the wildflowers until Thoren's wizards could do the rest, and you'd think he'd be grateful—but no, now there are reports and battle plans to write and County Clio is overrun (did you know?) and I'm quite lucky if he says good morning to me when I bring him figs—sigh!

But he lived, through my hands and yours. Thanks.

I'm not supposed to write to you of course. My brother would have a fit if he knew, but you saved the day and I think you deserve more than silence. Walworth is busying himself with his new duties and says little to me now, or to anyone—but I know he remembers what you did for him, and if there was any way he could arrange your freedom, I'm sure he would.

But there isn't—at least not now. The trial is too recent and even up here in my duchy people still speak of it—and of you! You are quite a local hero, especially to my parents, who still know nothing of our special friendship. But you know the moment you disappeared El would inform the king and Thoren would have to send his guards to find you and if you showed up anywhere near us, well . . . As my brother says, there's a war to fight now, and even if we could arrange for your release where could you go? To your sister in Hala who no doubt works for Roguehan if she's still in Hala? To Sunnashiven? Should we risk jeopardizing Threle all over again when your freedom will do nothing for the cause? And Walworth is so busy commanding the Threlan army that he doesn't even have the time to consider how to get you out, and of course he must think of the kingdom first. At least, that's what he told me the one time I brought the subject up. But he does think of you and I'm sure he wonders how you are.

So that's the war. Sometimes I wonder why we even have to have countries. Don't you? Llewelyn, if I could do anything to get you out, I would in a minute—no matter what my brother says.

I think of you every day. Please, please, write back to me—anything at all. My messenger shall be in the same place at the same time three days hence. You may trust to her discretion.

Love, Cae

First I put down the letter. *For Threle he'd sacrifice a friend*. Hadn't Cathe once said that? No, something wasn't right here.

Caethne had not "gotten past" Helas. From what Trenna had told me, she had clearly sought an audience with him in the middle of the night. From the timing of Trenna's arrival at the monastery I knew Caethne had told the duke about the town's destruction. And surely Caethne could have gone straight to her "wizard friend" without disrupting Helas at such a late hour. And as to the name stones—wouldn't Mirand have noticed if any of the fragments were missing? Where the hell had she kept them for six months without his noticing? *Damn her lying, deceiving tongue*. So she knew that I knew about her visit to Helas and she felt she had to deceive me about her intentions.

So many things made sense now. Her quickness to adopt me into the household and gain my trust had been nothing more than an effort to use me as a tool to link herself with her old master. All her interest in my studies. Her words about us being fellow scholars. Her eagerness to involve me in the operation by leading me to eavesdrop on that courier's report and explaining everything to me as if we were family. Damn her! And of course she had gained no influence over Mirand through me—quite the opposite. So she'd sold her loyalties to Mirand's old master, Zelar. Nothing else explained her actions: using her power to flag Grendel that night at the headquarters, her seeming immunity from prosecution at the trial, her unspoken marriage to Cathe, who I was sure now was as evil as El. But Cathe had said that happened a year ago. So she had been flirting with evil then—for all I knew, she had arranged for Cathe's escape from Sunnashiven. The marriage could explain Mirand's distance toward her, which I'd never understood, but Mirand was more attached to learning than to people—he was distant with everyone. I could readily believe that it was his habitual distance that drove her to play goddess-knows-what games with Cathe in the first place. And wasn't it Zelar who had wanted Cathe to change Mirand's alignment? And Cae, who cared nothing for alignments and everything for having Mirand's love or, barring that, something resembling his love, had personal reasons for cooperating. Wouldn't Mirand be most vulnerable to her charms in his new state—at first, anyway?

Why Cae? Why? I loved her—my special more-than-sister. I believed in her songs and words. I would have done anything for her. We all loved her, didn't we? Weren't we all a glorious team working to save the kingdom— even Mirand, in his own way, loved her as much as he could love—I had seen him close his eyes when he held her. *If it were within my power to make Mirand love her in the way a man loves a woman, I would—anything to get us all back together again as we were*.

I looked at Devon. I thought of how it would take more than pleasure apples to bend the affections of a master wizard such as Mirand.

I wondered if Caethne had always been a "lady"—that is, a liar, which is what the word means in Sarana? But was it all a lie? I could believe that

Walworth and Mirand weren't speaking to her, if they had finally surmised what I had. But if Caethne could get a message through to me, then Walworth certainly could. And he hadn't. I thought about the story I had made up for El, my beautifully crafted anger at Walworth's alleged willingness to let me rot in monastic limbo. What if it was really true?

"Are you all right, Luvellun? Are you mad at me?"

"No, Devon. You're too fine a friend."

"What does the letter say?"

"Nothing worth reading." I no longer wished to die. After sending Devon to steal some food from the cook, I stole some paper from Cristo's desk and composed the following response.

> *Dear Lady,*
> *No need for explanations, sister. I understand you perfectly.*
> *Love, Llewelyn*

When Devon returned I had myself a fine meal of bread and cheese. Then I took out Caethne's letter and wrote across the back of it.

> *Comrades,*
> *This was delivered to me a few days before Midsummer. Without problem, presumably. Does Caethne speak truly concerning your silence?*
> *If she speaks false, I shall assume that your messages have been intercepted and I shall walk out of here and join you to fight, law or no.*
> *If true, I shall certainly be thinking of you and your activities for a very long time.*
> *In either case, I thought you'd take an interest. I know I still do.*
> *Llewelyn*

Then I stole an envelope from Cristo and addressed it to Caen Walworth, Master Wizard Mirand, and Baniff the Gnome, through Their Excellencies the Duke and Duchess of Walworth, Duchy of Walworth, Threle. If my comrades were in Loudes, Walworth's parents would forward it. Then I put a wizard seal on it, a seal Mirand would have no trouble opening but Caethne would. "Come on, Devon." His mouth was full of bread. "We're going for a walk."

I led him out of the building, down the footpath, and out the gate leading to the main road outside the monastery grounds, not caring a fig for who saw me. If anyone in town tried to stop us and return us to the monastery, so be it. I probably should have broken this cardinal rule of not leaving the monastery months ago, but I had feared becoming a liability to Walworth. *Well*, I thought, *we shall see.*

It took us two hours to walk to the village, but we found the post immediately. I paid with one of Freda's coins and watched the postmistress mark the envelope with the seal of the Duchy of Kant. Good—there was tangible proof to Walworth that I had no problem leaving the monastery if I chose, that I feared no punishment and he need only say the word. I was not a prisoner of the damned clergy. The postmistress didn't even ask if we were from the monastery.

And then Devon and I returned to a fine dinner. I amused him with stories of gnomes.

Three days later Caethne's messenger showed up in the wine cellar as promised and I gave her my letter to deliver. I don't know what it is with gnomes and drink, but she had a half-depleted bottle of red wine in her hand and was singing and swaying a little against the barrels. I asked her in Sarana if she'd like to take a barrel home with her and she asked me in all seriousness if this was a possibility. I suggested that if she crawled inside one and drowned herself, she'd be home soon enough. She laughed for a solid five minutes, as if this was the funniest thing she'd ever heard. Devon watched her in puzzlement. Then we walked out, leaving her with the bottle against her lips.

I made up my mind to find some Sarana books and keep myself from getting rusty in this language. It was something to do while I waited for a response, and it was possible that the gnome had laughed so long because she didn't understand my meaning.

"What did you say to her, Luvellun? Was that gnome-speak?"

"In a fashion."

The response came from Loudes a month later. I had spent the time studying Sarana, practicing Kantish, meditating, honing my magical skills, and doing whatever chores I decided were worth the exercise in doing. And I ate well. So I was as strong as I had ever been in body and mind when I read the following words, delivered through the courtesy of the wine keeper.

I think it would be best for all concerned if you stay where you are.

W.

It didn't bear my name or any date. I burned it, and stared through the window at the angry summer sun as the scent of the smoke cleared. I stood there for about five minutes, breaking with my past, bidding good-bye to my dream of a life. Then I took three meditation breaths, long and low. I was betrayed. So be it.

When I entered El's apartments unannounced he was rustling papers and lecturing to Cristo. I banged open his door and interrupted him in mid-sentence. "I wish to try my calling."

"Yes?" He looked up, showing absolutely no surprise that I was speaking Kantish. Cristo looked startled that I was addressing his master in such a peremptory manner.

"Now," I insisted.

"We're busy now."

"So am I."

"Come later, Llewelyn, and we'll talk."

"My Kantish name is Luvellun," I corrected him.

"Yes, of course," said El in a tone of hasty annoyance. I looked hard at Cristo and he responded by slouching out of the door. El sighed as if I was inconveniencing him, which I was. He threw his reed pen on the desk and it splattered ink all over his papers.

"I'm waiting, Master."

"For what?"

"For you to ask me the name of the deity I would dedicate my soul to and follow to the grave and beyond."

"Yes, Luvellun," he hissed. "And if you take your dedication under me, you start taking orders from me. No more life of leisurely study, using Devon as a personal servant and doing as you please. You are entering the path to your goddess through me. That means your spirit becomes mine to do with what I will for all your years of study, until I am satisfied that it has become Hers. You will eat when I tell you to, you will starve when I tell you to, you will live as I tell you to live, and you risk your spirit's damnation if you disobey."

"I'm ready, Master."

"Take off your cloak and burn it!" I did so, and even though the smoke smelled beautifully of winter nights and witchworkings as it exhaled its birth all over the room, I shut it out. "And the rest of your clothes. You shall make your dedication sky-clad, as you were born." I did so without hesitation.

I didn't even feel a surge when El called down his goddess's power. First the power wasn't there and then it was, cleaner and sharper and more possessive than anything wizardry could conjure or call upon. We were locked. I spread my arms and opened myself to it.

"What is the name of the deity you would follow?"

"Habundia-Christus." Without thinking I added the suffix that had come to me in the dream vision I had once created. "And my name for Her is Hecate."

"Yes. To you She is Hecate. For Hecate loves a scholar's sacrifice. The Goddess has blessed your palm with Her sign." I clenched my fist and opened it. "And she has blessed your life from the beginning, for all your best works and days have been sacrifice. And it shall be through Hecate that you find Habundia, and it shall be through me that you enter Hecate and become one with Her. The path is long."

"I am on it already."

"Ever and always. It is your path. You are dedicated."

"So be it, Brother." And then the power was gone.

El pulled some clothes out of a drawer and threw them at me. "Wear these. You are now a novitiate." They were the simple black shift and pants worn by beginning clerical students. "You may remain in Cristo's rooms."

"Thanks. I intend to."

"Yes, right. You carry a ban against using your full individual powers."

"And against traveling north of the Drumuns. What's your point?" He made no mention of the bans Mirand had removed against my working magic for reasons other than aiding Sunna or working magic to help myself. But of course those bans were no longer relevant.

"I shall have to remove them at some point in your training. Here's a reading list. You will know these books before second harvest, at which time you will take my classes and only mine. I may allow you to take another cleric's instruction later, but that is for me to decide. Here's a letter giving you permission to use the libraries. Not that you seem to need it." I started to leave. "I didn't dismiss you yet. You will restrict your diet to fruits and grains. Habundia is a grain goddess and tolerates no meat, and a true devotee of Hecate should have a wan ascetic look about him. If your Goddess has taken your dedication, and I have no reason to believe She hasn't, She shall preserve your health."

"I don't eat much meat anyway."

"Good. First assignment. See what you can do about getting my boy Cristo to kill his wretched owl. Perhaps that will hurry his scholarship along, and such a deed would be an appropriate way to mark your dedication."

"An owl is Athena's bird, isn't it? And Athena is Hecate's opposition, the benevolent aspect of the Goddess who oversees scholars?"

"Yes."

"As you will, Master."

El began rustling his papers again. I was in the hall before he dismissed me. Strong and easy as the plummeting moon.

Eighteen

I killed Cristo's owl for him.

That was my first understanding, for it turned out that Cristo really did have some affection for the thing. Killing one's own affection was supposed to be the point of the exercise. Every cleric who chooses to work with the evil aspect of a deity must prove that he is willing to perform a supreme act of self-sacrifice, which is not suicide but the deliberate destruction of something he loves in which the good aspect of the deity is manifest. And so a cleric who works with Hecate must destroy something of Athena's that he has grown to cherish.

Cristo dutifully wrapped the remains in a towel and asked me to come with him to El's apartments, where El himself watched Cristo eat them and duly recorded it. El never asked Cristo if he himself had murdered his pet, but I'm sure he had to notice that my hands were red and that I was still holding the knife. I noticed that Cristo was eating quickly out of fear of displeasing his master, but not with the abandoned gusto of one who has experienced love and willingly rejected it. When we got back to our rooms he threw up in a bucket, which should have made me question the strength of his bond to Hecate. For although Hecate's clergy must forgo flesh for the mind, I later learned that there were approved ways to partake of flesh under rare circumstances, such as sacrificing Athena's bird as a prelude to initiation. Cristo should have been competent in those techniques by this point in his training.

Anyway, Cristo now owed me one. Most evil clerics do not kill the thing they love until the eve before their initiation, when the dedicants and clerics of the deity the initiate would embrace usually plan an elaborate, well-attended ritual around the killing. But Cristo had now earned credit for the required deed, which put him on strict notice to finish his academic papers before second harvest or be turned out of the monastery without record. And so he finished. He stopped his incessant talking, and developed a rather hollow, owl-like look around his eyes. Shortly before I was to take my entrance exam, El performed the expected rite of initiation on Cristo and marked him down as having officially entered the service of Habundia-Christus as a priest of Hecate. Whether Hecate Herself recognized him was anybody's guess, but his papers were now in order.

I expected that Cristo would then find a job teaching in another monastery and I would be rid of him, but El kept him around with a cruel sort of lightness. Since it is customary for a high priest to present his students with an appropriate gift upon initiation, El's gift to Cristo was a temporary teaching position that carried none of the job security and privileges the other clerics enjoyed, which El said was the shadow-light condition Cristo's spirit had long aspired to, the condition of being a professional scholar without really being a professional scholar. The high priest knew that the one thing Kursen *had* effectively taught Cristo was that he must hate himself as a failure if he ever dirtied his hands and mind by working in any nonmonastic employment. Cristo was not really a scholar, but I sensed that at one point in his life he had liked reading and knowing things, before he ate the monkish promise that what he happened to enjoy doing in his odd moments was a legitimate area of work that he could make a living at.

And El, with his disgust at incompetence and his almost dangerous passion for a calling that demanded one kill one's passion daily, took intense pleasure in having led Cristo to sacrifice more than half of his life for the privilege of having to live constantly with the terror of being turned out and becoming his own definition of failure. Simply letting him go or finding him permanent, secure work was not the way to keep Cristo on the rack. Keeping him on through seasonal work with well-timed promises of a permanent, secure position any day now kept him in a delicate state of torture. El was nothing if not thorough about such things.

El also bestowed on him the additional duties of advising younger students on their studies. This was a brilliant move on El's part, because Cristo had so little ability and interest in finding any student's particular path that he gave sublimely wretched guidance and managed to strangle away many years of young lives, much to El's personal enjoyment. To my mind, the destruction would have been prettier for El to watch if Cristo did his damage with intent, but El seemed amused with the raw primitiveness of Cristo's methods of execution and with his unthinking instinct for waste, and so he kept him around. Cristo was his instrument of torture on the other dunces who aspired to the sublimity of evil, and El's gift of temporary work was his torture in kind to Cristo.

Anyway, Cristo owed all the exquisite misery of his new situation to me, and since it was a misery he had been converging on for years, I suppose one could argue that his debt to me was as large as life.

Devon continued to live with me and Cristo, and so I had a household within Kursen Monastery to darkly mirror the one I once had believed I had in Helas, only to my mind a household more honest in its cruelties, which I could respect. Devon's little cruelties had no more intent in their execution than Cristo's panoramic ones, but the primitivism that was so inexcusably slipshod in an allegedly initiated priest such as Cristo was strangely incisive in a rough, untutored boy like Devon. Devon's favorite cruelty was mowing down wildflowers just before their buds blossomed, because somebody had once told him that you could catch a fairy that way and make it do whatever you wanted, and Devon proclaimed that he wanted to make it hurt. Of course he knew nothing of my attraction to fairies and flowers or of what Caethne's long-lived wildflowers had meant to me, but when I told him I disapproved he stopped. Or at least he stopped if he thought I was watching.

In his search for fairies, he began to focus his attentions on the dead. On dead animals, that is, which really sickened me as I progressed in my studies of Hecate. Not that Devon ever actually killed the animals. He would find their corpses in a corner of one of Kursen's herb gardens, where monkshood grew and snakes and rodents and other small animals would poison themselves on the leaves. Devon would then cut open their corpses looking for fairies, because he had heard that fairies sometimes took animal form.

He'd tell me about it and then he'd want to know if there was any way the dead animals could come back. Not that he missed them or anything, but he would have nightmares about armies of bats and mice returning to hurt him in his old age. So I would make up nice sunny stories about animals who talked and sang and loved. Animals who lived in pretty towns and rode in fine carriages and had friends and families. Animals who were just as sweet and helpless and innocent as pie and knew nothing of hurt or revenge.

Instead of shaming him away from his new fascination, my little fictions only comforted him for the next assault on whatever corpses he happened to find in the garden. And in time he left off his interest in fairies in favor of an interest in merely destroying things. I suppose, from the standpoint of evil, that was my first clerical healing, although I didn't know enough to think of it in that way at the time.

I was doing everything in my power to keep my own mind green and growing, despite El's best attempts to thwart me. You see, my spirit really was in his keeping, and we both knew that if El chose to bring down Habundia's power, he could force me to obey his will. El needed to restrict his students from being themselves as a means of teaching them the finer aspects of self-sacrifice, as a way of slowly seducing novitiates into perpetual self-denial. Once a student proved capable of living on the edge of his or her own self-destruction the real bonding with the deity could begin, which El of course had to preside over. I also knew that as a high priest of Habundia Christus, El *needed* to restrict others as part of his path and calling. The act of restriction pleased Habundia and served to increase El's own power. But as far as I was concerned, that was what the other students were there for. I resolved to be special.

The simplest and cleanest way to avoid becoming El's spiritual property was to make it cost him something dear if he tried. And with El being a high priest, about the only thing he could hold dear was his relationship to Habundia-Christus. So how does a novitiate who is completely under the power of a superbly trained, dreadfully experienced high priest even begin to threaten his master's relationship with the deity? By constantly creating conditions in which El had to choose between controlling me or pleasing the aspect of Habundia that was the very essence of his spirit. And this took some creativity on my part, since Habundia-Christus is the divine force that manifests most palpably in all acts that restrict the spirit. Under normal conditions El would draw strength and score points with Her by transforming me into something that I wasn't.

So I annihilated normal conditions whenever and wherever possible. One of my earliest annihilations was executed on second harvest, the day I was supposed to prove that I had learned the reading list El gave me at my dedication. Most of the books he had assigned me were repetitions of each other, so I had read three or four, skimmed the rest, and used the rest of my time to make good my resolution to keep up my private study of Sarana, even though I had no one to speak it with.

The questioning took place before a small assembly of clerics. El was technically the only one allowed to ask me questions. The others were there as witnesses, according to the rules. The whole process was just a formality to ensure that I was ready for actual classes. It was supposed to take no more than an hour or two. I decided to see if I could stretch things out for a full day and night. Why not start things right? And I played the whole thing as if I were merely out to prove, like any other scared and obedient entering student, that I was "serious." At least as "serious" as Cristo had been in his critiques of broken relics.

"Brother" Cristo was there, by the way, although he looked as though he wasn't sure he should be. So were Sister Elwyn and Brother Styrn. As soon as everyone was comfortably seated I suggested that we bring in the doorkeeper and the chief cook. Everyone laughed politely except Cristo, who seemed unsure as to whether he should laugh, his own position being so precarious. After all, he could laugh one day and get thrown out the next and then the laughter would hurt him. So he kept his face poised in a dopey sort of neutrality. The general mood was pleasant enough, however, and El breezily began to open the questioning. I immediately interrupted him to insist on including representatives of the servant class as witnesses. This time my voice sounded pointedly and uneasily self-righteous and I succeeded in making everyone uncomfortable.

"It's never done. The board is here," said El.

"I am most sorry for that, Master. I have prayed a good deal over this . . . blessed event." El looked impatient, but, after all, one was supposed to pray over these things, so what could he say? "And I have felt more strongly than ever that my life is not my own. It is Hers. I wouldn't be here if She had not led me to become a servant of the monastery as well as a scribe, and since in all humility it is out of service that I come into Her greater service, I believe it only fitting that I should share this blessing with other servants. None of us is better or more intelligent than anyone else in the eyes of the Goddess, are we, Master?" I paused so long that a fine expectation billowed upward through the room, a collegial pressure to which El had to bow by giving the correct answer to my question.

"No." Pause. "Hm." He spoke the latter into his collar.

It was beautifully ridiculous. Once El had properly proven his humility, everyone had to follow suit, so they all contented themselves with hiding their discomfort at my earnestness and nodding. Except Cristo. He was giving benediction by whispering loudly, "None of us." El glanced sharply at him. My speech had stirred him into a fleeting semblance of personality.

I continued sanctimoniously, "I am not special. Master El here is not . . . special." El's eye's started to bulge. "My master knows that none of us are special, that we are all lucky recipients of Her bounty, accidents of Her womb."

"Yes," said Elwyn devoutly. Everyone looked misty and pious, including Cristo.

"And I want to remind myself of how lucky I am that dear Master El has allowed me, of all servants, this opportunity to grow into Her. I beg to let my dear comrades from the kitchen and the cellar partake of this event, to remind me of where I came from, lest I get too full of pride in my new status and offend the Lady whose servants we *all* are." You see, I knew that the chief cook smelled to the gods' own abode at this time of morning, and that even though the doorkeeper would amuse Cristo, he would drive everybody else crazy with his imbecile hand motions and bobbing. Also, there was a rule that anyone entering the room before the exam would not be allowed to leave until it was over. I pretended to wipe away a tear. "Hail Christus."

"Most impressive," said Brother Styrn, nodding encouragement. He complimented El. "You are to be commended on your choice of dedicant, Brother."

"Hmmm, of course." He tried to cover his pique with a say-the-right-thing-and-get-it-over-with tone. It came out sounding confused.

As he said it I buried my head in my arms as if I were going into prayer, just to make it look as though no one was listening to him.

Anyway, I had requested only two servants. The board, not to be outdone by my commitment to humility, sent Cristo to round up as many servants as he could. I spoke my humble gratitude in prayer, murmuring into my arms that Kursen was such a . . . *spiritual* house. I thanked the Goddess and Sister Elwyn for Elwyn's tender care when I was sick and had no place to go. I thanked the Goddess and Brother Styrn for all his kindnesses. I thanked the monks for accepting me as one of their own and for their kind concern for all who enter Her house. I thanked Brother Cristo for being himself. I deliberately paused as if I were drowning myself in prayer and couldn't be disturbed. Then the afterthought: "Oh, yes, and Master El." I looked up solemnly.

El "hmmd" with pseudo-grace and looked up at the ceiling to avoid looking at me. I glanced up at the ceiling and appeared puzzled. Then everyone else first stared up at the ceiling and then looked questioningly at El. He was thoroughly annoyed now but couldn't show it without offending his colleagues. "Needs paint," he murmured helplessly. The ceiling needed more than paint. It was full of holes, and pieces of rush were dropping through from the floor above. I knew that El had work to do and really wanted to get this over with. I said seriously that perhaps the falling reeds were a gift from Habundia Herself, which made El's comment about paint sound thoroughly unobservant. I cradled my head back in my arms and breathed and shuddered audibly.

Half an hour passed. I asked everyone to pray with me, which they did. Elwyn led us in a hymn, and I kept adding verses so that everyone else would have to. El was intoning a verse solo when Cristo interrupted him by strolling in with about a dozen apprehensive-looking servants. He had rounded up all the cooks and the stable boy, as well as the wine keeper and Cristo's special buddy the doorkeeper. The doorkeeper was not apprehensive. He was wagging his head and doing a sliding sort of dance in time to El's singing, which caused El to stop his carefully constructed verse in dismay. I saluted the doorkeeper earnestly and he responded by raising his hands at right angles to his sides and spreading his fingers the way the younger students were supposed to. I believe Devon had been teasing him with the gesture. He also widened his eyes and puffed out his cheeks in a show of great pride as he stared pointedly at El. The doorkeeper knew the rules. He wasn't going to move until the high priest saluted him back.

So El quickly made the gesture and he looked so ridiculous it was all I could do not to laugh. Elwyn was not so skillful but she managed to cover her giggle in a broad smile. Styrn quietly chuckled but, being the oldest cleric present, he could get away with it. His chuckle gave everyone permission to laugh and poor El had to bear it. And Cristo, of course, had to laugh along with the majority. So El nervously twitched his shoulders and pulled at his collar and forced himself to smile at his colleagues while Cristo lined the servants up against the walls. Cristo then looked toward the other clerics for approval. He sat next to El and prayed. El stared glumly into space and drummed his fingers until Cristo had finished.

It was obvious that some of the servants were drunk. They smelled of bad beer. The cooks smelled of stale garlic and onions. None of them had washed recently. None of them understood what any of this was about. All of them avoided the doorkeeper, who ended up leaning against the wall in back of El. I didn't blame them, as the doorkeeper had a horrible spitting cough.

The other clerics began a light prayer for his health, so what could El do but join in? Finally he smacked his lips with great annoyance. *"Can we begin?"*

"Yes, Master, I earnestly desire it."

"First question—"

I stood and interrupted him to thank the servants for their presence and the happy times we had shared working together in service to Kursen Monastery. I spoke at length on the deep pleasure I had in making good plain sorrel soup with the cooks, in doing inventories with the account maids, in sweeping the servants' quarters to a fine gleaming morning polish, in running errands for the stable boy, and on and on and on. None of the servants had ever worked with me before. All of them had seen me about the grounds and no doubt wondered what I did. So they listened to me crow about the special bond we all shared, and glanced uneasily at each other, each one convinced that he was the only one who hadn't worked with me. And no one could protest without tacitly admitting that perhaps he *hadn't* swept the floor that day. And El wasn't about to announce to the board that his newfound prize had done about as much servant work as he had over the last few months. Cristo looked as if he believed me. He was trying to figure out where I had found the time to do all these chores and he was jealous of my efficiency. I knew I was driving him crazy. The board acted impressed with my dedication to work, although I could tell they were all getting tired and uncomfortable. The room really stank by the time I was finished. I closed by solemnly telling the servants that they couldn't leave until the questioning was over, making slow eye contact with each one. Then I sat.

"First question—"

"I didn't steal the spoon, Master High Priest! Honest!" blurted out one of the cooks in a quavering voice. "It was him that done it. I saw him." He pointed to the wine keeper. The wine keeper denied it and kicked him. This was better than expected. Now El would have to hold court over a lousy spoon! The exam would never begin.

"What spoon?" said El tiredly, since it was his job to ask. The doorkeeper made more bird motions with his hands and then pretended to drink from a spoon. El looked away.

"A spoon to send to his sister at the front. For rations," insisted the cook.

"I don't *have* a sister, you cud!" The wine keeper looked plaintively at El. "I don't, Master."

"Where *is* the front now?" asked one of the clerics. His interest was unbecoming but decorum seemed to have fled with the comfort level in the room. Styrn nudged him and then did his best to hide his own interest by looking at the floor. Anytime news got into the monastery it took precedence over everything else because it was forbidden. Clerics were not supposed to sound interested in outside events because they were not supposed to know anything about them. They were supposed to be too busy with their callings. The brother had lapsed. He had publicly admitted that he had time to care about the state of the world. He should have collared the fellow in secret and pumped him for information. That was what anybody else would have done.

The wine keeper could feel El's gaze on him. He was too scared not to answer. "Somewhere near Hala. The capital is holding, but the southern portions of Helas—I mean South Walworth—have been lost. Merchants make lousy soldiers. They all ran to the capital for protection. And the farmers along Kant's border are sending their surplus up here, where people have money to pay. All the influx in Hala is refugees who have lost everything. Not a copper do they have. And luxury foods aren't selling to those who can buy. More profit in shipping up to Kant than in giving everything away free to the soldiers." He spat. Some of his saliva hit El. "Sorry."

"How do you know this?" asked El.

"He got a letter from his sister hidden in the last shipment of blackberries. That's when he sent her the spoon."

"Did not. Heard it all from you and you know it! You're getting letters every day!"

"Come on, man! Where would *I* get letters? I know the rules. Besides, the only sister I ever had was yours, buddy, and believe me, I'd rather have the blackberry thorns!"

A scuffle broke out again until El asked, "Aren't there spoons enough in Hala?"

"It was the relic spoon from the vestry. The gold one, Master, as makes the food of plenty appear during service."

He meant the Harvest Spoon, a sacred item that initiated priests and priestesses of Habundia used to produce the Fruits of Communion during service. I had no idea what the wine keeper's sister would use it for, but the crime of stealing sacred relics carried the death penalty under monastic law. There were gasps of outrage from the board. Even Elwyn looked grave. Cristo looked scared. The wine keeper went pale. El sent Cristo to look for the spoon.

"I suppose we could start the exam while we are waiting," I said brightly. "First question, Master?"

El made a dismissive motion with his hand. No one else wanted to begin. The clerics were all murmuring and Styrn was sputtering about how affronted he was and how doubly affronted the Goddess Herself was. I'm sure he took it as a personal insult, as he always ate more fruit than anyone else when it did appear at rituals. The servants were trying to look frantically innocent.

I assumed guilt and asked the wine keeper why he had done it, which focused everyone's attention on him, so he had to answer. He looked aghast at me and began softly, as if he were trying to tell me something under his words. "The city is starving. A city used to plenty. Soldiers fight ill on empty stomachs. I would hope the good brothers and sisters of Kursen Monastery who profess to carry out the charity of the Mother Goddess would want to feed the hungry." His voice lost its edge of fear and became more clipped. "I am sorry if I have offended your sensibilities."

"Why don't the Helan farmers feed their compatriots?" I asked. "They've got surplus to send up here."

He looked at El.

"You may answer, hmm."

The wine keeper decided he'd better, as the truth was sure to get dragged out of him one way or another. "It ain't all Helans as want to fight Roguehan's forces. It ain't all Helans who care to take arms against their southwest kindred, who speak the same language and everything. The war is not as popular in some places as it might be in others." He looked at me with deep resentment and I responded with a look of studied mildness. He continued, "After all, the old duke kept the economy in good order, so nobody wanted for cakes and bread until the recent fighting broke out. And there's some who say if it weren't for the new lord's son meddling where he shouldn't have been, there'd be peace and plenty still, that the old duke never did no real harm. Smeared his gloves a bit for the good of the duchy, but then who wouldn't? Them's politics, and a good lord understands how to work 'em. Certainly didn't deserve to hang for it. Loudes is far away and shouldn't be meddling neither. The people liked their duke well enough, and now that he's dead and times are bad he's grown some in their estimation."

"Yes, hmmm," I said noncommittally, trying my best to sound like El just for the hell of it.

"Well, one likes to have causes to chew on when food's scarce for the same. And since the hunger is as new as the duchy's present management, well . . . Some grumble that maybe Caen Walworth's activities *provoked* an attack. Some say maybe it's time the Duchy of Helas should join the rest of the Botha-speaking world, like County Clio has already had the good sense to. Lot of 'em got relatives in the southwest anyway. And as to the farmers, they only want to make a profit, same as the next fellow. And some say who can blame 'em?"

"So who's fighting?" My questions were strictly out of order but no one was stopping me. The clerics all wanted news and I was doing their dirty work for them.

"Some Helans are fighting, but they're quickly losing heart, as their decision ain't popularly supported. People see them as prolonging the war. Some soldiers are going down from other parts of the kingdom—"

I guessed from his tone of voice and the way he was looking at me while he spoke that I was supposed to care. He was easy to crush. "Like your sister?"

"Yes, all right, so I do have a sister and like her, and so what? But those are powerfully resented. Most of the southern towns gave up peacefully. Been enough violence since one of them blew up. And there's still some talk over where that one came from. And so far Roguehan seems a kind enough lord. Promising a return to plenty next year. Open southwestern markets."

"So why aren't you working for him?" It seemed like a logical enough question on my part. El chuckled.

The wine keeper spat. "Seems I might as well be. The duchy is as good as gone over to the southwest. No one wants to defend it. People just want to live and trade and be left alone."

"If no one wants to defend it, then perhaps it's not worth defending," I said in my softest, most designed-to-irritate voice. "And deserves no aid from Kursen."

"Nicely put," said Brother Styrn, applauding me as Cristo returned. Cristo had found the spoon. He placed it on the table and resumed his seat.

"Thank you, Brother," said El, picking up the spoon. The wine keeper stared at the floor. Rushes dropped. Cristo was catching them in his fists. El sighed and looked at him, so he stopped. "So have we wasted our time with false accusations?" El asked the cook.

"I . . . I saw him take it, Master."

"Then perhaps his sister sent it back? Hm?"

"Or perhaps it is a replica, Master El," I offered. This really put him out. Now he had to test it. He grumbled and put his hands over it and mumbled and mispronounced the words because he was tired and the room was uncomfortable. Styrn corrected his pronunciation. El really didn't like being corrected and had to start over again. So *I* offered to help, just to be annoying—I didn't know any clerical magic at this point. Because I interrupted him El had to start for the third time. The best part was that this holy relic worked only intermittently anyway, and so El had to struggle with it awhile trying to get a clear reading. The wine keeper spoke up.

"Don't bother, Brother. It *is* a replica. I'm guilty of the theft."

"Then you die," El said stonily, pushing the spoon away with relief. The man nodded. At least he was being Threlan about the whole thing. He knew the penalty. "How do we get the real spoon back from your sister?"

"You don't, Brother. She doesn't have it."

"Then who does?

"A high priest by the name of Lord Cathe. Understand he's feeding half of Hala and then some with it." *Beautiful! Better than pleasure apples for Sunna.* Explained a lot about the people's current mood. I wondered if Walworth, desperate to feed the Helans at any cost, had ordered the theft.

"Isn't Lord Cathe Commander Walworth's cousin?" I offered brightly. "Northern branch of the family, I believe. High priest from Sunnashiven. Child of the gods and everything. Didn't he make first rank at the age of seventeen, Master?"

El scowled. "And so am I to understand that the commander of the national army is stealing from monasteries to feed his troops?"

"I did the stealing, as I said," said the wine keeper. "This priest Cathe has the spoon from my sister. I wanted to help her. The commander himself isn't in it, far as I know."

"Yes, enough." El ordered the other servants to take the man to an underground cell and lock him up. They gratefully cleared the room.

"First question." Since the day was wearing on and El didn't want to sit through another speech, I gave long detailed complex answers to all his questions and then graciously asked everyone in the room to comment. Which they all did, because to refuse would have implied an ignorance of the subject at hand. And Sister Elwyn, who couldn't be outsweeted by a mere student like me, had to make up more questions for her colleagues to show her interest in their opinions and so it went on and on until night and then some. And El, of course, couldn't speed things up without offending his colleagues, who all had to speak their worn-out lecture notes and so it was morning again before we were finished. I congratulated myself on meeting my goal.

And they passed me with high distinction and admitted me to formal studies as they dragged themselves off to bed, leaving me with Cristo and the spoon that the wine keeper had to die for lying on the table. Cristo was yawning. "You did really well. That was good." He stretched. "You going back upstairs now?" He was really asking me for permission to do the same. He didn't want to go anywhere in the building by himself.

"No." I was playing with the spoon and watching the room lighten as the candles sputtered. I covered a candle with the round part of the spoon to put out a flame and was surprised to feel the flame burning my skin through the spoon's handle as the fire spurted and flared around the edges of the round part. Fascinating. Replicas don't conduct energy because solidified magic resists everything around it. Perhaps clerical replicas acted differently. Cristo was watching me through bleary eyes. "How'd you find the time to read all those books so fast? It took me a solid year and a half. You were really good."

"We're not here to be *good*, Cristo. Besides, *you* weren't reading with a war on." I threw in the latter statement just for the pleasure of making him think he had missed something, but Cristo was too stupid to be confused about some things.

"Yeah, too bad about there being a war and all." Cristo thought he was supposed to say this, even though he clearly had no idea what the war was all about. He was chagrined over his improper use of the word *good* and he was trying to gain my approval with the sort of statement he thought nobody could possibly object to. All of Habundia's organized priesthood, save those who openly align themselves to Ares, is supposed to oppose war. Not because war is bloody and violent and kills people, mind you. We honor that. But war belongs to the realm of action, the base world in which we must not sully our fine minds. Cristo was certainly not about to sully his.

Organized violence didn't seem to move him one way or another. He didn't understand the issues. He only wanted approval. I was supposed to absolve him of his discomfort by agreeing with his sentiments. I said instead, "Yes, well, it's a rather tame sort of war as wars go, I suppose. Not much fighting. People getting fed divine dole off a stolen Harvest Spoon. The Threlan commander trying his hand at creating a believable enemy. Brother Cathe is probably making lots of converts."

"Do you know him—Lord Cathe?"

"We've met. He was one of the first people to encourage me to take up this profession."

"How can he be a high priest and everything and not be associated with a monastery? You said he made high priest at the age of seventeen?" Cristo could not comprehend this. "How can that happen? He must have been really lucky."

"Well, let's say he had the right sort of circumstances surrounding his birth. And at one time he was associated with Habundia's temple in Sunnashiven. I think he's doing government work now."

"He's feeding an entire city." The thought completely depressed him. "Must be nice. All those potential converts."

"Yes, well, Cathe is quite a fellow." I tried to put out the other candle flames without success. There was some kind of magic in the spoon that prevented the flames it covered from snuffing out. Interesting. I pocketed the spoon. The candles would sputter themselves out into morning light soon enough. "Knows how to fight a war. He'll probably have his own temple by the time he's twenty."

"Yeah," said Cristo dolefully. "That's really good—I mean great."

"Well, I'm off to rest now. Would you care to extinguish the lights, old boy?"

"They're out," he said, sounding puzzled. As far as I could tell the candles were all still burning, although one was gasping its life out. As soon as I saw the flame die completely I held the spoon over the puddle of wax and willed the flame to come back. When I removed the spoon all I saw was the wax puddle hardening in the cool morning air. "Hey, it's burning again," exclaimed Cristo. "The gods must be pleased."

And so they are, I thought. *For they've dropped a fine illusion tool in my lap. No illusionist can see his own illusions, so that explains why I saw flames when I wanted the spoon to snuff them and can't see the flame I just willed to come back, while in each case Cristo saw what I expected to see. Perhaps this very spoon has been working intermittently in ritual for a long time, as it apparently produces illusion in accord with the user's will. Its success in ritual must have depended on whether the user believed Habundia would bless that particular working. No wonder El couldn't get a reading on it. And didn't the wine keeper stop him from trying?* Now I had something worth thinking about.

I left the dying candles and started for my room, Cristo following. He was wishing peace and plenty on everyone he saw.

Nineteen

*W*hen I put the illusion spoon in my pillowcase I did not dream. When I kept it hidden near the hearth the dreams invaded. So every night I got to choose between oblivion and illusion. No illusionist can see his own dreams.

Sometimes Isulde got tangled in my visions, spoon or no spoon. That's how I knew she was real. I always called her Isulde now, not Genna. Isulde was her North Country name. I had no idea what attracted her fairy presence into my visions, but there she was, like a cloudy evening wind kissing memory out of memory, like an embodiment of the pieces of daily beauty that once had captured my heart in Helas and broke my heart now. She spoke or sang in her beautiful Northern language, which felt distantly like Sarana, but older and more powerful. In my visions I too spoke her language, willing the words to come as they did. She said once that the strange cold depths of my heart had drawn her on that empty winter night when she first came to me, but she also said it was the night itself that drew her. Set this down: Isulde came in visions when I wasn't looking. That is all I can say.

But that was a night thing. Days were for annihilating normal conditions, for keeping my mind strong and healthy, especially since after considering everything backward and forward I now had reasons to believe that the wine keeper was Baniff: the theft, the illusion spoon, the quickness to prevent El from discovering that the spoon made illusions, the way he had looked pointedly at me as he related the latest news from Hala. I had no idea when he had switched places with his friend the real wine keeper, but my guess and belief was that it had been sometime *after* I sent my reply to Caethne. It was hard to imagine Walworth stealing holy relics from monasteries, but hey, war was war and perhaps he was driven to it. Walworth had told me to stay here. Was it possible that he had planned the switch then?

But my mind was racked toward breaking, for as often as I would convince myself that it was Baniff under death sentence in Kursen and I needed to plan my own strategem for saving him as he had once saved me, it would also occur to me, in dark clutches of disbelief, that it was an impossible feat for any illusionist to keep his appearance and accent altered for weeks on end, and that the story about having a sister didn't make sense. But then I would shred doubt by telling myself he was trying to throw El off, as I was with my questions and cold demeanor. Perhaps the story about Cathe's feeding the city of Hala was another false lead. And despite Mirand's injunction that belief is not a choice, I willingly chose to believe, so desperately did I *want* the wine keeper to be my old friend.

Devon had missed me the previous day and was violently desperate for attention, so I promised him a long walk around the grounds if he'd go and gather as much information as he could about the wine keeper. Prudence dictated that I not compromise whatever Baniff intended to accomplish here by making my own inquiries.

"Why are you so eager about the wine keeper, Luvellun?" Devon would ask petulantly when I'd hit him with questions that were beyond his ken to answer. "Do you like him better than me?" Devon seemed so put out at the possibility that I might show interest in anyone besides his own royal personage that I had to pretend to a desperate neutrality concerning Kursen's new prisoner.

"No, Devon, I just want to see what kind of spy you'd make and how well you can tell me things without letting anyone else know. This is to be under secrecy. Understand?"

He seemed to, and I made myself scrupulously praise him for his discretion every time he brought me a bit of news.

In the meantime, I decided I would continue to keep my mind as strong, healthy, and independent of El's influence as I could, against the increasingly likely possibility that Baniff was here for me. The way I chose to do this was by teaching El's first class for him. I made sure to arrive in class a few minutes early, ostentatiously brandishing my papers and gravely greeting the other new students in the name of Habundia. The other students were displaying their hopeful nervousness by having arrived even earlier. Hell, some of them had probably camped out—anything to be serious. I could tell that my manner threatened them because even though I clearly was a beginning student, I was going to teach a class, and that made me more hopelessly serious than any of them could imagine. Somebody asked me my name.

"Luvellun," I said without further explanation, setting down my papers and glancing quickly around the room as if it were time to get to work. I was starting to assume a prayer stance I had read about when someone else, emboldened by his classmate's courage, asked me where I was from. He had probably noticed my accent. Everyone looked hard at me, breathlessly anticipating my answer, hoping to be able determine why *they* weren't teaching classes on their first day, trying to right what they feared was their first failure.

"Sunnashiven," I said smoothly, as if they were supposed to be impressed. They were. They all assumed I was from the temple. Then, without further ado, I turned my hands palm upward, making sure to flash my scar. This action elicited a few properly amazed gasps. Clearly they were in the presence of someone who had been marked by the Goddess from birth. There could now be no competition between us. They were mine to teach. I adopted a look of benign solemnity and began to pray to Habundia. Nothing too fancy, just a basic prayer that could be modified for good or evil. None of them questioned me. All of them took notes. All of them chanted the prayer back to me precisely as I told them to. Their collected energy was weak and hesitant, but that was probably to be expected, as many of them had never practiced any sort of magic before. I made them chant the prayer three times, waving my hands around in a thickly pretentious solemnity, conducting their voices, getting them to slowly increase the sound.

"Lovely, lov-e-ly, lov-e-ly," I intoned officiously as El jauntily strode in. He was puffing his cheeks and whistling, a pile of books under his arm. The class was picking up the prayer for the fourth time as he entered, intoning toward me, "Habundia, Habundia, Your many forms are blessed," as if I were the Goddess Herself. El's whistle faded as he stopped in midstride, left eye bulging. A book slid out of his grasp and crashed onto the floor.

"Hail Habundia." I nodded affably. A young woman motioned him toward an empty seat and looked brightly at me to make sure I was noticing how helpful she was. I picked up El's book for him and repeated her gesture with painstaking humility. "Master. Please. We should *all* be most honored. We are *all* here waiting for your instruction. Learning and waiting. Like winter fish." The young woman sighed audibly at the last phrase to show that she knew the allusion. "Please, Master." The other students all picked up on my cue and looked at him, wanting the high priest to notice that they were all brightly obedient and working extremely hard to make themselves worthy of the monastery.

I had no idea what El would do. I had neatly divided him against himself. I had created a circumstance in which he could control me *or* he could control the rest of the incoming class. It cost him less to sit. He watched me continue to lead prayers for about a quarter hour, hmming up a show of good humor and trying unsuccessfully to gaze me into nervousness. It wasn't working. Nothing less than Habundia's force was going to make me stop and he knew it.

At the end of a short prayer of thanksgiving to the grain he finally spoke. "Hm, yes, you've done a fine job. I shall remember it. But now it's time for me to take over." He started doggedly for the front of the classroom. I wasn't finished yet.

"Is that what you *want*, Master?" I asked softly, inclining my head.

"Yes, Luvellun, it's what I *want*," he snapped. "Enough. Sit down."

"No, Master, I can't do that." Audible tension snapped through the room. It was beginning to dawn on some of them that I wasn't supposed to be teaching after all.

"What?"

"I should greatly fear for my soul in giving you what you *want*. And I would fear for all of us. If I were to help you get what you *want*, I should be responsible for helping a high priest of Lady Christus stray from the path of self-sacrifice. And the rest of my classmates could be implicated for letting it happen. Humble or exalted, we are all responsible for each other's spiritual welfare, are we not, Master?" I waited for an answer. The whole class was looking at him and nodding vigorously to show that they were up to their divine responsibilities.

"Yes," he had to say.

"And it is our duty to keep Her laws, is it not, Master?"

"You have done your duty. I am pleased," he said sharply. "Now sit."

"Are you testing us to see if we are worthy, Master High Priest?" asked the young woman who had offered him a chair. For a dedicant of Habundia-Christus she looked unbecomingly proud of her question. The other students looked scared at the possibility of being tested. "Do you wish to see if we would knowingly break Her laws?" Everyone looked intently at El.

I milked her suggestion for all it was worth. "Dear Master, I certainly hope that by sacrificing my very strong desire to be a student and learn worthwhile things to the strict demands of monasticism, to your own honored calling as a high priest, that I am acting in accord with Her dictates. And my classmates, who would certainly prefer your instruction to mine, are also sacrificing their own preferences. As they should. Please tell me, tell *us*, if the sacrifice of one's strongest desires is *not* in accordance with Her laws."

I paused, and before he could answer, the young woman called out excitedly, " 'For you must destroy your very selves to follow me.' " Her tone was irritatingly self-congratulatory, a tone that conveyed, *I am just so spiritual and so insightful and this is so beautiful and why doesn't everyone else just notice how smart I am?*

I knew El was irritated with her too but he hid his irritation under a pleasant blandness that he intended her to take as approval. "Excellent quote, young lady. Most impressive. Thank you. What is your name?"

She pretended to forget her name. You can't be bothered with a name if you are truly serious. But without a name you can't get credit either, so she stumbled over her words for effect and then said shyly, "It's . . . uh,

Mirra," as if her prodigious book reading made it an effort to remember anything merely personal.

Anyway, I followed up El's empty praise by smiling at Mirra as if I were in total agreement and saying, "Yes, and I am teaching only because I care so little for the exercise."

That should have put her in her place, but she had to interject, "Oh, so do I. I know what you mean."

I turned to El. "Please let me respectfully ask, Master, on behalf of my classmates, that you absolve us of any infraction we might be committing should we let you act in accordance with your desires. And please absolve us from acting in accordance with our own, for we all truly crave your instruction but fear to displease the Goddess by attaining that which we truly crave."

What could he say? I had created a context in which El could not bring down Habundia's force to constrain me without acting against Her self-sacrificial nature. In a way I wished he would try an invocation, because the rebound alone would have been worth getting up early for. But he let me continue for the rest of class. And he saved face by pretending that we had passed his cleverly designed first-day test. Which meant that Mirra and I had to be singled out for special praise to keep the game going. When I dismissed class he told me sternly to stay behind.

I disobeyed by walking out with everybody else, basking in their grateful chagrin. I had gotten them all a pass when, left to their own devices, they surely would have failed. But now they all viewed me as competition because I was a student again. Except Mirra. Mirra tried to impress me by waving her books around and letting me and everyone within ten miles know that she was off to the library. I guessed that she wanted me to go with her. We were now supposed to be solely worthy of each other's company due to the superior nature of our minds, while the others were supposed to fall back and worship us. Or worship *her*, rather, for knowing there was a test that day.

I announced that I was retiring to my rooms to have tea with the Sun King and a member of the teaching staff. After the astonishment died down someone reminded me that El had wanted me to stay after class. "What do you think he wants?" The question held them all around me. None of them could stand *not* knowing what sort of special attention they were missing.

I looked idly toward the classroom and noticed that El was standing quietly inside the doorway, watching and listening. Mirra noticed him too, so she lectured loudly in his direction, "But we must never give our master what he *wants*. Remember, that was our test. We are all dedicants of Habundia-Christus now, and responsible for each other's maintenance of Her laws." She probably thought she was going to get extra credit. What she got was a tangible amount of popular support from her classmates; a heady yet uncertain anticipation of freedom started perking here and there through the crowd. Sanctioned, nay, *required* disobedience—what a concept! Monastic training was nothing like any of them had expected it to be. Maybe it was even okay to steal food.

I caught El's eye, a breaking storm in a dangerous calm. It was time to pull in the reins. "I have no idea what our master *wants*. But I do know that I, for one, am going to be careful about putting my desires before his in the name of some speculation about disobedience. Today was *one* test, and we all passed it, but that may be an end. I will assume that a high priest such as El is in the Goddess's keeping and that he is to us even as the Goddess should be. It is my path to deny myself without reference to anyone else's wants and to obey Her above all." I looked over at El again. "Let *him* worry about not getting what he wants. That's his job." The momentary burst of freedom fell into the passive comfort of being told what to do. I had given them all support for the safer path, so they bolted to it. The crowd broke up and I left for my room. I never did go to see him. He never pushed the issue.

But I noticed that after this El was scrupulous about treating me as a favorite and greeting my comments with a good deal of praise. It was preferable to risking another scene. El was not stupid. He knew full well how to make the best of a bad situation, and he clearly used his praise of me to deftly enhance the other students' insecurities. And I helped as often as decently possible, because I saw no reason to let El believe that he was controlling his charges solely through his own efforts.

So I pretty much ran the monastery for a while, at least as much of it as I cared to. Once El had designated me as his pet, it was damn near impossible for him to change the public nature of our relationship, because to do so would be tantamount to admitting that he had been wrong in his assessment of my work. And besides, it was obvious to all that I was bright enough to merit praise, so there was enough reality behind our dismal little charade to keep it going.

And besides, he made the grand mistake of "allowing" me to take other clerics' classes long before anyone else was allowed to, in an attempt to discreetly put some distance between us. He might have been hoping I'd turn my attention against Brother Styrn, who had a way of annoying El in conversation by constantly lecturing him on academic trivia that the high priest had long ago forgotten. I made such a favorable impression on Styrn and Elwyn and the rest, through studied praise of their efforts and practiced humility, that El could not disparage me without disparaging their judgment.

So it was possible to keep something of myself. El had my spirit, but there really wasn't much he could do with it. Within the confines of the monastery I continued to grow as I would and do as I liked.

And one of the things I liked to do best was keep tabs on the outside world. Like where illusion spoons got made and how wine keepers came by them. Devon had discovered that the wine keeper was being held in an underground cell beneath the wine cellar, that sometimes he was guarded but most times wasn't, and that his enemy the cook was the designated guard and that he brought him bean broth twice a day. "And I put a rat in his soup," said Devon proudly. "The cook thought it was funny."

"Did the wine keeper like it?" I asked with a steadiness I didn't really feel.

"No, he choked big." Of course Baniff would sicken over a dead rat. And yes, anyone else might do the same, but there was something in Devon's description that made me think the rat had been an especially pungent torture to the prisoner, as it would be to any gnome.

When I found my first safe opportunity to pay the prisoner an unobserved visit I was bearing a sack containing a bottle of good red wine, some thick corn stew, a steaming loaf of soft bread, and an unlit candle. If you spend enough time in a monastery you get used to stealing. We're all supposed to share everything anyway, so theft is painfully easy to justify. The cook was sharing the key to the cell with me. Which is to say, Devon had "borrowed" the key and I had manifested my own copy so that it wouldn't be missed before Devon returned it to its proper place. I had brought the spoon to help me see through his disguise, but by the time I got to the cell I realized that the spoon would only blind me to any illusions I created with it, not make me impervious to some other illusionist's magic, as I was not actually an illusionist myself.

The cell was dark, of course. The prisoner thought I was the cook when he heard me unlock the door and enter, for as soon as I locked the door behind me he asked, "What's this, cookie—back so soon? You mean I get a *second* bowl of dredge for my dinner tonight? Mmm-mmm."

"No." I lit the candle with wizard fire and set it on the floor. There was only floor, no benches. The cell was fairly clean, but the wine keeper looked sickly and diseased. It was clear that he hadn't been eating well. It was cold underground and he sat huddled in a corner with a blanket around him. I set the sack on the floor and laid out the food on it, waiting with the gods' own intensity for him to recognize me. "Enjoy, man," I said with a tight, grand sort of eager edge that surprised me. Now that I was here I felt strangely uncomfortable but I wasn't sure why.

"Is this my last sup?" He leaned toward the food, clutching his blanket.

"Probably not. Would you like it to be?"

He was ravenous and fell to his eating with such alacrity that it was several minutes before he was able to speak. "I thank 'ee, lad."

"What are you doing here, Baniff?" I spoke his name a little self-consciously, although the fact that he had just called me "lad" made me absolutely sure it was him.

The wine keeper held the bottle to his lips for the gods' own amount of time, draining every fume and drop. It *had* to be Baniff. "Sorry there's no Krygon," I said with a mechanical, knowing smile. The joke sounded harsh and out of tune in there. Something went sad in me as soon as I said it.

"I'm not. Damnable stuff to inventory when we had it. No sooner did I stack it on the shelves than it would sour and have to be thrown away. Gave it to my friend the cook." He was breathless from having taken such a long draught. There was nothing left in the bottle but air, but the man wiped his mouth on his sleeve and took one last swallow at that. I tried to find Baniff in his words but couldn't.

"Damn you, Baniff! Talk to me! What's the real story? I've got a key. Do you want to go? Now? Look at me. I'm here for you!" And I was—all my rage at being rejected had become a ghost at the possibility that one of my friends was really here.

"Who's Baniff?"

"I don't know—who's Baniff?" I repeated sarcastically. "Come, do I have to probe your mind to force the truth out of you?" I meant this as an affectionate joke, but in the excitement of the moment it came out sounding like a threat. I was never that careless with my demeanor.

He looked as frightened as he had during the exam. "No, lad, that's okay, really. I'm whoever you believe I am. Call me Baniff if you like. Knew a gnome by that name once. Fine illusionist." He looked at the cell door. "Want to go?"

"Sure." I picked up the candle and started for the door. "Here, take my hand. It would probably be best if we made our escape invisibly." *Yes*, I thought, *just as we once escaped from Sunnashiven, only this time we will not have our adventures compromised by a passel of monks! Surely there is a cleric aligned to the positive aspects of Habundia who can retrieve my spirit from El, and then all will be right again so long as I remain hidden from the king's guards—and I'm sure Walworth can easily manage that one!* My companion looked hesitant and uncertain. "Oh, of course. You're probably so tired from keeping up appearances for so long that you don't trust yourself to cloak us both. But I thought of bringing the spoon with me. Baniff, will that help?"

"I'm a little tired, lad. And drunk. Let's just go."

I put the key in the lock and suddenly withdrew it. "Hey, buddy, it's not like you to let a little drink stand in the way of illusion." He was silent for a fraction too long. He was thinking of a response. My blood blew like a dying gust and settled into my feet.

"Uh . . . it's been a while since I've had a drop. My tolerance is low."

That was the wrong answer. So wrong I felt a sudden rage. Then I heard myself saying somewhere beyond myself, "I take it you don't care if the cook gets your punishment when your escape is discovered." I was in control of my demeanor again, although only the gods knew how, because that wasn't my intent, and I actually said this merrily and conspiratorially, key in hand, as if sending the cook to his execution was all a grand game between us.

"Not in the least. The cud deserves no less." He spat. Baniff would not say this. Damn the life, but sometimes things are exactly as they appear to be. I returned to the floor and sent a probe into his mind with all the force of an iron punch. The wine keeper, never having invested himself with wizardry, did not respond physically to my force. I learned that his name was Welm. A good Kantish name. I pocketed the key.

"What's wrong, lad? Thought it was time to go and all."

"My name is Luvellun. No one calls me 'lad' anymore."

"Oh. Sorry. You look like a lad, is all. No offense meant. You want *me* to unlock the door for us?" He held out his hand eagerly for the key.

"No, Welm. I want you to tell me your story."

"So you no longer choose to believe me to be Baniff, huh, Luvellun?"

"Belief is not a choice, damn you!" I screamed with all the rage of raised and shattered hopes. I did not care who heard me. "Do you *choose* to believe you are our prisoner, or do you accept the fact that here you are, chilling your last days and nights in this underground cell? Do you *choose* to believe I can take your damn story from your mind if *I* so choose, or have you reached the inescapable conclusion that if I can get your wretched name, I can get everything that goes with it? Do you *choose* to believe you've just filled your belly on a fine feast, or does the fullness in your gut belie all choice?"

Welm looked at me aghast, not knowing how to respond. "I—I don't know. I guess there's always a choice," he said lamely.

"Yes, well, I'll give you a choice. Start talking. What are you doing here?"

He pulled his blanket tight around himself and shuddered. "Spying for Roguehan."

So Roguehan was able to get his people inside Kursen and Walworth did not see fit to even try! I made a heroic effort to control my demeanor and was splendidly unsuccessful. A pulse of anger escaped from somewhere in my emotions and pummeled Welm against the wall. I hissed over Welm's cry of pain, "What does Lord Roguehan need to know about Kursen Monastery that El isn't telling him? What does Lord Roguehan need to know about Kursen Monastery, anyway?"

"Your master can't be relied on to tell my lord Roguehan anything," he gasped. "Like most monks, he's more interested in exploiting the emotional highs and lows of an experience than anything else. He'll help us if there's some kind of emotional payoff in it. Otherwise he's off in search of other amusement." He rubbed his head and put up his arms, as if he could shield himself from another blast.

I got impatient. "What does Roguehan want El to do that El can't be relied on to do?" This was something worth knowing. This was worth all the rest. If I could be of use to Walworth's enemy here in Kursen, well, praise Habundia for life's little gifts.

"Voluntarily change his own alignment."

I laughed like madness at the thought. For minutes. "It's not so absurd as you seem to think," Welm said. I was still laughing. "It is just as evil to compel good to be evil as it is to compel evil to be good, for it is a mark of evil to force anything against its true nature. But using force on an evil priest is not much fun. Compulsion is juicier on those of good alignment, who tend to embrace free will and abhor force. Yet my lord would take great pleasure in watching a jaded high priest of evil such as El *voluntarily* break his spirit against himself, as evil abhors doing anything voluntarily."

"To force evil into freedom. A rare entertainment," I said slowly and deliberately. "Lord Roguehan is wondrously free about sharing his personal fantasies with his underlings."

"Well, a spy has to know what to look for." He met my eyes and smiled encouragingly.

"I suppose I could do worse than *voluntarily* offer my services to your liege lord in that way." I had done worse. I had offered my loyalty and service and risked my wretched life for Walworth's cause and ended up here. I smiled coldly into Welm's eyes at the thought of meeting up someday with my old compatriot in the course of working for Roguehan. I had a score to settle.

"I suppose," said the wine keeper. "You could also do worse than trust your humble servant to deliver your offer." He reached for the key.

"Not so fast. Something like that could easily take years. But then again, I'm not going anywhere. And I do have a certain aesthetic interest of my own at stake."

"Well and good, Luvellun." He stretched out his hand again. "If you want it, I'm sure the job's yours."

"I shall require a higher payment than the experience itself. After all, I shall be devoting years of my life to creating a fleeting circumstance for the pleasure of Roguehan's tender palate. And I understand full well the consequences of promising something to a lord such as Roguehan and failing to deliver."

"What shall I tell my lord is your price?"

"First, I should like regular missives delivered here on the state of the war. For my eyes only, of course. I'm sure Lord Roguehan is capable of getting news smuggled into a monastery."

"He is."

"Second, if I succeed, I should like a permanent position with his court. I don't care what that position is, so long as it involves life and action and adventure. And if he wishes me to complete my training here first, so be it. It may take me that long to uphold my end of the deal anyway. But in the end I want to dirty myself with the world in Roguehan's service. May it be the *new* world." I smiled. Welm wanly returned my smile. "I do *not* wish to complete my training here and end up rotting away in some other monastery or wasting away on my own uselessness."

"Understood."

"And if that same position should involve working against any of his sworn enemies, well, I won't object."

"Of course. That is the least that he would expect. Anything else?"

"No. Except that I expect to hear whether my terms are accepted before I begin work."

"Reasonable enough." He reached for the key. I picked up the candle and the remains of Welm's dinner, then unlocked the door and let us both out, locking it behind us and keeping the key for possible future use. "I'm curious about something," whispered Welm. "How do you know you can trust me to deliver your terms now that I'm free?"

"I don't trust you. Maybe you will and maybe you won't. But either way I've got nothing to lose by it. I'll await your lord's confirmation."

"Understood."

I led Welm out through the darkness, extinguishing the candle as we emerged into the night. The yard was empty except for a few students in the distance huddling themselves into libraries, so I was fairly confident he wouldn't be noticed. So was Welm—for different reasons. As soon as he had put about six feet between us I watched him smoothly become invisible.

The response to my offer arrived fairly quickly, within two weeks. Devon brought it to my room from the man who had been hired to replace the unfortunate cook, for the first cook was now awaiting execution for letting the wine keeper escape. The paper was sealed with black wax. The wax was imprinted with an *"R."* Of course I had had no idea that Lord Roguehan himself would respond directly to my offer, if he responded at all, so I was surprised to read in neat firm handwriting:

You're on.

Roguehan

That was all. The missive indicated no place of origin. Well, as the merchants in Helas say, "Coming home is always an act of belief." As far I believed, we were home.

*S*o it was now my job to study El more carefully. And the first thing I discovered was that he really did care a great deal about those students who had sincere callings to evil. To keep track of the spiritual needs and progress of dedicants of Hecate, Apollo Who Slays, Bacchus Who Destroys All Thought, Hermes the Liar, and other assorted evil deities and demigods is enough work for six high priests, but El was energized by the challenge. He always had time to counsel a distressed student who thought she might have committed a transgression against her deity, or to pray with another student over a personal crisis. And he never missed an initiation—including those of dedicants who belonged to other clerics. Once he had established his authority over his students he would even occasionally relax into a jovial, avuncular mood, although he always frowned on familiarity being returned. He inspired a distantly comfortable respect. He liked being a monk. And it's hard, even for votaries of evil, to resist someone who is spending his life doing what he likes.

Also, there was nothing base or cruel in his patient creation of self-hatred in each of his own students, unless the student happened to be an honest dunce such as Cristo. He was simply doing what needed to be done in the most sensitive way possible, and he took an odd, quiet joy in his work, a joy that gave me pause to wonder about his relationship with Habundia. It is the nature of evil to sacrifice the self, but it was El's nature to honor and augment his self by honoring his evil calling. From a strictly theological standpoint that might be considered a weakness, but it was a weakness I had no idea yet how to exploit, and it was a weakness that didn't seem to affect his clerical power or his relationship with his Goddess.

In fact, El impressed me during my first season of formal study at Kursen when a would-be initiate balked at destroying something he had come to love. El was surprisingly understanding.

This initiate was a young man named Jekan who had spent years learning how to heal with a lyre and, as a result, had fallen in love with his own music—which is a dangerous thing for an aspiring priest of Apollo Who Slays to do, even if falling in love was supposed to be part of the exercise. Jekan was supposed to destroy his instrument at his initiation dinner. And for months he couldn't bring himself to do it. There was a good deal of gossip about him during my first few months of classes, for apparently he had put in for initiation three times already and backed out at the last minute each time. His academic work was complete. He had to be initiated by Sunreturn or lose all credit.

His lyre was his own creation. He carried it everywhere, as artists will. He kept it slung over his shoulder so that it lay near his heart. I'd see him kiss it and hug it and whisper names of pleasure to it under the trees. And he wasn't a half-bad musician. I heard him playing it once as Mirra walked by. She spat on him because she found his music beautiful and El was watching. Jekan cried a little and wiped the spit from the strings with his sleeves. El walked over to him and gently ordered him to play a hymn of destruction. As Jekan did so two branches cracked and fell off the tree, and I heard El say, "Come along, hmmm? There is a fine burst of pain between my heartbeats as you play. Surely you are ready now, yes? Tomorrow eve?" But Jekan bowed his head and turned away and so El moved on.

Anyway, it's a scandal how things eventually came about for Jekan, although El did exactly what he was supposed to do and handled the whole tense situation with superb sensitivity. He let Jekan alone, and Jekan, who literally had nothing to do, would play night and day under the tree whose branches he had cracked. He slept little, ate less, but ye gods, would he play: dirges to the dawn, well-tempered love ballads to the failing light, rousing drinking songs to the receptive night sky, spiral dances to the falling leaves, and who knows what. He kept the music going strong and sure for hours at a time. And when the weather turned cold he went inside and played for the doorkeeper, who had something to dance and bob to for weeks. It was a pleasant enough diversion to stop and listen to Jekan occasionally, and he did draw a regular audience, although I suspect that most of his listeners were drawn more by his tattered, taut emotions than by his music. I remember thinking that his music was pretty and skillfully executed, something to listen to for a few minutes between the library and lunch. My own concerns prevented me from giving his performances much consideration. They were there for the taking and so I took whenever my path happened to cross his, but I never missed them when it didn't.

Anyway, Cristo was all excited about Jekan. Apparently El had put Cristo in charge of arranging for Jekan to perform a concert for the entire monastery on the night of Sunreturn, at which time Jekan would have his last opportunity to destroy his instrument and accept initiation. "It's going to be something really special. Really good—I mean great, Luvellun. You've never seen anything like it."

"Jekan is giving a concert for the monastery night and day now," I said tiredly. "Other than taking bets on whether the old boy will finally become a priest, what's the deal?"

Cristo looked as though he couldn't wait to share his superior knowledge with me. He closed the door to our room and whispered, "I'm not supposed to tell anybody this—"

"Then don't."

"But Ellisand is coming. El told me to get him special." Cristo waited for me to start looking as absurdly enthusiastic as he did. He was so slap happy you'd think El had promised him a permanent job. "You wouldn't believe this guy, Luvellun. You have to hear him. You just have to hear him. He came once before. You won't believe it."

"I won't believe what?"

"How good this guy plays. Well, not good in the moral sense, maybe, but really well—excellent—really—good! The lyre, the mandolin, the lute, wind instruments, *anything*! Once he gets going he can make frogs jump out of a drum."

"So can I."

"Without magic, though. With just the music."

"What's the difference?"

"You don't understand. This guy can make you see visions. He's part elf, you know. He's like nothing else. He's great."

*I*t was sometime after the above conversation and before Sunreturn that the Duchy of Helas went over to Roguehan. I say "went over" because outside of the capital there was more capitulation than fighting. And the fighting around the city was conducted mostly by volunteers from Medegard and Kant. I got a brief note via the new cook informing me of the fall of Hala and another note a few days later stating that Helas was now the newest province of some monster entity calling itself the Empire of Roguehan. So my new liege lord was no longer making any attempt to keep a low profile. He was openly the sole ruler of all the kingdoms of the southwest reaching up through Sevalas and Sunna, as well as County Clio and the Duchy of Helas. I wondered who was minding the store in Furnesse; perhaps King

Furna had cheerfully rolled up his sleeves and assumed all bureaucratic duty for his young warlord. I wondered if King Sunnas and King Sevalas had gotten good desk jobs.

And I wondered if the southeast kingdoms were starting to squirm. If Walworth couldn't motivate his own countrymen to fight, maybe he could seek a military alliance with foreigners.

So if there was to be any kind of fighting soon, it would probably be in Kant, and since Kantish volunteers had been willing to take up arms and go south to fight in Helas, I had every reason to believe that the real war would start here.

But Sunreturn brought no fighting and no notes. Devon was led out solemnly in the chilly dawn. There was no ice pillar this year, so Elwyn tied his wrist to a slender tree. I magically shielded him with warmth, and by sunset he was none the worse for the experience. Hail Sun King of the coming year.

Once Devon was released at sunset and properly clothed for the coming year, an unusually large crowd ran into the spacious room where initiation dinners normally took place. I don't think there was anyone in the monastery, from servant to high priest or priestess, who wasn't there. And there was much shouting and high expectation, for, after all, this was to be an initiation and it is always acceptable to show enthusiasm for someone who finally makes priesthood. It is a little like applauding someone who has withdrawn from being your rival.

And so when El crossed the dais with Devon in hand there was a small eruption of generous shouts of "Soonkin! Soonkin!" peppered with applause. El smiled down at Devon and the Sun King clumsily took his bow and ran down to the front row to sit next to me. Cristo was sitting on the other side of me, nudging my arm and whispering, "Just you wait. Just you wait. You really won't believe this. Ah, here it comes." El was raising his hand for silence.

"And so. Yes, well . . . ahem, thank you. Yes. Happy Sunreturn to you all. King Devon rules again."

More applause. Polite, expected applause from a politely expectant audience.

"Tonight there is one among us who would take his initiation into the priesthood of Apollo Who Slays." Loud, ostentatious clapping and hooting from Apollo's people. "Jekan by name. Jekan, whom you all know. Come, Jekan." El extended his hand and Jekan ascended the dais, tightly clutching his lyre. The clapping subdued into widespread politeness and a few muffled shouts of encouragement, done more to impress El than anything else.

Jekan bowed his head and blushed and smiled a little. "Master."

"The goddess Habundia will no doubt pardon my pride when I say that I am most proud of Jekan's steady progress toward Her Apollonian manifestation. I have had the keeping of your spirit for many years, Jekan, and

I have felt it harden and crack into itself until it has become more than ready for what must follow. You *are* ready?"

"Yes, Master El."

"You do wish to become a brother of Apollo Who Slays?"

"Yes, Master High Priest."

"Then before you play for us, before you play your lyre of healing for the last time, I shall alter the normal course of events and present you with your gift now. Before you are initiated."

"Thank you Master," said Jekan humbly.

"Please sit, my son."

As Jekan sat on a stool on one side of the dais, El motioned grandly toward the ceiling, using Habundia's force to light a circle of candles set in holes in a narrow wooden platform that encircled a suspended cage. The light revealed within the cage the cook who had been sentenced to die. The cook was looking understandably dour about his seating arrangements. He was holding the bars and grimacing at the audience, which immediately began shouting "Lousy cook! Lousy cook!" Even Cristo got into it, shouting, "Lousy cook!" because everyone else was, and looking at me for approval. I wasn't shouting anything. I was too intent on studying El.

"Jekan, we all know how much you love your instrument. We have heard you play it for nearly a season. And your love for your music is only fitting, of course, part of the grand plan, yes? But now is the night to sacrifice all you love. And I understand full well that such a sacrifice constitutes an execution of your past, a death to a way of being. You are strong and brave to trod the path of priesthood." Cheers. "And so my gift to you is the pleasure of watching a human being literally die to music, before you symbolically die to your own."

The cook groaned and swore and rattled the cage. There were sounds of "oooh, ooooh, luscious" arising from the audience. I thought it was kind of funny, as the cook didn't seem as though he had had much acquaintance with music, except maybe with the rattling of pots. He didn't strike me as having enough sensitivity to even feel music, let alone die to it. I supposed someone would stab him through the cage or El would blast him one as soon as Jekan started to play.

"This is better than a war, even," commented Cristo.

"Jekan, son, I am sorry only that my gift to you must be so poor. I cannot offer you the death of a king, or a duke, or a highly trained, sensitive wizard, because such lives are of higher energy and worth than the music you are about to destroy. I can offer you only the life of this poor, ignorant cook. For such be your circumstances as the Goddess reveals them to me. For the music you destroy, this poor life is held worthy. No more." El said this softly and intently.

"It is enough," said Jekan uncertainly. "Thank you, Master." There was a space of silence, and so Jekan took up his lyre and prepared to play.

"Hold," said El. "The gift is not complete. I want you to meet the executioner. Welcome, Ellisand."

And the audience exploded into shrieks and screams and whoops and unrestrained applause as a fair-complexioned man carrying a lyre tramped easily across the stage and sat on a little stool, facing the audience with his back to the cage. His features and coloring were definitely elvish, although he did not look to be an elf.

I wasn't certain Ellisand was aware of the cook hanging behind him, or of El, or of Jekan, or even of the audience. I wasn't sure that he was aware of anything. He probably was from Gondal and had kept their insulated ways. Or he was just self-absorbed. Jekan settled his own instrument in his lap. He wasn't moving. El positioned himself in a high-backed chair off to the side between Ellisand and the cook. He wasn't moving either. I was deciding whether I should stand up and conspicuously walk out as a show of independence when Ellisand began to play a soft melody on his lyre.

And I knew I wasn't going to walk out. Ever. The music was a sacred space and I was lost in it. Between the worlds and into the next and the next and the next one after. Somewhere I heard the cook moan with pain, and I dimly felt that El was taking the music and transforming it into power thrusts of torture, which he was directing at the cook. That was the performance we were all supposed to watch but I didn't care. It was all music to me, and within three or four measures there was no El, or cook, or Jekan, or Cristo, or even Ellisand.

There was only . . . how can I say this? Beauty.

Beauty is not truth. Beauty is when you stumble across truth accidentally outdoing itself.

Do you want to know the beauty of a sunset?

A sunset quietly and matter-of-factly closes the day. Truth, call it. The way nature works. There is no beauty in that. But if it's early evening and you *happen* to find a handful of rubies carelessly forgotten in the corner of a jewel merchant's window, or a warm orange cat slowly crosses your path on the way to its dinner, or you see a stranger holding a mead glass to the sky, and your life has happened along a certain way, then you'll know the beauty of that sunset. In such remnants of accidental existence the truth of the sunset outdoes itself, for the rubies will be righted come morning, and the cat will jaunt through its day cycle again, and the stranger will return— perhaps tomorrow—for another glass of mead. And so you know that moment, in its red and orange and yellow happenstance, is all the sunset's beauty, its one brief overdoing accident against the common day.

Ellisand played the sunset's beauty.

Ellisand played careless rubies and affectionately hungry cats. He played wildflowers kissing my hands, and my first dream of sunlight. Under the notes I heard Grana giving birth before belief became a hard white pea. I ate the pea and it bruised my dreams. And he played belief in the forms of maiden sylphs rising out of the east. And discontented summers danced hazily where the bruises made tears. I twisted myself into them. And no one could touch me, for my life was pure belief. Gold-and-blue birds sang me awake. I ate their speckled eggs and spoke. Silver-tongued trees taught me ancient poems. Their roots went north. I drank their mud and the mud was a river bottom entangled in spiny weeds. And I heard river bubbles exploding in the realm of the fairies to which the roots of the river weeds led, and I followed them down through the chords—the mud, I mean—until the bottom made something cool and round like a cave of dancing lights, and in the music I could either believe I heard the song of the water fairies or I could know it was all a beautiful accidental dream. And still he played, somewhere, but I was beyond the music now. I chose belief—I chose the fairy song and dashed myself against the dancing lights, and grew sharp fins and ate them, and in my naked freedom lost the cave to liquid darkness. It was a crystal cave and it too went north. And out of the cave, singing in the dreamy darkness, was Isulde, a darker dream, the dark of the moon holding me new and kissing me up to infinity as it waxed from below. And she said between kisses, "This is the love of spring. This is the love of spring when the lilacs bloom for the evening star. This is the love of—"

I was moaning and crying in ecstasy when the music stopped, but then so was everyone else in the audience, except the cook, who let out one final earsplitting shriek and died to applause, and Mirra, who was doing her best to look impatient and put out by a general enthusiasm that clearly was not intended for El's adeptness at torture. She kept sighing in annoyance and trying to catch El's eye. For credit, presumably.

El stood and grandly bowed as the cage with the corpse in it swung back and forth. Ellisand was unmoved, still sitting because he was comfortable where he was. Jekan looked flushed and nervous.

El gestured to Jekan and commanded, "Now you." There was a noticeable drop in the energy level of the room. Ellisand looked idly in the younger musician's direction. He was bored and didn't care to disguise the fact.

"I—cannot, Master."

"Play for us. We are waiting. This is your night."

"I cannot play."

"What?" said El in mock disappointment. "You tell us all"—he made a sweeping gesture toward the audience—"that *you* cannot play? *You*, a lyrist of so many years practice and training, cannot *play?* We are waiting for you to rend the night sky to shreds with your music."

"I cannot."

"You cannot rend the night sky to shreds. Hmmm . . . well, then, can you make the stars of our several births dance again for us, as Ellisand did?"

"No, Master, I cannot."

"Can you compel our hearts backward into their very first desire?"

"No, Master."

"Well, can you make us new dreams, then?"

"No, Master."

"Can your music make a rain cloud blush? A lion become a desert? A plowman's axe hear the singing of the gods?"

"No," Jekan choked out.

"Well." El shrugged. "What can I say? You have played your lyre night and day. You have refused initiation out of love for your music. You have kept us waiting through love of your music." Jekan was sobbing. "As if you could command worlds. As if your music were *special* . . . worth waiting for. Worth giving up a priesthood for."

"No!"

"Worth losing Apollo Who Slays for. And aren't there legends of great musicians who *did* live and die for their art? Who gave up all for music without a backward glance? Whom we remember and honor forever for their talent?" Jekan was silent. "Well?"

"Yes." Jekan was barely audible.

"A *great* musician might act as you have acted, but a great musician would act out of his or her talent. Are you a great musician, Jekan? Look at Ellisand and tell us."

Ellisand was idly smoking chaiaweed and gazing in the opposite direction. Jekan looked at his back and said, "No, Master."

"But you thought acting like one made you one. You were supposed to want nothing but music and we were supposed to admire you. Jekan, the immortal lyrist who cannot turn a cow to milk—"

"Noooo!" Jekan was screaming and screaming and smashing his lyre all over the dais. Stomping on it and kicking it and burning it into nothing with the fire of his rage. "I'm not worthy to sacrifice my life for it! I'm not worthy to sacrifice my life for it! Now! Now I hate you! Die!"

Ellisand was nonchalantly strumming his instrument, which only infuriated Jekan more, for he ran over and grabbed the stool out from under him, seeking to smash him into silence. I'm sure that if the chaia hadn't relaxed Ellisand's muscles, he would have been hurt by the fall, but El pulled Jekan off and Ellisand exited the dais unscathed. And Mirra, alone in the audience, stood up and applauded.

"Give me your rage and I give you back your spirit. For now I name you priest of Apollo Who Slays, with all rights and privileges appertaining to that position," and El brought down Habundia's force and Jekan, crying and breathless, was made a brother. He kissed El's ring and El kissed the top of his head.

"I love you, Master."

"Yes. Sit, Brother." And as Jekan did so El delivered his homily.

And since El's gaze happened to be drawn in my direction I made it a point to stand up and walk out in the middle of his speech, even though I was genuinely interested in what he had to say.

Anyway, I left the building and saw a stab of light floating off in the darkness, away under the tree Devon had been tied to earlier. As I approached I saw it was the end of a stick of chaiaweed that Ellisand was smoking. He was leaning against the tree. I remember trying to determine what my feelings were about Ellisand, and my strongest impression was that it would be an excellent thing to play as well he did and then go off in the darkness and lean against a tree and smoke chaia, as if playing brilliant music was just another job. I watched Ellisand out of the darkness before I spoke to him, and the language I hailed him in was Kantish. "Ellisand," I began. He glanced at me without curiosity. "I must tell you—you are the greatest musician in all the worlds. I've—I've never experienced in my life what music is until I heard you tonight—"

He interrupted me in words that sounded like Sarana, only accented in odd places. "I don't speak Kantish." He turned his back and started to walk away.

"Ellisand." I ran up to him and began speaking in Sarana, repeating what I had just said and describing all my visions to him at length, including my vision of Isulde and who she was. I closed with, "I could live and die in your music, I could give birth to my best self there."

"Oh, yeah?" he said coldly and disinterestedly, throwing a butt of chaia on the ground and walking away again. I felt my stomach drop into the ground with the chaia. I also knew suddenly that it was midwinter and I felt the air gnawing at my eyes.

I ran up to him again. "I'd give my life to be able to play like you did."

"Then why didn't you?" He wasn't really interested. He kept walking away from my increasing sense of devastation.

"Are you staying here tonight?"

"No, got a girl in town. Gonna screw." He stopped as if he was warming to me some and then asked, "Know any good inns? Her father ain't too keen on it."

"No. Ellisand, will you be back? Will you play for us again? Maybe next time El won't be executing a prisoner with your music."

"You mean he killed some guy while I was playing? Oh, wow. That's pretty cool. Who was it?"

"The guy in the cage. He was executed for letting a thief escape. The thief replaced an old relic with illusions—oh, never mind." I didn't know why I was giving him the details.

"No, please," said Ellisand, suddenly interested. "Tell me more. You mean he died while I was playing?"

"Sort of. El changed the energy in your music."

"Cool. Come show me the corpse." Ellisand was already on his way back into the building and it was all I could do to keep up with him.

"Well, the corpse may be gone now," I said, but we stomped back through the halls and into the initiation room, where invited guests were now feasting on dried peas and cardamom pods to celebrate Jekan's initiation. Everyone else had left. Ellisand left me at the door and walked right up to El, asking to see the cage. He was speaking Kantish, which irritated me. El graciously pointed out the remains of the cook to him.

I left and went slowly back to my room by myself. Ellisand's music was still with me. I took out my illusion spoon and used it to light a fire I couldn't see. Then I made a real fire to displace the illusion. Then, shielding my hands against heat, I bent the spoon in the flame and fashioned for myself a small plain gold ring, which I put on my finger before extinguishing the fire.

I crawled into bed with a book and a candle and it was almost an hour before I heard Cristo and Devon returning. I willed flames to spring back up while directing my will through the ring. I saw nothing. Cristo complimented me on preparing a fine fire and then complained that the light was keeping him awake. So I knew that the power of illusion held in the ring. And that night I learned that as long as my ring hand wasn't in my pillow I was able to retain the power of illusion without sacrificing my dreams.

Not even Baniff had been able to manage that one.

*T*he weeks held heavy and sluggish for me after Ellisand's visit, for I found it necessary to become a willing prisoner of academic work. I knew I needed to excel beyond excellence if one day I was to command enough clerisy to convince El to voluntarily change his alignment, so I studied until my spirit hurt with study and then I studied more. But at night, just before dreaming, I would look at my illusion ring and remember the beauty and freedom I had found in Ellisand's music and the ecstatic dream walks with Isulde he played for me. The contrast between his performance and the rest of my life killed me a little.

But although most of my time was lost in the vastness of books and papers and my slow patient scrutiny of El, there were shreds of life even in Kursen that were not entirely blotted out in the blankness of study.

To begin with, there was the war, which frenzied and pulsed and throbbed and crested and scabbed over and burst in glorious violence. Roguehan remained true to his word in that he kept me informed of all developments. I was also privy to some firsthand information, for Kursen Monastery is quite close to Kant's southern border and following the Sun-return of Jekan's initiation battles frequently broke out within sight of our walls. This would have been the winter and spring preceding my nineteenth birthday, to keep the telling straight.

Even though war produces the gods' own plenty of pain and sorrow and delectable dark joy and we monks are climbing the walls of our monasteries to get at it, we can't. War belongs to the realm of action, the base world we must not sully our minds in. There are exceptions for those who aspire to join the priesthood of Ares, and of course a fairly untouchable high priest such as El could concoct secret letters to lick and suck the honey from a juicy wartime event such as Walworth's treason trial, but for most monks it is simply not done to forgo academics for real life. Yet war is so sweet and savory a feast of horror that an embarrassing number of monks cannot pass it up, and there is considerable pressure to get a piece of it without violating monastic vows to abjure the mundane world. That is why for very special events, such as war and famine and plague, the temple in Sunnashiven issues proclamations urging everyone to stand publicly against the destruction of life, and it also provides special dispensations for entering the world. Evil clerics and their students are urged to justify their involvement in worldly concerns by pretending to be so outraged that they are willing to sacrifice themselves to bring peace. And so we dutifully condemn war up and down for its violence. It's the only decent way to get involved.

Anyway, first violence is monk-right, as they used to say at Kursen, and before I even got a letter informing me that the first border skirmish was imminent, the special dispensation came down and the "peacemongers," those clerical students who craved the taste of battle but publicly condemned war, were flying out of Kursen's walls and drooling and howling for blood and death like packs of under-fed hounds.

Mirra was first among them. Mirra was only in her second season of formal study, just as I was, and I knew she hadn't a raindrop's notion of how to absorb violent feelings, let alone find their sources and drink them fresh. My study of wizardry had made me sensitive to the energy levels within different emotions, but in terms of the spiritual appropriation and sophisticated enjoyment of emotional energy I still had quite a ways to go. Mirra's much-touted sensitivity was really more like feeling-by-numbers than natural talent. If a book told her she was supposed to react a certain way to a line of poetry, she would do so on cue, breathlessly quoting the critic's phrases as if they were her own and pretending to be surprised by El's empty praise of her natural ability to copy.

I used to like to finish the quotes for Mirra, and I was always careful to mention that I had been inspired to find those passages because I saw her reading them in the library. Getting credit for being studious and well read isn't nearly as exhilarating as passing yourself off as a natural genius. And Mirra would squirm and look down at her books while El politely intoned that it was "all right" or "fine enough" to consciously adopt another's argument. Nothing deflates the Mirras of the world more thoroughly than faint praise.

I once annoyed El by asking him who his favorite critics copied from. He waved his hand airily and shrugged and talked at length about mystical "ideas in the air" that everyone had access to but only some got credit for.

Intellectual greatness was kind of like a lottery. And that was as much as he ever had to say on the subject. "And so," he concluded, "here we are. Next assignment . . ."

Monastic life teaches one never to underestimate the need to impress. Mirra did know there was probably merit in publicly imitating the older students and clerics who lolled their tongues after the war, and so she quickly learned to parrot their rhetoric. As a result, she soon became more annoying than Cristo, because she clearly didn't understand the uses of slogans any better than he did. As I have already explained, the older students were taking advantage of the special dispensation against the war in order to partake in the violence. Mirra was against the war because she thought she was supposed to be.

None of this would have been my concern if Mirra hadn't decided otherwise by barging into my rooms with a cohort of five older students, all of whom were wearing ridiculous paper masks, pointing their fingers, and chanting, "Shame! Shame! Shame! Shame!" Cristo, who naturally thought the chanting was for his benefit, was terrified. I told Devon to order them to remove their masks and make themselves comfortable. Before the Sun King could open his mouth they all ran away, leaving Mirra bowing abjectly to Devon. After three bows she promptly informed me that she wasn't afraid of threats.

"Under the special dispensation I am acting according to law. Monastic rules are suspended for those who protest the war."

"Then why bow? We're just plain folks here. Right, Cristo?"

"Right," said Cristo, slowly recovering.

"Bow again." Devon giggled.

She nervously did so, despite her newfound fearlessness. "Great Sun King. Brother Cristo. I bear a message for Luvellun that Master High Priest El wishes me to deliver in private."

"So deliver it," I ordered. "And get out."

She looked defiantly at Cristo as a way to show courage without facing me. Then she stammered, "W-well, it's not really a message from the master, Luvellun, it's from the Student War Committee. We formed last night. And we feel unanimously that everyone who has the privilege of studying at Kursen Monastery has the obligation to join us in protesting the war. You weren't with us today."

"With you where?" I said this like a contemptuous comment. I didn't really care.

"In town. We were burning buildings and carriages to make people aware."

"Aware of what?" Now I just sounded annoyed.

Mirra didn't like my annoyance, but it did give her an opportunity to sound superior. "Aware of violence. The war. A lot of people don't care or don't want to get involved and we think it's important to make people aware about what's going on. One of our members is now adept at drawing destructive fire from his god. We destroyed seven carts and two streets of shops and then urged everyone to do something to stop the violence."

"Why would a passel of evil monks want to stop the violence? The war has brought us life. I haven't seen more excitement around here since Devon burned the cots."

Devon grinned.

"You don't understand. You are very insensitive. Violence is delicious and incredibly empowering."

"How would you know?" I was thinking of my own finely developed sense of violence here. "You can't even derive a violent feeling from a line of poetry without memorizing someone else's response from a book."

"Look, *I* happen to feel things," she whined. "But we can't just go by our own feelings when all emotion belongs to the Goddess. And we certainly can't just go out and say that violence is power. People aren't ready to hear that yet. So we make vague demands about 'doing something' and spreading awareness. My sensitivity and compassion are reserved for the needs of my brothers and sisters in Habundia Christus, as yours should be. It is our duty to make people aware."

"And the war club's belief is that no one besides themselves is aware of the war?" I asked. "How does a mob of cloistered clerical students come to know more about the war than the residents of a town on the front? Don't tell me you're smuggling in news."

Mirra sighed impatiently. "Well, the townspeople are aware, but many of them don't really know what violence is. We're just making sure that they learn."

"Do *you* know what violence is?"

"I'm learning. I'm getting involved." Mirra sounded defensive and uncertain.

"Lesson one: 'Making people aware' is code for making converts. If there's anyone in town who finds himself fascinated with violence, he might follow the terrorists back here, and we all know the value of increasing the fold. But since I already am here, I can't properly be considered a convert. I'm surprised that one escaped your quick and sensitive mind. But then again, it isn't in the books. Lesson two: Your friends aren't *urging* people to 'do something' to stop the war's violence. They're issuing a dare to the townspeople to stop the violence that the students are causing. It's more fun. And if the people take them up on it, it's more violence. Have some real awareness, Mirra. On me."

"Look, that's not the issue. So what if I'm not really a peacemonger? At least I know that I *do* have an obligation to be out there with the others. I'm very concerned about the many students here who, due to their temperaments and alignments, really cannot help but imbibe as much violence as possible. Not everyone can follow bookish Hecate."

"It's hard," said Cristo.

Mirra continued, "And I am *aware* that while those among us who cannot help but indulge their taste for violence hearken to the war, you are sitting here in comfort studying. It isn't fair for you to take advantage while there's a war going on. You outperform enough students anyway, and now you have an unfair time advantage over those whose spiritual principles lead them to get involved with war issues. The committee feels that no one should study until the war is over and that way no one will excel unfairly over anyone else."

"Sounds logical to me," said Cristo, ever hoping for a reason not to prepare for classes.

I thought of Jekan trying to smash Ellisand with the stool. "Besides," continued Mirra sanctimoniously, "in the eyes of the Goddess it is not right for anyone to be better or more intelligent than anyone else. We are all one. We are all the same. The committee will determine how much you can study and how much you should protest until the war is over. No one is to outperform anyone else."

"Well, determine this. Since we are all one and the same in Her blessed sight—thank you for reminding me of this fact, dear sister—then I'm sure you and the rest of the club won't mind giving up *all* your productive study time in favor of protesting. As long as the time is given up by someone, then, being one and all, we'll all get credit. Divine Goddess credit, Mirra. Can't you just taste it? In fact, your sacrifice of sounding semi-intelligent in the classroom would probably be much appreciated by many of your less fortunate colleagues, for they would immediately rise in rank above you, and we know that as a daughter of Habundia-Christus, you take joy in self-sacrifice and all."

"Luvellun, we're all here to be educated. You're not being fair. It's only for the common good—"

"The common *what*?"

"Good. Well, you know, it's just an expression."

"Here's my expression. Tell your masked henchmen that once I find out who they are—and I will—that they are heartily encouraged, nay, *commanded*, isn't it Devon?"

"Commanded," agreed Devon.

"They are commanded to refrain from attempting to excel in the classroom. I don't want them out of the monastery, mind you. But I expect their class rank to fall with yours before Midsummer."

"Luvellun, that's not fair," she pleaded.

"Call it my private protest against the war."

"If that's to be the case, why don't you just throw us all out?" she whined through a mess of tears. I had hit her vital spot. No more impressing the master. "You clearly don't care about education."

"Perhaps I *will* throw you all out. But it's closer to my sense of justice to force mediocrity on you the way your communal jealousy sought to enforce it on me. Let's put it this way. You can all be average—shudders—or you can spend your lives running messages for the baker's boy despite your high and fine minds. But since you're all one and the same anyway—what a concept—you should be grateful that I am forcing mediocrity on you. For really it is only for the *good* of all that you cease to excel. What a blessing the Sun King has bestowed this very day. You should really kiss his shoe, Mirra."

"You know, not everyone here is as fortunate as you," she whined. "All we have is our education."

"Tell me about it. No, on second thought don't tell me about it. Get lost before Devon here makes you take classes with Cristo." She bowed and fled.

"I don't want her in my class," said Cristo. "Too ugly."

"Yes, Cristo, enforced mediocrity is pretty ugly. I prefer the natural kind, don't you?"

"You bet. Every day." Cristo started pacing again. "Luvellun?"

"What? I'm busy destroying a love sonnet."

"Do you think Mirra might be right? About people needing to be aware of violence and all?"

"Mirra isn't even aware of her own violence."

"I mean about no one being able to excel more than anyone else. It's kind of a nice ideal—in a way."

"Would the world be a better place if Ellisand played like Jekan?"

"Yeah—I don't know. Hey, I think Ellisand's coming back near Equinox." He was all excited again. Of course, at the thought of Ellisand coming back so was I, although I succeeded in hiding it.

"Hey, Luvellun," interrupted Devon. "Will you teach me a special way to love things and make them die?"

His question startled me, not least because it was the same question my heart asked every day. I wondered if this hapless little boy in whom I had artificially created as strong an attachment to me as I once naturally felt for my Threlan friends had somehow overheard my soul's secrets. "Every once in a while you come up with a winner, Devon," I said lightly. "You'll make priest yet."

"Devon's got a ways to go to make priesthood," said Cristo, suddenly defensive about distinctions.

"So do you."

"Yeah, but I'm thinking maybe there shouldn't be priesthood. Or anything. Like with Ceres."

"So stop thinking. Or I'll tell El." I picked up my pen to close the conversation and went determinedly back to my work, breaking the image patterns, thinking of El's strange passion for evil, anticipating Ellisand returning at Equinox, and hoping to see my lovely dark lady in my later dreams.

Isulde was bathing my hands in a river of starshine and I was crying happily for sweet light and life when something knocked me out of bed and into morning. It was Cristo clumsily trying to dress himself. He had tripped over his own feet and slammed against my bedpost. I started swearing like a fishmonger. The light in the window told me it was later than usual but I didn't much care, as my work had kept me up later than I'd intended the previous evening. Devon was now curled up like a cat in front of the ashes from the night's fire. Cristo was hopping around with one foot in his hand. He had stubbed his toe when he fell. "Damn! Gotta get to class. Gotta get to class," he hurriedly apologized.

"Why? You won't miss anything." I crawled back in my blankets.

"Aha—some joke. Goddess, but this hurts. Christus!" He sat on my bed because he happened to be close to it and I kicked him off through the blankets. "Hey! Thanks a lot," he complained.

"No problem."

There was a light rap on the door, which startled Devon awake. Ten stumbling Cristos couldn't wake him but a rap on the door could. I told Devon not to answer it. Then I pulled the covers over my head and tried to throw myself back into my dream. At which point, of course, Cristo opened the door. "I gotta answer it. I gotta go to class," he sputtered as he crossed the room and pulled the damn door open.

"Goddess damn it! Go away, we're preparing for class," I groaned miserably from under the blankets to whoever was out there.

"Who are you?" Cristo asked politely at the same time.

"Who cares who it is?" I complained loudly through my blankets, thoroughly awake now. "Ask something relevant. Like 'Why don't you get lost?' "

"Why don't you get lost?" asked Devon.

"And miss all the fun?" It was Lord Cathe. "I came to see Llewelyn." He was speaking Kantish but he was using my Botha name. As I heard him enter the room I swore, threw the blankets off my head, and sat up in bed. I supposed I should get dressed. Isulde had vanished into waking and there was now no help for it. I manifested some clothes under my blankets.

"He's right here. Come on in," said Cristo, exiting.

"Hey, Devon, go keep Cristo this side of trouble," I ordered as I threw a shirt over my head.

"Get him *in* trouble. Nicely," crowed Devon as he yanked on a day shift and hurried after Cristo, banging the door closed behind him.

"What a truly joyful kid," said Cathe in Botha, promptly sitting on my bed. I got up immediately and crossed to the window. It really was time to be up. It looked to be about midmorning. When I turned around Cathe was reclining on my pillows and lazily tracing patterns in the air with his staff. "Anyway, greetings, coz. Lovely war, isn't it? Far too lovely to slug-a-bed away the morning minutes. Late days, late dreams, you know." He kept punctuating his words with his staff. "Yes. Yes, by our Lady. Right here. Ah, the very place of the Goddess, such dreams She dreams as round out your flattened life—" He suddenly looked surprised and startled. "Really, Llewelyn, not too bad, now . . . not bad at all, hmmm . . . I'm sure I should be jealous to own *these* dreams. And what is her name? Isulde, is it?"

I was making myself a tea out of the odd packets Devon had pillaged from the kitchen. Making tea and creating fire prevented my hands from breaking his staff over his head.

"And well and a day and a glistering night, but don't you find that the sun really perks up your blood lust when you know it's about to shine down on a battle somewhere? Yes, by my Lady's juicy ends I find that the slow flowering of violence gives each morning just—just something fine and gray and oh so—so—*mousy*—*dead* mousy, three days old, I believe—they get so soft and sweetening then—ah yes, like leftover candy, sweet and stinking the dust on a cold morning road, spoiling its ease near a colder toad—it's there for the plucking, and the beggar child will lick it and grow sick—ah, not die, mind you—" He briefly pointed his staff at me and then leaned back to resume tracing patterns. "—that would be too heavy a touch, but a light, bouncy sickness to take him through the week and spread amongst his kindred in hues of fever white and yellow. Have you ever been inside a dying, a real dying, to lick it? Lovely—hmmm—and I was thinking—perhaps when the fighting starts I could gather a pretty bouquet of sugary violence and scatter it fit to freeze a beggar's smile. War is so delicious." He looked at me pointedly. "Everyone should have one prime war in their lives, don't you think? Else why bother having a life? *I* do find that war makes waking worth the day."

"What do you want?"

"Nothing." He sounded as though my question surprised him, as if it were the most natural thing in the world to show up at my door and flop into my bed. He continued tracing meaningless patterns in the air and sighing loudly, as if he were privy to some secret beauty.

"Well, coz," I said, sitting on the window ledge and sipping the concoction I'd stirred together, "nothing comes of nothing, late dreams or no."

Cathe closed his eyes and loudly smacked his lips. "Yes, but I never do *want*. That one's for the Lady. Oooh, and when you drink that marvelous mussy brew, really it does slosh against my own tongue as I lay upon your bed—I do declare I could stay a week."

The thought of inflicting Cathe on Cristo for a week brightened my mood considerably. "Be my guest, coz," I said affably. "Let me bring you to class. Introduce you to my teachers." That would also be a wondrously fine way to annoy El. "My poor little life is yours. Can I offer you tea and moldy biscuits?"

"No." He waved his hand. "To taste your tea is—*moldy* biscuits, did you say?" He smacked his lips again.

"Why, yes, wouldn't think to give you any other kind."

"Why, yes then, coz, if I could just lick the mold a little, to complement the taste of the tea . . . You are most kind." I gave him some of Cristo's old bread. "*Green*—oh, how truly saucy." He kept holding the crust to his tongue and removing it.

"You wouldn't happen to have a spoon, would you?"

"A *spoon*, now. As a matter of fact, I did have a spoon. Lovely little thing until the rats ate it. Sent it back to your master sticking out of a hard little rat with my love. Mentioned *your* name and how we were the next best thing to family, now that I think about it. Suppose that clears the day, hmmm?"

"You know something, coz of my heart? I do find that your very presence makes waking worth the day. In fact, the instant I woke this morning I said to myself, 'Wouldn't it be a fine thing now if my good friend Cathe should happen to pay a call? Haven't seen him in a while and I do wonder how the old boy is keeping his life and spirit up.' "

"Did you now? Did you really say that?" He sat up excitedly and leaned on his staff. "Well, the dear Lady be damned and damned again. May She bless the seeds of my baggy tumors and damn my own heart to blessings besides. May She hang cracking like a bloated leech upon the outer reaches of inner thought! Well, well." He smacked his lips. "And here *I* was in all my squashy shyness thinking perhaps you had forgotten me. Sour mother of goats!" He leaned back against my pillows and started tracing patterns again.

"Forgotten *you*? I'd sooner forget myself. How blows your precious life?"

"Neatly and full. Thanks for asking." He gave the bread back to me, sticky with his saliva. I threw it in the fireplace to burn. "Aah, you're scalding my tongue!" He held his tongue out in the air between his fingers and gasped and sweated until I put the fire out.

"Ashes, ashes, and don't we fall down?" I sang softly. "So tell me truly, coz, how does your precious wife?"

"Ah, Habundia the Lady—"

"I meant Caethne."

"So did I. Caethne does as she does. North and south. And that, of course, is why I am here. Caethne needs your help."

"Then Caethne can ask for it."

"Well, she can't ask for it if she doesn't know she needs it. You see—" he waved one hand around in the air—"sometimes life is logical that way. And really, she has no more idea than a pumpkin's bleeding dam that your help is worth the asking, but to my mind and soul you are just the person to come to my damsel's distress. So—say you'll do it." He threw up his staff, slapped his hands against each other, and sat bolt upright on my bed. The staff became a snake that slithered back up onto his lap and hardened into a staff again. He kissed it lightly. "Sweet hissy baby."

"Say I'll do what?"

"Say you'll make Master Mirand fall in love with her. I'm sure she'd greatly appreciate it." I was nonplussed. "No, really, coz, I mean it. I truly think you're the man for the job. Caethne would absolutely love it—and well, think how much it would mean to the whole family, coming from you."

"I am."

He walked over to the window and inspected my books, opening a few at random with the point of his staff. "Yes, keep up your study of Sarana—nice!" He exhaled confidently and extended his hand. "So it's a deal."

I refused to take it. "Why do you want me to help your wife commit adultery?"

"Why be possessive?" Cathe shrugged. "Love's a bird and cousin Caethne's only my wife in play."

"So why be extravagant? Caethne's a witch. Let her take care of it. Her wretched love saga's getting old."

"Well, she really can't take care of it, you know. Mirand taught her the rudiments of wizardry before she learned witchcraft and so he knows her heart well enough to guard himself against it."

"And who do you think taught me?"

"Yes, for all of six months. But you see, he practically raised her. And it's been nearly a year now since he's even seen you. Longer since you've worked together. Stop being so *serious* about friendships, Llewelyn. Save serious for your studies." He leaned close and said sympathetically, "Come, coz, do you really think Mirand ever thinks about you with a war hanging 'round his neck? Now, if someone were to mention your name—well, maybe briefly. And as the war continues through the years—and it will—it will take more than your name to conjure back memory. You're probably fading fast now. First friend, favored apprentice, housemate, and comrade. Then former student. Then, stray lad I used to know, whatever happened to him? Then who? oh, yes, right, that was a long time ago, now I remember. And then just plain who? It happens. Natural as clouds." He drew back and studied me.

I thought about Caethne's letter. "Yes, I know."

"And I know you know." He tapped me lightly with his staff. "And hence your study of Sarana—and secret deals with Lord Roguehan, all of which I find most touching. Really I do. In fact, I put in a word or two for you on that one. Tickled me orangey blue till the day of doom when I heard Welm's message. Lady, but you know how to live."

"I'm not interested in solving Caethne's little problem. And frankly, I wouldn't even know where to begin. Why don't you do it if you care so much?"

"But I am doing it. I am. I was raised a high priest of Habundia Christus, however, and I've never had anything to do with the sort of love dear Caethne craves. It's all quite foreign to me. You see—" He leaned on his staff, meditated for about ten seconds, and continued. "It's like this—"

"Let me guess. Roguehan wants to watch."

"Oh, no. Oh, no." He sounded affronted. "Bloody my stars on a dewy morn, but this isn't his sort of thing at all."

"Is it yours, then?"

"Really, Llewelyn, what do you take me for? I'm a man of *simple* tastes. No. It's just that—might I have another lick at the mold?"

"Here." I tore off more of Cristo's bread.

"Thanks. It's just that—mmm, this is most fine, yes." He returned to my bed and looked at me with deep sorrowful eyes. He hesitated. I waited. The silence was long enough for the sun patches to visibly stretch themselves along the floor. He looked down at the speckled light and traced sad little patterns with his staff. "I grow old." He sniffed.

"So what do you want from *me*? A bloody prize?"

"I can feel the hours and days wriggling in and out of my gut like worms. I grow sick with time."

"Well, don't do it here. I'm busy." But he looked so despondent I added, "Hey, if the clerics in Sunnashiven hadn't stopped your growth, you'd be even older now. What do you want out of life?"

"Beautifully put. I want out—of life." His eyes puddled sadness.

"You just said you wanted nothing."

"Then I just said true. It's all much the same. Look, Llewelyn, what can I say to it? It's a poor deal. My body is decaying. It doesn't show yet, but I can feel death beginning to conceive itself between my skin and muscles. Every breath brings the taste of my last breath closer. Soon. Not tomorrow or next month or next year or even in the next ten years, but soon—in the teaspoon measures of infinity—the day will come when I won't be able to take my simple pleasures, to suck mold or eat the wind or grow hard upon another's anger. My own increasing sense of dying will blot all else out and really—"

"Poor baby."

"I *am* a poor baby." A tear ran down his cheek. "Help me keep my youth. The Sunnashiven clerics merely stopped my growth to match their own. I want you to help me stop it completely." He kept looking at me like a Sunnashiven beggar.

"By making Mirand fall in love with Caethne? I'm fascinated."

"By helping me to claim my cousin-wife's promise should he do so. Caethne," he sobbed mournfully, "could make all the deathy stuff stop if she chose, sweet lady." He kept crying. "And she swore it all upon Ceres that she would if I could get her her own heart's desire. And so I will and so I must. You *do* understand?"

"No."

"It's like this." He sighed. "Caethne and I come from the same place in a sense. Caethne's great-grandmother, meaning her dear old sickly father's granddam, started life as a little patch of weeping heather in the mouth of a crystal cave up north. It's quite true. Our family has North Country roots. But the dear old girl—the great-grandmother—grew backward into the soil and spread and so, you see, her seeds emerged in Sunnashiven—and in northern Threle. And the heather was a woman—two sisters—and so dearest darling Grana became yours and mine and Anarg, her sister, became sweet Caethne's grandmother. She was a witch too, and worked the land, and grew leaves in her hair like a fairy princess, and married a duke.

Caethne's grandfather was a peasant himself, and as he loved and worked and defended the land he won the heart of Arnag, who indeed *was* the land."

"Well, that solves that mystery." I had no idea what to say.

"No, it doesn't. Not really." He sniffed a little and sat up. "You see, here is the point and thrust of it. Only Caethne can keep me young because only Caethne stands to me in the same relation Ceres stands to Christus. My sweet wife, and only my sweet wife, has the power to oppose my natural processes, to create me over as I would, so that I need never die and live to grow old again. I could leap beyond the Lady into All That Is—I could be all things and never change."

"How divine."

"Yes, it is, really. I do so want to be a god. Manifestations are fine in their place—but I do so wish to *be*."

"And how does Caethne propose to give you eternal youth?"

"Well, she's not a bad hand at keeping things alive and youthful. She's promised to bathe me tenderly in the blood of her brother while chanting secret spells under a new moon. It's the only way to do it. You see, Walworth, being Caethne's twin and Arnag's other descendant, has fairy blood in his veins too. And he is the lord of the land, or will be soon. Caethne says she knows the right magic for opposing my life energy with his and creating—well, a stand-off, a life without energy, without movement, without the ability to age. I should be complete in myself—a son of forever." He sucked his knuckles and looked pleadingly at me.

"This is getting interesting. Why not use the old man's blood?"

"He's too old. And he's very sick now. Walworth is closer to Caethne's own energy level because they're twins. She would have more chance of success with his."

"So she'd murder her own brother to satisfy her passion. Nice! And then she and my old master would become duke and duchess upon the death of her parents?"

"That all depends on the outcome of the war. But really, who cares?"

"I do."

"Lamentable, that." He thumped his staff enthusiastically on the floor. "Picture this. Caethne murders—ahem, disposes of—her brother. We—you and I—will know all about it, of course, and as the time approaches we can involve further witnesses as we see fit. So Mirand and milady live in bliss—until you quietly let King Thoren in on all you know. Or, as is equally likely, if Roguehan is victorious, he makes the scandal so public that the two of them die for shame. Think about it. If your magic can cause Mirand to love, it can also restore him to his senses once the damage is done, and if you want to watch them both suffer, I really can't think of a better way."

"What about Baniff?"

"Well, I can't bring everyone into your revenge. But you're smart enough to think of something. I won't rush. I know my proposal could take you years. Besides, in the aftermath I would be the only one left with a claim to ruling the duchy, and being duke doesn't appeal to me. How would you like the position, coz? You'd be a strong candidate for the office no matter who wins the war."

"What is Caethne's current relationship to Roguehan?"

"She's hiding from him. Or from Zelar, rather, who's too busy right now to care. Caethne was not averse to helping Zelar reclaim his prize student with the understanding that she could work her charms on Mirand in his new state. But since that plan went slightly awry—"

"Yes. About that. Why aren't *you* hiding?"

"Because Roguehan himself does not have a personal interest in Mirand's alignment. It would have been nice if I had succeeded, but that whole thing was really Zelar's concern. He sold Lord Roguehan on the idea of using an evil Mirand to direct Walworth into working to destroy his beloved Threle, and with the promise of a base and the recovery of the key and the wand, well, why not? Entertainment's entertainment. The loss of a fine little market town more than made it up to Roguehan, especially since it was Mirand who destroyed it. And my liege lord was just as happy to no longer have to protect Grendel and Sina from his other henchmen. Keeps peace in the family. No, as far as Roguehan is concerned, I do valuable work in other areas."

"Like poisoning popular opinion with the holy spoon."

"Like that. So what do you say?" He extended his hand again.

"Nothing. The more you talk the more confused I get. Why not get Zelar to do the job? He'd probably at least have a shot at being successful."

"Because Zelar owes me no favors. He expected me to convert Mirand for him. I'm far too useful to Roguehan to have to concern myself with Zelar's disappointment, but I'm sure that Zelar would rather *not* see my deification. And he's not in any sort of mood to reward Caethne either. Besides, Zelar's not an ogre about the issue. I believe it would actually hurt him deeply to see Mirand suffer in the way I've described. He merely wants him over on his side of the universe. Which in a way I can understand. At one point in history they were rather close."

"So he won't mind your destroying the thing he seems to love?"

"Lady, what a mind you've got! Sharper than Medusa's spit! All right, so he'll mind. So what? What will Master Zelar say to a brand-new demigod? I don't care a bird's lost egg for Zelar and neither should you."

"And Lord Roguehan approves?"

"He will when I tell him about it. Really, Llewelyn, why bother the man? He's got a war to run and once we succeed he'll get a fine show of destruction. Probably give you extra credit after bringing in El. Which, by the way, I'm more than willing to help you with. No, this one's between you and me. For now."

"One last question before I agree. What does Walworth think of Caethne's secret deals with the enemy?"

"Not much. But he's got a war of his own to run and is in no position to pursue the issue right now. And the old duke is very ill and needs Caethne to care for him, the old duchess not being skilled in herbs and healing like her daughter. Walworth understands full well why his sister did it, which means he also understands why Zelar is not eager to make any more plans with her. Caethne is probably as much afraid of her twin as she is of Zelar but they've both got more important matters than Caethne to attend to right now. Walworth's fairly confident she can't do any damage to Threle, and that's all he can afford to concern himself with at the moment. In fact, I was present during a heart-to-heart talk Walworth had with his old tutor about the issue and they both decided that if Caethne was busy attending to duchy concerns, she wasn't likely to jeopardize the cause. And it's damnably hard to stay angry at someone who had a hand in saving your life, and Caethne did act rather heroically riding to Hala to save Mirand's."

So that much of her letter was true.

"Besides, it's not as if her sympathies lay with Roguehan. And under the present circumstances she'd greatly prefer not to see Threle lose. They're all doing their best to regard the incident as family business to be taken care of later, if later ever comes. I don't know—I'd put money on Caethne charming her way back into everybody's good graces yet. She's highly adept at that sort of thing. And like it or not, she is joint heir to the duchy. Walworth would prefer to have her performing administrative duties up north so that he can fight unencumbered. Which, given Caethne's disposition, might be considered punishment enough. Also, let's be practical. Even if Walworth saw fit to bring his sister up on treason charges, which might be a stretch considering her actual activities—Caethne could spend the next decade telling her life story without pausing for breath and, what's more, probably would—Walworth's too much the strategist to waste his time on it now."

"How did you come to be present at this private conversation?"

"I'm her husband. I was invited. It was the gentlemanly thing to do." I looked quizzical. "Really, Llewelyn, it's not as if *I'm* making secret deals with the enemy. I don't particularly care what the outcome of the war is. And like it or not, I am family."

"I can tell. You're so obvious about it. And I thought you were loyal to Roguehan."

"So does Roguehan. I'm loyal to myself and to Habundia-Christus. I may be Sunnan born but I've got Threlan attitudes."

"No, you don't."

"Well, look, if I knock about here and again in Roguehan's camp looking for a bit of sport, who can say me nay, poor wandering cleric that I am? And if I bring my cousin the commander an occasional useful tidbit, it's no worry to him where I go, and if I do the same for the other side—really, Llewelyn, it's war, and wars are meant to be enjoyed. Walworth was grateful to me for feeding the Halans. Roguehan was grateful to me for affecting public attitude. *You* ended up with a fine illusion spoon and I made a few converts for Habundia. Who could possibly object?"

"The cook we executed here might have had a few thoughts on the subject."

"Yes, but we know who let Welm escape, and you didn't concern yourself too much about the cook then. And even in that one there was a fine entertainment all 'round, from what I hear."

"Do you know what happens to double traitors?"

"Yes, the clever ones end up living their ease in monasteries. I don't concern myself with the rest."

"All right, coz, deal." I extended my hand and we shook.

"Oh, by the way, you needn't spend years here. Drive El into embracing goodness as soon as you can, take initiation, and leave."

"I'd like to speed things up. But how? El keeps my spirit and I still keep my bans from Sunnashiven against using my full individual powers and traveling into the North Country."

Cathe grasped my hand, looked me in the eyes, and gasped like an overblown fish, "Trust me to pray for you, then. Trust me to help those matters. Remember, I can initiate you when the time comes. And once you're free of El I can remove your bans. Trust me, coz, we'll be in touch."

"I'm sure." And with that he bounced up and down on his knees, spun in a circle with his outstretched staff, and danced away into wherever he went.

I didn't go to class that day. I washed my bedclothes, which now smelled faintly of dead insects, and worked on translating Sarana poems into Botha. Then I paced the floor and thought about what I had just agreed to.

I also thought once again of Caethne's letter detailing how little my former comrades cared for me, and of Walworth's terse confirmation that I was to stay in monastic hell. I considered it terribly un-Threlan of them to take a half-deadened heart from Sunnashiven, warm it into youthful exuberance, and leave it to rot without paying for the emotional damage, even if there was a war on. Well, I had a war on too, an internal one. Mirand had taught me to honor the self, to know that my life mattered, and I had long ago decided that I sorely wanted to take his lesson to heart and make my life matter to them, to let all of them know I would never forget or forgive the pain they caused me.

But it is one thing to fantasize about revenge and another to have the actual means dropped in one's lap. Welm had never hinted at anything more concrete than Roguehan's expectation that one day I would work against his enemies, which for all I knew might or might not even include Walworth directly. Could I find it in myself to be the cause of Walworth's death? Well, if dear Caethne could, then far be it from me to blanch. I decided I could do worse than to adopt a Threlan attitude about the whole thing. Caethne had made the deal. Caethne had chosen to commit murder in return for a certain favor. I was merely working a high-powered love spell against a powerful wizard and doing my duty by turning in criminals to the proper authorities. In the rawest, most basic sense I was merely providing the two of them with a temporary happiness they didn't deserve. The rest was really none of my affair. I liked it. I wasn't even sure the whole plan was illegal, if one wanted to get technical about it.

Roguehan might even be pleased, but so what if he wasn't? There was nothing in our agreement prohibiting my accepting Cathe's proposal, and as to Zelar, well, I wasn't going to live my life in fear of him or anyone else. Clerics don't have to worry about trivia. In fact, any cleric who knows how to live never has to worry. Period. It was about time I took that lesson to heart. Besides, even El felt comfortable bucking Roguehan from the safety of his monastery. Hell, El once bucked the whole Threlan kingdom when he found it amusing enough to do so. Look at the havoc the peacemongers could raise. Clerics do not take orders from mundane governments. I was a priest in training and *all* I needed to concern myself with was Hecate's protection. And Hecate would probably bless me for wreaking such awesome emotional destruction on Mirand, considering that Mirand was locked such a fierce celebration of Athena, a celebration no doubt made more pungent by his generous sampling of death. The whole thing sounded like a fine game to me.

And if the duchy ended up in my lap, well, at least *I* would manage it according to true Threlan principles—like loyalty. One way or another, I would be a presence in Walworth's family. Cathe had given me a plan. All I needed now was a strategy for execution.

Twenty-one

𝓘t was the doorkeeper who found the body on the morning following Cathe's visit. It was Sister Elwyn who found the doorkeeper, who was holding the corpse's hands in his own as he swung the body in semicircles along the ground, making bird patterns in the melting snow. And it was Cristo, of course, who first told me all about it. When he stomped unexpectedly back into our rooms as Devon and I were breakfasting on dark bread and honeyed black tea, he was so breathlessly excited I thought perhaps the peacemongers had gotten their way and canceled classes. He was talking in great spurts about the doorkeeper's corpse, and Elwyn's corpse, and everyone's corpse, until I began to think we'd been attacked overnight by someone's battalion. But finally Cristo made it clear that the wondrous event that had precipitated his excitement was the corpse of one the peacemongers. Apparently the peacemonger had stolen a dagger from an encampment of Kantish soldiers near town during a war protest on the previous night and plunged it into his own breast upon his return. He left a note that read *Peace at last.* Cristo didn't know anything more about it except that his name was Riven and that he had been a year away from initiation into the priesthood of Ares the Aggressor.

I was more annoyed than intrigued, especially since I wanted to be left in peace to mull over the best way to get through Mirand's considerable magical defenses. Cristo's chatter was making careful thought impossible, but then, that was the sort of thing Cristo did.

"So aren't you coming out to see the corpse? There's going to be a crowd if there isn't already."

"Then Riven won't be offended if I miss the show. Bring me a souvenir."

Devon stuffed the remnants of his crust through his sticky lips and spoke through a full mouth. "I'll go, Cristo. Take me to see."

"Yeah, all right. Luvellun, are you sure? Everyone'll be there."

"That's the point. *I'm* not everyone, Cristo. *I'm* fashionably unconcerned."

"You're going to miss it all," he eagerly warned me, leaving quickly with Devon so as not to miss anything himself. I sipped my rapidly cooling tea in the comfortable silence and glanced through the window for signs of the crowd Cristo was predicting. I saw nothing but the blank spread of muddy ground and dirty snow patches. The attraction must be on the other side of the building. I supposed I'd be hearing all about it and nothing else for the next six months. I had no idea why Riven had taken his own life so close to initiation, especially when he now had a war to live for and everything, but I did know that his suicide would become an inescapable subject of discussion and I wanted to make use of it for my own ends. A really well executed suicide is more likely to inspire envy than admiration within monastic walls, and I wanted to determine how much envy Riven's sad little gesture was causing and how I could best shape that envy to my own advantage. I was considering the problem backward and forward when Devon returned with a small red cloth in his hand.

"Hey, Luvellun, look at this! I got you a souvenir! Just like you wanted!" He smiled like a sun viper and held out the cloth, which was wrapped around something long and narrow.

"You got me a what? Oh, Dev, that was just a joke." The cloth felt stiff and knobby.

"Open it quick. Sister Elwyn wasn't there and I sent everyone away so I could get it for you." Devon sat cross-legged on the floor and smiled up at me in anticipation of my pleasure. I set down my now empty mug and unwrapped the cloth to keep him happy. There, lying stiff and yellow and repulsive in my palm, was a dirty index finger. Sweet little Devon had managed to break it off the corpse. He was still smiling, waiting for praise and approval. "Do you like it, Luvellun?"

I gingerly laid the cloth down on my writing table and quickly gulped half a pitcher of water. The fact is, the unexpected gift of a suicide's finger first thing after breakfast sent my newly awakened clerical senses reeling, and I wanted the water to flush away my rising sickness. I had been faithful to a vegetarian diet and faithful to my academic studies and I had recently become quite pleased with my ability to feel the death in things. So of course I no longer had any urge to touch meat. El had not formally taught us to feel death yet; we were still learning to destroy the feelings in poetry and to caress the abstraction of death as we desecrated some poet's lines. But apparently I had gone beyond these exercises without realizing it. The finger contained enough of the suicide's final nerve-ridden shudders to thicken my stomach into shuddery knots. The water was soothing. I supposed the peace-monger crowd, or someone with a more sanguine alignment, would probably be having a private orgy over the finger, the death throes in it were so fresh and strong. Well, maybe not just the peacemongers. The war was certainly making it fashionable for everyone to be "moved" by physical violence, hence Mirra's posturing. Perhaps she really was a budding young peacemonger, but I sure as Hecate wasn't. To manifest Hecate is to renounce flesh in favor of the mind—that is the crux of Her evil. This particular piece of flesh was cutting me unawares.

"Don't you like it, Luvellun? Everyone was talking about getting a piece." Devon sounded crushed.

I coughed. "It's beautiful, really it is, Dev. How clever of you to get it for me. Best present I've ever had—"

"Really? The very best?"

"Sure, I'll remember it always. Your butterflies and snakes are prettily done too. I really like those—but this is certainly special, Devon. Well done." I swallowed a rising lump of honey in my throat. "Why don't you go back down—"

"And get another?"

"No, sweetie. Go find out what people are saying and come back and tell me about it." He left and I slowly recovered. If I was progressing this fast, perhaps I should remind El about removing my bans. I shielded the finger as I covered it, slowly easing myself into calmness. There was a knock on the door. "Come in," I called, not caring to disrupt my recovery by rising to answer it. It was Mirra.

"There has been an incident outside and Master El has decided to hold class there now." Her voice sounded vaguely like a reprimand.

"What incident? You mean Roguehan's invaded the monastery and given us the day off?"

She looked annoyed. Humor always made Mirra look annoyed unless she was in class and trying to show El that she was intelligent enough to understand a witticism or an in joke. She never made witticisms of her own. "I've done my job and I've other students to inform." She left before I could question her further.

Well, we'll soon see what the deal with the corpse is. I dropped the shielded finger in my pocket. A prize like that would no doubt increase the envy of the war set toward me, and that alone could have its uses.

Physical violence was really fashionable that season, thanks to the war. Even El, for all his infatuation with rarefied emotions, couldn't resist sampling the body's death aura. I emerged into the day in time to see him order a fairly large crowd to disperse and to wave his own students over to have a look. Cristo remained behind to show El how serious he could be about such things, just in case there was a permanent job in the offing. I noticed that Devon had had the rare good sense to move the desecrated hand under the body.

Once our class was assembled along with El's more advanced students he grandly demonstrated to us why the body was in a particularly attractive pose, and how one day we would all wean ourselves away from critiquing literary texts and learn to appreciate sights like this one, sights that comprised what he blithely called the "splendiferous living world." Yes, hmm. Each of the more advanced students got to make a speech. Mirra was standing stock-still with head raised high as if the suicide were her accomplishment and she was proud of it. Then El praised the living end out of his advanced students and started speaking again about the exquisite loveliness of physical self-slaughter, of suicide as the ultimate destruction of one's desires to honor one's deity, and of Riven finding "peace at last" in Ares.

As soon as El stopped speaking the peacemongers started an ostentatious chant and Mirra nervously stepped forward and bowed low. "*Lord Master Most Exalted High Priest,*" she began abjectly. Where the hell was she getting "lord" and all the rest of it from? This would be good. El waved his hand in acknowledgment of her address. He really did get off on slavishness. "Our fallen comrade, Riven, was a victim of oppression. He was a true son of Ares. He loved war—"

"So what?" I made a voice say out of the crowd. I loved my illusion ring. There were several giggles, and El lost control and smiled for a second in spite of himself. I remained solemn and straight-faced, but I made sure to look around sharply at the affront as if I were personally offended. Mirra sighed loudly and the rest of the war club looked piteously at El, as if he was supposed to do something. El got control of himself and told her solemnly to continue.

"All war lovers share in Riven's oppression"—*can't let poor Riven take all the glory, can you, Mirra?*—"for while we are compelled to swallow the battle violence as it flowers, others"—she looked at me—"devote their time to studies and refuse to help their brothers and sisters who cannot help themselves away from violence. The lesson we have today is that we are all one, Master, we are all responsible for each other—and *we* are all responsible for and deserve credit for this great sacrifice. Riven died for us all, war lover or no. Today we are all Riven."

There was some uneasiness in the crowd at Mirra's blithe assertion that we were all Riven, who was really looking mottled and stiff at this point, but no one was about to risk seriousness by contradicting her, especially since El's face was now so bland and hard to read. Besides, if there was going to be free credit for the taking, well, why object? El turned his gaze on Mirra and said evenly, "Continue, daughter."

Mirra's nervousness made her bellow. "My brothers and sisters in evil, if you all truly be such, listen to the true nature and meaning of Riven's self-destruction. Our brother, who soon would have been priest, was faced with a cruel choice, a choice that *no* student of this monastery should ever have to make: a choice between excelling at the studies he loved, and following the irresistible call of his god to war. And so he took the higher path and under the special dispensation followed Ares to wreak destruction before the battle while others continued in their papers and books." She looked at me hard and then looked over at El. "One might say that Riven, like the rest of us peacemongers, sacrificed the very thing he loved to follow Ares."

"It's good practice," said El officiously.

Everybody nodded approval, so I made sure to repeat obnoxiously, "Very good practice. We should all aspire to such holiness, Master."

"Yes, we should," said Mirra shrilly, "and I'm glad you agree. For you"— she pointed her finger at me—"are very much responsible for the loss of our comrade!" Everyone was staring at me now, fully alert and completely puzzled. Mirra's shrillness was not earning her points with the crowd, but my superior classroom performance had earned me everyone's envy, and I could sense my fellow students dividing themselves between annoyance with Mirra and gratitude that someone was openly accusing me of something, even if it wasn't particularly clear as to what that something was.

"Does that mean I get full credit for the sacrifice, then?" I asked. Cristo laughed but stopped laughing when he noticed the widening silence around him.

"Continue, Mirra," said El blandly.

Mirra explained how I had used my well-known influence over the Sun King to damn the war club to mediocrity. In between burning soldiers' tents in "protest" of the violence, Riven had declared to every peacemonger who would listen that he simply could not sacrifice his academic standing to the Sun King's whim and that he felt it nobler to die than to fail in any aspect of his monastic training. "And so, out of his great sensitivity to violence, he took his life. But all of us who are compelled to feed off the war might have done the same."

"Go for it," I sent out through my ring, to peals of laughter.

"Riven was sacrificing his academic work to the god's call," insisted Mirra, "like a true son of Ares. But when a certain person unfairly decided that wasn't enough, Riven sacrificed his life! It was all he had." Mirra then made sure that everyone knew that, unlike herself, poor Riven's studies had been slipping on account of following the call to war. That was one of the hazards of peacemongering, and of course that wasn't fair either. Mirra left out the war club's own clumsy attempt to prevent me from excelling. Then she preached self-righteously that if the rest of us really cared about physical violence, none of us would be doing anything but aiding the war protests until the fighting moved on.

"So it was easier to commit suicide than write a paper," I interjected. This thought was not original. While Mirra was speaking I had opened myself to the thoughts around me to gauge the impact she was making and learned that nearly everybody was devoutly wishing for the courage to take their own lives as an honorable out from studying.

El's eyes bulged bigger than potatoes when I said this. He gave Mirra a tensely eager command to continue. Which she did, at excruciating length, claiming that she was bringing up the subject of my influence over Devon only for the good of the monastery and for the welfare of poor Devon, not because any of the peacemongers needed to excel. They were all too humble for that. But everyone should know that my cavalier cruelty had been the cause of Riven's death and might cause the death of other hapless victims. Furthermore, they were all *deeply* concerned for the spiritual welfare of yours truly, because I never seemed to sacrifice anything and always got everything I wanted through Devon. I didn't act humble enough. Oh, and I had enjoyed the music too much last Sunreturn, which didn't look good. We were supposed to be watching an execution and an initiation, not blubbering over beauty; anyone would think by the way I'd acted that I was a goddess-damned dedicant of Ceres. She concluded with a nervously noble statement about the war club's willingness to show humility by obeying the Sun King in all things. Then she folded her arms across her chest and looked most put out. She clearly wanted El to do something.

"Thank you, Mirra," said El quietly. Everyone was breathless, waiting for the high priest's response.

I broke the silence. "We all just sacrificed half an hour's worth of corpse kissing to listen to Mirra complain about me. Really, Master, if it's sacrifice—"

"Enough! Silence! First of all, the sacrifice of one's love is the highest rite that a dedicant can perform and must be taken *by choice* at initiation—not through the Sun King's command. If you love academic excellence, then academic excellence may be required of you at some point, but for you, Mirra, that point has not yet come." Half the crowd, including myself and two or three peacemongers, doubled over with laughter at El's unintended pun. "I absolve you and the others of the command." For someone who didn't care about excellence, she looked most relieved, for she sighed, smiled self-consciously, and dropped her arms.

"Master," I asked innocently, "why would followers of a war god even care about academic excellence?"

"We don't. Not really," sang out Mirra. "We care about higher things, like morality."

"Yes, well . . . Master, if I may speak?" El nodded coldly. After all, he would be fair. "Never mind me. I'm nothing, as the Lady Habundia says in holy writ. But it seems to me that Riven's 'supreme sacrifice' is a bit of a sham, a lamentable piece of self-indulgence in one so advanced in his studies. Here is a young man who clearly preferred wreaking violence to studying for initiation, long before Devon's little whimsy ever entered into it. Whether his preference was his god's call or fashion, it is no matter. His preference is clear to all. And our sister Mirra tells us Riven was not much of a student in the first place but loved the war. The way I see it, he didn't sacrifice anything. He embraced the violence he loved into his own person; he took everything he loved and made it his own. That *is* against the rules, Mirra— your comrade Riven may even be damned from evil for so doing."

Howls of outrage and cries of "Insensitivity!" from the peacemongers.

"But if the war club needs to claim some sort of credit through having a martyr in their midst to make up for neglected studies—why, it's wonderful work if you can get it. Now we've got a peacemonger who would have been brilliant but for me, and by association a whole club that would excel but for me." I launched into Mirra's own proposal that I should avoid excelling until the war was over. "So who is influencing whom? Riven is not a sacrifice. He's a putrefying blasphemy. He *wanted* to die. I've seen better sacrifices from artichokes at harvest time."

El had no intention of letting things continue as they were, so he ended our pleasant little class by blasting a loud hole in the muddy ground. And he made an unnecessary production out of it, by loudly calling upon Habundia and making sharp jabbing motions with his hands that caused the ground to rise and swell and throw everyone off balance. As the ground opened up it disgorged a storm cloud that spit snakes and black lightning before dissipating back into ether. This got everyone's attention, but I couldn't help noticing that this wasn't El's usual style. Clerical magic rarely needs embellishment and when done correctly, especially in a place of power such as a monastery, the energy is clean and sudden and arrives without warning. One second the deity's energy isn't tangible and the next it's inescapable. El's display of pyrotechnics struck me as, well, a bit sloppy, but it made an impression on everyone else. "Papers due tomorrow. Mirra and Luvellun, see me now." And so to sporadic catcalls from the dispersing crowd Mirra and I followed our high priest inside.

El's work area startled me with mess. Something was wrong here, deadly wrong. I had not been here since my dedication during the previous summer, so it felt odd to see that the chair and writing table I had used as a scribe were buried under great stacks of papers. El's own desk was paralyzed with parchment. His sacred censer was on its side, spilling a cold still pile of sand. The fireplace was damp and moldy and held a pile of ashes so thick that smoky pieces lifted and invaded the dust-laden air as we slowly moved to where El motioned us to stand. It was cold here, colder than outside. The window was dirty enough to subdue the morning light, and I wondered how El and his scribes managed to see to write in the late afternoon, when the light weakened considerably. I also wondered how El could even begin to think and practice clerical magic in this workplace, which no longer conveyed any of the efficiently evil power that the high priest invariably showed in his public persona—at least until that morning's strangely overdone display of power. Something was killing him, for there was destruction in the barren bureaucratic feel of the dust and immobile papers. El was buried alive in his beloved work. Some outside force was using this work as a weapon against him, as a means of wearing against his strength. I feared for a clench of time that some unknown rival was beating me to Roguehan's favor, but then I forced myself to study the situation and banish the fear lest El find it despite the deadening effect of his work area.

I was also surprised to observe that up close, El's face was taut and gray like an old corpse's. There was a dullness in his eyes that made my nerves crawl. His skin was the shade of tired that seeps into once-brilliant lives strangled with trivia. His was the nerve-wracking distance of one whose mind was forced to be on too many boring matters at once but nevertheless desired nothing more than to finish the work it loathed so that it might get back to the work it loved. The contrast with his sharp classroom persona was startling. Someone or something was wearing his life down around the edges, and he was valiantly fighting to preserve it in public. My job was to find those edges.

He clearly begrudged the time our coming reprimand would take. Mirra cried enormous tears as we stood waiting in the dusty chaos which swirls and chokes the life out of much-loved work until El looked up at us and dourly spoke. "Daughter."

Mirra's chest trembled miserably and she had trouble meeting El's eyes. "Yes, Mas—"

"—You have dedicated yourself to Hecate. So. And yes, I have known for some time that your dedication has not taken. Your spirit is too frenzied for Her path. And your actions are not in keeping with Hers. Therefore I return your spirit to you." He sounded so matter-of-fact that it was sad in a deadly sort of way, because he spoke in the voice of one who was constantly fighting for time and energy to experience his strange forbidden love for his self-sacrificial calling.

El began to raise his arm but Mirra set up a wail and then instantly bit her lips to stifle it. "Master, please don't send me away." She fell on her knees. "Please, I want to study and read and learn."

He dropped his arm. "You want to progress on the path of evil. And you thought book learning would take you along that path." El sounded very tired and impatient. "It sometimes happens that a person dedicates to an incompatible deity!"

"I love to read, Master," she whined.

"That is not clear. You crave esteem and notice, yes." Mirra sobbed and hugged herself into a pathetic little shaking ball. "And since you've read more than most, you found booklearning to be a way to such esteem. But now there is a war and a special dispensation and so—you wish everyone to esteem your sensitivity to violence. Well and fine, except rather than take the logical consequence of your formal studies falling to your new interest, you seek to make others fail so that you might maintain your own academic status. I think of the line from holy writ, Habundia's line, 'All must die so that I might live.' " Mirra could not speak. "Cry not, daughter, for I account your actions evil," El added consolingly. "Your heart is where it should be, if only you knew it. But I do not see for you the priesesshood of Hecate or of Ares the Aggressor."

"What do you see for me, Master?" whispered Mirra, a little calmer now that her master still considered her evil.

"Your true calling is to be accounted better than others, no matter what the medium. You are called to demand that others view you as more intelligent or sensitive or moral than anyone else. That others sacrifice themselves for your standing." El's words choked inside me a little, for they reminded me of Mirand's parting words to me, although El, unlike Mirand, sounded quietly approving.

"No, Master, I do not love myself in that way. I seek only to follow the Goddess."

"I know. And so it is the Goddess Habundia-Christus in her highest manifestation that you must follow. For you there is no other way."

Mirra looked up, her tears dried instantly, and she beamed in spite of herself. "Master?"

"You shall spend many years of your life in Her lower manifestations—one to the other as your spirit leans—but in the end I see you becoming priestess of Christus and perhaps beyond that archon. You may even live to become high priestess."

Mirra stood up proudly. "Master, I shall always follow the Lady's call. I shall rededicate myself to Her now. Without question. Here. With you."

"No. You shall take your spirit from me and resume your studies in Sunnashiven, for that is the highest temple of the Goddess. That is where one clings to Habundia-Christus."

"Sunnashiven," breathed Mirra, as if El were sending her to paradise.

"You'll love it, Mirra," I said.

She ignored me while El raised his arm. She followed the arc with bright expectant eyes and staggered a little as she took her spirit back. "I send you to your own life's path. You have no more business here." He wrote something on parchment and gave it to her. "Give this to the chief cook and the stable boy and they will provide for your journey. You may take a servant with you as escort if you wish. I shall write letters of introduction for you tonight, and as you are no longer a dedicant of the monastery, you shall leave us at first opportunity. I am sending you to study with a former student of mine named Salan. He can instruct you in the language and culture of the southwest."

"Master, I am so grateful I know not what to say," she gushed.

"Then give me your word of evil that you will say nothing to anyone save that you must leave," he ordered. "And aside from making preparations for your journey you shall seclude yourself in meditation until you leave our walls. For your path is the higher one and shall not be lowered through even the thoughts of others. And should you cross another's path it would be well for you to appear reticent and humble, for you are receiving a very great honor."

"Yes, of course, Master. No one shall know. Upon my word of evil." And she struck her fist upon her chest.

"May you prosper in Her keeping," said El warmly. He rose and extended his hand to her. She kissed all his rings several times over and bounced around and cried. El smiled and motioned her toward the door, and she exited as though she were a little southwestern queen.

The door closed behind her and El's smile vanished. He *hmm*d and coughed and settled himself stiffly back in his chair, briefly pressing his fingertips together before resting his palms on two piles of parchment. Now it was my turn. "Luvellun." For a high priest he really was in terrible physical condition, from which I concluded that something I needed to know about was disrupting his power and attachment to Habundia. I noticed his skin now had a yellowish tinge underneath the gray and that he was having some difficulty breathing. His fingers looked puffy and swollen against the parchment. "As far as anyone else is concerned, you managed through your cleverness and considerable wit to get your rival thrown out of the monastery in disgrace. I shall say nothing to contradict whatever tale of vengeance you wish to create."

To give myself a moment to digest this little surprise, I walked over to the hearth, cleared away a space from the considerable bundles of papers, and sat. His voice was harshly earnest. He was both giving an order and hiding an inner discomfort that I sensed was relatively new to him. It made me think of the contrast between his public and private personas, a contrast I needed to study. "Suppose I give out the truth, Master? That Mirra is on her way to more exalted studies in Sunnashiven?" I wanted to gauge El's reaction.

He sighed and shook his head like a great shaggy bear-dragon. "Suppose we get it clear between us right now that I'm running this monastery," he half thundered.

"Of course you are, Master High Priest." I deliberately rose and started for the door. "And you clearly don't need my help."

"Sit down," he commanded.

"Master? You mean you do need my help?"

"Please, Luvellun." He sounded faintly as though he was begging. He motioned to the hearth and I resumed my seat. He didn't speak but glanced sadly around the room at the stacks of paper. "The work, it never ends, hmmm?"

"I suppose it's a way of life. Not everyone could manage this." I said this gently to try to sound comforting, to draw him into revealing something useful about himself. By my tone I was encouraging him to believe that there were really no games between us, that brilliant as I was, I still had the utmost respect for him. The strange thing was, I sort of meant my tone at the time. El may have been an evil high priest but he wasn't really a bad sort, if you know what I mean. I could find it in my heart to feel something like a grudging respect for him.

Anyway, he wasn't about to share confidences. He glowered at me through heavy eyelids but said without rancor, "I want you to keep the war people in the monastery and out of trouble."

"How?" I asked automatically. "The Goddess Herself couldn't keep them in the monastery now that they've got this special dispensation to wave around, Master."

"By doing what you do." He seemed unruffled by my insolence concerning the dispensation. "Use Devon. Use your illusion ring." He glanced at my finger. It surprised me less that El knew what it was than that he didn't particularly care that I had it. "Use your sophistry and charm and anything else at your disposal."

"Master, I am sure you need only command them to sacrifice their taste for blood."

"No. As dedicants of Ares, they must make the choice. And I would prefer that my orders be carried out without violating the dispensation. I cannot command restraint in these matters without breaking monastic law and having to answer to Sunnashiven for it. You, however . . . can find a way to . . . *discourage*, shall we say, peacemongering, and to do so without reference to me or the law. I shall properly reward your success." This last sentence had a strange plaintive undertone to it, although it sounded fairly confident on the surface. El dismissed me by pointedly resuming his paperwork.

I wasn't about to leave. I let him work for a few minutes, watching him cough in the ashy dust-filled air. "Blessings on you, Master. Would you like me to open your window?"

"No, Luvellun, you may go."

"Your chimney flue, then, to let in a little air?"

"It's too early in the season for that. You may go. I'm looking forward to reading your paper." He coughed a little and kept scratching the parchment with his pen.

"Master El, might I ask why you have honored me with this little request?" I waited with bated breath. Here was the answer that would help me fulfill my deal with Roguehan.

He looked at me pointedly. "Because I would prefer to keep Lord Roguehan out of Kursen Monastery." For a second I thought perhaps he knew about my secret deal with Roguehan, but his next words convinced me that he didn't. "He's already trying to kill me with paperwork."

"I'm sure Lord Roguehan doesn't want to *kill* you, Master," I couldn't resist saying.

"Well, then, his cursed Sunnashiven temple priests are doing a fair job of it. Twenty years master high priest of my own monastery and every time the blessed sun rises and falls I now find myself having to account to Sunnashiven for it." He swept his arm in an arc to indicate the menacing piles of paper. "I'm a cleric, not a Sunnan clerk!"

"Yes, Master, this is pure scribe work. You deserve far better." The irony of him once having said something similar to me was lost on his usually sharp mind.

"Roguehan has no respect." El doggedly shook his head. "No respect for tradition, for spiritual principles, for the freedom of the clergy to follow their call without outside interference. To him monasteries and holy places are just another arm of the state, to be used at his pleasure for his own ends."

"Are your sympathies leaning toward Threle, then, Master?" I asked softly.

"My sympathies are with Kursen, Luvellun. As yours should be now. Roguehan has placed his own clergy in charge of the Helan monasteries and does not blush to empty the sacred places of their holy relics. He's defiled some of the monasteries by turning them into military bases. I'll be damned from evil if he gets his bloody hands on Kursen, but that appears to be what he wants. The dispensation from Sunnashiven had his mark all over it. It's Roguehan who is using our students to attack Threlan strongholds for him—notice they don't go burning down his camps. And of course it's not his style to destroy civilian towns if he can help it. In Helas he sought and got capitulation from the merchant towns and I'm sure would prefer to do so here if your old commander weren't so successful in organizing a fighting force."

"Well, Master, the Kantish people are less squeamish than the Helans about taking up arms against the southwest. And Roguehan's imperial intentions are much more clear than formerly. He can't rely on rhetoric to do half the job for him now."

"Precisely. So if the students can destroy the town for him, well, the locals would be very happy if he took Kursen Monastery into his own hands. Roguehan's already sending the townspeople promises of peace from the 'tyranny of the clergy' and this of course appeals greatly to the Threlans' innate sense that no one should have special privileges. Roguehan would prefer local sentiment to favor his having a base here. The townspeople are already frustrated that your old commander refuses to give permission to attack the students."

"He's probably conserving resources for the battle. And whatever crimes they commit under the dispensation, it is no different from committing crimes within monastic walls. The commander of the Threlan army must respect the law. . . . How do you know all this, Master?"

El tugged at his collar. "Brother Cathe dropped me a friendly warning yesterday, hm? And it tracks everything I know about Roguehan. So keep the peacemongers in bounds." El seemed to regret his lapse of protocol, for he suddenly pulled rank again. "It's against the rules to receive visitors, clergy or no. You'll not be seeing Cathe again." He tried to resume work.

I did not move. I was determined to prolong the unexpected informality as long as possible, so I pretended that I hadn't heard his last remark. "Why send Mirra to Sunnashiven? Why not just throw her out for some infraction unrelated to the war or to the dispensation? Make her an example for the war club."

"I'm counting on you to make her an example," he said dryly. "I will not violate the trust of my position. The Lady has called me to bring others in Her path. Mirra truly belongs in Sunnashiven. She is a daughter of the High One, and I am merely doing my duty by the Goddess Habundia-Christus, who is all." The way he said this sounded as though he truly wanted to confide in me, or in someone, but couldn't bring himself to do so.

"Master, it's no secret that Mirra's more irritating than Kantish poetry. And wouldn't we both like to see her fall?" He chuckled a little and then hid the chuckles in a cough. "My critic's sense tells me that through my words and wit I am about to create an illusion of what you would like the rest of the monastery to partake in—Mirra's disgrace. I am to make it possible for you to in effect deny your desires to teach Mirra a life lesson in true dedication, and through doing so save Kursen from Roguehan, Kursen being what you truly desire and love." This was bold, I'll admit, but the opportunity was ripe for such a thrust. I remembered El's proclivity for torturing the most incompetent students and how that seemed to spring from his genuine love of evil, and I couldn't imagine that he truly felt Mirra's eternal aping of her betters constituted anything resembling real talent for clerisy.

"Kursen is for the Goddess, not me," he said coldly, but without dismissing me. I was sure that at any other time he would have blasted me for my impertinence. That is how I knew I was hitting a vulnerability in his personality.

"Then why does it matter who it belongs to?" I asked.

El looked hard and colorless, his skin mottled dark and light like the surface of the moon. "Go! Do your job!"

"Don't worry, Master, I'll carry out your request. Kursen is yours, as it should be. And I won't tell. About your desires, I mean."

"I have no desires save duty! Damn you! I teach because I have to, as the Lady commands."

"Of course, Master. Of course. We all respect and honor your dedication to the path." I had clearly gone too far. I bowed very low and started for the door. I felt him watching my every movement, my every breath, through dull, thickly bulging eyes. Then I felt my hand on the door, and the hard wood was softer than his rage. El's anger made my scarred palm throb with pain. It was random energy, unusual for a cleric. El was too rattled to direct anything right now, of that I was sure. But I was also sure that it would behoove me not to leave him like this, that I should placate him somehow. I bowed again. "Master High Priest, I almost forgot. I had Devon get this for you and I would very much like you to have it as a sign of my great respect." I drew the shielded wrapped finger out of my pocket and quickly placed it on his papers. He was unmoved. "Master, I hope you like it. I am not able to stomach it, of course, so I used a shield that—someone else once taught me. And as a high priest, you are probably more capable of deriving enjoyment from it than I am." He was still staring; my palm was still pulsing with his anger, but more slowly now. "Actually, Master, due in part to your excellent instruction and in part to Lady Hecate and my work I find that I am becoming quite sensitive, to a lot of things. I have made so much progress under your teaching, Master, that I was wondering if you in your great divinely inspired wisdom felt it was time to remove my bans."

I felt his anger draining with my implicit acknowledgment of his superiority. He liked the idea of my needing him, especially after I had made it clear that I understood his weakness. "I suppose it's the least I can do," he grumbled. Then he looked around at the piles of paper that were strangling his life out of time. "But I'm not up to it now. Pray about it for a month and remind me again."

"Yes, Master, you can be sure that I will." I started to leave.

"And take your gift back. I suspect you will put it to better use than I will."

"Yes, Master. May Habundia Christus bless you." And with that I pocketed the finger and left him to another day of murdering himself in paperwork.

Reflections. El was already a divided man, and not just in the theological sense of loving evil so much that he was not truly sacrificing himself to follow it. He loved Kursen so much that he was half tempted to violate the dispensation to save it, a major infraction for a high priest. So tempted that he threw himself on yours truly as the only possible means to accomplish his end without violating his calling. Since I had just seen El's weakness and strength in its dark glory, I knew I had also seen the weapon I needed to fulfill my bargain with Roguehan. I had no idea how to bring it about yet, but I now knew my path was to convince El that the only way to save his monastery for evil would be to sacrifice his calling to evil. Roguehan was easing my way by having a hand in the dispensation and the killing paperwork that was slowly eroding El's power, although I had no idea if the emperor intended this. I also thought of Mirand's willing self-sacrifice for Threle and his last cold teaching to me and decided that I would learn from that too. It would be a brilliant application of my first master's lesson in self-sacrifice.

There was to be fighting within three days. I had this piece of intelligence direct from Roguehan himself, via his man the cook. Roguehan had set up a large camp across the border in what was formerly Helas and more recently South Walworth, and I supposed he was waiting to see if

Walworth would make the first move. There was no reason for Roguehan to show himself the aggressor, especially since his emissaries were telling the Kantish people that their Helan neighbors had secretly invited him to take up residence.

And there may have been more than a shade of truth against the Emperor's lies. It was plausible that many Helans, living on empty bellies for the first time in anyone's memory, now had nothing else to believe in except Roguehan's promises of prosperity. Welm had practically said as much at my exam. Also, the Helans were still outraged by Thoren's treatment of their former duke, who had found his way into Botha ballads and folk stories and, absurd as it sounds, really had become something of a hero figure who sought only the good of his duchy and was martyred by meddling Thoren for it. Roguehan had the good sense to keep their outrage alive by appealing to their historical and linguistic connections with the southwestern kingdoms. As an embarrassment to Walworth, there had been demonstrations along the southern border near the wasteland that used to be a market town, both against the commander himself and against his family's recent acquisition of the duchy.

So Roguehan was in a position to wait. If Walworth attacked first, then Roguehan's peaceful empire would merely be defending itself against aggression, and Walworth himself would be thwarting the will of the Helan people, with whom he was none too popular anyway. And if the local townspeople in Kant were to invite Roguehan to cross the border with a few token soldiers to save them from the war club's acts of terrorism, then so much the better, and three days was a plausible amount of time for such an invitation to be given and considered. Once Roguehan's troops crossed the border Walworth would certainly have to repel them, but he would then have to explain to the unhappy Kantish merchants why he appeared to want the peacemongers to burn down their shops and destroy their livelihoods and yet was willing to fight Roguehan, who had come to save them from terrorism. The Threlan commander might be a stickler for Threlan law, but the Kantish people would just as soon not lose their businesses to a bloodthirsty crowd of mad clerical students and might be persuaded to see Roguehan as a hero.

That is why, after considering the issue backward and forward for about a night, I decided to "encourage" the peacemongers to embark on a burning spree in Roguehan's own camp.

Roguehan would never expect it, but if he happened to win Kant in spite of the damage they caused and if Kursen was that important to him, he would be smart enough to see the propaganda value in painting himself as the victim and taking the monastery in hand to prevent further destruction. He and the Kantish merchants would then have a common enemy— the Kursen clerics. I merely had to be sure that Roguehan never discovered who spurred on the peacemongers to attack his stronghold. I would use what El called my considerable wit—nay, my skill with magic, what the hell—to get one of my brethren to take all the credit for it. And I might even go with them if the fancy took me. My illusion ring would allow me to travel invisibly. Really, no one in the monastery would ever be able to accuse *me* of being a peacemonger, especially since as far as anyone would know I had gotten Mirra thrown out in retaliation for the war club's efforts to get me to abandon my scholarly pursuits and join them. But the point of the plan was that a peacemonger hit on Roguehan's forces would really push El over the brink of insanity if I made sure he knew about it in advance. Now that I knew Kursen was his weakness, the thing he loved, I was convinced I could use his agitation to gain more power over him, which I could use toward fulfilling my deal with Roguehan. And if Roguehan was going to win Kant, I wanted to fulfill my deal with him as soon as possible. Cathe was right about speeding things along and about pursuing my own interests regardless of those of either side.

And if the peacemongers' actions helped ensure a Threlan victory, why, then I was still ahead. Kursen would be protected from outside interference, I would be safe from Roguehan's wrath in the unlikely event that my role should be discovered, and El would be relieved and happy enough to heap all kinds of spiritual rewards on me. Cathe might even convey my involvement to Walworth if he felt it would help further our own plans and if I decided it was in my interest to let Cathe know anything about my involvement. The way I saw it, having a high position in Roguehan's court was a fine thing, but ruling Walworth's duchy was even finer, and instigating the war club to harass Roguehan's forces could only speed things up one way or another.

My reflections kept me awake most of the night, and I had just fallen into a deadening predawn slumber when El sent Mirra to tell me to see him. And so my head and eyes felt like crumbling rock salt as I stumbled down to El's apartments. I stood in the close grimy darkness of El's work area, coughing not so much from the ashy air as from the finger-sweaty tone of waking up into close quarters that had sheltered grubby paperwork all night long. As far as I could tell, El hadn't slept much either. He had not bothered to make a fire, so his space felt chilly as well as grubby, the air contrasting irritatingly with the recent warmth of my bed. The tip of a small rush light was glimmering in and out on his desk, and I knew with my magical senses that the rush had been his only light all night.

Mirra stared at El with huge, froggy eyes while he explained to me with an air of great paternal concern that fearless Mirra, the votary of violence would surely feel better traveling to Sunnashiven with an escort. I sat on the hearth and dozed a little while El blathered elegantly about our esteemed little sister who didn't speak Botha, didn't know the way, and—horror of horrors for the champion of peacemongers—feared that battle might break out any day now. He sharply pulled me into near wakefulness by adding pointedly to me, "I've no intention of disrupting your studies by sending you, of course, as I know how much you have to attend to here. But I thought you could make yourself useful by recommending someone both discreet and fluent in your native language. As I said yesterday, our sister's path is the higher one, too high to be profaned by general knowledge."

"Then send Cristo," I said groggily, trying my best to gouge the heavy salt feeling out of my eyes. He was the first person I felt like volunteering. "He couldn't profane his own foot through general knowledge."

"Cristo?" whined Mirra, who already saw herself as better than the lower clergy. "Does he even speak Botha?"

I sank back against the fireplace stones for a few seconds of lovely unconsciousness. Why was I being dragged out of bed for this nonsense?

"Cristo talks too much. I'd rather go south with the doorkeeper. At least he wouldn't profane my new status with gossip."

"So go south with the doorkeeper," I mumbled. In Botha, "to go south" is a rude phrase meaning "to have sex." It's used mostly in northern Sunna. "He might even give you credit," I couldn't resist adding with a yawn. Then I dozed off again.

"Luvellun. Show respect," commanded El, but his command was thin enough to expose a hint of amusement guiltily strangling in the gray air between us.

I was closer to being awake now, but not much closer. I forced my eyes back open. "Come to think of it, Mirra, the doorkeeper isn't a bad choice. His command of Botha isn't *much* better than Cristo's."

Mirra sighed and folded her arms. "El, don't you think that we really need to do something? Everyone knows it's only a matter of time before the real fighting starts."

El clearly disliked being addressed familiarly, but since he had returned her spirit to her and was no longer technically her master, I supposed Mirra was not out of bounds. He cleared his throat, tugged his collar, and said to me in Botha in a tone that could cut light out of granite stars, "Llewelyn, who do you think would be an appropriate choice to accompany Mirra to Sunnashiven? You've made it your business to know Kursen under the ground and over. Is there anyone whose absence would be . . . helpful to your work?"

"Cristo's absence is always helpful to my work," I replied in Botha, emphasizing Cristo's name to annoy Mirra. "But since you put it that way, Master, I would recommend sending the new cook. I know he speaks the language." I was thinking that since I had the option it couldn't hurt to clear the monastery of Roguehan's courier while I went to work on the peace-mongers. Not that it particularly mattered to the success of my plan, but why pass up extra precautions? And I knew the cook wasn't the type to gossip.

"Interesssting," said El softly. "You *do* understand my meaning."

"Of course, Master. You want to send someone who speaks Botha and won't talk."

"Not many of our servants speak your language," added El grandly. "And with you and me resident here, we can certainly . . . hmmm, *spare* other Botha speakers, yes. Thank you."

"Thank you, Master," I said, too tired to care. "May I go now?"

"You may go tell the cook to meet us by the gate."

"Right." I really didn't come fully awake until I delivered El's message. The cook looked at me quizzically but said nothing. He followed me outside where El and Mirra were waiting.

Mirra was mounted on a little black donkey with a wreath of nettles around its neck. It was tied to a slightly larger, meager-looking horse. There was something queer about the horse, a fuzzy breaking darkness around it. I realized it was cursed. Then I realized that El had cursed it, that my link with Roguehan was not going to return alive, and that I had carelessly revealed through my choice of escort who that link was.

El briefly and earnestly explained to the man that he was to accompany this fine young lady to the temple in Sunnashiven. Then he ordered him to mount.

As soon as they were out of sight I ventured to say lightly, "Waste of a decent horse, Master."

"Yes, hmmm. But no sacrifice is too great to purge Kursen of Roguehan, is it?"

"Oh, surely you're not suggesting *that* man is a spy?" I said contemptuously.

"No," said El, chuckling maniacally. "I'm suggesting that he is an ex-spy. Remember it."

I decided the best thing to do was to laugh with him. Laugh *loudly* with him. Laugh and shriek and pretend to have no idea of my master's cleverness and perception, until El had to interrupt me to say stiffly, "You wanted him out. He's out. Know that whatever you need to do your job is yours." There was something freakish about the way he said this.

"Master, you may depend upon me to save the thing you love." I said this softly and sympathetically, as if he were a hurt child I wished to indulge. His eyes narrowed against the dawn sun. I had caught him in a secret sin. "And you may depend upon my silence, for . . . I—I love Kursen too, with all my heart and soul, Master, and if I may say so, I desire nothing save her self-sovereignty and freedom. Trust me."

"I do. I will." It was hard for him to say this. And then his mood instantly changed into flowers and sunshine the way a madman's might. "Come and watch me burn papers," he said excitedly, very much like a little boy. "On what's left of Riven's corpse, yes? We'll show Sunnashiven."

"Yes, Master, with great pleasure."

And so that's what we did. And I pretended not to notice as the flames leapt through the papers whose sole purpose was to immobilize El's own life and time. And I pretended not to sicken as the smoke combined their stultifying purpose with the remains of a peacemonger who lived for activity and violence. And I pretended not to hear as El laughed and laughed and cursed Riven's spirit from Ares and commended it to the peaceful dawn sun, and the white wings of divine serenity, eternal calm, icy tranquility, and ponderous biting inactivity forever and ever without end.

Not that I cared much for peacemongers, but really, there's a certain slant of cruelty that breaks up the boundaries of good taste.

Twenty-two

*O*n El and his psychic contrasts.

Try to keep all world energy, everywhere, flowing in one direction and your efforts will burst and fail into enemy glory. Send energy in one direction long enough and it will rebound against you and compel you to face your opposing force. Extreme goodness fetches extreme evil and extreme evil rebounds with goodness and so it goes back and forth until the cows come home to roost. Evil is the energy of decay, the widening dark of the waning moon, but decay needs growth to feed upon. Good is the energy of growth, the opening light of the waxing moon, but growth needs decay to feed upon. The two Habundias are abstractions of the opposing flow of universal energy and all creation is a distant echo of their eternal dance. Reverse the current or flash it forward like a well-oiled serpent, and out of the random patterns and tensions in the energy's casual oppositions comes the scream where the goddesses claw and kiss and the world happens.

The scream is eternally present. I know this apart from theory, for I have heard the scream many times over, and often without even realizing it. There is an exercise in which we clerics must listen for the scream, holding ourselves against places where graceful white swans devour struggling bleating frogs piece by bloody piece and fuzzier places where the fierce heat of the sun roughly chews up the tender grass. I have held myself against beats of time that come between the full moon at the climax of her strength and the reversal of her energy, when she pulls herself back into shadow— beats that soar and break themselves between my steadiest surges of logic. And there are other places to hear the scream. There is a birth scream between music and silence, without which neither exists. And between poetry and truth. And every living heartbeat screams the scream of life and death.

El held the scream in the space of soul between his love for evil and the demands of Habundia-Christus that her votaries continually sacrifice all they love.

I understood the theory, which is why I didn't even flinch when El cheerfully strutted around his best classroom persona later that day. To me, the contrast with his morning bout of madness was as natural as numbers. It was somewhere within that contrast that I knew I could drive in my wedge and hear in him the world scream as he turned toward his energy's opposition. So I studied and memorized his actions as if they constituted a mathematical formula, for on the higher levels they did.

He had called an afternoon class of all his students, including his dedicants to Ares, because he had decided to lead us in special prayers for Riven's death. "Our son's body has made a holy disappearance," El began devoutly. Everyone buckled down to seriousness. Seriousness is the next best thing to caring. "His body is now ash. I have seen it myself. And each of you has thrown his ash upon the still air. And thus is the body disposed."

"The doorkeeper moved some of it around with a thigh bone," said one of the older students seriously and helpfully, hands clasped in prayer.

"Yes, hmmm. Yes. Thank you. And so what is there to say? Except that we know from holy writ that the god fire took our brave son into eternity, into some new and glorious blessed state, in which he shall remain ever and forever without end."

"Forever without end," the class obediently repeated.

"And furthermore, we know that all of us together, as one, must pray to hold Riven's spirit in its new divine state—wherever and whatever that is."

"Yes, Master High Priest."

El piously led us in secret incantations that I knew were designed to force the peacemongers to pray against their own god—incantations in a light rippling language that none of us knew but which I was sure affirmed Riven's separation from Ares and ensured his eternal hellish existence in the peace he loathed. I didn't pray and I didn't go through the physical motions because I found the exercise so distasteful. El did not rebuke me. Everyone else prayed heatedly with all the fervor seriousness could provide. It was sickening. The peacemongers cursed themselves in Ares's keeping by unwittingly praying against their brother and their god. The more fiercely they prayed to fulfill their own seriousness the stronger their offense became.

El really stretched it out too, with a torturer's skill if not a torturer's cruelty. I sensed more pragmatism than cruelty. He was in effect using Riven to weaken the peacemongers as a group before Riven could inspire them with the strength of martyrs. The peacemongers would be having trouble getting blessings from Ares the Destroyer for a while. And El was counting on me to use Mirra's absence to continue to weaken their morale. All the better for me to manipulate them, I supposed. Also, El was clearly unprepared for teaching. I could see that the ferocity of paperwork had kept him awake during the previous night. Even a high priest cannot command the day to bring forth extra time. And so El was cutting down his own teaching demands by combining classes and taking up the time with prayers.

The prayers finally subsided into a strangely normal silence. The silence gave birth to shuffling feet and whispers while El appeared to collect himself for whatever was next. "Fine. Well done." He locked the fingers of both hands together and stretched his arms together in front of himself. "Riven is disposed of. Now, then. Papers, please."

Only two or three students besides myself had finished papers to turn in, the rest of my colleagues' intellectual exercises having been waylaid by the suicide and the war and the peacemongers and the weather and the color of the sky and who knows what. The master seized the day. He grandly took the finished papers, bowing long dramatic bows over each one that were calculated to rebuke the rest of the class. Then he stared at all of us for a half minute with a hint of contempt. The shuffling stopped as gazes fell to the floor. El quietly thanked us for our essays. Then he casually began to thumb through mine, hmming and sighing respectfully and nodding in approval, which served to fan sparks of jealousy throughout the room. The sparks burned audibly in everyone's breathing patterns as El took up more time by heaping all kinds of flowery praise on my dedication to my work. "Please, Luvellun, please," he said jovially, as though we were close relations or equals, "come up here and read this most excellent paper—and discuss, yes, *discuss* it with us. Such a paper deserves to be shared with all. A veritable model of right thinking and brilliant argument. It is so rare that I am graced with such high-quality work, work that easily puts some initiated clerics to shame," and so on, with many references to my discipline and dedication. El was shaping jagged resentment into an inferno of envy, for the more he praised my dedication the more my colleagues felt their own dedication to their own paths disparaged. In a monastery praise of one student is always interpreted by other students as an implied reproach to themselves.

So I read my paper and made a fine speech and made very sure to swagger around and make loud, pious references to "our former sister, who is no longer with us." Mirra's absence was already as conspicuous as monk's mirth, but since no one dared to mention it, I made sure to make everyone uncomfortable by doing the honors. El kept his trust by saying nothing concerning Mirra. Her absence was mine to define. So I concluded by mentioning how happy I was to be once again surrounded by students who truly loved their deities and I looked pointedly at Mirra's empty seat while declaring my wholehearted endorsement of Kursen's high standards. "May none save the truly evil, the truly serious, and the truly *dedicated* remain among us." My use of the word *dedicated* rubbed in the fact that most of the members of my audience hadn't done their papers. I bowed and sat self-righteously, consciously adopting Mirra's mannerisms.

Jealousy from the others engulfed me as El declared my classroom performance more impressive than anything he'd seen in twenty years.

"But we are all one, Master, as the children of Ares have been reminding us lately," I said in my very best voice of seriousness. This made my colleagues more upset than ever. "And because we are all one, I am sure that anyone here can reproduce what my esteemed Master is pleased to call brilliant. It is sorrowful that so few of my classmates have decided to pro-duce . . . something, but then, if I can write a humble essay, well, by Hecate, we all can."

"Yes," said El, quick to take the hint. He stroked his fingertips against his palms. "And so my best-beloved son has fixed the standard. I expect the rest of you to produce two papers, just as brilliant as this one, by next week. To make up for having nothing now." And to avoid showing himself as un-prepared for class, he dismissed us.

I made an issue over my immediate plans to go to the library, as Mirra used to do, announcing my intent far and wide. I was largely ignored. The war club was on its way outside, chanting and whooping up a storm and ordering everyone who cared to come with them to town to protest Mirra's expulsion. I followed them outside to keep myself informed. The chant was not drawing anything terribly energetic, thanks to El's actions in class, but a few curiosity seekers were now swelling their ranks. A force of twenty marched through the gates and off to wreak destruction, and under the circumstances there was nothing I could do to stop them. I turned and went slowly back inside the building, where I ran into El, who was standing next to the doorkeeper and watching the war club's antics through hard glittering eyes.

"Do something," was all my master said. His mouth didn't move. It was a silent plea to my spirit.

*W*hen I returned to my rooms that evening I learned from Cristo that Ellisand was no longer expected to play at Equinox. Cristo was sure it was because the fighting around the monastery, and all along Kant's border for that matter, would be too fierce and full to permit of travelers for the rest of the season. I had an idea that El was trying to mollify the peacemongers by censoring the only source of life and beauty Kursen had ever contained. No one could enjoy the music "too much" if the music wasn't there to enjoy. El, of course, probably knew that it was in his interest to avoid anything that might seem improper to Sunnashiven, although burning all the bureau-cratic paperwork on Riven's corpse seemed the height of impropriety to me. I had no idea how he was going to explain that one, when the flame kissed the wick.

Cristo also thought that Ellisand might give another concert at Midsum-mer, after the fighting had moved elsewhere. Poets and musicians generally share with clergy an absolute refusal to recognize political boundaries. Even though wandering minstrels generally have right of passage everywhere, I've noticed that the best ones never wander southwest of County Clio. So Cristo assured me that no matter whom Kant belonged to in a few months, Ellisand would be free to perform at Kursen. I was not convinced that Ellisand would ever cross into Roguehan's territory, should the emperor win. The southwest had a way of repelling artists not unlike the way the Drumun Mountains repelled the banned of Sunnashiven's wizard school. Most people who know something of how to use a musical instrument or sing a poem and who are content to fumble out weak energy for weaker applause will fumble in Sunna or Sevalas as well as anywhere else. But if a real musician, such as Ellisand, were to play in the southwest, he would trammel up the source of his own inspiration into something sense-dulling and ugly. *I* couldn't bear to listen to him down there. But as an artist, Ellisand would certainly have the right to cross over into Roguehan's territory unmolested should he choose to play again at Kursen.

The way Cristo tossed this disappointment at me, his bulging cheeks noisy with stale bread and his hands brushing crumbs from his chin to his shirt and from his shirt to the floor, made me want to slap him. There was a time when Cristo had been as worshipful about Ellisand's music as he was about talking. Now he sounded almost relieved that there would be no concert.

He was reading some absurd notice from the war club that was making the rounds. I sighed and stared out the window. Ellisand was playing out there somewhere, bringing strangers into dreams of their best and brightest loves, making starlight crumble between the heartbeats of old men. If only I could have just one of those heartbeats. I'd give it to Isulde to tend to over a North Country fire. I had really wanted to touch Isulde again through Ellisand's music and to dance over plains and forests with her at the moment spring entered the world. Isulde and I had whispered heart secrets in our now nightly dream and made great plans for Equinox, when the music would live for us again. She had spoken of "riding the smoke of the lily," by way of naming the spring—*our* spring—through elven music. "Naming the spring" was another of those strange shadowy phrases that ran through my dreams. It was a line not of her or my making, but Isulde liked it and so we made brazen songs out of it.

I had a notion that Ellisand's music was about as elven as music ever got. I had planned to manifest lilies all over my rooms and to make an offering of lilies to Ellisand as he played, a humble request for something seasonal, if he'd take it from me. And now there would be nothing outside my dreams save the monotony of work and study for the foreseeable future. *Damn! Is music too much to ask?*

"The peacemongers are holding a protest in town tonight," Cristo said enthusiastically. "I'm thinking of going."

"It's a lot of fun, isn't it? Thinking, I mean," I said dolefully.

"Ha, ha, Luvie, very funny. I really might go. Just to see."

"You're a little late, Cristo. They marched off a few hours ago. Heave it ho for Ares and all that."

"I could still join them," he said in a tone that threatened ambition.

"So go," I said suddenly. "It might be a wonderful experience for you. Prove you're decent and moral and all that. Prove you care. Prove you're willing to do something. Prove you're somebody." *And leave me to whatever dulled beauty I can cull from my poor dreaming of dreams!*

"Yeah, I think I will. I will go. I'll tell you what you're missing."

"I know you will, buddy. I'm counting on it."

*W*here were *you* last night, you ugly sonuvabitch of Hecate?" taunted a peacemonger as I made my way to class the next morning. He was blood drunk and his breath reeked greasily of bad meat. He had been harassing the doorkeeper, who was cowering and cooing in the entranceway, but he was interested in me. He tottered up behind me and Cristo as we passed the entrance. The only reason Cristo was up this early was because he had just returned from his night on the town, and he was trying to have everything both ways by pretending for El and the rest of the teaching staff that for once his only interest was in teaching his class. But with the peacemonger at our back professionalism lent no protection. Of course I would have preferred interrogating Cristo in private, but time was running out, so I had no choice but to garner what I could from him on the fly without appearing to be morbidly curious about the club. It was imperative that I maintain a public distance from the peacemongers as a safeguard against being suspected of influencing them to attack Roguehan's camp. So I found myself following Cristo in the hopes that he might need someone to brag and complain to. I needed a spy, so for once in my life I encouraged him to talk to me. And life being what it is, for once in his life Cristo declined.

"It was all right—it was decent," Cristo kept repeating.

"*What* was decent?" I kept asking impatiently.

"Huh. Well, you know, it was all right. Different." Cristo looked around nervously, as if he might get caught red-handed in the act of having an opinion. The peacemonger was listening to us, so I didn't want to sound overly interested in the club's activities.

"So what did *you* do, Cristo?" I asked sarcastically. "Wave around a sign for peace while someone else sliced the hooves off horses?"

Cristo looked over at the peacemonger, who was gasping rage against us. "No, I helped. One guy kept trying to burn three homes together and failed to raise more than smoke and mist, so then—" He was glancing nervously behind us at the peacemonger, who was trying to get us to notice him by loudly whooping our names. "But someone lit the thatch with a candle," Cristo added loudly, as if to mollify our companion. "So there was still burning and damage and all."

"Where? What part of town was the burning in, Cristo?"

"All over it, cud," boasted the peacemonger. "All over the god-bedamned townie-down it burned." The peacemonger pushed my shoulder hard to force me to turn and admire the dimness of his wits.

"See you later, guy," said Cristo, bravely hurrying down the hall and out of sight.

Ares's prize moron was swinging something red and spongy around his head, and the action was making it difficult for him to keep upright and balanced. "Mace! Mace! Mace! I gotta mace you, bleedin' son of Hecate."

"Congratulations. Do you know how to use it?"

Actually his mace was a sheep's bladder that he had tied with a leather thong to a pointed stick. "Getchyer face wet with fairy blood, you cudder-cud!" He had filled the bladder with something's blood and in his clumsiness managed to splatter its contents into an intricate chaos against the wall. My warrior friend looked confused as the blood trickled thickly down toward the floor, as if he couldn't understand why it didn't grow wings and fly up to the ceiling or turn itself into a singing cow. Then he picked his plaything back up in wonderment, recovered from his lapse into curiosity, and started singing. "Drank its bones. Drank its lousy bones, the foul new thing. Cracked its thighs like blackened corn in my own god fire." He made proud eye contact with the doorkeeper, who had come over to us and was now cooing in counterpoint as if he were entranced by the singing. "Tasted right last night," the peacemonger said into the doorkeeper's lips. There was a crowd gathering now. The doorkeeper turned his face from the peacemonger's foul breath in disgust and coughed. The drunk wanted notice. He roughly held the doorkeeper's head and forced the empty bladder to the man's lips, as if it contained something more drinkable than air. The doorkeeper whined softly as the peacemonger chanted, "Riven's eyes taste like flies. Crunch like old foul jelly they do. Woooo! Woooo!" He started howling some indecipherable battle cry right in the doorkeeper's face. The doorkeeper spit at him and the peacemonger pushed him to the floor and ran for me again, making motions with his hands as if his stick and bladder were a bow and arrow and he was trying to shoot me down. "Got high enough to see Ares's head bursting, you lousy son of Hecate! Had a *real* time last night. Twang! Twang! Ares got you—I'm gonna get you—for Ares Ares Ares—you book-be-damned cud!"

I decided then and there that if I was going to use anyone to manipulate the peacemongers into attacking Roguehan's camp, I would use him. I made a show of clutching my belly, as if his words were sickening me, thinking it strategic to maintain as much distance as possible in public from all aspects of peacemongering. I would deal with him later, but I would deal with him. "Oo-oh-ho-ho," he jeered. "So my lord master Hecate is sufficiently advanced in evil now that his tender stomach cringes at the sounds of death?" El apparently heard this polite inquiry into the state of my health, for we were closer to the classroom now, and I saw El quietly emerge from his classroom and stand in the doorway, watching the drunk. Several other people saw El too but the peacemonger was so blinded by his own frenzy to get me for Ares that he failed to notice. I made sure to position myself near El so that the drunk's words appeared to be targeted toward the high priest. "Aren't you the bloody sensitive one? Aren't you *advanced*? You think you're so much better than the rest of us because you write a pretty line? What ya gonna do, little Hecate, get *me* in trouble like Mirra?" The drunk punctuated the last two words with two draws from his imaginary bow. I thought it would be fun to create an illusory bow and an arrow to land near El's head. So I did.

There were three beats of silence during which the peacemonger noticed the arrow quivering in the door frame, noticed the bow in his hand, and slowly dropped open his mouth and noticed El, who was smiling. Everyone stood whispering excitedly that it was a sign from the god, that Ares was displeased with the high priest. Everyone except the peacemonger, who kept standing in terrified dismay, heaved his stomach twice in and out like a great beached sea dragon, and took El's blast, which was the master's only response to the furor. It seemed to me that El quietly enjoyed punishing the guy, for his eyes regained a little of their accustomed sharpness as Master War Moron fell writhing and shuddering to the floor.

El ordered the drunk to be taken to a prison cell, the same one Welm had occupied. Then he taught class in perfect time, with all the beamy brightness of his strange and strangling grace—the strange grace I had set myself the task of learning.

*T*he drunk was easier to turn than milk. First off, I made sure at the end of class to loudly and publicly and self-righteously declare that I was truly sorry that things had come to such a pass among the children of Ares. My words inspired subdued groans and hisses. "And Master, wouldn't it serve this offender right to starve on his own fury, to be refused all meat and drink for a day or two, that he might fast as those of other alignments continuously fast, and so that he might learn that all of us are truly one? After all, Master, is it really *fair* in the eyes of the Goddess for anyone to eat meat when there are some among us who positively sicken at the sight of dead flesh and really can't help it?"

El followed my suggestion and declared that he would starve the peacemonger's heretical disobedience into submission. We would not treat the incident as a sign from the god, although many were still convinced that something fine and holy had happened. El then grasped each of our hands as we left class and gave us all a personal benediction. He used the opportunity to look hard at me and at my ring, so I shot at him through my spirit the words "Trust me." It was all he had.

Outside class there were hisses and grumbling about my running the monastery, and how the gods were sure to be displeased with my arrogance, and hadn't I refused to pray for Riven the day before, and wasn't it most unfair about having to write papers with a war on? But as no one saw fit to bring these concerns directly to my attention, I ignored them and went back to my rooms, where I knew I would find Cristo cowering from the peacemongers. The drunk had scared him so much he was actually preparing for his next class. "Hey, buddy," I said in a high and happy voice.

"Huh."

"Huh? Really, Cristo my comrade, your Botha's improving every day. I understand there's to be another fine protest tonight. After dinner."

"Yeah? Where?"

"Outside the wine cellar. Our morning companion's been locked up in Welm's old quarters."

"Oh, yeah? Why?" Cristo was all excited now, so he dropped his work. Really, it didn't take much.

"I don't know *why*. I only know there's to be a big one. Why don't you go find out? I understand there might even be job announcements and everything."

Cristo ran out and spread the rumor. We all have our uses.

I waited till evening mealtime, using the hours to translate some essays into Sarana for the practice.

When I left the building near sunset there was already a crowd beginning to gather outside the wine cellar, so I willed myself into invisibility, walked easily into the cellar, and became visible again. Then I willed myself to look like Riven, minus one finger, and descended toward the cell, thinking how much energy and concentration this particular illusion took. I immediately thought about how serious—in the best sense of the word—an illusionist Baniff was to successfully pass himself off as the captain of the guards the way he once had in Sunnashiven, for even with my ring it was taking an enormous amount of energy to hold things steady. My admiration for Baniff caused me to lose my concentration, for I felt the ring go cold. I stood for a few seconds, steadied myself, decided on invisibility, and descended to the cell. I opened the cell with my key, the key I had saved from my dealings with Welm.

The cell was completely dark, and the prisoner no doubt assumed from the sound of the opening door that a jailer had been sent to him. Still invisible, I thoroughly frightened him by using wizardry to light a real candle I carried with me, and I set it on the floor. The cell was as barren as I remembered it, and once my eyes focused in the light I saw that the staunch and brave dedicant of Ares was trembling in the corner. He was shaking his head like an old horse. I supposed he was sober.

I appeared as Riven, unshielded the finger, ignored my ensuing nausea, and held the finger out to him so that he could smell it. Because he hadn't been fed, the effect was potent. Saliva burbled up all over his lips. I snatched the finger away and stood grandly over him as he looked up and gulped out semi-intelligent noises that sounded like, "Huuhm—huuhm—I—I—you're dead—"

"No, I'm not," I said slowly and deliberately. Terror tends to prolong one's experience of time, so by keeping the cadence of my voice slow I was hoping to make this incident seem especially long to the prisoner. So long that left to himself he would have to believe in the illusion of time really changing, believe that the god's messenger had really spoken. "Not to you, my friend, who prayed so well for the health and love of my spirit."

"I . . . uhhh, I . . . uhhh . . ."

"Come, friend in war, fear nothing. Be calm now. Be calm and hungry. Easy now . . . relax into your natural appetite and you shall have the prize. Relax. I bring you Ares's blessings. You of all His children are honored with this sign of His favor. Come, relax and let me in. There are no defenses to the frenzy of the god." My voice was calming and soft and seductive, a voice for a spell I had read of and wished to try. But I shied away from using the actual spell. I was hesitant to use any more magic than I needed to keep up the physical illusion, for illusion had a way of swallowing up my concentration.

"Riven—Ares, yes, of course, come in, come in," said the prisoner, opening his heart and eagerly nodding to whatever would come.

"Suck sweetly on my bloody wound, then, and listen to me," I gave him the hole where the finger once was to suck, and he swore and cried it was fine blood. Good, his own belief was carrying him through. I would need no wizardry.

"War brother."

"Yes, lord."

"Am I in your heart and in your mind, as Father Ares wishes?"

"Yes, oh, yes."

I knew I wasn't. I knew it didn't matter if the war moron believed I was. " 'Best-beloved vessel of my hate and wrath,' saith Ares. 'To you I give this finger. Do not eat of it yet. It is a holy sign. You are to obey me.' " I took back my hand because I couldn't keep up the taste of blood much longer. I circled him softly. There was no vortex to my circling, for I had no energy to spare, but the action would strengthen his easy belief. " 'Leave this cell, walk into the freedom of my violence, and tell your brothers and sisters, whom I love and bless, that tonight they must leave Threle. Hasten with them to Roguehan's encampment across the border. Lead them, my strong one—lead them to destroy it, all of it, without quarter or mercy. Now! Tonight! For that is my will. Do so with cymbals and trumpets, with all foul noise. And loudly boast of your work for succeeding days. And should anyone ask . . .' " I knelt down, took his teary chin in my open palm, and gazed in his eyes. " 'Should anyone question you, my son, say proudly that Father Ares led you into battle, and that Father Ares gave you the full cup of violence from which to drink, and that Father Ares is sole lord of Kursen.' "

And I tossed him the finger and left the cell wide open, gratefully becoming invisible in his sight. Invisibility is a blank and takes less energy to maintain than other disguises.

The peacemonger, who believed I was who I said I was, left the cell in a stupor, stumbled outside into the now considerable crowd, which was chanting for his release and Mirra's return, and held the finger aloft. He let out a boarlike groan that was greeted with earsplitting cheers. "I have seen— a ghost! Riven—Riven our blood brother, came to me! To *me*!" He pounded his chest and marched around to more cheers and exclamations of awe.

"The god Himself gave *me* His holy weapon. Yes! Riven gave me suck from his finger—like mush, like sweet and holy decay, my brothers and sisters— and gave *me* the words of Ares the Destroyer, King of War, to give to you. Now! Tonight—*tonight* we attack Roguehan's own camp!"

Cheers and cheers and cheers. It was a lousy speech, but it worked, for the crowd started eagerly for the gate, banging their cymbals and drums and causing a great din. The best part of the whole affair was El, who was watching from a dark clump of trees in the distance. I knew he would be watching from somewhere, and I was only slightly surprised that he had chosen such a location, for the tree that sheltered him seemed nothing if not fiercely sad. Unbudded. Too early for life. Something like an almost-rainbow. I approached him in my invisibility for better study. He had turned away from the crowd and was staring stoically through the branches. Then he was counting the stars with soft throaty choked sounds as the stars brought in the night. I took his hand as if I were a warming cloud out of the storm. I did not become visible. I whispered in beats of time against the next four quickening stars, "Trust me, Master." He squeezed my hand.

It was a good three hours' march to Roguehan's camp. Horses would have reduced the time to less than an hour, but there was no use wishing for horses. If the night was inclined to grant wishes, better to wish for fighting ability. I was worried that what with El's prayerful sabotage and the late hours the war club had kept in town the night before and the physical energy expended during the march itself, my troops would not be able to wreak much destruction when they finally arrived at their destination. That was why I had decided to come with them. Cristo's news that one of their champions couldn't raise anything more deadly than smoke and mist the previous night did not inspire confidence. If their efforts at violence were stymied by Ares's displeasure, at least I would be on hand with wizard fire. And if exhaustion threatened to turn them back, I was prepared to inspire my troops with illusions to keep the faith. I was most encouraged by the knowledge that not everyone in the crowd was a peacemonger. As I said, violence was in fashion that season, and the rumors and events of the day had attracted quite a throng. I was counting on the throng to carry out most of the destruction, since El had done his best to sap the regulars. I looked for Cristo in the crowd but it was now so dark I had no way of knowing whether or not he was there. There was no moon that night, but I still thought it the best side of caution to remain invisible.

As I marched softly behind my battalion, pacing my steps to the crash of their cymbals and the cadence of their battle songs, I thought about the torment El must be going through. I had absolutely no interest in remaining anywhere near El that night, for he was sure to be more anxious without me than with me. And of course he didn't dare touch me through my spirit lest he somehow interfere with what he could only hope was a workable plan to save Kursen. Since El's love for Kursen made him completely dependent on me, it was more than likely that any ill he did to me spiritually would rebound on him. Until his mood passed he dared do nothing to me, and until he knew the outcome of our little raid his mood wasn't likely to pass. So I felt reasonably safe from his wrath for the moment. The trick would be to keep him emotionally dependent on me for the long term—and to get him to remove my bans and restore to me my spirit before I went to work on him, for I trusted El with my bans more than I trusted Cathe. That is, if I ended up deciding it was in my interest to go to work on him to complete my agreement with Roguehan. After all, Threle might win.

But once I had run through my thoughts on El and hardened my resolve to do my best with the troops I had, there was nothing for it but to notice the night. The night was clouding over and so it was dark, dark, dark as we marched, sometimes more by the feel of the road than anything else. When the last few stars were covered the battle songs ran off into tired old silences. Then a cloud would break open a star pattern and the songs would rouse themselves again. This happened several times, to my great relief, for as the long as the troops were spontaneously hymning to Ares once or twice an hour they weren't getting tired or thinking of warm beds at home. I sensed no blood lust among any of them yet, but that was just as well. I wanted their frenzy to peak during the actual raid, not play itself out early. *That is, if they still have frenzy. Damn El for doing me favors! I need warriors tonight, merciless sons and daughters of the God-King of Destruction, not defanged kittens.*

After an hour or two I felt it was safe enough to drop behind the battalion and resume visibility. I wanted to conserve my own strength for the raid and there now appeared to be no danger of my troops turning back, for their chants were getting longer and higher. A ghost of war frenzy was getting raised after all. So I stood alone in the center of the road until the sound of the march vanished, knowing that crowds move much more slowly than individuals, knowing that I could catch up to them whenever I chose. They would reach the camp within an hour. I walked slowly and silently under a newly cleared sky, a black thing on a blacker road, until I came upon a crossroads. Then I sat. Stiff within the center of the crossing, I wrapped my clerical robe around me and prayed to Hecate for success. Crossroads are accounted sacred to Hecate, so it seemed the decent thing to do, even though my Lady doesn't concern Herself with battle violence. I asked Her to intercede with Her brother Ares for me, as I intended to cause the gods' own amount of destruction that night, and destruction of course was of His essence. I reminded Her that I had refused to pray against Him or Riven, that I was unused to His force and violence but hoped my clumsy attempt at peacemongering might be viewed with some favor. Then I cut my scarred palm on a sharp stone and made an offering of the blood of my hands. Then I cut my temple and offered Hecate the blood of my head, commending myself to Her keeping. When I ceased praying, I leaned back heavily upon my arms. My cut palm stung a little as it pressed against the dirt in the crossroads and I found the sensation pleasant. Then I came out of myself and looked leisurely upon the night.

Winter was fading all around me. The air was warmer here where I was sitting—settling near the hard ground where I thought it would stiffen and chill. Instead, the air warmed the ground without thawing it, for the dirt was too dry to become mud. I found myself attracted to the stretched packed dryness of the road, which was caressingly private. The night sky was for me now, clear and pressing its spotted immensity forever. I could actually hear the sky in snatches. Then I looked along the dark, which was like ground, and suddenly I felt the strangeness of being alone. I was outside Kursen's walls. I was outside, and the natural world was changed to me. I had forgotten that my life would be different here on the outside once I stopped to feel it. It was surprisingly comfortable here, where I was half reclining.

I suddenly realized that I had no desire to destroy the camp or return to my studies or do anything but walk somewhere into the darkness, as if I had never had another life. It was idle, but something in me felt that Kursen and Roguehan and Cathe and everything would cease to exist in my world if I merely stood up and began walking. I could just leave my life. I didn't feel particularly clerical or bound to monkhood. I didn't feel like a dedicant of the priesthood at all. I didn't feel like anyone's friend or enemy. I didn't feel like anything except maybe the night. There was something akin to magic in maybe feeling like the night. And then I didn't even feel like walking. I felt like living right there on the road—not as a beggar or a highwayman or a wandering monk or anything, but simply as part of the place. And I sort of believed that I could live there if I really wanted to. That I had found a moment within which, if I stayed, no one would ever come this way, neither dawn nor spring nor my heart's own needs. The wind was cool now, the stars gracious before the next bank of clouds rising on the horizon. I stretched my arms to the stars as the clouds took them. It didn't feel as though I was going to cause people to die tonight. I felt too full and innocent.

The night was calling me out of my funny birth. The night was outside now—outside of me, clouding over into an aloof existence like nothing else except its natural distant self. And then I could only know this night as ever and always apart from me. The strangeness passed. I had a job to do.

I heaved myself up and strode swiftly along again under the cloud-dark sky. I grew sweaty and tense before I heard the sounds of tramping feet up ahead. There was no singing now; all song energy had transformed itself into silent frenzy. Any step now, any second, and we would be upon the camp. I faded into invisibility and hurried to the front of the troops, which was splitting off from the rest. There were distant lights like bonfires—very distant, and I could see that my battalion was going to form a circle around the lights before it attacked. That is, if my troops could hold back their blood-frenzy for that long. There was blood lust sticking all over the air and under my robe, as if my prayer had worked. *May Ares go with them. May Hecate go with me. May our raid be deadly.*

And may Roguehan's clerics be preoccupied in prayer. If I could feel the sweltering fury, there was no reason to think that they couldn't.

I left my troops and walked straight toward the lights, which I knew belonged to Roguehan's camp. It surprised me a little to see so many bonfires everywhere, until I realized that Roguehan was in effect proclaiming that here was no secret headquarters of a sinister enemy but an open encampment of a friendly neighbor with nothing to hide. And the base was nothing if not friendly. Roguehan had managed to recruit so many Helans into his force that his camp felt more like a market town than a military base on the verge of a major battle. The only horror I felt in those lengthy minutes before the slaughter was the horror of walking invisibly in the Empire of Roguehan and stumbling over broken pieces of the Helas I remembered.

I moved swiftly past tents and loud, careless chatter, not sure what I was looking for, if anything. Not three feet away from me a lean man with a Helan accent was taking a bottle out of his shirt. He was standing before a large fire. "My sister ran a cloth business. Good merchant sense, my sister. Good cloth too. Used to export to County Clio. I used to weave for her before the troubles. She used to say I could weave a wizard's dream out of a spider's web, she did."

"What's a big-deal weaver like you doin' in the emperor's army, then? asked a Sunnan standing near him. He sounded annoyed.

"Same thing as everyone else." He shrugged. "No work. And Roguehan—"

"*Emperor* Roguehan, comrade. You're in uniform, *soldier*." This wasn't exactly true. The Helan had his shirt off because the fire was warm and he didn't appear to be in any hurry to put it back on. "Or ain't our cloth as good as yours?"

"It's rougher. Feels like fools' cloth." Helans aren't much for diplomacy.

"Guess His Excellency just ain't got the benefit of a great weaver like you. If you were really so fine with cloth you'd be weaving for the good of the empire, wouldn't you? Benefiting us all with your great talent?"

"Perhaps I will. We're all expecting to do business with Furnesse soon. Building up the new empire and all that. And your *emperor's* declared that soldiers are getting first dibs on government contracts once Threle recognizes our right to self-sovereignty and the armies all go home. Be sellin' you real cloth." He sipped gingerly from the bottle and grimaced.

"Don't you like Krygon?"

"No." The Helan spat and poured the contents on the ground. "Let the gods take it. You guys ought to learn how to make ale before you take Roguehan's gold for it."

"Come on, man, that was rude. It's our only ale. You're *supposed* to like it. Some of us poor soldiers without nice businesses to return to really missed the stuff when we couldn't get it. But then, you wouldn't know about that."

So much for the unity of the southwest. So the Helans were regarded as uppity well-to-do merchants come to play soldier. And some Helans clearly were playing soldier, doing whatever they felt would help business later. I moved on and saw three soldiers roasting a rabbit and leeks over a fire. Incredibly, they were singing "My Heart Is in Threle." One of them had fashioned a puppet out of his imperial uniform and was amusing his friends by making it sing along in a mock Sevalan accent.

> *My heart is in Threle*
> *I looks like an eel*
> *And thinks like one too*
> *When I think I'm a fink*
> *I probably am.*

"What's that?" bellowed someone out of the shadows, someone who looked and sounded very much like the puppet.

"Hey, Cap'n, what's the deal?" asked one of the soldiers.

The man with the puppet crawled behind the captain and began to mimic his every move. If my knowledge of the coming raid hadn't been pressing on me, the whole situation would have been too funny for words.

"What do you got there?"

"A rabbit on a stick, sir."

"On a big stick, sir. Got stuck that way, Cap'n." All Threlans have a wonderful way of making titles sound like insults.

The puppeteer made the captain's double hop around like a rabbit.

The Helans were laughing. So was I. There was really no help for it. Fortunately enough bystanders were joining the amusement to cover the sound of my laughter.

"I heard a song."

"What song? How did it go, Cap'n?"

The captain grew red. "That song you were singing."

"We're not *supposed* to be singing, Cap'n. You know that."

"Damn right! I'll authorize all singing." The puppet saluted. One of the soldiers made a face. "Is that supposed to be funny?"

"No, it's supposed to be dinner, Cap'n." At the word *dinner* the puppet dropped its drawers, squeezed its buttocks, looked around in mock ecstasy, and patted its belly, which caused the soldiers to lose all composure and resulted in the puppeteer himself laughing and drawing the captain's attention.

The captain turned and grabbed the puppet, throwing it in the fire.

"Why, Cap'n, you're destroying an imperial uniform. We'll have to write you up to headquarters."

"Give me the rabbit," said the captain, grabbing the stick from off the fire. Suddenly the laughter stopped.

"Hey, *I* caught that," said the puppeteer as the captain disappeared with his prize. "I caught that, you poor excuse for fun! I caught it. Expect us to live on southwestern rot?"

"Come on, man, calm down. This is supposed to be an army."

"So what? Does that mean I have to work for my supper and he gets to eat it?" *Welcome to the southwest*, I thought.

"Calm down, buddy. You've got a point. But just remember, after things settle with Threle the whole southwestern empire is going to be dependent on Helan know-how and we'll be running things. Two-goat Sevalan brutes like him will be toadying to us. If they're lucky."

We'll see, I thought. *At least the captain left you the leeks. If I know Roguehan, you'll soon be grateful if he leaves you alone.* The man did not calm down. He huffed off in a fury.

I moved on and watched a large group whooping and playing at dice.

"Two says there won't even be a battle. Two, gents! Haha! Three says why should the Threlan army attack us when we're willing to trade as an independent nation? The Kantish know how to make a gold piece. They'd rather trade than war. They've got brains. Five says three and I take the pot! And it's five to three! Yes! Do I have a wrist or what?"

"We're not really independent. We're part of the empire now," said someone who had just lost.

"Well, yes and no. For now, the Halan temporary council is glad to have Roguehan's protection but the empire doesn't grow without us. And Roguehan knows that. He needs an economy. He's just waiting for Thoren to send his general home. Then Roguehan will go back as he promised and we'll all get rich on Furnesse gold. You really think the Duchess of Kant cares a butter vat about warring against the southwest when she can make a gold piece by contracting postal services to Roguehan? C'mon. Six, gents! Sixes again and Lord Luck be mine!"

I didn't wait to see if Lord Luck was going to be his. Two female soldiers came careening out of a large tent, nearly knocking me over. They were half undressed and clearly drunk. They were giggling and spinning a blindfolded young man between them. He was wearing nothing but earrings and a dopey smile. Another woman came over and painted his arms blue and brown like the Helan flag, to many whoops of general approval.

A few tents away a man was smoking chaia and complaining to all who'd listen that he missed Hala. "Going home tomorrow," he declared. "No reason to stay. *I* only joined the army to prove a point to Thoren."

"And you think Thoren noticed?" a Sunnan called out of the crowd.

"Sure as Sunnan soldiers suck geese he's noticed. He knows there's an army against him. Now we can go home. In six months to a year he'll be begging to trade with Helas. The *Kingdom* of Helas. On our terms."

"Sunnan soldiers suck *what*?" called out the soldier who had caught the rabbit. I was sure the whole camp heard him. There were jeers and insults enough to annoy the speaker, who was high on the weed and wanted to be heard.

He broke through the noise. "Geese, sir, geese. All Sunnans suck geese. Fat geese as lay—as *lay*—I mean, as the Sunnan lads and damsels go south with—" Loud laughter. In control of his audience again, the man continued, "For everyone, including Roguehan, knows that the army is merely a symbol." The man was now an expert on world affairs. Chaia does that. "A symbol of a free and independent Helas. No need to invade Kant. The Kantish can take care of their own civil problems. They always do. Let them secede and form their own country for all I care. Then they can trade with us too. If they need someone to meddle, let 'em ask Thoren to meddle. He'd probably be glad to. He's got *his* army all over their duchy anyway, so what do they need our army for?"

"That's the point, man," a Sunnan called out. "What are you going to do when Thoren's army does invade? Sell them horseshoes and tablecloths?"

"Sell 'em your sister's goose for fun," called out the soldier who had lost his dinner to the Captain. A scuffle broke out, drawing the crowd's attention once again away from the lecturer. The man swore and went into his tent as five or six more people joined the fistfight.

So this was a sample of the imperial army preparing for war. Good job. No one had a clue about anything, everyone had a different theory of why they were there, and none of them was going to see another dawn. If Roguehan's entire fighting force was like this, it was small wonder that he was relying so heavily on propaganda before invading Kant. What else could the poor man do?

A Sunnan smacked a fellow Sunnan on the jaw, presumably by accident. The injured party lit into someone else, who went reeling into the nearest tent, causing it to fall over. More people joined the free-for-all, and it wasn't even clearly Sunnans against Helans because everyone was suddenly fighting everyone, so I couldn't be sure whether what I suddenly felt slithering through the air was a result of the nearby violence or my own precious troops approaching for the kill. *Wait—there. Good, close now, and clear as winter's thunder—there's frenzy in the air. Here it comes, here it comes . . .*

Yes! Screams and war whoops rising and rising from the edges of the camp. Then rising again. Louder. The scuffle near me had drawn in more people, and the hapless captain was trying to break it up, so the soldiers near me realized they were under attack about half a minute after I did. And even then they didn't stop their own fighting until I hit the three nearest tents with a blast of wizard fire. A neat, self-contained blast, I might add. If I hadn't been concentrating on keeping invisible, I probably could have hit half a dozen tents, but the fire did what it was supposed to. It scattered the mostly weaponless inhabitants in a panic toward the outskirts of the camp and spread all over nearby structures before consuming itself in darkness. There was no way to maintain invisibility and launch enough energy into my own fire to keep it burning for more than a minute or so. And it took some concentration to put up my shield against fire and take it down again when I needed to blast something, because by shielding my own power I risked visibility. A shield could easily interfere with the illusion I was generating. And all the while I had to keep careful attention on the action around me to keep out of harm's way. It wouldn't do to get caught in the middle of a physical combat.

I moved swiftly toward the nearest part of the camp's perimeter, which was west. Someone was yelling incomprehensible commands. It was another captain, and no one was listening to him. He jumped up on a log near a bonfire and flashed his sword around while swearing at his troops at the top of his voice. This attracted a small group of peacemongers, who stood still in the shadows listening and stirring their blood lust. The captain, who couldn't see into the darkness from the bright light he stood within, kept urging the shapes "to fight, to kill, to bring the enemy down, to hack his limbs to nothing!"

Needless to say, they did. Clerics love to take orders, even if they don't understand the language they're given in. One of my colleagues axed the captain in the back and the rest finished the job.

Which was all right by me, except that they started fighting among themselves over the captain's corpse. Such bickering would have been deadly had the camp been less confused. The fight ended when one of them threw the corpse on the bonfire to spite the others. The fire went out. The peacemongers raised a chant to Ares to draw down god fire and nothing happened. Then a group of soldiers rushed them and they scattered, whooping and howling. I noticed one of them had taken the captain's sword.

It disturbed me that there were no explosions or smells of burning flesh anywhere. There were plenty of whoops and yelps and crashing tents, and the weaponless soldiers who had fled the center of the camp were falling all around, but all of the fighting felt mundane and earthy to me. I saw a soldier and a peacemonger stabbing each other simultaneously in the chest, and that for me was an image of how the whole raid seemed to be going so far. Without the divine spark we were sure to do poorly once the soldiers got organized. *Please, please, Ares, be kind this once. Your servants did not know the nature of their prayer.* The peacemongers were motivated by their lust for violence, by their spiritual need to draw upon the energy of destruction. If Ares were to absent himself or thwart their ability to draw joy from their own destruction and ride it through their hearts as lustful abandon, then they might give up the raid and go home. And if the peacemongers fled, the rest of my troops would follow.

Yes! Praise Ares for a sport! Somewhere along the northwest edge of the camp a tent went up in flames. And then another. I moved closer in this direction, shielding myself. At first I thought some of the peacemongers had managed to draw down the god's favor after all. It was only when I got to the camp's perimeter that I noticed they were using the bonfires to burn the tents with—and failing miserably most of the time. The problem was that some of the more squeamish members of my battalion were contenting themselves with uprooting tents along the outskirts of the camp and throwing them on nearby fires, which resulted in most of the fires being put out and only an occasional tent bursting into flame. It also resulted in the camp soldiers having time to slice the tent burners into the ground. I scattered the soldiers with a blast of wizard fire, but not before they had pretty much decimated the raiders along the northwestern perimeter.

I saw more fires due west, so I moved back in this direction, intending to augment the burning with wizardry. The more experienced war club members already had the west under control and were using the tent burnings to slice down the soldiers, for as soon as a group of soldiers fell on a timid group of tent burners, the real warlovers fell upon the soldiers' backs with axes and spears, chanting, "Peace, peace, peace!" The tactic was working well enough for me to conserve my fire, but I soon realized that most of the bonfires were being suffocated through falling tents and ineptitude and the peacemongers were not getting any aid from the King of Destruction. And as more fires got put out it got harder to see, of course, so sometimes the peacemongers fell on each other. Or the soldiers did. But I was cheered to see that my own troops were moving slowly in from the perimeter, hacking toward the center person by person. As long as they were winning I had hopes that morale would hold in spite of Ares's apparent disfavor. Or perhaps excessive destruction would win back the god's favor, or the peacemongers would be too excited and dim-witted to notice that they were going this one alone as mere laity.

Damn El! May he rot in goodness! More and more peacemongers were stopping confusedly to ride the violence, leaving themselves open to counterattacks. This was the whole bloody problem. Without the god's blessing the violence was not to be ridden. The peacemongers couldn't find the kick they were looking for, and the more confused they got the more confusedly they fought. Or they just stood swaying like idiots until a sword thrust put them out of their misery. *Damn them for dolts.* At least the soldiers fought. Sort of. Sometimes they just chased off the peacemongers, which was really stupid, because the peacemongers, having gained a safe distance, just returned running pell-mell with maces. The whole thing was dark and confused. I needed to weaken the center again or the soldiers would definitely outfight us. Confusion and darkness are useless unless you can take advantage of them, but some of these peacemongers couldn't take advantage of their own brains. That is, if they had any. You can't fight a battle on emotion alone. Also there was no way of telling who was killing whom at the eastern perimeter and I knew that the center of the camp would be armed by now. I needed a system. I needed to keep the center confused and disarmed so the soldiers couldn't organize effectively enough to repel the raiders.

So I made my own way back to the center, burning whatever I could with wizard fire, which meant letting my own shield down. I was trying to form an inner ring of fire while still leaving myself escape room. I succeeded in pacing out enough wizard fire to form a half ring between myself and the western perimeter, which forced most of the armed soldiers toward the east. I ran with them, but I could not stay invisible and use more magical energy just then. A few more minutes and I would catch my breath, then perhaps I could pull down more fire—if my eastern flank hadn't killed itself by then.

I dropped back behind the soldiers and leaned against a pole to catch my breath and steady my own power for my next assault. It was hard to stay invisible with so much to think about and with the physical exhaustion I was now contending with. As I waited to recover a little strength I saw my wizard fire dying into itself, leaving the west open again. Perhaps I should risk visibility and simply rely on the dark confusion around me for cover. I could see and hear nothing in the west, but there were faint cries and the sounds of clanking weapons in the east. My own space was strangely quiet and empty, the swirling blank inside the storm. For a few seconds I thought the western raiders had given up and left and the others were soon to follow. Then there were fierce screams. The soldiers were turning in my direction now, running from the east, running from an immense curtain of growling ravenous flames taking down the sky and earth and air and everything else in its path. I'd never seen or read of anything like it—wizard fire, as I knew it, was nothing to this. And wizard fire is pretty deadly stuff while it lasts. Had Ares hit the east? Anyway, I was now in as much danger as the soldiers, who were screaming and falling before the approaching flame.

Hecate help me. I ran toward the west. Here, with my back to the yelping flames, it was too dark to see in front of me, and I tripped over moaning and sobbing injured soldiers as well as dead bodies. When I reached the outskirts I turned and saw that the flame appeared to have stopped halfway across the camp. Now by its glaring light I could see that most of the western portion of the camp was in ruins. A few soldiers had taken up a position near me. They were too shaken to be worth much as fighters. One was holding his gut and vomiting.

A sizable group of soldiers who had also outrun the flames was now approaching the west. I exhausted myself again by putting up a pillar of wizard fire in front of me, something to drive them back into the center. Then I prayed to Hecate to ask Ares to drive the pillar forward. There was nothing else I could do.

The pillar tightened, wavered, and burst forward, red and nervous. And it spread, sweeping the camp before me into the nothingness of angry light. *Praise Ares and all his kin.* Well, why shouldn't the god hear my Lady's intercession? I hadn't prayed against Him in class, and there was a fine lot of destruction to be had here. And I had lived faithfully within Hecate's narrow path. I stepped back into the darkness as far as possible. The heat was so terrific I put my shield back up but it did nothing for me, so I dropped it once more. I opened my robe and shirt and then closed them again because my skin was getting singed. Thunder. The sound of the two walls of fire colliding and crashing and grinding into a whirlwind of ash and heat. I sat back and watched the spectacular fire bursts against blank black sky while the ground sweated beneath me. In the horrid flashes of light I didn't dare regain visibility, for I had no idea how many soldiers or peacemongers had taken cover near me, if any. The camp was gone, that much I did know. Most of my battalion was gone too, if not all of it. And since El couldn't help but feel the release of each spirit he kept, he was no doubt intimately aware of the scale of loss. Well, I supposed I could get him to blame himself for weakening the peacemongers. Guilt could be a wonderful lever for increasing my control over him. I had not planned on losing so many troops, and I supposed I should have felt some kind of regret, but really I didn't. The peacemongers had followed their own hearts to come here. This whole event was no different from previous assaults in other places, and the newcomers—well, if you have to follow the fads and fashions, far be it for me to stop you. War is war.

It occurred to me that if Cristo had come with us, he might very well be among the dead. Then it occurred to me that try as I might, I couldn't feel anything about that. So I gave up trying and watched the fire. Sometimes there's a mild regretful sadness that comes when you realize that you should miss something or someone you are leaving but that you really don't miss them at all. But I learned as I studied the weird blaze that if Cristo was dead, I wouldn't even feel regret over *not* missing him. It was a valuable state to keep close—the knowledge of feeling nothing. I should apply it to all my waking life.

The mass of flame was now swaying into itself, as if it had expended the bulk of its energy, so the air around me was cooling rapidly. As the flame settled, its noise did too, and I heard voices floating out of the northwest and several less insistent thunderbursts of flame and mild sizzles tossing noise all over what used to be the camp. The fire had broken itself all over into random piles of light and was softly falling into ashes.

I listened for more voices but as far as I could tell there was silence everywhere else. So I stood and circled in a northerly direction at the edge of the weird light, keeping shielded and invisible, looking for what might have survived the destruction. As I moved closer the voices stopped. And then I heard voices close behind me whispering in Kantish. So I stood stockstill and invisible at the edge of light, watching the end of the destruction and listening for whatever I could learn. But the voices stopped. I don't know how long I watched the light fail, minutes maybe, before I raised my hand in a quiet salute to the western half of the wasteland. Then I turned my palm downward and silently thanked Ares for His power. I knew enough to thank the god, because after all Ares was not my deity and the force I had brought down had more to do with Hecate's intercession and the night's circumstances than my own clerical development.

I tore open the cut in my palm that I had made earlier for my blood offering and let my blood run down my arm, bright and lurid in the erratic, pulsing light. And as I brought down my palm the western flames went out in acknowldgment of my thanks, but the eastern flames remained, spreading high for a second and falling back down to ash and earth, where their remnants would no doubt burn until morning. That was it. And whether the eastern flames were of the god or not, there was nothing to do for it here. I would have to research what happened. I had best start back for Kursen anyway. The voices did not pick up again. Any survivors were bound to be on the road.

The rest is strange. I pulled my robe around me in the cooling wind and turned to my right. There in the weak light, sitting still and cross-legged and partially obscured by a leafy bush, was Welm. Welm, who once had disappeared before my eyes; Welm, the illusionist who was having no trouble seeing me, for invisibility is pure illusion; Welm, who had no reason not to let Roguehan know what he had just seen. And he wasn't alone. There were two or three imperial soldiers with him. It must have been their voices I heard. Welm looked blankly curious but made no move to approach me. He was evaluating. Since he had had ample time to make a move, I supposed he wouldn't. Perhaps he had some idea of blackmail in mind, in which case I would handle him. I might even be able to turn the situation to my advantage, depending on the events of the next few days.

As I stepped back I saw his attention focus suddenly behind me, so I followed his gaze. And there, standing in the shadow of an oak tree and gazing intently at me, was Baniff. Baniff had watched me put the fires out with blood and a gesture of evil. Baniff no doubt knew that the students of Kursen Monastery had been attacking Kant and could only assume—why not?—that here was their general. And standing behind him was Mirand, who was looking curiously at Baniff as if waiting for an explanation for the gnome's interest in what to Mirand could only be shadows in the air. Then I saw Mirand glance over at Welm.

I spread my arms open to Baniff in a mock take-me-if-you-want gesture. Our eyes locked in the flickering light for an excruciating minute. We knew each other. There was no mistake. And then Baniff flicked the back of his hand in a gesture that clearly meant "go."

Then I looked to Welm and spread my arms to him in the same gesture, probably more for Baniff's benefit than anything else. Welm responded immediately as Baniff had. I had been fairly sure he would. Other than that nobody moved. And nobody prevented me from joining in the fun. I could have stared them all down all evening if I chose. But there was El to attend to now, so I went off into the darkness and began the journey back to Kursen.

Like I said, it was strange. Strange to be so trusted. Strange to be so free and in the world once more.

———

I'm dying, my lord. I can feel the sickness again. A little only. A first suggestion."

Walworth ceased writing. His face betrayed no emotion concerning my role in destroying his enemy's camp, gave no sign if he accounted my story a defense against his charges of treason or a self-damning account of my guilt. He glanced impassively at the fisherman, who was staring through heavy-lidded eyes at the slow-burning remains of the yellow candle. Although I had ceased speaking, the fisherman was still listening to the remains of my telling, for I could feel the echo of my words in his mind. His lips moved in a dark prayer to Isulde, gurgling her name to the dull light, but he was also praying to me to continue my story. In his dreamful drunken state he was confusing her beauty with the poor power of my words, as if he somehow found my telling beautiful and hadn't the wit to distinguish between his foster daughter and a Northern night's amusement, as if here in the North it was all one.

"More." He banged his spoon to end his prayer, or perhaps to emphasize it.

I would have continued speaking, but his banging made the North Country night lurch and scream like a new ghost clawing for entry into its now-decaying body, or like a dark mirror of my sickness clawing for possession of mine. I knew that Hecate was dancing out of Habundia-Christus and screaming behind the Northern screaming, screaming for my ban to break into death and my spirit to break and suffer upon Hers. There was darkness screaming in long dark spirals between my heartbeats, and then my heartbeats spiraled down into the banging, and then they stopped when the banging stopped. I might have gone dead. I might have gone dark and dreamful. I might have become a curse or a prayer or a twist of fiction or the dull light of a shattered Northern poem.

> And one more time I was breaking to fall toward Mother Hecate and her dogs.
>
> And out of the scream of the fall I remembered I might have been a storyteller, but somewhere young my flower was poisoned and all my words went gray.
>
> And so the life I was meant was burst like Grana's promises of magical gifts.
>
> And Grana is welcoming me in Hecate's dress. Her old lips lean to wrinkle the life out of mine.
>
> And now in my mouth the poisoned flower tastes of kingsfoil and monkshood.

And my enemy, Walworth, is forcing into my mouth the medicine that keeps me alive to speak, and the point of his sword is a broken star on my chest. I am heavy with sickness, but I am alive. I am heavy with my ban, but back behind the Northern screaming, my entry into death half closes, and there—it fades into the fisherman's pious mumbles, Walworth's diligent violence, and the weakness of my still-living heart.

And so I'm strong enough against this space of dark to speak my plea once more.

Author's Note:

So paused Llewelyn in his telling,
and so pauses the first in a series of books
about Llewelyn and his adventures.